Don't Shoot! . . . I have another story to tell you

By
Elen Ghulam

Book cover design by Elen Ghulam.
The cover shows "Hanthala Makes it to Sistine Chapel" painting by Elen Ghulam.
Photograph by Douglas Hayes.
Back cover head shot photographed by Dr. Marwan Hassan.

ISBN 978-1-4303-0201-8

For My Parents Alexandra Ghulam and
Malik Ghulam

Acknowledgments

To Rebecca Klady, for working hard on editing this book. I cannot fully express my gratitude to my father Malik Ghulam, who read each chapter as it was written and provided valuable feedback, guidance and encouragement every step of the way. My gratitude to my friend Alyson Quinn, who proof read the manuscript during her vacation; but more importantly encouraged me to continue writing when I wanted to give up. My gratitude to Deborah Cambell, who read an early draft of this book and gave me valuable feedback on how to shape it to what it is today. A thank you to my brother Ibrahim Ghulam, for continuing to remind me of our childhood together. For showing me how to approach book cover design, I wish to thank Avril Orloff.

To my three children, Rawan Hassan, Yarra Hassan and Yusuf Hassan, who inspire me by their mere presence.

And finally, to my husband, Marwan Hassan – without a doubt the most astonishing man I have ever known.

There is a way between voice and presence
where information fows

In disciplined silence it opens
with wondering talk it closes

Rumi

Introduction

Don't Shoot! ... I have another story to tell you is a collection of stories of a Czech-born Iraqi woman who walks the tightrope between East and West. Each story stands alone, yet is part of a tapestry of real-life tales from the heart of a conflict. Watching a Palestinian man get shot in the chest during a house demolition in east Jerusalem forces reconciliation with the world and coming to terms with apathy about world events. Yearly trips from the Middle East to the Czech Republic lead to an identity transformation – from being the lightest-skinned in the crowd to the darkest. The haunting specter of Saddam Hussein imposes harsh realities on daily life.

These stories arise from my life and experiences. At age nineteen I immigrated to Canada, where for the very first time I was able to read censored Arab authors, leading to a new understanding of my country of origin. Later I married a Palestinian professor and together we lived in Scotland and Israel. In Israel, I learned Hebrew, worked for an Israeli company and experienced the military occupation of Palestine first hand – albeit from a perspective within Israeli society. I take an Israeli friend to visit Palestinian East Jerusalem and the West Bank for the first time in her life, and later take a Palestinian friend to visit Israeli West Jerusalem for her very first time. Living between two worlds, yet again. In the process of crossing cultural divides, I have gained four languages, several passports, a unique perspective and the stories in this book.

Identity Crisis

Eight Conversations About One Thing

When I immigrated to Canada, I went to the Motor Vehicle Office to apply for a Canadian driving license. I showed the employee my Kuwaiti driver's license. Here is the conversation that followed:

Employee: Ah! You are Kuwaiti.

Elen: No! I am Iraqi.

Employee: Ah! So you were born in Iraq and then you lived in Kuwait?

Elen: No! I was born in Czechoslovakia (Czech Republic now).

Employee: ....looks puzzled..... (Ok, is this woman crazy? Either that or she is just pulling my leg!)

Elen: Look! I know this is all confusing, I find it confusing myself, but it is a long story and you don't want to hear it.

A few days earlier I was standing at a bus station, waiting for a bus. A young man starts chatting with me. After a while he pops the question.

Young man: So! Where are you from?

Elen: Iraq.

Young man: Which province is that?

Elen: Iraq is not a place in Canada; it is a country in the Middle East.

Young man: Oh!

Those were the good old days when people didn't know what Iraq was. "Is that a kind of food?". Now everybody knows where Falujah is. Lucky me, I don't have to explain that Iraq is a country in the Middle East any more. Thank you, Bush.

A few years later, I am married and my husband didn't have his Canadian citizenship yet. We were about to take a trip to the U.S. and since I worked downtown, he asked me if I could apply for a visa for him. So I went to the American Consulate in downtown Vancouver and stood in the line to apply for a visa, holding his passport in my hand. A man with a red beard approached me, smiling.

Red Beard: moof, moof, blem, blem, blem.
Elen: I am sorry, I didn't understand that. Can you please repeat what you said?
Red Beard: moof, moof, blem, blem, blem.
Elen: I am sorry. I didn't catch that, can you repeat? (Now I come really close to him and try to listen attentively.)
Red Beard: moof, moof, moof, blem, blem, blem.
Elen: (realizes he is speaking in a foreign language). I am sorry I don't understand what you are saying. Can you please speak English?
Red Beard: (yelling) How dare you speak to me in English you bitch! (Other profanity followed, walks away in a huff).

I stood there completely shocked. I didn't understand? What did I do? Why was he upset? After about 5 minutes, I finally looked down and

I saw my husband's Israeli passport in my hands. Aaaah! He thought that I was Israeli; he was probably speaking Hebrew, which I didn't know at all at that time. When I got home I told my husband the incident.

Husband: He thought you were an Israeli pretending not be Israeli.
Elen: But why would I do that?
Husband: Some Israelis when they move abroad pretend that they are not Israeli and attempt to blend in. Others become annoyed with such people because they feel that they are selling out.
Elen: But If I was an Israeli and I spoke Hebrew, why would I pretend not to speak the language? I still don't understand.
Husband: You have to be Israeli to understand Israeli logic; I don't know how to explain it.

When I first moved to Canada I was living in student housing on the campus of University of British Columbia. Sometimes I would stay late in the library or the computer lab to finish an assignment. Afterwards I would have to walk to the residence in the dark. It was only a 20 minute walk, but I always felt a bit afraid. There had been several rape cases on campus reported in the news. So, I bought a huge, sturdy umbrella. One of those annoying umbrellas that take up too much space when opened. I bought it not because of the rain, but rather as a weapon. "If anybody tries to attack me, I will hit them with this umbrella." I assured myself. I named the umbrella Saddam, like you would name a pet. Dogs were not allowed at the student's residence. I thought it was an appropriate name considering what I bought it for - banging somebody over the head. In the end, I never did use it for that.

I carried Saddam with me everywhere. The first American-led war on Iraq happened and Iraq was mentioned on the news every single day. In Canada they keep talking about Iraqi terrorists that will try to do nasty things in North America. I am standing at the bus station holding Saddam and leaning against him. A big, tall, strong man starts chatting with me in a friendly way. We are laughing about something, when he decides to pop the question:

Tall man: So! Where are you from?
Elen: Iraq.
Tall man: (takes a few steps back, looks horrified, puts his hands on his head as if somebody is about to hit him), Oh, my God!
Elen: (thinks to herself) Hey! this is cool, it is amazing that a woman can scare a big guy like that just by saying the word "Iraq". I don't need to carry Saddam with me anymore. If anybody bothers me, I will just tell them I am Iraqi. That will scare them away.

After that, I discovered that I could have lots of fun by telling people I was Iraqi, I could make them gasp, choke on their food, run away, and strike the fear of God into their hearts. Thank you, Bush senior, for giving me these superpowers. It has been so much fun. I have put them to good use; well, . . . most of the time!

Person at a cocktail party: So where are you from originally?
Elen: I was born in the Czech Republic.
Person at a cocktail party: Ah! Beautiful country, been there once.
Elen: (thinks to herself) Now I understand why red beard yelled at me at

the American consulate. Maybe he could see my future selloutedness in my eyes.

But then there were the people who reacted to my newly acquired superpowers in scary and unpredictable ways. Let me illustrate with an example: I am sent with my co-worker Steve, to attend a five-day training class in San Jose, California. There are about ten people in the class. All of them professional geeks like me. Steve elects to sit next to the pretty girl in the right row and leaves me sitting on the left row by myself. I get the hippy looking dude with the long pony tail. Thanks, Steve. Well! We are in California after all.

Hippie dude: Where are you from?

Elen: I am from Iraq.

Hippie dude: (looks at me adoringly) Wow! you are a wonderful person, I want to get to know you better.

Elen: How about we go get some coffee. (We stand up to go to the coffee table, I introduce hippie guy to Steve.)

Hippie dude: You are so lucky to be working with such an amazing person.

Steve: (gets a smirk on his face, he has been working with me for a year and knows how plain un-amazing I am).

Steve: Yes! Working with her has been . . . ehm! . . . interesting.

Elen: (gives Steve a look that says, "please come sit beside me . . . help me")

Hippie dude: (spends the next 5 days looking adoringly at me and listing attentively to every single word I say, as if a simple hello coming from me becomes a divine word of wisdom. Maybe he is expecting me to produce a flying carpet.)

From adoration to revulsion, I have encountered the full spectrum. However, once in a while there are encounters that make it all worth it. My husband and I were visiting Jerusalem on a vacation. This was my first visit to the city and the country. We were on a public bus driving through Jerusalem's city center. It was a day before Eid Al-Adha (Muslim holiday). My husband and I are chatting in Arabic. An elderly Jewish woman is sitting in the seat in front of us. She is wearing a head scarf and a long skirt customary to Jewish women of eastern origins. The woman turns around and says to my husband.

Elderly woman: I wish you well on your upcoming Eid. May you spend it in joy and happiness.
Husband: Thank you.
Elderly woman: Where are you from?
Husband: I am from Nazareth area.
Elderly woman: (looks at me) Are you from Nazareth as well?
Elen: No, I am from Iraq.
Elderly woman: (her eyes widen and shouts) I am Iraqi too! I left Iraq in the fifties as a young woman and came to live here. My children and grandchildren were born and raised in this country.

The elderly woman starts touching my hands, touching my face and caressing my hair. As if she can't believe that she can see a real Iraqi in front of her.

Elderly woman: I grew up in Baghdad. Here in this country we just spend the days, one day after the other. In Baghdad I was really alive.

An elderly man wearing grey jacket, striped shirt, kipah (head scalp customary for Jewish men) and holding a walking cane gets up from his seat and walks towards us.

Elderly man: I am Iraqi too, I left Iraq about the same time.

Me and elderly woman stand up and all three of us stare at each other. After few seconds we all hug. A triangle hug, as if we are all long lost friends. We stand there for several seconds while the bus bounces us back and forth and sideways.

Husband: We reached our bus stop, time to get off the bus.

[Advice to kids: Do not give hugs to strangers you don't know on a public bus, a professionally trained wacky Iraqi was involved in this incident.]

Recently, I have accidentally lost my Saddam, the huge umbrella, I mean. I left him at a bookstore near Alma Street and 4th ave in Vancouver. I'm gonna miss him, he has traveled with me to many countries and held the repository of my sense of security for a long time. To whomever found my lost Saddam, please keep him. He never shielded me from bothersome people, not even once. The one time I was almost physically attacked, he wasn't there. A strong kick to the assailant's leg helped me get out of that sticky situation. I was rather surprised by how well I could protect myself without my trusted umbrella. He wasn't completely useless though. I remember, vividly, long

21

walks under the rain while holding my husband's arm. My husband explaining something about his work or world events and me looking back in adoration, listening attentively to every single word my husband uttered. I can still hear the tapping of rain on top of the umbrella as we huddled together underneath. Sometimes an umbrella is just an umbrella. Those were moments of tenderness and sweetness.

I have no regrets.

Presidential Dreams

I had a dream one night; I was standing in a room in front of a projector, giving a business presentation. Saddam Hussein was sitting in the audience; he asked stupid questions, looked impatient with my presentation and showed very little interest in what I was saying. I kept it short, collected my stuff at the end and before I left the room I said respectfully, "Thank you, Mr. President". I woke up greatly disturbed by my dream. You see, this is the first time I have had a dream about Saddam in a long time. I thought I had exorcized him out of my dreams.

Let me explain: I am an Iraqi citizen who grew up in Kuwait. Even though I never set foot in my country, as a child I was exposed to Saddam's personality cult on a daily basis. In our living room, my parents had to have a picture of Mr. President on a corner table. People working at the Iraqi embassy had criticized my father because there were no pictures of the president in our house. My dad, afraid of retribution, bought the smallest one he could find and placed it in a prominent place in the living room so that all visitors would see it. This might sound ridiculous to a North American, but all other Iraqi families had huge pictures of Saddam in every single room. Our neighbour had a huge poster of Saddam plastered on the wall; the wife would sit on an armchair next to the poster and go on and on: "Saddam is our father, Saddam is our protector, where would we be without him, ...etc." Everybody sitting around would nod his or her head saying nothing. The rumor was that our neighbours were associated with the Iraqi embassy. Later on, the same people had to leave Kuwait in a hurry; the rumor was that they had some sort of a disagreement with embassy people. My mom met the wife many years later, she sat in an arm chair in our living room and went on and on, "Saddam is a criminal, Saddam is a dictator, why doesn't he send his own son's to fight his stupid wars? ... etc."

My dad was a rebel with his single small picture. He tried to shield me from the propaganda as best as he could. Once in a while he would make a vague comment, like "Don't always believe everything you see on TV." Explaining that statement further was too dangerous.

As a child I had many nightmares involving Saddam Hussein. In most of them, I am running in a field, Saddam is chasing after me, I find a ditch or cave to hide in. Sometimes the dream involved my whole family being chased. I never met the man in person, but experiencing the fear that the mere mention of his name evoked made me realize that he must be a scary man. Normally, intelligent people would suddenly turn stupid in the presence of his picture. I used to watch him giving speeches on TV, his eyes piercing through me like an X-Ray machine. I would imagine him reaching out of the TV set to strangle me. Could he see what I am thinking about him through the TV?

I immigrated to Canada in 1989. Aaah, the freedom! No pictures of him, no long speeches on TV, nobody even knew who Saddam Hussein was. The only time I would hear his name was when I would

24

come in contact with another Iraqi. All Iraqis have what I call the Saddam Obsession. We can go on for hours talking about how much we loathe the man and what a horrible person he is. Each has his own favorite story of horror to tell, from the time Saddam assassinated his own cousin, to the women he raped, to members of parliament shot on the spot for criticizing the president, the list goes on. I have heard these stories told and retold with varying degrees of dramatization. Like folk tales that take you on a journey to a fairy-tale world, passed on from one generation to the next.

I have a theory that Saddam Hussein doesn't exist. We citizens of Iraq invented him. We placed his picture and statues everywhere, taught our kids to fear him and bestowed magical powers on him. We imagine his eyes and ears spying on us even in our sleep. Like the Wizard of Oz, he has magical powers because everybody around him believes he has. He can be a fireball one minute and a scary beast the next. Oh yes! He might have nuclear weapons too. I think that Saddam objected to weapon inspections because he knew they would find nothing. His status as the regional boogyman would have been diminished.

Before you pounce on me, I assure you that I am familiar with the history of my ancestral land. I am painfully aware of the Kurdish people massacred in Halabcha. I know about the war against Iran that killed 1 million Iraqis and Iranians. In 1990, I read an Amnesty International report that summarized human rights conditions in Iraq. Tales of torture, multitudes of people that disappear never to be found again. The report stated that Iraq is the only Arab country that tortures men and women equally. In Egypt they have the decency to leave the women alone. Iraq is an equal opportunity torture country. I cried for a week non-stop after reading that report.

However, Saddam is a single man. Thousands and millions of people had to cooperate with his plans to put them into action. Perhaps like Dorothy, before we uncover the true face of the wizard, we must destroy the Wicked Witch of the West. Oh, she is scary and she has those winged monkeys disguised as soldiers, and black bees disguised as smart missiles. Not to worry; she will be defeated with a simple bucket of water.

I had hoped that one day the people of Iraq would take down all those pictures from their walls. I had hoped that the average soldier would say, "I am sick of dying to defend the ego of a single man." I had hoped that the torturers in the prison cells would say, "I refuse to obey orders; I take responsibility for my own actions." The person on the street would reclaim his dignity. Saddam would lose all his magical powers and we would see a helpless and a scared man. You can't achieve that by simply exchanging the guy at the top with yet another wizard. You can't bomb and starve a population into empowerment. I hope that day of awakening comes soon because Saddam obsession is spreading into North America.

What did my dream mean? Perhaps I am scared of that business presentation I am about to give. At least in this dream I was able to look him in the eye and speak directly to him. In my next dream I will say "Mr. President, you're a humbug".

Lemonade

"An Iraqi and a Palestinian moved to live in Israel," starts the joke. Except that in 1996 when I moved to live to Jerusalem I didn't know the punch line, not yet, anyway. Let me explain: I am an Iraqi citizen married to a Palestinian. My husband is a member of a minority of Palestinians possessing an Israeli citizenship. He was offered a job to teach at the Hebrew University as part of a new affirmative action initiative at Israeli universities to prove that they are not racist. I had great doubts about the move. With all the conflict in the region how can an Iraqi and a Palestinian live in Israel? It sounded like some sort of joke. My husband in his usual calm manner assured me, "It will be a bit of an adjustment, but it is going to be fine, I promise!"

So we packed our things and decided to try it out. We were young and carefree. "Why not? it will be an adventure, " I told myself. I managed to get a job within weeks of arriving in Jerusalem. I was to manage eight people at a software development company. Three of them were immigrants from Russia with no knowledge of English, and the rest spoke it very poorly. Imagine explaining job assignments in hand waves and head nods. The whiplash created strong motivation for learning Hebrew. I immediately started intensive Hebrew classes. When asked about my country of origin I simply answered that I was from Canada, and avoided mentioning the bit about my Iraqi origins. Everybody

29

bought it, thinking that my accent was just a funny Canadian accent. I didn't bother to correct them. With Saddam Hussein threatening to use chemical weapons on Israel, what if somebody decided that shooting the Iraqi in his own backyard was easier than shooting the Iraqis far away? Many of my co-workers came to work wearing guns, adding to my feeling of nervousness. Several of the people I managed had recently been released from the army. One was a tank commander; the other was an explosives expert. It was easier pretending to be a Canadian with a funny accent.

Within a year I was able to pick up the language and speak it comfortably. I had to remember to speak the right language at the right time. At work in Hebrew, with North Americans in English, in the west bank Arabic only. One day I was chasing after my daughter trying to get her dressed. The phone rang. I picked it up in a hurry. Should I start by saying Hello, Shalom or Marhaba? Which language to use when I haven't identified the person yet? In my confusion I yelled "Aaaah!" into the phone. My friend on the other end asked, "Elen, are you feeling ok?" I was feeling ok, just a little uncomfortable in my own skin.

One day, during lunch hour at work, my co-worker declared that all Palestinian children should be killed. While munching on a chicken breast, he added: "They will all grow up to be terrorists anyway. We might as well kill them now and save ourselves lots of trouble later." Did that proclamation include my daughter? I wondered. She was only 3 years old at the time. My co-worker Uzi was a friendly intelligent person, he

30

simply wants to kill my daughter, and otherwise he was a very nice guy. The expression "The personal is political" gained a whole new meaning. I suppose life threw me a few lemons. Uzi and me got along just fine at work; I just never discussed politics with him.

The sour taste lingered for a while. "The Iraqis are not regular people like us," yet another co-worker told me on a different occasion. She saw Iraqi people on TV marching in Baghdad in support of Saddam Hussein. I mentioned that maybe these people were marching in the street out of fear of a dictator. "They are born with a violent mentality, you don't know these people, they are not like us," she tells me. How I wanted to let out a loud laugh, like those evil laughs that Jack Nicholson's characters are capable of. It was so tempting to say: "Have you ever danced with the devil in the pale moonlight? Boo!" Instead, I smile with hidden mischief. I thought I was so smart having fooled them all. And realized only later that the joke was on me.

I am a big fan of Jack Nicholson. I love his evil laughs and menacing looks. My favorite performance was in the first Batman movie as the Joker. As a result of a plunge into toxic waste chemicals, the joker's hair turns sickly green and his face becomes ghostly white. Most frightening of all is the big smile frozen on his face. Smiles and bad jokes abound throughout the movie. The Joker laughs while killing others, he laughs while being killed. The Joker has no choice but to laugh. I laugh lots and loud, so some people call me the Giggler; they can't see the toxic waste I've been through. After seeing Jack Nicholson's movie, *About Schmidt*, I go to Calahoun's, a coffee shop frequented by university students. In the ladies' washroom somebody had scribbled on the wall: "Your life is a joke without a punch line." . . . The Giggler disagrees.

"An Iraqi and a Palestinian moved to live in Israel. One day as they are taking a walk in downtown Jerusalem, the hot sunny weather takes effect. The Iraqi man faints and falls to the ground. The Palestinian man starts shouting, "Help! help!" An Israeli man runs over; "What is wrong?" he asks. The Palestinian man says, "I am not sure if this Iraqi man is dead or alive." The Israeli man says, "No need for alarm, I will take care of the problem." He takes out his gun and shoots the Iraqi man in the head twice. "Now we know he is dead for sure."

Liberation Stories

When Nelson Mandela Smiles, my whole being smiles with him. In all the film footage I have seen of the man, he has a warm passionate smile. I frequently ponder what keeps him going. I zip back to my grandmother, a tormented and broken spirit. My grandmother is Russian, and was forced to work as a slave laborer in Nazi Germany. She has great difficulty talking about her memories of that period. She doesn't need to say much, the pain and horror is evident in her eyes. My grandmother is a bitter and paranoid person. She thinks the worst of everybody, always complaining about how unfair life is. Many of her opinions are racist; for example, she believes that white skin is superior to black skin and she hates all Germans with a passion. My earliest memory of my grandmother is of her telling me that she will die soon and asking me if I would feel sad in that event. That was 25 years ago. She is alive and well today. Sometimes I wonder about her sanity. I haven't a single memory of her smiling. Who can blame my grandmother? With all the hardship that she has been through, is it any wonder that she is cynical? Yet certain people go through enormous difficulty and come out the other side whole. I remember in the first speech that Nelson Mandela gave when released from prison. He said, "South Africa for all South Africans." My grandmother would have said, "Let's stick it to the white people, time for revenge."

In Nelson Mandela's autobiography, "Long Walk to Freedom,"

there is a story that is embedded in my imagination. Nelson Mandela as a young man is walking home, and on his way he sees a white woman digging through a garbage dump looking for something to eat. He is so moved by the sight he immediately takes the money in his pocket and hands it to her. When he goes home he reflects on this incident. He realizes that he sees black women in that same predicament daily, yet he is never moved so strongly by the experience. Nelson Mandela realizes that by growing up in a racist society he has internalized the idea that when black people suffer it is just a fact of life, yet when white people suffer it is unbearable and it must be remedied immediately. Nelson Mandela has to fight the apartheid inside his emotions, inside his thinking and inside his soul before he is able to effectively fight the apartheid on the outside.

My grandmother, on the other hand, was liberated by the American Army. One day they showed up and told everybody that they are free now, even offered my grandparents a ride out of Germany. What my grandmother remembers most about her saviours was the neatness of their uniforms, how well fed they were, the fact that the soldiers would take time to shave every morning. "It is as if they weren't touched by the ugly reality of the war in any way, as if they were above it all," my grandmother told me once.

Shortly after the fall of Baghdad, President George Bush broadcast a taped message to the Iraqi people telling them that soon they will be free. Since electricity was knocked out in most Iraqi cities, I wonder how

34

many Iraqis got to see and hear the message. I wonder what sort of freedom President George Bush has in mind for the Iraqi people; the sort of freedom that Nelson Mandela was able to achieve or the sort of freedom my grandmother got? The burning oil wells sure looked happy to be liberated. As the shooting flames danced in the wind they looked like they were greeting the American soldiers. No words can describe my feeling of despair and helplessness. I have been to countless anti-war rallies. I have heard the speeches and shouted the slogans. I feel so defeated. I feel humiliated as a human being. I feel that my efforts have been in vain. Will I be able to free my heart from this feeling of defeat? . . . That is another liberation story.

My goal in life is not be famous. I don't want to be mentioned in any history books. I don't want to be a hero. I just want to be able to smile even when I am 90 years old and give my grandchildren passionate hugs, assuming I live that long. I don't judge my grandmother for her behavior, I am just glad she wasn't the leader of the ANC.

My Small Thin Multi-National Wedding

Some people like to collect stamps; in my family we collect passports. Would you like to see my impressive collection of passports? Not one of them is forged and each one has a picture of me wearing my signature smile, hey, hey!

My mother was beaten black and blue when her dad found out that she was dating my 'Dad'. "You are forbidden from seeing that Mohamadan (Czech speak for Muslim) ever again," were my grandfathers instructions. So my mom married the Mohamadan and followed him around the world, first to Algeria and then to Kuwait. How she managed to fall in love with a person she had no common language with is beyond me. My mom tells me that I get my stubbornness from my dad. Yeah, right!

My grandmother was beaten black and blue when she became pregnant with my mom. She was in a Nazi work camp and my grandfather worked in the kitchen. He used to sneak food to the starving Russian slave workers in the factory. So, if the shortest road to a man's heart is through his stomach, then the shortest road to a woman's heart is what? Well, you can guess what happened next, they fell in love and she became pregnant. The Nazi soldiers wanted to know the name of the father so that he would be executed. When my grandmother wouldn't tell them, they decided that they would let her have the baby and execute her after the birth. Luckily, Germany lost the war on the day my mom was born. My grandparents got married and lived in the Czech Republic. Hurray!

I wasn't beaten black and blue when I met my husband, though it would have made this story more interesting. Instead, I got a long speech from my Mom about how I should marry a young man from one of the nice (Mom-speak for wealthy) Iraqi families that we know in Vancouver. I reminded my Mom of the nice fiancée she left back in the Czech republic for an Iraqi political refugee that she met one day at a lakeside resort. "That was completely different," my Mom insists. Ehm! Ehm!

My husband was referred to as "Hatha ele beihki zei el yahood," (Arabic for the one that speaks like the Jews), by a participant at a charity for Palestine. See, I couldn't just marry the average Palestinian man: a refugee or one living in the occupied territories, no, no, no, no, no! That would be too average, too ordinary, too boring for a Palestinian, that is. I had to marry a Palestinian who grew up inside Israel, held an Israeli passport, and spoke Hebrew fluently.

I sometimes fantasize about traveling with all my passports. When the customs officer at the airport asks me for my passport, I spread them all in front of him and then say, "Pick one." I remember the good old days, when traveling with the Iraqi passport was preferable to traveling with the Czech passport. Iraq was America's ally and communism was the world's greatest evil. That was then, this is now. Today I travel mostly with my Canadian passport.

So, the Palestinian Who Speaks Like the Jews married the Czech/Iraqi concoction in April of 1991. On our wedding day we were all in pain over the recent bombing of Iraq during the first American-led war. We didn't know if our relatives in Iraq were alive or dead. Although I found the invasion of Kuwait to be an outrageous act, it was still hard to see my homeland being bombed. I oscillated between the happiness of a young woman in love and the depression over seeing the most powerful countries in the world bombing a third world nation.

I wanted to cancel the wedding and go to Iraq and get bombed with the rest of the people. I told my dad I wanted to die with the rest of the Iraqi people. My dad talked me out of it, he told me: "You must go on with your life and get married".

We had a small wedding, 12 people, only the closest friends and family. We celebrated quietly in one of the fanciest restaurants in Vancouver. The mood at my wedding was somber, but we all tried to make the best out of it.

With my husband, I ended up living in Glasgow, Scotland and Jerusalem, Israel, not the most logical places to live in for a Palestinian and an Iraqi, but love is blind. Finally we moved back to Vancouver. Where we live happily ever after.

When my first daughter was born, I told my mom that when she grows up it would be unacceptable if she brought home a nice average

Canadian boy. No, no, no, no, no! My poor daughter has to find some nationality not encountered by my family yet and do a masochistic trip around the world with him. I don't know, maybe a Buddhist monk, or a tribal chief from Zimbabwe; the nice Canadian man would be totally unacceptable, we have family traditions to uphold. The hunt for fresh passports must continue.

Discovery in Foreign Lands

My friend told me that he is planning to go on a year long trip all over Europe in order to "find himself." I told him; what if you find yourself and discover that you don't like what you find? You will have to spend many more years wandering around aimlessly until you lose yourself again. I didn't tell him that I was speaking from personal experience.

I remember vividly the first time I walked into The University of British Columbia's (UBC) bookstore for the first time. I had recently moved to Canada to continue my undergraduate studies after ninteen years. So many books, so much variety! I wandered around for hours, picking up books and reading a little from each one. I didn't buy anything on that day because there was so much I wanted to buy. Later on I discovered the main library. It's not that I haven't been to a bookstore before, I have been to many, it was the variety of the books that struck me, the fact that I could read about anything I liked, left wing, right wing, any religion, any philosophy and any perspective. I wanted to absorb it all. I spent my first year at UBC in the library, not doing my computer science home work that I would do in hurry in the computer laboratory, but reading books about history, philosophy, politics, religion, literature, . ., etc. And then I decided I would read about the Middle East. I thought I understood the Middle East very well, since we studied our history and Islam at school for 12 years. I was curious about how it was described in English by English speakers; "let's see what these foreigners say about us", I told myself as started my research.

As a kid growing up in Kuwait, I was taught in school that we, the Arabs, are the best nation that God has created on planet Earth. For we have spread our fair religion all over the world out of the goodness of our hearts. "Futuhaat," they were called in our text books, liberations. We liberated the Persians, Turks and many other nations, we salvaged them from darkness. And who can revile our strong family values, beautiful language and our plain goodness? I used lay in bed at night feeling sorry for all the people that were born non-Arabs. How unlucky for them!

Back at the main library at University of British Columbia I found a publication that held an in-depth report of current events in the Middle East. I opened the publication randomly somewhere in the middle; the article was talking about terrorist attacks at Kuwait University that blew up the cafeteria building in the Kuwait University Campus. The fact that the building was destroyed was no surprise to me, I was on the campus when the building fell, we all ran over and saw the rubble of the destroyed building. The fact that it was done deliberately was a shock to me. The respectable news reader that night told us that the building fell as a result of structural flaws and that construction materials were being stored on the roof which led the building to collapse. We all believed the respectable news reader person on TV; I didn't doubt his words, not even for one second that night. I was there in person and had no idea of what was going on around me, whereas people half way around the world were privy to the information about what happened that day. I have been lied to; what else have I been lied to about?

I started to read about the early history of Islam and realized that the Persians, among other nations we colonized, and were not very appreciative of our liberation. They didn't like being enslaved, forced to learn Arabic, converted to Islam by intimidation and being treated like inferior human beings. In Kuwait Persians were called "Ajam;" it turns out that this word originally meant "the dumb animals that can't speak properly." You see, the Persians tried to adopt Arabic but would speak it with an accent, so the Arabs called them dumb animals. Later on, Persian was adopted as the official language in Iran, instead of Arabic. Oh! Those Persians are so ungrateful for their liberation! Shame on them!

Ignorance is bliss. How I long for those days when we were the good guys and the bad guys were them. And you could feel good to be part of the "we" and not the "them.". That first year in UBC, I would lay awake at night feeling sorry for myself wishing I wasn't born "us." I didn't want to become "them", I just didn't want to be "us" anymore.

"I want to live a life of integrity," is what I wrote one day on a piece of paper and hung on a plastic tree. I was on vacation in Edinburgh, Scotland. While walking around the city, I noticed a big sign announcing a Yoko Ono exhibit. Since I had nothing better to do, I decided I would check it out. The exhibit was not very impressive; many pictures of Yoko and John. Several of the exhibits were titled "John and me." Ok! I get it; she was married to a super famous guy, but show us something about Yoko. There was one piece, that wasn't about John, "The Wish Tree". In one corner of the gallery, stood a white plastic tree with many branches. On a small corner table were placed long pieces of paper and pencils. The idea being, that each person would write a wish and hang it on a tree branch, the wish notes forming the tree leaves. I stood under the tree surrounded with everybody's wishes. One woman wants a man to notice her. A young man wants to pass his final exams; another wants to win a million dollars. What did I want? What did I wish for?

At age 27, I had it all. Good health, loving husband, healthy and beautiful daughter, rising career as a computer programmer, and decent looks. While no millionaire, I lived comfortably. While all my friends complained about how hard the dating game was, I came home everyday to a husband that I love and respect. While some women struggle with infertility or early pregnancy, I had my daughter exactly at the time that I had planned. So why is it that just a few weeks earlier, I told my husband that I needed a vacation. I needed a vacation from everything; I told him: "I need a vacation from my job, vacation from being a mother, vacation from being a wife." I don't know why I chose to go to Scotland for this mission, I just felt drawn there. As I read the wishes of other people, I realized that I had lots of what other people wished for. Yet here I was standing under a fake tree feeling broken. "What is wrong with me?", I thought to myself, "Why can't I enjoy what I have?" As I wrote my wish, tears welled inside me, I dashed out of the gallery before anybody could

44

see me.

When I arrived in Edinburgh, I took off my watch and never put it on for the duration of the vacation. In the morning I would wake up, have breakfast and dash out, purposely leaving my map of the city in my room. I would wander around in the streets of Edinburgh at random, not knowing where I was or where I was going to. When it rained, I would keep walking until I found a coffee shop. I didn't want to carry an umbrella, so I would sometimes get wet and then dry out while walking again. This was the first time that I enjoyed getting lost in a foreign city; usually I feel panic when I am lost. Wandering around not knowing where I was, in a city where nobody knew me. Nobody looked at me, nobody talked to me, I spent my days in delicious silence. Nobody wanted anything from me. I had nothing to explain or justify. I was a nobody. I was lost. I didn't have to rush home to prepare dinner. When I got tired, I would just get a taxi and give my address.

There is one advantage to spending a couple of weeks living inside your head: you start noticing all the garbage that is going on in there.

During this aimless wandering in Edinburgh, I came across a proper English tea house. Nothing like embracing the traditions of your former colonizer. I ordered sandwiches and tea, the sandwiches were rather bland but the tea was delicious. Across from me sat two elderly women in their 80s, enjoying their afternoon tea. Both were dressed up, flower print dresses, proper hats, delicate purses, grey hair. They were chatting about something trivial and gossiping about somebody. One of them was wearing tons of make up, hot red lipstick and blue eye shadow. The conversation inside my head went something like this.

. . .

Look how silly she looks.

I wish they would stop yapping.

Does she realize how silly she looks with that red lipstick.

Who the hell does she think she is, the Queen?

Listen to how stupid their conversation is?

Look at that silly hat!

. . .

Stop!

Stop!

Stop!

. . .

What is wrong with me?

Why do I even care about her lipstick?

Why do I notice such stupid things?

Why don't I just enjoy the meal in front of me and forget the other stuff?

. . .

That was the day I realized that I have to lose myself, being lost in a foreign city for few weeks was not enough. I need to get lost completely. I rarely wear my watch these days. I keep hoping that one day I will lose track of time.

I Am Losing It

Losing Reason

I have read many articles on alternative media websites. Frequently, I see words like "anti-war", "anti-poverty" and "anti-corporate control". Article after article is condemning the American war machine and the corrupt capitalist system. Something feels missing. There is a lack of agenda in the whole thing. Rarely do I read "and here is what we are going to do about it." "Here are the steps we will take to improve on it." I can't just define myself as being anti-this or anti-that, I have to be pro something. A better alternative, a vision that I can rally behind and support.

I lived in Israel for 4 years starting in 1996. Living there was difficult for me but it taught me, many valuable lessons. I met with many crazy fanatics on both sides of the conflict who believe God is on their side and anybody who doesn't agree with them deserves to die. On the other hand, I met with lots of so-called intellectuals, so-called moderate people. Many of them are intelligent, well educated, and each one had his or her own philosophy and complex analysis of the situation. People that claim they want peace and that they are against the use of violence. What struck me most is the relative inaction of this group. I would go to a meeting and people would go on and on about the brutality of the Israeli army, the historical context of the conflict, the unfairness of the whole situation, ... Very rarely did I hear somebody say, "and here is what I suggest we do about it."

I don't blame the Israeli army, they are doing their job (killing people). I don't blame Hamas, in their minds they are doing what God wants them to do. How can you say "No" to God? I blame myself, my husband and all the millions of so-called intellectuals, so-called reasonable people who watch. We shake our heads, talk about how bad things are, and then do nothing. Today for a Palestinian, on one hand there is the Palestinian authority that is completely corrupt and lacks all credibility, on the other hand there are fanatics who use mental as well as physical terrorism to further their goals, but at least are doing something to combat the Israeli occupation. It is us, the so-called left wing, reasonable people who failed to create or verbalize a third alternative, a third vision. I went to a political meeting in Nazareth where all these very smart people started discussing if Trotsky was right or not. I wanted to shout at them, "People are starving to death in the Gaza strip, what are you talking about?" I sat politely in the meeting and said nothing.

Two weeks after my second daughter was born in Jerusalem, I left her with my mom and decided to go for a little walk. I ended up walking around the Hebrew University to a part that looks over Essawiya (a Palestinian village). There was a gathering of Israeli army and police. They were about to demolish a house inside the village. Women were shouting, children were crying. A young Palestinian man was standing on the side watching. He was just standing there with his arms crossed in front of him. Then, for no reason, an Israeli soldier shot him in the chest. No reason at all. Later I found out that this young man wasn't even one of the inhabitants of the demolished house, he wasn't even related to the family. On the news it was reported that he was throwing rocks.

Do you know what I did?
Nothing.

I just stood there watching, it is not a pretty sight seeing somebody shot in the chest. I kept thinking, if I do something crazy I might get shot too. I am a mother, I don't want my children to grow up orphans. I went back home, It was a nice day in my affluent Jewish neighborhood, "French Hill." People were walking around, children were playing. When I told my husband about what happened, he told me "Elen, be reasonable." My neighbor and close friend told me to be reasonable. Don't be crazy, you did the right thing. I heard that about 100 times. If I did the right thing, then how come I feel so rotten about it. Yes, I can blame the army, the Palestinian authority, Hitler, the Ottoman Empire, and a whole bunch of other parties. I blame myself. I failed that man, I watched him get killed and I did nothing. I am a coward. A very intelligent, well educated, very reasonable coward.

When I came back to Vancouver, Canada, I simply wanted to forget about the Middle East. I avoided listening to the news, didn't want to meet anybody from there, neither Israeli nor Arab. When my husband wanted to hang some Palestinian embroidery on the wall I told him that looking at it is simply too painful; it reminded me of Jerusalem. I insisted that he take it down. I wanted to forget about it all and put it behind me. I felt very bitter and upset. Upset at myself for wasting 4 years out of my life. I was talking to a friend of mine who happens to be a therapist and she told me that I sound like a traumatized person. I realized that she was right; I have witnessed great injustice and inhumanity. The memories were haunting me. I felt like such a coward. Here I was in the middle of it all, witnessing the occupation first hand, and what did I do about it? Did I raise a voice? Did I scream, "This is wrong?" No, I was busy adjusting to it, looking the other way, pretending it was going to be ok.

Most of the Israelis I met were just regular people, just like me. The families I socialized with were not different from my own family. On the other hand, I was shocked by the horrible atrocities and inhumanity that I saw in the West Bank. Who are these monsters? Why doesn't anybody care? Am I any different? Am I capable of committing such acts? Would I be able to shoot somebody? I asked myself these questions a thousand times. It was driving me crazy. I think the problem was rooted in my perception of the world. I remember watching Czech and Russian movies about WWII, the Nazis were depicted as pure evil. They had evil smiles, faces carved from stone, showed absolutely no empathy, were psychopaths. In most movies the super evil guy looks super evil. That is a big lie. The pure psychopaths do exist, but they are very rare. Average people just like me commit the real evil, not psychopaths, but then, not complete saints either. I realized that the problem is not Hitler, Sharon or Saddam Hussein. It is all the millions of people who follow blindly like sheep, or if they question, do so quietly. We are enabling and empowering these mad men to get away with it, because we lack conviction in the alternative. I also realized that the reason I was feeling

54

rotten about my whole experience in Israel, was not because of anything that Israel Defense Forces did, rather it was my feeling of guilt about how I reacted to it. My lack of action and conviction is why I felt so much pain. The only way to deal with all these emotions was to do something positive and constructive with it.

I have been active with a local grassroots organization. I avoid people who whine and complain, yet do nothing. I am not afraid of Ariel Sharon or Osama bin Laden, at least their agenda is clear and they do as they say; I am afraid of all people who shake their heads and do nothing. We need to verbalize and create an alternative viable vision; if our leadership won't do it for us, then people like you and me need to do it ourselves.

I am still Elen Ghulam, but I am no longer reasonable.

Losing a Friend

My friend is upset with me. Why do you criticize Israel? My friend asks. Israel is the only democracy in the Middle East. Israel has the right to exist. Israel has the right to defend itself. Don't you know about the holocaust? Why don't you criticize Arab regimes? Why don't you criticize Saddam Hussein? Why don't you criticize Osama Bin Laden? You are defending and excusing terrorism. Arabs are using Israel as a scapegoat for their own failings.

My dear friend, you are telling *me* that Arab society is brutal; you see, I don't *think* that Arab society can be brutal, I *know* it. I have lived in the Middle East for 22 years and I have seen that brutality first hand. You are telling me that Arab regimes are corrupt, I know that very well my dear friend, for I have lived in Saddam Hussein's shadow for many years and I still get nightmares about it today. You are telling me that many Arabs blame Israel and the U.S. for their own failings. I haven't read that in some article, I have personally heard the pathetic "U.S. does this to us, and Israel does that to us," a million times. When you read the translated transcript of something that Osama Bin Laden said and it scares you, I understand what he is saying in his own words, I understand the historical references he is drawing on and when he quotes the Qur'an I know which sura he is referring to. Believe me his message is much more terrifying in Arabic than the translated English you read. The most terrifying of all is that I can feel some of his anger inside me. So what do

57

we do with all this knowledge, what do we do with all these facts? We have two choices, we can use them to demonize all Arabs all around the world and call for complete annihilation, or we can decide to take constructive action and attempt to reach people's hearts, minds and souls. Ask yourself what is it that I am trying to achieve? Kill, destroy and maim. Well, congratulations, the world situation is so ripe for that. Have a blast. Because if you believe it is justified to deny basic human rights to millions of people because of the fact that they are imperfect, the problem is not your intellect. I can see you are a very intelligent person and you know your history inside out. The problem is not in your emotions; I can see from the passion you display about this issue that part of you is alive and well. The problem is inside your soul. Get spiritual guidance, and I can't help you with that.

"If only there were evil people somewhere insidiously
committing evil deeds and it were necessary only to
separate them from the rest of us and destroy them.
But the line dividing good and evil cuts through the
heart of every human being. And who is willing to
destroy a piece of his own heart?"- Aleksandr Solzhenitsyn

Losing My Religion

My husband told me a funny story that happened to his friend the hydrologist; let's call him Jim (not his real name). Jim and another person were doing research on a certain river in British Columbia. The river runs parallel to a highway. They used a small boat to sail through the river, until they reached a section that contained large boulders lying on the riverbed, right underneath the water's surface. The two men decided to dock the boat and step from one boulder to the next, to take their measurements and collect samples. They were using the boulders as stepping stones, and moved briskly along the river. While they were working away, Jim lifted his head up to see a group of people gathering around. Each person had parked his car to the side of the highway and was staring in the direction of the two working men. From a distance, it looked like Jim was walking on water. The crowd thought they were witnessing a miracle. The fact that Jim is a slender bearded man probably contributed to the confusion with a certain Biblical figure.

"I am a Christian," I declared in first grade. I was attending Amal, a Catholic-run private school in Kuwait where half the students were Christian and the other half Muslim. Amal means hope in Arabic. The Muslim kids had to attend a weekly class on Islam as mandated by the state curriculum. We Christian kids got to play outside. Being a Christian was good: one less class, less homework and less studying. Until my father had to ruin it for me by telling the teachers and nuns running the school that I am a Muslim. I could no longer join the Christian kids playing in the courtyard during Islam classes. I had to stay in class and learn to recite the Qur'an. "Bismillah al rahman al raheem," the teacher would say, and we would repeat after her as loud as we could, "Al hamdo lilah rab al alemeen." In the name of God most gracious most merciful, Thank God the ruler of all the worlds. I understand what these verses mean today; in grade one I just repeated them over and over again. Nobody explained what it meant, just that we had to know it.

"I am shi'a," I declared in grade 5. I had transferred from the private catholic school to state-run public school where the majority of students were Muslim. On my first day there, I was asked about 10 times if I was sunni or shi'a. I had never heard those words before, I didn't know what they meant. At Amal we only spoke about Christians and Muslims; this was a new classification system that I was not aware of. At home I asked dad the question. My dad told me that our ancestors were shi'a, so shi'a I was. At school when asked the question, I had a clear and concise answer. People seemed happy with my answer and would nod knowingly. The "I don't know" of the first day at school seemed to confuse and irritate people. Now that they could fit me into a well-defined category, everything was simpler. I never understood the difference between Sunnis and Shi'as, the two major sects of Islam, until I became a university student and decided to do some reading on the subject.

"Islam is the only true religion," my primary school teacher told us one day. It is obvious that Islam is the only true religion; anybody who thinks about it would realize that fact. She didn't explain why Islam is the only true religion; it just is. Questioning the teacher was not allowed. Even as a child I had my doubts. There was a faint voice in the back of my mind that said, "It is not obvious to me." Would I still believe in Islam if I was born and raised in Holland or China? I would dismiss those thoughts and try not to think about it too much. Everybody around me seemed to concur with my teacher's proclamations, grownups and children alike. In Kuwait doubting the existence of God or Islam is punishable by law; furthermore it would make me an outcast within my own society. I would pray but feel nothing except the physical movement of the prayer. I would fast Ramadan and feel nothing except the challenge of conquering my hunger and thirst. I had faint doubts about my religion in the back of my mind, but was too afraid to acknowledge them. "Maybe there is something wrong with me," I thought. I wanted to believe, I wanted to have faith.

In 1996 I moved to live in Jerusalem, Israel because of my husband's work. I thought that living in the holy lands would help quell those doubts; I was expecting to have some sort of a spiritual experience.

"I am Jewish," an acquaintance of mine in Jerusalem told me one day. "And that means that I have a right to this land. It is the holy covenant between God and Abraham that we, the Jewish people, were promised this land." "But what about the Palestinians?" I ask him. "They don't matter, they can stay or leave, but this land is ours because it says so in the Old Testament." In my mind I was thinking, "But use your head, use your heart; does it seem right?". I don't say anything, he doesn't seem very perceptive anyway. He has faith.

In Jerusalem, you can tell a person's religion within the first second you lay eyes on him or her. Muslim women wear a small Qur'an hanging on a golden chain, Christian women a cross and Jewish women a Star of David. Everybody is wearing their religion around their necks, but is any of it getting inside?

One day there was an explosion in a coffee shop in Tel Aviv. Among the dead, a mother of a newborn baby girl. The baby was injured but survived. Somehow the story of this young mother touched a chord with me. I remember the stressful and overwhelming first year when my daughter was born. I would go for a walk while pushing a stroller in front of me. When my daughter would go to sleep I would go to one of the local coffee shops and have a cup of coffee; sometimes I would have a dessert with that. It was a prized treat that I gave myself. Somehow I could imagine this young woman walking around with a stroller, all tired from too many sleepless nights, her daughter finally goes to sleep and she decides to go relax a bit, have a cup of coffee and enjoy a stress-free 15 minutes. Then boom! She dies. Her crime being that she was enjoying a cup of coffee on beautiful, sunny day in Tel Aviv. A few days later a religious and bearded man from Hamas gives a speech telling people not to feel sorry for this woman. "Her death was necessary; we must be steadfast in our fight against the Israeli occupation. Rip any sympathy for this woman or her baby out of your heart, leave no room for such sympathy." He repeats those statements several times. I feel a piercing pain going through my heart, this man is asking me to give up on my humanity in the name of God and in the name of religion. If religion is not humanizing us and making us more compassionate, then what good is it? I can be a hate-filled person without any religion at all.

One day I decided that I would visit the Holocaust museum in Jerusalem (Yad Vashem). My husband said, "Don't go, you will be depressed for a week and I will have to deal with you." I insist that I should go to a holocaust museum at least once, I think I am ready to face it. Off I went, with trepidation. The museum is very silent, there is this stillness hanging in the air. A section displays works of art by children that lived in concentration camps. Handmade toys, children's drawings, children's clothing is on display. Under such difficult conditions kids still managed to find joy and play. As I walked out of the museum I felt crushed. It was a beautiful, sunny day in Jerusalem. I looked down from the mountain where the museum is situated; I could see cars driving below. A flock of birds was flying below in the valley. Such beauty surrounding me, yet so much ugliness in the world. I kept asking myself, "Oh God , what does it all mean? What does it all mean?" I do believe that what happened next was divine intervention; I think that higher powers decided to answer me. A Jewish ultra-orthodox man approached me, white beard, black suit and a black hat. He had a pleasant smiley face. He looked like Santa Clause in a black suit. I think he could see the distress that I was feeling. He starts chatting to me and I was happy to talk to somebody. He says that atrocities like the Holocaust are difficult for us human beings to comprehend, but that we must not lose faith in God. There is a reason for everything, even the holocaust. We must not question the wisdom of God. I listen attentively to every word. I want to believe in what he is saying. Listening to his calm voice is pleasant. He asks me about myself, my family situation and my work. Then he tells me that he is married with seven children. "Me and my wife have a very special relationship, we are close like this," he gestures by placing two fingers parallel to each other. Then he proceeds to say that even though he loves his wife very much and is dedicated to her, he enjoys having extra-marital affairs. He asks me if I would be interested in having such an affair with him. I can't believe my ears. I think to myself, "I must have heard that wrong." I ask him to repeat what he said and again he tells me that he would like to have an affair with me. "We can meet once a week at your place while your husband is at work," he adds. I get up abruptly and say that I have to go home because I am late. I quickly get into the car and drive away. I feel shock but also I feel anger. "Who the hell does he think he is? Why did I even waste time talking to him? Is it my fault for being friendly with him initially?" I think to myself as I drive. While I am rebuking myself, I start laughing, I laugh so hard tears stream down my cheeks. I have to park my car to the side because I am laughing so hard. It suddenly dawns on me that a religious man can't go to the bar to pick up chicks, he would look out of place there. What better place to pick up a women than the holocaust museum? Tourists in distress after seeing images documenting one of the worst atrocities in human history. Mr. Religious can offer comfort, a few words of wisdom and score. Perfect! I bet that trick worked often for him before. Hilarious!

At home, I start dinner. My husband comes home early and gives me a hug. How was your day? He asks me. "Fine," I reply. He looks a bit surprised. He was expecting me to be depressed, instead I have a smile on my face. That night I go to bed with a very light feeling, like a heavy weight has been lifted off my shoulders. I realize that I don't believe in religion any more, not Islam nor Judaism nor any other religion. From now on, no bearded man holding a religious book will tell me how to live my life. From now on, I will rely on my gut feeling to know the truth. The answer to my question "What does it all mean?" is that it means nothing. It means what I want it to mean. It can mean that life is beautiful or it can mean that life is ugly. It can mean that human beings are doomed and beyond saving, or it can mean that children always offer us hope for the future. What do you want it to mean, Elen?

"I am not Muslim, not Christian, not Jewish." This I declare today, knowing full well what each word means. Not Sunni, not Shi'a or any other category. I believe that all religions should come with an expiration date. "Valid for consumption until"….. Beyond this date this religion will turn into poison if consumed. Since everybody is creating God in his own image anyway, I think that from now on I will create something that I like.

When asked by friends why I no longer pray or fast, I reply that living in the Holy Land has cured me of religion. It always shocks people and shuts them up. After that, people tend to change the subject and talk about something else. I no longer get the speech on how as a good Muslim I should cover my head with a scarf.

A Catholic friend decides to visit me in Jerusalem. I decide that I will take her to all the religious sites relevant to Christianity. I do research on the Internet and I buy tourist guides. We visit the church of the Holy Sepulcher, the Garden of the Tomb in Jerusalem. We visit the Church of The Nativity in Bethlehem. And last, Tiberius lake. We visit a little chapel on the northeast part of the lake. Monks in dark robes are walking around. Pious worshipers look profoundly moved. Apparently this is the place where Jesus performed the miracle of walking on water. I walk towards the edge of the lake and look into the horizon. Fog was starting to lift in the early morning while white birds fly around in circles. It feels incredibly peaceful with the soft chanting in the background. There is magic in the air. I exhale deeply and then I look down. There are huge boulders, lurking right underneath the surface of the water. Many of them! Stretching well into the lake . . . . "I don't think that having a laughing fit in this place would be appropriate," I think to myself as I rush to the car.

Losing My Mother in-law

My husband has the weirdest looking nose in the world. It is round the way baby potatoes are and slightly raised up, the ridge of his nose is fairly short. His nose is not his only unique characteristic. He is mild mannered, patient, good-natured, and very compassionate. He gives money to every single panhandler we encounter on the streets of Vancouver. To the point where some panhandlers know us already and smile at us from a distance. He can't say no to anybody who asks for help. I mean, he has put up with me for 15 years, for Pete's sake. My parents believe that he deserves a medal for that. I am really not that bad, plus I think that my husband enjoys the challenge of taming a wild woman. One day he will figure out a way.

I used to think that my husband was pretty unique until I met his mother. It was a bit freaky meeting her at first. I felt I was talking with a shorter version of my husband only he was wearing a dress and a head scarf . . . I mean she. He looks like his mom, not just the nose but the same eyebrows, the same eyes, the same thick short fingers.

I met Alia (my mother in law) for the first time after two years of marriage. We decided to visit my husband's home town of Mash-had, which is a small Palestinian town out side of Nazareth in the Galilee, north of Israel. To say I was nervous about meeting my in-laws for the first time would be a major understatement. We were picked up at the airport by a brother and a cousin. As we drove into Mash-had, Alia was standing in the doorway of their house waiting to greet her son, apparently she had been standing there for an hour. My husband jumped out of the car to greet her. There in the doorway she hugged her son, only because of the height difference she was hugging his waist. They embraced for about 10 minutes. It was very sweet.

"I am not from Mash-had", was one of the first things she told me." I am from Kufer Kana." Kufer is colloquial Palestinian Arabic for "village" and Kana is the biblical Kana where Jesus performed the miracle of turning water to wine. She told me how difficult it was for her to move to Mash-had at first, how things here are different and the people are different too. "It is hard being a foreigner all my life, but I got used to it," she told me. Yeah! I could relate to her feelings, I have been a foreigner all my life as well. Turns out that Kufer Kana is a 15 minute walk from Mash-had. Since Mash-had in on a hill top you could see Kufer Kana by standing on the top of the house roof. Essentially she can wave to her sister in Kufer Kana from her house roof every morning. The two villages didn't seem that different to my tourist eyes, but to her they were worlds apart.

Alia raised nine children, 5 girls and 4 boys. In 1948 when Israel confiscated lands from Palestinians, the land left wasn't enough to support the family. My father in-law had to look for work in far away cities like Haifa, Tiberius and even Tel-Aviv. He would be gone sometimes for weeks. Alia would be left alone to raise the kids and farm

68

the remaining land. In the early days she had to walk an hour every morning to get a daily military permit to work in her own land, then walk home, and get the kids ready for school before she started farming work. At night all the kids would sit around a kerosene lamp doing their homework. My husband remembers that it would get so noisy sometimes that he couldn't hear himself talk. He also remembers that his mother rarely ever raised her voice at any of her kids. There was no rest for this woman, even on days she gave birth, she had to get up, get dinner ready and work the land the next day with a new born baby in hand. In a town where it is common for boys as young as twelve to join the work force, Alia pushed all her children to finish their education. Eight out of nine finished high school and most of them went on to get higher education. Alia has the highest percentage of educated offspring in all of Mash-had, something that has been a great point of pride for her. The fact that she herself was illiterate and didn't receive any schooling makes me admire her that much more.

"You married the best of my children", she told me once while we were alone in the kitchen. She told me that my husband as a boy was the most mild mannered of the children and that he caused the least amount of trouble. He also would help her with the house work from a very young age. I wish I had told her that he is the one most like her. Alia spoke in very low voice, it was more like a whisper. You had to strain in order to hear her talk. She had a very unique laugh. She would start by making this sound "hmmmmmmm," and then laugh with her whole body, like little children do. One day she asked me to show her the gold that my husband gave me upon our marriage. It is customary in Arabic culture for the groom to buy piles of gold for the bride. When I showed her my wedding ring, "That is it!" she exclaimed. "I wouldn't have agreed to marry him just for that." I tried to explain to her that we didn't have much money when we got married and couldn't afford to waste much on jewelry. A few days later she presented me with jewelry she bought for me. "Every bride should have new jewelry. Here, this is for you."

Alia had many unique characteristics. Besides the nose, she never gossiped about other people, a very unique feature for an Arab women. I never heard her say anything negative about anybody. When she couldn't think of anything positive to say she would say nothing. She was kind and generous to everybody, including young children. When I asked about how difficult it must have been to raise 9 children, she told me that if it was up to her she would have had 9 more.

Wow!

Alia passed away on Dec 19th , 2003. None of my children inherited the unique nose, but hopefully they will inherit some of her other unique characteristics. I will always remember her standing in the doorway of her house waiting longingly for her son.

Unlosing My Gender

I sometimes think that I am a transvestite trapped in a woman's body. Right now I am a woman, plain, simple, boring. Considering how interesting every other aspect of my life is, wouldn't it be more fun to be a man that wants to be a woman? Plus transvestites get to wear those super-feminine clothes and mile-long eyelashes that no average woman would dare to put on. Oh! Those high heels and long nails. Even more interesting would be to be a woman that wishes she could be a man that wishes to be a woman. Confused yet?

On other occasions I think, I wish I was a lesbian. I wouldn't have any guy problems. Plus, I could get a wife, now that same sex marriage is legal in British Colombia. I used to work with this guy, Ken. Everyday he had this yummy lunch packed for him by his wife. Hey! I would like to have a wife like that as well. Somebody that packs lunches for me, makes dinners, takes care of the kids and cleans the house. Hey Ken! Does your wife have a sister? I used to wish for a person like that in my life for years, and finally I was able to hire a wife. When my third child was born, I hired a nanny to stay home with the kids. For years my husband rejected the idea of hiring somebody to do house work. It goes against his principles; he thinks that if you hire somebody to clean your house then you are somehow taking advantage of them. I used to rush from work to go pickup the kids from day care and school, rush home to cook a dinner in 30 minutes or less, while my kids were whining and hitting

71

each other. Then I would have to give them a bath, help them do homework, do the laundry, clean the house, prepare for the next day. I would go to bed completely pooped. When my third child was born, I put my foot down: "I need help." So I hired a nanny to stay home with the two youngest. What a difference that made to the quality of my life! Now I come home, the house is clean, the kids are bathed and fed and the laundry is folded. I just cruise in and take over and the nanny goes home to her own family. Wow! what a difference. I feel like I hired a wife . . . minus the sex. I have to admit that I am in love with the nanny, she is a godsend. I will really miss her when we have to let her go, when all the kids are old enough to go to school. I think hiring a wife is better that marrying a wife; wives are not what they used to be in the olden days and the hired wife doesn't nag at you. So maybe it is a good thing I am not a lesbian.

I am just kidding; I have no desire to be either a transvestite or a lesbian. It's just that being a plain heterosexual woman is hard sometimes. Being a woman from the Middle East sucks. Being a woman in North America sucks, too, but in a different way.

As a teen going to high school in Kuwait, we had to learn home economics. This was taught to girls only, the boys didn't have to learn this subject in their schools. One year we were taught baby care. I strongly resented the implication that we would all become baby producers and I resented the implication that the young men didn't need to know any of this stuff. I made it my mission to make sure I learned absolutely nothing during home economics classes and commit small act of sabotage whenever possible. For child care, we were given a baby doll that had realistic life size and weight; we were supposed to use it to practice holding and bathing the baby.

While the teacher went outside for a little while, I detached the head of the baby doll and placed it on top of the door. When the teacher walked back in, the head fell on top of her head. The teacher was livid; she couldn't believe that a nice girl would commit an act of such cruelty. "You are going to be a failure as a mother and a wife," the teacher told me. She was near tears.

In sewing class, I made sure I learned nothing about sewing. We were supposed to make a skirt as part of the class project. I asked the girl setting next to me to do all the work. In return I helped her in math and physics. Why bother making a skirt when you can just buy it at the store? When our project was finished, our sewing teacher handed each of us our skirt with great pride. While getting home in the school bus, I waved my red skirt out the school bus window, much to the amazement of passers by. I finally released my skirt into the heavy traffic where it flew in the air like a balloon. That moment was the only enjoyment I got out of my sewing class.

I found it hard to embrace my role as woman; it is not that I wanted to be a man, it just that being a woman sucked. Can I have choice C please? Everywhere I looked, I saw depressed women. "My kids are driving me crazy," "My husband doesn't love me any more," "I am so bored with being at home all day long," . . . on and on the complaints go. What happens to the happy women? Do they all suddenly die when they get to 21 years of age? I looked around and couldn't find a single happy, middle-aged woman. Such is the lot of women in the Middle East. In Kuwait it is legal for a man to beat the crap out of his wife; the police won't get involved because it is his right. A women's sole purpose in life is to get married and produce babies. Women who fail in their mission are looked down on. Women who succeed in securing a husband and producing a baby become mildly depressed and bored house wives at best, and abused at worst. My only salvation was to get an education and be able to work. If I am financially independent I won't be at the mercy of whomever I marry.

Then I moved to Canada and started to work at a software company. I found that many of my male co-workers were obsessed with my physical features. You see I had something they didn't have, curves. One time I was talking to a guy who was staring straight at my bosom the whole time. So I bent my head over to one side so that my head was at the same level as my breasts and waved hello to him, "Hello! I am over here!." It is not that I didn't like having curves, it is just that I wanted to be treated like a person. A bit of dignity please. So I started wearing baggy clothes, no makeup, hair pulled back. I wasn't trying to be a man, I was only trying to become a Non-Gender-Specific-Entity (NGSE). I thought if I became unfeminine, people would be able to see me as a person. I would wear grey and black trousers, wide t-shirts, and try to look like the generic geek. Unfortunately, my eye sight is perfect so no eye glasses for me. Doh!

Years of happy non-gender-specific existence passed, until one day as I was working at a small startup company my boss told me that he likes hiring women, because women have a greater sense of intuition and women find creative ways to solve difficult problems. I think he was trying to tell me that I was doing a good job. It was the first time that I realized that I have something valuable to offer because I am a woman, not despite it. Sometimes you hear a kind word and it transforms you. Later on, my friend Justine took me to a flamenco dancing performance at Kino Café on Cambie street. The women dancers were wearing colorful colors, tons of makeup, big, bright earrings. They were shaking their hips and stomping their feet forcefully. It was captivating, enchanting and a bit vulgar. I was hooked. You mean a woman can be sexy and strong at the same time? Why didn't anybody tell me that before? A few weeks later I started going to flamenco dance classes. And a few months into the class I started wearing a bit of makeup and decided to put a bit of color into my wardrobe. For this year's performance, we are each supposed to make a colorful dress; most of the women know how to sew. I wish I paid more attention at the sewing class back in high school; I will have to find a seamstress to help me out. Hey! being a woman is so much fun, why would I want to be anything else? All this hard work and in the end all I had to do is learn to enjoy the things I already had.

Losing Racism

How many times have you heard somebody say, "I am not a racist but, . . . " Fill in the blank with some mildly racist comment. Examples would be, "Those people expect too much," or "They are simply too sensitive." Frequently I wish I could revise that statement to, "I am a racist and . . . . " At least it would be honest.

When I was about eight, I became best friends with a girl in my class. We sat next to each other in the classroom and spent many hours playing and chatting. At home I frequently talked about my friend. Several months later, I invited my friend for lunch at my house. We had a wonderful time, playing with dolls and watching TV. After my friend was picked up by her mom to go home, my mom asked me, "How come you never mentioned that your best friend is black?" I paused, I had no answer, I never noticed that my friend had darker skin than myself. Until my mother mentioned it, it never occurred to me that my friend was placed in a different category than myself. I simply never thought about it. At age eight I was completely oblivious to race. I can honestly say that at that point I was not a racist because I didn't notice people's race. I reacted to people solely based on their personality and behavior. I am not so innocent now. Something happened while growing up.

Don't get me wrong. On an intellectual level I fully believe that all people are equal and that everybody is equally entitled to all the good things in life. However, every once in while a small subtle incident happens and I have to question myself. For example, few years ago I was in San Francisco on a business trip. I was walking around the Down Town area. A group of 4 young black men were walking past me. They were chatting to each other and laughing about something. I immediately clutched hard onto my hand bag, as if I was afraid they would try to steal it. Later, when I went to my hotel room, I kept thinking, "Why did I do that? Would I have behaved the same way if they were white?" "Did they notice my behavior? Were they offended?" I know I would be offended if somebody reacted that way to my mere presence. While this is not the kind of racism practiced by the Ku Klux Klan or a Neo-Nazi groups, it is racist nevertheless. It is a more subtle kind of racism. It is subconscious; I don't do these things on purpose or with the intention to hurt somebody. It just seems to happen and afterwards I ask myself, "Why did I do that?" So I call it subconscious racism: it's when you behave just subtly differently in reaction to somebody's race.

In Nelson Mandela's autobiography, "Long Walk To Freedom," there is a story similar to mine. Nelson Mandela was traveling all over Africa attempting to raise money and support for the ANC. He was at the airport about to travel from one destination to another when the pilot and crew arrived. The pilot was black. Nelson Mandela was struck with a panic attack, he was afraid that the airplane would crash. Intellectually he understood that a black person could do any job as well as a white person, it's just that in South Africa he had never seen a black pilot before. Nelson Mandela forced himself to board the airplane despite his fear, and he arrived at his destination safely. I reached the conclusion that when you grow up in a racist society some of it seeps into your psyche no

78

matter how much you oppose it. Like pollution in the air, it does end up in your lungs.

Rian Malan is another South African struggling with his own racism. In his book, "My Traitor's Heart," he recounts many moving stories. One in particular about a white woman who one day finds a bleeding black man in her own backyard. She takes him to hospital, but the staff at the emergency department ignores the injured man simply because he is black. The woman yells at them and abuses them until they provide him with adequate treatment. The story travels all over town and from then on, whenever a black person is in need of medical care, they show up at her doorstep, she becomes the ambulance service for the black community despite the fact that she has no paramedic training. She spends many evenings driving bleeding people to the ER and yelling at the staff to get them to provide care.

It seems that you can't ignore racism, you have to face it head on. As long as it is part of our society it is poisoning all of us. As for me, I haven't owned a TV set for years. I believe that my TV set was a source of negative stereotypes planted in my head. I focus hard on treating each person as an individual.

"I am a racist, but I want to change."

Losing Credibility

I have a credibility problem. People don't believe the things that I tell them. There must be something about me that makes people not believe me. It all started at a young age.

I was a teen, maybe 13, and I was spending my summer holiday in the Czech Republic with my family, as we did almost every year. I was hanging out with Tomash, the next door neighbor kid. He tells me that when he grows up he will travel to the U.S. or anywhere in the West and become rich. I tell him that not everybody in the West is rich. I tell him about the homeless people I had seen on the streets of Paris. I tell him about how in the U.S. some people are so poor they have to eat out of a garbage dump. I tell him about the prostitutes I had seen standing in the streets of Madrid. He shakes his head, "I don't believe you, you are just saying these things" he tells me. I swear to him that these are things, I had seen with my own eyes, and that not everybody that lives in the U.S. is wealthy. "How come they never talk about these things on Voice of America?" he asks me. "You are making it up." It bothers me that Tomash won't believe me since we essentially grew up together. We spent many summers climbing on trees, playing hide and seek and sharing meals; you would think he would have learned to trust me by now. You would think he would rather believe me than a propaganda radio station. To this day, Tomash continues to live in the same town and the same neighborhood he grew up in. Some people prefer to live in a fantasy world.

Many years later, I was talking with a dear friend in Canada. Somehow we got on the subject of socialism. He tells me how socialism will solve all of the world's problems. I tell him about my personal experiences in the Czech republic. How everybody hated the socialist regime. He mentions how he visited the Czech republic himself few years earlier, how under the socialist regime streets were clean, there were no homeless people on the streets, no prostitutes on the streets, free health care and everybody he asked told him that they loved the socialists. I tell him that people told him that they loved the regime because of fear of imprisonment and that, although you didn't see prostitutes on the streets, prostitution did exist. I tell him how although the health care was free, each person was expected to pay a fortune in bribes to doctors and nurses if you ever expected decent care. I tell him how when my grandfather got sick we had to bribe everybody who came in contact with him to ensure that he would get decent care at the hospital. I tell him how you could bribe almost anybody in the Czech Republic. Yes! To a tourist spending just two weeks things looked just fine, even great. But to anybody who lived there a different picture would emerge. That is why I love the Russian movie, "Burnt by the Sun." It depicts a super happy, almost dream-like reality that is only interrupted for brief moments with little glimpses of awfulness. To me the socialist regime was exactly that. Everything was wonderful until you scratched the top layer. By the end of the movie your stomach is churning even though most of the movie is one happy scene after another. I also like the play on words: socialism was often described as the "rising sun" by the regime. Surely, if the majority of people were miserable under such a regime it is a good indicator that there was something wrong. My friend is shaking his head, he tells me that I have allowed my brain to be corrupted by the capitalist and imperial propaganda. I want to tell him that if socialism was so great, why not move to one of the socialist countries, but I don't, because I don't want to offend him. Socialism was great, nay, wonderful! . . . on paper and as long as you didn't live under it.

When you are an immigrant you invariably end up meeting other immigrants and you invariably will have the Nostalgia Discussion. The discussion where everybody goes on and on about how things were just perfect back home and how everything sucks in Canada. On one of such nostalgia talks I had, with my friend who is originally from Egypt. He starts with the standard nostalgia stuff: food tasted better back home, people are warmer and kinder back home, . . . etc. Then he graduates to the, "Canadian society is sick and depraved because of all the homosexuals," argument. I mention that probably there are just as many homosexuals in his home country of Egypt. My friend gets deeply offended and tells me that he has lived in Egypt of over 20 years and that in all that time he hasn't encountered a homosexual, not even once. My friend is certain that there are no homosexuals in Egypt, not even one. I tell him how homosexuality exists in every culture, throughout human history. I try to argue that the only reason you never see homosexuals in the Middle East is because no homosexual would dare be open about it for fear of persecution. I tell him about all the famous Arab people in our history who were probably gay. My friend shakes his head. He tells me that there is no way there are any homosexuals in the Middle East and certainly not in Egypt because of our superior religion of Islam. Islam protects us from the depravity that exists in Canada. He tells me that I have allowed my brain to be corrupted by western Christian media which is bent on discrediting Islam. I wanted to tell him that we Muslims do such a good job of discrediting ourselves with our own idiocy, others don't have to do it for us, but I don't. I have already offended his national pride by suggesting that some of his country men might be gay. Plus we all just enjoyed the delicious fish dish he made for dinner, so it would be rude to insult him any further after eating his food.

I must have the most corrupt brain in the world. Capitalist and imperial propaganda, followed by the western Christian corruption. I wonder if there are any further corruptions I could possibly add to that. Why stop now? A corrupt brain is a terrible thing to waste.

When I traveled to Palestine with my husband, I met his uncle for the very first time. The uncle welcomes me with open arms. Hello, hello, hello he says. I hear you are Iraqi, I love Iraqis, I love Saddam Hussein, welcome to my house. I tell him that I hate Saddam Hussein, that Saddam is a terrible tyrant who has caused harm to his own people. Uncle says, "that is no good, that is no good at all." He then looks at my husband and tells him that he doesn't like me anymore. My husband responds by telling his uncle, "Yeah! but she is religious and fasts Ramadan." I was religious at the time, it was before I renounced organized religions. The uncle responds by saying "your wife is half good then."

I was surprised by how positively many Palestinians thought of Saddam Hussein. Many bought the idea that he is some big Arab hero who wants to liberate Palestine. I spend so much time telling people about the horrible crimes that Saddam committed against his own people, the fact that he used chemical weapons on the Kurds. I would argue that any leader who treats his own country so badly can't possibly be good to any other nation, that Saddam's support for Palestinians is nothing but empty slogans and efforts to boost his image. Most people would shake their heads and refuse to believe me, you would think they would believe these words considering the fact that they were coming from an Iraqi. I never understood the source of support for Saddam among the Palestinians: was it desperation? Was it a desire to believe that somebody somewhere cared about their plight? Was it the fantasy that some powerful heroic leader would show up and give them freedom? Was it ignorance? My father-in-law was one of the few people whose opinion on the matter shifted. After many discussions between him and me on the subject I would hear him arguing with his brother and other friends telling them what an awful dictator Saddam is and that they shouldn't pin their hopes on him. I was very flattered to hear my father-in-law use the same arguments that he heard from me in our discussions. I have the coolest father in law in the world. He is the "salt of the earth" kinda guy. The fact that he had only 4 years of schooling makes me admire his ability for critical and objective thinking even more. For an uneducated man, he has more wisdom and smarts that many educated people I know.

The real surprise came when I joined the local anti-war crowd in Vancouver. There was a quiet support for Saddam among some individuals. I was frequently criticized about my vocal denunciation of the Ba'athist party. I was told that I am playing to the hands of the pro-war gang. I was told that I wasn't being committed enough to the anti-war ideal. It was implied that I was a traitor. I was told that the crimes of Saddam were exaggerated in the media to support the war. I heard one person say that Saddam was the only world leader who dared fight imperialism. I would argue with people and tell them just go and talk to any recent refugee from Iraq, I guarantee that you will get nightmares for weeks. I would quote amnesty international reports on human right abuses in Iraq, I would mention history books and personal accounts. You would think that people would believe an Iraqi on such matters, you would think that the activist community would have an open mind. People would just shake their heads and tell me that I got it all wrong.

To all the people that send me hate mail, telling me that I got it all wrong, you might be a bit surprised by how little I argue back and by how little effort I exert in attempting to convince you of my point of view. It is because I have learned the following lessons the hard way:

1. People believe what they want to believe.

2. The majority of people don't want to know the truth, they want to know things that they already know.

3. The vast majority of people are too emotional to form opinions based on objective thinking.

4. There is nothing I can do, absolutely nothing, to change the view of somebody who is not objective.

5. I couldn't even change the mind of a childhood friend despite my innocent tender age of 13. What makes me think that I could change the mind of anybody at my cynical, jaded age of 37?

    To the rest of you reading this book, consider yourself sufficiently warned. I have a credibility problem, I have had it all my life; you should take everything you read here with a grain of salt.

Losing Sleep

If I hear one more American say that they are sorry about the pictures of the abuse of Iraqi prisoners, I will gag.

Before the American occupation of Iraq, each time you said you were Iraqi, people would transpose the head of Saddam over yours in their imagination's Photoshop abilities. Nowadays, each time you say you are Iraqi people imagine you standing there with a bare bottom. I don't know which one is more humiliating, the Saddam head transplant or walking around in public with a bare bottom? When I was a University student I had a recurrent nightmare. I am doing one of my final exams. The professor hands me the exam papers. I look at all the questions and I can't answer them, not even one. I start sweating. I look down at the dripping sweat to realize that I am completely naked. I am sitting in the classroom 100% naked. In my hurry to get to my exam on time, I forgot to get dressed. I start debating with myself if I should run out to the dormitories and get dressed and rush back to finish my exam, or whether I should just sit there and do my exam and hope that nobody will notice that I am naked. At that point, I would usually wake up to great relief. I am in my room, I am fully dressed in my comfy pajamas and it is only 4 am in the morning. Three more hours of sleep. I would frequently assure myself that the nightmare could never happen because I always went to bed in very modest pajamas, so even if by some miracle I forgot to change one morning I would show up to the exam in my pajamas and fuzzy slippers, which is much less embarrassing than showing up naked.

So the nightmare could never become a reality.

Another recurring nightmare of my youth is of running in a field.
The sun is shining into my eyes. I look behind me, Saddam in chasing me
with a machine gun in his hand. I run as fast as I can. I look for a ditch
or a cave to hide in. Eventually I fall. I am lying on the ground waiting
for the bullets to penetrate my body. In most cases I would wake up at
that point to the great relief of discovering that it was just a dream. I
would touch my stomach and chest to assure myself that there are no
bullet holes in my body. On few occasions the dream continues, I get
sprayed with bullets and then I just lay there on the ground. Finally, there
is no fear . . . just an eerie sense of quiet. I sleep through the nightmare
and remember it the next day. I haven't had either nightmare in many
years. But lately I keep thinking about those horrible pictures of torment
we saw from the prison of Abu Ghraib. I keep thinking about it, I can't
push it out of my mind. I am worried the nightmares will come back.
Only this time I will be running in the field naked with a hood over my
head, Saddam, Bush and a U.S. marine are chasing after me and after I
get shot I stay alive, the agony continues. My two nightmares become a
single unified Mother of All Enduring Freedom nightmare.

I used to dream of Iraq without Saddam and without the rule of
Ba'ath regime. It was a rosy and hopeful dream. Now I have to imagine
Iraq without the Ba'ath coming back to power. Without religious clerics
taking hold of the government, without a civil war, without the control
and influence of Iran, without the interference of Al Qaeda and other

crazies out to destroy the world, without the American occupation, without psychopaths that make grotesque porno movies using us as loyal subjects, without capitalists who will sell our kidneys on eBay and without a genocide. To tell you the truth, I am having a hard time visualizing it all in my head. On Friday I was sitting on the couch after dinner, with a big frown on my face. My husband asked me; "why the doom and gloom? You look like a woman that has just buried her husband." I told him that I just realized that things will be a mess in Iraq for many generations to come and there is nothing I can do about it. Last week I had hope that things will get sorted out in my life time. I am mourning the loss of the beautiful dream I held in my imagination for such a long time.

We heard Rumsfield and Bush say that they are sorry about the abuse of Iraqi prisoners. Isn't democracy and free media great? We never got to hear that Saddam was sorry about all the things he did to the Iraqi people and we never will, I suspect. Just imagine Saddam coming on TV saying, "Sorry about the mass graves, sorry about the wars, sorry about the mess, sorry I am such a dork, sorry that I exist." Naaah! it will never happen. Would it make a difference? So is this what democracy and free media is about? You get to hear a powerful man say he is sorry once in a while. Well, I am not very impressed.

People tell me they are sorry when they accidentally step on my toe. People tell me they are sorry when they are late for a meeting. Once in a while I hear a sorry from my husband. He wants to avoid a fight so he will say he is sorry even though he doesn't mean it.

The time for being sorry has long past. It is time for you to get mad. Start getting angry.

The darnest things have been said about Iraqi people. Take this speech for an example.

" O people of Iraq! You are like a pregnant woman who, on completion of her pregnancy, delivers a dead child and her husband is also dead and her period of widowhood is long and only a remote relation inherits her. By God, I did not come to you of my own accord. I came to you by force of circumstances. I have heard that you say about me that I had spoken lies. May God curse you! Against whom do I speak lies? Whether against God? But I am the first to have believed in him. Whether against his Prophet? But I am the first who testified to him. Certainly not! By God, you failed to appreciate what I tried to say, and you were not capable of understanding it. Woe to you. I am giving out these powerful expressions free of any cost. I wish there were vessels good enough to contain them. "

No it wasn't George Bush who gave this speech, but rather Imam Ali. The man who married prophet Mohammad's daughter and is highly respected as a close follower of the prophet by all Muslims, and is especially revered among the Shi'a. Imam Ali gave this speech when he got fed up with Iraqi people that were dragging their feet at supporting him in his fight against his rival. This speech is recorded in the book Nahj al Balaga "Path of Eloquence" that records the most famous of

Imam Ali's speeches and sayings. The book is considered to be one of the top examples of eloquent usages of the Arabic language.

If this is said about us by the people we adore, can you imagine what is said about us by the people we loathe?

"O people of Iraq! O people of divisiveness and hypocrisy.
I see before me heads that have ripened
And I see that the time has come to harvest them. I am going to be that harvester.
Already I can visualize the blood flowing between your turbans and your beards.
The Prince of the True Believers has spread before him the arrows of his quiver and found in me the cruelest of all his arrows."

This is a small part of an address of the brutal governor of Iraq, Al-Hajjaj ibn Yusuf, having come to Iraq to quell a rebellion during the Umayyad dynasty. The "prince of true believers" is a reference to caliph Abd al-Malik ibn Marwan, who sent Hajjaj to Iraq to suppress the rebellion against him. The speech must have sent shivers down the spines of his audience. He proceeded to rule over Iraq for about 20 years with an iron fist. It is reported that he liked to gouge people's eyes out with his own hands and chop ears off. After his death many rulers had difficulty ruling over Iraq because he was a tough act to follow. Saddam came close. After Al-Hajjaj, the Iraqi people kept assassinating their rulers and rebelling against them, earning us the dubious reputation of being supreme trouble-makers. Al-Hajjaj promised and then he proceeded to deliver.

Luckily not all those wishing to rule over us deliver on their promises. Like George Bush promising us peace and prosperity. Oh well! You know what they say about something sounding too good to be true. On the weekend I heard on the radio George Bush say that Iraqi people are not used to freedom and that force is necessary to deal with us.

Mon Dieu! We must be the most miserable nation on earth. Sometimes it does seem that way. It seems like we are inherently violent. We are cursed. But then, I remember violence in hockey in Canada, Los Angles riots in the U.S., mob lynching of Nazi collaborators in the Czechoslovakia after WWII, and I force myself to remember that we are inherently human.

Here is a speech that I long to hear and so far haven't:

"O People of Iraq. One day you will become the people of mediocrity and boredom. We have been at the forefront of major historical events for far too many times and we have paid a heavy price for it. The time has come for us to take our leave and sink into obscurity. Let us give away our oil for free to the U.S., in fact let us deliver it to them for free with no extra charge, for this wealth has been nothing but a curse upon us. The land of the proud and free are more deserving of it, anyway, we are neither proud nor free, so we have no use for it. Let us tell Iran that they are welcome to their fight against Great Satan, for their quest is brave, but we shall ask them to conduct their blood bath against Americans off our lands. We shall tell the Americans that their war on terrorism is fair and just; however, we shall ask them to conduct it far away from us. We have no desire to liberate Palestine, though we wish our Palestinian brothers and sisters well on their own quest for obscurity. Furthermore, we have no desire for the Messiah to come back. We do not wish to be a model democracy in the Middle East, because we think that Israel is doing a fine job of it; the slow genocide against the Palestinians is a nice Middle Eastern twist to the concept of democracy, but I digress. We simply want to raise our kids and spend our time taking care of our families. In the afternoons we shall sit around drinking tea and chat idly away for hours. We will be so bored that we will have to make up stories and riddles in order to entertain ourselves. O People of Iraq, the time of national pride is over, we have pioneered dreams of Arab nationalists and Islamic idealists, but now we must leave all that behind. We shall become the most boring nation on earth. But wait a minute, that might become something to base national pride on. Ok! I revise that, we shall become the almost most boring nation on earth. We will allow a country like Holland earn the first prize in that category, but we will be a close second. My goal is to ensure that all our lives get into a rut. From now on, our country will not be mentioned on CNN, history books will ignore us and powerful world leaders will find nothing to say to us. The time of grandiose visions by powerful men is over. "

Losing Innocence

"My name is Ba'ath," said my class mate at Kuwait University. I wanted to laugh. Ha ha ha ha. That woman must have a great sense of humor. She is Iraqi and when I asked her what her name is, she replied by saying Ba'ath. Ha ha ha ha, Iraqi people are so funny. Luckily one second before I was about to burst out laughing I looked at her face. She looked dead serious. Oh my God! her name is Ba'ath. I better not laugh. If I am seen as making fun of the word Ba'ath I might get into serious trouble. I hid my face in my hands and pretended I was reading from a book laid out in front of me, on the desk. I was trying to hide the bizarre contortion forming on my face as one part of me wanted to laugh and the other was painfully trying to wipe any hint of a smile off my face. Her name was Ba'ath, no joke. No need to ask about the politics of her parents. That must be the ugliest name given to a woman I had ever heard of. Even uglier than the name the woman that frequents my gym in Vancouver gave to her daughter. My gym-mate called her daughter "Equity"; I wanted to laugh at her, too. Instead I nodded my head, even though I won't get beheaded for making fun of somebody's name in Vancouver; I thought it would be rude to laugh anyway. But Ba'ath is by far the ugliest name given to a woman. Ba'ath is the name of the ruling party in Iraq before the fall of Saddam. It also means resurrection. Why would somebody call his daughter resurrection? The birth of a new baby makes me think of life, hope, future; it does not inspire the thought of ghosts or zombies resurrected from the dead. If I am dead, why would I want to be resurrected anyway? Considering the fact that we live in a world where an unarmed and tied-up young man gets his head severed in the name of religion, why would anybody want to come back once they left? I certainly don't. No resurrection for me, thank you.

The daily news of killings and mayhem in Iraq reminds me of the year I realized that I was living in a rotten world. I was 14 and studying in a Kuwaiti high school. That year was marked by three events that made me realize that I was living in a horrible and scary world. First off, I read Roots, translated to Arabic. It was the first grown up book I had read. Everything I'd read before that had happy endings and the good guys won. All the grown ups were talking about Roots the TV series, but my parents would not allow me to watch it. They felt it was too harsh for my age. But when I decided to buy the book because I was curious to find out what the buzz was all about, my dad didn't say anything. My dad is an avid reader and he always encouraged me to read. The tale of Kunta Kinte captured into slavery and transported from his native Africa to America is haunting. I almost felt I was in the slave ship watching the wretched conditions the slaves were enduring at the first taste of their enslavement. I would read and cry, I was depressed for a whole week, but I couldn't put the book down. The story was so compelling. My mom kept saying, stop reading that book, it is upsetting you. Although the story is a work of fiction, it is based on a reality that did exist. "How could any human being subject another human being to such injustice?", I kept asking myself. How could anybody be so cruel? The knowledge that everything in the story actually happened made me sad. At night, before going to sleep I would fantasize that I was able to travel back in time and rescue Kunta Kinte and transport him back to his native town in Africa.

The second event happened while I was at the library. I was reading a book on the Second World War. Half way through there was a picture of some of the atrocities committed by the Nazis during that time. There was a picture of a pile of dead bodies, stacked up in a pyramid. That picture shocked me. The dead people looked like average people no different from me. I had to close up the book and leave the library right away. I felt nauseated, I felt I was about to faint. To me war conjured up images of heroic actions by heroic men and women. That image made me realize the flip side of the war. The death of thousands and millions of average people at the hands of other average people. The picture from that book kept haunting me. I kept wondering what sort of a world I was living in. But all this had happened in a different time in different lands. Surely I was safe in Kuwait. Everybody around me looked like they were not inclined to inflict pain on others.

One day in my high school, the vice principal summoned me to her office. This was a big deal, to be summoned to the vice principal's office. In her office she handed me a notebook and asked me to write down the name, address and phone number of each student in my class room. "We need that information in cases of emergency", she said. I took the notebook and did as I was instructed. Few days later I handed back the notebook proclaiming "mission accomplished." I had asked every single student in my class to write down their name, number and address in the note book. She opened it and glanced at it casually. "Very good!" Then she handed it back to me. Now, on top of each page I want you write down the name of one these girls. Allow several pages per girl. I want you to write down everything you know about that girl and then I want you write down what that girl talks about, things she tells her friends, her interests, her thoughts, what are her parents doing and so on. I was being asked to spy on my class mates. I took the notebook and stuffed it my school bag. This was a dilemma. On one hand, I didn't want to spy on my class mates. On the other hand, in Kuwait you never said no to a teacher, and this wasn't just the teacher, this was the vice principal. The whole culture at the school was that of obedience, you simply weren't allowed to disobey.

At home, my father noticed that I looked disturbed at the dinner table. When I told him the story, he brilliantly gave me the solution to my dilemma. He told me to tell the vice principal that my dad forbade me from spying on my classmates. While disobeying a teacher was considered an aberration, disobeying your parents is an even worse offense in Arabic culture. "If she gives you any trouble about it, tell her that your dad will come and speak to her," my dad instructed me. The next day, I walked into the vice principal's office, I apologized very meekly and handed the notebook back. I told her that my father told me that I am not allowed to do this. She simply nodded her head, said that is fine and gestured that I should leave the office. I left her office with huge sense of relief. I felt like a rock had been lifted off my chest. I was so grateful to my dad, having rescued me from this terrible situation. But then new thoughts entered my head. Why was the school spying on its

100

students? Are there other spies? Will this notebook be handed to somebody else who might agree? Is there something sinister or dangerous going on in the school? Why did she pick me? Is it because I was popular and I had many friends and had good relationships throughout the school? Or was it because there is something in my character that would indicate a willingness to be a spy? Is it because I was the class clown? I felt a sense of guilt for having collected the names, phone numbers and addresses in the first place. I never talked about it with anybody. I felt a sense of shame for having marginally participated in something sinister that I didn't understand. I was worried that if I told anybody, I would then be accused of being a spy or that suspicions would circle around me among my class mates. That year the high walls surrounding the school seemed more like prison walls. I kept waiting for the school to build watch towers around the school perimeter and place watch guards and snipers in them. I felt my school was a prison. There was a sense of danger in the air, only it was mysterious and you never knew where it might come from. Everything seemed strange and new. Everything was the same but different.

Ba'ath was a whiney young woman. She whined all the time. The course material was too hard, the professor was not explaining things properly. She had a constant frown on her face. She would tell me all the time how things were better in Iraq. She was unhappy living in Kuwait and wanted to go back to Iraq. Ba'ath was never excited by anything, she was always mildly unsatisfied with something or another. She told me she didn't like to eat in restaurants because she didn't know how to use a fork and a knife properly and always felt embarrassed when she ate in restaurants because of it. Seems like a silly thing to worry about, but Ba'ath worried about it each time we went to the cafeteria. Ba'ath wasn't very intelligent, but she got by in her class work, barely getting a passing mark. She didn't look like a dead zombie as her name would indicate, she looked about average. On the day I met her, I went home and told my dad about it. I told him that I met an Iraqi girl in class, I told him her name and then I started to laugh. My dad looked very alarmed, "You didn't laugh in her face? did you?" "No dad, I wanted to but then I managed to stop in time." My dad shook his head, "You must be careful, are you sure you did not laugh at her name, not even a little bit." "No dad I did not laugh, I swear, I did not laugh." "You must be careful, promise me you will be careful." "I promise dad, I will be careful."

Losing the Desire to Read

"It got good reviews in both Israeli and Arab press, it must be good," says my husband. Usually Arab and Israeli press are mirror opposites. If one side praises something, then the other thinks it is the true embodiment of evil. The source of this unique harmony in the Middle East is a book called "the Alchemist" by Paulo Coelho. My husband runs out of the coffee shop we are sitting in to go to the bookstore next door. "I just got to buy this book," he mutters as he runs out. He then runs back into the coffee shop and plunks this little book into my hands. "You got to read this," he tells me. "You got to read it," he repeats several times.

I am still struggling with my vow of reading deprivation. As an avid reader, I had just realized that I am very knowledgeable about world affairs, the human condition, politics, history, philosophy; you name it, I know about it. However, I am not putting any of this knowledge into good use. "I have read enough," I declared a mere two months earlier. I will stop being an observer and become a doer. I will do something about all this knowledge inside my head and make a difference in the world. Reading about it and then having interesting discussions at dinner parties is for idiots. For two months I have watched my husband finish one juicy novel after the next while I held steadfast to my vow of abstaining from reading. Now the ultimate temptation: a book so highly recommended, plus it is so small, it won't take long to read. I have been so good for two months. Would it really hurt if I deviate just a little and made an exception just this once? Oh yeah! Addictions are hard to break and mine is the hard-core kind. My name is Elen and I am a book addict. You are supposed to say, "Hello Elen," at this point.

I started reading the first page right there in the coffee shop. Santiago, a young man has a happy and content life. Then he meets a mysterious figure who tells him that he must follow his dreams. Santiago must give up everything that he has in his current life in order to take a long and risky journey towards his dream. A few weeks later, I quit my highly paid job, though I don't have an alternative job offer. I decide to start my own project. My family thinks I am crazy. My husband thinks that I am experiencing mid-life crisis in my early thirties. Such rash behavior from a "mostly reasonable person." Ex-mostly reasonable person by now.

Shortly after Santiago starts this journey, he falls flat on his face. Splat! Ouch! But now he is stuck in the middle, he can't go back to his comfortable old life style and he can't get to his dream either. Oh man! What was I thinking? What craziness took hold of me? I should have been realistic. All this talk about following your dream and living out your personal legend that is nonsense. There is everyday reality to contend with, there are bills to pay. Wake up! You can't just fantasize about something crazy and then expect that it will just happen. Nobody has that kind of a control over their destiny. Ok! That was pretty stupid, back track, let's work hard on getting back to that comfortable lifestyle we had before. Let's go back to square one. Lesson learned: don't trust crazy mysterious people that tell you to follow your dream. People like that are dangerous. Dangerous, I tell you.

Santiago has to work hard in a crystal shop for a whole year in order to save enough money so that he could go back to where he started and go back to his original life style. He finally saves up enough money and is ready to go back home, when suddenly something grips him again and he decides that he can always get back home later; Santiago's risky journey continues.

Just Like Santiago, I have found my way to a safe crystal shop where I have been for a little over four years. I have gathered my strength back, but what now knowing about the ordeals Santiago faced after he leaves the Crystal Shop? Do I have the courage to continue with the original path I set out upon, more than four years ago? Now that I know how difficult this road is, do I have the courage to walk it again? I will probably fall flat on my face again. I think I need a kick in the behind to get me out of the crystal shop. On one hand I am terrified, on the other hand I know that if I stop following the omens they will stop appearing.

I no longer have a desire to read any more books; they all seem to be saying the same things. The ultimate and most exciting story is the one I am creating right this minute, every minute of my life, with every breath. The book addict has encountered the ultimate fix. I am a book reader no more.

Don't read this book, it is dangerous. It will make you do crazy stuff like yearning to dance and believing that your craziest dreams might come true. You will start believing that you can change the world around you and that you are not a passive passenger in this life. You will fall flat on your face again and again but keep going on. You have been warned, don't read this book. Go back to your safe, sane and predictable life.

Losing Weight

I myself hoped that Adnan Pachachi would be the next Iraqi president. Anybody whose last name is that of an Iraqi national dish has to be ok. Pacha is a slowly cooked combination of sheep's head, stomach, feet and a variety of other meats in broth. It might sound disgusting to you to look into a pot and see a whole sheep's head looking back at you, but we Iraqis love all our heart attack inducing dishes. In fact, I think that all heads of state should be named after national dishes. Imagine Fettuccine Alfredo, prime minister of Italy, Gordon Bleu, President of France, Seashell Paella for Spanish president or Zucchini Tempura for a Japanese prime minister. Doesn't that sound more palatable than their real names? The Russian president is already ahead, only he is residing in the wrong country. Poutine is Canadian for French fries smothered in gravy and melted cheese. Mmmmm!, digusting. If heads of states were named after food, it would make deciding on who to vote for during election time that much easier. Instead of thinking about complex policy issues and figuring out if you trust the promises of the candidate and then deciding if extra marital affairs should weigh on your decisions, we all know what our favorite dishes are. Deciding between two dishes is so much easier. Ok, who would you rather vote for:

Ice cream Sundae or Jalapeno Nachos?

Cheesecake New York or Colonel Kentucky?

Tahini Shawarma or Baba Ghanough?

We each could decide without any hesitation, who our favorite is. Plus, imagine how much fun election campaigns would be. Instead of the boring speeches we would have cooking shows. Instead of empty promises, instant gratification, feed me now. "The proof is in the pudding" would have a whole new meaning. As in, feed me pudding and I will believe you. Who cares about foreign policy, just make international potluck dinners. Forget about armies and make mean chili sauce for export to the enemy. The country that makes the most deadly chili will rule the world. The only drawback is that Ronald McDonalds might win elections in the U.S. That would be a real farce.

Plus people would talk about their president or prime minister in whole new way. "I find him way more appetizing that the other guy". "I can't stomach that candidate". "He gives me diarrhea". "She is a real dish". "That last election campaign left a bad taste in my mouth". "Tart" will become a good word for a politician, so will the word "fruitcake." Do you see the potential here? It is endless.

Ok, ok, ok. I confess. I am obsessed with food. Gluttony is my favorite mortal sin. I have never met a cuisine I didn't like. It really is my downfall. I like it all; Italian, Japanese, Indian. Can you tell that I started a diet only two days ago and now all I can think about is all the food I am not supposed to eat? I know what your are thinking. Surely a serious person like myself, somebody who is preoccupied with important world

108

affairs can't possibly be wasting her time with that futile womanly quest called "diet." But, believe me, this serious lady has asked her husband: "Does this dress make me look fat?" more times than she cares to admit.

[Advice for married men: When your wife asks you the question "Does this dress make me look fat?," telling her that it is her lovely ass that makes her look fat, and not the dress, will not flatter your wife. It might be a guaranteed method for ensuring she won't ask you that stupid question again, but it won't be healthy for your relationship.]

If I was running for any public office in Iraq I would change my name to Dolma Fasanjoun. Dolma is an Iraqi dish that consists of stuffed grape vine leaves and stuffed vegetables, like zucchini, eggplants and other vegetables. It is an amazing dish that is popular all over Iraq. Fasanjoun is a dish common in the south of Iraq. It is Chicken that is simmered in this brown-purply sauce. The sauce contains walnuts and pomegranate juice. I don't actually know how to make either dish, but I am good at the eating part. For my election campaign I would forget about leaflets and posters and instead give out small tupperware containers with dolma in it. "Vote for the candidate who feeds you best," will be inscribed on each package. Everybody in the whole of Iraq would vote for me.

Losing Myself in Your Love

One day I went to bed next to my handsome Palestinian husband. The next day I woke up to find lying next to me an Israeli man with a hairy back. He was sleeping on his tummy, drooling on the pillow and snoring. How did I end up next to this man? Where am I? What is going on?

Aaaaaaaaaaaaaaah!

Before I explain to you how I ended up in this Kafkaesque nightmare turned into reality, I need to tell you the story right from the beginning. Let me start right back when it all started. Many moons ago, I met a dashing dark young man who captured my attention right from the moment I laid eyes on him. He had beautiful dark curly hair and an intense look about him. I was one of those silly people that didn't believe in love or romance. I never read romantic novels because I believed that all love stories were Hollywood fabrications with no root in reality. I considered myself far too serious and far too intelligent for silly idle pursuits like love. Only pathetic helpless and naïve women sat around dreaming about the knight in shining armor to come and rescue them. I myself planned to roll up my sleeves and fulfill my own dreams with my own hard work, without the aid of a man.

I nicknamed the dashing young man Za'atarah. Za'atar is a herb common in Palestine similar to oregano only with stronger taste. If you never had za'atar, then you are in for a treat. A'antarah is a pre-Islamic Arab hero. He was a black slave who fell in love with A'ablah, the daughter of a tribal sheik. So I combined the words za'atar and A'antarah and created the nickname Za'atarah. Seemed appropriate considering the fact that Za'atarah was Palestinian, dark, and looked larger than life to me. Plus anything to do with food is good in my books.

The evil father would not allow A'antarah to marry A'ablah and instead kept promising her in marriage to other men of higher stature. A'antarah had to travel all over the Arabian dessert, sword fighting with all the suitors so that A'ablah would be his. A little bit like Romeo and Juliette, only A'antarah and A'ablah did really exist. All stories and movies about A'antarah close with the happy ending of a happy wedding between A'antarah and his beloved. In real life, they did get married – only they were miserable together after marriage. A'ablah continually put down A'antarah because of his slave roots and treated him in a haughty way, like the daughter of a tribal sheik that she was. A'ablah could not have children and, therefore, A'antarah had to marry another woman because of his desire for offspring. Apparently, they spent most of their time together fighting. No movie has been made about that part.

My Za'atarah, on the other hand, did not carry a sword, nor any other weapon, but his eyes were as sharp as Excalibur. One glance from him would make me break into sweats and make my heart race. Two weeks after meeting Za'atarah, you would find me walking around with a huge smile on my face, like an idiot. There was a skip in my step and I constantly felt the urge to break into song. Yada, yada, yada, yada, insert all the pathetic romantic spiel you want here. Yes, it's true, when you are in love you feel like a bird that will fly any minute. Like everything in life is beautiful and like everything is possible. ....Pathetic! Ha?

Well! To my credit, Za'atarah is an exceptional guy. For one thing, he carried the complete poetic works of the Iraqi Muthafar Al Nawab in his backpack, and whenever the fancy struck him he would pick up the book, stand up and start reading poetry. He had large portions of it memorized by heart.

How could I resist?

As if that wasn't enough to rock my world, Za'atarah was radically different from all the Middle Eastern men I had met before. For one thing he was completely unpretentious. For example, even though he had a Ph.D. and taught at the university, he insisted that everybody call him by his first name. Whenever somebody called him Dr. he would just wave his hand and say don't be silly, call me Za'atarah. In the Middle East titles are very important. People who have earned the prized Dr. title are deeply offended if you forgot to address them by it. Za'atrah dressed very modestly, too. He wore plain pairs of jeans and plain T-shirts. You might think, what's the big deal with that? Well, for an Arab guy that is a very big deal. Most Arab men able to afford it would be decked out in their best Armani suit, fancy Italian shoes and a Pierre Cardan pen placed strategically in the pocket to impress. Za'atarah was the antithesis of Arab middle class pretension and snootiness, the snootiness that I grew up with and was familiar with.

Za'atarah is a brutally honest man. He had no problem telling someone that he is an idiot straight to his face. Arab culture is all about saving face. I grew up in a culture where people I only met 5 minutes ago would tell me they loved me like their sister. I am talking major white lies, huge unwarranted compliments and massive face-saving action. Za'atarah was none of that. Every word uttered by him was precise and measured. Everything he said he meant deeply; otherwise he would say nothing. Hence, I got the feeling that everything he said he meant; when he said something nice it meant something, it wasn't yet another figure of speech, he deeply meant every single word he said. How un-Arabic! Visitors to the Middle East find all the compliments and words of endearment friendly. They leave the Middle East with the impression that people are Oh! so friendly. But when you grew up in a culture hearing "Oh! how are you? I have missed you. Why don't you call more often?" from a person who won't answer your phone calls and you know that she hates your guts and can't stand the sight of you, it gets nauseating after a while. The insincere compliments always got on my nerves.

When I first met Za'atarah, he told me he was the son of simple peasants. That, too, surprised me, because Arabic culture is class-conscious. People from upper classes look down at people from the lower classes. People from lower classes pretend that they are from higher. I knew many people who would live lavishly, drive expensive cars and wear expensive clothes they couldn't afford, trying to create the illusion of being wealthier than they were. I knew many people who came from humble origins, but who as soon as they were able to get a good salary, denied their origins, pretending to be something they were not. In Canada, it would have been very easy for Za'atarah to claim that his family was some educated, middle-class bunch. Instead he seemed to almost brag about his humble origins. How un-Arabic! To be proud of who you are instead of what you are supposed to be.

Everything about this man was radical and admirable. Plus, he was an amazing cook. He would make me kusa mahshi (zucchini stuffed with meat and vegetables). He introduced me to avocado, which I never ate before because I thought it looked weird. What a treat to taste avocado for the very first time! I wouldn't say that my stomach is the shortest path to my heart, but that path is fairly short. I think it was the poetry that impressed me the most, but the food didn't hurt. Like most Hollywood movies, you should be able to predict the rest of this story. We fell in love, got married and lived happily ever after.

The End

And then the rest of our life together started. Five years into our marriage we moved together to Israel pursuing an academic career for Za'atarah. I had grown up in a country where the word "Israel" was rarely uttered; it was always referred to as the "enemy." The state of the enemy, the prime minister of the enemy, the Zionist enemy were all part of the everyday vocabulary in Kuwait at the time. All maps of the Middle East would show "occupied Palestine," but no Israel. I had never seen the state of Israel on a map. Somehow in my mind, Israel was this entity hovering in the air somewhere. Imagine my surprise when I discovered that Israel is yet another country that actually exists on the ground and they don't refer to themselves as the enemy; they all have names. Wow! How radical! Well! I was determined to put away all that "enemy" propaganda taught to me in school, leave it behind and keep an open mind and adjust as best as I could. But childhood conditioning dies hard.

Jesus said, "Love your enemy as you would love yourself." I always assumed that only a select few, a special breed of people were capable of that. I always assumed that it would take massive effort and discipline in order to achieve that. I always assumed that it would be something that people would engage in out of choice; maybe a hint of masochism mixed in with that as well. I myself am not too fond of the principle. It doesn't make much sense to me.

Israelis are the most brutally honest group of people I have ever encountered. In Israel, I realized right from day one that if people didn't like me they would tell me that they hated my guts right to my face. There was no pretending, no white lies, no room for saving face. Nobody pretends to like you if they don't. At first it was shocking, but later on I found it refreshing. No need to beat around the bush. Additionally, Israelis have complete contempt for pretension. Nobody wears suits or fancy clothing. When people want to look casual they put on old pairs of jeans and old stretched-out T-shirts. Nobody wears Gap or Tommy Hilfiger in Israel. The highest executive to the lowliest garbage sweeper

116

on the streets dress in a similar fashion. In Israel you can't tell the difference between the wealthy and the poor by appearances. What you see is what you get, from an Israeli. The socialist past of the country still affects it today, making hard work and hand labor points of honor rather than things to be looked down upon.

The things I admired most about my husband were the things he learned by growing up in Israel. I didn't want to love my enemy; but I was already in love with the enemy. I was angry because I felt that I had no choice in the matter. That morning when I woke up realizing that I was sleeping next to an Israeli guy, I told my Za'atarah that I didn't want to be married to an Israeli, I wanted to be married to a 100% Palestinian. I would have never married an Israeli man and I am not going to settle for an Israeli husband now. Za'atarah placed his hand on my shoulder and told me, "I never lied to you, I told you about my background right from the beginning. I am who I am. There are things I can't change about myself. This country is my country. I grew up in it. I don't care if it is called Israel or Palestine. It is part of my identity." I shook my head. "No, no, no."

Given my own messed up identity, is it any wonder that I attracted a man with a psychotic identity?

I was called the gypsy kid. In my childhood I spent most summer holidays in the Czech Republic. All my cousins on my mother's side are blonde, fair and have blue eyes. I am considerably darker than the rest of them; therefore I was the gypsy kid. We would play in the front yard and neighbors passing by would say half jokingly, "How did you get that gypsy kid mixed up with the rest of you?" The other half was malice. And then I would travel back to the Middle East and I would suddenly turn blonde. Ok! I didn't actually turn blonde, but that is how the other kids referred to me, "that blonde girl" was a common way to refer to me at school. Everything in life is relative. I learned that at age eight. Not because I am so smart, but because I had no choice. The constant relativity of my being was hard to ignore.

What right did I have expecting Za'atarah to be 100% when I wasn't 100% anything either?

And so love my enemy I had to, because hating the person closest to me would have killed me. For you, my dark beauty from the land of milk and honey, I will learn to love the whole world, even my enemy.

"It may be that God will ordain love between you and those whom you hold as enemies. For God has power over all things; and God is Oft-forgiving, Most Merciful," Surah Al-Mumtahinah Qura'an 60.7

What is Left Behind

Dragon Woman

For most of my career I worked in companies where I was the only woman. There was always me and the receptionist and maybe the bookkeeper. Everybody else was male. All my coworkers, bosses ...etc. In every single meeting I was the only female in the boardroom. There were times when I felt like a freak. Why am I the only woman interested in computer programming? Why can't I like nursing or teaching. In this super male environment I frequently found it embarrassing the way some guys would talk about women. Commenting on the size of their boobs and thighs, making disgusting noises, taking about how wonderful or not they are in bed. The more I blushed the more they seemed to delight in it. The self-righteous speech about "women are not sex objects" only made matters worst. I felt depressed. I want to be treated with respect and dignity; I want to be treated as a person not as a potential sex conquest. Eventually, I found a method that solved this problem completely. This method is so effective and has worked for me so many times that I should patent it. But I will share it with you for free. Before I explain it to you let me give you a few examples.

Story #1

I am sitting in the lunchroom eating a sandwich. My coworkers, Steve and David are discussing the difference between fake and natural breasts. They are guessing which actresses have natural and which have fake. An inappropriate topic for discussion at the office lunchroom in the presence of a women, don't you think? Steve asserts that natural boobs feel completely different from boobs that have been enhanced with breast implants. I ask him how does he know all this. Steve smiles in a sneaky way and says "I just know". I say, "I think I know how Steve knows the difference between the two. I bet you he has purchased a pair of fake breasts implants, which he fondles at home at night. He probably has them in his brief case right now." Everybody in the lunchroom is laughing his head off. Steve's face turns red and he never discusses boobs in my presence ever again.

Story #2

I ask my coworker who to me to write a report on a technical matter. A few days later I ask him if he has finished the report. He answers "Oh, when you asked me to write the report I thought you were faking…… you know…… the way women fake the other thing … ha ha ha ha". An inappropriate answer, don't you think? I look straight into his eyes and tell him. "Honey, maybe you are talking from a personal experience, maybe this happens to you all the time, the faking is entirely dependent on the man, you know!". The guy's face turns red, he goes back to his desk and writes the report right away. Afterwards he tells me that I am mean and that he wants to go home to hide under his bed and cry. In any case, I never hear about faking or anything remotely related to sexuality from him ever again.

Story #3

    I start a new job with a coworker who is older than me, yet I am hired into a more senior position with higher salary. It is obvious right from day one that this is irking him to no end. One day as I am sitting in my office, he stands behind me and start massaging my shoulders. As in, yeah! You have the more senior position, but I am a man and I can put you down and make you feel uncomfortable. So I move his hands away and ask him politely not to touch me. The next day he does the exact same thing. This dude is asking for it, don't you think? So I get up to face him and I shout as loud as I can, "DON'T TOUCH ME AGAIN OR I WILL KICK YOU." Everybody in the office stops in mid conversation or in mid whatever they where doing and stares at us. The guy's face turns red and he walks out of my office and sits at his cubicle. From then on, me and him get along just fine and he never gives me a hard time.

Story #4

    I am at a pub with many of my co-workers, at a company social. Paul, who has just come back from a long business trip abroad, is telling everybody that he hasn't had sex in a long time (the whole time he was away) and that he is ready to jump on the first woman he meets. Then he brags about the long list of women he has slept with. Jennifer gives him the self-righteous speech about, "women have feelings, women are not sex objects, yada yada". Paul says "But these are not real women, one day I will meet a real woman and marry her; these women that I sleep with are not real women." A downright condescending comment, don't you think? I look very innocently at him and say, "Aaaaaaaaaah! You mean you have been sleeping with a wide collection of plastic dolls, which you left home while on your trip." Everybody bursts into laughter, men and women. Jennifer is laughing so hard tears are streaming down her cheeks. The laughter lasts 20 minutes. The look on Paul's face is worth a million dollar. Yes you guessed it right, Paul never brags about the number of unreal women he has slept with ever again.

I don't get depressed, I get even. That is my moto. My method is simple. When somebody is putting me down or attempting to embarrass me because I am a woman, I go for the jugular. I insult his manhood in the most painfully embarrassing way possible and I do it with humor and wit while keeping my cool. The bigger the audience, the bigger the humiliation.

Smile

I lived four years in Israel, so that makes me an expert on the Israeli/Palestinian conflict, Right! I am afraid the matter is much more complicated than that. In order to understand the situation you would need to understand the 2000 years of Arab and Islamic history and 4000 years of Jewish history. You would need to understand events of the WWII, the holocaust and how that contributes to modern Israeli thinking today, as well as the colonization of Britain in the region and how that acted as a backdrop for events today. You would need to understand America's long-standing interest in the region and its attempts to protect those interests. Finally, you would need to comprehend what happened when European Jews fleeing prosecution came to the Holy Land, mixing with Yemenite and Moroccan Jews and the indigenous Palestinian population. East meets the West in more than one way and Boom! You have the very unique Middle East conflict. Speaking Arabic and Hebrew doesn't hurt either. In short, it is very complex. There are about nine million people living in Israel and the occupied territory, and almost each one of them has an expert view on the situation. When I moved to Israel I was surprised how even six year old children have an understanding of the political climate surrounding them and pointed opinions about it. No doubt, if you have been following the commentary on the conflict, you have heard various experts mention historical events and statistical data in an attempt to make sense of it all.

One day I was sitting in a coffee shop in western Jerusalem, sipping coffee on a beautiful sunny day. A Palestinian boy about 10 years of age approached me selling some trinkets. The expression on this boy's face was that of a 60-year-old man who has lived through catastrophes. I never saw so much desperation on a child's face. I gave him some money hoping to illicit a smile. The boy placed the money into his pocket and stared back at me, not even a hint of a smile. I placed my hand on his shoulder and shook him gently saying, "Smile for God's sake, you are only a kid." He stared back at me with that same desperation and simply walked away. The expression on that boys face has haunted me until today. I frequently wonder what this boy's life must be like for him not to be able to smile. What sort of a world are we living in, when even children can't take joy in living?

My own kids frequently play pretend games. My eldest daughter likes to pretend she is a teacher and the two younger ones are her students. Sometimes, they play fashion show; they wrap themselves in blankets or towels and march back and forth pretending to be fashion models. In Ramallah, Palestinian children play pretend funeral. One of the kids pretends to be dead and the rest walk around in a procession carrying him on their shoulders. You can also catch kids playing pretend demonstration, where half of the kids will pretend to be Israeli soldiers and the other half pretends to be demonstrating. Then the pretend Israeli soldiers beat up the pretend demonstrators and then they switch roles.

I don't have a Ph.D. in Political Science nor History, but I know

126

that this situation must end. If I had the chance to meet Israel's Prime Minister, Ariel Sharon, face-to-face, I would place my hand on his shoulder and gently shake him while saying, " For G-d's sake, withdraw the army from the occupied territories." Maybe one day even Mr. Sharon will crack a smile. The sort of warm and sincere smile that usually comes from a child.

Writing Letters

I used to feel frustrated with the way mass media covers the Middle East. I would read our daily newspapers and feel just so mad with superficial reporting. Here is a sample of letters I have written to The Globe and Mail, Canada's leading newspaper. This is only a sample; I have written many more, and not just to the Globe and Mail.

September, 2002

Dear Globe and Mail Editor,

In an article titled, "The Palestinian Intifada Has Been a Disaster", Palestinians are urged to stop the intifada for their own sake (Editorial, Sept 3, 2002). The article fails to mention that Israel is a country that spends 11 billion dollars a year on its security, and uses its fine arsenal to oppress a largely hungry and unarmed population. Had black South African's stop fighting apartheid, had the Civil Rights Movement fighting discrimination in the U.S. stopped we would all be worse off in this world. Perhaps the next advice column for Palestinians should be titled, "Get used to oppression with the use of drugs and alcohol". Just look how well that advice has worked for our local Native Indian population.

September, 2003

Dear Editor,

Our media mogul Izzy Asper decides to bank roll the visit of Mr. Benjamin Netanyahu, in order to raise funds for a state that already spends billions on oppressing a largely hungry and unarmed native population. When activists decide to challenge the ex-Prime Minister, who by the way is a vocal proponent of the so called "transfer solution" for the Palestinians, surprise, surprise, all the media outlets belonging to the Media Lord call these activists goons and compare them to terrorists without any mention of the denial of basic human rights to 3.5 million people living in the occupied territories. Yellow journalism at its best. Why bother with journalism school when dog obedience classes will suffice.

October 2002

Dear Editor,

I am writing with regards to the article titled, "Settlers Fear Prospect of Palestinian State", by Timothy Appleby, on October 29, 2002. The article never mentions the fact that Israeli settlements inside the West Bank and Gaza strip are

illegal settlements according to international laws. The article also

fails to mention that Israeli settlers are involved in a daily harassment campaign against Palestinian civilians. Their actions include, shooting at civilians including children, damaging property, uprooting trees, burning mosques and preventing farmers from going to their fields. I believe that these facts deserve a mention in any discussion about Israeli settlements in the west bank and the Gaza strip, to help provide the reader with some context.

June 2002

Dear Sir,

I am writing with regards to the article about the baby dressed in a suicide bomber outfit, published by Paul Adams on June 29. The Israeli Government pounced on the photograph as proof that the Palestinians are brainwashing their young. It has long been trying to convince the outside world that the real reason Palestinian suicide bombers are murdering Israeli civilians is not primarily because of Israel's actions: occupation, settlement building, curfews, assassinations, the killing of hundreds of civilians, and the destruction of property or farmland, but because of the wickedly, fanatical Palestinian mentality. The killing of six Palestinian children in a week, several as young as six years old, by Israeli forces might have had some bearing on the timing of the baby bomber photo's release. The question that needs to be asked is why the Israeli army is going through the personal photo albums of a Palestinian family? Why is a newspaper like The Globe and Mail publishing this photograph without the permission of the child's family?

June 2003

Dear Editor,

I bet you got a chuckle while looking at the cartoon published on Saturday, June 14th. On Father's Day, an Arab father gets an explosives vest. What amazing sense of humour. When I look at the cartoon, I see years of colonization that have passed and many years of military occupation to come. I see a road map to nowhere and copious quantities of lies and mass destruction. I suppose I would find it funny too, if my family wasn't suffering with thirst in Baghdad and my friends in the West Bank weren't being shot at for sport. So go ahead, laugh at us. Laugh at our misery. Perspective is everything.

The more I wrote, the more frustrated I felt. Then I realized that I was causing my own heartache. I stopped reading the daily newspapers and stopped writing letters. Criticizing is easy, actually attempting to do something about the things that you believe in is much harder, so I started writing articles and making efforts to publish them.

Now that I don't read the newspaper on a daily basis; every once in while somebody brings an article to my attention that is a nice surprise. Like an article about a talented young Palestinian man from the West Bank that was not able to get to university due to the closures. The Globe and Mail published a story about him in August, 2003 and subsequently The University of British Columbia (a local university) decided to give him a scholarship to study here. I met the young man in person. A brilliant young man, full of ideas, oomph and zest for life. Meeting him made me remember myself when I first arrived to study at The University of British Columbia at the age nineteen. I wish him all the best and my heart aches for all the talented young men and women living in the occupied territories that will never get a chance.

Good job Globe and Mail, you made a difference for at least one person. Sorry about the nasty letters.

Tough Girl

"You are a tough Iraqi girl", my dad tells me at age sixteen as I am about to undergo a minor surgical procedure. "I am a tough Iraqi girl", I repeat after him. My dad gives me the thumbs up and smiles. "That's my girl," he says, "Don't worry, it is a minor surgery, everything is going to be fine," he continues. As the nurse hauls me away on a bed on wheels towards the surgery room, I look back. My dad looks like a deflated balloon. He is hunched over and looks worried. The smile is gone. He doesn't look all that tough any more.

I am a tough Iraqi girl. I have told myself that through out my life, especially during trying times. At age 8 I decided that I wouldn't cry anymore, because crying is a sign of weakness. Initially it took an effort to fight the urge to cry, over time I lost the ability to cry completely. I have a tendency to smile or giggle even in the most stressful situations; a reaction that puzzles and sometimes disturbs people around me. It took even more effort to regain the ability to cry later on, but that is another story.

In September of 2000, I was 8 months pregnant with my third child, had recently moved back to Canada and was working my tail off at a high stress job. My husband was traveling all over the world with work. Finally, he comes back from what I thought to be his last trip for a while. I felt relieved to have him back home. He can help me bathing the kids in the evening as bending over has become hard, he can also help me

135

carry the 1.5 year old to the car in the morning as she is becoming too heavy for me. One evening, right after dinner, his graduate student calls from Jerusalem. He is writing his thesis and freaking out, as many students do during this stage. My husband tells him not to worry; I will grab the first flight to Israel and spend a week with you. Later he tells me that his student needs emotional support, he has to be with him. "What if the baby comes a week or two early? You will miss the baby's birth" I tell him. "I am starting to get tired and I need some emotional support too," I continue. My husband chuckles and says, "I am not worried about you at all, you are as strong as a horse." Damn! I fooled even my husband with the tough act, so strong as a horse I had to become.

[Tip for married men: Don't tell your wife that she is strong as a horse when she is 8 months pregnant and asking for your help.]

One year later my co-worker comes into my office and asks me, "how do you do it? You have three young kids, a more difficult job, yet you come every morning with a smile on your face and you look great. I have a much easier job, just one kid and there are times when I think I am going to go crazy. So how do you do it?" "Oh piece of cake," I tell her, "You just need to be organized, that is all." She leaves my office looking even more puzzled. I don't tell her how I get up at 5 in the morning to get everything ready and run around like crazy till 10 pm. I don't tell her that there are days when I don't feel like getting out of the bed, but I force myself. I don't tell her that there are days when I feel I am about to go crazy too, but I force myself to smile. That is the tough girl's trick. When everything is falling apart, smile and keep saying, this too shall pass. This too shall pass, this too shall pass.

A few days before the second American led war on Iraq, we call my uncle in Baghdad. We try to be cheerful, but everything we say sounds like we are saying good-bye. My uncle asks my dad if we are doing well. He had heard over the news that in North America people of Arab decent are being harassed. "I am worried about you", he tells my dad. Uncle is in Baghdad, days before the war, and he is worried about us living in Vancouver. My dad asks Uncle why he doesn't move out of Baghdad before the war, as the fighting is bound to be the most intense in Baghdad. "My son is in the army and he is stationed in Baghdad, how can I run to safety and leave him? If Baghdad is nuked I want all of us to die together," is his response. We hang up the phone and look at each other, "Do you think we will hear his voice again?"… the question hangs in the air. "This too shall pass, this too shall pass. We have been through this once already, no problem, piece of cake," I tell myself.

The war starts. At night I go to my parent's house and we see aerial footage of Baghdad getting bombed. The heartache of being an Iraqi; can't be described. I mask the pain under a poker face and thick layer of makeup. I go to work, attend meetings, look into daily tasks and discuss schedules and work assignments. In between meetings and emails I sneak to the washroom to cry, then I wash my face, apply fresh makeup and put the tough Iraqi girl face on. Back to my busy work schedule. At the end of one meeting, one of my co-workers says, "I was watching the war last night, isn't it cool?" Does he realize that thousands of people are getting killed and that many more are being maimed? What could possibly be cool about that? Later on the same day yet another co-worker starts telling me some of his personal problems, he is unhappy in his job and other aspects of his life are not going as he would like them to be. I want to tell him that his problems seem incredibly trivial at this point, but instead I listen carefully. I give him the pep talk about how life has its ups and downs and we need to face each stage with courage. Later I email him Gobran Khalil Gobran's poem "Joy and Sorrow" from his book "The prophet". I am sending the poem to my co-worker; really I am sending it to me. I really want to believe that there is joy at the end of this sorrow; I want to believe that there is a flip side to this coin; I want to believe that there is light at the end of this tunnel.

I secretly hold a grudge against both co-workers because of their lack of humanity on a very difficult day in my life. Sometimes I think it is not their fault, I do the tough Iraqi girl act so well.

And then, the ultimate tough Iraqi guy gets captured. Only he turns out not to be tough at all. In fact he looks pathetic, he looks disheveled. I should be happy, I should be celebrating. How I dreamt of this day, how I fantasized about Iraq with out this man. Only now I feel depressed. It takes me a long time to figure out my strange reaction. Fair trial, not a fair trial, I don't care. I hope they hang him upside down and kick his head in. Why did we let this pathetic loser rule our lives?

138

To all of you who know me in person, I have a confession to make. I am not tough at all. It is all a big act. Really, I am a big wimp. Perhaps I should spend a week or two feeling sorry for myself. Yes! I know that feeling sorry for myself is unproductive. But, I have been productive since I was 8, I deserve a break. I am contemplating not taking a shower the next time I feel in distress, perhaps if I look and smell like horse shit, it would give people a good indication of how I feel on the inside.

Hijab Story

Let me tell you the story of my experience attending Hussieniya (a lament for the death of Imam Hussien performed by a sect of Shi'a Muslims every year). The year was 1995 and I was living in Galsgow, Scotland. My husband and I became good friends with a religious Iranian couple, K. and S. Both became incredibly excited when they heard that I come from a shi'a family and decided to invite me for a Hussieniya held at a mosque in Glasgow by the Shi'a community living there. I have never attended a Hussieniya before. I have read about it in books though. While living in Kuwait, the Shi'a performed such ceremonies in secret to avoid persecution from the government. I would sometimes hear other girls whisper about it to each other in school. Since my father is very secular we were not involved and hence my knowledge of various Shi'a ceremonies was restricted to things I have read or heard from other people. Nothing like exploring your religious roots in a foreign city that has absolutely nothing to do with it.

On the day of the Hussieniya, I decided that I would wear Hijab the whole day and not just during the period while at the mosque. I thought it would be an interesting experience, to see how people would react to me when I was wearing a head scarf, a long skirt and long sleeves. That was the first time I wore Hijab in my life. On that day, I placed my daughter in her stroller and did grocery shopping, went for a little stroll in the park and walked around the city center. Everywhere I

141

went, there would be another woman wearing Hijab who would walk towards me, smile and whisper "Salam Alaikum sister". I would smile back and say "Salam Alaikum sister". Glasgow, has a large immigrant community from Pakistan and many of them are religious. I never noticed how many Hijab-wearing women were around until that day. I felt like there was this whole sisterhood action going on; I must confess that I enjoyed that aspect of it. I didn't enjoy the way people looked at me in the neighborhood grocery store though. I went to the CD store and asked the person attending the shop if he had a CD for "Ani Difranco"; he was so shocked it took him several seconds to finally respond. He probably didn't think that a woman wearing Hijab would know who Ani Difranco is. I must confess that I got some guilty pleasure out of surprising him like that. I am such a trouble maker.

As the time to the Hussieniya approached, I started to feel nervous. What if I do or say something stupid and offend everybody at the mosque? What if people can tell I am not religious and kick me out of the mosque? All sorts of dark thoughts like that started to cross my mind. Then I remembered a book I read a year earlier, "Guests of the Sheik: An Ethnography of an Iraqi Village by Elizabeth Warnock Fernea". Elizabeth Warnock Fernea spent the first two years of her marriage in the 1950s living in El Nahra, a small village in Southern Iraq, and her book is a collection of stories about the life of a western woman attempting to adapt to living in super conservative society. Her husband is an anthropologist and instructs her that she must learn about the lives of the women, since as a man he has no access to that world. Many of

142

the village woman befriend her and help her adapt to the local customs. In her book she describes in vivid detail many Hussieniyas and other Shi'a processions she had attended. I thought to myself, if an American Christian like Elizabeth can go through it, so can I. At the mosque, I meet S. outside; she complements my proper Hijab. She seems happy to see me dressed like that. Later on she told me that she was worried I would show up wearing jeans and T-shirt. We go into the mosque together. The women are sitting on one side and all the men are setting on the other, everybody is sitting on the floor, and kids are running all over the place. I sit down in the middle of the crowd and seat my daughter next to me. On the other side I can see K. with the men, as soon as he sees me he jumps up and runs towards the women's side, something he is not supposed to do. He looks at me with amazement, he tells me that my Hijab is very proper and tells me that I look great. This is so out of character for him, K. is a super demure, shy and modest person. Usually he never looked at me straight in the eye. When he talked to me he would look away according to Muslim modesty customs. But now he was staring straight at me with a big smile on his face, he looks like he can't believe that the jeans and T-shirt girl can be transformed to proper hijab girl. His wife instructs him to go back and sit with the men. Which he does promptly.

The Imam starts telling the story of Imam Hussien, his voice is melodic and sad. Once in a while he breaks down into crying. People around me start crying. Something very surprising happens next; I start crying too. I think I am overcome with group hysteria. My daughter looks surprised:

Daughter: Mommy, why are you crying?

Elen: I don't know.

Daughter: Why are these other people crying?

Elen: They are sad because somebody very important died a long time ago; his name was Imam Hussien, he was the grandchild of the prophet Muhamad.

Daughter: Who is prophet Muhamad?

Elen: Shh! (I don't want people to know that my daughter doesn't know who prophet Muhamad is). I will tell you about him later. Here are some crayons and paper to play with.

Daughter: Ok! (she looks happy with the crayons).

I make a mental note, I must tell my daughter the story of prophet Muhamad and afterwards about Imam Hussien. She should at least know about it. After a while some of the people start swaying from side to side and hitting themselves on the chest. The hitting is symbolic, I myself stick to crying. I have read in books about processions where people would beat themselves until they bled. I have read about chains, rocks over the head, but none of that happens in this place. Just gentle hitting over the chest, nothing too dramatic. This lasts for a couple of hours, then everybody moves to another room where food is served; everybody eats and then sits around chatting. All the Iranian Shi'a are on one side, and Iraqi Shi'a are on the other. Maybe it is the language barrier thing. I end up chatting to two older Iraqi women who tell me about how much they miss living in Iraq and why they had to move abroad. A fairly sad story.

The next day, I got up to go to work. I wore a dark suit, short skirt, white silk blouse and a colorful silk scarf. Panty hose and black shoes. Makeup. I looked at myself in the mirror; I looked professional, as in "get out of the way Aggressive women on the move" professional. I went to the office and said good morning to my co-workers.

good morning
good morning
hello
hello
how do you do?

Nobody called me his sister on that day.

Operation Enduring Purchase

It is time for Plan B.

I am going to buy Israel. Yes! you heard that right. That is my plan. I will buy the whole country and convert it into a state where each person has a single vote and each person is equal. It will resolve the conflict and everybody will be happy.

I have been an activist for several years, I have gone to numerous demonstrations. I have been part of a small but active group, we have hosted forums, contacted politicians, the media, tried to raise awareness about the human rights violations against the Palestinians. I have spend many weekends standing on the streets giving out leaflets, I learned to speak at public forums and give presentations, something I wasn't very good at in the beginning and I have learned to refute every argument slung at me with concise yet razor sharp rebuttal. I wrote hundreds of letters to editors of our major newspapers, pointing out their biases. I got so frustrated with our major newspapers that I eventually gave up writing letters to the editor and started writing my own articles and had limited success getting some of thier published. The plan was to create public pressure in North America that would force Israel to give basic human rights to the Palestinians. The thought was to use the same tactics as with the Apartheid government in South Africa, that by creating international pressure on the South African government there was an impetus for change, that we could do the same with Israel. In fact many people involved with the pro-Palestinian movement have been involved in the anti-Apartheid movement as well. We wrote up pamphlets and other literature, we built a cool website and we had a Yahoo newsgroup to spread the news. We have had our small successes, and there were times when I felt the message was getting through, but in the mean time things have only gotten worse for the Palestinian people. During the last few years, Israel had started to build the separation wall, which will encircle Palestinian communities into little isolated islands. The policy of targeted assassinations had started and on most days at least a few Palestinian civilians died. Recently we have heard the American President give Israel the green light to do as they please and the rest of the world doesn't seem to care, not beyond words anyway. We have seen Sheik Ahmed Yassin and Abed Al Azziz Rantissi assassinated, and nobody seems to care. So I think it is time to acknowledge that despite of all the hard work of the last years it really made no difference.

I felt so mad at first when I heard George Bush over the radio commending Ariel Sharon and giving him backing to do everything he has ever dreamed of. And then I realized that I have no reason to be mad. President George Bush simply had the courage to clearly and honestly outline the American policy towards Israel and Palestine. This has been America's policy all along, under Clinton, Bush the father, Reagan. They all paid lip service to the Palestinian right of self determination while allowing Israel to do as they wish. I read in a newspaper that this is drastic change in the American policy towards the Middle East. It isn't. This is exactly the American policy in the Middle East all along. I admire President Bush for being honest; I admire him

148

for having the courage to get real. I finally realized it was time to stop paying lip service to my own beliefs and get real as well. It is silly to think that you can keep doing the same thing over and over again and expect different results. I think it is time to abandon Plan A and envision a new plan. Ladies and gentlemen I present to you my Plan B. A plan that will create a revolutionary peace in the Middle East without shedding a single drop of blood or engaging a single soldier.

My plan is to do a Bill Gates stunt, develop some software and convince everybody in the world that they have to buy it. I will become a bazilionaire and use the money to buy the state of Israel. I will simply buy everything there is to buy in that country, land, media, and businesses. Whatever is up for sale, I will buy it. It's not a very big country so it is not that hard to buy either, all or most of it. I figure I will need about 85 billion dollars to accomplish the task. Once I have majority ownership stake in the country I will create a quiet revolution. I will fire the Knesset (Israeli parliament) and remove the Prime Minister from power. Megalomaniacs like myself should not rule countries so instead I will instate my good friend Alyson as the interim ruler of the state for a year. Alyson is a Zen New Age type of person, very concerned with justice and equality in the world. However, because of our special friendship and since I am the one that placed her in power, I would expect that my ideas would have some influence on the new government. Alyson will assemble a transitional government whose members will represent all the various ethnic groups living in Israel: Jewish, Palestinian, Badu, Druze, people who believe they are the next messiah, all the different groups. During that year a provisional constitution will be drawn - guaranteeing equal rights to everybody, one-citizen-one-vote. The provisional constitution will be subject to the approval of the transitional governing counsel, but I am already sure that will adopt the constitution that I have drawn for them because it is so great, I can't imagine they will possibly be able to improve on it. That year will also be used to prepare for elections and re-educating people about concepts of human rights, justice and equality; yes, even the Palestinian deserve equal rights, what a radical concept. We will call the new state Israstien and create a new flag that is representative of the entire ethnic group rainbow. The transitional government can choose a different name if they like – hey, I always said I believed in democracy and freedom of the individual.

In fact I was raised in a democratic family. When I was a kid my dad always said that we were a democratic family. To teach us the principles of democracy he would let my brother and myself vote on decisions like which restaurant to go to on the weekend, or what activities to do during the summer holidays. I frequently called my dad's democracy a one-legged democracy, because we only voted on the things of little consequence. All important matters were decided in my father's head all by himself. My father would always respond by telling me that as the head of the family he maintains certain veto rights. I am only telling you this story to illustrate that I was raised with democracy flowing in my blood. But I digress, back to Plan B. The West Bank and Gaza strip will become part of Israstien. All hostilities will end and there will be nothing to fight over, once everybody has equal rights. Eventually, democratic elections in the end will have a big party. Dance, music and plenty of

150

ululations. We will party for days as if we are in some perpetual weddings the party will go on until everybody is too tired to party anymore, one long rave, beats having a genocide, but is equally tiring. Finally, everybody will go home to sleep it off, and when they get up there will be peace, just like that.

Anybody wishing to make a donation to my free Israel fund please make a donation, each dollar will get me closer to my goal. All you skeptical lefties shaking your heads at my idea, Capitalism rocks! We just haven't seen it applied appropriately until now, but I intend to change that. Wealthy people of the world, unite!

Alyson will be moved to rule over my next purchased country.

Having Fun - The Angry People Stories

The man honked at me as I was about to take a left turn. He was trying to rush me, as in "turn already!". Instead, I stop the car and look in my rear view mirror. Now, he is even angrier, his face is turning red and he starts honking repetitively. Honk, honk, honk. It was a beautiful sunny day in Vancouver, Tracy Chapman was playing on the radio and I was in a good mood. I can't remember why I was in a good mood, but I distinctively remember the sense of serenity that I felt on that day. The guy comes out of his car, his face is red and he tells me to kiss a certain body part of his. I ask him if he would like me to do that in the street right there and then, or if he would rather we go somewhere else. Now his face is all contorted, he starts calling me all sorts of names which I don't wish to repeat in polite company. I blow him a kiss, "love and peace brother, have a nice day" I answer him. Ok! Now I am ready to take that left turn, now that he looks like he will start frothing at the mouth at any minute. I think what annoyed him the most is the fact that he couldn't wipe the smile off my face. Yeah! I am annoying like that.

Remember how I told you that I don't get depressed, I get even. Well the next story is a perfect example

When I lived in Scotland, we had your typical busy-body neighbour. He would stick notes on the entrance to our apartment with a list of his complaints. We made too much noise, my daughter cried too much and we didn't pick up the newspaper from our door step promptly enough in the morning. So one day when I got fed up with his notes. I took a sheet of paper and drew a big and colorful smiley face on it. I wrote underneath it, "Smile, life is too short". I stuck the paper in the exact place where he usually stuck his notes. He became the butt of jokes in our apartment building and we never saw another note from him ever again. Not to me and not to anybody else in our building. It is funny how you can turn somebody's anger against them and still maintain your cool.

So next time you meet an angry miserable person, don't miss your chance to have some good clean fun. If you are mad at me, I will teach you a lesson on how little I care about what others think of me.

Like when somebody calls me a bitch. I always respond by saying, "Now that is original, I have never been called that before …….. Not!". Then I start laughing. It always drives the person mad.

Non-Gently into a Good Night

I walked into the living room to find Latifa standing on the window sill from the outside from our sixth-floor apartment in Jerusalem. She was holding on with one hand. Latifa was not attempting to commit suicide, she was merely cleaning the windows from the outside, using the free hand to wipe away layers of sand and dirt. I gathered all my strength in order to suppress my urge to scream. With the softest voice I could muster I said, "Latifa, come inside I want to tell you something". I watched as she gathered her robe around her in order not to trip on it, she held with both hands and then swung her body into the balcony with an agility that seemed out of character for her 60-something year old body. As soon as her feet were planted on the floor of the balcony, and before she had the chance to straighten her self up, I started to scream.

Elen: What in heavens name are you doing?

Latifa: I am cleaning the windows from the outside.

Elen: We are on the sixth floor, you could have slipped and gotten yourself killed.

Latifa: But the windows are dirty and they are too big and heavy; I can't move them out of the window frame in order to clean them properly and so I have to go outside. There is no other way.

Elen: In that case leave the windows dirty and do your best cleaning them while standing on the inside.

Latifa: But when people visit you and ask you about who cleans your

155

house and windows they will say that Latifa didn't clean those windows properly. They will say that Latifa is dirty. They will not look clean if I only wash one side. This is what I do in all the other apartments as well. Don't worry, I never slip.

Elen: I don't care. This is my apartment and you are not allowed to get yourself killed in it. Get yourself killed in somebody else's apartment. Leave the windows dirty. I want my windows to be dirty. Do you understand that.

Latifa: (she waves her hand in a dismissive fashion and nods her head). Fine! fine! you can have your dirty windows. I will do as you say. But if it was God's will that I die today, then I will die today, regardless of whether I stand on the sill of the window from the outside or not.

I go into the kitchen to have a glass of water to calm myself down. It was the first time of only two times that I raised my voice with Latifa. She was the domestic help I hired to clean the apartment in Jerusalem. Latifa was a Palestinian living in the occupied territories, she is living in a tiny village right outside the city of Ramallah. Most of the time I was too intimidated by her. She had a fierce personality. Her face looked like one huge wrinkle that had slithered all across of what used to be a face. Her hands were so rough from years of physical labor you could grate parmesan cheese on them. A constant frown adorned her face and frequently when she thought that nobody was listening she would mumble to herself. She always seemed to be mumbling to god to have mercy on her and to make her life easier. She had a sturdy and tall body and looked like she could punch the crap out of anybody given enough provocation. There was something thuggish and menacing about her. When she stood in my living room with her hands crossed, wearing the traditional headscarf and traditional Palestinian dress, she looked like a rock. No, more like a mountain. Most of the time she gave me orders and told me what to do, not the other way around. For example, the second time she came to my apartment she opened the china cupboard and yelled at me. "I cleaned and organized this last week. Now look at it, it is messy again. You don't expect me to organize it for you every week, do you? I will organize this again but you need to keep it in order from now on." She set up a specific order in my cupboards, a place for the large plates, small plates, cups and serving. Everything had to be in its place. Otherwise, watch out for the Wrath of Latifa. You would think I was working for her. Woohoo! those Palestinian women. Let me tellya.

I really like my Canadian domestic help here in Vancouver much more. She comes every morning with a smile on her face. She greets me with a pleasant "Good morning". She does everything I tell her without any objections and no arguing. I ask her, "can you clean the cupboards please?" and the answer is "yes". Then I say "Thank you", and that is the end of that. My Canadian domestic help is dedicated to her job and does it very well but her dedication to her job is not suicidal. She would never stand on the sill of a window from the outside, no matter what. Furthermore, she never tells me that my skirt is too short and that as an Arab woman I need to dress more modestly. She never tells me that I should spank my kids in order to teach them respect. And she never tells me that I must produce a son in order not to lose my husband. In fact, my Canadian domestic help never interferes with my personal life. She never tells me that I should do anything. When I have guests or friends over, the Canadian domestic help doesn't give her running commentary about them. I don't think I miss Latifa at all. In fact, I have to confess that of all the cities that I have lived in, I like living in Vancouver the best. However, I have to give credit to Latifa for one thing, besides making me realize that I am a wimp and a push-over; she is the one that made me realize the source of my infatuation with the Palestinian people.

When I was a little girl growing up in Kuwait I used to always say that I would marry a Palestinian. As young as eight my mind was made up about this fact. You can ask my parents and they will confirm this fact to you. I frequently wondered why I made that determination at such a young age. The advantage of living in Kuwait was that I got to meet people from all over the Middle East. Kuwait had a large percentage of Arab nationals from everywhere in the Middle East working and living there. The Kuwaitis drove the expensive cars and wore the fancy Ray-Bans. The Iraqis were the most macho and had the most heroic tales. The Egyptians were the funniest and had the best jokes. The Palestinians were the geeks at school. So why did I want to marry a Palestinian, but not an Iraqi and not a Kuwaiti? How funny, that in the end that is exactly what I ended up doing when I grew up. It was one of those secrets about my life that I frequently contemplated, but never quite understood. Was it destiny? Was it the cosmic joker playing yet another one of his tricks on me?

158

Latifa means the gentle one in Arabic. There was absolutely nothing gentle about this woman. Her parents couldn't have chosen a less appropriate name for her. There wasn't much gentleness in her life either. Forced to marry at age 13 to a man in his 40's who proceeded to beat her regularly and sponge off her paycheck. Twenty years into her marriage her husband died, which Latifa didn't consider such a horrible disaster, if you catch my drift. At least she was free to use her money to raise her seven children. Upon her husband's death one of her daughters had a nervous breakdown, an event shrouded in secrecy. I never got a good answer as to why her daughter had the nervous breakdown, only that after a short stint in the hospital, the daughter now spends most of her time staring into the void at home. Latifah was made a refugee twice, courtesy of the Israeli state. As if that wasn't enough, Latifah had to support her younger sister who was abandoned with four children by her chivalry-laden husband. Plus, her oldest daughter was divorced from a psychopath of a husband and so Latifah was supporting her and a grandson as well. She was most proud of one daughter that worked as a nurse and seemed to be having a happy and stable life.

"Sometimes being a bitch is all a desperate woman has to hold on to." Latifah taught me that. She never said those words, I actually heard that in brilliant movie named "Dolores Claiborne". But Latifah was the true embodiment of these words. In the movie Dolores Claiborne, Kathy Bates, plays a tough housekeeper whose life has been a series of re-occurring miseries visited upon her from many sources. She becomes a defiant bitch, who is not expecting any gentleness from the world and

159

rarely ever receives any. Really, if you want to know what Latifah is like, go see Dolores Claiborne and imagine Kathy Bates with a head scarf, many more wrinkles and a long hand-embroidered robe for a dress. It is as if Kathy Bates had based it on the non-gentle character of Latifah.

I remember the news announcing the complete sealing of the occupied territories after a suicide bombing or some other threat, some real and others imaginary. The news would show the army blocking people from entering into the not-so-occupied territories. "The West Bank is completely sealed," the news announcer would declare. "Not even a rat can cross through." Latifah would appear at my door steps anyway. "Latifah, how did you get through? How did you pass?" I would ask her. Latifah would just wave her hand in dismissive way. "Nah! They don't scare me. Their stupid tanks with their stupid soldiers and their stupid machine guns. I have a job to do; a woman has to support her family." And you ask me why I was intimidated by this woman: the fourth strongest army in the world couldn't stand in the face of her determination.

In the Middle East we have all learned to eat shit from a very young age. The poor before the rich, women before men, but eventually we all learn the lesson very well. Just keep your mouth shut and look the other way. Don't ask why. That is just the way it is. The Palestinians always had at least a tiny defiant flick of hair or a slight dismissive rolling of the eyes. They would eat shit just like the rest of us but at least they didn't pretend they were liking it.

160

Latifah liked to socialize with my friends whenever somebody would come over for a visit. Once, a Palestinian woman friend from East Jerusalem came over for a visit. N was from a well to do family of merchants. Like all snotty Arab upper middle-class women, N was always dressed up and decked out in gold, layers of makeup and the latest fashion. I made some coffee and invited Latifah to take a break from her work and join us. N was horrified by the prospect of socializing with the uncouth, illiterate Latifah. N. whispered to me, "you sit and have coffee with her?". I said "Yes all the time, she has magnificent stories" . Well! you could see the look of shock on N's face at the prospect. Latifah sat down in my living room, made herself comfortable and starting chatting with N Asking her questions about herself and her family. I could tell that Latifah understood that N was not used to socializing with people from a lower social class, and she seemed to delight in the whole situation. She held her head high and seemed to enjoy making my snotty friend uncomfortable. I sat back and observed while sipping quietly, joining the conversation on occasion. Eventually N left. Latifah commented afterwards: "Your friend is very beautiful." I said, "Yes everybody says she is a beauty." Latifah replied "But you are much more beautiful than her, in a natural way with no make up." It was the first time of only two times I heard her say something kind.

I don't miss Latifah at all, but I appreciate the lesson she taught me.

The Adventures of a Boring Sinner in Lotus land

"Let him send me to hell" I thought to myself.
"That pompous arrogant tyrant! ….. who expects me to worship him. Since I am going to hell for refusing to obey; I might as well earn a deserving place in there." I was determined to go to hell in style. But how? What do I have to do in order to go to hell in style? I had no idea.

Shortly after losing my religion in the Holy Lands of Jerusalem. I faced a dilemma in my newly found religion free life ; one which I had no idea how to tackle. I was certain I was going to hell for my act of disobedience, and I wanted to be sure it was for a worthwhile reason. How do I mark my new identity as a sinner? How do I make sure that I would make my hell bound path count?
The questions dogged me night and day.

I drew comfort from the thought that as I was losing my religion I was planning to move from the Holy lands of Jerusalem into the sin city of Vancouver, Canada. "Surly after the move I will be able to find creative ways to express my new identity", I told myself. I wasn't sure how yet, but I was sure that with enough determination I would find a way.

Sin city! ….. here I come ….. this time with open arms.

Vancouver, BC, Canada is frequently called the sin city of North

America. Gay marriage is legal, churches sit mostly empty Sunday service after a Sunday service, Downtown Vancouver east side is the proud host of the highest concentration of drug addicts in the world, additionally, Vancouver is renowned for marijuana growers, nightclubs and strippers.

Oh! what pleasures awaited me. All those years of religious piousness, surly have deprived me of awesome adventures and delights and now I was free to sample and explore to my hearts desire. As soon as I settled down in Vancouver I sat down pondering my next steps as a sinner.

"What sins I should tackle first?", I pondered.

Drugs? ….. Anybody who has lived in Vancouver and has walked passed the junkies on East Hastings streets with their twitching arms, skinny figures and bulging eyes, could not be more turned off by the prospect. The thought of joining them one day horrified me. I had never used drug in my life. When I say I never used drugs, I don't mean "I never inhaled" like when Clinton wasn't using drugs, I mean I never touched the stuff, didn't hang out with that crowed and never had anything to do with it. Surly committing sins should be enjoyable and not terrifying, seeing the drug addicts in their pathetic state didn't appeal to me at all. And so drugs were ruled out.

Fornicating? …. But I was already married to the most handsome man I had ever met. His sight made my heart skip and his touch was pure pleasure. The mere thought of even looking at another man seemed revolting and surly being sinful was supposed to be pleasurable. Had I met him after my religion loosing experience, I might have allowed for our love to be expressed physically before we were married. But, it was too late for that, we were already married both legally, according to Canadian law, and religiously by a Muslim imam. "Doing it" before marriage would have been a perfect foray into sin-hood; worthy of going to hell for, but unfortunately I had missed the boat on that one. Now it was too late. Had Islam been one of those puritanical religions that demanded sex between husband and wife take place for procreation only, I would have achieved the most pleasurable opportunity to be a sinner. But my understanding of Islam was that sex for pleasure between husband and wife was perfectly sanctioned ….. damn you Islam! ….. must you make my life hard even when I am trying to rebel against you. I wished I was born a catholic at that point.

Desperate times requires desperate measures. I had no choice but to break the big taboos of Islam: alcohol and pork. Both are not only strictly forbidden, but so ingrained in the culture that even non-religious people feel shame about breaking those taboos. I went to the supermarket and looked at the pork chops laying there in the meat section. I always would pass over the pork section in the meat department in the past. This time I looked at the various kinds of pork cuts and contemplated bringing the pork chops back home and frying them. Just looking at the pork chops with their pinkish color made me want to vomit. While I understand that this is a cultural thing and that many people would look at those pork chops and think yum …. yum, I couldn't bring myself to cross the boundary of revulsion after years of brain washing that taught me to think of pork as yuck!.

Sigh! This sin committing thing isn't easy.

I discovered however that now that I no longer cared about religion I could eat in Chinese restaurants without being the one that is a pain in the neck and always asking to ensure that there is no pork in any of the ingredients. I could eat the dumplings and sweet and sour soup and as long as nobody would point out to me that there was pork hidden in the shredded bit of thingies floating in there I was fine. I applied the don't ask, don't tell policy at restaurants and I was able to relax and enjoy myself more. I wouldn't order the pork chops from the menu, but on the other hand I stopped asking questions like "are you sure there is no pork in the Swiss meat balls dish?".

I still remember the look of joy on my husband's face after I told him that I was ready to let go of the strict "no alcohol in the house" rule. "You mean I can have a beer?" was his first thought. For 10 years he has respected my religiosity and not bought nor drank alcohol out of respect for my feelings. I sincerely admire my husband for putting up with my prudishness all these years. I also informed my husband that I was ready to try it myself, at which point he looked a bit concerned, but was willing to go along with the idea. I couldn't stand drinking hard liquor, a single sip made me want to choke and it all tasted like dissolved soap water. Beer tasted fine but bubble for bubble, I still prefer a diet coke to a beer on any day. But then I tasted red wine, and I started to understand why people like alcohol. With a good meal it really is nice. For the first time my husband told me about his favorite kind of wine, turns out he likes white wine …. very very dry. I also finally understood what gave cream mushroom sauce that special taste in French restaurants. At home I tried to make it many times and it never tasted quite right. But add a few drops of white wine and walla! …. like magic …. the right taste. After I sampled a little bit of this and that I was ready to try getting drunk. I told my husband that I wanted to get drunk but he rejected the idea. He would only allow me one drink and with food, each time he would remind me to drink slowly. In restaurants, whenever I wanted to order more or drink fast he would say no and instruct me to "GO SLOW". So one Friday evening while he was on a business trip I dug up a wine bottle and drank half of it fast and without food trying to see what would happen if I got drunk. In Canada people constantly talk about how they had fun at parties by getting drunk and I wanted to experience that fun. But all I experienced was that I felt dizzy afterwards, so much so that I had to go to bed immediately. The next morning I woke up with a headache and felt icky on the inside. I don't get what is fun about that but I am not going to do it again.

Besides Chinese sweet and sour soup which may or may not include pork and that wonderful French cream of mushroom sauce, which I absolutely adore, I haven't discovered anything worth going to hell for. It seems that gluttony is my favorite mortal sin, however I have to admit, it is an area I indulged in even in the pre losing religion era.

In desperation I went to my husband explaining to him my dilemma hoping he would give me good advice. I explained to him how I wanted to do something big, something monumental to mark my new reality as a non religious person, yet so far I haven't found anything that felt right or that felt so enjoyable as to merit losing religion over. Surely there must be something out there, some pleasure, some sin, that I can commit that is worth the whole exercise. I live in a liberal society that gives me the freedom to do whatever I want. I don't have to worry about what people will say about me or what the neighbors think of me. What do I do with all this freedom? …. nothing. I must be the most boring person on earth. What is wrong with me? Am I just a pathetic person?

My husband listened carefully while I detailed my dilemma and then he gave me the answer I was looking for. He said: "You are going about this the wrong way, you are trying to do the things that you think are bad or frowned upon by religion and really non of it is in your nature. What you should be doing is thinking of something you deeply desired or deeply wished for in the past but were prevented from doing because of religion. Surely there must be something that you fantasized about but not allowed your self in the past. Think back, think of something you deeply desire"

That is when it hit me. I should go buy my first pair of pants.

Up to this point I had always dressed modestly with skirt below the knees, long sleeves and baggy shirts. While I never covered my hair in proper hijab as is common to Muslim women I made sure to observe strict modestly rules which I imposed on myself since the age of 12. Deep down I wished I could wear a pair of jeans but in the past I always denied those thoughts even to myself. I still remember that first pair of jeans I wore as a grownup, they must be the baggiest pair of jeans in the world. They had so many pleads around the waist I might as well had been wearing a skirt. But I felt radical whenever I wore them. The thing with wearing pants is that it freed me in so many ways. Now that I allowed myself to wear pants I could skip, run, ride a bike, go to the gym and even go for a hike in nature. All these activities I didn't allow myself in the past because you can't do them wearing a skirt. At least you can't do them wearing a skirt and not look silly. Oh the fun I had in those pants. The many many joys, I can't describe them in words. To be able to move and feel your body, to be able to throw away the demure feminine walk. But the most enjoyable of these activities was discovering nature. And if there is one thing Vancouver has plenty of it is nature. The sea from one side and mountain on the other side and now that I was a pant wearing member of the public I could discover it all. They don't call Vancouver lotusland for nothing you know.

Odysseus (in greek mythology) and his men discover a magical land of lotus eaters. Some of the sailors eat the delicious lotus and forget about their homeland, pleading to stay forever in this lotusland. (It is likely that the lotus in question was a real plant, the jujube, whose sweet juice is used in candy making and which has given its name to a popular fruity candy.) The label "lotusland" is now applied to any place resembling such an ideal of perfection, but it also carries connotations of indolence and self-indulgence, possibly derived from the way the sailors refused to work once they reached the original lotusland.

I definitely had reached my own lotusland once I discovered hiking and kayaking around Vancouver. Having lived in a city all my live, nothing prepared me for the sensation of being in nature. I would go on for several days where I never saw another human being, I was surrounded with trees, the sounds of branches swaying and birds chirping. The joys of week long hiking and camping trips in complete solitude is that you stop caring about what other people think because there are no other people around. There is just nature, the mountain, the river, the sound of my breathing and heaving, the smell of moss ….. and that is when it happened. I can't describe it in words.

Oh how cruel this cosmic joker is. He sends me to the holy lands to lose my religion and then back to lotus land to experience spirituality. He must have watched too many monty python episodes or something.

Few weeks ago, my daughter was learning about world religions in her social studies class. She asked that I give her some things from our Muslim heritage for show and tell for her class. I dig up my old prayer rug from the closet, find a copy of the Qura'an in the library with the beautifully decorated test, I find a piece of dirt from holy city of Najaf that all shea'a seem to carry. Suddenly I find tears in my eyes. I wipe them off and dismiss them as fake sentimentality.

170

My husband predicts that I will go back to religion. I keep telling him "no way". I refuse to give up my pants wearing freedom. He also wants to go back to our old "no alcohol in the house" rule. While he enjoys the occasional beer, he thinks that we should set a good example for our kids ….. hmmmm! is my husband turning religious on me?

Two weeks ago I had a parent teachers meeting with my daughter's grade four teacher and one of her suggestions for me was to buy my daughter more books about Islam, because she is very interested in the subject and has already devoured all the books on the subject available in the school library. Now that has to be the ultimate sin, when the infidel Canadian heathen who has nothing to do with Islam tells me that I should buy more books on Islam for my daughter. I am certainly going to hell for that.

I think I have achieved my objective

Hassan

Usually the coffee fortune telling is composed of poetic imagery that you are free to interpret according to your circumstances. Examples would be:

"I see a journey ahead of you, one which will take you to new and unfamiliar places"

"I see you next to a white snake, you should be careful of the snake, but on your right I see a bird, the bird will be your salvation"

"The evil eye is upon you, but don't worry, I see three feminine figures watching over you and protecting you"

The language is vague enough so that almost everybody could interpret it in a meaningful way to his or her personal circumstances.

Rarely does Arabic coffee fortune telling include a precise statement that says: "You will marry a man whose name is Hassan."

"But, I don't want to marry Hassan," I exclaimed in exasperation, upon the seeing the coffee cup with my own two eyes

Many years ago, before I met Za'atarah. I knew an Egyptian man named Hassan. He was doing a Mamasters degree in Engineering while I was in computer science in Vancouver. I could tell right away that he liked me. The way he looked at me ... the way he smiled each time he saw me. But we pretended that we were friends. Hassan, me and my brother and a group of Arab friends were constantly hanging out together. Going to the beach, movies and such as a group ... never just me and him ... since I was still in my religious phase. I was flattered by his attention to me, but I didn't share his feelings. I thought he was a nice guy and everything, but I wasn't in love with him. Hassan looked ok, not too handsome, but not bad looking either. He was smart and funny. You could tell that he had a bright future ahead of him. Our arabic "shellah", or gang, as we liked to call ourselves, we had lots of fun together.

Then one day Hassan said that he wants to talk to me in private. So I met with him at the Student Union building after my classes. It had been a long day and I was tired after too many classes and a three-hour chemistry laboratory. So we sat and Hassan mumbled and mumbled, he looked nervous. Finally I said: "Tell me what you want to talk to me about in private," and Hassan said:"You look visibly tired, I will talk to you about it some other time when you are not tired." Ok, fine.

I suspected that he wanted to tell me that he loves me but I pretended to be stupid and not understand what was going on.

Then two months later, the shellah agreed that we all meet in Hassan's apartment and then all of us as a group would go see a show together and then go for coffee and cake afterwards. I arrived at Hassan's apartment to discover that I was the first person there. It turns out that Hassan told me to arrive a full hour ahead than everybody else. He said that he wanted to talk to me in private .... again.

Ok!

Again he mumbled and mumbled and talked about all sorts of things that didn't seem to make sense. He looked nervous and his hands were shaking.

Again I pretended that I didn't know what he was about to tell me.

Finally! He said it.

And then he proceeded to tell me his full plan for our life together. That we would get married in Egypt so that his family could be at the wedding and that he applied for immigration to Australia and that after we both graduate we would both go to Australia and that he doesn't mind that I work after we get married. He even calculated how much everything would cost, our wedding, tickets to Egypt, tickets to Australia ... everything. He had estimated how much both of us would earn in our jobs in Australia and he calculated that it would be enough for both of us to live well together. He had my next five years of my life planned out for me.

Ha? What? What are you talking about ..... I didn't agree to marry you yet. What about what I want to do? .... What if I don't want to get married in Egypt or immigrate to Australia. I happen to like living in Vancouver..... Wait a minute .... why am I even thinking about these things? I don't want to marry you to begin with, so why discuss the details.

Hassan was sure that if I would spend some time alone with him that I would fall in love with him and agree to marry him. He suggested that we date for a while, go for walks together and go to restaurants alone.

I told him that I couldn't do that because I was religious and that would be inappropriate.

Hassan told me that I was too conservative and making things too complex. And that even in the Middle East people dated before marriage and that I am too backwards.

I got mad at him and told him he was an idiot

But then we made up and he apologized. He asked me to think about it and I agreed that I would.

Later that day I went home and decided to think about it seriously. Here was a nice man that would make a good husband and probably a good father and anyway I wasn't in love with anybody; finding eligible Arab husbands in Vancouver was hard .... so why not? But then when I tried to imagine myself living with him everyday of my life, waking up next to him every morning, I felt appalled. I liked talking to him, he was nice and all, but only in small doses.

Two days later I told him that I didn't want to get married at all, that I was too young and that I think highly of him but don't love him and blah, blah, blah.

He told me that I was pretending because I was shy, that in his heart he knows we will end up together, that we were made for each other. And that with time I will realize that I love him too.

I tried to tell him about how I felt but he was in complete denial about it. He kept insisting that it is my destiny to be with him.

Later I discovered that he had told many of our friends that him and I are going to be married. Which made me very mad. I couldn't believe his audacity. How dare you talk about it to other people without getting my approval first?

So after all that, when I saw Hassan pop up again in my Arabic coffee cup, the one I just finished drinking from, I was massively annoyed. How did he manage to write his name in my Arabic coffee cup in the privacy of my parents' house?

"I don't want to marry Hassan!" I yelled at my coffee cup. "I already said Nooooooo!"

A few weeks later Hassan severed his relationship with myself and all our mutual friends and essentially dropped off the face of the earth. His friends who tried to contact him could not reach him and he wouldn't return their messages. He disappeared .... just like that.

One month later I accidentally bumped into him on the street, he looked at me and in a hurry ran away to the other side of the road to avoid me.

"What an idiot" ... I thought to myself at the time ... "Good thing I didn't agree to marry him."

I felt hurt by his behavior.

I heard rumors from somebody that he did immigrate to Australia.

Today, when I look back I realize that I made the right decision to wait until I met somebody I loved;, I am also grateful that when I met Za'atarah the feelings were mutual. But now that my heart has been stung with the bee of love and I have experienced that desperate feeling of being hopelessly in love, I realize that I should have acted a little different with Hassan. I wish I was a little more forgiving with some of his crazy behaviour, and I wish I had made things easier for him. I wish I didn't pretend that I didn't know when it was obvious. I wish I made it easier for him to talk to me. I wish I was a bit nicer to him. I wish we had stayed friends.

I hope he is doing well wherever he is.

A Wedding in Galilee

About 14 years ago, as part of attempts to broaden awareness on Palestine we would organize Palestinian movie showings here in Vancouver. Whenever the issue of Arab-48 was brought up, there was a single movie whose name would come up.

A Wedding in Galilee.

At the time, there seemed to be no other movie by and about the Palestinians who remained inside Israel proper after the establishment of the Israeli state in 1948, commonly called Arab-48 or "Arabs of the inside" or "Israeli Arabs".

As a result I have seen that movie more than 10 times. Don't get me wrong …. it's a good movie …. it's just not the sort of movie that you want to see more than 10 times ….. believe me. There is no Julie Andrews singing, "The hills are alive with the sound of music," nor a chilling classic scene of a murder in the shower with a sharp knife. However there is a skillful and realistic depiction of a small Palestinian village. It talks about both the positive and negative aspects of that society through the prism of a wedding being attended by the Israeli Military Governor of the time. Many interesting interactions happen and you are left with a fairly accurate idea what it is like to live in that small village. The movie contains some harsh scenes, so if you are the sensitive type you might want to avoid it.

For all of you silly North Americans who will run out and go see the movie, let me clarify a very important point. Those scenes are not about homosexuality in the Arab society. All you silly homophobic North Americans don't understand that same sex friendships in other societies can be deep and meaningful. In Arab society men friends frequently hug or even hold hands as a show of friendship and this does not imply that they are gay. Just because your society assumes that all closeness between same sex people must be sexual, please don't make the same assumption about other societies.

Phew! …. now that I got that off my chest, once and for all, I can continue with the story.

My husband would watch the movie as if he was looking through the family album.

"Look! …. that is the street I used to walk on my way to school everyday"
"I know that actor personally"
" That is exactly the way my mother used to cook when I was a kid"

He would exclaim throughout the movie. It was both charming and annoying at the same time.

Thankfully, there have been new movies made by Palestinians living in the Galilee and so I have been pardoned from having to watch the same movie over and over again.

180

For those of you who didn't catch the drift, the name of the movie is a reference to the Wedding in Galilee mentioned in the Bible. Where Jesus attended a wedding in the village of Cana and performed the miracle of transforming water into wine. Cana now is called Kufer Kanna, Kufer means village in Palestinian dialect, and is visited by Christian tourists every year who buy really bad wine that is made at the village, so that tourists can go home and brag to their friends that they got wine from the village of Cana mentioned in the bible. My attachment to Kufer Kanna has nothing to do with the bible, nor bad wine, but rather with the fact that many of my husband's relatives live there. My husband was born and raised in the neighboring village of Mash-had, which is about a 15 minute walk from Kufer Kanna. Mash-had is not mentioned in the bible, and is not visited by tourists, not Christian nor any other kind, and does not have an awful wine factory. However, while living in Jerusalem we would visit there frequently and attend many of the local weddings. I came to realize why A Wedding in Galilee was worth a mention in a holy book; because weddings there are truly unique and worth attending ..... even by Jesus.

While the rest of the Middle East have gone the way of the West in wedding ceremonies, by embracing silly white dress, silly white cake and food banquet at a fancy hotel with a band; the Palestinians living in Galilee have managed to maintain ethnic authenticity and local customs in their weddings. A wedding there is typically celebrated over three days. A day to celebrate the bride, a day to celebrate the groom and a day to celebrate them both together. The wedding is held in the streets of the

181

town and everybody from the town and neighbouring towns are invited.

I used to like waking up early on a wedding day so that I would go watch the women doing the cooking for the wedding. A group of elderly women have been designated to do the cooking for all the weddings in the village. Youngsters like myself are not allowed to participate in any aspect of the food preparation, we are only allowed to sit and watch and clean the dirty dishes and pots afterwards. These elderly women cooked in huge pots on an open fire in the yard of a designated house. These were the hugest pots I had ever seen in my life. They looked like water tanks, only they were round. Wedding food is always the same dish ..... mansaf. Mansaf is a traditional Palestinian dish of rice, cooked lamb and yogurt sauce. No need for a miracle by a holy man since the food these elderly women cooked would easily feed thousands.

Dancing and music provided by the participants and performed in the streets and main square of the town, these weddings were tiring but fun.

While living in Jerusalem, I always enjoyed visiting my in-laws in Mash-had and the neighboring city of Nazareth. These weekend visits provided a welcome refuge from the psychotic Jerusalem.

I remember a Palestinian friend who was named after a famous

Islamic battle; I secretly called her Mrs. Battle. The nick name fitted her personality. Mrs. Battle was born and raised in Jerusalem, East Jerusalem, the Palestinian Jerusalem. I remember taking Mrs. Battle to West Jerusalem for a girls' night out. I took her to the trendy neighborhood of Emik Rafaeem. We sat in the trendy coffee shop of Kappeet, the one people go to be seen. The one Israeli celebrities and politicians hangout in. Mrs. Battle was amazed. The scenery, the ambience, everything was new to her. She was slightly uncomfortable. You see …. this was her time visiting this side of her home town.

I remember my co-worker Rachel, also born and raised in Jerusalem, West Jerusalem, the Jewish Jerusalem. I took her one weekend to East Jerusalem for a day-long adventure. We walked around the Old City. Visited a bunch of churches. Walked around Salah al Deen Street. We did some shopping and had humous at Abu Shoukri. Rachel enjoyed our little excursion enormously, this was also her first visit to this side of the her hometown. She too seemed a little uncomfortable.

Jerusalem is a unified city …. my foot.

Jerusalem must be the only city in the world where tourists can introduce the locals to their own hometown.

But Nazareth was none of that. Despite the Israeli State's effort to build another Nazareth, calling it the Upper Nazareth, everybody knew where the real Nazareth was located and that is where everybody

183

would hang out. I used love walking around the narrow streets of Nazareth. I would wander around in the old market, visit the clothing shops, a mandatory to visit to the Arabic sweets shop where I would have my favorite dessert in the world, knaffeh. Knaffeh is sweetened white cheese topped with shredded filo pastry that is dyed orange and the whole of this is drenched in sugary water called qater. I know that the concept of sweet white cheese and filo pastry might seem weird to some of you, but trust me you have to try knaffeh to discover what heaven must taste like.

But my favorite place to visit in Nazareth is the Basilica of the Annunciation. I usually find churches depressing and don't enjoy visiting them, but this church is different and unique. For some reason, which I can't explain, I always feel something when I go in there, a feeling I can't describe, a feeling of peace and contentment. This is the only church in I have ever been to that gave me that feeling. I always go in there for a visit whenever I am visiting Nazareth and I always ask my husband to visit the church for me when he goes to Nazareth without me. The church looks like no other church I had ever seen. It has a very modern design, yet you would never mistake it be anything other than a church. The Italian architect, Antonio Barluzzi, was heavily criticized for his design. Most churches built in the Middle East were built by European, Russian or Greek money and hence look like churches that have been transplanted from those far away countries. I have a feeling that the architect was trying to design a church that looked local, as if it was built by the local

184

population, as if it was Middle Eastern …. people seem to forget that is where it all began. Jesus wasn't European … you know! In the back courtyard of the basilica there are wall murals that depict images of virgin Mary and baby Jesus made in various countries around the world. It is a very interesting display because the images change drastically from county to country. Mary and baby look black when depicted in African countries, blonde from European countries and look Asian when depicted in South East Asia countries. It is interesting to walk around and contemplate how people create religious icons in their own image. The contrast is almost provocative. A church with a display that makes you think and question? ….. How radical?

Two years ago, our local newspaper, The Vancouver Sun, published an image that some scientist made up trying to guess what Jesus looked like from analyzing skulls of people from the same period. I took one look at the composed picture and gasped. The similarity was astounding. It looked just like my beloved husband Za'atarah.

If You Are Insane ... Move to Vancouver

"I want to know if I am crazy or sane,"

I said to my family doctor, immediately after the usual greeting and after he asked me his usual, "Sooooo! What can I do for you today?" The doctor looked surprised.

He didn't know what to say.

He asked me to explain.

I reminded my family doctor of my brother's first psychotic episode, that had preceded my visit to the doctor by about two months. The doctor nodded to indicate that he remembered. So I continued to explain how since my brother's hospitalization in the psychiatric ward, all the meetings with all the doctors, the medications, time spent observing the other crazies in the psychiatric ward made me start thinking

"What if I am crazy too?"

"Perhaps I am insane like my brother, but nobody has noticed"

"Perhaps I am mentally ill, but in milder form and hence nobody has noticed it"

"Perhaps this thing is genetic, perhaps it runs in the family, perhaps we are all insane"

"If this thing is genetic then perhaps if I have children they will have the mental illness as well" (I didn't have children at the time, but was thinking about having children)

"Perhaps I am sane now, but will become insane later"

Doctor! …. I have so many questions that I need answers to.

The doctor took a deep breath and started asking me questions about my job, my marriage, my relationship with my family and relationship with friends.

Then he explained to me that mentally ill people have a hard time staying in the same job for a long time, staying in a marriage, maintaining a good relationship with friends and family.

The doctor said: "From what you have told me about your life it seems that you have a fairly stable life, you have been in the same job for years, you have been married for years as well, you have a positive relationship with many people, you are telling me that you don't take drugs nor drink alcohol, most people that experience metal illness start displaying symptoms in their teens or early twenties, since you haven't displayed any symptoms thus far there is a very small chance you will have mental illness later on in life. So I don't understand why you have these concerns."

I explained to the doctor how I sometimes feel down, even depressed, how I sometimes feel sad even though there is no particular reason for it, how I sometimes I wakeup in the morning and wish I didn't have to go to work.

"And when you experience the feeling that you don't want to go to work, what do you do?" asked me the doctor.

"I force myself to go to work anyway," I told the doctor.

"Aha!" said the doctor. "That is the difference, all of us experience those feelings, but some of us know how to function in spite of it, but for

188

others those feeling take control."

So the good doctor assured me that I am most likely sane, that I shouldn't worry about it.

But back in my mind for years there was a little nagging voice.

Family friends have the most interesting cure suggestions for my brother's insanity. My favorite is:

Ali: Why don't you find him a bride and marry him off to somebody?

Elen: My brother is schizophrenic, what woman would want to marry him?

Ali: You know! …. Don't you have an eligible cousin in Iraq that is marrying age?

Elen: Yes, we have many female cousins that fit the category, but don't you think that it would be unfair to inflict a man who hears voices inside his head and needs his family to remind him to take a shower on a young woman of any nationality?

Ali: Yeah! but maybe if he got married he would feel better.

Elen: The man can't take care of himself, how is he supposed to take care of a wife?

Ali: You can help him.

And they say that my brother is crazy …. sigh!

Then there are those that after deep thinking come up with a brilliant explanation for my brother's predicament.

Sa'eed: You know, I figured out why your brother is not feeling well.

Elen: (thinks to herself: oh boy! here we go again) Aha! Please tell me.

Sa'eed: Your brother received a shock to his system when he moved to Canada; the cultural change was too much for him and that affected him. It's living in Canada that drove him insane.

Elen: Aha! ….. and ….. what do you suggest we do now?

Sa'eed: You must get him to move back to living in the Middle East.

Elen: In the Middle East they lock up people like my brother and throw the key away. People like him are kept out of sight. If we were living in the Middle East we wouldn't be having this discussion because we would all be pretending that we don't know my brother. If you are going to be insane, Canada is probably the best country to be insane in.

(I rattle off about the long list of services available for the mentality ill in this country).

Sa'eed: But while I lived in the Middle East I never heard about schizophrenia. It's only since I moved here; therefore, it must be this country that is causing it.

And they say that my brother is crazy …. sigh!

Then there is all the crazy stuff that we his family do thinking that we are helping him.

Like the time my brother's therapist chastised me for continuously bugging my brother about his smoking.

190

"He is battling suicidal thoughts, do you think he needs the added pressure and anxiety that comes when people try to quit smoking?" he told me.

What a self righteous prim and proper asshole I can be sometimes. "But smoking is bad for his health," I wanted to reply …. luckily I managed to stop myself from saying it.

And then I say that my brother is insane …. sigh!

10 years later from my appointment with the good doctor and many more psychotic episodes and trips to the psychiatric ward, I have learned to accept my brother as is, craziness and all.

So in the last episode he decided to attack a policeman and was arrested before he was moved to the psychiatric ward. In our family we have the standard routine for such an event. I go over to my parents house. My mother prepares the standard bag with the standard stuff in it: a change of clothes and cigarettes. No need for food, they feed them up the ying yang there, but don't provide them with cigarettes. Then my dad and I go to visit him. We already know the visiting hours and all the dos and don'ts at the psychiatric ward. My mother never comes with us; she spends all the time crying and causes the other crazy people there to become even more upset.

Do not mention the word crazy, nuts or insane in the psychiatric ward. It doesn't bother the crazies, but it seems to deeply offend the nurses working there.

Do not attempt to strike up a conversation with any of the other visitors, the newbies are usually so distressed they don't want to talk to anybody.

You can tell the newbies from the hardened family members from the look on their faces. Shock, disorientation and disbelief versus the "Here we go again" look.

The doctors and nurses never wear the white lab coat as in the Hollywood movies. One nurse explained to me that the white coat has too much of a stigma attached to it and the mentally ill are terrified of the white lab coat wearers and so all the staff wear regular street clothes.

Do not ask any of the other patients why they are in there, they actually will tell you and frequently you will hear stuff you didn't want to hear.

Finally, everybody knows that you do not mess with the big burly security guards; they can put you in a straight jacket faster than you can say, "I am a visitor".

So my dad and I walk into my brother's room and see that he has bruises all over his body.

"So, the police decided to teach you a lesson you will never forget?" … I asked my brother. My brother shakes his head, the police didn't do this to me, I did it to myself. I started banging my head against the wall in the detention cell they placed me in at the police station. When the psychiatrist couldn't calm me down they brought me here in an ambulance.

How lucky that we live in Vancouver, because in the middle east if somebody had attacked a policeman they would certainly receive a lesson they would never forget.

When my brother is released from the hospital, I go to visit him at his apartment and I am pleasantly surprised when I walk into a clean and neat one bedroom apartment.

Elen: "Hey! brother ….how come your apartment is so clean?"
Brother: "I knew you were gonna come."

I feel rather flattered that he bothered to clean his apartment just because of me. "He must be feeling well; this must be a good day," I think to myself.

After we chat for a while I notice that there is no food in his apartment and so I suggest that we go do some grocery shopping. I take him to the corner grocery shop and try to interest him in various produce.

"yum! yum! Look cookies ….. would you like cookies?"
my brother doesn't look interested but I place the cookies in the

shopping basket anyway.

"Hmmmmmmmm! Look instant noodles in a cup ..... surly even crazy people like those."

My brother gives me a sly smile.

"What else should we buy? Bread, cheese, milk, cereal, what else do you want?"

My brother doesn't care and shows no interest. So I just buy what I think he might need and we go back to his apartment.

Afterwards I decide to take my brother for brunch at the Elbow Room Café in downtown Vancouver. This place is full of character. It is run by these gay men whose motto is "The customer is always wrong and the abuse is free". The waiter is greeting all the male customers by calling them doll or queen, he calls me a sweetie. I usually like going there because the food is good and the place has character, but as soon as we walk in I realize that I made a mistake. While going to a funky place is fun, bringing a mentally unstable person to such a place can be difficult. For one thing my brother is confused by why the waiter is calling him doll; I keep explaining to him that this is part of the gay atmosphere of the café. When the waiter comes to take our order, my brother asks a question about one of the menu items, then he asks the same question about three times in different ways. Typical behavior for my brother. In cafés where the motto is "The customer is always right" the waiter would patiently answer the same question four times, but this isn't one of those cafes. The waiter gets annoyed and says, "What is wrong with you? Did the doctor drop you on your head after you were born? Are you crazy?"

194

My brother and I look at each other and start laughing hysterically, we are both thinking the same thing. "Yes! I am crazy," my brother says. "Yes!, He is crazy," I say. We keep on laughing.

The waiter looks surprised, he didn't know that what he had said was that funny.

I am absolutely certain that my brother is crazy; as for me, I guess I will live forever in doubt about my sanity. But a wise doctor taught me, worrying too much about it is a waste of time.

Cheap Shots

"Since they are using generic brown people, why not hire generic brown people that can speak the language?" I kept thinking to myself as I heard the Arabic language being butchered in the movie Hidalgo. In that pathetic Hollywood movie, not famous brown actors pretend to speak Arabic and unfortunately the director has chosen to put lots of Arabic dialog with English subtitles. Their language was so bad and so pathetic that I had to block my ears with my own hands because it was hurting to hear such a monstrosity. Aside from Omar Al- Shrief who speaks the language beautifully, the rest of the Arabic speaking roles go to people who have no clue and make no effort to speak it in an understandable way. The result ….. a total travesty. Serves me right for renting a Hollywood movie that has a depiction of Arabs or Muslims in it. In Hollywood Movie Universe …. Arabs and Muslims are either crazy pure evil fanatics the strategically placed so that the All American Hero can get his hero shot at the end, or stupid simpletons who provide cheap comic relief breaks into an otherwise serious movie.

I rented the movie Pitch Black, a horror sci-fi movie starring Vin Diesel, recommended by a friend. The movie included a Muslim father whose name is Imam and three of his sons. Had I known that the movie included a Muslim character I would have not rented it, as I have vowed after watching Hidalgo never to watch another American movie with Arab or Muslim characters in it. Why pay money in order to be insulted, humiliated and leave frothing at the mouth? Why waste my time to see myself depicted in ways I can't relate to nor feel any connection to my reality? But, I must say that the movie Pitch Black offers a considerable improvement over Hidalgo. For one thing, the three young boys seemed to speak Arabic fluently; I suspect they are native speakers of the language. One spoke with a Lebanese accent, the others with Palestinian or Jordanian accents, but at least they knew the language. The actor playing Imam, the father, spoke Arabic with an American accent, but I could tell that he had put an effort into learning the phrases in his dialog well enough so that at least I could understand what he was saying. I appreciated his effort. At least they didn't butcher the language and make my ears hurt. I wondered early on in the movie why the writer had placed four Muslim pilgrims in the movie. "Either they will turn out to be the source of pure evil that needs to be eliminated or the stupid idiots that mess the situation up for everybody else in the plot," I thought to myself as the first half-hour got underway, but my guess was wrong. In fact this suspense-filled movie keeps twisting and turning in most unexpected ways. In the first half-hour I thought I would be watching a science fiction version of Silence of the Lambs, but I was wrong. Then after 45 minutes into the movie I thought I was going to be watching a science fiction version of The Birds, but I was wrong again. The movie is one suspenseful moment after the next and leaves you guessing to what will happen until the very last minute. Turns out the four Muslims are just four stranded passengers on a harsh planet, trying to survive like everybody else ..... Wow! ..... what a unique and radical movie .... on so many levels. Creative indeed.

198

Many years ago, while living in Glasgow, Scotland, I saw a painting entitled "Seeing Ourselves the Way Other People See Us" at the Museum of Modern Art. It is a painting by a Scottish artist whose name I can't remember. In the painting you see a hairy legged man wearing a kilt with a head that looks like a soccer ball. He is sitting on a chair upholstered with tartan fabric watching TV like a couch potato. Beer bottles and shortbread wrappers strewn all over the room. The wallpaper in the room is yet another tartan print. Ironic, funny, painful. The painter is at once criticizing his own society, yet at the same time making fun of all the outsiders and tourists who want to see Scotland in a certain way. So many thoughts compacted in one painting; introspective, loud, vulgar, annoying, rude, offensive, how dare you? critical, hilarious. That painting is so many things. While living in Glasgow I developed a relationship with the hairy legged, soccer head man. Each time I was in downtown Glasgow, I would make a quick trip to the Museum of Modern Art to say hello to my new friend.

Elen: Hello! Hairy legged soccer head Scottish man, how are you today?

Hairy legged, soccer head Scottish man: Hello Elen. I am smashing. Still sitting here on my arm chair and watching TV. How are you ihath?

Elen: I am fine. Still lost. Still not sure what I am doing on this planet.

Hairy legged, soccer head Scottish man: That is jolly good my lass. I must go now. Time for the next Coronation Street episode.

Every nationality should have at least one "Seeing Ourselves the Way Other People See Us" painting. It would be good for the soul of every nation to do that. But I am not in the mood for the hard work of introspection and the grueling work of being self critical. Today I am in the mood for deep shots made at the expense of the other guy.

Warning: Cheap shot ahead

Disclaimer: The following story is fictional. Any similarities to real events or people living or dead is completely intentional

In honor of the spirit of cheap shots and easy way out, I would like to suggest to all Arab film makers in the Middle East to start incorporating American characters into their movies. Payback time! …. I say. For starters lets hire white French actors who will speak English with that heavy Parisian accent to play the role of Americans. After all … all gringos are the same, aren't they? Make them squirm while they hear their own language being twisted and turned by those that pay it no respect. Then make sure to create plots where the American characters are always the weirdoes. Put them on the defensive ….. I say. Here is one film idea that I am willing to donate for free to any Arabic movie maker provided he or she promises to hire Parisian actors to play the main roles. So here it is.

The Da Falihi Can

A secret society of weirdoes that are obsessed with taking nude pictures of unsuspecting victims is having a meeting at their secret hall. After they perform secret hand shakes they sit down to have their discussion. After they are finished with planning their evil plan to dominate the world, they move on to the next item on their agenda; difficulties faced with taking nude pictures of unsuspecting people. Recently several members have gone to jail and have been scandalized for their god-given obsession. It is becoming increasingly difficult to take nude pictures of people who do not want to be pictured in the nude. For one thing, the number of people refusing to expose themselves in the nude is sharply declining in America. As we see in home movies and American college video, American people are willing to take their clothes off for a glass of beer, for a smile or even to get 5 seconds of fame of passing attention. Even the big celebrities are willing to take their clothes off. And for this secret society, taking pictures with cooperating subjects is a no-no. It's just no fun if the subject is willing. Secondly, laws of privacy in the land of the proud and free are becoming ever stricter and harder to work around. In the past, priests, police men and politicians were above scrutiny and when they took those pictures people looked the other way. But in today's sad and skeptic society people look with suspicion even onto the clergy. They all shook their heads at their sad state worrying that their ancient society of weirdoes will become extinct. That is when Freddy, the bright one in the group, came up with a brilliant plan. And it went something like this.

Let's create a powerful lobby group that pretends to embody good Christian values that influences to put an unsuspecting poor soul into the White House. Then we convince this God-fearing poor soul to invade a country because it has weapons of mass destruction. And then we need to liberate that country and give them democracy. Then we infiltrate those silly left wing groups and whisper in their ears that it is all for oil. So that all sides are confused about the real motivation. We must select a conservative country with very modest population. A country where people never show up nude, not even in front of their own family. A country where women are covered up from head to toe and men are covered up from neck to toe. For example, Iraq. Then when the war starts, we all will volunteer as soldiers claiming patriotic feeling. We make sure not to fight and keep our heads low and volunteer to guard the prisoners. And there we can go wild, take nude pictures of modest Iraqis of all shapes and sorts. Then we will create a scandal and those picture will be published in every newspaper and TV station so that our comrades back home can enjoy as well. I predict that even the most respectable of news agencies won't be able resist publishing those pictures when they have their hands on them. We might even get new recruits into our secret society, as looking at nude picture of Iraqis will become the new American past-time. We will have a free hand. We will gain a new legitimacy that we never had before. Taking all the nude pictures we want. Heck! I even predict that we will be able to get nude pictures of their President ….. that man they call Saddam. They call us perverts, now but they will start calling us heroes who were a bit confused under the strain.

Everybody in the room looked unconvinced.

"But that is is too complex and elaborate," said one of them

"I can't believe that a mainstream news agency like CNN would broadcast nude images of Iraqis against their wishes .... I just can't see it happening," said another.

"You think we can fool all those intellectual Left Wing people to believe that it is all for oil?" said the third person.

Freddy was annoyed, "Unless one of you is able to come up with a better plan I suggest we stick to mine. These are desperate times and we need desperate actions."

Who knew that the wacky plan would work so well. The Weirdoes Society was very pleased with the progress it acheived in very short time.

The whole Middle East was plunging into despair and humiliation. Nude pictures of Iraqis were popping up in mainstream media on a daily basis. The shame was destroying the spirit of this once modest nation. Nobody was safe and nobody knew when it would be their turn to have their pictures taken and have to live out the rest of their life in shame.

That is when our hero Falah comes in. A historian and scientist, Falah comes across a set of secret documents reveal to him the existance of the Weirdoes Society. He then walks around the Louvre in Paris and sees all the paintings of nude people done by all the great masters. Falah puts two and two together and figures out that the war was not about oil, nor about weapons nor about democracy, it is about our nude assess. He tries to expose the conspiracy, but nobody believes him.

The director of the U.N. named Slofi Banan, tells him that since the gravy train of food for the oil program ended he has to live off of his meager U.N. salary and has no time to think about wacky conspiracies.

The director of the C.I.A. assures him that the American public is not interested in hairy Iraqi ass.

The director of Al Jazzeera refuses to air the story because talking about ass and nudity goes against their moral code.

In despair, Falah returns to his Iraq knowing that he has to take matters into his own hands. He works day and night in the laboratory of his house until he discovers Falihi spray. Falihi spray is a substance distilled from the sand, that when applied to human skin produces ultra-violet light undetectable to the human eye, but deadly to cameras. It's effects are that it jams all camera, regardless of their make and model, and inplace of a nude body the picture appears with a black blob instead. Falah travels all across Iraq disguised as a holy man, telling the people that the Falihi spray is a holy substance blessed by all religeous clerics. All the people start applying the Falihi spary and all nude pictures of Iraqis appear with big black blobs in place of nude bodies. The Weirdoes

Society starts withdrawing from the army because their plan has failed.

A group of Islamic terrorists discover the true nature of the Falihi spay and steal huge quantities of it. They travel to the U.S. and apply the spray on all American actresses and fashion models and porno stars. This causes a complete colapse of American pop culture and Hollywood producers vow to make movies in accordance to Islamic shria'a laws.

Falah becomes a popular figure and is votted to be the next Iraqi president. During his inaguration he announces his love to Fahima (whom I forgot to introduce earlier in the story in order to make this more of a complelling ending). Fahima accepts his marriage proposal. Fahima and Falah get married in a big ceremony in the middle of Fardous square dancing and singing all night long. Their wedding photo is one big, happy, black blob.

Both American and Iraqi people live happily ever after and the Weirdoes Society go to therapy to help them heal from their evil ways.

The End

Jeans

My favorite scene in the Lord of the Rings movies, is the battle outside the city of Minas Tirith where it ends with the ghost like deads storming the city at the last minute and rescuing it from the wrath of orcs. The city of Minas Tirith looked so glamorous with it's seven circular layers, each smaller than the other and reminding me of the tower of Babel. It was once a city of great kings, thinkers and civilization. But now it is a place of decay and stagnation, as its people spend more time remembering the past and glorifying the Forefathers than living their own daily lives. The little bit of remaining courage among the few is not enough to save her beauty. That is when the haunted dead are summoned to the rescue. Having broken their oath to a king of old, they are unable to join the after life in peace. A new battle offers a second chance to fulfill their oath and be free of the curse. ….. What a brilliant story plot. Only a genius story teller would come up with that.

While in Washington D.C. I had one of the most embarrassing moments of my life. I was walking around in yet another art gallery in awe of the art exhibits, when one of the security people walked up to me and said,

Security guy: Mam! ehm …. ehm ehm

Elen: Ha? ….sorry I didn't hear that.

Security guy: Mam! ehm … ehm …. errrrrrrrrr!

Elen: (I walk closer to him) ha? …. What?

207

Security guy: ehm! …. cough! …. errrrr! (while he keeps touching his zipper)

Elen: (thinks to herself: is this an obscene gesture?): what?

Security guy: mam! ….. ehm! … ehm! … ehm! (keeps touching and pointing at his zipper)

Elen: (I finally look down and realize that he is telling me that my zipper is undone) Oh my God!

My face turned red.

I wished the ground would split and swallow me whole.
I have never felt so embarrassed in my whole entire life.

I remembered that I visited the washroom 10 minutes earlier at the gallery. It must have happened there and I simply forgot to do up my zipper. Luckily I was wearing very solid underwear underneath, non of that skimpy, lacy stuff I bought two days earlier. I tried to console myself by thinking that I am in a foreign city and I will never meet any of the people that saw me ever again. I will probably never see that security guard ever again either. Still, I felt so embarrassed I wished I was struck down by a bolt from the sky that would make me invisible. I am such an idiot. A hillbilly. A disgrace to my race and gender. What would my husband say if he saw me now? What would my father say if he saw me now? What would my co-workers say if they saw me now. I could imagine everybody that I have ever met in my whole entire life standing there pointing at me and laughing. At least the gallery was nearly empty.

Surely only a few people saw me with my zipper undone. But still, how embarrassing. Luckily there were no children in the gallery. Imagine how their parents would have felt about their children seeing a lady with unzipped pants? They would have been offended that their children were being exposed to such a sight.

I thanked the security officer and walked away in a hurry so that he wouldn't see my face red with embarrassment.

And so I walked over to the Smithsonian. They had an exhibit of American First Lady dresses. "O how kitsch? They are just dresses," I thought to myself as walked around. Other people were ogling them in admiration. There were other kitsch Americana exhibits that I didn't care about. Then I walked into the science and technology exhibit. They had the first computer, the first IBM mainframe and other cool old machines ….. Oh my god! ….. what do I see? …. Apple IIe on display in the Smithsonian. "Hello old friend," I wanted to say. Apple IIe was my first computer. I bought it when I was 13 years old, as a hobby. Never expecting that computer programming would become my life-long profession. I can't believe that something I used is on display in the Smithsonian as an historical relic. I am not even that old. Yet an object with fond memories from my teens is on display in a museum. Now embarrassment was replaced with depression. But that computer was state of the art back when I got it. That was the bestest and the greatest and now it sits like a monkey on display in a zoo, to be ogled by the same ignorant masses that just finished ogling a Jacky Kennedy dress. What is happening in the world? How much have things changed? When I graduated from university there was no internet ….. can you imagine life without internet? …. I can't ….. yet it wasn't that long ago that it didn't exist at all. How much my life has changed. Growing up in Kuwait, then moving to Canada, moving to Israel, then back to Canada. Learning different languages, adjusting to different cultures, marriage, motherhood, which hit me like a hurricane. How I have changed in very short years. I have lived a life at the speed of the internet. Each coolest technology made obsolete within a few years, constantly learning new things, new buzz words, are there any constants? Where am I now? Where did I come from?

revolution
revolution
always painful
always blood shed
somebody always gets his head chopped in a revolution
What bits of myself have been assassinated in the last few years?
Discarded away, extra baggage that was thrown overboard in order to preserve life?
I don't believe in the revolution any more.
From now on I will walk the path of evolution.
Old things will be recycled into new things.

"The revolution ate its own children" – said Maximilien Francois Robespierre, referring to the French Revolution. Had he been talking about the Battle of Karbala he would have said, "The revolution ate its

210

own grandchildren."

The Battle of Karbala is a bit of a historical misnomar, since it actually was a murderous assault on a defenseless caravan of the Holy Prohpet's family which merely had few dozen able-bodied men. It took place on October 10, 680 AD, in Iraq. The battle saw the large and professional army of the ruler at the time, who surrounded the family and few friends of Imam Hussein (grandchild of prophet Mohamed), which, consisted of 72 men, a number of children and women. The moral stature, charisma and popularity of Hussein was so tremendous that there was a serious chance of a massive revolt against ruler at the time. A massive army of 30,000 was sent to nip the rebellion in the bud.

Massacre in the name of power is nothing new. But the interesting twist in the story is the people of Iraq. Having urged Imam Hussein to travel from Mecca to Karbala, promising to support a rebellion, Imam Hussein risked his own life and the life of his family and few suppors to stand up for the revolution. For the principles of Islam that prophet Mohammed stood for, for the people seeking a ruler that hasn't seized power by force.

Upon arrival, the people ran out to greet the Imam only to see a huge army camped behind him. All but a few ran back home and negated on their promise to support their king in his hour of need. Massacre followed and all were crushed. Forever doomed to shame, forever cursed, forever haunted by the heroes of the olden days.

Baby

"Not another baby!" …. was my first thought when I realized that I was pregnant for the third time, in the year 2000.

The youngest was still in diapers and a third baby was not on the agenda. My marriage was on the rocks, as I was preparing to tell my husband that I was leaving Israel with or without him. A pregnancy was absolutely the last thing I needed while moving countries, jobs and changing my life inside out.

My husband wasn't overjoyed to hear the news either. He just got a scowl on his face and didn't say much.

But how?
Oh yeah! …. Remember that night.
Aha! It must have happened then.
We should have been more careful.
Aha! Yes. We should have been more careful.

I was taking birth control pills as I was certain that two was my limit, but destiny or higher powers had a different plan in mind. My monthly cycle, which is always 100% regular, was suddenly disrupted. Worried I might be pregnant, I had to stop taking the pill because I didn't know what was going on. One pregnancy test after another turned out negative, and that is when I became pregnant.

In hind sight, I think that it was my destiny to have three children instead of the two I had planned.

"Abortion" …. my husband mentioned the word once as a suggestion.

I told him that just thinking about it caused me so much mental anguish that I didn't want to think about it or even consider it.

Yet another pregnancy, yet another giving birth event, breast feeding once more, sleepless nights …. I spent all my days contemplating all the hardships already familiar to me that lay ahead, and I was not looking forward to it. I had been through it all already twice.

I was depressed about it all.

And then I went to my first medical checkup. The doctor listened to my belly and told me that he can't hear the baby's heart beats. "The baby might be dead, in which case you will have to have a miscarriage. You need to take an ultrasound to verify the state of the fetus," the doctor told me.

I left his office alarmed. I tried to make an immediate appointment with the ultrasound people but I couldn't get the appointment until the next day.

214

I went to work, but I couldn't get anything done, my mind was distracted by worrying about the state of my unborn baby.

I went home by the end of the day a nervous wreck. I was crying the whole night, not able to sleep not even a wink.

"God is punishing me," I told my husband. "It's because I didn't welcome this baby into the world with the same happiness, joy and anticipation that I did my earlier two pregnancies. God is punishing me. Or maybe the fetus felt unwelcome and decided that he or she didn't want to come into a world that doesn't want him."

My husband held my hand all night through and tried to reassure me that everything will work out somehow.

The next day he came with me to the ultrasound technician holding my hand; I was shaking with fear at the news I was going to get.

The ultrasound technician told me that the baby was fine, heart beats, movements, size …everything was fine. She told me that at two months of the pregnancy it is not unusual for the doctor to not be able to hear the heart beats, since the baby is still moving around and might be positioned in a way that doesn't allow for the heart beats to be heard.

I was crying tears of joy as I heard the good news.

I left the ultrasound place realizing that I cared about this unborn baby already. It was unplanned and very inconvenient, but I loved the baby and cared about it already. I also had an urge to go over to the doctor's office and kick him in the behind for putting me through 24 hours of hell.

Perhaps higher power wanted to teach me a lesson on accepting events of fate.

My whole attitude changed after that. From doom and gloom and feeling sorry for myself about the hardship I would face, I decided that I will welcome this child into the world with the same joy I did with my other children.

"Poor little me."
changed to
"Everything will work out somehow."

I suddenly had the feeling that this child was meant to be, despite all my best efforts not to get pregnant, and that he would bring good fortune into my life. Everything would work out somehow, I just didn't know how yet.

When I told my husband that I was going back to Vancouver; he told me many things

"But I might not find a job in Vancouver."

"Everything will work out somehow," I told him.

"But you might not be able to find a job in Vancouver either now that you are pregnant."

"Everything will work out somehow," I told him.

"But if both of us don't find a job, who will support us?"

"Everything will work out somehow, I just don't know how," I told him.

I developed an "Everything will work out somehow" attitude about everything. Moving, job search, travel, child care, housing …. no need to worry….. things will work out, my instincts told me.

And my instincts were right …. things did work out …. in amazing and wonderful ways that I couldn't have imagined at the time.

Recently I was having coffee with my mom, we were chit chatting about this and that when suddenly my mom said something that shocked me; I never thought I would hear these words coming out of her mouth ……. ever.

"You are a better mom than I was," … my mother said.

"Ha? What? Where did that come from?"

"You were pregnant in a difficult situation, yet you were

determined to go through with the pregnancy and you managed to put your life in order at the same time; I admire you for it," my mother explained.

"You are stronger than me, I didn't have your strength when I was your age," … my mother continued.

My mother went through an abortion twice in her life.

Nowadays, I look at my son and imagining life without him is like trying to imagine my life without one of my legs or arms …. absolutely impossible.

He has brought so much joy and good fortune into my life

Suits

Gollum is my favorite character in the Lord of the Rings movies. For one thing, he is neither with the evil side nor with good side, he has no quest, no mission; he is simply looking out for his own interests. He is neither with us nor against us, he is himself. He neither wishes to destroy planet earth nor liberate it from itself; all he wants, is to exist in a dark quiet corner and stroke his precious …. is that so bad? Of all the characters in the trilogy I found him to be the most compelling. His face transformed from sinister to angelic within seconds. Frodo the goodie two shoes and Sam the wimp got on my nerves. Aragon is handsome and brave and all that but he falls in love with a woman with pointy ears ….. something must be not right with him. Gandalf is wise and smart and has lots of experience, but he talks the talk and let others walk the walk for him. Gollum, on the other hand is a naturalist, he doesn't attempt to wear clothes or disguise his true nature in any way. He lives in harmony with his surroundings and his own ghosts. Let us not forget that it is Gollum who gets the ring into the pit. If all that wasn't enough to convince you to like Gollum, it is enough for me that he has good taste in food. Sushi is my favorite food in the world. Maybe Gollum is not pretty, but at least he has taste with regards to food, none of the disgusting looking elfin bread …. yuck!

I have a secret to share with you. My last name when written in English and pronounced by English speakers sounds lots like "Gollum"; only the spelling is different.

Alright!

Now back to my trip to Washington. In a previous story I told you about how I spent my first day in Washington, now here is how the second day went:

Turns out that even the geeks dress in suits in Washington, I discovered much to my chagrin. I went to attend the first talk at the conference to find out that I was grossly underdressed in my jeans, T-shirt and a baseball cap. Luckily I arrived early and had plenty of time to run back into my hotel room and change quickly into more suitable attire. The geeks were still geeky, which I found comforting. They still walk around with their laptops, two pocket PCs, the blue tooth ear piece and all, but in Washington they wear fancy suits. Must be an East Coast thing. Luckily I always bring a variety of clothing with me just in case. My husband always complains as I am packing "Why do you need to carry that much clothing with you?". "You never know what you might encounter while on a trip," I always answer. And this time I was glad I was prepared for the emergency.

I was determined to avoid discussing politics at any price. I thought that an Iraqi visiting Washington shortly after the war better keep her thoughts to herself. I tried very, very hard to chat with people about things not political.

"So, what is it like to live in Washington?" I asked one lady attending the conference. I thought this was the perfect question for light, non-political, safe small talk.

"It is so hard being a single woman in Washington, all the men are too important and don't have time," the woman responded. Then she went on a rant about how all men are assholes in Washington, and that reminded her that George Bush is an asshole too, and then she went on rant about how much she hates and despises Bush.

So much for the light, small talk.
I thought I would try my luck again,

"What is it like to live in Washington?" I asked a young man at the conference. After I ditched my first small talk encounter.

"Living in Washington sucks big time, all the women are gold diggers who expect to be wined and dined all the time," the man responded. Then he went on a rant how everybody he knows wants to become a lawyer and then they become corrupt self-centered human beings; then he told me how much he hates the Washington Post because of its friendly stand on Bush and the war, and then he went on a rant about how Bush and his administration is the source of all evil in the world.

I was tempted to introduce the man to the woman I was talking to earlier, since they were both complaining about the hardships of being single in Washington, but then I thought it might get me into trouble. I might be accused of participating in the Iraqi conspiracy to confuse single

Americans with weapons of wrongful matchmaking.

I think I had better change my opening question. I wasn't trying to ask loaded questions, but it was getting me into loaded answers.

For lunch I went to a nearby restaurant and ordered something called Cobb Salad; it sounded healthy. Holy Molly what a feast. Imagine a salad topped with strips of bacon, sliced steak and chicken breast smothered in blue cheese dressing. I proceeded to have Cobb Salad for lunch every single day for the duration of my stay. My only complaint is that it shouldn't be called a salad, it should be called heart attack with greens on the side. Good thing I don't live in Washington because I would have to eat heart attack with greens of the side for the rest of my life, and I would look like a whale. If you are planning a visit to Washington please have a Cobb Salad at least once.

Washington is very different from all other American cities I have visited. People are generally friendly and polite, everybody was wearing a fancy suit, there is sense of history and culture in the city, and everybody I met would somehow mention how much they despise George Bush regardless of how hard I tried to steer away from the subject. I almost felt like I was in Europe. If you took away the bit about friendly polite people, you could almost imagine that you were in Europe. Down to the art galleries.

I opened the entertainment newspaper, trying to see if there was something going in the city in the evening that might grab my attention. Madeline Albright was giving a talk that night. The thought of hearing Ms. "Killing 500,000 Iraqi children during sanctions was a worthwhile price to pay" made my stomach churn. There were other important politicians talking at different venues. Part of me felt that I wanted to soak in the Washington experience, but the other part remembered events of the previous day and I thought I had better avoid any politicians of any sorts; it is hard enough dealing with the average Washingtonians who all feel compelled to express every political idea they ever had within 5 minutes of meeting me. So I decided to go to an art gallery instead. I always liked art galleries. I ended up going Freer Gallery of Art. I didn't expect much from an art gallery in the U.S. having visited plenty of art galleries in Europe, but I was in for a shocking surprise.

I was enjoying the interesting exhibit there until I walked into the Peacock Room. A dining room designed by American Artist named James McNeill Whistler, whose name I had never heard before. I was stunned, awestruck, flabbergasted and transformed.

I stood there for 30 minutes in awe, admiring the perfection of what is called "Harmony in Blue and Gold". I was not prepared to view that day an object of such beauty and such perfection that my whole existence would be transformed by it. As I left the dining room I was in tears. I have no doubt that I had come face to face with a work of art that had a touch of divine inspiration. I felt sorrow. I wish I could create something so perfect and so beautiful in my life. I might never do. If I could do one thing in my life, just one thing that is as beautiful as the Peacock Room I would die a happy woman. There was a sense of deep yearning, yet I felt spiritually uplifted. I can't describe how I felt at that moment. It was similar to the feeling of falling in love, delicious yet terrifying at the same time.

As I walked outside the dining room I could see a homeless man sitting on one of the benches of the gallery; he was hunched over, head down. He must have gotten past the security guards somehow; he looked like he just wanted a peaceful refuge for a little while. As I passed him, the thought crossed my mind that I might never be able to create a work of art as inspiring as the Peacock Room, but I might be able to make the day for a single homeless man. I walked up to the hunched over man and tapped on his shoulder. He looked up at me. I realized that this was barely a man, he looked like a 16 year old boy, he was merely a kid. A slew of questions passed through my brain: "Why are you on the streets? Where are your mom and dad? Don't you have any relatives that could help you?" But I didn't ask any of them. In the distance I could hear the security guards marching towards us, mumbling incomprehensible codes on their walkie-talkies. They were coming to shoo this kid away, to tell him that he didn't belong in this posh gallery. There wasn't much time. I handed him 20 dollars. He looked at me, perhaps he had a whole bunch of questions for me as well "Why are you giving this to me? What are you doing in this snotty place? Don't you find all this artwork boring?" But he didn't say anything. He smiled. A beautiful smile that revealed a set of white teeth that shined like a string of pearls.

224

We parted in silence, no exchange of words, only a 20 dollar bill changed hands.

I returned to my hotel room, exhausted and drained yet again, but this time it was a different kind of exhausted.

Underwear

I was sitting in my hotel room feeling various sorts of pain. I was emotionally drained from a day full of events. I was physically tired from too much walking, but too wired to go to sleep. I tried to watch a bit of T.V. to amuse myself, but the reality show whose name I can't remember was so pathetic I couldn't stand watching it more than 5 minutes. Worse of all was the physical pain I experienced as a result of my newly purchased sexy underwear, which I was wearing under my super comfy and super modest flannel pajamas. The questions, "Who invented G-Strings?" and more importantly "Why?" was crossing my mind several times. I wanted to cry, but couldn't. I felt lonely and wished my husband was there to give me a hug, but I wasn't going to see him for another ten days. I missed my kids. I didn't know what to do with myself. Should I start reading the bible guaranteed to be found in the drawer of the nightstand next to my bed? ....but, but, but, ... I have never sunk so low .... not in any of my travels.

Let me tell you how I got to that low point in my life.

In November of 2003, I was on my way to the airport traveling to Washington DC to attend a conference related to my work. There were so many thoughts going through my head as I was heading towards the airport. It was the day after the story of Maher Arar broke on mainstream Canadian media. The Syrian-born Canadian stopped in New York on his was back to Canada, only to be interrogated and shipped to Syria were he was imprisoned and tortured for a whole year. All the newspapers and radio stations carried detailed accounts of Maher Arar's ordeal and horrid details of his torture in Syria. I was starting to have second thoughts about my trip to Washington. On several occasions I was close to telling the taxi driver to turn around and take me back home. I could see and imagine myself being interrogated and then shipped to Abu Graib prison in Baghdad where I would be tortured daily. I could imagine my poor husband with the children having to protest in front of the Canadian Parliament Building, demanding that the Canadian government intervene to release me. I could imagine my poor children having to stand in the cold, day after day, demanding that their mom be released. Was it worth it to take such a risk just to attend a conference? I used to think that having a Canadian passport made me immune to the fates of the less fortunate masses, those unfortunate enough to travel with an Iraqi passport. The rules have changed recently; what once was a ticket to no visa required, dignified treatment guaranteed, is no longer enough. These days having Arab origins is more powerful than my elegant, pocket size, beautiful Canadian passport. It didn't help Maher Arar that he had a Canadian passport.

I have an intense relationship with my Canadian passport. I love my passport. You will frequently find me holding it and stroking it in admiration the way Gollum (from Lord of the Rings) stroked his "Precious". I even talk to my passport.

"Hello dearie, nice to see you oh beautiful green one, we are about to go on a trip this morning. Yes we are. Are you ready? Oh! I remember traveling with those other green ones. Nasty, nasty green ones. But you are different, you are special, you are my precious. Those other passports I had to use in the past. But traveling with you is so much nicer. You have elevated me from the realm of the Iraqis to the realm of the anonymous Canadians. You spare me the humiliation, make me invisible, give me special powers that bestow dignity and respect on my poor person. Before you, I was one of the other ones, the suspected ones, those that get the odd looks and extra handling."

But on this trip, as I stared at my precious … ehm! ….. I mean my passport, his shine was gone and he seemed less powerful and less magical. Do I have the courage to venture into the world without the magical powers? I suddenly felt like an impish elf about to travel from Middle East …. ehm! ….. I mean Middle-Earth towards the Dark Tower without the aid of a magical toy that made me invisible. Will the watchful eye of Sauron detect me? Will the spotlight be placed on me? Will I be sent to the Abu Graib dungeon? After all, isn't it suspicious that an Iraqi is traveling to Washington just months after the war?

Well! This Gollum tried to put on her brightest elfish smile and most innocent look, so as not to arouse suspicions. Everything went well, Smeagol was working double time in order to behave himself and look as innocent as possible. But, Gollum would not rest; he would raise his sinister head every once in a while. Towards the end of the flight as we were approaching Washington, the pilot announced that we are about to land in Washington and that within the next 30 minutes as a security precaution we all have to remain seated. If anybody gets up for any reason at all he will change direction and land the airplane at some other destination. Suddenly I was gripped by the urge to stand up and yell "I am Iraqi, I am Iraqi, I am Iraqi, I have fooled you all, ha ha ha ha." I tried to imagine what would happen if I had done that. Would I be shot or arrested or what. Thinking about all the crazy surreal scenarios in my head created an irresistible urge to laugh. I wanted to laugh hysterically, but I knew that laughing would look suspicious. I had to gather all my strength to get my Smeagol facial expression again so that I looked perfectly harmless before landing.

I decided that I would not visit any monuments, including the White House, while in Washington. Too much negative feeling, too much turmoil going on inside me. All the feelings of distress that accompanied the first war, the sanctions and the second war. There was simply too much bottled inside me and I thought that it might all unravel if I visited any of those places. So I decided I would not get a map and would not look up any of these places and just go for a walk to clear my head. Even though this was my first visit to Washington I discovered that I have all this knowledge about Washington city floating inside my head. I seemed to know street names and places, names like Dupont Circle and George Town. I realized that all these names I learned from watching "The American President"; the lousy, schmaltzy, super yick Hollywood trash-of-a-movie, starring Michael Douglas. I didn't enjoy the stupid predictable love story, but at least all the names of places in Washington

230

stuck in my head. And so I walked and walked and walked and walked, and suddenly I found myself in front of a big, white house surrounded by a tall fence.

"This can't be the white house….it looks too small", I thought to myself.

But then I saw all the police and security people all over the place and realized that I had reached the white house without meaning to.

"Oh Man! This is exactly the place I wanted to avoid. Damn you Gollum!"

There was a crazy looking old lady camping in front of the white house in a tent with peace signs and anti-war slogans. There were Japanese tourists with cameras, families with their children, a bunch of people looking like journalists and many people hovering about in fancy suits. I decided I would walk around the white house and get a good look from all sides. I am here already; I might as well get a good look. So I walked slowly in a steady pace, thinking about all the decisions that have taken place in this big, white house and have affected my life. There was the decision to support the ba'athists in order to defeat the communists in Iraq; there was the first war, sanctions, and a second war. How many have died as a result of these decisions? Hundreds of thousands? millions? Yet this house looks whitey white, as if it has been recently bleached. The lawn is immaculate, everybody is smiling while having their pictures taken.

I finally stopped and starred directly at the white house with an intense look

"I curse you, I curse you, I curse you, I curse all your residents and I hope that they all get diarrhea tonight. I hope that George Bush gets diarrhea tonight. Please God give them diarrhea, Strong One, make them all sick for one day." And then I heard the siren of an ambulance in the distance

"Oh O! The curse had started to work, I had better get away from here"

Anyway cursing people is a pathetic thing; it is the vice of the weak.

And so I walked and walked and walked some more feeling exhausted and drained until I saw a Victoria Secret store, which again my Gollum-possessed legs compelled me to go to.

I spent 45 minutes admiring all the overpriced satin and lace items. I never buy such things, nor do I ever spend time in such stores, but for some reason I felt compelled to buy at this store at that precise moment.

"Depressed about all the injustice in the world? ….. Go buy underwear, it will help you feel better." That logic seems silly now, but it made sense at the time.

232

And happy with my loot and exhausted from a day of walking and psychotic Gollum/Smeagol transformations, I went back to my hotel room.

On the news I discovered that George Bush was visiting Turkey that day so he couldn't have received the wrath of my curse.

I lay on bed contemplating the sad state of the world and the loss of magic in my world.

Suddenly, I remembered the Captain Underpants stories that I read to my children before bed time. The superhero wearing diapers that saves the world with a toilet plunger from alien-possessed talking toilets. I remembered how my kids would roll on the floor laughing as I read Captain Underpants books to them and I realized that I don't need magic in my life after all. Here I am staying at a $ U.S. 250 dollar a night hotel. I will spend the next 10 days dining in some of the finest restaurants and mingling with like-minded geeks. The torture devices have been self administered: must be the shi'a side of me that tends for self mutilation. I changed into my regular underwear, thought about the super hero in underwear, forgot about tales of doom and gloom, good and evil from Lord of the Rings and read from my Rumi book until I fell a sleep.

And thus ended another day in the life of a non-super hero.

If anybody got diarrhea in the white house in mid November of 2003, I profusely apologize, I promise never to do it again.

Humiliation

She: So.....are you thinking about marriage?

He: No, not at all. I am penniless, drifting through life, without a future. I can't go back to my country and I have no idea where my life is taking me. How can I possibly think about marriage?

She:So.....do you at least love me?

He: No, I have dedicated myself towards the political struggle in my country. There is no room for love in my life.

This very romantic exchange happened between my parents when they first met.

Promising start for a love story, eh?....... It only gets better.

When I was a little girl, I would soemtimes ask my mom,

Elen: Mom?......How did you marry dad?

Mom: When I met your father, I chased after him and he tried to run away. I ran and ran and ran. He kept on running and running, and running trying to get as far away from me as possible. The faster he ran the faster I ran, until finally he dropped to the ground in exhaustion. He couldn't run anymore, he was too tired. I jumped on top of him while he was lying on the ground breathless, struggling to take his breath. I shook him violently, "Are you going to marry me or what?" Gasping for air he replied, "Ok, ok, ok. I will marry you......I can't run anymore"..... and that is how me and your dad got married.

When I became older my mom told me the more detailed version of that story.

Sasha was a young woman of 22 years, living in the city of Liberec north of Czechoslovakia and was engaged to be married to a young man from her home town. Working as a clerk in a bank, she happened to meet a wealthy German man who drove in a fancy Mercedes.....which was a rare sight in the socialist country. The wealthy German man took a liking to Sasha and started showing up at the bank for made-up reasons all the time.

One day, Sasha was going on a date to see a movie with her fiance; at the end of the date the fiance walked her home and tried to plant a kiss on her lips before parting, but she pushed him away and ran into the house. Her father, Joseph, saw the kafuffle taking place at the door steps.

Joseph: Sashenko?....... Do you not like it when he touches you?

Sasha: No.....Yuck!......I can't stand it.

Joseph: So....how will you live with him once you are married?

Sasha: I guess will have to get used to him touching me once we get married.

Joseph: Since you are not getting married for reasons of the heart, why not get married for reasons of the head. Since you are about

236

to marry a man you don't love, then why not marry a man you don't love that has money. Why don't you marry the German that chases after you all the time.

Sasha: Ha?.......I didn't think about that.

So Sasha went on a vacation to a lake side resort. Her plan was to use that time to think and decide about which man she will spend the rest of her life with. Her curent fiance, who is nice, or the older German man with the fancy car.

And there she saw an Iraqi man sitting under a tree by the side of the lake reading a book. While all his Arab friends were ogling the young women in bathing suits and flirting with anything wearing a skirt; this young man seemed serious and was completly engrossed in his reading. Sasha was so drawn to this man that she took his picture from a distance without his knowledge that very first time she saw him. She has cherished and kept that picture till today. All her efforts to meet this man and talk with him were met with a lukewarm reception. Still, upon returning from her vacation she broke off her engagement without giving a specific reason and would keep going back to meet with this young man that she saw at the lake side resort. Once the young man made his intentions clear - he had no intention to get married and he was not in love - Sasha was heartbroken.

On her way home, she went to church and kneeled in front of the statue of Virgin Mary. She paryed and prayed and prayed that the holy mother of Jesus would grant her wish and let her have the heart of the man she was madly in love with.

"Holy mother of the lord, I have come to church every Sunday for the last several years despite the fact that I live in a socialist coutry where going to church on a regular basis is heavily frowned upon. I have attended mass time and again with the handfull of 80 and 90 year-old ladies who are the only people still coming to church in these times, never doubting you once. I have knelt here and prayed at your feet many many times. Will you not grant me this one wish this one time? Will you please place love and tenderness in that man's heart towards me." In tears, my mother looked up upon the statue of virgin Mary and swears to God that she saw the head of the statue nod in agreement, as if telling her that her wish would be granted.

Elen: Mom?......Didn't you think that it was odd to ask Virgin Mary to grant you a husband that wasn't Christian? Don't you think that the Virgin Mary would rather you married a Christian man?

Sasha: When you are in love you don't think about such practical matters.

Elen: Mom?......wasn't that humiliating...you being in love with a man that didn't have the same feelings?

Sasha: Off course it was humiliating. I was heartbroken. Each time I would see him I would tell myself that I would never ever come see him again. But then I would tell myself I will go see him one more time, just one more time and it will be the last time. But then I would go

238

see him agian. I couldn't help myself....I was drawn to him by powers beyond my control.

Elen: But, what did you see in him? He is not even handsome.

Sasha: To me he seemed like the most beautiful man on earth.

Elen: That will never happen to me. I will never allow myself to fall in love. It seems terrible.

Sasha: One day, when you meet the right guy you will have no choice......you will see.....when the time comes I will remind you.

And she did remind me of this conversation when I met my husband.

Elen: Dad?....So why did you marry my mom?

Dad: I was touched by her sincerity. I told her I was penniless, I told her that I couldn't even go back to my country, I told her everything and she kept coming back to see me. I was flattered that somebody was in love with me, no woman has ever been in love with me before.

Elen: Didn't you have a sweetheart back in Iraq?

Dad: No, off course not. There were no women in University back in those days. There was maybe one woman in my whole class and she was ugly.

Elen: But, wasn't there a neighbours daughter or a young woman you met on the street that caught your eye?

Dad: My generation ..... we were different. We were serious and dedicated group of young people, not like young people these days. We didn't have time for love and other such nonsense. The revolution was our love.

Elen: So how did you change your mind? What made you finally decide to marry my mom?

Dad: Well! I started thinking, here is this young woman who really, really loves me. I am in my thirties. I can't go back to Iraq to get my mom to find me a bride the old fashioned way. So I thought, why not? It's not everyday some woman falls in love with me. Plus it was about time I started a family.

Elen: So did you fall in love with her eventually?

Dad:Yes, your mom kinda grew on me after a while.

On their wedding day, my dad didn't know enough Czech to be able to understand the service at his own wedding. He worried he wouldn't know when to say yes when asked "the question" because he wouldn't understand the question. And so he agreed with my mom that they would hold hands and when it came time for him to say "ano" (yes in Czech), my mom would squeeze his hand and he would know it was time to say ano.

Judge: Do you take this woman to be your wife for the rest of your life?

Sasha: (hand squeeze)

Dad: ANO!

The other day my daughter asked me,

Daugther: Mom? ..... How did you marry dad?

Elen: Well!.....When I met your dad he gave me a lecture about the state of the Universe. The things he said made perfect sense and explained many things that I was wondering about. I was so impressed with how smart he was and how wise he was that I decided to give him a gift in appreciation. I thought I would give him a book, but he had many books and I was worried I would give him the wrong book, and he would think I was stupid. Your dad has high intellect and I was worried that I would give him a present that would expose my ignorance. Then I thought I would give him a CD, but you know your dad, he has no appreciation of music. So after a long and agonizing thinking, I decided that I should give him something that he needed and not something that he would necessarily like. Being the super logical man that he is, I thought he needed a wife that would drive him a little crazy. I went to him and told him that I offer him myself in marriage as a token of appreciation. He looked me over, walked around me to take a good look from all sides and finally smiled. He told me that he liked the gift and that it was the best present ever.

One day I will tell her the full version of the story.

Sweet Dreams

The men where crying like little babies, hitting themselves with grief; they looked distorted, confused, completely defeated. You could feel the distress in the air

The year was 1967, and my father was in the Czech Republic taking a language class as part of his graduate studies. He was studying along with a group of other Arab students. When Egyptian president Jamal Abed Al Nasser announced the loss of the Six Days War to Israel, the Egyptian students became so grief stricken that my father worried they would have nervous break downs. The other Arab students were also depressed, but the Egyptian young men took it the hardest. That moment is frozen in my dad's memory because he has described it to me many times. The moment of defeat, the loss of a dream.

But, it was the era of broken dreams, and loss of the Six Days War was only one of many.

My dad in his youth had many sweet dreams.

The son of a wealthy merchant in the city of Al-Shamiya, south of Iraq, he dreamed of a new Iraq, a better Iraq, an Iraq that was completely different from the Iraq he grew up in. He dreamed of an Iraq were everybody would be equal and have the same rights. He dreamed of an Iraq were nobody went hungry and nobody was poor. He dreamed of an Iraq free of British occupation and free of the current regime left behind by them. He dreamed of a country where everybody could express themselves freely and without fear for their life. Dreams of pride, victory, Arab nationalism, Arab unity, progress, modernity and better life. Dreams of rebuilding the whole country.

And so.......he joined the Iraqi Communist Party against the expressed wishes of his father. The Communist Party was going to achieve all these dreams.

Did you ever notice how all the leaders of communism come from privileged backgrounds? Carl Marx, Lenin, Fidel Castro. Yet they claim to be fighting for the rights of poor and hard working. My theory is that all these overeducated, privileged young men became communists in order to rebel against their fathers. ... just a silly theory....don't take me too seriously.

When the forces of darkness reined in Iraq and those that objected got killed, arrest orders were issued for my father. Hiding in the apartment of a friend, the police came to arrest him anyway, somebody must have spotted him and informed on him. As he was being arrested, he remembered comrades that were arrested like him only to show up dead with holes and burn marks few weeks later.

"I have no idea where the courage or the idea came from, but I decided to give it a try," my dad told me. While he was being driven in a

244

jeep to his dark fate, he decided to try to b.s. his way out of it.

"Do you know who I am?" he asked the arresting officers.

"You are making a huge mistake, I am a high officer in the army, all of you are in big trouble as soon as this mishap is cleared up, I will have all of you arrested and punished," he belted at them with confidence.

The arresting officers looked worried; somehow this display of haughtiness was convincing. They decided to let him go and come back after verifying that they had the right man. My dad was long gone when they came back the second time.

After that he went into hiding in the basement of an abandoned house. His first brush with death convinced him he should never be seen in public and so he never left the room for months, eating nothing but canned food the whole time. Going out to buy fresh fruits and vegetable seemed too risky. Until this day my dad can't stand canned sardines because it was his main stable for months during that period.

Later he arranged for a fake passport and used it to get out of the country. He simply walked with confidence into the airport hoping he wouldn't be discovered. "I was shitting in my pants, knowing that if I was discovered I would be dead, but pretending to be walking in all confidence," my dad told me about his unusual exit of his country.

And so the son of the wealthy merchant would arrive in Kuwait penniless, without papers, without ID, without a way to prove his education; the one who wanted to defend the poor and the hard working would soon join them. It was the first time in his life that he would experience hunger and poverty but not for long. Soon the party would arrange for him to study in the Czech Republic.

In the Czech Republic he would experience an even bigger heart break. Seeing the corruption rampant in the socialist country, he soon started to doubt his ideals. He wasn't sure anymore if this was something that was worth risking his life over. It all seemed very different in his dreams than the actual application he witnessed. "But some are more equal than others" didn't have the same ring to it.

Here he was, depressed, away from his county, exiled from a country that wants to kill him, his beliefs shaken, no longer sure what he believed in, all his sweet dreams broken, drifting through life, nearly broke, no job, doing a degree he didn't care about, Life seemed very very dark indeed.

And so............He got married and had two kids.

In my childhood, I was discouraged from having dreams about rebuilding countries.

Such dreams can be a serious risk to your life.

Preacher

What makes a good preacher?

Effective Christian preachers have a compelling vision of Jesus Christ, which they communicate forcefully to their listeners to lead them to view their circumstances differently and to respond with strengthened faith and commitment.

(Zuck, R. B. (1996, c1994). A biblical theology of the New Testament (Page 370). Chicago: Moody Press) need to talk about the refernce

I believe that to be a good definition of what a good preacher is. The same definition can be adopted for a preacher in any other religion or ideology. Notice that the definition of a good preacher doesn't include strength of one's own faith.

Now let's analyze it a bit. First, the preacher must have a "compelling vision". The preacher must be able to verbalize and communicate a crystal clear vision that the listener is able to imagine in his own head. He must be able to talk about some idealistic world or some perfect place and describe it to you in such detail that you start believing that such a place does exist. Once that is done you are hooked, you will do anything to follow him into that perfect place. For example, you have to say "I can make you become thin, I can make you become happy, I can make you find comfort, I can make you feel good, I will take you to a beautiful place." You can't just talk about happiness or comfort or whatever else it is you are selling, you have to describe it in detail. What does it look like? How does it feel? What does it smell like? Once I am in that state how will I be different, will people perceive me differently? Will I look different? Will I be more successful?. You need describe that person so that I can even imagine what they will have for breakfast for the next 10 years.

Second, "communicate forcefully". The preacher must be a good communicator, he must be able to communicate not only clearly, but in a forceful manner. It's not good enough that the preacher communicate in clear language, he/she must communicate in a manner that can't be ignored. He must be entertaining, his words must be gripping, he must be charismatic; when he talks you just want to listen and can't ignore him. Very few people know how to communicate in such a seductive manner. For example, you can use one-liners which are radical yet memorable, so that they will stick in a person's head for a long time: "Jesus love you", "Islam is the solution". It doesn't matter what that means, it sounds good and once you hear it a few times it sticks in your head and the next thing you know everybody is repeating it like a mantra. Humor is a good communication tool, if you can get people to laugh then you have them; it is hard to ignore somebody once they give you a good laugh.

Finally, he must relate to the personal circumstances of the listener. It is not enough that a preacher paints a beautiful picture of the

248

ultimate goal. Most people will say, yes but I am flawed; perhaps some other people can reach to that idealistic place, but I can't. A good preacher will address your own particular short-comings. He will say I can see that you have sinned, I can see that you have suffered, I can see that you have been through tough times, I can see that you have failed before and that is ok. What that does is help the listener to believe that even they can achieve the required goal. For example, you must be able to sense what the person is looking for and then promise that you will give it to them. This person wants to lose weight, another is having marriage problems and feels completely overwhelmed by it, this person is afraid of social gatherings, another is looking for lasting love. To each person you need to say I will give that which your heart desires. To each person you must deliver a customized message that speaks to their individual yearnings. You might think, but hey! isn't that manipulative and perhaps a little dishonest. Well yes it is, and quite frankly it only works on feeble minded people; objective and self confident people are not swayed by such techniques. The good news is that majority of people are the feeble minded category and only a minority are the objective kind. Most people allow their feelings to sway them.

Most people will say that they hate being preached to, I believe that what they mean is that they hate being preached to by bad preachers who don't follow the basic rules of conduct of preaching and give other preachers a bad name.

You my friend are a bad preacher. You simply suck at it. You don't communicate a compelling vision at all, you keep telling me about how am I going to go to hell, well what is so compelling about that? You communicate in the most boring, tedious and obnoxious manner that even a believer will defect after listening to you. I am willing to bet that even your own mother can't stand your sermons. Finally, you are not even attempting to relate to my personal circumstance. Heck! you don't even know anything about me nor are you willing to take the time to find out.

Please do everybody a favor, either quit preaching or take the time to do it right. Like most things in life, preaching is a skill that can be taught and with practice you can actually become good at it.

Condolences Letter to My Democrat Friend

I wrote this letter the day after the U.S. presidential elections.

Nov 3rd, 2004

Dear Friend,

A few days ago Sheik Zayed El Nehyan passed away. He was the president of the United Arab Emirates. Many people in that country are genuinely mourning his passing. He was a leader who cared about his people and attempted successfully to create a comfortable and privileged living for his fellow country men. I have read about people crying about his death and feeling depressed for days. In a region where corrupt dictators installed by the CIA like Saddam are the norm, Sheik Zayed was a rare exception. While I myself am not a big fan of Sheik Zayed El Nehyan, who was one of the most wealthy people in the world, can you guess where that money came from, and who got to power by getting rid of his brother? I can sympathize with the mourning of the UAE people over their loss of a rare Arab moderate leader who actually cared about his country.

As for you my friend, I have a hard time sympathizing with your pain. You are walking around looking like somebody who got a kick in the stomach, mourning the fact that Kerry is not your president. Was Kerry really such a great man? If he was, then he will find some other way to do great deeds for his country. He is neither dead nor sitting in a jail somewhere. Just look at president Jimmy Carter, he did more for his country after his presidency that during the presidency. But somehow, I doubt we will ever hear about Kerry ever again. You woke up yesterday, went to the same job, your kids went to the same school and even though you voted for the guy that didn't win, no police showed up at your house to haul you off to some dungeon. In fact, you life didn't change that much. In the Middle East each time there is a new president or a change of power it is associates with massive bloodshed and everything in the country needs to be scrapped and rebuilt from scratch. Thousands end up in jails and everybody's life is disrupted.

Yes, yes, I know that you are hurt by all those French people that use George Bush as an excuse to make fun of Americans and call you a nation that lacks culture and sophistication. Well! As a part European myself I have a secret to share with you: we Europeans made fun of Americans long before George Bush arrived on the scene. You guys are a newer country and you do have less history, but that means you are young and hip, so if I was you I wouldn't pay much attention to what those snotty Europeans say about you. Shall I remind you of the not so distant European colonial past? .... Nah! Let's not talk about that.

Oh yes I know, you are upset about the thousand Americans that died during the war on Iraq. But how many Americans die in road accidents every year? How many Americans die in homicides every year? We Iraqis when we waged wars we ended up loosing hundred of thousands and even millions of deaths; really, that number is not that high as far as wars go. At least now I can send money to my family in Iraq so that they could buy the necessities of life without fear of imprisonment, because it was illegal for me to do so under the sanctions. This I have Bush to thank for, not Clinton, not Bush Senior, not Kerry, but George W Bush. Some estimates state that about one million Iraqis died as a result of the sanctions, but no American were dying then....but oops! I must be boring now, talking about something that you don't care about. I will try to stay focused and talk about your feeling and not mine.

Think of all the things you have to celebrate. You just participated in democratic elections where you got to cast your vote and so did your fellow countrymen and fellow countrywomen. In the end the majority got their way. Oh! What would I give to be able to do that in my native Iraq. Even if the religious fundamentalists would win, I would still be happy about the fact that I got to have an equal and fair say in the matter. Iraq would be 100 times better off than where it has been for the last 35 years.

To the United Arab Emirates people, my condolences, and to you my friend I say: Take your wife out for dinner, have a glass of wine on me. Chill out. You have plenty to celebrate. If things get really bad you can move to Canada.

Writing

Two years ago, had somebody told me that I would want to write, I would have laughed at them. Me? Write? But I can't write, I am just a computer geek, plus I have nothing that I want to say, nothing that I want to write about. And then, just like that, in one moment all of that changed. I remember that moment vividly; there was electricity in the air, everything felt intense and multiplied by 100. I wrote a letter to somebody that came straight from the heart. I was expecting that person to ignore my letter and throw it away, instead he reacted is such an emotional way that it completely surprised me. I realized that when you write straight from the gut that it can influence other people in positive and constructive ways. I realized that the keyboard can be mightier than a tank. And that was that, I never stopped writing since. It all was just a fluke. It came out of nowhere. I never dreamed of nor wanted to be a writer before that.

And then I published the first article in a magazine. Seeing my name in print gave me a rush, I have no idea why. But I just wanted more. Welcome to the crazy house of writing. Self doubt, self loathing, I am too stupid to write this, everything I write is trash, people will laugh at me, nobody would want to read this garbage. When I started writing I went to see the movie Adaptation. It is a movie about the messed up crazy process called writing. It made me realize that I am not the only one who finds it torturous. Writing requires hours and hours of being completely inside your head, listening to your own inner voice. Spending that much time inside your head can drive one crazy. My friend Alyson tells me that I should quit my job and dedicate myself to writing alone. I completely disagree with her. I thank god I have a job, kids, and other activities that provide some sane, normal life balance to my life. If I was doing nothing but writing I know I would go crazy. I would become one of those weird people that talk to themselves on the bus. In fact, I don't think that writing is my ultimate goal, dream and passion. My ultimate dream is something else. I think I just have a limited number of things that I feel compelled to say and explain and once that is done I will stop writing. One thing for sure is that I will not write for the sake of writing. In fact I think my ultimate dream and goal is something completely different, which will require complete dedication when the time is right.

And then came the letters. I got fan mail that was so sweet and so wonderful that I sometimes have to wonder if it wasn't intended for somebody else, but ended up in my hands by a mistake. I sometimes read the fan mail to my husband, hoping he would be impressed by his wife once he hears what other people write about her. Most of the time he just shrugs his shoulders and tells me not to let it get to my head. "That person says such wonderful things about you only because he doesn't know you in person," was one response my husband had for a particularly lavish fan letter. There have been many more surprises along the way as well. When I started writing I expected that only women would respond to my writing because of the inwards and emotional nature of my writing. I was surprised time and again by long letters from men who were sharing with me similar experiences, thoughts and feelings. Turns out that the inner world of men is just as complex as the inner world of women….who knew?.... what a gift to discover that. Then there was the playful fun that I discovered I could have once I started writing. Many of the stories are really aimed at a single person. They contain keywords and references that only that person would understand, disguised as yet another story or article to everybody else. It has been so much fun. I discovered that a publishing something in the public sphere can be a great way to pull somebody's chain. I also discovered that people now fear me, because they are afraid that if they annoy me I will write about it and cause them public embarrassment. I frequently hear from a friend, "You are not going to write about that, are you?" right after he says something really stupid. Wow! It is like I have this power or influence that I never had before. Then there is the positive influence it had on my family. I print out my articles and give it to my mom and dad, usually the article becomes the source of lively discussion on our family weekly lunch get-together. My mom says it has helped her understand me better, and we had a few cries together. My husband thinks that I use my writing in order to get back at him for the few times he did to upset me. My dad delights in finding factual and historical mistakes in my writing. When I started this I told each member of my family that they have a veto right to remove anything from my writing that concerns them if they find it upsetting. My family frequently disagrees with me, but none of them have used their veto right, not even once. Which made me realize what a cool family I have.

There are also unanswered questions: are virtual friendships real friendships, or are they more like having imaginary friends?.... I am still thinking on that one. As a result of getting published I had the previlage of having long and deep email exchanges with complete strangers who write to me about their personal lives and share with me things that they haven't shared even with their family. These are people that I have never met and I might never meet in real life, yet I feel as if we know each other somehow.

George Orwell wrote thought provoking stories. But more importantly he bravely lived out his beliefs. He participated in the Second World War against the Nazis and volunteered in the Spanish Civil War against Franco. He actually wrote very little, but wow! what impact. George Orwell wasn't a writer, he wasn't a man of words, he was a man of deeds. His writing wasn't even that great from a pure literary sense.

I went to a party at a friends house. It was during the time Iraq was being bombed in this last war. I met a woman there and started chatting with her. She was telling me about her husband, who is an American and was serving in the army and was involved in the Iraq thing somehow. She told me that his real dream was to write a book. That when he retires from the army (which was due in a short time), he will take a whole year off and finish his novel, which he has been thinking about for a long long time. Later, this woman asked me where I was from; I told her that I am from Iraq. She looked nervous after I told her that. She then started to apologize. She told me that her husband didn't believe in this war and in fact was only participating in it so that he wouldn't lose his pension. I wanted to ask her, "What will your husband's book be about? Will it be about a man who went against his beliefs in order not lose a salary?" I didn't say anything. I just nodded my head. Needless to say I am not going to read his book.

If I am going to be a writer, then I want to be a George Orwell, not the wimpy military guy. To tell you the truth, I don't think I have that sort of courage or strength. When push comes to shove and things get tough and bullets start to fly, I am just a big chickenshit. So, I don't think that I am going to become a full time writer. I will finish up the few remaining things that I have to say and zip it.

Fantasy

When I feel down I will listen to the song "I will survive", It has magical powers over me. I just have to listen to it once to turn everything around in my mind.

My favorite part in the song is when she says "Oh now go. Walk out the door." That is when I imagine myself dancing, wearing big leather boots ready to kick somebody in the behind. That is the turning point in the song, for that is the point where darkness lifts and hope begins. " Just turn around now. You're not welcome anymore."

Speaking of sick fantasies, I sometimes fantasize that I am driving in car when a rocket hits my car. CNN reports "Writer named Elen was assassinated today by the CIA on her way to work this morning, she was suspected of corrupting the minds of our youth with her writting." Images of the burning car and firefighters in the background. I figure, if I am gonna go, I would rather go with a bang. It seems so glamorous to be assassinated by the CIA or the Mossad.

One person who didn't have to fantasize is Sheik Ahmed Yassin. An Israeli strike helicopter fired three missiles at the wheelchair bound, blind and nearly deaf quadriplegic Hammas leader and his entourage while on their way back home following the dawn prayers.

I will always remember the first time I heard Sheik Ahmed Yassin's name. I was at work in Jerusalem and one of my co-workers had the radio on and was listing to the news. It was September 25, 1997. The news reported that several Mossad agents were caught red handed after an attempt to assassinate Khalid Meshal (another Hammas leader) in Amman Jordan. They managed to hit him in the neck with a dart that contained a deadly but untraceble poison; somehow the Jordanian police were able to catch them. Apparently this poison makes the victim dies few days later in what appears to be a heart attack. In return for the release of the mossad agents, Jordan was asking Israel to provide an antidote for the poison injected into Meshal's body, and also a demand was made to release Sheik Ahmed Yassin from prison. The reason this news release drew my attention had nothing to do with Hammas, Meshal or Yassin, I was worried about my husband whom I had just said goodbye to that very morning. He had just boarded an airplane to Canada going through London. The Mossad agents used forged Canadian passports to enter Jordan; my husband was carrying a Canadian passport as well. A Canadian passport that states he was born in Israel, he has an Arabic name, brown skin and he is traveling on the same exact day Mossad agents have been caught in an assassination attempt. Surely my husband will be a suspect in something or other. I kept praying that my husband gets to his destination safely with minimum harassment.

Later on, my husband told me that in London Heathrow airport he was interrogated, except he hadn't heard the news and thus had no idea why they were interrogating him. He thought that maybe the Engli security officers were looking for drugs, he kept telling them, "Just search my luggage, let's get this over with." But they were not interested in his luggage. They kept examining his passport carefully and took photocopies of each page from it. Eventually he was able to board the plane. Once he arrived in Canada he heard the news and finally understood the extra handling.

Few days later Sheik Ahmed Yassin was released from prison. On the news they showed him being carried by supporters. He looked frail, weak and all shriveled up. His wife was standing in the door in anticipation, a huge smile on her face. Later on, he gave an interview with a journalist, he could barely speak, he would pause between the words, the simple act of talking was putting him out of breath. I thought to myself, this guy will die in few weeks, he looked nearly dead already. Weeks later he looked invigorated and more energetic, as if the release from prison breathed a new life into him. In some Arab media Yassin's release was likened to the release of Nelson Mandela. I am a big admirer of Nelson Mandela and it always irritates me when people compare lesser men to him. Sheik Ahmed Yassin was a demagogue. He believed that establishing an Islamic state was the only solution; he believed that secularism was the enemy and I can't imagine that his views on women's rights were all that enlightened. In short, he disapproved of everything that I believe in. Everything, except for one thing.

I didn't grieve the death Sheik Ahmed Yassin. The man lived by the sword and died by the sword. I won't miss his speeches. I grieved because I knew what would come next.

If I am gonna go I would rather go in a big blast.

Surprise

It was the day of the talk.

I was about 15 or 16 riding on a train in Europe, far away from the Middle East. On a vacation. Since we were going to be in this train for few hours with nothing to do, my father decided that it would be a good time to have The Talk. He decided that I was old enough to know the secret.

No, I am not adopted. And no, my dad didn't have another wife back in Iraq with older brothers and sisters that I never met. It was nothing like that. But, what he did tell me, had an equivalent amount of identity confusion associated with it. I might as well have been adopted, I might as well have discovered siblings I never met before.

It was a day of stunned silences. Gasps. One heck of a story.

"I am a communist," said my dad.
I am the daughter of a communist. Surprise!

"Communism is a sinister ideology invented by Jews in order to corrupt Islam," I was taught at school in Kuwait. Just one tidbit of nonsense out of many I was taught and believed while young.

"Communists are infidels."

"Communists are dangerous."

"Communists are evil."

"Communists will go to hell."

Given the valued education that I have received in Kuwait, it should be no surprise that I had a tough time adjusting to the idea of being the daughter of a communist. I was a good Muslim right wing girl, brought up with proper Arab nationalistic values. That is what I thought I wanted to be at the time.

I guess the signs were on the wall. I should have figured it out on my own. Why else would my dad be studying in the Czech Republic? Why else did my dad leave Iraq in the Sixties never to return again? There were also other siging. Like the fact that servants in our house always ate with us on the same table despite the strong objections of all family friends, who thought this to be odd. There was all the lecturing about how all people were equal. The way my dad would be deeply disturbed if my brother or I treated somebody from a minority group in a derogatory way as was common in Kuwait.

At that point I had a choice; either continue to believe that all communists are evil and will go to hell, and by default my dad would be with them, or adjust my beliefs and learn a little bit more about it. It was very hard for me to continue believing that the man who raised me and taught me that I was equal to any man, despite the society around me

266

indicating otherwise, could possibly be evil.

I found out many things about my dad during that train trip that I never knew before. He couldn't talk about it earlier because it was dangerous to tell a child information that could get you killed. You thought my life story is amazing? Wait till you hear my dad's life story. But that will be in another book.

Ten years later, I am living in Vancouver and I get a phone call from my dad. He asks me to go shopping with him on Saturday. I agreed to meet him at the time and date he specified. When I hang up the phone I have the following discussion with my husband:

Elen: I just had the strangest conversation with my dad.

Husband: What?

Elen: My dad asked me to go shopping with him.

Husband: What is wrong with that?

Elen: My dad hates shopping, plus my mom always buys all his clothes for him. The man hates the shopping mall and he is asking me to spend the whole afternoon with him in the shopping mall. You don't think that is strange?

Husband: Maybe he just wants to talk with you about something.

Elen: So why wouldn't he just come over and talk to me?

Husband: Maybe he wants to talk to you in private.

Elen: Must be something serious then, do you think that maybe one of my parents is ill? Do you think that maybe my parents are getting a divorce? It must be something big. He sounded really odd on the phone.

Husband: Don't think about it like that. Just wait until the weekend and you will find out. No point in speculating.

The dark thoughts wouldn't leave me alone. I kept thinking about all the dark things that my dad might want to tell me. Perhaps I was adopted? Perhaps, I do have siblings I never knew about?

Saturday finally came and I met my dad in the shopping mall. "Ok dad, so what do you need to buy?" I asked him eagerly, pretending that I bought the bit about me helping him do shopping. We walked around looking at trousers, jackets, sweaters, and shirts. My dad would look at different things and never showed much interest. He didn't try on anything and didn't buy anything either. When we finished looking at all the men's clothing my dad said. Let's go find a coffee shop; I will buy you a cup of coffee.

"Ok, this is it, he will tell me now." "It must be something that is really tough to say," I thought to myself.

In the coffee shop we had a generic discussion about world affairs.

"Come on dad, spit it out, you are driving me crazy. Just tell me already, I am dying here," I kept thinking, but I thought that I should just let him tell me when he is comfortable. I thought I should not push him.

Then my dad got up and said: "let's go to the makeup counter."

Oh my God! My dad is losing it, I never heard my dad say he wants to go to the makeup counter, I thought to myself.

So we go to the makeup counter and my dad keeps asking me which lipstick I like, which perfume I like. "Do you like this one? Would you like me to buy you this one?", my dad kept picking up different articles of makeup and showing them to me.

Ok, something is definitely wrong. I have never seen my dad even notice makeup in my whole life and now he is recommending the Christian Dior Sumptuous Fuschia lipstick, something is definitely up.

Suddenly my dad looked at his watch and said: "Ok it is time to go home. I will give you a ride".

Maybe my dad didn't feel comfortable telling me in the mall; maybe he wants to tell me at home where there is more privacy.

So he drives me home and he parks the car, telling me that he wants to come in with me to say hello to my husband.

Ok, maybe he wants to tell me and my husband at the same time,

I thought to myself.

So we walk together into my apartment.

Hey! What are all these people doing here.
My friends, my mom, what is going on?
    "Surprise!" they all shouted.

It was my 25th birthday and my husband and my dad devised this whole plan together in order to give me a surprise party. I started to laugh hysterically, I was so relieved that my dad's odd behavior was nothing more that a stalling tactic to keep me out of the house while my husband prepared food for the party. On one hand, I wanted to hug them both for making such a huge effort; on the other hand they nearly gave me a heart attack in the process.

Hey! Families! Full of surprises. You think you know somebody because you have known them all your life and then you realize that there is a surprise in store.

Yeah, he is a Commie, but he is still the best dad in the world.

Losing Sanity

I love it when people give me advice. Especially when it is from complete strangers. Usually those are the best kinds of advice. Over the years I have benefited greatly from advice given to me by various people.

Take the advice given to me by Abdullah (not his real name), an acquaintance of the family. We socialize with Abdullah about once or twice a year. He was sitting in the living room after a festive dinner and we were chatting about world affairs as all us Middle Easterners like to do, when Abdullah suddenly said that he has been thinking lots about my brother, who has been suffering with mental illness for many years. Abdullah said that he spent many hours attempting to figure it out why my brother was ill, and after long thinking and contemplation he has finally figured out. Wow! Abdullah you are a genius, all the best psychiatrists and therapist haven't been able to help my brother, please tell us why my brother is in his tormented state. Abdullah said, "Your brother is sick because of you Elen. You are so successful on many fronts, career and family. Each time your brother meets with you, he feels inadequate because in his mind he is comparing himself to you. It makes him feel inadequate and then he feels depressed as a result." Wow! What great advice from somebody who barely knows me.

I have spent fifteen years watching my brother deteriorate from bipolar disease to schizophrenia. I have been to every psychiatric ward, half-way house and group house in the City of Vancouver in order to visit my brother, because he was housed in all of them at one point or another. I have talked to a bazillion psychiatrists, nurses and therapists and heard them tell me the same nonsense. I have watched him take medication after medication, each with such vile side effects that it made me doubt if being insane wasn't better. I have watched him gain lots of weight until he looked like he would explode and then lose it again with amazing speed where he looked like a skeleton. I have spent hours listening to him tell me about his dark illusions and fantasies, how he walks around for hours and everybody seems be a devil-possessed human, how he can actually see horns on their heads, how all these people are after him and want to kill him and he is constantly trying to escape. I have visited my brother in the psychiatric ward where he was locked up in a room with nothing but a mattress and a stainless steel toilet. When he is in that state, I need to be accompanied with two body guards that look like Vin Diesel on steroids, for my own safety. I have watched my parents plunge into their own depression over this and I had to tell them over and over and over that my brother's illness was not their fault. All this torment could have been spared had I listened to the valuable advice of Abdullah. I will mess up both my professional and family life so that my brother will no longer feel inadequate next to me. I figured that the quickest way to mess up my life would be to take hard drugs. From what I hear it seems to be a guaranteed way to mess up everything. Since I don't have much knowledge about the matter I need advice. Which kinda drug should I take? I hear drug names in Hollywood movies like crack, LSD or cocaine; which is best and fastest at ruining a life? Is there a way to take this drug without needles? I am really squeamish about needles in general and cannot imagine injecting myself with a needle. I get dizzy when the doctors gives me the flu shots.

Off course, Abdullah's not so successful career and recent divorce contributed nothing to his sincere advice to me. There is no way that this bright middle-aged man feels inadequate next to me. There is no way that he was projecting his own feelings onto my brother. No, that is absolutely not what was going on in his mind.

I love the fragile ego of some Middle Eastern men; it can be such a hoot.

So, as I have illustrated with the above example I get valuable advice from people already. So all of you who send me emails about how I should live my life and what I should think, just make me laugh. You pale in comparison to the wonderful advice of Abdullah. Unless you can top the brilliance and deep wisdom of Abdullah, then I recommend that you don't bother sending me advice. I get able advice already.

My favorite emails are the ones where the sender diagnoses me with mental illnesses that I have never heard off. Considering that I have read several books on mental illnesses after my brother's affliction, I am constantly amazed by new illnesses that I have never heard of. One person diagnosed me with Stockholm Syndrome. Another concluded that I must suffer from evilitis – a chronic state of evil. All this time, when my brother was really ill and he would start imagining that I was one of the devil-possessed, horn-wearing people, I thought it was because he didn't take his little blue pills on time. Turns out he was right all the way. Hey! The amazing things that you discover from complete strangers! All this time I had no idea. Been going to the family doctor on my yearly checkup and he never mentioned a thing. Finally, I get free psychoanalysis for free from people whom I never met. Isn't this internet thing just wonderful?

Despite all the advice I have gotten, I myself am rotten at giving advice. In fact if I ever give you advice on anything you should probably ignore it. Had I known any good advice I would have given some to my brother, but none of the advice has worked thus far.

Perhaps if I take drugs, I will be reduced to a psychotic state as well. There probably is a drug out there that can induce that. One day, both my brother and I will be sitting on a couch in the psychiatric ward. We will both be wearing those flimsy hospital gowns that show your behind when you stand up. We will talk about the devil-possessed, horn-wearing people and devise escape plans together. At last, my brother won't feel lonely in the dark world that he lives in. At last I will be able to understand what he is going through. It will be like the good old days, when we were both kids and we would spend hours sharing our fantasies and hopes for the future.

Yearly Challenge

My father laughed. My brother was laughing so hard he was swaying forwards and backwards. My mother placed her hand on her head and said, "Oh no! What now!" My husband suppressed the laugh, but only because he knew that he would have to go home with me that night.

In 2000, I announced at the family weekly get together lunch that I would do the Vancouver Sun Run, a popular Vancouver ten kilometer run.

There were head shakes with disbelief.
There were, "But you need to be an athlete to run ten kilometer."
There were, "But you can't run around the block, how will you run a ten kilometer race?"
There was, "But people train for that sorta thing."

In defiance I said, "So I will train and do the bloody ten kilometer race. I don't see what the big deal is?" Despite my nonchalant exterior, I wasn't surprised at my family's response. I would run for five minutes and feel like I was about faint and collapse. A few days following my proclamation, I enrolled in a running clinic that is for complete beginners. The premise is simple, you start by running 30 seconds and walking for four and half minutes, repeat for an hour. Every week, you increase the running time and reduce the walking time by a bit until you are able to run the whole hour. I would meet with the group nine am every Sunday and do the routine with the group, and later you are supposed to do it on your own twice during the week. The first meeting was easy. Those 30 seconds went by so fast that I would hardly notice the time going by. Hey! Even I could do it and with ease. Good start.

The next day it snowed in Vancouver. And when it snows in Vancouver you don't get that nice powdery ice cream-like fluff you get in Montreal. You see, in Vancouver it snows, then the temperature goes up, which means the snow partially melts forming a slushy substance, and then it rains on top of that, forming wet vastness of murky goo. After people walk on this murky goo for a day the icy part is compacted leaving the water on top of the compacted murky goo. Water on top of compacted ice-like murky goo is the perfect recipe for breaking your neck. How was I supposed to do my two walk/run routines during the week? It snows very rarely in Vancouver, about once or twice a year. That year the snow was particularly unusual because it happened in October. I felt that the whole universe was conspiring to stop me from training for the Sun Run.

Even God was laughing at me and telling me "Elen, you can't do this".

But being the stubborn Iraqi that I am, I was adamant that I would do it. Since I work full time and have three small children to care

276

for, my days are pretty full, making five am in the morning the perfect time for training for this working mother. I woke up at five am and looked out the window. It looked dark, cold and miserable outside. I put my running shoes on and went outside anyway. If you think that walking on the murky goo is dangerous, try doing it in the dark when you can't see... much more fun. I was the only person outside. As I ran and walked I kept telling myself "I am the most insane person in the world". Definitely, an A-type personality. I spent more energy looking where I was going and balancing myself on icy patches than actually running. I think I got more muscle toning than cardio on that day. But, I did it anyway. When I got back home my husband was awake. "You are the most insane woman in the world," he told me.

I knew if I would drop the ball at the beginning I wouldn't continue with the running clinic and I would have to bear the teasing of my family for many years to come. I could imagine the weekly family lunch, week after week, year after year hearing, "Do you remember the time when Elen said she would run the ten kilometer Sun Run? hahahaha wasn't that a hoot?" Who says family can't be the source of your motivation?

The next week, I showed up for the group run and it was snowing heavily on that day. About 20% of the group showed up only. Most people didn't bother leaving home on that morning. But I was there, ready for the next stage. "Go ahead God! Have a good laugh."

We ran walked for an hour and it snowed so heavily that I could hardly see in front of me. Anybody who lives in Vancouver will tell you how rare that is. There was something beautiful and surreal about walking and running in the snow. At least with the fresh powdery snow it wasn't slippery.

Three weeks of running/walking on slippery goo were where followed by five am running/walking in the pouring rain. And I mean I would come home dripping water from every limb. I would walk through the back door into the kitchen of the house so wet that I had to take all my clothes off in the entrance so as not to wet the carpets in the house. I would find my husband in the kitchen about to make coffee and he would look at me and shake his head. He had already given up on talking me out of it at that point.

For my birthday that year, my husband bought me the full running gear. The trousers, the technical shirt, even the running jacket thing. All Sugoi, a popular running name brand. All in my favorite color of eggplant purple. I guess he figured if I was gonna fall flat on my face, I might as well do it looking good. I saw this as an awesome gesture of encouragement. Even though he didn't support what I was doing he supported me anyway and I loved him for it.

The night before the race I got a concerned phone call from my dad. It went something like this.

Dad: So are you going through with it?

Me: Yes, off course.

Dad: Honey, I am worried you will hurt yourself, running ten kilometer is no joke.

Me: Don't worry, I trained.

Dad: You know, I won't think less of you if you quit, I promise that nobody in the family will make fun of you if you quit now.

Me: Dad, don't worry, I will do fine.

Dad: Listen, if you feel hurt half-way through, don't push yourself, just stop half-way through and go home, ok!

Me: Dad, don't worry, I will do fine.

Dad: Ok, just promise me you won't push yourself, if you feel pain you will stop.

Me: Ok dad, but don't worry.

Dad: I promise you nobody will make fun of you if you stop half-way through.

That night when I went to bed I tossed and turned. I had nightmares where I am running and then I fall flat on my face. I couldn't sleep well. My husband kept telling me "You will do fine, now go to sleep".

The next day, I did it. I ran the ten kilometer and I didn't fall flat on my face and I didn't stop half-way through. When I crossed the finish line, I started to cry.

I had finished university, balanced career with family, gave birth to three children, learned foreign languages and traveled around the world. None of these things were easy, but they were all expected of me. They were things that I myself and my family expected of me. This was the first time that I had done something that nobody expected of me. I surprised them all, including myself.

I went home to find my children cheering "Mommy we saw you running". My husband gave me a hug. My dad called to say, "I take my words back, I am sorry I made fun of you earlier. You did it and I am proud of you."

From then on, every year, I have resolved myself to do something that I don't believe that I can do. Something that I am terrified of, something that I have never done before. So far I have done, running, dancing and this years challenge is writing a book. The fun just never ends.

My Ph.D. Thesis

I always said that my mother gave me the best preparation for married life. She taught me nothing about house work cooking or cleaning. So when I got married my husband had to do it all. It was great.

At age ninteen I had never used the oven, never vacuumed a carpet and never ironed a shirt. I was your typical spoiled princess, expecting to snap my fingers and see other people jump to my commands. It's not easy growing up spoiled because you eventually have to face reality. As a teenager I was used to throwing my dirty clothes on the floor of my bedroom and they would magically reappear clean and folded in my closet the next day. I would come from school and a hot meal was ready on the table. Imagine my shock when I went to university and would throw my clothes on the floor and find them lying there the next day? The day after, the pile kept on getting bigger. Oh no! You mean I have to do laundry? Maybe, I should throw away the clothes and buy new ones, but I figured that would get too expensive so I introduced myself to the laundry room at the university dormitory where I was living. I approached the task with lots of trepidation. That big machine thing with the huge hole in the middle was intimidating. It was mocking me. "You can't do this, you can't do this, you can't do this, nah nanah nananah!" It seemed rather obvious that you should stick the dirty clothes in the middle, put some detergent on top. How much detergent? O! I don't know. Maybe this should be enough, a scoop or two, a third won't hurt. And then I pushed a button and it starting buzzing. I could hear the sound of water woshing around in there. Hey! This isn't so hard. This is dead easy. Even I could do it. One hour later, I learned the lesson about separating your clothes based on colour. Everything came out a pukey shade of pink. At least I didn't have to worry about colour coordination since everything was the same color now.

At least I didn't have to cook. The dormitories I lived in had a cafeteria that served three meals a day. Yeah! So when I got married I knew how to colour separate but couldn't fry an egg. I didn't know that in order to fry an egg you should heat some oil in a pan and then break and egg in the middle, that was too hard for me. Luckily, my husband is a great cook and he seemed happy to make great meals everyday. Until one day I had the following discussion with my mom over the phone.

Mom: What did you have for dinner last night?

Me: Take away pizza.

Mom: Doesn't your husband mind?

Me: No, why would he mind, we like eating pizza straight out of the box.

Mom: But you are married now, you can't keep doing this.

Me: But I never ate pizza straight out of the box before, it is rather liberating to be able to do that.

Mom: Well, your husband doesn't mind now, but later on he might appreciate it if you prepared him a nice meal once in a while.

Me: Hmmmmmm!

282

Ok, I was determined to learn to cook. I mean how hard can it be? I am a university graduate, surely I can figure out how to cook. So I went to the bookstore and spent 2 hours examining all the cook books on the shelves. After careful examination I settled on buying this one: The New Basics Cookbook, by Julee Rosso and Sheila Lukins

Which turned out to be a good choice since it teaches all the basics, yet it contains a variety of interesting recipes. Every night I would sit for hours studying the book to try to settle on a simple first dish for me to prepare. My diligent studying of the book got me the mocking remark, "Is that you Ph.D. thesis?" from my husband. He said that each time I opened that book I got a serious look on my face that reminded him of students when they are revising their Ph.D. thesis. From then on, that book has been called Elen's Ph.D. thesis; we still call it that today. Finally, I settled on a pasta dish. It seemed easy. You boil some pasta, make a sauce to go on top. How hard can it be? Only problem was that my Ph.D. thesis didn't mention that you should put the pasta in already boiling water. I instead placed the pasta in a big pot of cold water and proceeded to boil. How was I supposed to know that the pasta would stick all together and come out a giant gew mass? " Why didn't the Ph.D. thesis mention that you should boil the water first?" I asked. "It is because everybody knows that you should do that," replied my husband.

My poor husband. When I remember all the disasters that I created in my kitchen on those first few months, my husband would eat it anyway and then try to give me compliments on my progress. There was the burned rice. The chicken that stuck to the pot. The mashed potato that was too liquid and the chili that made you wanna call 911.

And then there was the pita bread incident. After several months of adventures, I decided to get really brave and make pita bread from scratch. Only problem I didn't calculate how long it would take and started making the bread around 9:30 pm. At 12:30 pm I was ready to start baking the bread in the oven. My husband was tired and wanted to go to sleep. He kept urging me to leave it alone and that he will buy me all the pita bread I wanted the next day, but being the stubborn Iraqi that I am I persisted: I would finish what I started. And then I burned my pinky finger while opening the hot oven door. Ouch! Ouch! Ouch! I cried in panicky pain. I burned my finger. I insisted I had to go Emergency right away. My husband got dressed and took me to the Emergency Department of a nearby hospital. We sat there in the waiting room for two hours while doctors and nurses attended to heart attacks, drug overdoses and accident patients. I sat there with my red pinky and started to feel a bit silly once I compared my "injury" to the very real injuries of the people around me. When the doctor finally saw me, I wasn't in pain anymore. It seemed to have gone away on its own. But since I was there I showed the doctor my pinky. I could tell that the doctor was resisting the urge to laugh. He was kind though; he placed some dressing on my finger and bandaged it anyway, instead of kicking me out for wasting his time.

On my way home, I remembered the wonderful Czech movie

"Pysna Princezna" "Proud Princess," but it can also be translated to the "Snotty Princess." It is a childhood favorite of a mine. A tale about a super spoiled princess who rejects love letters from a king in a far away kingdom. The king disguises himself as an average man and decides to teach the princess a lesson with both tough and tender love methods. That night I felt like the silly "Pysna Princezna". But, for the first time, I didn't like playing that role anymore. It was time for me to grow up.

When I got home at 2:30am, I finished making the pita despite my husband's urging to go to bed. I think he was afraid I would detonate a weapon of mass destruction in the kitchen by accident. I persisted and it actually tasted alright.

Now that is what I call determination.

Losing the Family Curse

My family is cursed by the most unusual curse, it seemed harmless at first but in truth its sinister cloud overshadowed most of my life.

We are cursed to buy houses we never live in. We all buy houses we plan to live in at some point in the future and rent an apartment on a temporary basis. The Cosmic Joker keeps playing his jokes on us and we never end up living in the purchased house and instead end up living in the rented place. Allow me illustrate with a few examples of this curse.

When I was a child growing up in Kuwait, my dad built a house in Baghdad. The plan was that he would work in Kuwait for several years and once he collected enough money the whole family would move to Baghdad to our beautiful five bedroom house. The two story house has a swimming pool, a garden with palm trees and custom-designed rooms. I never got to even see the house let alone live in it. I have seen pictures of the house and grew up in rented apartments in Kuwait for 18 years instead. As the political situation in Iraq kept getting worse the likelihood of us returning to Iraq got slimmer and slimmer and so my mother decided to purchase a house in the Czech Republic so that eventually when we would immigrate there, we would have a nice house waiting for us. This house I did get to visit. Only because my mom's family lives in it, I always get to stay in the attic on brief vacations. It is a really nice house, too bad we immigrated to Canada instead. Shortly into my marriage I realized that the curse is stuck to me no matter what I do. My new husband proudly showed me pictures of the house he built in Mashhad, his home town outside of Nazareth. Only problem is that he is an academic and there are no universities in the area of his hometown. I asked him why he built the house. He told me that when he finished his B.Sc. he had some extra money and his dad advised him to use the money to build a house on the family's property, so that he would have a nice house waiting for him when he decides to get married and have children. At the time my husband didn't think he would end up in Canada pursuing an academic career. When we lived in Jerusalem we lived in a rented apartment and about once a month we would drive to Nazareth to visit my in-laws and we would stay in this beautiful house on a hill top with an unobstructed view of the valley underneath it. Three fair sized bedrooms, a beautiful marble entrance. The outside of the house is decorated with amazing rocks. Too bad we will never live in it and my kids won't get to grow up in it. What a tease. This Cosmic Joker is cruel. If you think that not owning a house is bad, try owning a house you can't live in. Try owning several you can't live in.

"I want my life to be boring; I want my life to get into a rut," I told my dad when I moved from Israel to Vancouver in September of 2000. All this traveling around the world, learning new languages and discovering new cultures seems all interesting and glamorous; few people realize the toll it takes on your emotions and psyche. I swore off adventures. I swore off interesting. I wanted dull, I wanted gray, I wanted ordinary. I wanted average. I am going to become the most boring person on earth. I am gonna buy a boring house with a boring backyard. I am gonna buy the most boring family sedan for a car and I am gonna get a boring job. Preferably in an office where I just push paper around aimlessly. Even my food will be boring; I will eat boring meat and potato dishes. No interesting people allowed into my life. If you are the least bit interesting then please don't talk to me. If there is a small smudge of excitement happening somewhere, then please be sure to exclude me from it. That was my objective on September of 2000. I set out on my mission by striking bravely at the source. I am going to break the family curse. I am going to take the radical step of buying a house and actually live in it. I am not gonna just live in it, I am gonna fully dwell in it. I will hang pictures on the wall and I am gonna plant flowers in the front yard, and I am gonna get me some of those boring lawn chairs for the backyard. I know this doesn't seem like such a radical concept but for a woman possessed by the gypsy spirit, it was a destiny-defying step. Dare I break the family curse? Dare I change my destiny in such a defiant manner? Will the Cosmic Joker leave me alone? Or will he punish me in retaliation?

As I moved into my newly purchased house I felt a tremendous trepidation. I woke up every morning expecting something horrible to happen. Surely I would be punished somehow, somewhere, when I least expect it. If I had believed in Arabic superstitions I would have bought 50 evil eyes and blue beads and hung them in every room in the house. If I was Jewish I would have bought 50 mezuzahs and placed them on every entrance of every single room of the house. If I was a Christian I would have bought 50 holy pictures of the baby Jesus cradled by the virgin Marry and crosses and hung them in random places in the house. But since I don't believe in any of that I had a dilemma. I knew I needed to do something to ward off the evil eye that was sure to strike me, but how could a heretical, non-believer infidel like me do that? What do you do to bring good luck and good fortune into your home when you are agnostic? I couldn't find anything, so I had to invent it myself.

One day while on a business trip to San Francisco, I was walking around looking at art galleries, of which San Francisco has plenty, when suddenly I saw this large hand-woven medieval tapestry. I fell in love with it right away; I didn't know why at the time, but I felt a sudden urge to buy it. The sales man urged me to buy it; I responded by saying that I had to consult with my husband first, and since he is back in Vancouver I won't be able to do that. "Surprise him!" said the sales person in the most mischievous way. What could I say other than, "Ok! Here is 900 dollars for it", after some haggling to be true to my Middle Eastern heritage

The beautiful tapestry depicts a merry medieval scene of music, food and dance. It is based on an antique that is hanging in some historical castle somewhere in Europe. When I got back into my room and examined it closely, I realized why I had such strong gut instincts that made me buy it on an impulse provoked by a clever sales man.

It has a woman, her husband and three children. The woman is sitting and playing an organ, the husband is holding a scroll and looks deep in thought and the tree kids are playing around. That is exactly like my family. I notice how each one of the children has a very different personality; the eldest is pulling a cat's tail, the middle child looks like an angel and stands adoringly between the two parents, and the youngest is goofing off and petting a dog. That is a very close representation of my three children. I noticed how they all look very bored; they all look like they are infinitely staring into the void. They look so serene and calm. I have found my good luck charm. I will hang it in my living room and stare at it every single night until my family becomes the family in that tapestry. Forever stuck in a bored stance.

Several years later. I continue to live in the boring house, walking distance from the beach in one of the nicest neighborhouds in Vancouver. In the evenings I sit in my backyard sipping herbal tea and watching the trees softly sway from side to side. In the morning I get up early, make breakfast, go to work in my character-deprived Toyota Corolla. Ahhhh! The bliss of living La Vida boring. The gypsy spirit is nearly gone, the Cosmic Joker seems to have finally given up on me.

Who says you can't change your destiny?

Epilogue

In the book One Thousand and One Nights. King Schehrayar started as a loving husband. One day after a hunting trip, he came home to find his wife in bed with another man. In a fit of rage he killed his wife and declared war on all women. He marries frequently only to kill the bride the morning after the wedding night. His heart is safely sealed behind a security barrier that no feminine intrusion can breach. The mother of all sex battles rages until he encounters the wise and enchanting Scheherazade.

That is how the story goes.

Printed in the United States
66858LVS00010B/47

INSIGHT GUIDES

WESTERN HIMALAYA

Edited by Manjulika Dubey and Toby Sinclair
Photography by R. K. Gaur, Toby Sinclair,
Joanna van Gruisen and others
Executive Director: Bikram Grewal
Editorial Director: Geoffrey Eu

APA PUBLICATIONS

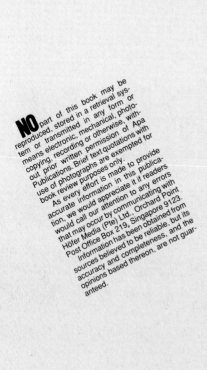
WESTERN HIMALAYA

First Edition
© 1992 APA PUBLICATIONS (HK) LTD
All Rights Reserved
Printed in Singapore by Höfer Press Pte. Ltd

ABOUT THIS BOOK

The publication of *Insight Guide: India* in 1985 has marked a major step in Apa Publications' coverage of Asia. **Bikram Grewal** who along with Samuel Israel edited this exceedingly successful volume, still continues to oversee the Indian program. He is again joined by **Manjulika Dubey** and **Toby Sinclair**. Manju who has several years of book publishing behind her, was the motivating factor for the team's *Insight Guide: South India* and the first Indian *Cityguide* to the golden triangle of *Delhi, Jaipur & Agra*. Toby, whose primary love is wildlife, produced *Indian Wildlife*, which marked Apa's departure into non-destination guides, and co-edited *Rajasthan* and the *Insight Pocket Guide to New Delhi*.

This team, co-ordinating actively with **Geoffrey Eu** and **Jennie Lee** in Apa's Singapore headquarters, now bring to you *India's Western Himalaya*: the seventh volume in the *Insight Guide* series on India and which bears witness to Apa's continuing involvement with the compelling enigma off this exasperating and enchanting country. It brings to its readers a comprehensive survey of some of India's greatest treasures – the land and people of the mountainous north-west.

Another innovation for this volume was finalised in discussion with publisher **Hans Höfer**. It was decided to include descriptive articles on selected treks that could be undertaken in this extraordinary part of the world and several specialists were invited to give the benefit of their experience. These along with specially created maps give this volume a distinctive meaning and special place in Apa's coverage of South Asia.

Two collaborators, **Sanjeev Saith** and **Vikram Malhotra**, both dedicated Himalaya freaks, allowed themselves cheerfully to be shanghaied into selecting appropriate authors and listing interesting treks. The benefit of their expertise to Apa readers is first-hand and up-to-date travel accounts of little-known areas.

Sanjeev's career as a photographer and writer emerged from his interest in mountaineering. Over the past 15 years he has participated in as many climbing and rafting expeditions to the Himalaya. His work has been exhibited in Delhi and London, and his film of the Indian Everest expedition was judged best documentary at the 1985 National Film Festival. His books include *A Journey Down the Ganga* and *Himachal Pradesh*.

Vikram is a civil servant, an Indian administrative service officer of Himachal cadre, with a keen interest in music, photography and ecology. His wife and co-author Rekha is an officer in the Indian Railways and has a special interest in Himalayan crafts and miniature paintings.

Many of the 19th-century records of India were compiled by observant civil servants posted in remote areas. This tradition is very much alive in this book, a major portion of which is the product of similar curious and sympathetic minds.

Janet Rizvi, who has contributed most of the section on Ladakh, lived there for many years with her civil servant husband. She is the author of *Ladakh: Crossroads of High Asia* (1983), the finest introduction to this fascinating region.

Deepak Sanan and his wife **Dhanu Swadi**, **Sarojini Thakur** and **Tarun Sridhar** are all IAS officers of the Himachal cadre, and (depending on length of service) have spent between 7 and 12 years working and travel-

Dubey   *Sinclair*   *Saith*   *Malhotra*

ling in the state, living in close proximity with the people. **Parvez Dawan**, a Kashmiri by birth, currently heads the civil administration of Jammu district. He has written libretti for opera (including a rock opera on the Ramayana), helped revive the celebrated Basohli school of miniature painting and published two books.

Three other writers with Kashmiri affiliations are **Jaya Jaitly**, **Brij Tankha** and **Marie D'Souza**.

Jaya, a regular contributor to *Insight Guides* on India, lived in both Kashmir and Ladakh for many years. She has written two books, *The Crafts of Jammu, Kashmir and Ladakh* (1990) and *The Craft Traditions of India* (1991). Marie, a freelance photographer and writer, author of a pictorial book (*Kashmir*, 1990), has travelled extensively in the state and recently married a Kashmiri. Brij, a Kashmiri by birth, teaches modern Japanese history in Delhi University and is due to publish two books.

Joanna van Gruisen, who has contributed to several Insight Guides, has spent the last 14 years in South Asia working as a photo-journalist and wildlife photographer. She has co-produced and made several films including *New Hope for the Hangul* in Kashmir's Dachigam National Park, followed by three arduous years filming the wildlife of Ladakh in both sub-zero winters and the bright, dry days of summer.

Most of the contributors to the trekking section have in common this enthusiasm for the wilds, though they are distributed through a range of professions.

Shouma Banerjee Kak is a designer specializing in animation films and digital videographics. **Hashmat Singh** leads trekking groups all over the Himalaya for an adventure sports agency. So does **Alka Sharma** when she isn't parachuting out of planes, skiing and para-sailing. Another daring young woman is **Pavan Sarao**, who works for a white-water rafting outfit and enjoys rock climbing. **Manish Kawlra** markets food products and **Reba Mukerji**, who lists music and modern dance as her primary interests, works as a Program Officer at the American Centre in Delhi. **Anirban Roy** makes advertising films and documentaries.

Paramjeet Singh and **Shubhendu Kaushik** are both architects who often abandon their drawing boards to go off rock-climbing, trekking and skiing. **Amitabh Dubey**, who compiled the Travel Tips with his classmate **Amit Agarwal**, is a college student who enjoys rafting, kayaking and skiing and plans to take up hang-gliding next.

Photographic contributions come from regular sources including **Pramod Mistry**, **Avinash Pasricha** and **Shalini Sara**. This book also introduces new photographers to the *Insight Guides*.

Ashok Dilwali has made the mountains his specialty and has published five photographic books. **Suman Dubey** has been in love with the mountains since his schooldays and was the youngest member of the 1965 expedition to Everest which successfully put nine climbers on the summit. **R. K. Gaur** took to photography during a long and successful career in the Indian Army from which he recently retired as a major-general. **Sondeep Shankar** is the picture editor of the *Observer* group of newspapers.

Thanks are also due to **Radhika Singh** and her team at **Fotomedia**, India's foremost photo library for their help in the picture selection. **S. Muthiah** of TT Maps and **Kaj Berndtson** in Munich supplied the maps.

Singh *Sharma* *Kawlra* *Roy*

CONTENTS

History & Culture

Places

Maps

TRAVEL TIPS

INTRODUCTION

Today, India's Western Himalaya are recognized politically as the states of Jammu and Kashmir and Himachal Pradesh. Centuries ago, however, this natural frontier was a junction, a difficult but crucial link on the ancient land-locked trade routes originating from as far away as the Balkans, from Bukhara and Yarkand, and from Lhasa and beyond, coming together at this elevated crossroads to meet the southern avenues that reached up from the Gangetic plain, from Rajasthan and from Central India.

Traders and caravans, saints and missionaries, emperors and armies, all representing a multitude of cultural streams, travelled along these classic routes. Most were transients; some, however, were permanently caught by the network of valleys, driven and directed by the crests and troughs till they came to rest somewhere in these scattered mountainous enclaves. This dynamic frontier eventually ceased to be in flux once political strife put an end to trade. The residue that emerged was a fascinating patchwork of diverse ethnic zones, where Mongoloid features inhabited one valley, and Aryan the next; where women took to the *burqa* (veil) in one, and took two husbands in another; and where some villagers spoke the language of the kings of Persia, while others, but a day away, understood a dialect used by the lamas of Tibet.

The simple, yet intense experience of such disparate Himalayan phenomena can surprise the traveller even today. In Ladakh, he can observe a pair of black-necked cranes perform their primeval dance of courtship at the edge of the turquoise Pangong Lake, and at the end of the day witness the more sombre display of the lamas as they step to the clash of cymbals. Exotic saffron blossoms carpet an exclusive habitat in Pampore in autumn when, elsewhere, the Gaddi shepherd guides his flocks back from the upper valleys to where nature is kinder. A snatch of a Dogri song carried by the wind in a deep valley can be as uplifting as the sudden sighting of a hangul stag as it flashes past in its ultimate preserve of Dachigam. The onslaught of a Kashmiri *wazwan* upon the taste buds, or the explosion of a vintage Kinnaura *anguri* on the palate are, of course, moments of sheer joy. And what can be more exhilarating than a horseride among the flower-bedecked meadows of Kishtwar in the company of a Gujjar? Or the ultimate expression of freedom – the last few steps on a pristine snow arête rising gracefully to the summit of a Himalayan giant?

Of such lasting traditions has been woven the intricate tapestry that is our Western Himalaya today, its fabric of physical geography worked upon over and over again by varicoloured human thread. Its rich surface texture provides enough reason to pass a few seasons within its folds. The subtlety of its hues, however, needs more than just one lifetime to be explored.

Preceding pages: awesome landscape of the Himalaya; Himalayan peaks; Leh Palace, Ladakh; Bhimakali Temple, Sarahan, Himachal Pradesh; Lama above Leh; Pang, Ladakh. Left, Kashmiri Muslim.

THE LAND

The physical map of the Indian subcontinent portrays the Himalaya as a thick drape of white, falling from north-west to south-east over 1,500 miles. What appears to be a continuous stretch of snow and ice to the common eye is actually a complex mountain system, comprised of a series of parallel, curvilinear ranges.

These ranges first began to appear after the drifting subcontinent of India, once part of Gondwanaland, collided with Eurasia a million years ago. Under stress from the elemental forces, the bed of the vast Sea of Tethys that once separated the two converging land masses was thrust upwards in a gigantic upheaval, and these Himalayan folds emerged out of chaos.

Perhaps the most complex region in this great mountain system is that of the western Himalaya, broadly defined as the section bounded by the basins of two rivers – the Indus to the north and west, and the Satluj to the east and south. Contained within the embrace of these waters are five successive mountain ranges that curve across the states of Jammu and Kashmir and Himachal Pradesh. From south to north, these are the Shivaliks, the Dhauladhar, the Pir Panjal, the Great Himalayan, and the Zaskar ranges.

The lowest of these five ranges, as well as the youngest, the gentle Shivaliks represent the crumbling edge of Lord Shiva's abode in the Himalaya. Rising only a few thousand feet above the dusty plains of Punjub, these accessible slopes have suffered severe deforestation under stress from increasing habitation as well as from the demands of the more developed regions below.

An older, wider zone, more contorted by uplift and sculpted by wind and water, leads up to the Dhauladhar, the first granite range in the system. Its crestline has an average elevation of about 15,000 ft (4,500 m), and extends with remarkable consistency across the breadth of Himachal. Often forming an imposing wall of precipitous rock that rises dramatically from the gentler slopes of its foothills, it can look spectacular, as it does

Left, Sindh Valley, Kashmir. **Above**, confluence of the Indus and Zanskar rivers in Ladakh.

from the district of Kangra. North-west of Dalhousie, however, it begins to peter out, and finally loses its identity among the Shivaliks somewhere near Batot in Jammu and Kashmir.

The taller Pir Panjal is a range sympathetic to the Dhauladhar. Their flanks run just thirty or forty miles apart, and sometimes almost merge, as happens in central Himachal where the longitudinal rib of the Bara Banghal massif links these two ranges, collectively referred to as the Lesser Himalaya. Like the

Dhauladhar, the Pir Panjal remains low in the north-west where it forms the jagged southern lip of the ancient lake-basin of Kashmir. Several high points do exist between 15,000 ft and 16,000 ft, but the range is perhaps best known here for the pleasant alps on its lower northern slopes, Gulmarg being the most frequented. Eastwards, the Pir Panjal swells as it passes into Himachal. Many summits rise above 19,000 ft, and as it approaches the crests of the Great Himalayan range, its icy peaks touch the 20,000 ft mark before the two ranges merge in a sort of confluence in eastern Himachal. Deo Tibba (19,685 ft/6,000 m) and Indrasan (20,410 ft/

6,220 m) are amongst the better known peaks of the Pir Panjal.

The Great Himalayan Range itself is the main axis and crystalline core of the entire mountain system. Its crest rarely falls below 18,000 ft/5,486 m, except at the deep gorge of the Satluj and at the well known passes. Though this range soars to 29,000 ft/8,800 m elsewhere, it remains relatively modest in this western region, with the notable exception of Nanga Parbat (26,660 ft/8,126 m) and the twin summits of Nun (23,410 ft/ 7,135 m) and Kun (23,250 ft/7,086 m). In fact, no summit rises above 20,000 ft between these two massifs, though there are many that are popular with climbers such as Kolahoi

west of Gya the Zaskar range curves into the state of Jammu and Kashmir, where it traverses the barren expanses of Rupshu and then extends into the district with which it shares its name, Zanskar. Here, several summits overlook the Indus valley to the north, the most familiar being the elegant peak of Stok Kangri. These are the five ranges that collectively constitute what we commonly refer to as the Himalaya. Further north, across the Indus, is yet another set of ranges. These, however, are not geologically considered to be part of the Himalaya.

Rising above Leh is the Ladakh range, named after the district on its southern slopes, though it is actually an extension of the

(17,794 ft/5,424 m) and Harmukh (16,872 ft/ 5,143 m). Beyond Nun-Kun it redeems its reputation, with a number of peaks above 20,000 feet as it dips south-east through Kishtwar and into Himachal Pradesh.

The last of the five ranges is the Zaskar which, like the Pir Panjal, is a subsidiary of the Great Himalayan Range. In the Western Himalaya, however, it retains a separate identity, and forms the north-eastern border of Himachal Pradesh, where its summits are the highest in the state. Leo Pargial (22, 275 ft/6,789 m), the second highest, has been climbed often, but Gya (22, 285 ft/6,792 m), the highest, has yet to be attempted. North-

Kailash range. In Ladakh it attains a maximum height of about 19,000 ft/5,790 m. To its north, however, lies the Karakoram range, the most heavily glaciated region outside the sub-polar latitudes. Forming the great watershed between the drainage to the Indian ocean and that to the arid expanses of Central Asia, its summits are among the highest in the world, and its glaciers among the longest.

In the furrows between these ranges flow perennial rivers that drain the snow slopes of the crests. Besides the Indus, this complex mountain region contains the basins of the five rivers of Punjab (*punj,* five, *ab,* water) – the Jhelum, the Chenab, the Ravi, the Beas, and of course, the Satluj.

Both the Indus and the Satluj gather their headwaters from the slopes of Mt. Kailash, north of the Himalaya. Then, flowing in different directions, they meet hundreds of miles away in the plains, having adopted very dissimilar methods of dealing with the mountains that stand between their source and the sea. The Indus never breaches the Himalaya. Instead, it continues to flow behind the range, draining its northern slopes all the way till Nanga Parbat at its northwestern extremity. Then, granted a passage around this gigantic cornerstone of Himalaya, it turns south towards the plains. The Satluj, on the other hand, shows scant respect for the

"middle kingdom" – locked between the Zaskar and Great Himalayan ranges. Thereafter it flows in the deep gorge that cuts through the Great Himalayan and Dhauladhar ranges in the district of Kinnaur, before passing through the Shivaliks where its waters are harnessed for power.

The longitudinal massif of Bara Banghal feeds two of these rivers, the Beas to its east, and the Ravi to its west. Draining both the Bara Banghal as well as the Pir Panjal, the Beas is pushed in a southerly direction by the transverse Bara Banghal rib, and flows through Kulu before pushing its way through the Dhauladhar. The Ravi drains the Bara Banghal to the west, threading its way through

impeding ranges. Beginning as the outflow from the sacred lake of Rakas at the foot of Mt. Kailash, it charts a direct course by carving out an awesome gorge through the series of mountainous barriers. Probably predating the Himalayas, its waters have held course as these ranges inched upwards, and today it flows against their general strike. Entering Himachal through the Zaskar range at Shipki, the Satluj is met by the Spiti, its main tributary which carries the melt from the remote district of Spiti – literally the

Left, high altitude lake, Kashmir. **Above**, terraced rice paddies, Kashmir valley.

Chamba, the trough between the Pir Panjal and the Dhauladhar, eventually piercing the latter west of Dalhousie to flow south towards the plains. Lahaul, the major defile between the Pir Panjal and the Great Himalayan ranges, forms the basin of the Chenab (also known here as the Chandra-Bhaga after its original tributaries, the Chandra and the Bhaga). The north-westerly furrow guides the river out of Himachal into Kishtwar, where it is met by the waters of the Maru-Warwan. Reinforced by the flow, it forces a passage through the Pir Panjal, and then curves around the truncated Dhauladhar to pass west of Jammu. The last of the five *abs* is the Jhelum, the river of Kashmir, formed by the confluences of a number of smaller streams that drain the different slopes of this lake-basin.

All these five rivers flow south of the Great Himalayan axis. Northwards flow the left-bank tributaries of the Indus, notably the Zaskar and the Suru. The former, predictably, flows through Zanskar and drains the Zaskar and Great Himalayan ranges, joining the Indus a few miles downstream of Leh. The Suru is fed by the northern glaciers of the Great Himalayan peaks as well as the final reaches of the Zaskar range before it exhausts itself near Kargil.

Where there are peaks there must be passes.

Thankfully, this hopeful statement is true for each of these major mountain ranges, which otherwise would have proved insurmountable. The passes were discovered centuries ago, and formed the vital links on all the trans-Himalayan trade routes. Most have continued to be used for commerce, though some have become the preserve of trekkers and shepherds ever since a road laid across the range elsewhere proved to be a more economical route. In Kashmir, the Pir Panjal pass (11,462 ft/3,494 m) gave access to the Mughal emperors in the 16th and 17th centuries, though it is the Banihal pass (8,985 ft/ 2,739 m) that now provides the lifeline between Jammu and Srinagar. Ladakh was invaded by the Dogra general Zorawar Singh in the 19th century via the Lonvilad pass (14,370 ft/4,380 m), a deep notch in the Great Himalayan range, while today it is the lower Zoji La (11,578 ft/3,530 m) that has the main highway across it.

Other well-known passes across the Great Himalayan range are the Umasi La (17,370 ft/5,294 m) linking Kishtwar and Zanskar, and the Baralacha La (16,050 ft/4,892 m) at the head of the Chandra and Bhaga on the old trade route between Leh and Lahaul. Parang La (18,300 ft/5,578 m) is the chink in the Zaskar range between Spiti and Rupshu, and of course, the Rohtang pass (13,050 ft/3,978 m) on the Pir Panjal is crossed often by traders and tourists alike who frequent Kulu and Lahaul. The river valleys provide the conduit through the Dhauladhar range between most districts, though the Gujjars and trekkers continue to use the passes between Kangra and Chamba for their seasonal migration. The Gujjar trail leads further over the Pir Panjal into Lahaul over the Kugti (16,000 ft/4,877 m), Chobia (16,400 ft/4,999 m) or Kaliche (16,720 ft/5,096 m) passes.

Flora: With the arid Tibetan plateau less than 200 miles (320 km) from the plains of Punjab, the flora on the slopes of these ranges spans a number of transition zones from the sub-tropical to the arctic. Towards the plains, broad-leafed sal and silk-cotton line the Shivaliks, giving way to sheesham, kail and the long-leafed chir pine on the higher slopes. The Lesser Himalayan ranges, the Dhauladhar and the Pir Panjal, rise from the temperate zone to the alpine. Dense mixed forests on their lower reaches include oak, spruce, fir, pine, rhododendron and the magnificent deodar. Around 9,000 ft (2,743 m) the vegetation thins out with scattered birches and clumps of juniper marking the tree-line. Beyond it are the alpine meadows which come alive after the melt of summer, when a few hundred species of flowers blossom below the passes. The Great Himalayan Range represents the arctic zone, with only the hardiest of species like lichen managing to survive the altitude. It is not surprising that the classical texts referred to this arid zone as the end of the habitable world.

Above, Dachigam rivulet, Kashmir. **Right**, Upper Warwan valley; water is the architect of Western Himalayan landscape.

THE PEOPLE

The Himalayan states of Himachal Pradesh and Jammu and Kashmir can broadly be divided into three socio-cultural zones. At the highest altitudinal levels, Ladakh and its neighbouring trans-Himalayan tracts comprise a region stamped by the dominant influence of its geographically contiguous and environmentally similar neighbour – Tibet. A second division consists of the valley of Kashmir, which of all the hill states had the most complex society and diverse culture. The least homogeneous is the wide sweep of country between Jammu and the Yamuna, encompassing a host of former hill stations which in size varied from a valley or two, to fairly extensive tracts like those of Chamba, Mandi, Sirmaur and Rampur Bushahr. The common thread binding this miscellany together is small subsistence-based economies neither agriculturally rich nor located on trade routes of any significance. The dominant strains in craft and lifestyle are relatively unsophisticated and utilitarian, reflecting the rigour and frugality characteristic of the life of the hill peasantry.

Ladakh: The bulk of the trans-Himalayan region of Ladakh and its neighbouring valleys has long been considered one of the last outposts of the religio-cultural empire of old Tibet. It is probable that the earliest inhabitants were migrating Tibetan herdsmen; as the political suzerainty of Guge (Western Tibet) and later Ladakh overspread Dard and Balti areas to the west and Lahaul, Spiti and Kinnaur to the south, other racial components were added on at the fringes of the Ladakhi heartland. The western areas of the Suru Valley (Purig), and Dras and the people of Da-hanu in the Indus Valley below Khalsi are purely Dardic, while Lahaul and Kinnaur have marked influences from the lower Himalayan hills. Leh, the capital town in Central Ladakh, was at the centre of important trade routes with trails leading to Kashmir in the east, Yarkand to the north, west to Tibet and towards the south to Kullu and mainland India. Travellers from these different regions have left their imprints on the racial stock of Ladakh, although it would still be true to say that central and eastern Ladakh, Zanskar and Spiti retain predominantly Tibetan characteristics.

In this high cold desert region with its harsh climate and forbidding topography, only assured irrigation can sustain agriculture. Human settlement is thus scantily spread in green oases of relatively flat terrain near water sources – a scattered mosaic in a vista of endless yellow, brown and grey, topped by the clearest of blue skies. Only on the rolling plains of Changthang and Rupshu (an extension of the Tibetan Plateau) is there no settled agriculture. Here the nomadic herdsmen tend their flocks of Pashmina goats and Humiya sheep and herd their yaks, in migratory cycles established over centuries.

The limitations of arable land and the fragile nature of the environment engendered forms of social organization which would enable the inhabitants to maintain a balance between the resources available and the demands placed on them. Systems of polyandry and primogeniture evolved in Ladakhi society in response to the need to keep population growth under control. The eldest brother alone married; younger male siblings either co-habited with his wife or entered monasteries or made their own way in the world. The eldest brother also inherited the family lands on reaching maturity, usually in his father's lifetime. The older generation then moved out to a smaller subsistance holding. Demographic changes and the spread of outside influence are now creating a disequilibrium in these traditional systems.

Ladakh society is more or less free of any caste structure, but a distinction does exist between the peasantry and the musician and artisan classes in the villages. The latter occupy a lower rung in the social order and their treatment in some ways calls to mind the casts prejudice prevalent in mainland India. In central and eastern Ladakh this group, called More (a word more or less synonymous with musician), is obviously a remnant of original Dardic populations. Class distinctions also exist to some extent, between a small aristocracy at Leh and Kargil and the ruling families in the outlying provinces being a cut above the general mass of the peasantry. Deference and respect are shown to these sections but there is no evidence of the kind of servility existing in typical feudal societies. In essence, Ladakhi society is democratic in character and equal status is enjoyed by women in all matters. This is no doubt a reflection of the tolerant nature of the Buddhist faith. This open society stands in marked contrast to the seclusion of women and the orthodox structuring of relationships found in the neighbouring Islamic and caste Hindu societies.

Buddhism came to Ladakh earlier than to Tibet proper, travelling up from Kashmir. By the 9th century it was probably widely accepted as far south as Lahaul and Spiti where it was spread by the great sage Padmasambhava. With the political hegemony of Guge in later centuries it was Vajrayana Buddhism of the Tibetan variety which established itself in Ladakh and came to influence thought and life style. Tibetan Buddhism is highly mystical in content; subjected to Tantric influences, it has evolved elaborate doctrines which can take years of learning to comprehend. It is not a homogeneous school but broken up into a number of orders.

The complicated symbolism and iconography of Tibetan Buddhism is beyond the understanding of the average Ladakhi soul and indeed even the ordinary lama. But the symbols of the religion are all around him. *Mane* walls, mounds of earth covered with stone slabs inscribed with the sacred invocation 'Om Mane Padme Hum' (Hail to the Jewel in the Lotus) line village paths and tracks. Between one and two metres in height and a couple of metres wide, they can stretch from a few metres to a kilometre or more in length. *Chortens* (stupa-like structures) of varying size and shape, to denote different aspects of the Buddhist 'way,' mark the entrance to a village or may dominate the village square. Prayer flags printed with texts and invocations flutter from flagpoles in houses and *gompas,* and the prayer wheel is set in walls and gateways for the passer-by to earn merit on his journey. Even on his person the Ladakhi will very often have a small prayer wheel and beads handy, and the murmur of the sacred *mantra* rises automatically to his lips as he carries on with his everyday chores.

Despite the overwhelming presence of Buddhism in daily life, the peasantry have not completely lost touch with elements of the animistic and pantheistic faiths which preceded Buddhism. Especially in the culture and life of the Da-hanus, remnants of the old faith, the Bon-chos, continue to be an important influence. Elsewhere, too, almost every village has a local deity and a medium to deliver its message and although monasteries frown on this practice, the local deities continue to command a following from those seeking deliverance from misfortune.

Besides Buddhism, both Christianity and Islam have a presence in Ladakh, and down in Lahaul the Swanglas are Hindu Brahmins.

Christianity has only a limited following, centred around the Moravian mission established in Leh in the last century. Islam maintains a much stronger and more vigorous presence, dominating Dras, the Suru valley, Pashkyum and Shagkar-Chigtan. Mulbekh and Bodh Kharbu have mixed populations, while small Muslim communities exist in Nubra, Zanskar and Leh. In the Suru valley and Dras the strong Shia orthodoxy imposes a strict code, secluding women, restricting contact with outsiders and frowning on music and art. However, the latter-day converts of Chigtan have a living tradition of dance and music, with women participating in community life. The affluent Sunni Muslims of Leh, a cultured community with a lifestyle akin to their Buddhist counterparts, have for centuries been an integral part of Leh's cosmopolitan community. The co-existence of Islam and Buddhism and even inter-marriage between the two communities have been common both in Chigtan and Leh, though of late signs of strain have appeared in this traditional harmony.

In the main, the languages of Ladakh belong either to the Dardic or the Tibetan group. In western Ladakh, inhabited by people of Dardic stock, dialects of the former hold sway. However, centuries of evolution in different pockets have resulted in various

the language of Central and Eastern Ladakh.

The traditional Ladakhi dress, like so much else, is inspired by Tibetan styles in clothing. The *goncha* worn by both sexes in central Ladakh is an enveloping woollen gown. Stylishly made, it is in effect a double-breasted calf-length coat. Its loose folds are pulled to the back in two pleats and it is tied with a brightly coloured cummerbund. It is fastened on the right side up to the shoulder with brass buttons and loops, and the stand-up collar has a silver brocade piping. The colour (usually a dark shade) and material of the *goncha* vary for the rich but in general it is made of coarse, homespun woollen cloth, dyed a deep maroon. In Kargil it is generally

dialects being no longer mutually comprehensible. In the Dras area, the language has been influenced by Kashmir and the Purig people can no longer follow it while the Dahanu Dards, influenced more by neighbouring Tibetan people, have a language which is virtually their own. In the south, the dialects of the Chandrabhaga valley in Lahaul and those of lower Kinnaur have little in common with the Tibetan dialects spoken in upper Lahaul, Spiti and upper Kinnaur while these latter areas differ only in accent with

Left, Kashmiri grandfather. **Above**, narrow boats continue to be the best form of local transport.

made from plain unbleached cloth.

The women's *goncha* has a full skirt gathered in a large number of small pleats and secured with a cummerbund. A goatskin (wool worn inside) may be tied over the shoulders by older women while the more stylish would use an embroidered multi coloured or brocade mantle with long fringes. In Lahaul, the pleat and skirt is stitched at the waist to the blouse above and a woollen shawl with brightly woven borders replaces the mantle. In Spiti and upper Kinnaur the women use a multi coloured woven woollen stole worn over the shoulders and fastened in front with a pin. The women in Ladakh use a hat or a *perak* as a head dress. The *perak* is the women's main item of jewellery; a strip of leather covered with cloth and stitched with rows of turquoise, reaching from the forehead half down the back. Silver jewellery set with coral, amber, turquoise and pearls is also worn around the neck and ears.

The food of the Ladakh seems fairly basic, but has provided nourishment to the robust peasantry of Tibet and its fringes for centuries. The staple ingredient is *tsampa,* parched barley flour. This is mixed with butter-tea *(cha-za)* or *chang* into a kind of gruel and drunk by all the Tibetan people. The butter tea is a mixture of tea, milk, butter and salt blended together in a *gur-gur* or *dongma*, a

Foundations are laid with stones from the ground and the thick walls may be composed partly of stone and partly of hand-formed sun-dried earthen blocks, often made *in situ,* each successive layer being allowed to dry before it is added to the wall. The only plaster used, if at all, is mud, white-washed with lime. The small square windows are outlined in black and maroon. Roof beams are usually poplar trunks over which willow twigs are laid neatly and covered with well-beaten clayey earth, adequate in an area where rainfall is virtually unknown and snow limited. Houses, palaces and the sprawling monasteries have all been built by these same time-tested methods. In Leh town, of late, glass is

cylindrical container with a churner, and drunk in copious quantities.

Curd and buttermilk and a kind of whey-cheese are important ingredients to the diet. Vegetables of a limited range are consumed in season, added to the *thukpa,* a clear soup of stock with *tsampa* and even noodles thrown in. Formal meals may have Tibetan dishes like *mok-mok, chow-chow* and *phing* added, while in Leh the cosmopolitan traditions allow for a more varied cuisine.

The Ladakhi house draws its material from its surroundings. A square built structure with simple, straight lines, it is both functional and harmonious with the environment.

being used increasingly to utilize the heat of the sun in the clear, cold days of winter.

Houses are usually two-storied, the lower floor being used to pen the livestock in winter. Household activity centres around the kitchen. In winter this large room also serves as living room and sleeping quarters. In the middle of the room is a stove of iron or sometimes baked earth, with the flue pipe going up through a hole in the ceiling. On one side is the cooking area, its walls lined with shelves containing shining pots and pans, the *gur-gur* or *dong-mo,* and china bowls from Nepal decorated with dragon motifs. The other side of the stove has low tables called *chokse,* and behind are even lower carpet-covered divans which function as seats in the day time and beds at night.

Ladakhis live in close-knit communities, at work, in the fields or in the construction of a house, mutual help is readily extended. The short summer is a busy time geared to producing necessities to last through the long winter. Even before the winter snows are gone, earth is spread over the fields and they are ploughed. Irrigation chanels are cleared to bring water from the mountain streams and the sowing done. A few weeks later the work of weeding and watering begins, the timing regulated by customary practice. Women perform most of the functions after

Winter is a time of leisure when the Ladakhi's love of dance and music is strongly in evidence. Most monasteries celebrate their annual festivals in winter, marked by the colourful pageantry of masked dances. The Tibetan new year, 'Losar', occurs in winter, and most weddings are celebrated in this season. Community gatherings don't necessarily require a formal fixture and a get-together for song, dance, and drink is almost a daily feature in winter evenings. Large quantities of *chang* (a sort of barley beer) and *arrah* (a liquor distilled from *chang*) are drunk, in some areas only by men and in others by both sexes. Winter too is the time when the Buchan, the lay lamas of the Pin

the sowing, right upto harvest time. The Ladakhi has learnt to husband carefully the limited resources available to him and one of the best examples of this is the system of sanitation. Human waste is collected from below the *chaksa* (usually on the first floor, in a corner of the house) and spread in the fields twice a year. Each household maintains some livestock; in summer they are usually sent up to high altitude pastures, and post-harvest they are left free to graze on the fields and leave natural manure behind.

Far left, Kashmiri beauty. **Left**, Muslim patriarch. **Above**, nomadic Gujjar family with their *samovar.*

valley in Spiti, wander far and wide from Kinnaur to Ladakh. The Buchan will stay many days in a village presenting charades and wonderful displays of swordsmanship and physical prowess. They sing beautifully, accompanied by a plaintive, single-stringed instrument, and by the village musicians on the drums. The Ladakh folk dance appears at first glace to be a monotonous, slow shuffle but its grace and infinite, minute variations grow on the watcher, while the songs have a haunting quality.

Two famous Ladakhi pastimes in summer are polo and archery. Polo probably came to Ladakh from the Baltis and its Central Asian version differs considerably from the international version of the game. It is wildly popular in the Muslim areas and in Leh. While in Kargil it has a certain solemnity, in Leh a game becomes an occasion for a carnival with music on the *surna* and the *daman* and wildly cheering crowds. Archery too, is conducted more in a festive than a competitive spirit. In the Pin Valley of Spiti archery is a winter pastime, while horse-riding feats on the famous Chamurti ponies are part of post-harvest celebrations.

The Ladakhi people have a remarkably sunny disposition. Not loquacious but always ready with a smile, their warm, generous nature contrasts sharply with the bleak,

scribed by routine; but the Ladakhi exhibits a tremendous ability to adapt, to absorb the new while retaining the underpinnings of his cultural world – a tribute perhaps to the tolerant embrace of the Buddhist faith.

Kashmir: The social order in the Kashmir valley exhibits a degree of stratification and complexity akin to the societies of the plains and with no parallel in the relatively simpler, scattered, rural hill communities found elsewhere in the Western Himalaya. The specifics of the local environment and the overwhelming conversion to Islam have lent distinctive twists to the traditional divisions of a caste Hindu society.

The most noticeable departure from the

harsh land their forbears chose to settle in. The stranger is always welcome and the householder does his utmost to make a guest comfortable. They are a sturdy people too, their unusual strength of heart and lungs a product of the rarefied atmosphere in which they live. Their lives are governed by the demands of the environment; summer is wholly given to work, while winter offers the opportunity to take in the sun in a sheltered corner of the roof, sing and dance through the evenings in convivial company, listen enthralled to myths and legends of *Kesar ling*, the Ladakhi saga, or watch the feats of the Buchan. It is a life in many ways circum-

norm has been the absence of any significant warrior class in Kashmir. Even in the days when a powerful Hindu kingdom existed, there is reason to believe that much of the army was drawn from mercenaries and neighbouring subordinated areas. By the end of the 14th century, barring small sections of the old Brahmin orthodoxy, the valley converted to Islam under the combined influence of Saiyyad preachers and the Muslim rule established in the middle of that century.

In the years to come, the remaining unconverted Brahmins, Kashmiri Pandits as they are called, largely took over the clerical and administrative tasks performed elsewhere in India by the Kayasthas. The bulk of the converted population, called Sheikhs, were the peasantry, the artisan classes, the menials and a significant boat community, owing its origin to the predominance of water-based transport in the valley. Another departure from the norm was the surprisingly limited trading class in pre-modern Kashmir. In recent decades members of all communities have come to play a part in the business opportunities offered by tourism, including the production and sale of the traditional crafts for which Kashmir is renowned.

Despite the massive conversion to Islam, the age-old caste-based divisions in Kashmir society continue to manifest themselves

where issues of marriage and close family ties crop up. Among all groups and classes, relationships are regulated by customary perceptions of location in the social hierarchy. In earlier periods, newcomers merged with the inhabitants, but the communities who arrived after the Mughal period have maintained a separate identity. Thus there are small groups of Sikhs, Pathans, Rajputs and, on the fringes of the valley, the nomadic Gujjar, all of whom have established their own niches in Kashmir society without becoming part of the mainstream community.

Left, Muharram procession, Kargil. **Above**, distinctive features of a Ladakhi child.

As elsewhere in India, religion occupies an important slot in the Kashmiri psyche. Shiva, lord of the mountains, is the most revered of the deities of the Hindu pantheon. Each year, a huge Amarnath Yatra winds up the Lidder valley, to worship the sacred *ling* on the day of Sawan Purnima (early August). Another difficult pilgrimage is to Gangabal below the sacred mountain of Harmukh, where Hindus go to immerse the ashes of their dead in the deep waters of the lake. For the Kashmiri Pandit, perhaps the most sacred place in the valley is the temple of Khir Bhawani at Tula Mula at the mouth of the Sindh valley. The spring at Tula Mula is said to change colour as a harbinger of good or bad tidings for the people.

Seeing divine portents in natural phenomena is not limited to Hindus alone. The Muslims of the valley, relatively recent converts from a pantheistic faith, have similar beliefs. Dragons and monsters, fairies and goblins, ghosts and demons all have their haunts and there are trees of ordeal where a lying witness is sure to be overtaken by blindness. Religious recluses and saints command great respect and have quaint legends attached to them. Their simple lessons and ascetic bearing have traditionally held greater appeal than the mysteries of religious orthodoxy. For the ordinary Muslim, the shrines dedicated to Shah Hamadan, Nurdin and his Khalifas, Dastgir and Makhdum Sahib are places of far greater reverence than the neighbourhood mosque (other than the Jama Masjid and the Hazratbal), and the Pirzada, Rishi and Baba invite more respect than the village Mulla.

Annual fairs held at the various shrines are red letter days for the Muslim peasant. Thousands crowd and spend the day eating sweatmeats and buying knick-knacks from the numerous kiosks which spring up. Alms flow into the shrine and before it devotees dance in ecstasy, chanting songs in praise of the saint. There is great faith in the efficacy of the shrines to fulfil a *murad* (wish): the sick will regain health, women bear children, litigants win cases, if a pilgrimage is made to any of these shrines in true faith.

Kashur, the language of the Kashmiris, differs considerably from those spoken in the rest of the Western Himalaya. Considered to have descended from Prakrit, a dialect of

Sanskrit, it is a polyglot of Sanskrit, Persian, Arabic, Hindustani, Dogri, Turkish and even Tibetan influences. The written script now is largely Urdu although at one time Devanagari may have been used.

The everyday dress of the Kashmiri, worn by both sexes, is an enveloping drab, woollen gown buttoned at the neck and reaching down below the knees called a *pheran*. The *pheran* serves to cover the *kangri*, a small wicker basket enclosing an earthernware bowl filled with smouldering embers, carried by Kashmiris of all ages in winter. A plain skull-cap usually covers the head of a villager and there is a grey monotony to his attire which contrasts sharply with the vivid-

and several other spices enrich the food, which must always include rice and kohl-rabi (*karm-ka-sag*) so dear to the Kashmiri palate. Nature has endowed Kashmir with a wealth of fruit, vegetables, spices and meat and the inhabitants have learnt to conjure epicurean dreams from the material at their command. The Kashmiris drink tea, sweet *(kahwa)* and salt *(shiri)*. Both are made in the Russian samovar and the *kahwa*, made with saffron and dry fruits, is a delicious beverage.

Houses in Kashmir are traditionally made of unburnt brick set in wooden frames using the timber of cedar, pine and fir with a pointed roof to throw off snow. In the loft

ness which Nature offers in the physical environment. Pandit women may wear maroon or blue gowns with a white cummerbund and offer a brighter picture. Their hair is often plaited with silken cords into many braids and covered with a kind of scarf falling down the back.

Community life in Kashmir centres round occasions of marriage, birth and death, the thread ceremony for the Hindu and circumcision for the Muslim. At these functions, depending on the affluence of the family concerned, the splendour of Kashmiri cuisine is revealed in the celebrated banquet called *wazwan*. Saffron, grown in the valley,

formed by the thatched roof, wood and grass are stored, so that they can be thrown easily in case of fire. Rice straw is favoured as a thatching material while near the lakes reeds are often used, and in the vicinity of forests wooden shingles may be laid over log walls. The first floor of the house usually has a covered verandah where leisure hours are whiled away in summer, and in winter it is festooned with dried turnips, apples, corn cobs, chillies and other vegetables. Sometime the roofs may be of birch bark, with a layer of earth on top; covered with iris and lilies in summer, these present a charming picture. The ground floor is normally reserved for cattle and sheep in winter and the dwelling is kept warm with the breath of the animals, travelling through chinks to the first floor, where the family lives. Each house usually stands alone, with its courtyard and kitchen garden ringed by a fence of earth, stones and wattling. Newer houses use corrugated and galvanized iron sheets for roofing and cement and stone in the walls.

The more affluent Kashmiri house has at least one room adorned with a *khatamband* ceiling. This consists of geometric patterned modules of pine or spruce wood fitted together by a complex system of grooving which entails superb joinery techniques. The finest example of *khatamband* can be seen at ruins at Matan, Payesh, Wangat, and Avantipura belong to the reign of Hindu kings from Gopaditya onwards. The impressive architecture of these stately ruins bears an unmistakable stamp of Greek influence and with their lofty pyramidal roofs are among the finest known examples of the Gandhara school. Of a later time, the work of the Mughal period is best seen in the gardens terraces, waterfalls and summer houses built by Jehangir. The pleasure haunts of Salim and Nurjehan at Nishat and Shalimar, Verinag and Achabal are among the most popular excursion destinations for most tourists.

Writers through the ages have extolled the natural beauty of Kashmir, but the inhabit-

the shrine of Naqshband Sahib near Khanyar.

The Valley has always possessed a sacred quality for the Hindu and almost every village reveals some relic of antiquity. Curious miniatures of old Kashmir temples, huge stone seats of Mahadeo (Shiva), phallic emblems (*linga*) and carved images heaped grotesquely near spring sources, are scattered profusely in the valley. The earliest of these probably date to the Buddhist Kushana period but the more impressive of the older

Left, Ladakhi crowd absorbed in watching masked dancers at festival. **Above**, vegetable sellers in Leh spin wool while waiting for customers.

ants of this paradise have not, by and large, received such favourable notice, mainly because the outsider's contact is limited to those Kashmiris who are selling him something. In the village and off the beaten track, one can still encounter the generosity and hospitality common to most rural communities. The Kashmiri can turn his hand to virtually anything, as the range and beauty of his traditional arts and crafts testify. He does not suffer from lack of self esteem either. He believes that no system or technique used by him can be bettered, and is always ready to quote a rhyming proverb to justify this. He is generally a family man and instances of divorce or departures from monogamy are rare. A husband may sometimes chastise his wife and talk boastfully of the need to maintain discipline in the house, but as a rule the Kashmiri lives in awe of his consort. Social gatherings are limited in the Kashmir village and both men and women spend their leisure hours at home. There is no tradition of sport or games but music is a part of their heritage and Kashmir has given the world the beautiful sound of the *santoor,* a stringed instrument with great depth and range.

Kashmiris love to exaggerate, and every spell of cold, heat or rain can become the worst ever and a tyranny of unimaginable magnitude. But surprisingly an extreme ca-

eastwards from the Jamuna to where the Chenab leaves India encompasses a wide diversity in climate and topography. From the foothills of the Shivaliks, where the seasons are scarcely distinguishable from the plains, to the snow-bound hills bordering the main Himalaya, is an environmental range capable of bringing socio-cultural variations even among a homogeneous people. But the points of commonality are perhaps still insufficient for the area to be considered together in describing the people and their life.

This region, it is often believed, was first inhabited by the Khashas, an ancient people of Aryan stock. However, traces of a pre-existing race are present among the lowest

lamity may be received with an unusual and intense silence. In many ways the Kashmiri character has a disarming pathos, sometimes likened to that of the Irishman. There is pure response to natural beauty in his soul and a song for every act of work or leisure. Often in need of a wash; with an amazing gift for malarkey and spontaneous wit; fond of ribald humour, children and old folk; capable of quick changes of temper; timid when faced with aggression; apt to suddenly plumb the depths of despair; capable of pulling a fast one – the Kashmiri is an often perplexing but always fascinating personality.

Himachal Pradesh: The tract stretching

castes even today, and it would be safe to assume that these poor and scantily populated hills have provided sanctuary to successive waves of dispossessed people.

This region has always fallen in the sphere of influence of a powerful outside kingdom. From the days of the Kulindas and Trigartha (which find mention in the Mahabharata epic) through the Buddhist period of Ashoka, followed by the revived Hinduism of the Guptas down to the Mughals and finally the British, ultimate authority lay outside. At the local level petty hill chiefs held away over small fiefdoms. Normally left to themselves, they were incessantly at war with one another in an attempt to expand their possessions. Only after the establishment of the Pax Britannica in the 19th century did internecine conflicts cease.

While the hill societies reflect the basic caste structure of orthodox Hindu society, they allow for a greater degree of flexibility and variation. Widow remarriage was uniformly permitted all across, while the custom of fraternal polyandry was widespread in the upper hills among upper and lower castes. In local belief the sanction of polyandry is derived from the Pandavas of the Mahabharata, but it obviously arose as a response to the limited availability of cultivable land in the hills and the need to control population

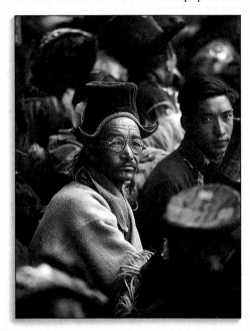

and prevent fragmentation of holdings.

The sanction to the remarriage of widows is an index of the importance of women in hill economy. Traditionally, barring the ploughing of the fields, a rite of fertility reserved for men, hill women perform every function in field and home, from the weeding and harvesting of the crop to the management of home and livestock. Their economic importance conferred on them a degree of freedom not generally found in conservative Hindu society, extending to the right to divorce and remarry – small compensation,

Left and above, Ladakhis, young and old.

though, for the drudgery of their everyday existence. This region is predominantly Hindu, with Muslim majority areas restricted to Poonch, Rajauri, Doda and Kishtwar, adjoining the Kashmir valley. Elsewhere small pockets of Muslims are to be found in Jammu, chamba and Sirmur.

Among the Hindus, as in Kashmir, the mountain god Shiva occupies a pre-eminent position. His shrines are numerous, and many are the fairs and festivals in his honour. In the Jammu region, the temple of Sud Mahadev commemorates the performance of the 'Tandav Nritya' (the cosmic dance of destruction) by Lord Shiva, and a huge fair is held in June every year. Manimahesh Lake in Bharmour in Chamba district attracts thousands of pilgrims in August every year and Shivratri is celebrated with special food in every household in the hills, while in Mandi it is the occasion for a huge festival.

Along with the Shiva cult, Devi worship is widespread in the hills. Pre-Hindu forms of the mother-goddess have been absorbed into the Hindu pantheon as incarnations of the goddess Durga. Many of these ancient divinities command a sizeable following in the plains. Among the more famous are Vaishno Devi near Jammu, Jwalamukhi and Chamunda in Kangra, Naina Devi near Bilaspur, Chintpurni Devi in Una and in the upper hills Bhima Kali and Hatkoti Mata. Each diety has stories and legends attached to her, usually involving the slaying of troublesome demons.

In the interior hills within the overall hegemony of Shiva and the major Devis, there is the happy co-existence of local deities. In fact these local gods, many of whom (like the Mahasu Devta) have elaborate and colourful mythologies attached to them, are far more important in the everyday life of the people. They have an almost tangible presence in the village.They communicate their wishes and desires and answer supplicants through mediums. In former times may of them had barbaric rites of sacrifice, now muted, as part of their rituals of worship.

At a broad level the language of this region is classified as Pahari and forms part of the Aryan group. But within this broad division is a wide spectrum of dialects known by regional names like Dogri, Chambialli, Kangri, Mandiali, etc. The relative isolation imposed by the terrain resulted in the growth of a maze of dialects, so that even these regional variations contain differences from valley to valley which often render them virtually incomprehensible within a relatively short distance.

There has been a considerable adoption to styles of dress common in the plains, in recent decades. Some of the features of the older forms of dress are still visible, but to a large extent it is in the interiors now that tradition continues to govern attire. In the lower hills, handspun cotton was the traditional clothing material and in the upper areas rough woollen cloth woven through the winter months met the needs of the people. Women wore brightly coloured skirts

cap with a plain velvet strip of green or maroon running half around the edge. The Kullu cap is similar, except that the decorative strip is brightly patterned. The men everywhere in the hills wear a buttoned-up coat of *patti* (woollen cloth woven on pit looms at home), over leggings of wool or cotton. In Mahasu, the *loiya*, a long, wide woollen cloak is worn on top in winter while in many parts the *pattu,* a long shawl, is wrapped around instead.

In valley bottoms and cultivated flat lands paddy cultivation is extensive and forms the staple food of the people. In fact in Kangra and adjoining areas, the traditional wedding feast is called *bhat* – literally, rice. *Bhat* must

and the *salwar-kameez* in the lower hills. In the upper areas drab woollen skirts predominated except in Kullu, where even now checked woollen shawls are wrapped sarong style by the women, and in Kinnaur, where the long *chodu* with its intricately woven, beautiful borders covers the women from neck to ankle. Head dresses vary from area to area. In Mahasu, women wear the *dhatoo,* a cotton scarf in blue, pink or yellow (black for widows) pulled back behind the ears from the forehead and knotted, the ends being left free to fall down the back.

In Kinnaur both men and women wear the Bushahri cap, a round, flat-topped woollen

include a *khatta* (sour), a *mitha* (sweet) and a *palda* (curd-based) dish, each to be eaten with rice. Cuisine has nowhere developed any elaborate forms in these hills. The peasant's normal food included maize, *sattu* (parched flour), pulses, beans or vegetables, all cooked in the simplest of ways. In the upper hills amaranthe and varieties of buckwheat were extensively cultivated in earlier years but now wheat, potato and apple orchards have supplanted these traditional crops. However, a feast in the upper areas still constitutes nothing more than boiled rice and meat cooked in a rudimentary style and a form of blood sausage.

Houses are scattered over the hillsides in small hamlets in some parts of the lower hills but in general they are bunched together in fairly large villages, specially in the higher reaches. The house is usually a small, sparsely furnished two-storied dwelling with the lower floor being used to pen the livestock. In the lower hills a separate *obera* is often constructed for the animals. In the upper areas where forests were abundant, houses are almost wholly made of wood, while in the lower areas local stone and a mixture of mud and straw packed into wooden frames, is usually employed in construction. Roofing material was traditionally slate, although in thickly forested areas where slate is scarce,

toil, relieved only by the occasional fair, festival or wedding. Nevertheless, the hill people have developed a vigorous folk culture of song and dance, in which both sexes participate equally. Folk songs record in graphic detail history, myth and legend, convey the beauty of hill and valley, forest and stream and describe the labour and events of daily life.

There is, particularly, a pathos in the songs recording the depredations of the Gurkhas, who pillaged the area in the early 19th century. Dances are colourful and vigorous with local variations in each major valley. The flute of the lonely shepherd in the pastures has inspired *ragas* in classical Indian music.

wooden shingles and planks are still used. There is, however, an increasing use of corrugated GI sheets in recent years. Wooden houses in the upper hills are generally left unpainted, but it is common to use a lime whitewash in the lower belt.

The hill peasant leads a hard life. The hills have never known abject poverty but putting together the basic necessities of food, clothing and shelter require a life of unremitting

Left, village deities taken in procession, Dussera festival, Kullu. **Above**, feathers of the endangered Monal pheasant still decorate the caps of Himachali men.

Art flowered to its zenith in the famous Basohli and Kangra paintings between the 16th and 18th centuries, but in general folk art form is limited to temple carving. The hillmen were once renowned bowmen, but archery is a virtually dead tradition now. *Toda*, a once popular martial game in Mahasu, is also dying today.

The 'Dogras', the generic name used by British army recruiters for the hill people, are a tough but not aggressive people. Warm and friendly, they are both trusting and trustworthy. They may have frugal means and limited comfort to offer, but they make the stranger welcome.

THE MAHARAJAH RUNJEET SINGH.

AGED 58.

King of the Sikhs & Ruler of the Punjab, Ladak, Kashmere & Peshawar.

From an original Portrait now in England and taken during the visit of His Excellency General Sir Henry Fane G.C.B. Commander in Chief of the Kings & Hon.ble Comp.ys Army in India to Lahore, for the purpose of attending the marriage of N. Nehal Sing the Maharajahs Grandson at the dáree in the Punjab on the 8th Mch 1837.

A HISTORY OF JAMMU, KASHMIR AND LADAKH

The *Rajatarangini* or River of Kings (1148-1150) is the only history written in India. Its author Kalhana traces in measured Sanskrit verse the history of Kashmir from its mythical origins to his own period of disruption and disarray. His chronicle is not a mere narrative of the successive dynasties which ruled this region; it is a vital work which provides a rich and varied picture of a country geographically isolated but open to influences, not only from the rest of India but Central Asia and China as well. Kashmir, though ringed by mountains, bordered three cultural regions: India, China and the Middle East, and from these diverse influences it developed its syncretic and tolerant culture. The history of this 'half closed eco-system, opening up slowly in space and across time' is marked by an evolving interaction, not always peaceful, between indigenous and foreign ideas and beliefs: Naga worship, Buddhism, Islam.

Origins of Kashmir: Jammu, Kashmir and Ladakh, though geographically distinct regions, share an interlinking history. Kashmir and Ladakh were bound through Buddhism and later the very important shawl-wool trade. Jammu has been a part of Kashmir occasionally, but was firmly joined by the Dogra rulers in the 10th century.

Legend has it that the Valley was an immense lake, Satisaras, or the Lake of Sati. Its inhabitants, the Nagas or serpents, were persecuted by a demon, Jalodhabhava (Waterborn). Their king, Nila, sought the help of his father, the sage Kashyapa, who in turn asked the god Vishnu to end the depredations of the monster. Vishnu sent Balabhadra to drain the lake by piercing the mountainside with a ploughshare, after which the god killed Jalodhabhava. The myth of a great lake is supported by archaeological evidence; drainage and water control continued to be vital activities in the subsequent history of the Valley.

Archaeological evidence indicates that this area was inhabited as far back as neolithic times at least. Near Srinagar, at Burzahom on the flood plain of the Jhelum, excavations have revealed neolithic artefacts: polished axes, hoes and bone implements, indicating a connection with the Northern Black Polished Ware culture of northern India. Further excavations have revealed even older habitation, a settlement of pit dwellers (290 B.C.).

These people produced a coarse and ill-fired pottery, but interestingly, their burial sites show that dogs were buried with their owners. This practice, as well as artefacts like jade beads and knives made of rectangular perforated stone, indicate similarities with finds in North China. All the evidence firmly points to human settlements in the Valley from the middle Paleolithic period, and from the second millenium Dardic and Indo-Aryan language groups entered this region.

Early History: The early history of Kashmir is fragmentary and unreliable. It is only with the advent of the Mauryan Empire in North India that the history of Kashmir can be reliably constructed. Ashoka, who brought most of the Indian sub-continent under his rule, is said to have built the capital Purandhistan (Srinagar) around 250 B.C. on the high ground behind the modern village of Pandrethan, and according to the historian Kalhana, this magnificent city with 'ninety-six thousand dwelling houses' was 'resplendent with prosperity'. Ashoka is reported to have sent Majjhantika to Kashmir to spread the doctrine of the Buddha. It was, however, with the establishment of the Kushan empire in the first century that Buddhism became the dominant religious system in this region.

Buddhism: The philosophical growth and development of Buddhism created a number of widely differing sects and from time to time councils were convened to bring order and preserve orthodoxy. During Kanishka's reign the Fourth Council was convened in Kashmir (78 A.D.) – an indication of the importance of Buddhism in this region.

The acceptance of Buddhism was not without opposition; of Kanishka's successors, Mihirkula favoured Shaivism. Kalhana writes, 'His approach became known by the sight of vultures, crows and the like, eager to feed on those massacred by the encircling enemy.'

Despite such setbacks, Buddhism became an integral part of Kashmiri culture and its spread thence to Ladakh, Central Asia and China was furthered by Kashmiri scholars. In the early 7th century the Chinese traveller Hiuen Tsang came to Kashmir to study Buddhism. He stayed for two years in the Valley before proceeding on his pilgrimage to the areas associated with the Buddha. He writes that there were over five thousand monks in the valley.

Imperial Expansion: Till the Karakota dy-

markable man called Suyya. Said to have been brought up by a low-caste foster mother, he offered to help the king solve the Valley's perennial problem of flooding by clearing the river beds and building embankments. Tradition has it that the ingenious Suyya had the king throw bags of gold coins into the river at selected points and the people, in search of the gold, cleared the river bed. Most remarkably, he changed the confluence of the Vitista, as the Jhelum was then known (in Kashmiri it is called the Vyeth). Suyya also had circular embankments built around villages and these rings *(kunda)* are still to be found in place names, such as Utsakundala. His flood control measures

nasty, Kashmir was under succession of nondescript rulers, but with Lalitaditya (724-761 A.D.) it entered a period of expansion. Lalitaditya's rule was marked not only by extensive military conquests but also a vigorous development of the Valley. He carried out extensive reclamation projects and built towns, temples and shrines. It was during his reign that the town of Parontsa (Poonch) was built, as was the famous Martand temple, the ruins of which still exist.

During the rule of Avantivarman (853-883 A.D.), the *damaras,* feudal barons, became an important political force. This reign is distinguished by the exploits of a re-

improved production and he ensured that fish and fowl were protected in the Wular Lake area. The modern city of Sopore is named after him.

Damaras and Queens: The power of the feudal barons continued to grow and from their fortified residences *(upavesana)* they exacted onerous taxes from the peasantry and challenged and circumscribed the power of the kings. By the time Queen Didda came to wield power, they were the real masters of Kashmir. Didda, daughter of the Simharaja of Loharu, became regent on the death of her royal spouse and from A.D. 981-1003 ruled Kashmir directly. Of all the queens who ruled Kashmir, she was the most strong-willed and able ruler, if contemporary chroniclers are to be believed, as well as the most licentious and cruel. With her lover Tunga, who was made Chief Minister, she subdued recalcitrant barons and left a stable and well run kingdom.

King Harsha (1089-1101), the next notable ruler, was an accomplished artist as well as a learned scholar, and his lavish patronage of the arts attracted many reputed poets and scholars. The famous poet Bilhana came from the court of the Chalukyan ruler in southern India. Harsha also introduced Carnatic music and instruments to Kashmir. But his unbridled extravagance and oppres-

sive system of taxation alienated the people, and the feudal barons led a revolt which led to his death, Kashmir saw 'the citizens deprived of all means, and the land overrun by numberless Damaras who were like kings.' The principalities of Rajauri, Poonch, Jammu and Kishtwar broke away till the 14th century when they were brought back under control by the Muslim rulers.

The story of Kashmir's first Muslim ruler is a romantic tale with three major protago-

nists: two adventurers, Rinchin, the Tibetan, and Shah Mir, from Swat, and Kota, the beautiful daughter of Ramachandra, commander of the armies of King Sahdeva. Rinchin came from Tibet and found a patron in Ramachandra. Shah Mir, told by a fortune teller that he would become king of Kashmir, came in search of his fortune. At this time the Tartar Dulchu invaded the Valley and Sahdeva, rather than face the prospect of battle, fled, leaving his commander to handle the situation. Dulchu, after spreading death and ruin, retired, and Ramachandra declared himself king.

Rinchin, who had risen in Ramachandra's service, next raised the banner of revolt. He killed his patron, seized the throne and persuaded the beautiful and ambitious Kota to marry him. It is said that Rinchin could not convert to Hinduism, so he became a Muslim. Following Rinchin's death, Kota, with the support of the Lavanya *damaras,* controlled the affairs of Kashmir. Shah Mir, till now a faithful retainer, had established his power and position through careful alliances and finally spearheaded a rebellion which ended with him not only capturing the throne, but Kota as well. However, in suitably dramatic manner Kota killed herself when she entered the bridal chamber in all her finery.

Since the 9th century Kashmir had remained in relative isolation, and with the decline in trade the exactions on the peasantry increased as the *damaras* grew in power and strength. Rebellion, intrigue and turmoil are the hallmarks of this period; 'shameless lust, fiendish cruelty and pitiless misrule,' as Kalhana described it.

Ladakh's Early History: It was during this period, around the middle of the 9th century that Ladakh began to emerge from under the shadow of Tibet. Its early history is a matter of conjecture and surmise. The work of scholars like Dr. A.H. Franche has shown that by the 2nd century A.D. the area was inhabited by Dards, an Indo-Iranian tribe, and that it was a part of the Kushan empire under Kanishka (120-162 A.D.). Ladakh's first contact with Buddhism was through Kashmir.

After the decline of the Kushan empire Ladakh was split into various independent principalities, and till the 7th century not much is reliably known about it. Then the

Left, prehistoric site at Burzahom, 10 miles east of Srinagar. <u>Above</u>, Shiva temple at Pandrethan, near Srinagar.

region witnessed the struggles of China and Tibet and the emergence of Arab power in Baltistan. With the decline of these three contestants, Ladakh emerged as an independent entity. The Ladakhi dynasty was established by Nyi-ma-gon, who gained control over Zanskar, Spiti, Lahaul, and Western Tibet as well. However, by the reign of Zain-ul-Abidin, Ladakh had become a feudatory of Kashmir, paying yearly tribute, till the monarch died. Lha-cha Bha-gan then re-established Ladakh as an independent state and his dynasty, the Namgyals, ruled till the Dogras captured it in 1842 and made them the *jagirdars* of Stok.

Muslim Rule: Traditionally, Kashmiri history has been divided on the basis of the religion of the rulers. In a society marked by syncretic trends, this seems a major anomaly. It fails to distinguish the changing character of social and political organization: the rule of the independent Sultans, for instance, has more similarities with the earlier era than with the centralized monarchy of the Mughals. Islam was brought to Kashmir by missionaries, and its intermingling with the existing religions produced features not always approved by the more orthodox.

Buddhism had created an ethos of egalitarianism which facilitated the acceptance of Islam, but just as Buddhist and Saivite beliefs coexisted, so did Hindu and Islamic practices. Intermarriage was common between the two religious communities, as was performance of Hindu religious rituals by the Sultans. Under Shahab-ud-din (1354-1375), the Kashmiri language was developed. This enlightened ruler is best remembered for having built the town of Shadipur, as well as for rebuilding Srinagar, destroyed by floods during his reign. He relocated the town near the foot of Hari Parbat and named it after his queen Lakshmi (one of the aspects of the goddess Sri).

He was followed by two rulers who have come to symbolize the two poles of bigotry and oppression and religious toleration and enlightened rule: Sikander (1389-1413) and his successor, Zain-ul-Abidin (1420-70). Sikander, it is said, ended the earlier tolerant policies and persecuted the Hindus. This *buth-shikan* (destroyer of idols) is said to have destroyed the famous temples of Martand, Vijayeshwari and Sureshwari. His forcible conversions and oppression

of the Hindus forced the Brahmins to flee. Yet Sikander could not have been merely a merciless tyrant. His policies were carried out by Suha Bhatta, a converted Brahmin, and it is likely that many Brahmins gained from converting to Islam. Sikander not only built mosques and hospices such as the famous Khangah-Mulla in Srinagar, but was instrumental in abolishing sati among the Hindus.

Sikander's second son Zain-ul-Abidin, known as *Budh* Shah or the Great King, is often compared to the Mughal ruler Akbar for his enlightened policies for he 'cultivated the society of all classes'. As a youth he had been sent as a hostage to the court of Timur

in Samarkand, where he was exposed to a world of sophistication and culture which he brought to his rule.

Before Zain-ul-Abidin, manuscripts were written on birch bark but he brought back with him craftsmen and settled them in Naushar, where pulp made at the nearby town of Ganderbal was brought and made into fine paper. Paper became an important commodity of trade and it was at this time that *papier mâché* was also introduced, though the skill of the *naqqash* took time to develop (the best products were under the Mughals). Zain-ul-Abidin also introduced carpet weaving which became an important source of revenue. He provided a stable administration which sought to alleviate the miseries of the people by proper flood and famine relief measures. His reign saw an active and vigorous cultural life.

The golden age of Zain-ul-Abidin was followed by strife and turmoil, marked by the clash between the Sayyids from Central Asia and Persia and the local nobility. Mirza Dughlat, a cousin of the first Mughal emperor Babur, took control of Kashmir in 1541 with Mughal support and till 1551, when he died, governed Kashmir under Mughal suzerainty.

Mirza Dughlat is remembered as a just administrator, a scholar and a patron of the

The Chak dynasty which followed ushered in a period marked by chaos, in which the romantic story of Yusuf Shah (1579-1586) is an arresting interlude. A scholar and musician and an ardent lover of nature and beauty, Yusuf Shah developed Gulmarg and Sonmarg as holiday resorts. It was while travelling here that he met the beautiful Zooni, who later gained fame as the singer Habba Khatun. His romance is enshrined in popular memory, but his rule was marked by neglect; his laxity led to his being driven out of the Valley he loved so much, and to a lonely death in exile in Bihar.

Mughal and Afghan Rule: The Mughals entered Srinagar on 14 October 1586, and

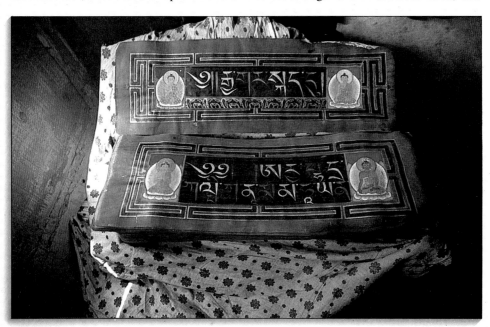

arts. He wrote the *Tarikh-i-Rashidi,* in which he writes of Kashmir, 'One meets with all those arts and crafts which are, in most cities, uncommon, such as stone polishing, stone cutting, bottle making, window cutting, gold beating, etc.' However, as an orthodox practitioner of Islam he castigated the Sufis of Kashmir for 'forever interpreting dreams, displaying miracles and obtaining from the unseen information regarding either the future or the past. Nowhere else is such a band of heretics to be found.'

<u>Left</u>, Mattan fragment, Kashmir. <u>Above</u>, Tibetan manuscript.

Kashmir became part and parcel of the Mughal empire. The Emperors, particularly Jahangir, were frequent visitors to the Valley. Akbar constructed a fort whose walls still exist. More significant were the land surveys which were carried out under his minister Todar Mal: taxes were fixed and a measure of stability introduced into the lives of the people. Akbar actually had workers paid for the work they did in construction but some of his governors were not so generous and famine, disease and epidemics continued to be the lot of the common people.

The Mughal rulers are today remembered for the gardens they constructed. Jahangir designed many himself, particularly the *char chinar* – placing maple trees at the four cardinal points to ensure shade at any time of the day. Among the many governors of Kashmir, Ali Mardan Khan has left a favorable record, but with the decline of Mughal power few were willing to accept the governorship as it meant removal from Delhi, the centre of power and intrigue.

The Afghan Shah Abdali wrested the throne of Kashmir in 1752 and his successors ruled till 1819. In the often oppressive rule experienced by the Kahmiris, this interlude was short but with few redeeming features. Kashmir was a milch cow, a source of tribute; power was exercised from Kabul. The

founded during the time of Alexander's invasion of India. The name of the people, 'Dogra', is believed to derive from two lakes which existed near the city, Sau and Dogirath. While the early history of Jammu is unclear its Raja is mentioned as a *mansabdar* during Mughal rule. By 1780 it was taken over by the Sikhs and formally annexed in 1803.

Gulab Singh (1792-1885) joined Ranjit Singh's service in 1809 and swiftly rose to a position of trust and power. In 1820 he was given Jammu to govern and, as a special favour, allowed to retain an army. He used this army judiciously, expanding his control over Kishtwar and Rajauri, and built up his ascendancy under the umbrella of the Sikh

Afghan governors levied onerous taxes, particularly on the lucrative shawl trade. Unable to endure their relentless oppression, a section of the Kashmiris appealed to the ruler of the Punjab, Ranjit Singh, and in 1819 the Sikhs brought Kashmir under their sway.

They ruled up to 1846 through their governors, and the Sikhs too proved to be 'hard and rough masters.' Like the Afghans, they saw Kashmir as a source of revenue.

Jammu and Gulab Singh: In 1839 Ranjit Singh died, and Gulab Singh, the Raja of Jammu, emerged as the ruler of Jammu and Kashmir. Historians and traditional accounts trace the origins of Jammu to principalities

state. He was ably served by Zorawar Singh, who rose from the ranks by dint of effort and an ability to command the army.

The Namgyals: Ladakh, since the beginning of Namgyal rule, experienced many vicissitudes. In 1532 Mirza Haidar invaded Ladakh and plundered and massacred its inhabitants, but with his death Tshe-wan Namgyal (1535-1575) became the ruler of Ladakh and expanded its borders into Guge, Lower Ladakh and Baltistan. However, these areas re-asserted their independence upon his death, and Ali Mir Khan of Baltistan invaded Ladakh with great destruction. Peace was restored by a marriage alliance between Ali Mir's daughter and the Ladakhi king. The sons of this marriage, Sen-ge (1600-1645) and Delden Namgyal made Ladakh into a powerful empire, and from this time on historical evidence becomes reliable.

Sen-ge Namgyal came into contact with the Mughals and agreed to pay tribute (but never actually sent any). His son, De-den Namgyal (1645-1675) invaded Baltistan but under Mughal threat agreed to accept their suzerainty; the emperor Aurangzeb in 1663 extracted a tribute of crystal, musk, jade and yak tails. The Ladakhi kingdom came to spread over Nubra, Dras, Guge, Spiti, Upper Kinnaur, Lahaul, and Zanskar.

The coming to power of the Great Fifth Dalai Lama would be a Kashmiri monopoly. Four Kashmiri merchants, living at Spitok, would handle supplies to Kashmir. Ladakh and Tibet agreed to exchange trade and religious missions. The Cha-ba mission brought tea bricks from Tibet while the Ladakhis, acknowledging the religious superiority of the Dalai Lama, would send their Lopchok or yearly salaam. The commercial benefits of this trade to the officials and monasteries was great, but politically Ladakh's power receded.

Zorawar Singh invaded Baltistan in 1841 and in the same year, attempting to extend Dogra conquests into Tibet, established a base at Lake Mansarovar. However, matched

Dalai Lama in 1642 saw the strengthening of Tibet and between 1681-1684 the Mughals, fearing the loss of the *pashmina* trade, helped the Ladakhis. The Tibeto-Mongol forces were defeated and in return De-ge Namgyal embraced Islam, calling himself Agabat Mahmud Khan.

Among the territorial and revenue stipulations he conceded was the demand that the entire wool export and transit trade of Ladakh

Left, Zain-ul-Abidin or Badshah's Tomb, Srinagar. **Above**, Henry Lawrence at the second Lahore Durbar of 26 December 1846, with Raja Ranbir Singh of Jammu.

by equally competent fighters and hampered by an over-extended line of communication and the onset of winter, his troops were decimated; only twenty-five survived to return to Jammu.

The following year he concluded a treaty which delimited the borders of Ladakh and Tibet. This aggressively expansionist policy was quietly tolerated by the Sikh governors of Kashmir, while the British viewed a stronger Gulab Singh as a counter-balance to Ranjit Singh. After the First Sikh War in 1856, Gulab Singh helped to negotiate the Treaty of Lahore. In a separate treaty the British gave Gulab Singh 'all the hilly or mountainous country with its dependencies situated to the eastward of the River Indus and westward of the river Ravi including Chamba.'

Kashmir, particularly after the last five years of Sikh rule, was in a sorry state. To an oppressive administration were added the effects of the famines of 1832 and 1838, which had reduced the population to living on water chestnuts, and raids from external marauders. Shawl weavers had been so heavily taxed that many migrated to Amritsar and Ludhiana. Gulab Singh tackled both these problems: the raiders were repelled and the shawl weavers taxed, not on the looms as was done earlier, but on their production instead.

The British, though willing to give Gulab Singh the trans-Satluj areas, attempted from the very beginning to impose their advisors; imperial rivalry with Tsarist Russia and the lucrative *pashmina* trade were the incentives. Ranjit Singh received an annual revenue of Rs 12 lakhs through their trade, and Zorawar's invasion of Ladakh was linked with an attempt to get the wool through Kishtwar.

Ranbir Singh: Gulab Singh was succeeded by Ranbir Singh, an able administrator who reorganized the civil and judicial administration, implemented a modern civil code, and greatly improved education and medical services.

The British, because of their concerns in Central Asia, were anxious to appoint a Resident in Kashmir. Through treaties they installed a joint Commissioner in Leh and a Political Officer in Gilgit. These officers provided information which enabled the British to play an important role in Central Asian politics.

Ranbir Singh was followed by Pratap Singh in 1885, under whose reign the British began to exercise greater control on Kashmir than they had earlier. This resulted in economic developments: a cart road down the Jhelum and one over the Banihal Pass; electrification of the big cities and improved communications. However, the main thrust of British policy was to oust the Maharaja. The British forced him to step down and replaced him with a Council of Regency headed by his more pliable brother, Amar Singh. Decisive power was thenceforth exercised by the British Resident.

Hari Singh (1895 – 1961), who came to the throne in 1925, introduced some social and educational reforms but remained politically hand in glove with the British government. As the nationalist struggle gathered momentum in India, he instituted harsh and repressive measures to still the independence movement in his state. Yet political associations and democratic institutions continued to develop, and with the emergence of the most important modern Kashmiri leader, Sheikh Mohammed Abdullah (1905-1982), the son of a shawl maker, the 'bulwarks of reaction' began to crumble.

In the wake of Independence in August 1947 came the partition of the sub-continent and the formation of Pakistan, an Islamic state. Erstwhile India's princely states were required to opt for either Pakistan or India, but Hari Singh, a Hindu ruler of a largely Muslim population, vacillated and sought time, perhaps hoping to remain independent. In October 1947, the infiltration of raiders into Kashmir from Pakistan escalated into a full-scale invasion, and Hari Singh invited Indian troops in after acceding to India.

The invaders were repulsed but in August 1948, with a substantial part of Kashmir still in Pakistani hands, the UN imposed a cease-fire and the state was effectively divided into two along a 'line of actual control'. It remains a matter of dispute between India and Pakistan.

Sheikh Abdullah headed the first popular ministry in the state, and the Jammu and Kashmir Constituent Assembly was formed in 1951. Several elections have since been held in the state assembly and the national parliament, but there have been frequent periods of unrest or political instability. Sheikh Abdullah was dismissed in 1953 and placed in detention, only to be restored to office in 1975. He remained chief minister till his death in 1982 when he was succeeded by his son, Dr Farukh Abdullah. The younger Abdullah has had two spells as chief minister but as Kashmiri sub-nationalism and religious fundamentalism came together to ignite a powerful separatist movement in 1989-90, the state has been virtually run from New Delhi. The flow of visitors to the valley has been reduced to a trickle and there seems to be no early end in sight to the turmoil.

Seventeenth century Patthar-ka-masjid (Stone Mosque), Srinagar.

Geological evidence suggests that pre-historic human life existed in the valleys of the Beas and the Satluj rivers in the late pleistocene age. Archaeological discoveries, however, reach back only forty thousand years. Stone tools like axes, chisels, picks and hammers found in the Shivaliks at Kangra, Bilaspur, Suket and Sirmaur indicate the existence of a settled community life in these areas.

The earliest identified settlers were actually migrants from the Gangetic plain, pushed into the hills by the growing Indus Valley Civilization between 3000-1750 BC The Munda-speaking Kolorian people, referred to as Dasas in the Vedic literature, spread themselves in groups over most of the Western Himalayan foothills, possibly as far as Kinnaur, Lahaul and Spiti. Around 2000 BC they were joined by the Khashas, of Aryan origin, who penetrated the Himalayas from the north-west after crossing the Hindukush.

By 1000 BC, about the time of the Mahabharata, a series of tribal republics had developed in the region, referred to as *janapadas* in classical texts. Some of the more important *janapadas* in Himachal Pradesh were those of the Kunindas, the earliest, extending from the Satluj to the Yamuna across Kinnaur, Shimla and Sirmaur; the Kulutas in the upper valley of the Beas; and the Trigarta and Audambaras, both of which flourished in Kangra. They retained distinct cultural identities, and most of them functioned as republics with elected or hereditary chiefs. Abundant numismatic evidence testifies to their economic affluence around the 2nd century AD, possibly due to their location on the trade routes from Central Asia to the Gangetic plain. Coins discovered in Chamba also reveal the presence of Greco-Bactrian settlements, probably the legacy of the Macedonian march across Himachal foothills. The departure of Alexander marked the rise of the Gupta empire in North India, including parts of Himachal. The Gupta conquests in the hills continued

Detail of Naggar Temple exterior, Himachal Pradesh.

till the 5th century, when their empire crumbled, to be succeeded by that of the Vardhanas. The Vardhana rule proved to be an era of relative political stability, and is described as such in the travelogue of Hiuen Tsang, the Chinese traveller who visited this region around AD 630 when Harsha-vardhana was in power.

The eventual collapse of the Vardhana empire saw the emergence of the Ranas and Thakurs, petty chiefs who controlled territories of diminutive sizes that were liable to change as one ruler triumphed over another. These warring lords were subdued by the powerful Rajput families who were attempting to reconsolidate their principalities in the hills. Some of these Rajput chiefs were expansionist adventurers who had penetrated the western Himalaya around the 10th century AD, while others had taken refuge in the hills from the Turkish onslaught in the 11th century.

The complex topographical features of Himachal, however, rendered it impossible for any one ruler to gain complete control over the whole region. Only small states could flourish here, bounded by the natural features of rivers and ridges, but enjoying varying degrees of independence. The Katoch kingdom of Kangra, once part of the erstwhile *janapada* of Trigarta, was among the largest as well as the most prosperous. On account of its proximity to the plains, it was subject to numerous raids from the Sultans, who conducted their forays primarily to pillage the legendary wealth stored in the fort and temples of Nagarkot, its capital. Mohammed of Ghazni carted off a fortune in gold, silver, and jewels in 1009 AD, and the shrines were plundered again in the 14th century by the Tughlaqs. Nagarkot changed hands several times during subsequent years, till its shrines eventually won royal patronage under the tolerant reign of Akbar. In fact, the 'loot and run' policy of the Sultans underwent a radical change with the coming of the Mughals in the 16th century, who made a serious attempt to expand their empire. However, the inaccessibility of the mountain enclaves, coupled with dogged resistance from Rajas like Chander Bhan Chand ensured that this annexation was never effectively completed. The Mughals managed only a shadowy supremacy over the hills of Himachal.

Till the 16th century, Kangra's chequered history of conquests and recovery ensured that this state acted as a sort of buffer between the military expansionists from the plains and the other hill states beyond. Chamba, for example, remained physically untouched by virtue of a formal accession to whoever controlled Kangra. This insulation nurtured an unbroken tradition of medieval Hinduism in the district, symbols of which are still in evidence today. The Rajas of Chamba were Suryavanshi (literally 'sun-

the smaller dominion of Keonthai further east in the same year. Mandi, now one of the major districts in Himachal, was actually an offshoot of Suket, formed in the 16th century. Bilaspur was founded around AD 900 by descendants of the Chandheri Rajas of Bundelkhand. The capital was situated on the eastern bank of the Satluj, and witnessed much strife in the 18th and 19th centuries when battles were fought between the kings of Kangra, supported by Maharaja Ranjit Singh, and the Gurkhas of Nepal.

Further east, between the Satluj and the Yamuna, lay the area that was divided into a number of petty states, classified as the Shimla Hill States. Two that were important,

clan', claiming descent from the sun) Rajputs, believed to be originally from Ayodhya. Among the earliest to move into the hills, Raja Meru Varman founded this principality at Brahmapura, or Bharmour, around AD 550. The capital was transferred to Champa, or Chamba, in AD 920.

Other hill states nearby that managed to retain more than just a passing identity were Suket and Bilaspur, also founded by Rajas from the plains. Suket was established as late as AD 1211 by Raja Vir Sen, a descendant of Lakshman Sen, belonging to the Sena dynasty of Bengal, who had fled north under pressure from the Turks. His brother Giri Sen founded

and stable, were Bushahr and Sirmaur, occupying the largest area. The remaining territory was fragmented into thirty minor dominions, known as *thakurais,* some as small as three square miles. Keonthal, Koti, Jubbal and Theog were among the more prominent *thakurais.* Bushahr, one of the older states in Himachal, was at one time spoken of as Bushahr-Kinnaur when its capital was at Kamru. In the 10th century the capital shifted lower to Sarahan, and later to Rampur. It owed some of its importance to the fact that its strategic location along the Satluj valley commanded trade movement to Tibet. Sirmaur, located in the Shivaliks bordering

Punjab, was established by the Rathor Rajputs. Some time in the 13th century, it overran the smaller *thakurais* to its north, and stretched its limits almost to the borders of Bushahr. Its capital, once at Kalsi, was moved up to Hatkoti in order to control these higher reaches, but was eventually relocated at Nahan in AD 1621. Sirmaur largely remained loyal to the Mughal emperors, till the advent of Guru Gobind Singh and Sikh power.

North of all these lower states were Kullu, whose ruling family, according to tradition, came from Haridwar in Uttar Pradesh. A cultured state, it had its capital at Nast, or Jagatsukh, and at the height of its prosperity

early suzerainty of the rulers of Ladakh. Later, Lahaul was annexed by the Rajas of Kullu, bringing to an end Ladakh's political supremacy over it. Once the beneficiary of the booming caravan trade from Mohhara, Samarkand and Lhasa that came together on its barren plains of Patseo and Losar, Lahaul continued to remain culturally linked with Ladakh. Spiti, across the Kunzum La, also owed its prosperity to the fact that it was a vital link on the great trans-Himalayan trade route from Lhasa to Kashmir. Once part of the West-Tibetan kingdom of Guge, it probably came under Ladakhi suzerainty as well when Guge became fragmented in the early 17th century. Thereafter it followed a course

at the end of the 17th century held Lahaul under its sway. Beyond Kullu lay the rugged mountain fastness of Lahaul and Spiti, once considered to be beyond the habitable world. These two districts existed as separate states in the medieval period. Lahaul was ruled by petty chiefs, similar to the Ranas and Thakurs of southern Himachal. Known as *jos,* they were of Tibetan origin, and submitted to the

Left, *Barselas***, engraved stone records of the rulers of Mandi. Above, goat and deer horns decorate the outside of a timber house in Malana, Himachal Pradesh.**

similar to that of Lahaul, being subject to rule from Kullu, and later from the Sikhs.

A new political force arrived in the Shivaliks in 1695. The Sikhs, organized as an army by their tenth Guru Gobind Singh, settled at Paonta on an invitation from Raja Medini Prakash, the ruler of Sirmaur. After the death of their Guru, the leaderless Sikhs became fragmented into smaller divisions, each beginning to encroach upon the hill states for reasons of safety from the Mughals, as well as territorial ambitions. It was only the rise of Maharaja Ranjit Singh at the close of the 18th century that reunited them under one banner and gave them nearly half a century of stable rule. Ranjit Singh swept across the hill states, amassing all the western dominions to his Lahore *darbar,* all the way up to Kullu. Raja Sansar Chand of Kangra, the most powerful hill chief at the time, was probably the only one who could have initially opposed the Sikhs, but he too was engaged in the expansion of his own Katoch empire.

Finally, seeking deliverance from Sikh dominance, some of the smaller hill states turned for help to Amar Singh Thapa, the commander of the Gurkha army, who had reached the eastern banks of the Satluj in his endeavour to expand the limits of Nepalese territory. Amar Singh Thapa crossed the river to fight the combined forces of Raja Sansar Chand and Maharaja Ranjit Singh at Kangra, was defeated, and turned back to reconsolidate his power over the Shimla Hill States, remaining in Rampur-Bushahr till 1813. The chiefs of the *thakurais* in turn sought protection from the British, who were only too pleased to help. After conclusively pushing the Gurkhas back into Nepal by 1815, they established their own supremacy over this part of Himachal. In fact, so enamoured were they of their salubrious acquisition, that they developed Shimla as a summer capital for their Government.

Predictably, the Anglo-Sikh war followed. A treaty was signed in 1846 by which the British annexed the territory between the Ravi and the Satluj. The hill monarchs thus lost most of their rights over their dominions, though they continued to be in possession of their land through *sanads* (grants). When India gained independence, both the zones of the Punjab Hill States and the Shimla Hill States acceded to India.

The twenty-one Punjab Hill States were integrated into a single, centrally administered unit in 1948, under the charge of a Chief Commissioner: the unit was named Himachal Pradesh. In 1954, Bilaspur was added, in 1956 Himachal Pradesh became a Union Territory, and in 1966, the rest of what we now recognize as Himachal Pradesh was merged into the mountain state. In 1971, Himachal Pradesh was granted statehood, and became the 18th state of the Indian Republic.

Evening promenade at Annandale, Shimla; nineteenth century aquatint.

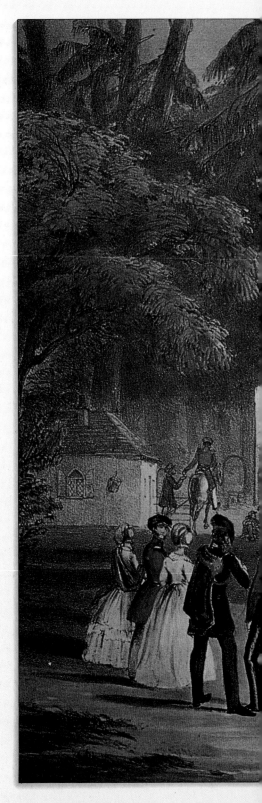

63

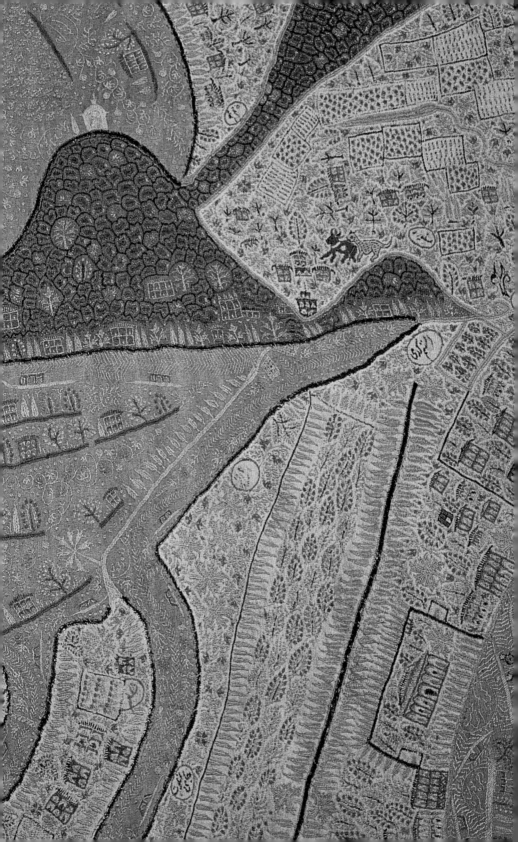

ARTS AND CRAFTS OF KASHMIR

The two major industries which sustain the economy of Kashmir are tourism and handicrafts. In no other state do nature and art complement each other more harmoniously; it is as though the patterns, motifs, colours and textures of the crafts were mirrored reflections of the environment. Yet the traditions of craft work are built as much upon the influence of major historical events and cultural movements dating back to the Indus Valley Civilization, as upon the inspiration provided by nature at its most idyllic.

From its first signs of settled existence to the majestic stone-carved 8th century Sun Temple in Martand, Kashmir received the most highly developed artistic influences from Buddhist and Hindu cultures. The dynasty of Lalitaditya developed the art and architecture of Kashmir. Craftsmen and painters added Kashmiri influences to their work and travelled onwards to Ladakh and Tibet to build their monasteries.

The golden age of arts and crafts, however, is inevitably ascribed to Zain-ul-Abidin, son of Sikandar, who ruled Kashmir from 1421 to 1472. He was called the Great Badshah for his contribution to the cultural enrichment of the valley. During his father's rule he spent seven years as a hostage of Timur the Lame in Samarkand, where he came across fine craftsmen from Turkestan, Persia and China. On ascending the throne he sent for skilled workers from different parts of Central Asia and Arabia who provided a remarkable cross-cultural fertilization of craftsmanship. Calligraphy, the art of paper making, papier mâché with its finely painted decoration, shawl and carpet weaving, silk cocoon rearing, metal work and jewellery, all flourished under his patronage. Most artisans and traders of Kashmir will answer "the great Badshah" almost by rote, when asked about the origin of a particular craft. Though this may not necessarily be accurate, it does acknowledge the tremendous enrichment that took place

during that period.

Carpets: What makes Kashmir carpets world-famous is the perfection that goes into their elaborate Persian designs, and the high level of skill attained by weavers. Apart from the age-old familiarity with weaving *(kalbafi)* that seems to be instinctive among peasants inhabiting mountain regions, the famed Kashmir shawl *(see box)* had already dazzled the courts of the Europe and the Middle East. Carpet weavers use the same weavers' alphabet, the *talim*, and work in *karkhanas* or

workshops. Visitors are welcome to hear them chant while they weave. The various processes of designing, drafting, weaving, washing and finishing can all be observed. Adjoining showrooms are stacked high with carpets in hundreds of designs, colours and sizes, from the small prayer carpet to grand pieces fit for royalty. Wages are paid per thousand knots, and training begins at a young age when fingers are small and nimble. Years of practice can make a young man of thirty a master weaver.

Carpets are woven in staple rayon, silk, wool and pure silk. A recent development has been the introduction of *zari* or metallic

Preceding pages: old Kashmiri shawl embroidered with map of Hari Prabat and Dal lake. **Left**, Kashmiri carpets draw upon an extensive Central Asian tradition. **Above**, dyeing woollen fabric, Kashmir.

thread in the weft with figures and flowers in wool appearing in relief. The *Shab-i-chirag* carpet has been embedded with pearls. Both have a special glitter and sheen when reflecting light in a dark room. The rule of thumb is that the larger the number of knots per square inch the higher the quality, but the yarn, dyes, pattern and selection of colours along with the strength of the border and quality of finish are essential ingredients in their gradation. Patterns on carpets are reproductions of Persian, Turkish, Turkman and Caucasian designs. Mughal patterns and adaptations of antique shawl designs have also enriched the Kashmir carpet weaver's repertoire.

The *namdah* and *gabba* are floor rugs dis-

What is particularly heartening is that the *namdah* suits perfectly the ambience of a typical Kashmiri home as well as the tastes of a sophisticated foreign clientele.

Woodwork: The walnut tree is a precious commodity both for its fruit and for its soft brown satiny wood. Bees and birds nestling amongst roses and narcissi; woodpeckers flitting between chinar leaves; fine Islamic calligraphy encircling a bowl: no form is too difficult to create for the Kashmiri wood carver. Seated on the floor accompanied by apprentices and the ubiquitous *hookah, samovar* and *kangri* (the hubble bubble pipe, tea kettle and chafing pot) the craftsmen uses a variety of indigenously developed tools to

tinctive for their embroidery. The *gabba* is made in the heart of the old part of Anantnag town. Family members usually work on a *gabba,* piecing together an appliqué of dark and light blanket cloth and embroidering floral outlines and borders with brightly coloured woollen yarn. The *namdah* is a floor rug made from pressed felt. Raw wool, or wool and cotton, is rolled out on a mat and pressed under foot after which it is milled, washed and dried. This work is carried out on the banks of the many waterways connecting the Dal and Nagin lakes. The *namdah* is then embroidered in a variety of bold designs in floral, geometric and even nursery patterns.

decorate the basic form of anything from a salad spoon to a vast table top.

Writing desks, jewellery boxes, models of houseboats, cigar boxes, nut bowls and screens are just a few of the walnut wood articles made for the domestic, tourist and export markets. There are innumerable workshops and retail stores particularly in the Rainawari area and around the Dal and Nagin lakes in Srinagar where visitors can observe, admire, photograph and shop. Since most craftsmen work with intense concentration and pride and combine their artisanal

Above, *shatush*, the celebrated 'ring shawl'.

68

THE KASHMIR SHAWL

No handcrafted article has been at the centre of such high politics, high romance, high tragedy and high fashion as the 'Cashmere' or Kashmiri *shal*. The Chinese traveller Hieun Tsang mentions a delicate and soft fabric found in Kashmir, and the famed Kashmiri historian Kalhana speaks of the woollen garment which the Kashmiri elite wore over their shoulders. A Persian tract, the *Risaleh dar fann-i-shal-bafi* claims that Mirza Haidar Dughlat, the Central Asian adventurer who occupied Kashmir in AD 1541, was the originator of the Kashmiri shawl. He apparently compared the coarser varieties of handwoven cloth found in Kashmir with the finer, warmer *puttoo* presented to him by the ruler of Tibet, and commissioned the spinning and weaving of this wool.

Pasham, the local name for cashmere wool, comes from the underbelly of the *pashmina* goat *(Capra hircus).* Its even softer counterpart, *tus,* is the fleece of the Tibetan antelope or ibex, which is rubbed off onto rocks and brambles as the weather turns warmer in Ladakh. Both the delicacy of spinning and weaving demanded and the rarity of the fleece makes the *pashmina* and *tus* or *shahtush* shawl a must in every aristocrat's wardrobe. Multimillionaires and Maharajahs boast of shawl collections of unimaginable value. The Emperor Akbar was an aficionado, according to the *Ain-e-Akbari.* By 1798, the exquisite *kani* shawls of Kashmir had reached Napoleon Bonaparte who after his Egyptian campaign carried one home to Empress Josephine. She was so impressed that she ordered 400 of them, and so began a fashion which spread like wildfire all over Europe.

The *kani* shawl at the height of its glory kept 30,000 looms occupied all over Kashmir. It was woven with a special technique of interweaving different coloured threads wound around wooden bobbins *(kani).* Today, the tiny village of Kanihama which lies on the road from Srinagar to Gulmarg is valiantly attempting a revival of these shawls. The weavers work from a coded instruction sheet called a *talim,* "lifting three, using red, lifting five, using green," according to one of 16 famed patterns. These are the vestiges of the shawl that formed part of the famous treaty of Lahore and Amritsar in 1846. The treaty states, "Maharajah Gulab Singh accepts the government of Great Britain and from his side as a gift will give every year one horse, twelve goats (six male and six female) and three pairs of *jamawar* shawls." *Kani* is the real name of the shawl, while *jamawar* actually refers to the length of *kani* fabric used to tailor court gowns – a subtle but important difference in nomenclature. Despite all the glory, the poor weavers suffered from overwork, heavy taxation and miserable wages. Many are said to have cut their fingers off rather than toil under such oppressive circumstances.

The embroidered shawl, *amlikar,* emerged as an innovation born out of necessity when the market for the *kani* shawl collapsed, after the French-Prussian War, and the mills of Manchester and Paisley took over the production of imitation *kanis* by machine. The *sozankar* (embroiderer) of today has a proud heritage of being amongst the finest male embroiderers in the world. Plain shawls in pale greys, browns and creams are decorated in silk thread with trellis and floral borders, medallions, paisleys and skilled *do rukha* (double-sided) patterns. Embroidering is done in rural homes by farmers during the leisurely winter months, as also in *karkhanas* or workshops in the myriad lanes running off the banks of the Jhelum in Srinagar. Groups of men work swiftly and silently in dark old wooden buildings bathed in light reminiscent of a Rembrandt painting.

The peasant shawl or *chadar* of Kashmir is the coarse, thick blanket-sized fabric with colourful narrow end-borders. Spun and woven in rural homes, *chadars* are slung over the shoulders of nomadic shepherds and farmers, summer and winter. These are woven in villages such as Bandipur and Gurez, the border indicating its local provenance by its colour and pattern. Simple and commonplace as this shawl may be, it is the age-old tradition of peasant spinning and weaving that provided the base on which the famed history of the Kashmir *shal* was built.

skills with an ability to be persuasive salesmen, visiting a *karkhana* is always an exhilarating experience.

Papier mâché: A special craft in Kashmir is papier mâché work, which evolved during Zain-ul-Abidin's rule. Closely connected with the development of paper-making and calligraphy, this art was at first used to make pen holders or *qalamdans*. Later, papier mâché packing boxes were ordered by French shawl agents. Decorated ceilings, wall panels and screen were commissioned for mosques and durbar halls. The 15th century Madin Sahib mosque and the Shah Hamdan mosque at Fateh Kadal in Srinagar are examples of papier mâché decoration.

embossed effect is created by painting the desired pattern in a mixture of glue and sugar and placing fine gold or silver leaf over it like a paper transfer. Commonly used colours are gold, cochineal, ultramarine, white lead and verdigris to produce rich, mellow colours, although today most craftsmen use commercial paints. Designs are taken from shawls and the influences of nature such as the hoopoe, woodpecker, deer, flowering trees, chinar leaves and a large variety of flowers. These are laid out free-hand from the traditional heritage of patterns lodged in the craftsman's memory.

Embroidery: While the finest of Kashmiri embroidery is seen on its shawls, the chain

The technique of production involves two processes. The first, *sakhtasazi,* consists of the preparation of the pulp and the mould and the second, *naqqashi,* is the application of the outer decoration. The paper paste is pounded manually for hours, after which wheat or rice starch is added for malleability. This is laid layer by layer over a clay, wooden or brass mould, smoothened, and then sawn apart to remove the inner mould. The two pieces are rejoined and brushed with glue and chalk. A layer of paper or cloth seals the cracked surface. The object is then covered with a ground colour. Designs are first painted in white and later filled in with colour. The

stitch or crewel work which goes into the vast production of fabric for home furnishings is a typical feature of its craft industry. Cream-coloured handloom cloth, commonly called *dosooti*, is elaborately embroidered with chinar leaves, trellises, roses, crocuses and all kinds of flowers that adorn a summer garden. The awl, like a crochet hook, pulls the yarn forward as embroiderers sit under trees beside streams in the countryside, or in workshops all over Srinagar, with meters of cloth spread about them.

The sense of colour imbibed by the Kashmiri embroiderer reflects both an aesthetic response to nature's palette and the influences of the European market of yore. Perhaps because Kashmir's seasons follow the European pattern, and the colours of the landscape merge softly, unlike the vivid hues so typical of the rest of India, it is the pastel sophistication of spring, autumn and winter colours that are evident.

Cushion covers, bedspreads and curtain fabric used in most *shikaras,* houseboats and hotels of Kashmir display the variety of designs and adaptability of this embroidery. Chain stitch is done with finer thread on garments and leather accessories.

Basket-weaving: Baskets tumble over themselves in shops all over the valley as they come in handy as excess baggage carri-

spread out on the pavement along with biscuits, bread, nylon ribbon and plastic buckets in a battle between tradition and modernity – where the latter obviously loses!

Fine willow basket making was introduced earlier this century, but local reeds and rushes have always been used all over the Valley to make baskets for agricultural use. The *kangri* is an indigenous handicrafted chafing pot made of a willow basket with a handle and a clay pot inside containing live embers. Kashmiris carry it around like a hot water bottle all day under their gowns *(pheran)* and slip it inside their quilts on cold winter nights. The *kangri* is decorated with shiny tinsel and brightly coloured willow

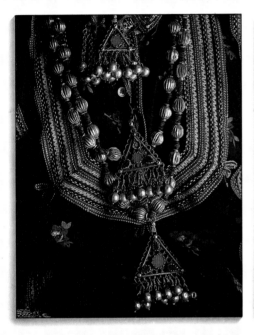

ers, picnic hampers and fruit holders for both tourists and the local Kashmiris. Made of supple rich brown willow, they are woven in and around Srinagar, with the best shops located beside the Hazaratbal Mosque on the banks of the Dal Lake. A wonderful market springs up here every Friday where, in addition to the permanent willow shops, pottery, copper kettles and wooden ladles are all

Left, finely decorated *papier-mâché* artefacts are an important source of income for Kashmir's craftsmen. **Above left**, Gujjar women wear fine silver jewelery; **right**, detail of Kashmiri timber construction.

strips woven in elaborate patterns. It is a ceremonial part of a bridal trousseau and is also given to priests on the coldest day of winter as a homage to ancestors.

The Nagin and Dal lakes abound in a type of reed known as *pits*. This is collected and woven into mats called *waggu* which are used as roofing for boats and flooring in homes. Just like the *kangri,* the *waggu* mat is an intrinsic part of the life of the common man and hints at where the long story of the crafts of Kashmir must have originated.

Metalwork: Serving dishes, tea kettles and *samovars* become important adjuncts in a society that loves lavish and elaborate feasts, endless cups of *noon chai* (salt tea) and *kahva,* a delicious green tea flavoured with almonds, saffron and cardamom. In the Haba Kadal and Fateh Kadal areas of old Srinagar, copper workers beat and engrave vessels of different types, carrying on traditions and techniques brought from Persia in the 11th century. It is said that Zain-ul-Abidin met his entire private expenditure from the proceeds of a copper mine in Kashmir. Designs on metal vessels are mostly calligraphic inscriptions or birds and animals nestling amongst foliage. The chinar leaf and lotus are perennial favourites, along with the ornamental *badam* (almond) motif taken from the *kani* shawl. Copper ladles with long engraved handles, glistening *samovars,* rice dishes, *surahis* for water and *aftabas,* technically for wine but in fact for decoration, hang in special shops all over the Valley, sounding a mellow and old-wordly note in the hubbub of rapid progress.

Ornaments have always been part of the traditional dress of Kashmir. The nomadic and rural people wear silver and white metal earrings hanging from long chains, bracelets, bangles, elaborate buttons, hair clips and necklaces, crafted by silversmiths in both villages and towns. In the old quarter of Srinagar hundreds of tiny shops, with two to seven craftsmen in each, reproduce traditional designs as well as new styles to catch the tourist's eye. Semi-precious stones such as turquoise, opal, garnet, tigerstone, onyx, lapiz lazuli and jade are brought in from other states to be cut and fashioned into trinkets. Old jewellery, cast off by peasant folk in search of modernity, is sold in sackfuls by weight, and it is possible to discover quirky pieces amongst them – rings decorated with foil from old cigarette packets placed under plain glass, or bracelets imitating wristwatches with a dial face and numbers – if you are lucky.

The real connoisseur of craft must be adventurous and patiently seek out the very best in the villages and workshops of the valley. A high quality of age-old skill exists at the craftsmen's fingertips; it is for the visitor to recognize it and demand it, so that Kashmiri craftsmanship never succumbs to the call of crass commercialism.

Kashmiri vernacular architecture is distinguished by the sensitive use of wood.

While the crafts of Kashmir have attracted attention for centuries, those of ethereal and isolated Ladakh have seldom found mention and frequently been confused with those of Tibet. Ladakh has its own syncretic culture, and the art and iconography of the region have been shaped by its own historical and religious currents.

Before Buddhism, the people followed an animist form of religion called Bon-pa, replete with spirits, demons and the worship of trees, rocks and supernatural beings. With Ladakh's prime position at the crossroads of the highways of Central Asia, it absorbed a variety of cultures – including forms and concepts flowing out of the Buddhist centres at Mathura, Taxila and the Indus Valley. Under the Gupta dynasty (3rd to 5th century AD) art forms such as scroll paintings were introduced into the Himalayan area and with local stylistic variations transported to Central Asia via Ladakh.

Between the 7th and 10th centuries, Tibetan and Indian influences finally changed the essentially tribal culture of this region into a feudal one. Ladakh was also flourishing as the meeting point of the famed silk route; caravans between Khotan, Yarkand, Kashgar and other trading posts between China and the Mediterranean, all passed through here. The art traditions of Vajrayana Buddhism with its rich iconography, *thangkas* (scroll paintings) and wall paintings gradually spread throughout the region. This process intensified during the reign of King Lalitaditya who had enriched Kashmiri art through the import of many skilled craftsmen after he conquered Kanauj in AD 733. The Kashmiri style, combining with the styles of Kushan, Kanauj and Magadha, greatly influenced the art tradition of Ladakh. The consolidation of the Buddhist cultural heritage by Kashmiri artisans can be seen best in the exquisite and ornate wall paintings in the monasteries of Lamayuru and Alchi.

In the 16th century Ladakh suffered under the plundering rule of the Mongols, and the

fortunes of its kings swung back and forth. Later, Tsewang Namgyal rebuilt many of the monasteries, making use of artists and craftsmen from neighbouring Kashgar, Khotan and Kashmir. Artists from these areas created the beautiful wall paintings in the Hemis monastery, built in AD 1602-1606 by Senge Namgyal, one of the most celebrated kings of Ladakh. Sober and delicate, with a dignified use of colour, the Hemis paintings depict Buddha's renunciation and various other episodes in his life combining Tantric

and Vajrayana Buddhist canons of art.

After the 16th century the painting of religious themes became a mode of worship. Artists began appending their names to paintings not for individual recognition but to demonstrate their efforts to gain salvation. The establishment of the Mughal empire at Delhi resulted in Ladakh, along with Kashmir, becoming part of Akbar's kingdom by 1585, and Buddhist art began to be affected by the stylistic features of the Mughal miniature schools. The later paintings at Alchi monastery demonstrate this. Finally, the Emperor Aurangzeb's puritanical rule brought about a ban on visual art and ended

Left, a silversmith at work in the Ladakhi village of Chilling. **Above**, clay tablet from a *chorten* in Ladakh.

the period of frescoes and large clay sculptures. The making of ritual objects and *thangka* paintings then became a secretive enterprise carried out by lamas from various monasteries.

Secular crafts: The craft forms of Ladakh are rooted in traditional peasant life. Most of the inhabitants of Ladakh are engaged in some form of artisanship, apart from their work on the soil or grazing their goats, yak and other cattle. Every man and woman carries around a spindle, *thulshing,* to produce yarn for home use from the local goat, and weavers set up their portable looms to produce long strips of *pattu.* The baskets carried on their backs are made in various

Namgyal. The exact location was identified by loosing an arrow in that direction and settling where it landed. Copper deposits were abundant and their work flourished. Today, despite their geographic and economic isolation the *sergars* or silversmiths of Chilling are prosperous and well engaged in producing ladles, tea kettles, water pots, lids and other ornamental containers commissioned by the well-to-do of Ladakh.

Watching a potter mould cups of barley beer *(chang)* or create a brazier and kettle out of the clay lying about his hut is like travelling back in time. No potter's wheel, kiln or electricity is required by the man wearing coarse homespun cloth and putting together

sizes from a local grass, *chipkiang.* The village potter and silversmith create elaborate cups, kettles and bowls in clay, copper, brass and silver to adorn kitchen shelves and aid monastery rituals. The wood carver is also a maker of clay stoves and the blacksmith of the Gara community constructs enormous decorative kitchen stoves, unique locks and keys, and even conch bangles for women.

Ladakh's elegant copper and silver ware are made by the most simple and primitive production methods in the remote village of Chilling in the Zanskar valley. According to its inhabitants, their ancestors were sent there by the kings Delden Namgyal and Sengge

or dismantling the simple tools which help him carry on his trade. Every Ladakhi home will have the potter's clay bowls to either burn incense, drink beer or light a lamp.

The division of labour in the production of yarn and fabric is curious: women only spin the wool of sheep while men spin yak hair and goats' wool. Unlike in Nepal, Spiti and Tibet, women do no weaving in Ladakh, perhaps due to age-old beliefs that they belong to the subterranean world of *lhu.* The wool of the local goat is spun into yarn for socks, sweaters and caps, or woven into strips about 20 cm wide, which are stitched together and tailored into *gonchas* (gowns) or blankets known as *chhali* in Leh and *pherba* in the Kargil area. Very similar to the hues of natural yarn blankets of Mexico or the Andes, these are produced in each home for family use and have never been part of the market economy. Thicker yarn of goats' wool is woven into sacks and grain bags in natural colours of grey, black and brown. Yak wool produces thick pile blankets or rugs called *balstuk*.

The concept of *lhu* is reflected in the magnificent headdress, the *perak,* worn by the women of Ladakh. These, too, are made exclusively by men and resemble a serpents' hood, fish fins and scales, all reminiscent of the gods that are supposed to inhabit the

motifs which distinguish Ladakhi from Tibetan designs. Women string seed pearls, coral and turquoise beads together at home to make simple necklaces for everyday wear. Earrings too are of pearls and beads. Men wear a single earring of small beads strung on thread. Plain silver jewellery is influenced by the styles of Baltistan and Gilgit. Today, silversmiths in Kargil or Srinagar can all produce these heavier folk designs to suit the needs of their clients.

The extent to which local craft activity is still harmoniously integrated with every day life can be gauged by watching the men and women who come to sell or buy vegetables in the main Leh bazaar. They will be dressed

subterranean world. Legend has it that this headdress was introduced by a queen from one of the neighbouring regions who had married a Ladakhi king. The ear-flaps were added when she once had an earache! A small filigree charm box made by the local goldsmith is attached where the *perak* goes over the top of the head. These and other silver accessories are made by *sergars* working in the by-lanes of Leh. They like to point out the subtle differences in shapes and

Left, ornate painted ceiling of *chorten* in Stok, Ladakh. **Above**, Lama applies finishing touches to a painted beam in Llkir Gompa.

in hand spun, hand woven, hand dyed *gonchas* with *pabbu*, the colourful felted tie-dye cloth shoes, on their feet; a *tibi* (cloth hat with metallic thread embroidery) or *perak* covering their head; on their backs will be the *tsepo*, a basket woven out of grass to carry vegetables, fodder or even babies; in their ears and around their necks will be the bead and pearl jewellery made at home; hanging from their waists by a thread or silver chain are ornamental keys made by the Gara, while their hands will be busy spinning yarn around a wooden spindle made by the village carpenter, or turning the copper and silver prayer wheel made by the *sergar.*

ARTS AND CRAFTS OF HIMACHAL PRADESH

Nestled in the seclusion of the Himalaya, the self-contained communities of Himachal have developed through the years a corpus of original and distinctive arts and crafts. The state of Himachal Pradesh remained largely distanced from the political upheavals experienced by the rest of the country. Bloodshed, invasions and destruction are not the shaping forces of its socio-political and cultural development. A gentleness pervades the hill people of this region whose life and art resolve around quiet pastimes such as sheep herding, weaving, growing fruit and worshipping their gods. It is not surprising, therefore, that the art forms embraced by these simple hillfolk reflect gentle themes of love, worship and music.

Painting: One the the clearest examples of this is the tradition of Pahari painting, commonly called Kangra painting because it was patronised by Kangra kings under whom a large number of works emerged from this region. Executed as miniatures in the Mughal tradition, Pahari miniatures are distinct enough in character to warrant an entirely separate classification.

The history of their origin is still obscure. However, it is largely agreed that Pahari paintings first emerged in the hills of Himachal during the 17th century. This date coincides with the dissolution of the Mughal court, which led to a dispersal of its court painters, some of whom found shelter in the alpine retreats of the Himalaya.

The intermingling of artists belonging to the old, indigenous Rajput school and the more contemporary Mughal school brought about the fusion known as the Kangra School. Apart from Kangra, many different centres were established: Guler, Chamba, Mandi, Suket, Kullu, Jasrota, Sujanpur Tica, Nadaun and Basholi. The style of painting developed in these centres came to be known respectively as the Kullu school or *kalam* (pen), Mandi *kalam*, Kangra *kalam*, etc. An inter-

mingling of artists belonging to different *kalams* fostered a stylistic unity in the paintings, but with distinct regional variations. Kangra paintings flourished during the reign of Raja Sansar Chand (1775-1823), who assumed power at the age of ten and went on to become the most renowned ruler of Kangra as well as its most generous patron of art.

Kangra paintings were inspired by the widespread cult of Vaishnavism, the doctrine of personal, passionate devotion to Krishna (the most popular of the Hindu gods).

Great poets like Jayadeva, Mirabai and Keshavadas popularised Krishna through their work, and Kangra paintings became another vehicle of expression of this deep love for Krishna.

The chief features of Kangra paintings are delicacy of line, brilliance of colour and minuteness of decorative detail. The central theme of all paintings is love, symbolizing the human soul striving to escape the trammels of the senses in its search for eternal peace, through a mystical union with God. The nuances of symbolism that Chinese art achieved in its exploration of landscape is here accomplished in the realm of human

Pahari miniatures from the Bhuri Singh Museum, Chamba. Left, miniature depicting the abduction of Sita, from the Ramayana, the popular Indian epic. Above, the eternal lover, the Hindu god Krishna, with his beloved, Radha.

love. Though many of the paintings were lost in the Kangra earthquake of 1905, thousands still exist in museums and private collections, and on palace walls and temples. The museum at Chamba has a large collection; others can be seen at the Himachal State Museum in Shimla and the National Museum in Delhi.

Textiles: As the art of painting flourished in Kangra, a different art form, namely embroidery, originated in Chamba. Known as Chamba *rumals* (handkerchiefs), these can be described as paintings translated into embroidery. The themes of the *rumals* are the same as of Pahari paintings, the only difference being in their execution: while

or decorating religious books and idols, and also for ceremonial exchange in marriage rituals. Chamba women are presently being trained in the intricacies of this art so that the tradition does not die out.

In the warm summer months the wild Himalayan goat sheds its fleece on high mountains. The wool is gathered by hill people and stored till winter comes and the fields are covered with snow. From this, people spin and weave exceptionally fine shawls. The most valuable of these is the soft shawl made from the hair of the *pashmina* goat. The colours most commonly used are mellow shades of gray, mustard, blue and black. Designs differ from region to region.

paintings were done by men, *rumals* are exclusively the domain of women.

Chamba *rumals* are generally square, ranging from 60 cm square to 120 cm sq. The cloth used as a base is a kind of muslin on which embroidery is done using a double satin stich so that both sides have the same image. One of the finest examples of this art is a wall hanging depicting the battle of Kurukshetra, presented by Raja Gopal Singh of Chamba to the British in the 19th century. The *rumal* now hangs in the Victoria and Albert Museum, London.

Rumals were not used for domestic purposes nor as headgear, but for covering gifts

Kinnauri shawls are known for vibrant designs and colours on the border, while Kullu shawls are duller with largely geometric patterns on the border. Each region has improvised its own style of draping the shawl, the most popular being the *dhobroo* and *pattoo*. Kullu woollen *topis* (caps) are also known for their distinctive style. They are worn by peasants as well as by rich folk. The caps worn on festive occasions are elegant, a proud symbol of the Himachal people.

Carpets: Brilliant hues, dragons, a garuda on a flowering tree, swastikas for luck, flutes and the lotus are traditional patterns found on Himachal carpets. These symbols hold a sacred meaning for the weaver: flutes signify happiness, while the lotus is a symbol of purity. The weaver creates carpets which are stories of luck and heroism, not mere random designs. Most highlanders use carpets for furnishing as well as carpet saddles for their ponies. A blanket known as *chuktu* is actually a modified version of a carpet. *Gudma* is a fleecy soft blanket made from the wool of Biangi sheep found in the higher reaches of Himachal. Hill folk rear these sheep and goats for the famous wool and hair that goes into the making of traditional blankets, rugs and *namdas* (floor covering). *Gudma* weaving is done mainly in the Giabong and Kullu valleys as these areas have the special

and baskets from the dried bamboo. This is a peaceful time when, with mugs of hot tea, shared laughter and folk songs, the hill people work with their hands to shape beautiful oval and lotus baskets with tall handles.

Music and Dance: Folk songs and the traditional Natti dance of Himachal are an integral part of its artistic heritage. Most of the songs are about love and courtship; however, every region has its own songs about farming, ploughing the land, wood sawing, harvesting, fruit picking and local legends. The Natti is performed by groups of 15-20 with an orchestra comprised of pipes, drums, trumpets and cymbals. The dancers wear traditional costumes and black woollen caps

clay used for cleaning and finishing. Usually, natural wool colours such as gray, beige, brown and black are seen in traditional *gudmas* which also have a warm red or black edging. *Thobi* and *namda* (floor coverings) and *kharcha* (mattresses) are made from goat hair, while the well known *pattoo* cloth is made from the soft wool of sheep.

All along the crystal streams of Himachal grow bamboo and willow trees. During winter months, groups of people sit around small life-giving fires, making intricate bowls, trays

with silver edging on which there is a badge of silver or gold shaped like a crescent moon. The tunic is covered by a sash made of silk, over which is worn a woollen shawl. While there are approximately fifteen variations of Natti, its characteristic blend of classical and folk idiom is recognised by all as representative of the Himachal people's spontaneous joy and integral spirituality.

In a typical Natti, everyone in the village joins hands to form a chain and circle in step, slowly at first but gaining momentum. Caught up in the tempo of the collectivity, the colourfully dressed revellers present a memorable spectacle.

Left, a weaver at his loom, Pangi village. **Above**, detail from the Bhimakali temple, Sarahan.

In the Chamba and Kullu regions one finds unique styles of footwear. Chamba *chappals* (open-toed sandals), embroidered with intricate designs, are extremely light and suitable for walking and trekking. Kullu *pullans*, celebrated for their warmth and comfort, are shaped like bedroom slippers and made of *bhang* (marijuana) fibre and goat's hair. Colourful designs are found on the upper part of the *pullan*.

Wood Carving: Although the art of wood carving is an ancient one in Himachal Pradesh, not many significant works have survived the rigours of time and the elements. The few visible remnants of this art form can be seen in some of the temples, palaces and houses in the higher ranges of Kullu, Mandi, Chamba and the Shimla Hills.

Mostly the wood of the deodar, walnut or shisham tree is used for decorative carving, and technique is determined by the grain and density of the timber – deodar and walnut being amenable to deep cutting, while only shallow relief work is possible with shisham.

Common motifs found in carvings are figures of local deities, floral patterns and arabesques, animals and birds, dancing girls, riders on horseback, etc. In the the temples and houses carvings are mostly found on doors and window frames, balconies, pillars and facades.

Temple Architecture: As many as six thousand temples are located in this tiny Himalayan state where devotion reigns strong. Their architectural diversity too is impressive. The earliest specimen of the *shikhara* design in the Himalayan region is the series of monolithic temples at Masrur in Kangra district. The main temple, 148 feet (48 m) long and 103 feet (31.5 m) broad, has been sculpted from a single rock. Such rock-hewn temples, common in western and southern India, are elsewhere unknown in the Himalayan region. Dating back to the 8th century, the Masrur temples are particularly remarkable for the deep-cut carvings that surround their doorways.

The Baijnath temple, 22 miles (36 km) from Kangra town, was built in AD 1204 in the *shikhara* style, and is considered one of the most beautiful temples of Himachal. The Lakshimnarayan temple complex in Chamba and the Basheshwar Mahadev and Jagatsukh temples in the Kullu valley, the Bhutnath temple in Mandi and the Trilokinath temple in Lahaul are other famous temples in the *shikhara* style.

The 'pagoda' style temples, located primarily in the Kullu valley, are a folk variation of the more sophisticated and intricate Nepalese court architecture. The most interesting examples of this style are found in the Hidimba temple at Doongri (Manali), the Parashar temple in Mandi and the Kullu valley temples of Tripura Sundri, Trijugi Narain and Adi Brahma located at Naggar, Diyar and Khokhan respectively.

The most elementary form of hill architecture is represented by the old temples scattered all along the mountain slopes of Himachal. The rectangular stone and wood temples with pent roofs are the most ancient of these. One immediately noticeable aspect of these Johari temples is the base, constructed with large, finely chiselled stones. Quite a few of these temples have verandahs encircling the upper storey, serving as a circumambulatory path around the cella. The finest wood carving work is also found in the temples of Kali at Mirkula (Lahaul), Shakti Devi at Chhatrarchi (Chamba), and Lakshana at Bharmaur. Other noteworthy examples are Bijli Mahadev in Kullu, Bijat at Sarahan (Chopal) and Magreshar at Kot (Kumarsain).

The Satluj valley has a variation of these Pahari temples which is a fusion of the pent roof and pagoda roof. The Bhimakali temple at Sarahan is perhaps the most spectacular example of this fusion; the Dhaneshwari Devi temple at Nithar is another. A further variation can be seen in the temples at Hatkoti and Jubbal, where the central tower is built on a square plinth and topped with a pyramid-like slate roof.

Through their folk lore, music and dancing, their painting and embroidery, building, weaving and various other crafts, the Himachali people express the common themes of love, chivalry and faith which have inspired the works of artists, poets, story-tellers and artisans over the ages. A gentle people, pursuing a life away from the frenzy and bustle of the plains, taking pleasure in creating objects of beauty, singing to themselves and to God, the Himachalis find inspiration in the mountains, trees, and streams around them to shape their arts and crafts.

Shiva temple at Hatkoti in the Shimla Hills.

The trans-Himalaya is an extensive area of about a million sq miles (2.6 million sq.km.), a small proportion of which lies in India. Most of the Indian trans-Himalaya lies in the states of Jammu and Kashmir and neighbouring Himachal Pradesh, 69,575 sq miles (180,200 sq km) and 2,300 sq miles (6,000 sq km) respectively. The trans-Himalaya occupies 81% of Jammu and Kashmir in the districts of Kargil and Leh in Ladakh and 10.7% of Himachal Pradesh in the administrative districts of Lahaul, Spiti and part of

Kinnaur. The severe climatic conditions combined with extreme aridity create an environment in which the survival of any form of life is very difficult. Indeed, an initial impression of the area is one of great barrenness and bleakness, but it is in fact a region of high diversity in both flora and fauna.

Flora: The vegetation of this region has a high altitude desert characteristic and can be described as being dry alpine steppe. Its desert characteristic is represented in species like *Capparis spinosa, Echinopsis corni–gerus, Ephedra gerardiana*, which are commonly found throughout the region. The typical alpine steppe plants commonly found

are *Stachys tibetica, Tanecetum sps., Artemisia sps., Caragana sps., Potentilla sps.* The plant community composition is dependent on altitude, aspect and steepness of slope. The southern aspects, being drier, have a more sparse vegetation, whereas north facing slopes can have lush plant cover as the snow remains longer on these areas and thus provides more moisture critical for the plant growth. In Zanskar, where the precipitation is higher, the vegetation has more of the alpine character and is more lush. Throughout the region, 17,000 feet/5,200 m is the approximate limit for vegetation; above this elevation permanent ice and bare rocks predominate. The small valleys where snowmelt streams flow in the warmer months have natural scrub vegetation of willow *(Salix sps), Hippopohae, Myricaria* and *Rosa* and *Lonicera* species.

In the major valleys where there are human settlements, species of economic value such as poplar, willow, apricot and apple have been introduced, changing the natural landscape. The only sizeable tree indigenous to the area is the juniper, *Juniper macropoda*, which can now only be seen around monasteries and some villages where they enjoy religious protection; in a few places relic forests remain, e.g. Kargil and in the Khurna valley where there is no permanent habitation.

The high-altitude plants have adapted to their extreme environment in various ways. Most of the plants found are perennials. Due to the limited growth period of the short summers they often flower early, prior to the completion of their vegetative growth, and have brightly coloured flowers to encourage quick and successful pollination. This region, therefore, has some of the world's most attractive flowering plants like columbine *(Paraqueligia sp)*, rose, geranium, buttercups *(Ranunculus spp.)*, anenome, *Wald–hemia*, asters, *Hydeserum, Pedicularis spp.* The peak flowering season is late June and July and though alpine blooms can be seen throughout the region, two of the best places for flora are the Rangdum valley in Zanskar and the Nimaling plateau in the Hemis High Altitude National Park.

Fauna: The fauna of the trans-Himalaya is

also surprisingly diverse and contains a high number of endangered species besides. As many as 15 mammals of this region are listed in Schedules I & II of the Indian Wildlife Protection Act.

As with the vegetation, the severe climatic conditions and the high altitude have brought about special adaptations in the fauna morphologically, physiologically and in behaviour. Thick fur, long bushy tails, large nasal cavities, hibernation and considerable seasonal altitudinal migrations are examples of these. In general, animal populations of the trans-Himalaya are of relatively low density and often have extensive ranges due to the paucity of food. The open landscape means

most widespread of these is the blue sheep or Bharal, *Pseudois nayaur*, which has characteristics of both sheep and goats (making its taxonomic position debatable). The Zanskar region is the westernmost limit of its distribution in Ladakh, but east of this it is found all over the Indian trans-Himalaya. It is generally found between 11,000 ft and 16,500 ft (3,400 m and 5,000 m) and in this range has a distinct seasonal migration from lower altitudes in winter to higher elevations in summer when the snows melt. Contrary to its English name, the Bharal is not blue in colour – more of a dark fawn with a greyish tinge, while the underparts are creamy white.

Both sexes have prominent black leg

that most of the animals have developed excellent camouflage to make them inconspicuous. For these reasons it is easy to overlook their presence and visitors to the trans-Himalaya can be unaware of the richness of wildlife that surrounds them. A good pair of binoculars, a keen eye and some knowledge of what to look for and where will, however, reward the interested observer.

Ungulates: Among the ungulates found in the trans-Himalaya, wild sheep and goats form the largest group. The commonest and

markings and tails. Adult males and sometimes mature females also have a black stripe on their flank and black chests. These are more prominent in the males. The male's horns are much larger than the female's and whereas the latter's grow straight before curving slightly out, the male's curve out and back and are of a much greater girth and length. The rutting season of the blue sheep is December/January and at this time they are most likely to be seen in the rocky and precipitous terrain of their wintering areas at lower elevations. The young are born in mid June, by which time many of the males have separated into bachelor groups and moved to

Preceding pages: snow leopard. **Left**, Kiang, or Tibetan wild ass. **Above**, Bharal, or blue sheep.

the pastures at higher elevations.

An equally common ungulate and the only true goat of the region is the ibex, *Capra ibex sibirica*. However, its distribution is limited to the Western Himalaya with the Satluj gorge in Himachal Pradesh forming its eastern boundary. Like all true goats, the ibex prefer the steeper, more precipitous rocky areas which provide it with suitable escape terrain. The male ibex can be easily distinguished by its prominent beard and impressive long, scimitar-shaped horns, jagged in front. The female's horns are fairly inconspicuous, being very much smaller and smooth. Both have rich, dark brown coats, but a mature male may carry a lighter saddle

patch. Their rutting season is a little earlier than that of the blue sheep, November/December, but they show a similar altitudinal seasonal migration. The upper Suru valley around Rangdum, and the Lugnak valley in Zanskar, are prime habitats in which to view them, as unfortunately the Pin valley in Himachal Pradesh, where they are perhaps most visible, falls in a restricted area.

One of the smallest of the wild sheep and also one of the world's most endangered is the Ladakh Urial or Shapu, *Ovis orientalis vignei*, sometimes referred to as the "red sheep" due to its reddish-brown coat. Only perhaps 1,000 remain in Ladakh and their

distribution is limited to the major river valley systems of the Indus and Shyok. Human disturbance, poaching and grazing by domestic livestock thus threaten this species even more than others, which explains its endangered status. The males sport a thick long black ruff and splendid curving horns.

One of the largest sheep in the world is also found in this region – the great Tibetan sheep or Nayan, a race of argali, *Ovis ammon hodgsoni*. Except for a small population around the Ganda La above the Markha valley, the Nayan is found only in eastern Ladakh and the adjoining area of Lahaul and Spiti, preferring as it does the smooth rolling mountains characteristic of the Tibetan plateau. It is a majestic, long-legged animal. Both sexes have large white rumps and the males have huge white ruffs and massive curving horns. Found mostly above 4500m, the Nayan only descend to lower elevations in the spring to feed on the early sprouting vegetation. Only 500 or so are believed to remain in the Ladakh region.

Among the other ungulates, the Kiang or Tibetan wild ass, *Equus hermionus kiang*, is the most common. It is found in the broader, open valleys of the trans-Himalaya like those of the Changthang region. It is a little larger and darker than its close relative found in the Rann of Kutch in Gujarat. The other ungulates of this region are the Tibetan gazelle or Goa, *Procapra picticaudata*, an extremely rare animal also only found in the Changthang area; the Tibetan antelope or Chiru, *Pantholops hodgsoni*, whose status is uncertain but which may still occur seasonally in northeastern Ladakh; and the wild yak, *Bos grunniens*, which may still occur here.

Carnivores: Less visible to a visitor than the herbivores, the carnivores are nevertheless represented by a number of different species. The brown bear, *Ursus arctos isabellinus*, is the largest carnivore of this area but its range is limited to part of the Zanskar region. A second member of the bear family may be listed, the Tibetan blue bear, *Ursos arctos pruinosus*, but almost nothing is known of it and there has been no certain record of it from this area recently. By contrast, the most commonly seen carnivore which also has the widest distribution, is the Tibetan Wolf, *Canis lupus chanku*. Locally it is considered as vermin as it frequently preys on domestic sheep and goats, although it has a wide range of wild prey species varying from the large herbivores to small animals like marmots, hares and pikas. Generally seen singly or in pairs, it does not here hunt in packs like another canid member found in the trans-Himalaya, the wild dog or Phara, *Cuon alpinus alpinus*. These roam the mountains in packs of three to nine, mainly preying on the large ungulates of the area. Compared to their plains relatives, these wild dogs have much longer and thicker coats but they are also red in colour with black tail ends, a feature which clearly distinquishes them from the white-tip-tailed red fox, *Vulpes vulpes montana*. This smaller predator/scavenger is found throughout the region and may be seen

is of course the snow leopard, *Panthera uncia*. Somewhat smaller than the common leopard, with a relatively longer tail, the snow leopard has thick fur of soft grey paling to buff white on the underparts. Its diffuse rosettes and inconspicuous colour enable it to merge in perfect camouflage with its environment. This, combined with its natural shyness, low numbers (an estimated 200 for Ladakh) and the inaccessibility of its preferred terrain, make it an animal near-impossible to see. Ibex and blue sheep are its major prey species, but it also feeds on smaller animals such as marmots, hares, snowcocks etc. and on domestic livestock. Occasionally it may enter a local cattle pen, killing as many as 30 or

close to human habitation as well as in the remote areas.

The rarest of the cats known to occur in the Ladakh region is the Pallas' cat, *Felis manul*. Indeed, there has only been one confirmed record from Ladakh. The other lesser cat found here is the lynx, *Felis lynx isabellina*, easily recognised by its short tail and prominent ear tufts. It is sparsely distributed throughout the region, except in the Nubra valley where it is still said to be fairly common. Most famous and glamorous of the cats of these areas, but also distributed sparsely,

40 sheep and goats and it is then in danger of being killed itself by local villagers. Happily, increased awareness worldwide and more stringent legal protection have reduced the demand for its pelt, and commercial poaching is now rare.

Smaller Animals: There are a host of smaller mammals found in the region, some of which are rarely seen, due to their nocturnal or secretive habits. Included amongst these are the stone marten, otter, weasels, bats and voles. Others are locally abundant and can easily be sighted – the Tibetan woolly hare, *Lepus oiostolus*, the mouse hare, *Ochotona roylei* and two species of marmot, the

Left, alpine flowers. **Above**, flowering shrubs.

Himalayan marmot, *Marmota bobak*, at higher elevation and the long-tailed marmot, *Marmota caudata*, at lower heights in Zanskar.

Whereas pikas are active throughout the year, the marmots avoid the harsh winter by hibernating. The only other mam-mal of the area to do so is the brown bear. By this ploy also three or four species of lizard surprisingly manage to survive at this altitude. Many insects also amaze with their ability to adapt to this high, extreme environment.

Birds: The trans-Himalaya region has relatively few resident birds, but its numbers are swelled by numerous migrants that flock here in spring for breeding. The rarest of

raven. Also easily recognisable are the Chukor partridge and snowcocks, Himalayan and Tibetan species, Tibetan partridge and Tibetan sandgrouse. Colourful and common smaller birds to be seen in the region are several species of redstarts, rose finches, accentors, snow finches, leaf and tit warblers, wagtails and larks. Both the brown and white-breasted dippers are found here, as is the crimson-winged wallcreeper with its distinctly butterfly-like flight. For the serious birdwatcher, spring and early summer are the most rewarding times to visit, as this is the time the migrants arrive and before the the residents move to higher altitudes.

Conservation: The trans-Himalayan region,

these is the black-necked crane, which favours the marshes of east Ladakh for nesting – though hardly half a dozen pairs come, and fewer than this nest. Thousands of ducks and geese also breed in the Changthang area; many of these will stop off en route along the Indus and may be seen especially at the Shey marshes. Of the resident birds, the most conspicuous are the great golden eagle and the bearded vulture or Lammergeier, whose enormous wingspans may appear dwarfed by the huge mountain surroundings. The Corvidae are represented by the ubiquitous and noisy magpie, red- and yellow-billed choughs, common crow and the wedge-tailed

geologically one of the most recent in origin, is also a fragile ecosystem, more vulnerable than most to intrusive human activity. However, the larger part of India's trans-Himalayan region is populated mainly by adherents of Buddhism: in proscribing all killing and exhorting a harmonious relation with nature, it has encouraged the human population traditionally to husband the limited resources of the area economically and thus the natural balance. But opening of the area to the outside world in 1974, the necessary presence of the army and the increasing population have had their negative influences. Over-demand for fuel wood, an increase in livestock numbers and greater accessibility, leading to easier poaching, are some of the problems that have surfaced in recent years. Other detrimental effects may be less obvious: extensive road construction entailing labour from outside the region has indirectly caused the local extinction of some animals like hare, fox, marten and marmots, who are being trapped for meat and for the fur market of Srinagar.

In recognition of the problem, the Government has proposed a network of protected areas for this region, of which the Hemis High Altitude National Park is the first to be informed. Named after the famous monastery, this park covers the entire catchment of

between Hankar and Konmaru La. Above Yuriche and around the Ganda La, look out for the small group of Nayan, great Tibetan sheep, as well as large bachelor herds of blue sheep. The wolf may also be encountered around these high pass areas. To see the Shapu on this trek, scan the slopes to the south as you cross the Spituk plain along the Indus and around Lhatho as you begin or end your trek.

Other major areas proposed as reserves are the Karakoram National Park in north Ladakh to provide further protection especially to the snow leopard, lynx, ibex, blue sheep and Chiru; the Changthang Wildlife Sanctuary in the east for the protection of breeding

the Rumbak, Alam and Markha valleys, covering approximately 600 sq.km., and further proposed extensions will increase it to more than 3,000 sq.km. The Markha valley trek through the centre of this park is one of the most popular for foreign visitors.

Although winter is in many ways the better time for wildlife viewing, summer trekkers may still expect to see large herds of blue sheep, many marmots, hares, snowcocks and pikas, especially on the Nimaling plateau

Left, hill fox, and above, musk deer; both are making a comeback thanks to conservation efforts.

migratory birds such as the black-necked crane, geese, ducks, grebes, gulls and other waterfowl as well as gazelle, Nayan and the Kiang. In southern Ladakh, providing a buffer to the Hemis National Park, is the proposed Lugnak Wildlife Sanctuary and Kanji Wildlife Reserve, both excellent areas for ibex especially. In upper Suru valley, the Rangdum Wildlife Sanctuary will provide added protection to the brown bear, snow leopard and ibex. In Himachal Pradesh an area of 675 sq km, the Pin Valley National Park was declared in 1987; an area of typical Tibetan cold desert in north east Spiti has also been proposed for further protection.

• Taxkorgan

AFGHANISTAN

HINDUKUSH MOUNTAINS

HINDURAJ MOUNTAINS

Thui Ah

Kilik
Dawan
Mintaka
Pass
Parpik
Pass

Khunjerab
Pass

Kampire
Dior

Disteghil
Sar

Kanjut
Sar

AGHIL MOUNT

Hunza
(Baltit)
Altit
Rakaposhi

Aghil Pass

C

Gilgit

Indus

K²

Gasherbrum ▲ Ma
I

Masherbrum

Saltore
Kangr

Chilas

Nanga
Parbat

DEOSAI MOUNTAINS

I

N

D

PAKISTAN

G
R
E

DEOSAI PLAINS

JAMMU

AND

LADA

Kupwara

Bandipura
Haramukh

Garhi Habibullah
Khan

Muzaffarabad

Wular Lake
Gangbal

Dras
Shargol
Mulbekh
Khalsi

Tarbela

Jhelum

Baramula 1A

Sonamarg

Umba
La

Sas

Havelian

Uri

Dachigam

Amarnath
Cave

II
Rasi
La

Lamayuru

Alchi
Gomp

Haripur

Khilanmarg

*Dal
Lake*

Kolahoi
Glacier

Nun Kun

Kanji La

Zaskar

Hasan Abdal
(Punjab Saheb)

Gulmarg
SRINAGAR

Pahalgam

Ma

Taxila

Punch

Yusmarg

Awantipura

Martand

Pensi
La

Karsha

ISLAMABAD

Rawalpindi

Achabal

Anantnag

Daksum
Kokarnag
Verinag

Zunkul
Umasi
La

Sani
Padum

Jawahar II
Tunnel

Banihal

Kishtwar

Bardun

Gujar
Khan

Mangla
Mirpur

Naoshera

Chenab

Chakwal

Jhelum

Riasi

Kud
Batoti

Katra
Vaishnodevi

Akhnur

Udhampur

Jammu

Ramnagar

H
I
M
A
L
A

Gujarat

Bilaur
Basoli

Chamba

Key

Sialkot

1A
Kathua

PUNJAB

Nurpur

Dalhousie

Ravi

HIMACHAL

Dharmshala

Manali

Gujranwala

15
Gurdaspur

Kangra

Palampur

Kullu

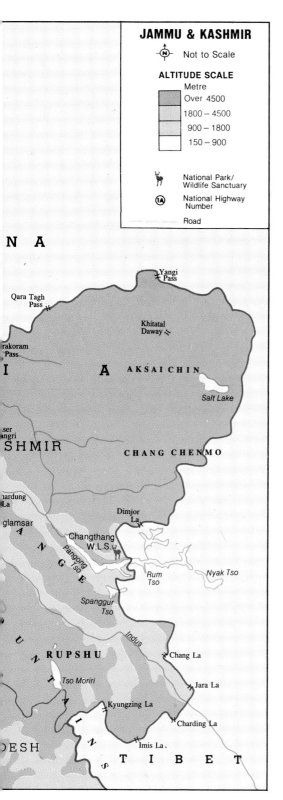

JAMMU & KASHMIR

-N- Not to Scale

ALTITUDE SCALE

Metre

Over 4500

1800 – 4500

900 – 1800

150 – 900

National Park/
Wildlife Sanctuary

National Highway
Number

Road

N A

Yangi
Pass

Qara Tagh
Pass

Khitatal
Daway

rakoram
Pass

I A AKSAI CHIN

Salt Lake

ser
angri

SHMIR CHANG CHENMO

ardung
La

glamsar

Changthang
W.L.S.

N G Pangong Tso E

Dimjor
La

Rum
Tso

Nyak Tso

Spanggur
Tso

Indus

U

RUPSHU Chang La

Tso Moriri

Jara La

Kyungzing La

Charding La

)ESH Imis La.

T I B E T

JAMMU AND KASHMIR

As the Jammu-Srinagar highway crosses the Banihal Pass to enter the valley of Kashmir, a roadsign confidently proclaims the proximity of paradise across the Jawahar tunnel. This rather fanciful assertion may be a reaffirmation of a Mughal emperor's feelings for the beautiful valley where he spent his summers, but it carries in its conviction some resonance of truth. Despite the well-worn tourist clichés, a visit to this idyllic Himalayan lake basin is indeed a matchless experience.

The alpine meadows of Gulmarg, Tangmarg and Yusmarg are prime attractions in all seasons, as is Pahalgam, the popular resort on the banks of the Lidder. Those who shun crowds prefer to spend time in the more secluded enclaves of Daksum and Verinag. There is a selection of lesser known places to consider for an undisturbed sojourn in picture-postcard countryside.

The trans-Himalayan journey to Ladakh and Zanskar is an odyssey in itself. Today, they can be approached by road through Kashmir, by the classic shepherd routes used to make a shorter, more arduous crossing of the ranges through the land of the Dogras, and then by the high pastures frequented by the nomadic Gujjars and Bakarwals. Lying within reach of the towering summits of the Great Himalayan range, these pastoral meadows have been the backdrop for a nomadic lifestyle that has continued unchanged for several centuries. Even now, in the warm months of the year, a tired trekker will pause awhile at the summer home of these transmigratory tribes for a sip of fresh buttermilk before carrying on along a trail that has been travelled by thousands before him.

Preceding pages: Stok Nullah, Ladakh; barley fields, Lahaul; Toshe Maidan, Kashmir; Hari Parbat across Dal Lake, Srinagar.

JAMMU

The Hindu goddess, Vaishno Devi, had her abode in the Trikuta mountains, at a place called Adkunwari, Eternal Virgin. When the demon Bhairo wanted to marry her and tried to force her to submit to his wishes, the goddess fled uphill to a cave, which later came to be known as her Darbar or court.

To this day some 2.4 million pilgrims climb up the Trikuta mountains every year from the village of **Katra** to visit the cave (5,577 ft/1,700 m) where Mata (mother) Vaishno Devi had sought shelter, placing it among the world's most frequented places of pilgrimage (and one of the country's richest shrines).

But apart from this short eight mile (12 km) trek, and treks in Kishtwar (which attract a few thousand trekkers, mostly from the West, every year) the vast, mountainous province of Jammu receives next to no tourists, Indian or foreign. The reason is that very little is

known about it. Most people tend to confuse the city of Jammu with the sprawling province spread over six districts. While the city (1,400 ft/426 m above msl) in the foothills of the Shivaliks is only slightly cooler than Delhi, the province of the same name is mostly mountainous and temperate in climate.

The earliest references to the region are in the Vedas in which the cave of Mata Vaishno Devi is mentioned. Evidence of ancient Indo-Greek settlements has been found in Ambaran and Mendhar (the latter thought to be named after Menander, the Greek general). The first kingdom based in Jammu city, however, was founded as recently as the 9th century AD, by King Jambulochan, after whom the region takes its name.

When the Mughals set out to conquer Kashmir in the 1580s they used the Mughal Route which passes through Rajouri, a north-western district of Jammu, and the entire province came under their sway. When the empire began to disintegrate, the then chieftain

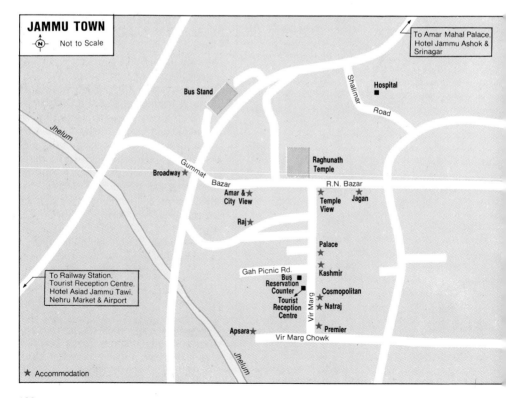

JAMMU TOWN
Not to Scale

To Amar Mahal Palace,
Hotel Jammu Ashok &
Srinagar

Bus Stand

Shalimar

Hospital

Road

Jhelum

Gummat

Broadway

Raghunath
Temple

Bazar

R.N. Bazar

Amar &
City View

Temple
View

Jagan

Raj

Palace

To Railway Station,
Tourist Reception Centre,
Hotel Asiad Jammu Tawi,
Nehru Market & Airport

Gah Picnic Rd.

Kashmir

Bus
Reservation
Counter

Cosmopolitan

Tourist
Reception
Centre

Vir Marg

Natraj

Apsara

Premier

Vir Marg Chowk

Jhelum

★ Accommodation

(and later, Raja) of Jammu, Ranjit Dev (1742-80), declared Jammu an independent kingdom. However, this independence was short-lived.

In the first half of the 19th century, following a military setback in 1807, the Dogra rulers of Jammu briefly came under Maharaja Ranjit Singh of Lahore. As Lahore's hold on Jammu loosened in the mid-19th century the Dogra army, led by the legendary General Zorawar Singh, started moving northward through Kishtwar to conquer Ladakh, Baltistan and western Tibet. (The last mentioned did not stay under them for long, though).

The 1846 Treaty of Amritsar with the British gave Maharaja Gulab Singh of Jammu control of modern India's largest princely state, Jammu and Kashmir (which included Ladakh and Baltistan). Hari Singh, his descendant, was the last Maharaja of this state when in 1947 it acceded to the Union of India. Hari Singh's son, Dr Karan Singh, a scholar, has been a minister in the Union Cabinet and India's ambassador to the USA. His palace in Jammu is now a museum, with one wing converted into a hotel.

A number of minor Rajas, sometimes with kingdoms no larger than a dozen villages, served under the Maharaja. **Basohli** (2,154 ft/657 m) is one of the best known of these subordinate kingdoms, chiefly because of its celebrated school of miniature painting, its palace (now in ruins) and its vivid nine-day Ram Lila (enactment during the festival of Dussehra of the story of the Ramayana) on several sites scattered about the town, including the palace and the lake next to it.

On the tenth day, people trek up to the hill pass of Banjal Galla (6,500 ft/1,980 m), to witness an animal sacrifice that the Hindus of the plains would condemn as pagan.

Beyond the Galla is an exquisite valley called **Banni** (mean elevation around 4,300 ft/1,300 m) that trekkers are only now beginning to discover. Till 1990 the only way to get there was on foot, so Banni has retained a unique ambience which includes colourful fairs, mystical medicine men, merry songs and distinc-

tive (i.e. liberal) marital customs.

From here one can branch off westward towards the dense, silent deodar forests of the **Lohai Malhar** region (mean elevation 6,500 ft/2,100 m) and thence to the tiny erstwhile kingdoms of Billawar (with its ancient temple, said to dislodge a stone each time a ruler is about to die), Bhaddu and Ramkot, and the Mansar lake.

Or one can trek up to the meadows of Sarthal (7,872 ft/2,306 m), climb the Chatter Galla (9,928 ft/3,027 m) and descend through thick, shaded forests to **Bhaderwah**.

Apart from its own natural charm (and those of its mostly literate people), Bhaderwah (5,427 ft) is an important junction; from here you can either take the bus to Doda and on to the Jammu-Srinagar National Highway, or the bus to Kishtwar. Using the town as your base you can trek to Padri Galli (9,200 ft), Kailash/Vas Kund (14,000 ft) where a pilgrimage takes place in early August), the green Chinta Valley, and Jaai, the anglers' paradise.

ck crystal
nga at
ambireswar
mple,
mmu.

Kishtwar (5,450 ft) is surrounded by waterfalls, the sacred shrines of the Hazrats (saints) Zainshah Sahib, Israr-ud-din Sahib and Akhiyar Sahib, and the temple of the 18-armed Sarthala Devi. It is also the starting point for journeys to Srinagar – motorable by two routes, as well as by foot through the Margan Pass – and to Zanskar (via two possible trekking routes).

Three well-known hill resorts are within reach from the Jammu-Srinagar National Highway: **Batote** (5,500 ft/ 1,676m), **Patni Top** (9,000 ft/286 m), almost always covered with mist, and **Kud**.

Heading towards Jammu City, the highway passes the Chenaini valley (3,500 ft/1,066 m), a tiny state with a large but rustic palace; a detour from here leads to **Mantalai** (5,500 ft/1,676 m) where Swami Dhirendra Braha-machari has his ultra-modern Aparna Ashram. Further ahead on the same detour is the Sudh Mahadev temple, displaying portions of what is said to be the Hindu God Shiva's trident, where a famous annual fair is held. From here some exciting treks go through dense forests to Majorhi and the kingdom of Ramnagar (whose palace is said to have been decorated by European artists) via either Basantgarh (6,717 ft/2,048 m) or the exquisite Charhi Bungalow (6,000 ft), located amidst a silent deodar forest.

Past the large cantonment of Udhampur on the way to Jammu lies Domel, from where we can take a detour to Katra, the base camp for the trek to Mata Vaishno Devi's durbar. Reasi, further ahead of Katra on this detour, is a favoured starting point for treks to Gul Gulabgarh (6,500 ft), Rajouri and Kashmir. Gulabgarh is famous for its equestrian statues.

Jammu is known as the City of Temples, especially for the Ranbireshwar, the largest Shiva temple in North India, and the Raghunath temple. The fort, temple and park complex at Bahu, the two museums and the Mahamaya City Forest are its other major attractions. The temples of Parmandal, the ruins at Babbaur, the temples with wall-paint-

Late nineteenth century Ama Mahal Palac and Museum Jammu, erstwhile winter residence of the Dogra ruler.

ings near the Jhiri fairgrounds and the Tawi river to the north are some of the spots of interest around the city. Indo-Greek artefacts discovered in nearby Ambaran are now mostly in museums.

To get to Rajouri and Poonch one has to leave Jammu by the Akhnoor road, past the famous forts of Akhnoor, built in the 18th century by the Dogras, and Chingus ('intestines'), where the entrails of the 17th century Mughal Emperor Jehangir were buried to prevent putrefaction. Also en route are the hot-water springs of Tatta Pani, the shrine of the sufi mystic Peer Baba at Sunderbani and the rock castle at Rachwa with frescoes of the Poonch school.

At Rajouri (3,094 ft/943 m) proper the hilltop Dhannidhar fort is the sole attraction. However, the town comes alive on Friday afternoons when colourfully attired Muslims with beards dyed red come down from the neighbouring villages to offer prayers. We are now on the fabled medieval Mughal Route. The powerful Sufi shrine at Shahdra Sharief, the largest of its kind in Jammu prov-

ince, is nearby. So are Thannamandi, where handicrafts are made of the rare chikri wood; the pass at the picturesque Dera ki Galli (7,022 ft/2,140 m); and the riverside Baflayaz (5,200 ft/1,580 m).

From Baflayaz one can trek to the 200 feet Noorie Chham waterfall at Behram Galla (8,000 ft/2,400 m) where Jehangir's consort, the Empress Noor Jehan, is said to have bathed, and to the beautiful Surankot Valley.

Poonch (3,300 ft/1,009 m) and Suran-kot can also be reached by bus or car from Baflayaz. Poonch was perhaps the largest autonomous kingdom within the confederacy headed by the Jammu Dogras. It has three major palaces, known for their woodwork.

Resorts near Poonch included **Loran** (6,000 ft/1,829 m), the site of an ancient kingdom, famous for its forests, waterfalls and the Amarnath temple, Mendhar, with its Mughal maidan (meadows), huge carved stones, monuments and pastoral folksongs; and Bhimber Galli (5,500 ft/1,676 m), known for its forests and streams.

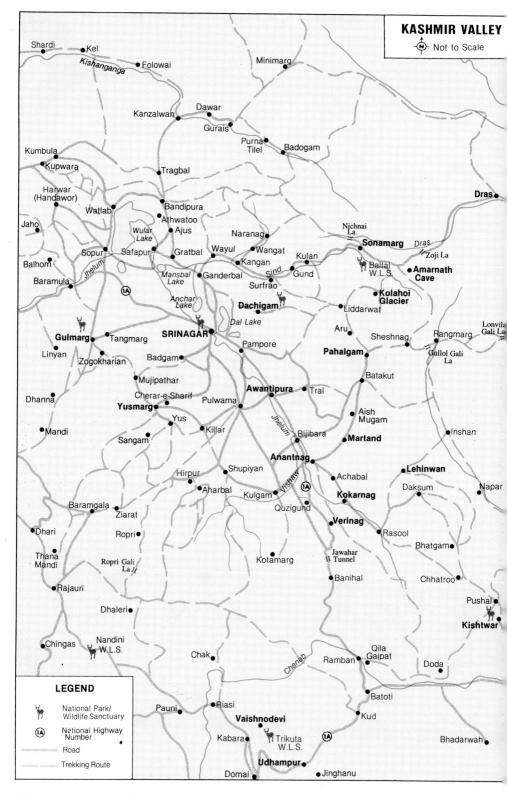

KASHMIR VALLEY
Not to Scale

Shardi
Kel
Folowai
Kishanganga
Minimarg

Kanzalwan
Dawar
Gurais
Purna
Tilel
Badogam

Kumbula
Kupwara
Tragbal

Harwar
(Handawor)
Watlab
Bandipura
Athwatoo
Jaho
Wular
Lake
Ajus
Naranag
Dras

Nichnai
La
Sopur
Safapur
Gratbal
Wayul
Wangat
Kulan
Sonamarg
Dras
Balhom
Kangan
Zoji La
Baramula
Jhelum
Mansbal
Lake
Ganderbal
Sind
Gund
Baltal
W.L.S.
Amarnath
Cave
Surfrao
1A
Anchar
Lake
Dachigam
Kolahoi
Glacier
Liddarwat

Dal Lake
Aru
Lonvila
Gali La
Gulmarg
Tangmarg
SRINAGAR
Pampore
Sheshnag
Rangmarg
Linyan
Zogokharian
Badgam
Pahalgam
Gullol Gali
La
Mujipathar
Batakut
Cherar-e-Sharif
Pulwama
Awantipura
Tral
Dhanna
Yusmarg
Aish
Mugam
Yus
Killar
Inshan
Mandi
Sangam
Bijibara
Martand
Anantnag
Hirpur
Shupiyan
Lehinwan
Aharbal
Achabal
Daksum
Napar
Baramgala
Kulgam
Vishaw
1A
Kokarnag
Ziarat
Quzigund
Dhari
Ropri
Verinag
Rasool
Bhatgam
Thana
Mandi
Ropri Gali
La
Kotamarg
Jawahar
Tunnel
Rajauri
Banihal
Chhatroo
Dhaleri
Pushal
Kishtwar
Chingas
Nandini
W.L.S.
Chak
Qila
Gaipat
Ramban
Doda

LEGEND
Pauni
Riasi
Batoti
National Park/
Wildlife Sanctuary
Vaishnodevi
Kud
1A
National Highway
Number
Kabara
Trikuta
W.L.S.
1A
Bhadarwah
Road
Udhampur
Trekking Route
Domai
Jinghanu

108

SRINAGAR

The capital of the state of Jammu and Kashmir, Srinagar lies more or less at the center of the Valley of Kashmir at an altitude of 5,675 feet (1,730 m). It is the entry point into the Valley for travellers by air, and the base for holidays in Kashmir: excursions to resorts outside the city all start from Srinagar, since no roads link one resort with another. Srinagar is almost implausibly beautiful – a river, three lakes, a ring of mountains, a quaint old city with a medieval flavour, terraced rice fields and tiny mud-walled villages.

The Old City: The original straggling city of Srinagar lies at the foot of Hari Parbat hill. With the river Jhelum and its network of tributaries forming the focal point, the Old City with its hump-backed bridges and tall brick houses has scarcely altered over the past few centuries.

In this part of Srinagar, the construction of the houses (burnt brick and wooden beams) and the dress of the people (baggy knee-length smocks worn over pyjamas) all strongly suggest Central Asian influences. It comes as no surprise to learn that merchants from Central Asia used to visit the Old City even up to the first few decades of the present century.

But if shops lined from floor to ceiling with copper utensils suggest a bazaar in far-off Bokhara, other aspects are peculiar only to Kashmir – its tracery of waterways, for example, teeming with wooden barges in which people live. *Doongas*, as these barges are called, are a throwback to when they were used as a means of transport for commodities from rural Kashmir to the trading centre of Srinagar. Both sides of the Jhelum all along the Old City are crowded with the houses of former merchants, who only had to peer out of a window to see if their consignment had arrived on time.

Today, with the advent of motorable roads and vehicular traffic, boats are no longer used as a means of transport, but those who plied them still live on the water as their forefathers did. Some

areas, notably those around Gow Kadal and Kani Kadal, are so crowded with barges, that the waterway is a series of sloping shingled roofs, with rosy matrons serenely picking over spinach greens on handkerchief-sized sundecks.

In the confines of the Old City, where space is at a premium, most houses are earthy brown – the same colour, in fact, as the river and its barges. This gives the cityscape a curiously monochromatic quality, and it is a closer scrutiny that yields interesting details. Mosaic tiles decorate houses around Zaina Kadal and at Makhdum Sahib. The back streets of Rainawari that line the Dal Lake are nicely embellished with wooden fretwork window screens and projecting balconies.

One recurring theme around the Old City is its craft connection. Newly embroidered tapestry rugs are hung out to dry on the railings of bridges; shawls are washed in the none-too-clean waters of the Jhelum; through the windows of a house comes the chant of a carpet design being sung out by the master weaver

to his apprentices. Zadibal, a locality in the bowels of the Old City, is the stronghold of papier mâché painters. Here, freshly painted vases can be seen perched on windowsills to dry. Gojwara, not far from the Jama Masjid, is the district where most of the city's *namdas* are made, woollen felt rugs gaily embroidered with folk artsy designs. On a sunny day, rug makers hang their creations on such unlikely places as the wall surrounding the Jama Masjid, and over tombstones in the local graveyard.

Frequently, horse-drawn carts are piled with bales of embroidery; cyclists carry silk carpets on their handlebars with easy nonchalance; a nondescript bundle of mousy brown fabric perched carelessly on a scooter could well be the exorbitant *shahtoosh* on its way to the embroiderers.

Tiny shops no larger than stalls on Nallah Mar Road and in Zaina Kadal sell skeins of silk and wool yarn for carpet as well as tapestry-weaving. There is another kind of embroidery, highly prized in Kashmir, yet seldom noticed outside it – *tilla* work, the silver embroidery that is done on the *phiren*, the rather shapeless garment that every matron wears over her baggy trousers. The embroiderer's hook creates a design in silver thread on the yoke and cuffs. *Tilla* workers are scattered all over the Old City, but there is a whole row of them in Khankahi Mohalla. Each shop hangs its finished work out on display, and the little street is dazzling with its rows of garments flashing with silver embroidery.

The Old City's shops are unique. Bakery shops are mere windowsills piled with a variety of Kashmiri breads. Some are shaped like buns and sprinkled with sesame or poppy seeds, others unleavened, and still others resemble shortbreads of an English high tea. Shops selling copperware do a roaring trade: local households use a bemusing range of bowls instead of plates; cups are stored in a copper basket; banquets are eaten off gigantic copper plates; and every family, however poor, boasts of at least one copper samovar and one

The Jhelum flows throug the old city Srinagar.

HOUSEBOATS

Marie D'Souza

Srinagar's most popular form of accommodation, houseboats, are far removed from the conventional hotel. Houseboats have no room numbers, room keys or menu cards; the guest is expected to chalk out the day's menu. Most have between two and four bedrooms, which means that a maximum of eight persons can occupy one houseboat. The glowing cedar wood out of which they are fashioned underscores the warmth and cosiness that these floating holiday cottages symbolise.

When, at the end of last century, the British came to Kashmir, they were forbidden by law to buy land on which to build houses. Nobody said anything about the water, however; so they set about imitating the half-amphibious families of Srinagar whose homes were on the lakes, converting *doongas* into homes fit for an Englishman: More than a century later, the keynote of the Srinagar houseboat is still the chintzy charm of a country cottage, complete with deep armchairs, formal dining areas and pine-panelled bedrooms.

Some things have changed in the interval, for houseboats are now of varying standards of comfort, from the downright hedonistic to the spartan, to cater to the budgets of a cross-section of holiday makers.

Locations, too, vary widely. Houseboats are strung out in sections of the Dal and Nagin lakes and along the banks of the Jhelum. In general, the river has less luxurious boats, the pristine Nagin principally deluxe boats, and the Dal offers the whole gamut. Within the Dal are areas that overlook the Boulevard, the most fashionable of Srinagar's roads, but there are other locations too, much quieter, overlooking panoramas of lotus plantations. Still other areas are crowded with shops that cater variously to tourists or locals, where the lack of solitude is compensated for by atmosphere.

There are a few common features for every houseboat, be it the top grade 'deluxe' class or the bottom of the rung 'D' class: the daily tariff includes three meals of the visitor's choice, as well as free boat rides from the houseboat to the nearest landing jetty and vice versa. Every houseboat has an attendant on call, more or less round the clock.

Houseboats provide a sybaritic holiday; there is no need to do a great deal unless you're feeling energetic. Simply laze away the day on the sun deck, or pick up a book from the assortment left by former visitors. When the weather is fine, a day-long *shikara* ride is a good idea.

copper *hookah* base.

The seven bridges of the Jhelum serve as landmarks, postal addresses, clotheslines, even informal bazars, as street vendors line up against the sides with an assortment of wares from roasted chestnuts to dried fish. Most of the seven large bridges and all the smaller ones are made in the same cantilevered style, using durable deodar wood.

The Fort: One of the few forts in the Valley was built in the early years of the 18th century, by an Afghan Governor, Atta Mohammad Khan, during Kashmir's Afghan occupation.

The fort, crumbling and dilapidated from the inside, is Srinagar's chief landmark, and can be seen from most parts of the city. The prospect of the hill caught the attention of Emperor Akbar when he conquered the Valley in 1586. A royal city was built containing a palace for himself, apartments for the ladies of the royal household, and quarters for his entourage, but nothing remains of it today. What has endured is the wall that surrounds the hill, commissioned in 1590 more as a famine relief measure than as a way of enclosing the new city. Akbar's wall has three main gates, the most imposing of which is the **Kathi Darwaza** near Rainawari. This gate bears a Persian inscription commemorating the year of construction. The two other gates are Makhdumi Darwaza near the shrine of Makhdum Sahib, and the slightly more difficult to find Singhin Darwaza at Hawal.

Emperor Akbar's great-grandson, Dara Shikoh, was also inspired sufficiently by the Hari Parbat hill to construct on its slopes a mosque in memory of his Sufi teacher, Akhund Mulla Shah. Built of smooth blocks of grey limestone, it stands in its own quiet garden, surrounded by a low stone wall with niches. This jewel of a mosque, perfect in its proportions, is largely unvisited except by a handful of locals who gather every evening in its garden, an oasis of tranquility overlooking the sea of rooftops of the Old City. Nearby, the shrine of Makhdum Sahib, reputed to have effected miraculous cures, draws

The Jama Masjid, Friday Mosque, is redolent of i Central Asia ancestry.

112

crowds from all over the city. The view of the Old City from this shrine is excellent, dominated by the lofty proportions of the Jama Masjid.

At the foot of the hill, just outside the Kathi Darwaza, is the **gurudwara** of Guru Hargobind Singhji, the sixth Guru of the Sikhs. Chatti Padshahi ('the sixth reign'), as he is called, reportedly visited Kashmir during the reign of Emperor Aurangzeb, and every spot that he stopped at to preach has been honoured with a gurudwara.

A ten minute walk from the shrine of Makhdum Sahib leads to **Jama Masjid** – the Friday Mosque – the nerve centre of this part of Srinagar. With the same dun-coloured walls as the buildings that hem it in on all sides, it commands attention with the sheer expanse of its walls and its soaring steeples. Each of its walls is pierced by an immense door leading into vast shaded prayer halls supported by columns of deodar trunks. Four steeples rise from the roof, one above each door. Elsewhere in the Islamic world, mosques are mostly crowned by domes and minarets. Throughout the Valley, on the other hand, mosques and shrines are surmounted by pagoda-like steeples. The Jama Masjid was built in 1398, destroyed three times thereafter and rebuilt, the last time being a faithful reproduction of the original building.

Before the arrival of Islam in the Valley, during Hindu rule, stone was the medium of construction. With the influence of Islam, this changed to burnt brick – of which the Jama Masjid is made – supported with timber beams, or timber alone. This has continued into the present times, the only exception being a few examples of Mughal architecture, one of them the **Patthar Masjid**. Built by Empress Nur Jehan on the banks of the Jhelum, this mosque has all the elegant grace and simplicity of the other Mughal mosque – Akhund Mulla Sahib. At that time, Patthar Masjid could, perhaps, be sighted from a distance as it was approached by boat, but today it is lost in the welter of three-storeyed houses that cluster around it.

Opposite the river, the shrine of **Shah**

Hamdan dominates the horizon, as its steeple soars above the straggling skyline of the riverfront. Shah Hamdan came to Kashmir from Hamdan in Iran first in 1370 and twice thereafter, converting much of the population from Hinduism to Islam. The spot where he perched by the river Jhelum, between Fateh Kadal and Zaina Kadal, is where a shrine has been erected in his memory. Made entirely of wood carved into simple yet striking geometric patterns, the shrine is decorated on the inside from floor to ceiling with papier mâché painting. Although women and non-Muslim men are not allowed inside, a visit to this shrine is certainly worth the effort.

Just down the road is **Zaina Kadal**, the fourth bridge near which is one of the city's enigmas: a red brick edifice surmounted by five domes, the only domed structure of antiquity in the whole of Kashmir. Some sources believe it to have been built by Sultan Zain-ul-Abidin, as a tomb for his mother. Others maintain that it was actually a Hindu

temple.

Kashmir's best loved ruler, Sultan Zain-ul-Abidin (1420-70) was from the first dynasty of Muslim rulers in the Valley. It was Badshah (as he is affectionately referred to) who brought in many crafts that to this day form the mainstay of Kashmir's economy. Badshah is credited with another innovation – the building of the first-ever bridge across the Jhelum, named after him Zaina Kadal. Before the 14th century, when stone was the medium of construction, citizens used to ford the river by a pontoon bridge – a row of boats lashed together. Subsequent bridges were named in turn after those who commissioned them.

Srinagar's only stone bridge is a quaint hump-backed one in the backwaters of Rainawari. Called **Puz Mohalla Mughal** bridge, it was obviously built by the Mughals. Each of its three arches bears an inscription in Persian. Beside **Saffa Kadal** stands a long, low two-storeyed building of no particular architectural merit. Until the 1920s

Yarkandi Sarai, as this building is called, was a sort of guest house for the merchants from Yarkand who would stop over in Srinagar. It was a long journey over high mountain passes, with yaks laden with dainty porcelain bowls. When the merchants arrived in Srinagar, in their long striped coats of many colours, their yaks would be sent to graze in the nearby Idgah, a vast open tract of land, and the merchants would settle down for a few days at Yarkandi Sarai, and sell their bowls in the bazaar around Saffa Kadal.

Near Khanyar, the crossroads that mark the beginning of the Old City, is the tomb called **Rozabal**. Exactly who is buried there remains a mystery, but it is widely held to be the grave of Jesus Christ. The shrine, a small, unpretentious shelter in a bylane off the main street, has been the subject of much speculation. Scholars claim that Jesus Christ visited Kashmir twice – once in the years preceding his public life, and the second time after his crucifixion, when his tormentors presumed him

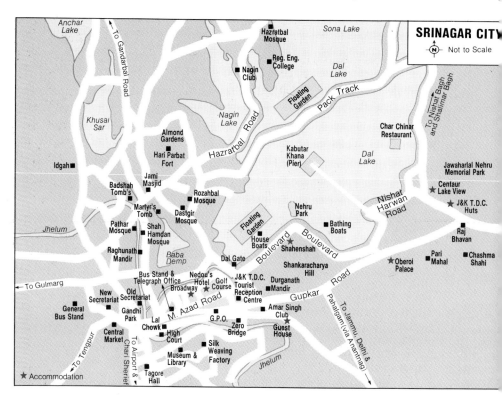

114

dead.

On the periphery of the Dal Lake is Kashmir's newest mosque – **Hazratbal**. Its gleaming white marble facade, surmounted by a single dome and minaret, is reflected in the waters of the lake. The mosque enshrines a relic – a single hair, believed to be that of the Prophet Mohammed – which is exhibited to the public a few times in the year, and on these days as well as every Friday, the afternoon prayer draws several thousand worshippers, some by boat. On such days, the area surrounding the mosque is turned into an impromptu bazaar, complete with streetside dentists and vegetable vendors.

The oldest known site in Srinagar is that of **Shankaracharya temple**. Atop a hill to the south-east of the city, the site, if not the temple itself, is believed to date from 2,500 BC when the original sandstone structure was built by King Sandiman. The philosopher Shankaracharya visited Kashmir about ten centuries ago and stayed at this hilltop site. A good motorable road leads to the top, just short of the temple. The climb is worth it, if only for the panorama of the city below.

The **Shri Pratap Singh Museum**, known locally as SPS Museum, is located between Raj Bagh and Lal Mandi, by the side of the Jhelum. Many of its exhibits are the Valley's handicrafts, of which woven *kani* shawls are the most notable. However, the museum is worth a visit chiefly on account of the sculptures from old Hindu temples and archaeological finds from various sites all over Kashmir.

Parks and gardens: Srinagar's best known and loved Mughal legacy are its splendid gardens. They are visited by tourists to recapture the legendary romance associated with them. Local families picnic in them to savour fresh air and greenery, so conspicuously absent in the Old City.

From 1586, when Kashmir was conquered by the Mughals, they were enchanted with its beauty. Paradise, repeats the Koran, is a lush garden watered by flowing streams. It seems as if

eft, Nishat agh, laid ut by the mperor hah Jahan the early 7th century. ight, the rnate terior of a eluxe ouseboat.

KASHMIRI FOOD

Because of Kashmir's geographical location, many of the components of its culture have been derived from Central Asia and Iran. The *wazwan* is one of these. It is essentially the term for a banquet served at all festive occasions, prepared by the male members of a community of cooks. The banquet has a few dozen, mainly meat-based, dishes in his repertoire, and between eight and thirty dishes can appear on the menu depending on the grandeur and formality of the occasion.

In a world of ever-changing values, the *wazwan's* popularity remains undiminished; one of the chief reasons for this is its versatility. The *waza* eschews the conventional trappings of a kitchen; the banquet is prepared over log fires in the courtyard of a house or in the open. This means that an outdoor excursion can be crowned with a sumptuous *wazwan,* many miles from Srinagar. The traditional *wazwan* is eaten off large platters around each of which four persons sit cross-legged on the floor, but state banquets hosted for visiting dignitaries are served buffet style. Many restaurants in Srinagar include a handful of popular *wazwan* dishes on their menus. For those who are unlikely to get invited to a full-blown *wazwan,* this is a good opportunity to sample the ever-popular **tabak maaz** – crispy fried spare ribs, **yakhni** – chicken or mutton curd-based gravy, and **ristas** or finely pounded meatballs.

By far the largest number of *wazwans,* however, are held in Kashmiri homes to celebrate engagements, weddings and births. The family *waza* is sent for, and the menu discussed. There are certain dishes so popular that only the most foolhardy host would dare leave them out. Mutton, all-important for the

feast, will be bought from the butcher and carried along in its live form by the *waza* and his entourage.

On the day of the banquet, the host family gather together their stock of copper platters and domed lids. Each Muslim family of status owns a few dozen, although they may be used only once a year. Meanwhile, the cooks outside in the courtyard go about their specific duties with the efficiency of an army.

Within a few hours, a mountain of rice and a bewildering assortment of gravy-based dishes are simmering on the log fires. One of the assistants stirs and tastes each with an oversized ladle. When he is satisfied, a sampling is brought gravely to the *waza.* All is well if he nods his head; if a dish doesn't pass muster, the *waza's* reputation is at stake.

When the guests arrive, they are seated in the Kashmiri equivalent of a banquet hall, men and women in separate rooms. The *wazwan* starts with rice and roasts – chicken, spare ribs and *kababs*, and goes on to an assortment of chicken and mutton gravy dishes thickened variously with curd, tomatoes and onions. Each dish has its assigned place in the *wazwan*; to start with *ristas* would amount to serving meat before fish at a formal Western banquet. The sign of appreciation is the amount of food left on the platter. Not to leave any indicates that the host has been too frugal. Invariably, the last dish to be served is a giant meat-ball supposed to be shared by all four seated around one platter. This signifies the banquet is over.

Not even the most accomplished housewife can ever duplicate the flavour and taste of a meal cooked by a *waza.* Few would attempt something so sacrilegious. The consummate skill of the master chefs is lauded by every Kashmiri who dreams of the next banquet he will attend ...

one emperor after another immediately associated Kashmir with Paradise, and sought to strengthen the connection between the two. History informs us that by the end of the Mughal rule, there were no fewer than 777 gardens around the Dal.

Today, the most often visited three are **Cheshmashahi, Nishat** and **Shalimar**, more or less along the same road. Cheshmashahi from (*cheshma*, spring, and *shahi*, imperial) is the first reached from town, perched on a hillside overlooking the lake. Shah Jahan, who laid out this garden in 1632, probably planned it to contrast with Shalimar and Nishat. Built on a series of steep terraces, Cheshmashahi is the smallest of the three gardens, whose source of water is a spring with delicious mineral water.

A road winds past Cheshmashahi up three kilometres to **Pari Mahal**. Built originally as a Sufi place of retreat, Fairies' Palace, as Pari Mahal translates, is full of secret nooks and crumbling stairways leading onto terraces.

As a place for spiritual discourses, Pari Mahal is unsurpassed for its inspired location and secluded recesses. Each of the terraces is planted with beds of flowers, and the exposed stone surface of the structure turns the colour of honey when the sun touches it. This garden is Dara Shikoh's other architectural contribution to Srinagar. Like the mosque on Hari Parbat Hill, it was built for his Sufi teacher, Akhund Mulla Shah.

Nishat Garden's masterful plan is apparent from the topmost of its twelve terraces – spacious lawns, formally laid out flower beds, a central watercourse, and in the distance, the backdrop of the Dal. Nishat's series of side gardens are planted with stately trees.

Further along the same road is **Shalimar**, laid out by the Emperor Jehangir himself. Like Nishat, it is located by the Dal and backed by hills, but there the resemblance ends, because Shalimar has fewer and shallower terraces, and its pavilions are its focal point. The march of time and less-than-sensitive restoration has not been kind

to Shalimar's pavilions, but one of them still has papier mâché painting on the ceiling.

Nissim Bagh, the Garden of Breezes near Hazratbal mosque, is the Emperor Akbar's legacy. Now part of the Kashmir University campus, Nissim Bagh as it exists today, is an enormous grove of chinar trees. Across the road is a fragment of a garden, enclosed by a stone wall. Perhaps once a part of Nissim Bagh, the garden is now private property but the owner, an ardent conservationist, is pleased to show visitors around.

Dal and Nagin: Just as Venice is never thought of without its waterways, Srinagar is unimaginable without the Dal and the adjoining Nagin lakes. They are not merely a picturesque body of water that forms the focus of the surrounding city; they are home to a community of river dwellers whose unusual lifestyle has been moulded by their surroundings.

Only towards the north does the Dal look like a conventional lake. Most of it

is crowded along its shores with mile-long rows of houseboats, while other parts resemble islands with houses, shops and schools. Still other areas look like vegetable patches encircled by willow trees. Human ingenuity and need have combined to create *demb* and *rad* plots on the lake. *Demb* consists of compost and silt built up from the bed of the lake to above its surface, while *rad* is layers of compost on a bed of twigs, so that the whole garden, no more than two feet deep, can be towed from one spot to another.

While neither sort of garden adds much to the beauty of the lake, the third type, the lotus garden, certainly does, with its display of large circular leaves and pale pink flowers. Like the vegetable gardens, lotus gardens have a sound commercial *raison d'être*, lotus stems being a popular dish everywhere in North India.

Village settlements exist all over the lakes in pockets. Typically, each village has a preponderance of people bearing the same surname, and each village is referred to by this name. No roads connect them to the outside world, but none are necessary – every one of their inhabitants, man, woman or child, can row a boat with a remarkable degree of proficiency.

Boats are used for every conceivable purpose – to convey children to school; to transport goods varying from live sheep to tourist bric-à-brac; to carry a bridegroom and his entourage to the *doonga* of his bride.

While some areas of the Dal bustle with village life, others are secluded spots, shaded over with rows of weeping willows. Still others are crowded service centres: the butcher, barber, tailor, grocer, each has in front of his shop a cluster of impatient clients in their boats.

Exploring the lake by *shikara* is one of the highlights of a trip to Srinagar. The *shikara* is a graceful gondola-like boat with a heart-shaped oar. The men who row them know the waterways so well that they can steer their way around the lake unerringly even on the darkest night.

Left, there is a belief that Jesus was buried at Rozabal, near Srinagar. **Right**, the newly built mosque at Hazratbal, housing the hair of the Prophet – a venerated relic.

118

THE WETLANDS

Long before the advent of motorable roads and vehicular traffic, the network of lakes, rivers and streams that intersect Kashmir served communication purposes effectively. It is believed that the entire valley was once a vast lake, now drained and dried out except for parts like Wular Lake. At the time Kashmir was conquered by the Mughal Emperor Akbar in 1586, Abul Fazl, his biographer notes, boats were the pivot on which trade and commerce moved. Even into the present century wooden barges used to ply down the Jhelum laden with fruit, grain, timber, sometimes live sheep.

There were boats of every size: *doongas, bahats* and *kishtis* provided storage space for grain and doubled up admirably as living quarters for the family. Each contained a couple of rooms with a shingled roof. Although for the most part the occupations of the boat dwellers have changed, their lifestyles endure, and they continue to live in barges moored all along the Jhelum. While the majority live in Srinagar, a few can be seen throughout the Valley's waterways.

Life on the water was, by and large, arduous, and the work of the boatman unenviable, punting laden barges upstream all day long. *Being* punted around, however, was another experience altogether, as the Emperor Jehangir and his entourage discovered during their many trips to the Valley. Jehangir and his Empress Nur Jehan soon made weeklong boat tours fashionable and the aristocracy of Kashmir eventually adopted this mode of entertainment, complete with a retinue of professional cooks and musicians.

Today's tourist can hire a *shikara,* the slim, long, canopied boat that has often been likened to the gondola of Venice, for a water trek. Two oarsmen come with the boat. For the duration of the trip – generally three to five days – simple meals are cooked on a primus stove in

A typical rura Kashmiri house, surrounded by mustard fields.

the boat, which is rowed all day long and moored at night, sometimes at a camping site. Equipped with reading material, a Walkman and perhaps a fishing rod, the modern sybarite will find it easy to recapture the indolent luxury of the *doonga* picnics of the past.

Kashmir's chief river, the Jhelum, commences in Verinag at the south-eastern tip of the Valley as a spring of deep blue, crystal-clear water. A few miles downstream, its turbid waters are unrecognizable as a continuation of that spring, and muddy and brown it remains throughout its course. It flows through the district of Anantnag into Srinagar where it joins the Dal, Nagin and Anchar lakes. The river goes on to cut a swathe through the districts of Sopore and Baramulla after joining the Wular and the Manasbal lakes, and flows out of Kashmir into Pakistan at the border district of Uri.

Two of the Jhelum's largest tributaries are the Lidder, which flows from Pahalgam, and the Sindh, from Sonamarg. Two well known minor

tributaries are the Bringhi which originates above Daksum, and the Vaishav whose source is above Aharbal. There are, in addition, scores of other streams which swell the current of the Jhelum into a mighty river. Many have their origin in the glacier-fed tarns that lie secluded in the remote upper reaches of the mountains.

Water treks commonly begin at Srinagar, where the Jhelum flows beneath wooden cantilevered bridges and between rows of brick houses tightly wedged together. All is commotion here: bundles of shawls and tapestries are washed in the river and hung out to dry out of windows and over railings of bridges. Barges, usually moored along the banks in tidy rows, sometimes crowd the river, leaving only a narrow trail of water through which the *shikaras* deftly maneuver their way. In this amphibious world, even the shops are small flat skiffs laden with an assortment of goods: vegetables, aluminium cooking vessels, bolts of fabric.

From the vantage point of a *shikara*,

The Hokase Wetland Reserve attracts many thousands of migratory wildfowl each winter.

the Old City as its stands today seems scarcely to have changed for the last few centuries. Almost immediately outside the city, a short way past the seventh (and last) bridge, the clamour and bustle gives over to quiet open countryside. In the occasional village that is encountered during a water trek, houses are traditional Kashmiri, but far more rustic – mud walls and thatched roofs being the norm.

As the river flows through Shadipora, it broadens out between raised banks planted with clumps of ashy green willow. Into the muddy brown waters plunge pairs of pied kingfishers – for fish is plentiful along the length of the Jhelum. A species of carp known locally as *Kashir gad* which translates as 'Kashmir fish,' forms an important part of the diet of those who live along the Jhelum. While trout which abound in mountain lakes and upstream rivers are prized for their delicate flavour, *Kashir gad* makes a wholesome through uninspired meal. Onwards from Shadipora, around Sumbal and Harjan, are a few barges which are the homes of fishermen who live off the river, setting out with their nets early every morning.

The Wular, the largest of Kashmir's lakes – in fact, one of the largest lakes in all of Asia – announces its presence miles away in Baniyar. From the far west come occasional flashes of lightning that send the villagers scurrying for shelter. The Wular's storms are as sudden as they are dangerous, and nobody can afford to ignore their warning signs.

During these frequent storms, the Wular rages under hills that loom menacingly. During fine weather, however, the lake is a picture of serenity. Hundreds of ducks inhabit the lake, and much of its surface is unfortunately covered with the picturesque water chestnut weed which grows wild here.

The 200 sq km lake is more or less divided into two unequal parts by a hillock, on the very top of which is a shrine. The lesser section is encircled by hills, on the lower slopes of which tin rooftops glint in the sun like crystals of sugar.

Water bodies and fields fringed by poplars and willows dominate the landscape of the Srinagar valley.

From the nearby hilltop shrine at Watlab in Bandipur district, the larger section of the Wular looks like a sea, and it is easy to believe local tales of how no fewer than seven cities lie buried in its depths. Across from Watlab, in the far distance, Sopore appears a faint smudge on the horizon.

Many miles to the east is a low hill like a camel's hump. It is towards that that one must proceed to reach Manasbal. Connected to the Jhelum by a mile-long neck of water shaded by willows, the Manasbal is the only one of Kashmir's lakes to be fed by its own spring.

Small and intimate in scale, the pear-shaped lake surrounded by fringes of poplars with quaint villages interspersed has a manicured scenic beauty. In summer its surface is covered with pale pink lotuses. Manasbal's bird life is rich and varied.

The lake was a favourite of the Mughals too, for there is a garden laid out at its edge. 32 km from Srinagar, it makes a delightful excursion quite apart from its route on the water trek. The

state owned tourist corporation has a bungalow here, but the area abounds in attractive camping spots.

The area also abounds in folklore, as interesting as it is hard to verify. Tales about holy men who have spent lifetimes making ropes long enough to fathom the depth of Manasbal Lake are popular, perhaps because Manasbal is deeper than any other of Kashmir's lakes.

From Manasbal to Srinagar, the common route is via Ganderbal, through which flows the river Sindh. This tributary of the Jhelum is a clear blue in colour all along its route, and the difference in hue is clearly discernible where the two rivers meet.

Another more circuitous route leads into Srinagar's third and least known lake, Anchar. The area surrounding the Anchar is open countryside, tranquil and echoing with bird song – though this may not be true after a few years, given the expansion of Srinagar. Its surface is already intersected by man-made strips of land on which rice is now planted.

e Wular ake, north Srinagar, the largest esh-water ke in India.

AROUND THE VALLEY

Achabal, Kokernag, Daksum, Verinag, Aharbal: each of these places in the south-east of the Valley is connected to the other, which means that it is not necessary to return to Srinagar each time. Aharbal, in the district of Shupian is the only exception; the route to it turns off the Jammu highway about eight miles (13 km) outside Srinagar.

Beyond the quaint old town of Anantnag is the Mughal garden of **Achabal**. Planned by Empress Nur Jehan, the consort of Jehangir, it is one of the most feminine Mughal gardens in the Valley, with its central theme of falling water. Flowing from a forested hill that towers over the garden, a spring here has been channelled into a cascade, fountains and ornamental pools, until it is the sparkling water that is the focal point of the garden, rather than the beds of flowers. History records Achabal as Nur Jehan's favourite haunt, and it is easy to see why.

Kokernag, a few kilometres further, also has a spring and a garden, but the contrast between the two could not be more marked. While Achabal is an intimate garden in the shadow of a steep hill, Kokernag sprawls in the flat of a valley whose vistas are bounded by low hills in the far distance. And if Achabal typifies the formal style of a Mughal garden which owes its beauty to its symmetry, and where water is a chief characteristic, Kokernag is a modern garden whose splashes of vivid flowers and lush expanses of turf are informally laid out.

The spring at Kokernag claims the distinction of having the most delicious water in all Kashmir, with amazing digestive properties. Kashmir has an awesome number of springs, each with its own claims, but there is little doubt that the waters at Kokernag are colder and possess more curative properties than those anywhere else in the Valley. At Kokernag the spring is hidden away, and first-time visitor can find it only by

Rocks collected from river beds make effective walls and windbreaks.

retracing the footsteps of those who carry jugs of what appear to be refrigerated water.

Anywhere else in the world, Kokernag would have been a much-sought-after health resort, with its tonic waters, fresh air, delightful surroundings and a few Tourist Corporation cottages, fully furnished and pine-panelled. It is a popular picnic spot with families living in the vicinity, but most tourists leave Kashmir without ever hearing of it.

The countryside surrounding Kokernag is flat, affording gentle walks, and the river Bringhi offers excellent fishing. It is the site for an ambitious venture: a trout hatchery. Trout, reared here, are fed into streams all over the Valley. Eventually, the project is expected to yield enough fish to be sold as table fish; currently, the delicate flavour of the trout can be savoured only by a few fortunate anglers.

Further up from Kokernag, lies **Daksum**, an altitude of 8,245 ft (2,513 m) squeezed between two hills with the snowy peaks of the Pir Panjal range visible all around. Daksum would be almost unnaturally silent were it not for the river that rushes through it. It is cool even during summer days, and woollens are warranted after sunset even in July.

Day-trippers to Daksum are somewhat pained to discover that there is nothing to 'do': no organized sightseeing expeditions, no snacks and drinks stalls, no shopping mall or even horse riding. Daksum is not a destination for such visitors. It is the long walks out of Daksum which are its chief delight, taking one through dense pine forests, and into upland flower-strewn meadows. There are many such rolling meadows around Daksum, fringed by giant conifers. The Bakarwals with their flaming henna-ed beards and weather-beaten features, nomads who herd their large flocks to graze on these slopes, are as much a part of the Daksum landscape as the mountains. It is possible to trek from Daksum into Kishtwar in the Jammu province crossing the Simthan pass.

Few places in the Valley are as inextricably linked to the Mughal Emperor Jehangir and his wife Nur Jehan as is **Verinag**, situated in the extreme southeast of the Valley on the road parallel to the Banihal tunnel. Of all the Mughal emperors associated with Kashmir, it was Jehangir who loved it the most, travelling extensively within it and making comprehensive notes on the places he visited and the things he saw. His memoirs leave one in no doubt that Verinag was his favourite place.

Verinag's chief claim to distinction is not its association with Mughal court, but as the source of the Jhelum. Its spring has for many centuries been regarded as sacred, but it was Jehangir who ordered an enclosure to be built around it. The pool of sapphire-blue water is enclosed with an octagonal walkway and brick halls with honeycomb ceilings. The structure, which has been extensively renovated in the last couple of decades, leads out onto a Mughal garden, in the centre of which runs the first few metres of the Jhelum. So pleased was Jehangir with Verinag

ying the lebrated shmiri illies for ture use.

that he had a palace built not far from the spring. Nothing remains of this, however, except for a few stones which were probably part of the foundation.

Through the districts of Pulwama and Shupian, the drive to **Aharbal** is along the first part of the old Mughal road, now no longer in use as a route out of the valley. After miles of flat rice fields interspersed with villages, the road inclines upwards, through sparsely forested hills with charming hamlets clinging to their sides.

Soon enough, the river Vaishav roars into earshot. Aharbal is a tiny village – its only teashop frequently runs out of tea leaves! The Vaishav runs through a narrow rocky gorge, sparkling as it gushes over boulders, and falling at one point over a drop of 50 feet. This is Kashmir's best known waterfall, and a path has been hewn out of the rock to reach within a few feet of the torrent. Aharbal is a delightful retreat, and the Tourist Corporation bungalow is seldom full. It might be good idea to supplement the not-always-inspired cooking here with tinned supplies from Srinagar.

The most popular walks from Aharbal are to **Kungwattan**, 5 miles (8 km) away and to **Kounsernag Lake**. Kungwattan is a charming meadow, with the occasional shepherd and his flock being the only visitors. Further away, Kounsernag is a mountain lake surrounded by mountains whose reflections are cast into the cloudy green waters.

Lesser known places: To the north-west of Srinagar, past the town of **Pattan**, is the apple-growing district of **Sopore**, with its headquarters in the eponymous town, which has grown to a bustling commercial center with all the trappings of affluence. Where rice fields dominate the landscape elsewhere in the Valley, Sopore and its neighbouring district, **Kupwara**, in springtime feature mile upon mile of apple orchard in a profusion of frothy white blossoms.

After Kupwara district comes the gentle valley of **Lolab**, its rolling hillsides dark green with pine forests skirting fields of rice. Lolab is quite off the

The spring a Verinag is t source of th Jhelum rive

beaten track, visited only occasionally by film crews. Sprinkled over this valley are tiny hamlets with sloping tin-roofed houses nestling in the shade of sprawling walnut trees. Autumn brings the entire population out of doors and into the fields for harvest. It is the busiest time of the year, for in the absence of machinery, paddy has to be manually separated from the stalks which are then piled into neat haystacks. Life goes on very much as usual, with lunch and tea being served out in the fields.

One of the commonest sights during autumn is *pheran*-clad women carrying enormous samovars out to the fields. In the samovar is salted tea, which in Kashmir is drunk almost with reverence. Brewed from conventional undried leaf tea, to which milk, bicarbonate of soda and salt have been added, *noon chai,* as it is called, is a vital part of life in Kashmir. Certainly, the families who cluster around the samovar in the fields drink it with much relish in the firm belief that it is responsible for their physical strength.

In preparation for the long winter ahead, every family in Lolab dries great quantities of chillies, shelled corn and turnips, this last being garlanded together like giant beads, and hung from open windows.

Historical Sites: The oldest by far of these is at **Burzahom**, 10 miles (16 km) east of Srinagar. Located on a vast plateau which commands a view of the surrounding countryside, it is an important archaeological site marked by three pits and a few curiously shaped megaliths which project out of the earth at angles.

The earliest date ascribed to this site is 2,400 BC; though the identity of the people of this period is uncertain, they are generally thought to predate the Nagas, the tribal worshippers of serpents, who are referred to in the *Nilamata Purana* as the earliest inhabitants of the Valley. Archaeological evidence indicates that the inhabitants of Burzahom lived in pits about ten feet deep, used hand-made pottery, and hunted with spears and harpoons. A few findings

TROUT FISHING

Water is the theme of the Kashmir landscape: rivers and rivulets, streams and lakes. The Jhelum, rising from a spring at Verinag below the Banihal Pass, bisects the valley. For a few miles it flows as a clear tree-lined trout stream before broadening out northward toward the Wular lake. From the valley's girdle of mountains many smaller rivers descend from glaciers and pockets of winter snow; many of these rivers, their tributaries and side-streams, hold trout.

Trout were first introduced into Kashmir in 1899 by a group of Scotsmen and now flourish in what is often considered an angler's paradise. Each year sees a few fish upward of 6 lbs (2.75 kg) brought to the bank; in July 1924 a 14.5 lb (6.6 kg) specimen was landed from the Upper Bringhi, one of the finest stretches. Over the years the Government has been able to manage the waters and control the number of fish caught. The rivers are all maintained by the Department of Fisheries and a Danish-guided fish farm at Kokernag is inducting new stock into the streams and lakes.

One of the attractions of fishing in Kashmir is the variety and quality of the waters. Each stream has its own characteristics, but falls into one of the three main types. The larger rivers like the Lidder, the Sind and Kishenganga are turned into foaming torrents by the melting snows during the warm afternoons of May, June and July. Here a weighted cast and a wet fly are needed to get the bigger fish lying in the gentle currents that flow back below the big boulders. By late July or early August, and into September, there is little snow melt to fill these rivers, so the angler needs to look at the side streams. It is often when the rivers fall dramatically in height that the best fishing is to be had. The snow-fed streams that feed these rivers are normally good for wet fly throughout the season. At this time of year the Bringhi and its tributaries, the Naubug, the Duisu and the Ahlan, offer some of the best fishing in Kashmir. The upper beats are often more difficult to reach but

fishing at 7,000 ft in such pristine surroundings makes the effort of getting there worthwhile.

The small spring-fed streams such as the Kotsu near Pahalgam, the Kokernag and the Verinag are good throughout the season, from April to the end of September, and take both wet and dry fly. Above the side valleys is a third type of fishing. Many of the high-altitude lakes, a few days' trek from the roadhead, were stocked with brown trout. These lakes, many of which are above 14,000 feet (4,250 m), are fishable from July to October. One trek from Sonamarg takes at least eight days (not allowing for days spent fishing!) and takes in the lakes of Vishansar, Kishansar, Satsar, Gadsar and Gangabal. During the winter the fish tend to keep close to the bottom but rise to the surface to feed once the ice melts. Spoons and spinners are allowed while fishing these lakes.

The rivers are divided up into beats of approximately a mile (2 km). A permit allows fishing on either bank anywhere along the beat and the local 'beat guards' or gillies are always there to help. There are over 100 beats along the valley's rivers and streams and most are within a two hour drive of Srinagar. It is however best to stay overnight in a nearby hotel or camp as the best fishing is in the early morning or late afternoon. The Fisheries and Forest Departments also have huts which need to be booked in advance. The huts are basic and serve as a base for a self-catered stay; many of them - such as the Dandipura Lodge on the Bringhi and the Batkut Forest Rest House on the Lidder - are well located but have few facilities.

Permits for all rivers and streams have to be booked in advance from the Department of Fisheries at the Tourist Reception Centre, Srinagar. Permits for the Lidder are also available at Yennar, near Pahalgam. The permits allow for up to six fish per rod per day on each beat. Only residents of Kashmir are allowed to fish on Sundays and there are a few streams that can only be fished once or twice a week depending on the size. Rods and reels can be hired from one of the many tackle shops in Srinagar (the three shops next to Grindlays Bank on the Bund probably have the best selection and advice).

from Burzahom are housed in the Shri Pratap Singh Museum at Lal Mandi, Srinagar, which is the Valley's chief storehouse of archaeological and historical finds.

Buddhism was introduced into Kashmir by Emperor Ashoka Maurya (273-273 BC), and for a time it flourished as the predominant religion, until in the 7th century AD it was completely succeeded by Hinduism. Hieun Tsang, the Chinese traveller, visited Kashmir during the Buddhist period, and from his accounts we learn that there were one hundred Buddhist monasteries and four chaityas or prayer halls. Today, only two sites date back to the Buddhist period – Harwan and Parihaspora.

Harwan is about 2 miles (3 km) beyond the Shalimar gardens. It consists of a water reservoir, a garden and a village, and to find the archaeological site is not easy, tucked away as it is on a steep hillside behind village houses. Like Burzahom, Harwan is chiefly of interest to archaeologists, being of no particular sightseeing value. At the time of its

discovery around 1895, however, it must have been spectacular. Buddhist remains were found at each of its lower terraces, and on the highest one were the ruins of an aspidal shrine whose courtyard was paved with concentric circles of rectangular terra cotta tiles. It is these tiles which added an important dimension to the site beyond the merely aesthetic, for the imagery depicted on them includes human figures, naturalistic and mythical animals, and abstract designs. The tiles have been removed from the site, some to be lodged in Shri Pratap Singh Museum, and today Harwan is no more than a series of terraces with stone foundations of what were perhaps stupas and shrines.

Parihaspora is even more obscure than the site at Harwan, not having a village around it for miles. On the Srinagar-Pattan road, a badly tarred road turns right leading to a magnificent plateau on which stand the remains of Parihaspora. On three sides, below a drop of some fifty feet, the view stretches many miles in all directions.

he Kashmiri
illow is
orld-
nowned for
s use in
icket bats.

The remains here include three plinths of stone held together by mortar, and a few rocks with bas relief carvings of Buddha. According to the *Rajatarangini* however, Parihaspora was once a large secular and religious complex, associated with the 8th century ruler Lalitaditya Muktapida.

The three plinths are of a stupa, a hall of worship and a communal residence for monks. The stupa was constructed by a Buddhist minister in Lalitaditya's government. Even the king, though a Hindu, is credited with the construction of the monks' residence which had, according to the *Rajatarangini*, a large image of the Buddha – a worthy testament to religious tolerance.

Lalityaditya's masterpiece, however, is the Sun Temple at **Martand** in the Anantnag district. The site is inspired, standing at the top of a hill with a commanding view of the surrounding countryside. The temple is dedicated to the sun god Martand and the site has been held in reverence for centuries.

Even in its ruined state, the temple is impressive: it consists of a central shrine, spacious courtyard and a pillared arcade built of enormous blocks of limestone fitted together without the use of mortar. Both the arcade and shrine are built on a dramatically high plinth. Viewed from a height, the elegance of Martand's proportions strikingly evokes a Greek temple.

Few of the carved images that once adorned Martand remain today, and those that do are, by and large, indistinct. Of the ones that can be recognized, the most important is that of Surya, the Sun God.

Insufficient evidence remains to determine the type of roof that the Sun Temple had. However, other smaller shrines of the Karkota dynasty, of which Lalitaditya was the best known ruler, all have steeply sloping roofs, and it is reasonable to suppose that this featured in Martand as well. The sloping roof formed by intersecting cross members is a distinctive feature of Hindu temples in Kashmir. They probably owe their origin to Parthian influence which

The Sun Temple at Martand against the backdrop of the Pir Panjal range.

scarcely penetrated into the rest of the country.

The best preserved of these is the Shiva temple at **Pandrethan**, just outside Srinagar, immediately after the army cantonment at Sonwar. It is thought to date to the 8th or 9th century. Made of large blocks of limestone, the temple in construction is quite unlike Hindu temples in the rest of India. Built on a square plan in the centre of a spring, it is referred to by historians as the "lantern" type by virtue of its sloping roof.

It is believed that the Pandrethan temple was, for centuries, submerged in the water of the spring, and hence escaped depredation at the hands of iconoclasts. Its most remarkable feature is the ceiling with its unique arrangement of stone slabs and classical sculpted figures.

The Karkota dynasty was followed in 856 AD by the Utpalas, the last Hindu dynasty of note before the advent of Islam in Kashmir. Avantivarman was the first ruler of this dynasty and established his capital at **Avantipura** on the Srinagar-Pahalgam route. Both the temples built during his reign are now little more than heaps of rubble, but it is possible to see the floor plan in each case quite clearly. The temples which bear the respective names of Avantiswama and Avantiswara were both dedicated to Mahadeva, one of the aspects of the great god Shiva. The style is roughly similar to that of Martand, but it is chiefly for sculptures and stylistic decorative motifs that these temples are considered the high watermark of the Karkota period. A great many stone sculptures from the Avantipora temples are housed at the SPS Museum.

The town of **Pattan**, on the Srinagar-Sopore road, has two temples constructed of the usual blocks of limestone. Each is made on the simplest plan and was probably surmounted by the lantern roof which has crumbled away long ago. The Pattan temples were built by King Samkaravarman of the Karkota period, and constructed by the simple expedient of transferring stones from Parihaspora, a few kilometres away.

etails of the
th century
hiva Temple
t
vantipura,
n the
rinagar-
ahalgam
ad.

PAHALGAM AND THE LIDDER VALLEY

Many decades ago, Pahalgam was a somnolent valley at the confluence of two streams, the Sheshnag and the Lidder. In its tranquil environs of forested hills and snowy peaks, practically the only sounds to be heard were those of the wind sighing through fir trees and the gush of the river. As the population of the village was largely made up of simple shepherds, it was called shepherd's hamlet or, in Kashmiri, Pahalgam.

Today, Pahalgam swarms with hotels, lodges and tourist huts, restaurants, shops, a golf club, weekend cottages belonging to affluent families from Srinagar, and institutional holiday homes. But the setting has not lost its charm. Sixty miles (96 km) from Srinagar, at an altitude of 6,988 ft (2,130 m) above sea level, Pahalgam is still lulled at dusk by the music of the river. The view is still framed by serried ranks of mountains ranging from deep green in the foreground to smoky blue in the background. Add Pahalgam's bracing climate to its natural beauty and it is little wonder that the resort is a favorite with everybody – honeymooners, trekkers and Indian movie moguls.

From Srinagar, Pahalgam is approached via **Pampore**, famous for its saffron fields that bloom in late autumn, and thence into Kashmir's largest district, **Anantnag**, whose headquarters are at the eponymous town. One road, 9 km longer, goes past the town to the Sun Temple at Martand. The commonly used route turns left at the quaint old town of Bijbehara, and goes steadily upwards along the left of the Lidder, passing apple orchards and villages cut into the hillside.

Finally as the road inclines steeply upwards, the panorama of the valley floor unfolds 50 feet below: giant walnut trees shading rice fields that stretch out on either side of the river as it tumbles over smooth, well-worn rocks. Two villages, **Yenner** and **Batkoote**, En route to Pahalgam: farmers take a tea break.

132

both by the Lidder, are popular fishing beats, as it is here that the river flattens out and slows down.

As Pahalgam approaches, the landscape alters dramatically: the wide valley floor narrows to a deep gorge through which the Lidder crashes its way down. On either side pine-covered hills rise sharply, and soon enough, Pahalgam comes into view. Pahalgam has a bus stop at its entrance around which are dozens of inexpensive eating places and a stretch of road referred to locally as "the town". All the shops and most of the hotels are situated along the length of this road. Pahalgam's market is the only tourist resort where it is possible to shop for handicrafts, film, books and periodicals, food supplies and chemist's sundries.

Pahalgam also has a range of hotels from the super deluxe down to flea-bag, catering specifically to Indian or to Western tastes. By far the best value for money comes from the resort's lodges; each caters to travellers on a budget, and because most of their guests are trekkers,

every arrangement can be made for treks, from planning a route to hiring a pair of well fitting trekking boots, all in a matter of minutes.

Although trekking out of Pahalgam is enormously popular, the resort itself offers a number of walks. **Baisaran**, at the end of a 4.5 mile (7 km) motorable road (the pony track is a mile (2 km) long), is a secluded upland meadow. Girdled by towering pine trees overlooked by rocky mountains, it is just the sort of retreat that Kashmir's sages and hermit must have sought.

Pahalgam's 9-hole golf course, too, has an inspired setting, and makes for an enjoyable walk when not in use.

Namleshwar temple is probably the oldest Hindu stone temple in all of Kashmir. Made on the same "lantern" pattern as the valley's other temples of the 7th century, that is to say, square and squat, topped by a sloping roof, Mamleshwar's construction suggest that it predates the others: unhewn limestone boulders bound together with mortar. (The valley's other temples are

nce a astoral taging post, ahalgam ow has a ange of otels and tores.

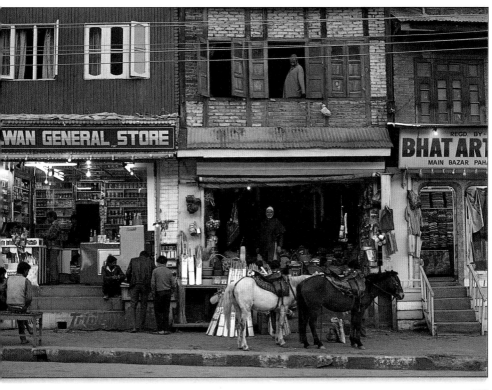

made of chiselled limestone blocks). The crystal-clear spring that wells up just in front of the temple is considered sacred.

Outside Pahalgam are a number of possibilities for day treks. **Tulian Lake** is a tiny mountain lake hidden away among the peaks overlooking Pahalgam. The trek is a moderately arduous one, approachable on pony except for the last couple of kilometers which have to be negotiated on foot.

Hargam, less than 6 km away from Pahalgam on the Chandanwari road, is where the Sheshnag flattens out from a crashing torrent to an aquamarine stream meandering through a wide valley of pine and meadows. When it is not being used as a film location, it makes a delightful day's excursion.

Further on, past the village of Fresluna and along the course of the Sheshnag stream, is **Chandanwari**, 10 miles (16 km) from Pahalgam. Both in its geographical features and flora, it bears a striking resemblance to Sonamarg. Chandanwari has become well known

as the last motorable point on the pilgrim route to the Amarnath cave.

Eight miles (13 km) from Chandanwari, steeply uphill most of the way, is the mountain lake of **Sheshnag**. Its waters vary from pale blue to pale green to deep sapphire. Seven peaks surround the lake, which is the subject of many legends and myths. The route to Sheshnag is along a well marked path, traversed by several tens of thousands of people during the three months long pilgrimage to the shrine of Amarnath.

The source of the Lidder is above **Lidderwat**, some 16 miles (25 km) from Pahalgam. Two mountain streams, from the Kolahai glacier and Tarsar Lake tumble into confluence below the wide meadow of Lidderwat and flow down through **Aru**, 11 kms from Pahalgam. Lidderwat and Aru are the base for several treks to surrounding mountains. It is interesting to compare the topography of the course of the Lidder to that of the Sheshnag stream, the former with its lush forests, the latter with its dramatic vistas.

Convivial hookah cheers a winter morning. Right, a Bakarwal child.

SAFFRON

There are not many places in the world where this aromatic spice is grown; Pampore, a small town outside Srinagar, is one of them.

Although saffron cultivation is a demanding process, it is highly lucrative, and nobody quite knows why other similar plateaux all over Kashmir have not been given over to saffron cultivation. Four hundred years ago, the Mughal emperors who visited Kashmir were entranced at the sight of carpets of gentle mauve flowers that bloomed for two short weeks at the end of autumn. But the earliest mention of Kashmir's saffron goes a good deal further back: Kalhana, the twelfth century historian of Kashmir, has mentioned its cultivation in his epic **Rajatarangini**, Chronicle of the Kings.

Come October, and the uplands of Pampore bloom for miles with fragile mauve flowers of the **Crocus sativus**. Each has six stigmas – golden and crimson. Although the golden stigmas appear saffron in colour, they are worthless. It is the crimson ones which go to make the precious spice.

Small landholdings in Pampore are owned by local families whose income is, not surprisingly, derived mainly from the saffron harvest. By the time farmers and their families have sorted out their crop, many grades of saffron emerge. The finest is known as **mongra,** and contains only the tip of the stamen. The next grade includes **lochha,** the white base of the stigma. **Lochha** is, by itself, worthless as a substitute for saffron, but so closely does it resemble the stigma that it is difficult for the untrained eye to detect the difference.

Perhaps the best place in Kashmir to procure saffron is in Pampore itself, from the innumerable shops that line the main road. Dealers are generally happy to show samples of both **lochha** and **mongra** and point out the difference in taste. The Pampore dealers are the first step in a long process in which the price goes up a notch every time the spice changes hands. Buying the same quantity eight miles (13 km) away in Srinagar is likely to be very much more expensive. On the other hand, it is well to beware of saffron being sold cheaply. The contents of such a transaction are likely to be suspect.

Partly due to the extremely high price of the spice and partly because only a few strands are required to flavour a dish, saffron is not sold by the kilo or even by multiples of grams. Five or ten grams is sufficient for a family for years, even with regular use.

YUSMARG

Given the plethora of running brooks, mountains, rice fields and small villages in Kashmir, it would appear that one excursion would be much like another. The drive to Yusmarg, 25 miles (40 km) south of Srinagar, however, yields different vistas and experiences, from the pear-tree groves immediately outside Srinagar with their white frothy blossoms in springtime, to the vivid gold of mustard fields set off by a backdrop of bright blue sky and snow-capped mountains. Soon, windswept plateaux come into view – mostly planted with almond trees, whose slender branches are wreathed with clouds of the palest pink blossoms.

Towards the town of Cherar-e-Sharif, the road begins to ascend and the valley drops away to an undulating patchwork of mustard fields and glinting rooftops.

Cherar-e-Sharif, 19 miles (30 km) from Srinagar, started out as a small village like hundreds of others all over Kashmir. Then, in the 14th century, it served as the burial place of a Sufi saint, Sheikh Nur-ud-din, and since then, many visitors from all over Kashmir come to pray at his shrine. Inside the small town, most of the roads are steep and narrow; vehicles have to be parked in the quadrangle outside the shrine.

The concept of saint worship is abhorrent to orthodox Islam, a creed which places God as the only giver, from whom all mortals must ask favours. In Kashmir, the shrines of saints are normally well attended, and none more so than Cherar-e-Sharif. The life of Sheikh Nur-ud-din, and his deeds and sayings, are revered by many. He drew a large following even during his lifetime, and when he died, Sultan Zain-ul-Abidin is said to have walked along with his funeral cortege.

Because of the widespread belief in the miraculous powers of saints, their shrines are lavishly decorated. Traditionally, everyone in the village contributed in cash or by working on the structure. But only one other shrine has been as ornately embellished as that of Sheikh Nur-ud-din, and that is Shah Hamdan's in Srinagar.

Cherar-e-Sharif is a testimonial to the sophistication of Kashmiri woodwork. Its carved corbels and pierced open-work window screens are masterfully wrought, and the walls are made of blocks of wood laid like bricks, presenting a facade of interestingly varied textures.

As is usual with shrines all over the Valley, a bustling market has grown around the entrance. Stalls selling everything from biscuits to prayer mats crowd the quadrangle and the pavement. However, it is the *kangri* shops that draw the most customers, for Cherar-e-Sharif is famous for these. The *kangri* is an ingenious clay pot enclosed by a woven wicker basket with a handle. Through winter, Kashmiris carry these portable heaters filled with live embers under their loose *pherans*, both within the house and out of doors. The *kangris* from Cherar-e-Sharif are made from a species of local willow, supple and hard-

Many local pilgrims come to Cherar-e-Sharif to offer prayers at the shrine of Sheik Nur-ud-din.

wearing. The more expensive kind incorporates a variety of intricate embellishments to the basic design. They are gifted by parents of Kashmiri brides to their prospective sons-in-law.

From the bustling town of Cherar-e-Sharif, the road climbs up to pine-covered hills where the air becomes progressively clearer and cooler.

Yusmarg itself is upland meadow, 7,790 ft (2,377 m) above sea level, whose grassy slopes are set off to perfection by dark fir trees and, further behind, by the snow-capped Pir Panjal range. There are no shops, hotels or restaurants to disturb the peace, and not much in the way of local habitation either. Nomadic shepherds live during the summer months in the charming log huts that dot the hillside, and the handful of clamorous ponymen around the tourist bungalow hail from villages nearby.

Yusmarg translates as 'meadow of Yus' (Jesus), from the widely held belief that the Messiah spent his last years here following the crucifixion and his subsequent escape from Palestine. The views from Yusmarg are superb and the weather pleasantly cool even during the summer months. It offers a number of delightful treks and refreshing rambles.

A one mile walk leads to a frothing river whose milky whiteness has earned it the picturesque name of Dudh Ganga or Ganges of Milk. Another walk in the opposite direction leads to **Nilnag** a small lake surrounded by low hills. There are a couple of one-day treks as well. One is to the foot of Yusmarg's highest peak, **Tattakutti**. The other is to **Bargha**, an upland meadow with a splendid view of the valley.

Those wishing to stay for a few nights – there are tourist bungalows and dormitories as well as camping sites – are well advised to bring tinned provisions from Srinagar, the menu at the tourist bungalow canteen being somewhat restricted. The same applies to anyone wanting to trek from Yusmarg, since very little is available in the town or in any of the hamlets neighbouring it. While there are plenty of guides and ponymen, few speak English.

Idyllic Yusmarg, the meadow of Yus (Jesus).

GULMARG

The rolling meadow of Gulmarg (literally, 'meadow of flowers') lies 33 miles (53 km) west of Srinagar at an altitude of 8,950 ft (2,730 m) above sea level. History records that a 15th century ruler of Kashmir, Yusuf Shah Chak, first discovered the charms of this resort. Thereafter, the British seem to have fallen under its spell, and it is easy to see why. The drive to Gulmarg is inspired: a long straight road, fringed by rows of stately poplars, flanked by endless fields of rice interspersed with picture-book villages. In autumn, strings of red peppers hung out in the windows of almost every house bring a note of gaudy cheer. These are *degi mirch*, the famous Kashmiri chillies, prized all over the country for their mildness and flavour.

From **Tangmarg**, 8 miles (13 km) before Gulmarg, the road climbs steeply upwards, along hills thickly forested with pine. Midway up the hill is a bend in the road popularly referred to as View Point. Fifty feet below, as far as the eye can reach, is mile upon mile of rice fields that change colour with the passing of the seasons. In the far distance, though often obscured by mist and clouds, is Nanga Parbat, every photographer's dream. On a clear day it is immediately recognizable as it towers above all its neighbours.

On the way to Gulmarg, a turn-off in the road leads to the shrine of Baba Rishi, a local saint. Visited by favour-seekers of all faiths, the shrine is well worth the short detour for its interesting wooden architecture typical of Kashmir. Around it have sprung up a cluster of quaint stalls selling an assortment of snacks, toys and religious books.

Gulmarg itself is a huge undulating bowl-shaped meadow, fringed with fir trees. It lies in the shadow of towering mountains on three sides, and on the fourth overlooks the plains. Because of its altitude, Gulmarg is delightfully cool even in the middle of summer, when temperatures peak around 25°C. By vir-

Gulmarg is one of the fe▸ Kashmir resorts that remains ope▸ throughout the winter.

tue of its proximity to Srinagar, it is used more frequently as a day's excursion than as a place to spend a few nights; every evening, when the busloads of tourists have departed, Gulmarg reverts to its somnolent self. Even in the daytime, most of the activity is centered around the small, straggling market, leaving pleasantly quiet stretches.

The market serves as pony stand and car park, and contains handicraft shops (of no particular interest to the discriminating) as well as inexpensive eating places. Most of the resort's hotels are situated nearby. The rest of Gulmarg has open meadows with plenty of lovely walks, and, even in the height of the season, enough secluded spots for a walk or a picnic.

For the six months of the year when Gulmarg is not covered by snow, its golf course attracts many players. Gulmarg's 18-hole course is one of the highest green golf courses in the world, and the adjoining club has been a local landmark since the days of the Raj. Mementoes of a bygone age abound – deep

horsehair armchairs and golfing trophies; and many of the club's regular members are army officers.

From the end of August, all the state tournaments and a few national contests are played at Gulmarg. Serious golfers carry their sets with them, but for those who are not, the club has a limited stock available on hire. Facilities are accessible for would-be golfers as well: attached to the club are a few professionals who claim to have taught many of the State's best players.

However, it is for delightful walks that a few days in Gulmarg are most rewarding. One road, about 7 miles (11 km) in diameter, runs right around the resort. Gulmarg's hundreds of ponymen inveigle most tourists to enjoy this spectacular circuit on horseback. Another popular pony trail leads steeply upwards to the picturesque meadow of **Khilanmarg**, 2.5 miles (4 km) away surrounded by giant brooding pine trees.

Kongdor, also called Seven Springs, is a large upland meadow a few miles up from Khilanmarg at the foot of

ulmarg ffers a nge of kiing, from ursery runs high-titude opes for eli-skiing.

Apharwat, Gulmarg's highest peak, and from here the view of the Valley is spectacular.

Four miles (6 km) onward from Kongdor, up a rocky path that even seasoned trekkers find tiring, is **Alpather Lake**, forbidding yet well worth the arduous climb. Unlike many of Kashmir's other lakes, Alpather is frozen over for the greater part of the year. For those not inclined to make the journey on foot, ponies can be hired from Gulmarg.

Most resorts in Kashmir close down in winter. It is unusual to see many tourists in Pahalgam, and the smaller resorts like Yusmarg are unapproachable after the season's first snowfall. Not so Gulmarg; its high season is from December to March, when its snow-covered slopes attract skiers and holiday-makers come to enjoy Christmas-card scenery.

Ski runs connected to T-bars and chair-lifts measure from between 200 metres to 900 metres, the former being used mainly by first-time skiers. Gulmarg's facilities for skiing are comprehensive: trained instructors can be hired privately; there are week-long skiing courses for groups; and shops abound from where equipment and suitable clothing can be hired by the hour. What most attracts visitors from the West are the prices. The cost of hiring skis, goggles, a jacket and ski sticks and the half-day ticket for the use of the T-bar is about as much as a meal in one of Gulmarg's less pretentious eateries.

For years, Gulmarg was better known as a skiing resort for beginners, with its gentle slopes and easy descents. All that is changing. For one, a gondola chair-lift now links Gulmarg with Kongdor, providing a ski run that descends for a couple of hundred feet, steep for the most part. Then too, heli-skiing has been introduced by a Europe-based entrepreneur, who arrives in Gulmarg with his helicopter and consolidated groups of bookings. The helicopter takes a group up to one of the neighbouring peaks, from where they ski down several hundreds of feet.

On the road ⬧ Khilanmarg.

DACHIGAM NATIONAL PARK

To enjoy a part of the beautiful vale of Kashmir in all its natural splendour and unspoilt beauty, the Dachigam National Park is the place to go. It is also unusually accessible, lying only 14 miles (22 km) from Srinagar and open to all with the appropriate permit available from the Chief Wildlife Warden's office at the Tourist Reception Centre in town.

First protected in 1910, this mountainous area forms almost half of the Dal Lake's catchment area. Its importance in supplying Srinagar with pure drinking water was recognised by the then Maharaja of Jammu and Kashmir who initiated steps for the preservation of this environment. Maintaining the well-wooded and grassy slopes, minimises erosion and ensures that the waters that feed the city are almost as clear and clean as in the Marsar Lake from which they flow.

The area was also protected as a hunting preserve by the Maharaja. It was declared a sanctuary after India became independent and in 1981, upgraded to National Park status. Between 1910 and 1934, ten villages were relocated outside the boundaries of the reserve, hence the name *dachi-gam*, "ten villages".

Within its two sectors, Lower and Upper Dachigam, spread over 55 sq miles (140 sq km), it incorporates a variety of vegetation types – riverain forest, grassland, broad-leaved woodland, coniferous forest, bare rock faces and alpine pastures – spanning heights ranging from 5,500 ft to 1,400 ft (1,700–4,300 m) above sea level. Two ridges rise steeply on either side of the park, forming a natural boundary encircling an area of great topographical variety – deep gullies, wooded slopes and huge rocky outcrops – and into Upper Dachigam where amidst 1,400 ft ridges nestles Marsar Lake from which flows the Dagwan river.

Paramount among the range of flora and fauna of the Dachigam area is the

ft, the ▪gwan river ▪ws from ▪per to ▪wer ▪chigam. ▪ght, the ▪lendid ▪ngul or ▪shmir ▪ag.

Hangul or Kashmir Stag (*Cervus Elaphus hanglu*), one of the most endangered species of red deer in the world. Dachigam is now the only place in the world with a viable Hangul population. But even here they have had a somewhat chequered history, due mainly to illegal poaching and competition from the grazing of domestic livestock. The population dropped between 140 and 170 in 1970, but with better protection in recent decades has now increased to around 600 individuals (census of 1989). The Hangul is a magnificent creature with an adult male sporting large antlers of ten or twelve points, though occasionally more may be counted. October is their main rutting month and the valleys reverberate with the deep roaring calls of the stags.

Although the Hangul may be seen at any time in the lower areas of the park, autumn and winter are the seasons when they are likely to be seen in greater numbers. In spring the males drop their antlers and with their new velvet growths they move to higher areas for the summer season. The females remain longer and give birth to their calves in the long grass of the lower slopes in May and June. The young are spotted and well camouflaged for their early days when the hinds leave them hidden and alone, returning only periodically to feed them. Later the calves move with their mothers upwards to the high pastures once the snows have receded.

In spring another large mammal for which Dachigam is justly famous makes its appearance – the **Himalayan Black Bear** (*Selanarctos thibetanus*). Having spent the winter hibernating in rocky shelters, it emerges hungry from its foodless sleep. The Black Bear is omnivorous and in these first weeks many overturned stones along the park's paths testify to the bears' search for ants and other insects and grubs. They will eagerly scavenge a leopard kill and may even bring down a very young or sick Hangul themselves. But the bulk of their diet is found on the variety of fruit trees and shrubs to be found in Dachigam; this makes locating these animals rela-

The Streake Laughing-thrush is on of the easie birds to see

tively simple as soon as you know which fruits are in season, from the early mulberry through to the blackberries, walnuts and acorns of autumn.

Indeed, Dachigam may be the best place in all the Himalaya for viewing this impressive animal. One will not be so fortunate, however, if looking for the **Brown Bear** (*Ursos arctos isabellinus*). This is a rare and endangered animal, found at higher altitudes than the forest-dwelling Black Bear, and in Dachigam, only to be found in the least accessible reaches above the tree line. Even there its exact status is uncertain and few sightings occur.

The **Himalayan Grey Langur** (*Presbytis entellus ajax*) is another creature of the Dachigam forest which follows a seasonal migration from the lower wooded valleys in winter to the higher ones in summer. It is an impressive long-coated sub-species of the grey langur to be found over much of the northern part of the sub-continent. In winter the langurs have to eat tree bark but as the leaves begin to sprout they are quick to take advantage of this new source of food. Being messy feeders, they drop many half-eaten twigs and branches to the forest floor. At this time the Hangul will frequently be found associating with these monkeys, waiting eagerly beneath their tree to feed on their dropped morsels.

Both the langur and Hangul form part of the prey base for the main predator found in Dachigam, the **leopard** (*Panthera pardus*). As the fortunes of the Hangul have improved, so have the numbers of leopards and, although they are by no means numerous, a visitor has a good chance of seeing signs of this most elegant of animals, perhaps finding a kill or even getting a glimpse of the leopard itself. The leopard's kills help sustain a host of smaller scavenging animals which in this area include the **Red Fox**, Yellow-throated Marten, **Jackal** and **leopard cat**. Wild Boar said to have been introduced to the area for hunting purposes by a Maharaja would also be found feeding on a deserted leopard kill until a few years ago. It

e Yellow-
lled Blue
agpie often
eds off
rrion.

seems, however, that unsuited to the harsh winter climate they have now died out. Birds also look to these kills for food – the **Himalayan Griffon**, the dapper lammergeier or **Bearded Vulture**, as well as the attractive long-tailed **Blue Magpie**.

The birds of Dachigam are a major attraction, colourful and various; what you see will depend on the month you visit, as many follow a seasonal migration within the park, while others come from lower altitudes than Kashmir when the snow and cold of winter is past. In winter flocks of **Cinnamon Sparrows** appear, and the **Black-and-yellow Grosbeak** presents a startling splash of colour against the white backdrop. Its clear call rings through the air mingling with the chattering of the **Black Bulbuls**, a vociferous species abundant in winter. Even the **Monal Pheasant**, the male splendidly multicoloured, may be seen at this time in the lower valleys.

In spring the lower forest blossoms into a profusion of delicate hues as the various fruit trees come into flower.

Wild cherry, pear, plum, peach, apple and apricot bloom white and pink amid the varying fresh greens of the new leaves. The main valley contains principally broad-leaved genera – oaks, elms, willows and poplars will be found there, while the side valleys become thick with the creamy flowers of the *Parrotiopsis Jacquemontiana*, a shrub of the witch hazel family which is interspersed with trees of walnut and Indian horse chestnut.

This time sees an appreciable change in birdlife too. The prominent winter species have disappeared to higher altitudes and others appear to feed on the new vegetation and begin their breeding cycles. The beautiful **Golden Oriole** suspends its cradle from a high branch; the **minivets** flash scarlet and yellow as they move in noisy feeding parties with **tits**, **warblers** and **finches**. Tree holes often house **Pygmy Owlets** and **woodpeckers**, most conspicuous amongst which is the **Himalayan Pied Woodpecker**, a smart black and white bird with red vent and, in the male, matching

Autumn display in Upper Dachigam.

red cap. Among the lower level shrubs and grasses hop the **babblers**, **buntings** and **laughing thrushes** – the **Streaked Laughing Thrush** being one of the most commonly seen birds of Lower Dachigam.

Upper Dachigam with its change in elevation presents a new variety of birds. The **Red-browed Finch** is an attractive one to look for in the birch forests; higher still, above the tree line, **redstarts**, **wagtails** and the **Himalyan Rubythroat** can be seen among the rocks edging Marsar Lake. **Alpine Accentors** are here, and the crimson-winged **Wall Creeper**.

Upper Dachigam presents quite different surroundings to those of Lower Dachigam, but this is an area without roads, recommended out of winter time for those who enjoy trekking and camping, although some shelters are available in the Sangargulu valley and at Gretnar, several thousand feet lower, where the **Koklas Pheasant** can be found. The views here are truly glorious: vast rolling meadows, splashing clear streams, waterfalls, silver birch stands, deep azure skies and high snow-dotted ridges combine in delightful harmony. The green summer grass of these highland meadows is all but eclipsed by the immense array of alpine flowers dispersed in it – crimsons, golds and purples are background to more detailed patterns picked out in blues, reds, orange and other more subtle hues. The delicately coloured **Blue Poppy** is here, several medicinal plants and many representatives of the rarer Himalayan flora.

Winter remains late at these altitudes and comes early, but during the few summer months, with the appearance of the abundant flora, come the fauna too. Also to be seen is another hibernating animal, the **Long-tailed Marmot** (*Marmota caudata*), an endearing rodent of the squirrel family. **Himalayan Weasels** may also be sighted scurrying among the boulders of the streams' edge.

Unfortunately this area is also attractive to the nomadic Bakarwals and Gujjars with their large herds of livestock, buffaloes and goats. Their presence has a detrimental effect on the environment and presents heavy competition to the Hangul in their traditional summer haunts. Although the herds are now restricted to a limited number of Dachigam's valleys, this is an ongoing problem for the Wildlife Department in their preservation of this spectacular and precious area.

Visits to Upper Dachigam necessarily take a certain amount of planning and preparation, but any one with a few hours to spare may enjoy the beauty, tranquillity and interest of lower Dachingam. Aim for early morning or late afternoon, as this is when the animals are most active and visible and the light at its best. Though you can drive through the lower valley on its short network of roads and tracks, it is far more rewarding to explore it on foot, and chances of seeing the more shy animals, like **otters**, **Levantine's Viper** and the **Jungle Cat** are increased. Limited accommodation is available within the park – details and bookings can be obtained from the office of the Chief Wildlife Warden in Srinagar.

achigam
rest
anketed
nder snow.

C H I N A

Movu

AGHIL MOUNTAINS

Aghil
Pass

Yangi
Pass

▲ K2

Haji Langar
(Qara Qash)

Gasherbrum ▲

Marpo
La

Qara Tagh
Pass

AKSAI CHIN

Masherbrum ▲

Shaksgam
Pass

Karakoram
Pass

Doghani

Kurma
Ding

▲ Saltoro
Kangri

Karakoram
W.L.S.

Daulat
Beg Oldi

Chip Chap

Salt
Lake

KARAKORAM

Dzingrulma

Gapshan

Burtsa

Amtogor

Goma

Skyangpoche

LINGZI TANG

Pilin

▲ Saser
Kangri

JAMMU AND KASHMIR

Kharmang

Ringdangdo

Nubra

Panamuk

Galiwan

CHANG CHENMO

Marlol

Mondri

Mandaltong

Kanutse

Kargil

Themisgang

Chhumed

INDIA

Tobo
Maru

Shargol

Bodh
Kharbu

Indus

Khalsi

Rizong

Domjor
La

Mulbekh

Lekir

Phyang

Lamayuru

Saspul

Basgo

LEH

Tisseru

Choglamsar

CHINA

Photosar

Spituk

Stok

Shey

Taktar

Changthang
W.L.S.

ZANSKAR

Singi
La

Ganda
La

Hemis

Markha

Sakti

Pangong
Tso

Khurnak

Nyak
Tso

Rangdom
Gompa

Zaskar

Kongmaru
La

Upshi

Rum
Tso

RANGE

GREAT

Shing
La

Rubrung
La

Likche

Spanggur
Tso

TIBET

Zunkul

Pishu

Charcha
Pass

Tanglang
La

Kiari

Sani

Karsha

Debring

Nalgubukla

Indus

Umasi
Pass

Padum

Bardun

TakTak
Gompa

Stagrimo

Mune

Phuktal

Sutak

Lezambo

Peldo

RUPSHU

Fukche

Chang
La

Atholi

HIMALAYA

Tzrap Lingti

MOUNTAINS

Jara
La

Dharwas

Tso Moriri

Shiukpe

Demchok

Alwas

Shingo
La

Thoyor

Charding
La

Tisa

Zing Zing
Bar

Kyungzing
La

Udaipur

Darcha

Imis
La

Chamba

HIMACHAL PRADESH

Keylang

Lashm

Kugti

Khoksar

Manali

LEGEND

National Park/
Wildlife Sanctua

Road

Trekking Route

LADAKH

Ever since 1974, when Ladakh was opened up to visitors, it has been a prime destination both for students of Tibetology and for lovers of the world's high places. Lying within the rain-shadow of the Great Himalayan Range, much of Ladakh is a high-altitude desert plateau. The western Zanskar region just beyond the main Himalayan range receives the maximum precipitation (50mm per annum), mainly in the form of snow in winter and spring. The barren terrain of Ladakh is in marked contrast to the rest of Kashmir – vast expanses of brown broken only by a shock of green marking the occasional village, much like an oasis.

Ladakh was once the cradle of Buddhism, from where the gentle creed initially spread to parts of Tibet. Today it is one of the last sanctuaries where the tradition of Tibetan Buddhism is to be found as a living, thriving religion. Repositories of Buddhism's treasures, gompas like Hemis and Alchi, are accessible to all, and are thronged at times of festivals, while others, like Lamayuru, are held in honour for their unbroken and uncompromising monastic traditions.

However, the topographical and cultural resemblances with Tibet are only part of Ladakh's appeal to travellers. Its historical location at the centre of important trade routes criss-crossing the Western Himalayas endowed Ladakh with its own distinct ethnic and cultural identity. The great wave of Islam, in particular, contributed to a traditional Buddhist society forms and idioms of artistic expression that are best exemplified in the marvellous mural of Alchi. The area around Kargil remains to this day largely Shia Muslim, with each small village in the Suru Valley centred around whitewashed mosques. The Dards of Dras and Da-Hanu are people of discernibly different, Indo-Iranian stock who have largely come into the fold of the two dominant religions but who continue in places to exhibit traces of their earlier animistic beliefs.

Modernization is bringing about changes in Ladakh, subtly but inexorably altering a way of life that has endured in harmony with nature over centuries. This process is bound to accelerate as this region is opened up to the intrusions of the outside world, but the hallmarks of Ladakh will certainly abide: its astonishing natural beauty, its adherence to religion as the guiding principle of life, and the fundamental character of its people – "kindly, cheerful and courteous", as an explorer remarked almost three centuries ago.

Preceding pages: Lamayuru Gompa on the way to Leh; young initiates at Thak-thak Gompa, Ladakh.

THE ROAD TO KARGIL

Although the option of flying from Delhi or Srinagar exists, the Leh-bound visitor, especially if coming for the first time, is strongly advised to stay on the ground. (There is something to be said for flying out at the *end* of the visit, taking the opportunity to marvel at the incomparable vista of the snowy summits, ridges and passes of both Himalaya and Karakoram.) The road journey not only provides a certain orientation – a sense of how Ladakh is connected with Kashmir and through Kashmir with the rest of India – but is also a spectacular and rewarding experience in itself. Driving time is about 16 hours from Srinagar: eight hours to Kargil and another eight on to Leh. The buses take a little longer. Movement of traffic on the Zoji La is controlled by the military, who impose their own timings according to the schedules of their daily convoys. Those with their own transport

might check up on this before embarking on the journey.

The gateway to Ladakh is the 11,385 ft (3,450 m) **Zoji La** (*la* means pass), a few kilometres beyond Sonamarg opposite the village of Baltal. The road approaches the pass by a dramatic series of hairpins known as the Captain Bends in memory of a captain of the paramilitary Border Roads Organization who lost his life at the time of the road's construction. Landslides and the ongoing work of realignment have tended to change the mountain face, but in a few places it is still possible to make out traces of the old summer route, for centuries the main link between Kashmir and Ladakh, following a rather steeper and more direct line than the present road. There are also fine views of the gorge above Baltal which, filled to the lip with avalanched snow, used to form the winter route up to the pass.

For, improbable though it may seem, the six to ten metres of snow that fall on the Zoji La every winter (which ensure that Ladakh is 'cut off' from the rest of the country except by air for seven months out of twelve) were not formerly an impenetrable barrier. Until the 1960s the wheel as a means of transport was unknown in Ladakh and, except during the periods of actual snowfall, the feet of hundreds of men regularly beat a path through the snow from Dras to Baltal. The most regular crossings of the pass were made by the mail-runners; but in Dras and its surrounding villages there was hardly a family in which one or more of the male members did not supplement its income by carrying trade-goods between Srinagar and Leh.

In summer they used horses; in winter the goods were made up into bundles of 1.25 maunds (about 45 kg) which was reckoned a man-size load, and a number of men would join together in a group to make the crossing, many of them doing it several times each winter. Even more incredible is the fact that in November 1948, during the first war between India and Pakistan, when the Pakistanis had taken Kargil and were entrenched on the Zoji-La, the situation was saved for India by the amazing feat – unparalleled

in the history of warfare – of bringing tanks up the mountain from Baltal. The Pakistani troops, taken completely by surprise, were forced to retreat beyond Kargil, and the Zoji La; hence Ladakh as we know it today was saved for India.

At the top of the Captain Bends the road flattens out, and the immediate approach to the pass along a high bleak corridor rises so gradually that if the crest were not signposted it would be easy to miss. But the observant eye may notice that it forms a watershed in the most literal sense of the term.

From the top of the Bends, as the mountains crowd in, shutting off the view behind, the landscape changes abruptly. On the Kashmir side, above and below, a sparse growth of birches has somehow survived the damage the construction of the road has done to the mountain slopes; even the steep sides of the gorge support a few trees and bushes. But here at the pass and over the other side, all seems windswept and desolate but for the grassy slopes that offer summer grazing for the sheep and goats

of the Bakarwals, nomadic herdspeople from the foothills. Even where the road as it descends passes a few settlements – Gumri, Machoi, Matayan, Pandras – there is not a tree in sight, only a few fields with stunted crops which may or may not ripen before the winter's first frosts.

And yet some of the pastures, especially the meadow of Meenamarg, have an astonishing richness of high-altitude wild flowers. It is only at **Dras,** an hour's drive beyond the pass, that willow plantations and smiling fields of barley relieve the starkness; and it may be here that the visitor first becomes aware of one of the most striking features of the trans-Himalaya region – its brilliantly clear, haze-free light.

The road between Dras and Kargil offers a fair enough introduction to some of the main features of the Ladakh landscape. Steep barren mountainsides rise abruptly from a narrow boulder-strewn valley down which pour the turbulent waters of the Dras river. Here and there local engineers using indig-

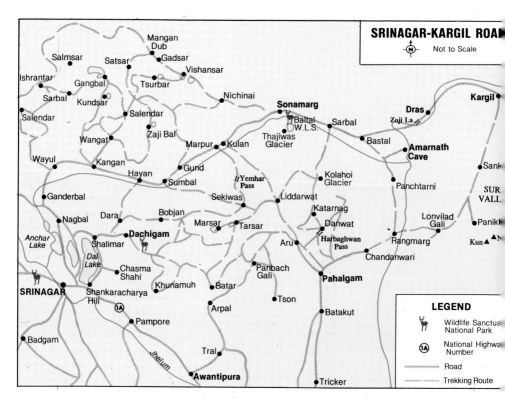

enous techniques have channelled the water of a tributary stream to a slope gentle enough to be terraced for cultivation, and a village has grown up. Despite the heavy winter snowfall, the houses are built on the flat-roofed Tibetan pattern, stone walls plastered with mud and roofs constructed of bunches of willow-twigs laid over wooden beams, the whole consolidated by a thick layer of stamped-down earth.

In winter these flat roofs have to be cleared of snow with special shovels, but they have the advantage of providing efficient insulation against the bitter cold, and also constitute storage-space for the fodder needed to keep the live-stock going throughout winter.

Past the villages of Tasgam, Shimsha Kharbu and Chanigund, the road follows the Dras river down to its confluence with the Suru which joins it from the south. Turning right up the latter it arrives very soon at **Kargil**, equidistant between Srinagar and Leh and the main staging-point on the road; also the take-off point for Zanskar.

Built on a narrow strip between the river and the mountain, which precludes all possibility of a bypass, Kargil's style is somewhat cramped by the heavy traffic, both civil and military, that pounds up and down its main bazaar. Traffic, on the other hand, brings prosperity, as witnessed by the new houses of wealthy Kargilis up the hill, and several recently built hotels. While lacking in obvious tourist draws, Kargil is still an attractive enough little town. Travellers with their own transport, not tied down to the exigencies of the bus timetable, or those obliged to stop over while making their arrangements to get to Zanskar, may enjoy a day spent there. A stroll across the footbridge will allow them an instant glimpse of a Ladakh village, in the fields and houses of Puyin, huddled at the foot of a stony mountainside. Up the hill, from the road to the Dak Bungalow, an easy walk along the track marked 'Goma Kargil' gives a birdseye view of the town, and a panoramic vista of the mountains to the east across the Suru river.

e Srinagar-
h highway
osses
ectacular
gh-altitude
sert
untry.

THE SURU VALLEY

Although most Leh-bound travellers bypass it altogether, the Suru Valley is more than just a stage on the route to Zanskar. It has a distinct personality of its own, and well repays a day or two spent lingering among its attractive villages and shy but friendly people. Tourist amenities are admittedly scanty although plans to develop them are afoot, so the visitor should be as nearly self-sufficient as possible.

The geographical interest of the Suru Valley is that for its whole length between Kargil and the Pensi La, the pass into Zanskar, it constitutes the divide between the Great Himalaya and the Zaskar Range, the limits of the latter to both south and west being defined by the abrupt right-angled turn the valley takes at Tangol. Below Tangol, the mountains alternately crowd in towards the river, and draw back to form wide flatlands; these are sufficiently well watered to allow extensive cultivation of barley, peas and a little wheat, together with plantations of willow, which give the landscape a greater softness than that of – for example – the Dras Valley between Dras and Kargil, or even the Indus Valley of central Ladakh.

Once past Kargil's modern suburb of Baroo, the road follows the Suru river through the villages of Minji and Trespon, then Saliskote, the last village where the summer is warm enough and lasts long enough to permit the people to take a second crop – usually of turnips or buckwheat – after the barley is harvested. Across the river from Minji, **Choskhor**, seen from a distance, demonstrates one of the most striking features of the Ladakhi village – the way in which its houses and fields stand out sharply from the surrounding barren hill-slopes. Water is too precious to allow any 'strip of herbage strown that just divides the desert from the sown'; the only division is a dry-stone wall. Beyond Saliskote the road leaves the river to cross a bare and dusty plateau

The Suru River, with the marshes beyond, offers rich opportunities for bird-watchers.

called Khumbathang and joins it again at Langkartse, scene of a decisive battle in 1835, during the Dogra conquest of Ladakh. After this comes the broad fertile tract of **Sankhu**. Although in this region the population is 100 per cent Muslim, there are occasional signs of the Buddhist religion that Islam displaced. The name Choskhor is one – a Tibetan term meaning 'place of religion'; another is the two immense rock-engravings near Sankhu. Six miles (10 km) short of Sankhu village an *Avalokiteswara*, shown with attendant goddesses and human devotees, is executed in shallow relief; the other engraving, *Maitreya*, in a style of deep bas-relief similar to the one at Mulbekh, is up a side-valley to the east of Sankhu, close to the village of **Kartse**, and accessible by jeep. Both date from the pre-Tibetan period of Buddhism in Ladakh.

Kartse was the capital of one of the small principalities, tributary to the kingdom of Ladakh, into which Purig – the Kargil area – was divided until the Dogra conquest. The ruined Kartse fort is down in the main valley, occupying a strategic situation on a bluff above the river at a point where the mountains draw close on both sides. It is approached by a rough track, or can be seen across the river from the road. The next village is Sangra; beyond it, where the valley after narrowing once more opens out into the wide fields of Yuljuk, the traveller gets the first, and perhaps best, view of the twin summits Nun and Kun, together with a third hardly less impressive belonging to the same massif. For as the road continues up the valley – past Te-suru village with its two mosques, their sheet-metal domes gleaming in the sun, past **Panikhar** – formerly a Dogra garrison-station and now a base for treks to Pahalgam and Kishtwar – the summits retreat behind a great ridge of alluvial debris, the last gasp of the Zaskar Range, in the angle of the river's bend that divides Panikhar from Parkachik. Once this has been turned, Nun, a soaring shapely pyramid, is shy and refuses to show itself again. Kun, though an aggressive mass of ridges

Kun of the n-Kun ssif which minates ﾠSuru lley.

and pinnacles, will be the companion of almost the whole route as far as Rangdum.

Round the bend at **Tangol**, the landscape begins to change. The heights of the Nun-Kun massif draw in to the southeast, prominent among them the subsidiary peak noticed earlier. Between these and the less dramatic slopes of the Zaskar Range there is no room for wide swathes of cultivation as at Sankhu or Panikhar; the villages of Tangol and Parkachik have to make do with a much smaller area of fields, terraced laboriously from the valley's gentler slopes. The river too is confined, way below the valley-bottom, to a rocky gorge which narrows to a mere crack just above Tangol, at the point where a bridge carries the road from the left to the right bank. This is a geologically fascinating spot. So narrow is it that at various points the crack is bridged by boulders tumbled down in some later upheaval.

Parkachik is both the last village where crops may reasonably be expected to ripen most years, and one of the easternmost outposts of Islam in the Himalaya. Just beyond it, across the valley, the great snout of the Nun Glacier, all grubby with earth and gravel, debouches straight into the river. Travellers who pause for a while can sense the uneasy movement of the great mass of ice, notice the plash of fragments into the river as the swift-flowing water erodes the snout, hear sometimes a sharp crack as the imperceptible onward motion fractures the ice. A little further up there is another glacier flowing out of the very heart of the massif. Gradually the valley opens out, and in contrast to the water-moulded contours of the lower reaches, the sweeping lines here show that this trough was originally hollowed out by the movement of glaciers. Stony wastes on either side give way to boulder-strewn meadows of short grass and an occasional profusion of wild flowers. The wildlife-enthusiast with plenty of time and patience, and a good pair of binoculars, may be lucky enough to spot ibex on the slopes high above.

Far ahead there now appears a strik-

Left, pillar decoration. **Right**, tantr wall paintin at Rangdum Gompa.

ing pyramid-shaped mountain, its face striated with sedimentary layers at an angle of about 45 degrees. This is the signpost for **Rangdum**, the gateway to Zanskar, a dead-level plain with several water-courses meandering across it. The village, Juldo, consists of not more than a dozen houses; and though the bleakness of the spot has a certain grandeur under the sun and fast-passing cloud-shadows of a summer afternoon, the cold of the night – well below freezing in early September – is a reminder of how hard life must be during the long months of winter, when snow falls to a depth of two metres or more and covers the ground for at least four to five months. It is only in an exceptionally warm summer that it is worth the effort to raise crops; even then there is no guarantee that they will ripen before the first frost. The people's wealth, such as it is, consists of livestock; virtually all their foodstuffs, apart from dairy products, have to be brought from down the valley, or from Zanskar. Since the road was opened some of the supplies come by truck, but even so horses continue to be bred for use as pack-animals.

The *raison d'être* of a settlement in such a bleak and unpromising spot was no doubt originally to service the *gompa,* situated on a hillock at the very foot of the striated mountain, and dating from the 18th century. A Ge-lugs-pa foundation, it draws most of its lamas from Zanskar. Its Du-khang, giving on to the main courtyard, has little out of the ordinary to show, apart from an old butter sculpture behind glass; but one of the smaller temples not apparently in regular use has a series of beautiful wall-paintings, looking as fresh as if painted yesterday, but dating – so the lama-guide avers – from the time of the monastery's foundation. They depict, besides the Thousand Buddhas on one wall, and some fierce divinities in *yab-yum* near the entrance, a stylized battle-scene, in which the warriors of the mythical land of Shambha-la issue out to repel attackers, their dress and accoutrements looking distinctly Mongolian.

e Suru
lley is a
ssroads
tween Balti
uslim) and
dakhi
uddhist)
tures.

ZANSKAR

The Zanskar landscape has a completely different character from the rest of Ladakh, the main valley being more open and grassy, and almost completely treeless. The region's main attraction for the visitors who have flocked to it since a road fit for jeeps and trucks was completed in 1980, are the still largely unspoiled simplicity and warmth of its people, its magnificent *gompas,* and the fact that it is the beginning or end of several popular trekking routes – to Manali in Himachal Pradesh; to Kishtwar in the hills between Jammu and Kashmir; and to Lamayuru.

Although there is the 14,435 ft (4,400 m) Pensi La to be negotiated between Rangdum and the upper reaches of Zanskar – a spectacular drive giving views from the top of the pass on to glaciers stretching far below – the latter is nevertheless a continuation of the Suru Valley, the divide between the Great Himalaya and the Zaskar Range. Zanskar is in fact made up of three main river valleys, two tributary ones joining near the capital, Padum, to form the Zanskar river proper. It is these two – the Doda flowing from the Pensi La and the Lungnok coming in from the south-east – that form the dividing trough between the two ranges, while the united stream makes a great gash through the Zaskar Range as it flows north to join the Indus. The broad open western valley and the central plain appear to have been hollowed out by the movement of glaciers. The Lungnok valley however, is for much of its length a savage, stony gorge.

Like Dras and Rangdum, Zanskar suffers heavy winter snowfall; the only route out is along the frozen waters of the Zanskar river, down to its confluence with the Indus at Nyemo. Even today many Zanskaris undertake this gruelling trek, six days out and six back, every winter, to sell their surplus butter, which is prized in Leh for putting in tea far above the mass-produced brands in India.

With its small population (currently estimated at something over 10,000) and its relative abundance of land and water, Zanskar has traditionally been surplus not only in dairy products, but also in foodgrains, which up till ten or 15 years ago its people used to barter for salt with the Chang-pa, the nomadic herds-people of the Rupshu valleys further east. The economy is divided roughly into two overlapping zones, the higher villages (above about 12,000 ft/ 3,700 m) being more dependent on live-stock – yak, *dzo* (the hybrid between the yak and the cow) and their females *dri* and *dzomo,* sheep and goats. They may also grow some barley. The people of the lower villages also keep livestock, much of which is sent up to the high mountain pastures in summer, but are mainly dependent on their crops of bar-ley, wheat and peas. Thus there is busy trade between the two zones, as between Zanskar and its neighbours.

Before the Pensi La road was built, the main line of communication with central Ladakh in summer was what is

eft, the
erak, an
laborate
eaddress
orn by
adakhi
omen.
ight, front
iew (worn
y the Rani
f Zangla).

today regarded as one of the most challenging of the trekking routes: that from Karsha or Zangla to Lamayuru, about a week's march. Apart from their winter journeys to Leh along the frozen river, the Zanskaris were in more constant communication with Paddar, in the upper reaches of Kishtwar, than with central Ladakh. Paddar, immediately to the south across the Great Himalaya, could be reached in three or four days by the (17,370 ft/5,294 m) Umasi La. Almost everything that they needed from outside (apart from salt) the Zanskaris brought in by this route, carrying it in loads on their backs, since the way was not fit for even the hardy local ponies. This included not only such household necessities as cooking oil, spices and tea, but even the wooden beams they needed to build their houses.

The commissioning of the road has thus made an appreciable, though perhaps not as yet a radical, difference to the people's life and economy.

In winter, despite the snow, they are still happy to trek long distances to the annual festivals of the *gompas*. Agricultural work comes to a standstill, and only the animals have to be tended, so there is ample time for song and story as busy hands ply spindle and loom to make the warm local cloth from the wool of their own animals. The rigours of the climate are more than compensated for by the liberal consumption of home-brewed *chang*, the barley beer enjoyed all over the Tibetan plateau.

From the middle of the 10th century, Zanskar appears to have been an independent kingdom, connected dynastically with Ladakh, but not subservient to it. The mini-kingdom of Zangla split off perhaps towards the end of the 15th century, under the rule of a junior branch of the Zanskar royal family. Ladakh's greatest king, Sengge Namgyal, conquered and annexed Zanskar about 1638; when his empire was partitioned at his death it fell to his youngest son Demchog Namgyal. In 1752, by the terms of a settlement of certain political and dynastic problems of Ladakh, only two vassal kingdoms

Cultivation i only possibl during the brief summer.

were allowed to remain in the Ladakhi polity, of which Zanskar was one. Zanskar suffered in the Dogra invasions of the 1830s, and the king, who resisted the invaders, was taken prisoner and died in exile in Jammu. The present royal family is descended from the kings of Heniskut. The Zangla dynasty seems to have survived the troubles of the Dogra invasion; thus the present king – though since 1752 'king' has been no more than a courtesy title – represents a very ancient lineage.

The Zangla raj consists of the four villages of Tshazor, Pishu, Pidmo and Zangla itself, which is some 16 miles (25 km) down the Zanskar river from Padum, and the first stage on the Padum-Lamayuru trek. There is a 'jeepable' track; but even for those not taking it as part of the longer trek, more rewarding than hitching a lift is to make the trip into a mini-trek on foot, with or without pony support, spending one or two nights en route. If the prospect of crossing the river by a suspension bridge consisting of three ropes of twisted twigs isn't too daunting, it is possible to go and return by different routes, taking in Karsha on the way. Much of the route is across barren stony plains; but the villages – **Stongde** with its cliff-top *gompa*, Shilingkit and **Tshazar** on the right bank of the river, Pishu and Binam on the left – are enchanting, and the people, though poor, welcoming and hospitable. (No offence will be taken if payment is offered for a cup of salt tea or *chang* and a bowl of *tsampa*, roast barley flour. But all necessary supplies should be carried along.)

A typical Zanskari village, **Zangla**, as befits the capital of even so tiny a kingdom, is both the biggest and the prettiest in lower Zanskar. Its houses, which include the king's 'palace', only slightly more imposing than the rest, are clustered at the foot of bare mountain slopes, and the fields spread away in front of them to the river. The main feature is the ancient fort atop a seemingly inaccessible crag, one room of which was home during the winter of 1823-24 to the Hungarian scholar, Alexander Csoma

zos and
aks are
sed to
ough the
nall fields
s soon as
inter is
ver.

de Koros. It was here that, shivering through the long months of sub-zero temperatures, he started to acquire the proficiency in literary Tibetan that was to make him the founder of modern Tibetan studies.

Apart from a handful of Sunni Muslims mostly descended from the garrison settled in **Padum** by the Dogra conqueror Zorawar Singh in the 1830s, the population of Zanskar is entirely Buddhist, and has been so, it would seem, from a very early date. Most villages have their own local temple, some with interesting old images and murals; and in many places rock engravings are to be found in a distinctly pre-Tibetan style.

There is one such near the very centre of Padum, beneath the old fort, of the five Dhayani Buddhas; close by there are niches cut into the rock, presumably to hold wooden beams, so this may well be the site of a monastery or shrines of which no other record remains. Otherwise the only religious foundation in Padum itself is the small *gompa* of Stag-

ri-mo; near it is the Photang, a residence for visiting ecclesiastical dignitaries of the Drug-pa order.

These apart, Padum has not a great deal to recommend it. The best things about it are its central position, which makes it the obvious base for the exploration of central Zanskar, and the wide views it affords. Transport is not easy to come by in Zanskar; but those without their own vehicles may with the help of the tourist authorities be able to hire horses for local sightseeing. Within easy reach are the *chorten* and temple of **Pipiting,** imposing on top of another glacial mound; and the prayer-ground and pavilion constructed for the visits of His Holiness the Dalai Lama.

One of the oldest Buddhist sites in Zanskar – and perhaps in the whole of trans-Himalaya – is **Sani**, some two hours' walk northwest of Padum. The belief in its antiquity rests largely on the evidence of a large *chorten* of unusual shape, whose name, Kanika Chorten, is thought to refer to the great Kushan king Kanishka, ruler of an empire stretching

A track hewn out of rock leads up to Karsha Gompa.

from Varanasi to Kabul around the turn of the 1st and 2nd centuries AD. The *gompa's* foundation, however, is attributed, like many others in the Himalaya and trans-Himalaya, to Padmasambhava. It is an unassuming square building right in the village, shaded by one of Zanskar's few stands of poplars; its lamas belong to the Drugpa order and own allegiance to the Rinpoche of Stakna. At the heart of the building, the Guru Lha-khang, dedicated to Padmasambhava, has some fine old murals.

There is also a temple to Naropa, with a unique form of wall decoration – painted bas-relief in stucco, with small niches for the images. Apart from the Kanika Chorten, Sani is famous for a ring of monoliths bearing engravings in a pre-Tibetan style, enclosing a piece of ground said to be particularly holy.

Although, seen from Padum, **Karsha** appears to be within easy reach, distances in the clear haze-free atmosphere of trans-Himalaya are deceptive, and it is a walk of more than two hours to the village at the foot of the *gompa.* (Best to check before setting out that the bridge over the river at the foot of the hill is functional; if not, it will be necessary to make a long detour by the steel bridge at Tongri above Sani.) Situated on a mountainside overlooking the central plain, the buildings of this impressive monastery seem to tumble down the slope till arrested a short way above the village. Tradition attributes Karsha's foundation too to the ubiquitous Padmasambhava; and ancient rock engravings near the Maitreya temple at the foot of the complex testify to the antiquity of the site. The oldest part of the extant fabric, however, is an Avalokiteswara temple known as Chukshik-jal, situated a little apart from the main *gompa,* across a gorge and beneath the ruins of a fort. This is decorated with fine wall-paintings in the same style as those of the older temples at Alchi.

The important temples at the topmost level are two Du-khang and a recently redecorated Gon-khang. The main Du-

he Zanskar iver winds s way past adum.

khang has only recent paintings, having been rebuilt after a fire some years ago; but the lower Du-khang – actually almost on the same level – is a little bigger, and has murals in the interesting late Tibetan style, showing distinct traces of Chinese influence, as well as others more purely Tibetan-looking. Halfway up is the Lha-brang, to which access is through a trap-hole in the roof, and which has some excellent murals, though these are reported to have been damaged recently by necessary repairs to the walls.

About three hours' walk from Padum on the Zangla road, **Stongde** Gompa is said to have been founded by the Tibetan master Marpa towards the end of the 11th century, and near it is a cave – where he is believed to have gone into meditative retreat. It was taken over by the Ge-lugs-pa during the religious ferment of the 15th century, and today the public buildings include no fewer than seven beautifully decorated and well maintained temples. Of these the most interesting is the Tshogs-khang, which has some paintings of rare beauty. It is home to some 60 lamas who – along with those of all the other Ge-lugs-pa establishments in Zanskar, including Rangdum – owe allegiance to the Ngari Rinpoche, in incarnation at present embodied in the person of the younger brother of His Holiness the Dalai Lama.

Apart from Sani, the only *gompa* in or near Zanskar's western valley between Padum and the Pensi La is the small Drug-pa establishment of **Dzongkhul** near the foot of the side-valley leading up to the Umasi La. Its foundation is attributed to Naropa, who is said to have meditated in the two caves round which it is built, and whose footprint is visible near the entrance to one of them. The temples are decorated largely with *thangkas,* and contain a large number of unusually lifelike images of Drug-pa lamas. Some of the paintings on the cave-walls are nearly obscured by the soot and smoke of the butter lamps; those which are relatively clean are good, and appear to be very old. Nearby Tsilatse consists of a single temple,

Bas-relief in stucco at San Gompa.

dedicated to the eleven-headed Avalokiteswara, and a large, beautifully decorated *chorten.*

The *gompas* up the Lungnok Valley are more inaccessible from Padum than those of central Zanskar, though they can be taken in by those doing the arduous trek to or from Manali. **Bardhan** is not much further from Padum than Sani or Karsha, but the narrow path running high above the Lungnok river across an almost perpendicular mountain face is somewhat alarming, and the going is much slower. The *gompa's* situation is dramatic. Jutting out from the mountain, a crag rises perhaps a hundred metres sheer out of the river, and the *gompa* perches high on the top of this. Attached to the Drug-pa order, Bardhan dates from 1618. The Du-khang has some fine wall-paintings, apparently dating from the foundation of the temple or soon after.

A little further up the Lungnok valley is the small Ge-lugs-pa *gompa* of Muni with its two Du-khang, both with recent murals. A Maitreya temple stands at the edge of the village, and scattered about the fields are a number of ancient rock engravings.

Phugtal is situated in a side-gorge, the last of Zanskar's major *gompas,* rivalling Karsha in the grandeur of its buildings, and surpassing it in the drama of its site. The approach is by a narrow footpath clinging precariously to the mountain high above the river; the main temples are embedded in a huge cave at a point where the mountain falls in a nearly sheer cliff to the swirling waters. Smaller buildings, tiny homes for the lamas, have been somehow constructed on the cliff-face beneath the temples. The whole amazing complex is linked by a system of ladders, ledges, and steps cut into the rock. There seems to be no record of this *gompa's* foundation, but certainly its paintings, especially those on the ceiling in the Ton-pa Lha-khang, are in the somewhat roccoco Indo-Kashmiri style, said to be identical in concept and execution with the ceiling panels at Rinchen Zang-po's famous *gompa* of Tabo in Spiti.

Phugtal, the southernmost of Zanskar's gompas.

KARGIL TO LEH

From Kargil the main road, after crossing the Suru, rises to the Kharbathang Plateau opposite the town. A great flat-topped mound of alluvium between the Suru and Wakha rivers, previously barren, Kharbathang has since 1989 been watered by a canal taken off the Wakha further along the road towards Mulbekh. Once the network of distribution channels is complete, much of the plateau will come under cultivation, while the sloping sides will be green with willow plantation.

Across the plateau the road descends to **Pashkyum**, one of the prettiest villages in all Ladakh, its fields occupying the whole valley floor where the surrounding mountains draw back a little. As the valley narrows to a gorge, the Kharbathang channel – a major engineering work – is seen contouring wildly along the slopes opposite the road and leaping tributary torrents by small aque-

ducts. Past the small settlements of Lotsum and Darket, the valley opens out once more – Shergol with its tiny *gompa* or monastery clinging to a cliff-face up a side-valley to the right – onto the broad fields and trim dwellings of **Mulbekh**. This is where exclusively Muslim Purig (the old name for the Kargil region) gives way to predominantly Buddhist Ladakh. Although there are a handful of Muslim households in Mulbekh, and even a small mosque, the village is dominated by the *gompa* high above it on a crag. Close to the road is an ancient rock-engraving of Maitreya, the Buddha-to-come, executed as a huge free-standing boulder; the lower part is hidden by the chapel of a small shrine recently built around it. From here on, the visible signs of Buddhism will be noticed everywhere. Prayer-flags like faded bunting flutter not only on the house-tops but across gorges and over bridges. In and around every village are the squat towers of *chorten* – the *stupas* of ancient Buddhist India – together with *mani* walls faced with stones en-

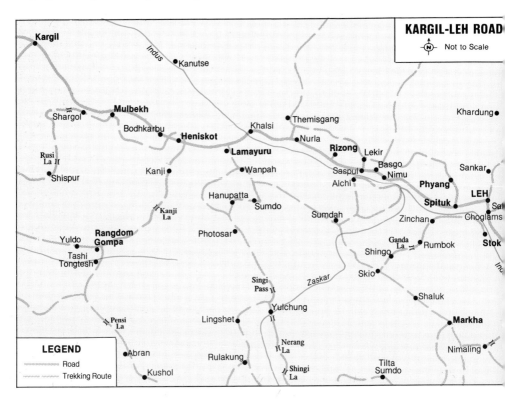

graved with endless repetitions of the sacred invocation *Om Mani Padme Hum*. These, in common with all other religious structures, are to be passed or circumambulated on the pilgrim's right; thus, the foot-path invariably bifurcates around them.

Ignoring the village of Gyal straight ahead, the road now abandons the Wakha river, turning left towards the (12,139 ft/3,700 m) **Namika La**. It rises up the west side of a valley down the middle of which runs a wide pebbly river-bed, while the sides are seamed with channels of its tributary streams – typical enough mountain terrain, its contours moulded by the action of running water. But the strange thing is that, apart from a meagre trickle in the main channel, there is not a drop of water to be seen. Like nowhere else, this section of the road brings home in a single *coup d'oeil* a fundamental truth about Ladakh – that here is a landscape shaped by water over unimagined ages, from which at some stage of geological evolution the water drained away, leaving the high-altitude

desert we see today.

The top of the Namika La is marked by the great rock-formation that gives it its name – 'Pillar of the Sky'; down the other side the road follows another valley, only less arid than the last, which at the village of Kangrail opens out into the Kanji river valley and the big scattered village of **Bodh-Kharbu**. A little ahead across the river is the ruined fort of **Stagtse**, and another, **Heniskut**, where the road leaves the valley to begin the ascent to the Fatu La. These fortifications bear witness to the fact that in the centuries of Ladakh's independence Bodh-Kharbu was the gateway to the kingdom's heartland in the Indus Valley. Two major battles were fought hereabouts in the first half of the 17th century.

As the road winds up to the **Fatu La**, at 13,450 ft (4,100 m) the highest of the three passes it crosses, the vista of jagged peaks becomes ever more spectacular; while from its windswept top a whole new panorama unfolds, of bare mountainsides in an amazing range of

eft, the ad etween argil and eh remains en most of e year. ght, Mane alls are a mmon ature of the adakhi ndscape.

colours, predominantly ochre and dull red, far ahead on the other side of the Indus. After the first steep descent from the pass the slope becomes gentler, and down to the right is the fairytale village of **Lamayuru**, dominated by the massive walls of its *gompa,* its houses spilling down the steep valley-slopes, while far below are the fields on which the life of the village depends. But the really extraordinary thing about Lamayuru is the astonishing formations all around it. For the Wanla river, way down in the valley, has cut its course through an immense mass of compacted earth, probably the deposit settled in a lake that existed here geological ages ago. And millennia of wind erosion have sculpted the crumbly sides of the resultant valley into armies of earthen stalagmites, a little reminiscent of the Grand Canyon.

There is no end to the marvels on this section of the drive. At the fifth kilometre-stone out of Lamayuru a glance to the right reveals, through a break in the mountains on the other side of the valley, a vista of ridge upon ridge stretching into the distance, and challenging the fact that the Zaskar Range is in Himalayan terms quite a minor affair. A little further on begins the descent to the Indus – a series of whirls, loops and hairpins which bring the road gradually and safely down, straightening out only on the approach to the bridge over the Wanla river, hardly a kilometre distant as the crow flies.

The Wanla brings the road out into the valley of the Indus, its very name redolent of history and romance. The Indus is geographically significant as the central channel of the great river-system that drains the area from Lake Mansarowar in Tibet to Karachi in Pakistan, from Kabul in Afghanistan to the Great Indian Desert. At this point, although it has already come 800 km from its source near the holy Mount Kailash in Tibet, it has received only one major tributary, the Zanskar, and is a river of medium size, its waters at most seasons brown and turbid with silt. The first village after the road reaches the Indus is **Khaltse**, where

lunch is usually available in rudimentary restaurants.

The road will now follow the line of the Indus for the remaining 62 miles (100 km) to Leh, departing from it occasionally when the valley narrows to a tight gorge, to cross a neighbouring plateau. Although the landscape continues wild and rugged, the main interest of this part of the drive is the villages and the glimpses they afford of the people and their way of life. After Nyuria and Ule-Tokpe comes **Saspol**, famous for its apricots, and the taking-off point for the ancient temples of Alchi across the river. From Saspol the road climbs on to a barren plateau, past the turning for Likir Gompa*,* to descend again to the wide plain of **Basgo-Nyemo**. In the 15th and 16th centuries Basgo was a royal residence, and a careful look at the eroded red cliffs above the village reveals the ruins of ancient fortifications, a palace which contains three temples. It is said that the fortress had a perennial spring, and that in the early 1660s, this is what enabled it to hold out for three

The ancient rock-engraving of Maitreya at Mulbekh.

years, checking the advance of an invading Mongol army from Tibet. On the outskirts of the village a side-stream tumbles down towards the Indus; its grassy bank shaded by willows is as good a place as any for a last halt before reaching Leh.

Beyond Nyemo – which is separated from Basgo only by a few kilometres of desert – the road rises again, but before it turns away from the river there is a striking view down to the confluence of the Indus and the Zanskar, the latter apparently contributing a rather greater volume of clear water to the turbid flow of the parent stream. For some distance after their meeting the two currents can be distinguished, until Indus silt obscures the limpid waters of the Zanskar.

One more last stony plateau remains to be crossed, its only feature of interest being a modern Sikh shrine over a rock where Guru Nanak is believed to have rested on his travels. Nestling at the foot of the mountains several kilometres away is the small village of Taru. The descent to the Leh valley is marked by a side-stream brawling down from the village and gompa of Phiyang. From this point the signs of a big military headquarters are everywhere – truck-parks, nissen huts, and a busy two-way traffic of all kinds of military vehicles. By now Leh, at the opening of a wide side-valley, dominated by the square outlines of its 17th-century palace, can be clearly distinguished some eight kilometres distant across the plain through which the Indus meanders in a number of channels. On the right is Spituk Gompa on a hillock, with its village beyond, right down by the river. Close by is the airfield, after which army structures give way temporarily on the left to the fields and houses of Skara, a village so close to Leh as to be almost a suburb. Finally the road wriggles up one last ascent, past the new hospital (one of the few Government buildings mercifully designed in the local style) and the Tibetan Hotel, past a big gaily painted *chorten,* and into the surprisingly broad main bazaar of the town – the heart of Ladakh's heartland.

ack ponies ll follow e ancient de routes.

LEH

It is the Palace on its granite ridge above the city – a building in the same architectural tradition as Lhasa's Potala, though on a more modest scale – that gives distinction to the little town of Leh, fitting it for its role as capital of a mountain kingdom. In earlier centuries Ladakh's capital was at Shey, and the other important royal seats were at Basgo and Tingmosgang; the first reported instance of special interest being taken in Leh on the part of the rulers is the fort and temple-complex at the top of the Namgyal Tsemo Peak behind the city, built by Tashi Namgyal in the third quarter of the 16th century. The Palace dates from the 1630s, and is the work of the greatest of the Ladakhi kings, Sengge Namgyal. It probably represents the final stage in the shift from Shey to Leh, whose situation at the foot of the Khardung La, the main summer route to central Asia, may reflect the increasing importance of trade in Ladakh's political economy. By the beginning of the 18th century Leh had far outstripped its rivals. The Jesuit Father Ippolito Desideri who traversed Ladakh in 1715 reports that 'there are villages but only one city in this kingdom, Leh or Lhata, which is the capital.'

The next European visitor was William Moorcroft who remained in Ladakh, based in Leh, from 1820 to 1822. His evidence shows that life in the town was largely dominated by the caravan-trade from central Asia; and though the trade had its ups and its downs, this remained true for the most part right up to the time of India's independence. This coincided with the political changes in China and Tibet that resulted in the closure of Ladakh's northern and eastern borders, and brought the centuries-old trade to an end. Even today elderly Ladakhis can recall the days when the bazaar was abustle with the arrival of caravans of horses and camels – the shaggy double-humped Bactrian variety – and in the absence of sufficient warehouse-space the footpath was all but blocked with great bundles of merchandise, and bright with carpets and felts from Yarkand spread out for sale. It must have been an animated and colourful scene, all the more so for the sprinkling of merchants from Yarkand across the Karakoram in Sinkiang, men remembered for their dignity and courtesy, striking in their ankle-length quilted coats, leather boots to the knee and fur hats.

During the heyday of the trade in the 1920s and early 1930s, between ten and 15 caravans reached Leh every year across the Karakoram, with loads of carpets, felts, raw silk, semi-precious stones, and *charas*, a narcotic resin derived from the hemp plant. (This was the only segment of the trade under the close control of the Government, which profited handsomely from it through the imposition of heavy duties.) In addition, the bazaar was filled with Kashmiri merchants come to buy *pashm*, and their Ladakhi suppliers down from their trading journeys to Rupshu and western Tibet; Indian merchants or their agents from the Punjab, doing business with the Yarkandis; and at certain seasons an influx of Tibetans attached to the official tea-trading Cha-pa mission from Lhasa.

Even the layout of the town was dictated by considerations of the trade, the unusual breadth of the main bazaar built in the 1840s surely having been planned for the convenience of the caravans. Distinctive landmarks of pre-Independence Leh were the two town gates, one at the southern end of the main bazaar, and the other up the old Khardung La road near today's Idgah – two-storey structures with an upper room where sat a clerk who called out from his perch to the caravan leader, and made a note of what goods were being carried. The gates were wide enough to accommodate benches along both sides, where the old men would spend an hour in the evening chatting.

Most visitors begin their stay in Leh by simply loafing up and down the main bazaar, a particularly attractive feature of which is the line of vegetable-sellers along the footpath. These are women from nearby villages, who have brought great basketfuls of fresh produce on their backs, and who make good use of the intervals between sales spinning woollen yard on portable drop-spindles as they exchange good-humoured conversation with one another and with the passers-by. The shops too have their own charm. Many of them, however prosaic their stock-in-trade of soap, cooking-oil, *dal,* brooms and other household necessities, are embellished with a dash of local colour in the form of a bunch of shocking-pink cummerbunds hanging from a wooden pillar, or a woman's waistcoat of fleece-lined brocade. Curio shops offer ritual religious objects like prayer-wheels, *dorje* or thunderbolts, small drums and cymbals; in some there may even be *thangkas* – icons painted on silk – or fierce masks in painted wood. Secular objects include locks of curious design, and carved printing-blocks, but many of the strangely worked jugs and boxes are said to have been fabricated elsewhere in India specially for the tourist-trade.

Then there are the jewellers' shops, offering a variety of semi-precious stones, especially turquoise, pearls and coral. A wider selection of such items is to be found in the shops of the narrow Chang Gali, which runs parallel to the main bazaar, and the stalls of the Tibetan refugees down the hill near the Dak Bungalow.

Towards evening the streets fill up with the local people, on their way home from work, or simply out for a stroll, or to meet their friends. The crowd, alas, is a good deal less picturesque than it was even in the 1970s. In summer, at any rate, the men tend to discard their traditional *goncha* – a stylish calf-length double-breasted coat with stand-up collar, the seams and borders embellished with contrast piping, and caught in at the waist by a brightly-coloured cummerbund – in favour of the more drab Western garb. Most of the women, more conservative, continue to wear the *goncha,* their version falling in gathers from the waist, and also tied with a cummerbund. Sadly, though, the bright

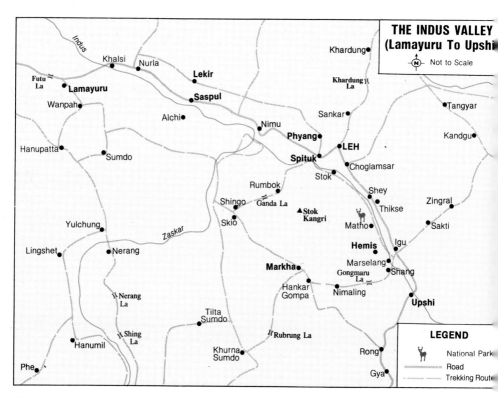

brocade mantles and jaunty quilted and embroidered stove-pipe hats with the brims cut away in front, that used to be *de rigueur,* have now almost disappeared in favour of the ubiquitous Punjabi-style *dupatta* – a simple chiffony scarf. Mantle and hat, and even more the ornate turquoise-studded headdress, the *perak,* are today worn only on formal and ceremonial occasions.

Between the main bazaar and the polo-ground, and on the slope up to the **Palace**, is Leh's old city, and the description that Moorcroft gives of it in 1822 shows that it has not changed all that much in the last 170 years:

'The houses of from one to three storeys in height are constructed of sun-burnt bricks laid in mortar of mud, the roofs flat terraced with earth, the outsides whited with a wash made of clay, and each Mansion is furnished with one or more Verandahs, but the buildings run into each other so strangely that from without it is frequently difficult to ascertain the extent of each mansion.'

Climbing up through a maze of al-leyways, the dwellings interspersed with *chorten* and short *mani* walls and giving fascinating glimpses of the people's everyday life, the visitor first reaches a complex of religious buildings – the **Gompa Soma** or New Monastery, and temples dedicated to Avalokiteswara and Maitreya – immediately below the Palace. The latter has been deserted since the early 1940s, when the then representative of the royal family – ex-iled to the village of Stok since the Dogra conquest – discontinued the ceremonies which had the Palace for centuries as focal point at the winter festivals of Losar and Dosmoche. It was then left to fall into decay, but latest reports are that some basic maintenance work, if not actual repair, is now being undertaken. Meanwhile, the dilapida-tion of the interior is such that visitors enter it at their own risk.

In accordance with the canons of Ti-betan architecture, the Palace is planned on nine levels, of which the three lowest had a largely structural function, and were used for storage and similar menial

THE TRADE ROUTES

Despite its inhospitable terrain, its remoteness and the enormous distances across it, Ladakh was for centuries a major entrepôt. Trade, in fact, was a decisive factor in shaping both the political history of Ladakh and the social and economic life of its people.

Four routes converged on Leh; two followed roughly the line of today's motorroads from Srinagar and Manali; from the east, several routes from different parts of Tibet joined at Karu, some 40 kilometres above Leh; and north was the Karakoram route from the Central Asian cities of Khotan, Yarkaod and Kashgar. This too was less a single line than a set of routes, converging at the bottleneck of the 5,600-metre Karakoram Pass, the choice of which line to take being dictated by the season and conditions in the mountains.

In winter, when there was little or no snowmelt and river waters were immobilized by frost, it was possible to take the river valleys, and for this reason many merchants considered winter the more favourable season for travel, is spite of the bitter cold. In summer, to avoid the turbu-

lent waters of the Shyok, the caravans, after crossing the Khardung La into Nubra, followed the Nubra River up to the formidable Saser Pass, an icefield spawning glaciers on all sides, which took the route across the Saser-Rime spur. Dropping down to the Shayok, it met the winter route which had come from Leh via the Indus valley to Karu, the Chang La and the Shayok Valley. The combined route then climbed up on the terrible, desolate Depsang Plain, 5,200 metres, dead level and 'as bare as a gravel walk to a suburban villa' where you could not walk more than ten steps without having to pause for breath; and from there up a valley to the Pass itself.

On the high-altitude stages of this route it was impossible to lose one's way, as the track was marked by the whitened bones of animals whose strength had failed them, and who had been left to die. Human fatalities too were common; a caravan could not afford to wait for the weak or for anyone who fell behind; the best they could do if someone died was to pile stones over the corpse, mutter a prayer, and hurry on.

A couple of stages on the other side of the pass the way similarly divided into summer and winter routes, meeting again at the town of Khargalik. Whichever route was chosen, it took 35-40 arduous days to reach Yarkand.

Between Leh and the Punjab, the Manali route was the main one in use during most of the 19th century, but as Kashmir was linked to the plains via Baramulla, Murree and Rawalpindi by a road first fit for carts, and later improved to take motor traffic, the bulk of the trade gradually came to prefer the Leh-Srinagar route. This had constituted the *pashm* trail from time immemorial.

Pashm – the downy winter undercoat of the pashmina goat – was brought to Leh from Rupshu, from the Pang-Gong Lake, and from western Tibet by Ladakhi traders, who took it from the Chang-pa herdspeople in exchange for foodgrains which the latter had no chance of producing themselves. In Leh they sold it to Kashmiri merchants who came for the purpose, and who arranged its transport to Srinagar.

Other commodities in which there was a brisk local trade were dried apricots from Kargil and Baltistan, and salt from the brackish lakes of the high plateaux to the south-east. Every September there was a market at Chemrey to which the Chang-pa brought thousands of sheep-loads of salt to barter for grain carried up by farmers from far afield. The absence of wheels notwithstanding, there was no lack of movement on the trails of old Ladakh.

purposes. The Ketuk-Chepmo, or Spacious Courtyard, where the main court and religious ceremonies were performed, overlooks the town at the fourth level, where there is a temple of Dukkar, the thousand-armed form of the goddess Tara. The next three levels have the royal living quarters and main throne-rooms and halls of audience, also more temples; but most of level 7 is taken up by an extensive roof-terrace, with the top two levels forming a kind of penthouse structure at one corner. From this terrace a glorious panorama unfolds. Immediately below, the roofscape of the old city appears, flanked by the straight line of the main bazaar; south across the sandy plain, varied by outcropping spurs, are the Indus and the mountains of the Zanskar Range dominated by the graceful **Stok Kangri** peak. The starkness of this is balanced by the view to the west and north-west, which shows the fields, interspersed with stands of poplar and willow, of the nearby villages – Skara, Changspa and Sankar, and further up Gompa and Ganglas, in the lee of the mountains towards the Khardung La.

Apart from the Palace and its attendant temples, sites worth a visit are the **Jo-khang**, a modern ecumenical *gompa* on the second section of the main bazaar (after it takes its right-angled turn); the **mosque**, founded in 1685, facing the little square at the turn; and, most striking of all, the fort and temples of **Namgyal Tsemo**, the Peak of Victory, far above the Palace.

Namgyal Tsemo can be reached by the zig-zag path visible from the bazaar, behind the Palace; by a direct path from the hamlet of Chubi on the north side (this is the one taken by the lama from Sankar Gompa who comes to light the butter-lamps in the temples morning and evening, the only times when they can be visited); or, longer but less steep than either of these, from the Khardung La road behind the Polo Ground, off which – at the point where it crosses the ridge joining the Namgyal Tsemo spur with the main range – an easy path leads to the complex. This consists of a Maitreya temple with recent wall-

paintings, and a Gon-khang containing veiled images of the fierce Guardian Deities. The main interest of this is the 16th-century wall-paintings, representing various deities and Bodhisattvas in their benevolent aspect. There are also vignettes of secular life, one of which is a court-scene with the first identified portrait of a king of Ladakh – Tashi Namgyal, founder of the temples. Above the temples are the ruins of Tashi's fort, traces of painted decoration on the walls and woodwork still visible; and behind it the remains of yet more ancient fortifications locally known, according to the scholar A. H. Francke in 1911, as the **Dard Castle**.

It is as well for any visitor to take things fairly easy on first arrival, as Leh's altitude of 11,500 ft (3,500 m) takes its toll on the human system, and not even youth and fitness guarantee immunity from its effects. High Altitude Pulmonary Oedema, a potentially fatal condition, is known to strike the young and fit at least as often as it does older people. Thus it is particularly important

for intending trekkers or climbers who will be going up to even higher altitudes, to spend at least three or four days in Leh, taking no more than gentle exercise, in order to acclimatize.

Luckily, Leh is a great place for strolling, and there are any number of interesting and attractive walks. Once the alleys of the old city have been explored, as good a direction as any to step out in is from the end of the main bazaar at Zangsti (the copper-workers' quarter in the old days), up the gentle slope, past a new line of shops which includes Ladakh's only bookshop, and a block of flats – built only some 30 years ago but looking as if it had been there for ever, so quickly does the local architecture weather and blend with the environment – to the Moravian church compound on the right. From here there is a choice of routes. To the right, skirting the church compound, an alley leads back towards the interior of the city. The road ahead forks a little further on, the left fork leading to the **Ecological Centre**, headquarters of the Ladakh Ecological Development Group, which has a small but choice library of books on ecology, environment, appropriate technology and Ladakh, and a restaurant offering mainly solar-cooked delicacies. The right fork take the stroller past the hamlet of Chubi to **Sankar,** which can however be reached more pleasantly by a paved footpath through the fields.

Those wishing to visit the *gompa* at Sankar should check up at the Tourist Office, as this is one of the few *gompas* to have regular opening hours. It is a small complex, the monks' dwelling surrounding three sides of a courtyard, of which the fourth is made up of the Du-kang and other temples. The images in these include Vajra-Bhairav, the special Guardian of the Ge-lugs-pa order, Avalokiteswara, Tson-ka-pa and Duk-kar. Their wall-paintings are fresh and bright, and the whole *gompa* has a pleasantly clean and well-maintained appearance.

Back at the **Moravian church**, a left turn along a rather countrified-looking

Archery is possibly the most popula sport in Ladakh.

lane takes the stroller past the Christian compound – where the missionaries of a century ago built their houses in the local style, and brought the waters of the nearby stream to irrigate plots of exotic vegetables like potatoes, spinach and cauliflower, and where in the last ten years a fine mission school has been established – past the old Residence of the British Joint Commissioner – now the Alpha Mess, lodging of the local military commander – to the village of **Changspa**. This is distinguished by a massive ancient *chorten* of unknown history, and on a hill above the village a new Japanese-built *gompa*, dedicated only in the mid-1980s. From Changspa a new road swings right to Sankar, making a satisfactory round.

Another charming walk is down past the Dak Bungalow to **Skara,** where the massive earth-built Dogra Fort, now a police barracks, can be admired from the outside. The District Handicrafts Centre is in a complex of drab Government buildings just out of town on the main road, near the Tibetan Ho-

tel. A little further afield, the delightful village of **Sabu**, some nine or ten kilometres from Leh, nestles between two south-stretching spurs of the Ladakh Range, its houses scattered across extensive fields and pasture-land. The small *gompa,* a daughter house of Spituk, consists of a Du-khang with good murals, surrounded by the dwellings of the monks.

Nearer town, about half a mile (4 km) off past the new housing estate, is the village of **Choglamsar**, with the Jeevan Sthal, the Dalai Lama's prayer ground, and the Tibetan refugee settlement. The latter includes an SOS Children's Village, some of whose buildings have been constructed with the benefit of solar technology. The hospital, for instance, is independent of any artificial means of heating, even in winter; there is also a solar bakery. In the workshops exquisite carpets in the Tibetan style are woven, and can be bought or ordered.

From Leh, local taxis can be booked for half-day or full-day trips to *gompas* and villages around the Indus valley.

LADAKH'S GOMPAS

From about the 13th century Ladakh, though never politically subject to Tibet, was an integral part of a religious empire that included, as well as Tibet proper, Sikkim, Bhutan and the trans-Himalayan regions of Nepal. Its monkhood was divided into different orders, several of which are represented in Ladakh. The Drug-pa are a branch of the Ka-gyu-pa or School of Oral Tradition established in the 11th and 12th centuries by a succession of Indian and Tibetan teachers – Tilopa, Naropa, Marpa and Mila-Respa. This was the order especially favoured by the Namgyal dynasty, kings of Ladakh from the 16th century to the eclipse of Ladakh's independence in the 1830s.

The Ge-lugs-pa, founded about 1400 by the reformer Tson-ka-pa on the basis of an earlier order, the Ka-dam-pa, are the only order of lamas to sport yellow hats on ceremonial occasions, all the rest contenting themselves with headgear of the same dull brick-red as their robes. To this belongs Tibet's highest religious incarnation, the Dalai Lama, though indeed he is venerated equally by the adherents of all the orders.

Orders represented in a small way in Ladakh are the Dri-gung-pa, another branch of the Ka-gyu-pa; the Nying-ma-pa, the most ancient order of all, based directly on the teachings of the Indian apostle Padmasambhava; and finally the Sas-kya-pa, at one time politically influential in central Tibet, but was upstaged in the 15th century by the Ge-lugs-pa.

Although the differences between these orders may be considerable, there is no sense of any kind of rivalry or competition among them today; it is a question rather of varying emphasis on different aspects of the teachings. These, however, represent an almost unimaginable elaboration of the simple message of the religion's founder, Gautam Buddha. No doubt the core remains – that the object of the mortal pilgrimage is relief for all beings from the infinite

suffering entailed by attachment to the endless cycle of existence, and that this can be attained only through Enlightenment, the state of complete insight into the true nature of things. But there is an enormous quantity of accretions, derived not only from the abstract philosophical speculations of generations of scholars, but also from aspects of Tantra, the esoteric manifestation of Hinduism, and from pre-Buddhist animistic beliefs.

Large numbers of local deities and spirits all over Tibet and trans-Himalaya were co-opted by the great teachers into serving the new religion. In the end, in one all-embracing synthesis, the universe has been classified into various hierarchies of gods; spirits evil or benevolent, fierce or gentle; Buddhas who after aeons have accepted nirvana, the final escape, the merging of the individual with the cosmic soul; Bodhisattvas, the embodiment of compassion, who have attained Enlightenment, but are willing to forgo nirvana until by their efforts every last soul

Images of Buddha are the focal point of worship in the gompas.

achieves liberation; and the visible realm of humans and animals, plants and stones. The relations between all these, and their influence on the quest of the individual soul, are expounded in the 108 volumes of the Kanjur, the basic scriptures, 'the translation of the Buddha-word'. The translated commentaries by Indian masters make up the other great canon of religious writings, the Tenjur.

All this is expressed in an iconography which the visitor will find in the *gompas* in the form of images and wall-paintings. Typically, the approach to a *gompa* will be signalled by *chorten*, squat towers sometimes surmounted by a tapering spire, recalling the *stupas* erected over the divided ashes of the Buddha. Sometimes they sit atop a gateway, and the passing traveller who glances up may notice the remains of ancient paintings on the stucco ceiling. The *gompa* itself will have one or more Du-khang, or assembly halls, in which the daily worship takes place; depending on its size it may have other temples

as well (Lha-khang, Lha-brang, Tshogs-khang), used for worship on particular occasions.

The Gon-khang, or temple of the terrible Guardian Deities, is a small dark building with red-washed walls (in contrast with the prevailing white of the other buildings); unless, as sometimes happens, the deities are veiled, it is forbidden to women. The rest of the buildings of a typical *gompa* consist of the monk's dwellings – tiny two-room apartments with a bed-sitter incorporating a small personal shrine, and a kitchenette.

The Kushok or incarnate abbot, whether or not permanently in residence, often has a penthouse set of rooms giving a wide view over the surrounding countryside, and including a private chapel. Although in most *gompas* the lamas are expected to find their own maintenance, and to do their own simple cooking, many of the *pujas* (forms of worship) involve the consumption of the Ladakhi staples, butter-tea and *tsampa* (roast barley flour), and there is

Winter festival of Stok Gompa.

a monastery kitchen to prepare these.

Iconography: In the earliest extant monastic buildings – of which Alchi is the prime example – there is a distinct emphasis on the cult of the five Dhyani Buddhas or Buddhas of Meditation, whose nature may be better understood if they are regarded rather as five manifestations of Buddhahood than as separate beings. They represent the four cardinal directions, and the centre, and as the cult developed each acquired his associated female deity and Bodhisattva.

Thus, for example, Amitabha, Buddha of Boundless Light, associated with the west and the colour red, has as his corresponding goddess Panduravasini; the Bodhisattva who emanates from him is Avalokiteswara (the Tibetan Chen-re-sig), who is incarnated in the line of the Dalai Lamas. These and other mystical relationships are worked out graphically at Alchi and elsewhere in the form of elaborate *mandalas*, circular representations aimed at guiding the initiated soul towards as intuitive awareness of the essential unity of all things.

Both at Alchi and in the later *gompas* there are vast numbers of paintings and images which, while they lack the elaborate symbolism of the *mandalas*, are intended like them to be an aid to devotion. As the cult of the Dhayani Buddhas waned in importance, increasing prominence was given to the concept of a thousand ages each with its own Buddha, of whom Sakyamuni, the historical Buddha of our age, was the fourth. The Thousand Buddhas are a recurrent theme of the wall-paintings in many *gompas*; of the 996 yet to come the most commonly portrayed – frequently with whole temples dedicated to him – is Maitreya (the Tibetan Chamba), the Buddha of the age next to come.

As prominent as these Buddhas in the iconography are the various Bodhisattvas, especially Avalokiteswara, who may feature in four-armed or eleven-headed forms, or with eleven heads and a thousand hands. These endowments were allowed him, it is said, by his father the Buddha Amitabha in consideration of the stupendous size

and complexity of his self-appointed task of bringing all sentient beings to Enlightenment and eventual nirvana. Only less popular than Avalokiteswara is Manjushri (the Tibetan Jam-yang), the personification of wisdom. Bodhisattvas can occasionally be represented in terrible as well as benevolent forms, in which case their five-pointed crowns are replaced by a headdress of five human skulls. Either way they can be recognized by the Six Precious Adornments – earrings, chains on the neck, chest and waist, and bracelets on the wrist and upper arm.

The great teachers – Padmasambhava, Rinchen Zang-po, Atisa, the Ka-gyu-pa masters, Tson-ka-pa and others – also figure among the paintings and images, usually in human form but occasionally portrayed as Bodhisattvas. The most popular among the goddesses is Tara, who may appear in a white or a green form (Tibetan Dolma Doljan, Dolma Dolkar), or in a thousand-armed manifestation as Duk-kar, the Lady with the White Parasol. She is the Deliverer, but

Novice monks watch a procession in Leh.

especially at Alchi appears to be sometimes identified with Prajna–paramita, Perfection of Wisdom.

All these beings may be represented as images, as wall-paintings, or on *thangkas*, silken scroll-paintings. The verandahs of most of the temples however have a different set of murals. On either side of the door are the Lords of the Four Quarters: Dhrisharashtra, Lord of the East, who is white and plays a lute; Virudhaka, Lord of the South, blue, holding a sword and a lotus, and wearing an elephant's head in place of a helmet; Virupaksha, Lord of the West, red and holding a *chorten* or a *vajra* (Tibetan *dorje*), the symbolic thunderbolt; and Kuvera, Lord of the North, also known as Vaisravana, who is golden and carries a banner and a mongoose. Despite the symbolism of these portrayals, they appear less in a transcendent religious light than as friendly, accessible – almost secular – figures, beckoning to us from a distant age of chivalry and romance.

The same cannot be said of the other main decoration of the temple verandahs, the Wheel of Life, Samsara Chakra, also known as the Wheel of the Law (Dharma Chakra) or the Wheel of Time (Kala Chakra). This is no *mandala*, yielding its innermost meaning only to the devout meditation of the initiated; rather it is a direct representation, simple enough for the unlettered laity to understand, of the chain of cause and effect in the affairs of the world. Other figures occasionally encountered on the verandah are the Old Man of Long Life, and the Four Brothers – elephant, monkey, hare and bird, in a pyramid one on the top of the other.

Immediately inside the temple-doors are the fierce divinities who guard the entrance; chief among them is Mahakala, Great and Black, known in Tibetan simply as Gon-bo, the Guardian. These fearful spirits are often portrayed in a state of *yab-yum*, or sexual congress with their female counterparts. It is they whose terrible images are housed in the Gon-khang.

The dos and don'ts for visitors to the *gompas* are few and simple, but important. Do in the first place remember that these are not museums, but places of living worship, and comport yourself with due decorum and reverence, even when images or paintings seem grotesque or surreal. Do observe restrictions on access and on photography. Do make the rounds of temples, *chorten* or any other religious structure in a clockwise direction. Do carry a good torch, as many of the temples are inadequately lit. Don't smoke within the *gompa* precincts.

The palaces and *gompas* of central Ladakh may conveniently be divided into three groups by location, though even with individual transport – the visitor's own, or a locally hired jeep-taxi – it may not be possible to 'do' all the sites of a group in a single day. In the group of sites on the north side of the Indus above Leh is included Hemis which, though situated in a gorge to the south of the river, is most conveniently approached by the bridge at Karu. This group consists of Shey, Thikse, Hemis, Chemrey and Thak-thak.

Women and children in traditional festival finery.

184

Shey: This is the ancient capital of upper Ladakh, and even after the centre of political importance shifted to Leh, Shey's special importance to the Namgyal kings is attested by the fact that it was mandatory for the heir apparent always to be born there. After the loss of Ladakh's independence in the wake of the Dogra invasion, and the royal family's exile to Stok across the river, Shey appears to have been altogether abandoned as a royal residence.

The most ancient survivals at Shey are the ruins of a fort on the top of the hill far above the present palace. Of the construction of the latter there is no record; it is similar in concept to Leh palace, but smaller. Almost equally dilapidated, it incorporates a temple housing a gigantic two-story Buddha image; ancient murals, once obscured by soot from the burning of innumerable butter-lamps over the centuries, have recently been painstakingly cleaned to reveal figures and landscapes of the utmost sophistication in wonderfully rich colours with much gold. This tem-

ple and image was erected by command of queen Skalzang Dolma, widow of Sengge Namgyal, in 1647-49.

Some 300 metres distant across the fields is a temple housing another enormous Buddha image. The temple itself, rebuilt around the image fairly recently, is hardly distinguishable as such from the outside. The image is rather more pleasing than that at the palace, and was probably ordered to be set up by Sengge Namgyal. Tradition avers that it was built by craftsmen brought specially from Nepal by Gyal Khatun, Sengge's mother, who were later settled at Chiling, to this day celebrated as the only village in Ladakh where fine metal-ware is produced. The temple is so constructed as to let in plenty of light, and the murals, which presumably follow faithfully those on the original walls, are bright without being gaudy. They represent the 16 *arhats*, original disciples of the Buddha, together with some of the great teachers – Padmasambhava, Atisa and Tson-ka-pa. Nearby are two small Tantric shrines, and an unrestored

The re-enactment of legends and myths as dance dramas is a special feature of Ladakh's festivals.

chapel of Amitabha.

Shey is rich in rock-engravings, most prominent a huge one of the five Dhyani Buddhas on the rocky spur hugged by the road at the foot of the palace hill, while a group of smaller ones is gathered around a *chorten* near the second temple. There is also an extraordinary number of *chorten*, presumably erected as acts of piety by a succession of kings.

Thikse: Dramatically situated on the end of a spur almost sheer above the road a few kilometres above Shey, Thikse was founded during the first phase of Ge-lugs-pa expansion in the 15th century, possibly on the site of an earlier Ka-dam-pa establishment. A motorable track delivers visitors to the very entrance of the main buildings at the top.

Immediately though the gate there is a new Maitreya temple, dedicated by His Holiness the Dalai Lama in 1980. The gigantic image is not, as Maitreya is usually depicted, standing or seated on a raised throne, but is in lotus position. The main Du-khang doubles as the li-

brary, and the whole of one wall is given over to the system of pigeon-holes in which the woodblock-printed volumes of the scriptures are kept. Most of the wall-paintings are of the terrible deities, some in *yab-yum*. A small dark chapel behind the main altar, with images of Sakyamuni, four-armed Avalokiteswara and Tson-ka-pa, has traces of murals in the free creative style of the 16th and 17th centuries. Women are admitted to the Gon-khang, because the images are kept veiled. Half-way down the hill is a second Du-khang, known as the White Du-khang, which has good murals in the Tibetan style. From the roof-terrace above the main Du-khang an extensive view is obtained of the wide flat into which the Indus valley opens here, with Stakna on its isolated hillock a little upriver, and an almost birdseye view of Shey; while across the river are Matho at the entrance to its gorge, and the long strip of cultivation of Chushot village.

Hemis: A drive of an hour or so beyond Thikse, Hemis is the *gompa* best known to visitors, on account of the fact that it

Rock carving of the five Buddhas of Meditation at Shey.

is the only one whose annual festival is celebrated in the summer months, thus allowing them a glimpse of an otherwise largely inaccessible esoteric tradition. Situated deep in a gorge, whose windings keep it hidden from view till the final approach, the *gompa*, clinging to the hillside, forms the focal point of an oasis created by the slight widening of the gorge to allow a growth of willows and poplars.

Belonging to the Drug-pa order, and founded by Lama Stag-tsang-ras-pa under the patronage of Sengge Namgyal in the 1630s, Hemis was in some sense the special shrine of the Namgyal dynasty, and a pavilion and walled garden just below the *gompa* served presumably as a rest-house for the royal pilgrims. Today it is converted into a restaurant and picnic-spot.

The annual festival takes the form of a dance-drama performed over two days in the *gompa*'s central courtyard. In it the lamas wearing rich brocade robes and grotesque masks and perform a series of solemn mimes, varied by comic interludes in which young novices cheekily caricature the solemn rites just enacted, to the great delight of the crowd. The drama reaches its climax in the dismembering of a human effigy moulded out of *tsampa*-dough.

This is variously interpreted as an enactment of the assassination of the apostate Tibetan king Lang-dar-ma; as the dissolution of the body after death; as the annihilation of gross desires in the individual soul and its purification; or as the soul's dissolution and merging with the totality of things. The lamas themselves offer conflicting interpretations; however, precise 'meaning' enunciated in words is clearly irrelevant to the impact of the drama on the imagination of the devout laity who flock to see it. Once in twelve years the festival includes the ritual exposition of Hemis's greatest treasure, an enormous *thangka*, embroidered not painted, and adorned with pearls.

Apart from the dance-drama, Hemis's most interesting feature is its secondary temple, the Tshogs-khang, which gives

ooking
outh across
e indus
om the roof
Spituk
ompa.

onto the main courtyard to the left of the Du-khang. It contains some beautifully worked silver *chorten*, the biggest set with huge flawless turquoises and said to date from the first half of the 18th century, and a fine Buddha image. Damaged paintings on the back wall behind the *chorten* seen to be of an early date and a correspondingly individual style; the side and front walls have paintings of the Thousand Buddhas and fierce divinities in the Tibetan manner. The Du-khang has no particularly interesting images, and its walls have been repainted in the last ten years or so. Other temples may not be open to the public.

Chemrey: Another Drug-pa foundation of the mid-17th century is Chemrey, north of the Indus in the valley leading to the Chang La. Also associated with Sengge Namgyal, it was established just after his death in 1644 as a funeral act of merit for him. Perched like so many other *gompas* on a little hill down which spill the dwellings of the lamas, it can be approached by a motorable track off the road giving access to the main temples at the top. The old Du-khang has images of Stag-tsang-ras-pa, the founder, and other important Drug-pa lamas, and a fine silver *chorten*; the paintings include mandalas of Kala-chakra and Akshobya. But the main treasure is an incomplete set of the scriptures – only 29 volumes – the title-pages lettered in solid silver of exquisite craftsmanship, and the text in pure gold. A smaller temple upstairs has intriguing murals from the period of the *gompa*'s foundation, unfortunately obscured by layers of smoke and grime from the butter-lamps. At the very top of the complex is a new Du-khang, built to house an ancient image of Padma-sambhava. The paintings on these walls were completed only in the early 1980s.

Thak-thak: A few kilometres beyond Chemrey, above the village of Sakti, is Thak-thak Gompa, the sole representative in Ladakh of the Nying-ma-pa, the most ancient religious order, but itself said to have been founded in the regain of Tshewang Namgyal in the 16th cen-

Wall paintin from Hemis Gompa.

tury. It is constructed round one of the innumerable caves in the Himalaya and trans-Himalaya where Padmasambhava is believed to have stopped and mediated during his journey to Tibet, and this forms the innermost shrine, while a little further down another cave serves as the kitchen. The small Du-khang has the usual paintings on the verandah, and on the inside walls recent murals, mostly of fierce divinities. A new temple outside the main complex was consecrated by His Holiness the Dalai Lama in 1980.

With transport it may be possible to cover the three sites south of the Indus above Leh in a single day.

Stakna: On an isolated hillock close to the river rises Stakna, the earliest Drugpa foundation in central Ladakh, though its exact date is unknown. This small *gompa* is beautifully maintained, though on the whole its paintings and artefacts are fairly new – the most noteworthy being a silver *chorten* of exquisite workmanship in the Du-khang, manufactured in Chilling as recently as the 1950s. The small chapel behind the *chorten* and images has paintings in the free and individual style of the period of the *gompa*'s foundation, but these are unfortunately so ill-lit as to be almost impossible to study in detail. As with Thikse, the roof-terrace offers stupendous views up and down the Indus, and across to the snow-capped ridges and peaks of the Zaskar Range to the south.

Matho: Although the *gompa* – situated on a spur above the village of the same name at the entrance to a gorge running deep into the Zaskar Range – has relatively little out of the ordinary to offer the visitor, except a collection of fine *thangkas* in its 'museum,' and presents a somewhat run-down appearance, it is said to be one of the spiritually most flourishing of the Ladakah *gompas*, with a healthy intake of novices. Its main importance in Ladakh's religious life is that it is home to a spirit which, entering every year into the bodies of two oracle-monks, is willing to answer questions about the welfare of Matho, and of Ladakh in general, and also questions put by individuals about their own spiritual and worldly concerns. The fes-

tival of the oracles takes place after the Tibetan new year, usually some time in March; and once possessed by the spirit the oracles are said to be able to perform amazing feats of balance on the *gompa*'s high ramparts, also to be immune to injury from the knives which they swipe at their own bodies.

Stok: The palace was built by Tshespal Namgyal, the last king of independent Ladakh, some time early in the 19th century; and it was to Stok that the deposed royal family was banished when Ladakh was formally incorporated in the state of Jammu and Kashmir, and which continues to be their residence. The present queen, Deskit Angmo, has turned part of the palace into a beautifully laid-out museum, in which the display of the royal family's treasures brings Ladakh's past alive. It includes besides the ritual objects – bell, cymbals and *dorje* – used by the kings in certain religious ceremonies, a set of *thangkas* said to date from the 16th century and authenticated by the hand-print of king Tashi Namgyal on the back of each. The

ompas *enerally* *ccupy* *olated or* *recarious* *tes* *verlooking* *abitation.*

same king is represented among the secular objects by a sword whose blade, twisted into a knot, is said to have been thus contorted by his enormous strength. Among the most fascinating of the exhibits – which also include objects from the ruling family's daily life, like spouted pots for serving tea and *chang*, and exquisite Chinese-made cups of jade and porcelain – are the personal ornaments of the queens, and the regalia of Ladakh, including a turban-shaped crown, with ceremonial gown and boots.

The small *gompa* at Stok is a daughter house of Spituk. The Du-khang contains some good recent murals, together with images of Tson-ka-pa, Sakyamuni and Maitreya. Down the Indus from Leh is a whole series of *gompas* – Spituk, Phiyang, Basgo, Likir, Alchi, Ri-dzong and Lamayuru. Of these, Spituk and Phiyang are within very easy reach.

Spituk: The first of the Ge-lugs-pa foundations in Ladakh, dating from the beginning of the 15th century, Spituk was probably built on the site of an earlier Ka-dam-pa monastery. Perched like so many others on a hillock, it is the seat of Kushok Bakula, the most important spiritual line in the Ladakh hierarchy. The *gompa* has a commanding view of the surrounding fields and villages below. The present incarnation, a member of a junior branch of the royal family, has had a distinguished career in public life, having represented Ladakh in the Indian Parliament for two terms. When in Leh, he prefers to reside at Spituk's daughter house of Sankar.

The main buildings, without having many features of particular note, may nevertheless stand as a 'typical' *gompa* – a maze of ill-lit passages and stairs, and unexpected shrines in odd corners. Prominent among the images in the Du-khang and other temples is the terrible Vajra-Bhairav, the tutelary deity of the Ge-lugs-pa. At the uppermost level are subsidiary temples, one dedicated to Tson-ka-pa with a library of his works, and another sacred to the goddess Tara and containing superbly crafted images of her 23 manifestations. The Gon-khang is above and a little apart from the main

A lama prepares the butter oil lamps in the chapel of Shey Gompa

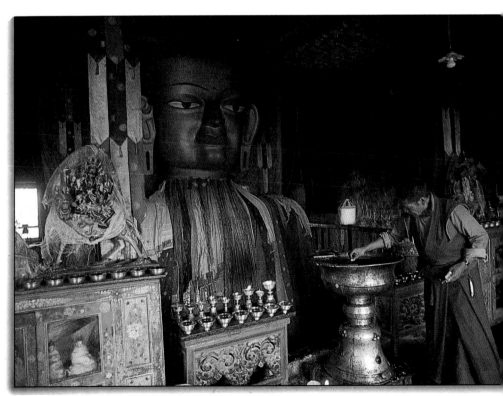

190

structure, near ruined walls which may be the remains of the earlier monastery. Down the hill a flat boulder has engravings in shallow relief, said to depict Tson-ka-pa and his disciples.

Phiyang: Up a side valley to the north, a little way down the Indus from Spituk, this is one of Ladakh's most charming villages. The *gompa*, affiliated to the Dri-gung-pa sect of the Ka-gyu-pa, was founded under the patronage of the energetic king Tashi Namgyal in the mid 16 century. More than many others, Phiyang *gompa* gives the impression of loving maintenance, the paintings on the temple walls being invariable replaced as soon as they being to show signs of becoming worn or grimy. Thus there is no chance of seeing ancient murals, but rather of appraising the best of religious art as practised at the present day. Apart from the Gon-khang, the temples are constructed so as to let in a lot of light. Phiyang's main treasure is a collection of Kashmiri bronze images dating from not later than the 14 century.

Basgo: Right on the main road, the village of Basgo is dominated by a precipitous mountainside of reddish wind-eroded rock. Among its ridges and pinnacles rise the ruins of an ancient fort, the capital of lower Ladakh in the 15th century when the kingdom was partitioned. Today the living apartments of long-dead kings are reduced to rubble, but the temples they built to their gods remain. There are three of them, all dedicated to Maitreya, and dating from the 16th and 17 centuries. Unrestored since then, their murals are the single main source for the study of the iconography of the period.

In the biggest of the temples, which has a particularly fine image, the guardian divinities are relegated to a position of secondary importance. Even the usual place of Mahakala above the main entrance has been usurped by the Bodhisattva Vajrapesi, with the Lord of the Quarters occupying prominent positions on either sides. Miniature paintings of court life show the temple's founder, king Tshewang Namgyal (c.1580) and his family, dressed in

Kashmiri-Mughal style. The side-walls are covered with benevolent representations of Buddhas and Bodhisattvas, the spaces between them taken up with decorative detail, mermaids and elephants, ducks, dogs and lions. The ceiling is also cheerfully decorated.

Entered through a fine carved doorway, the Ser-zangs ('Gold and Copper') temple is so called on account of a fine set of the Kanjur and Tenjur in these materials, copied as an act of merit at the instance of Sengge Namgyal. The walls are taken up by the wooden racks in which these are stored, and some small images in bronze and brass are kept in a glass case. The Maitreya image is too tall for the main structure of the temple, and the head reaches up through an opening in the ceiling. It can be viewed from an enclosed verandah upstairs, the walls of which have interesting, rather secular-seeming paintings in poor condition, of Buddhas in an ideal landscape. A third much smaller Maitreya shrine near the Ser-Zangs temple was dedicated in 1642 by Sengge Namgyal's queen, Skalzang Dolma.

Likir: Situated above its village in a side valley off the road between Basgo and Saspol, in a position very similar to that of Phiyang, is the Ge-lugs-pa *gompa* of Likir. At the time of its foundation in the 12th century it must have been associated with the Ka-dam-pa order; it was taken over by the Ge-lugs-pa in the 15th century. The present structure dates from the 18th century, the earlier one having been destroyed by fire. The head-lama is the Ngari Rinpoche, an incarnation at present embodied in the younger brother of His Holiness the Dalai Lama. He heads a number of *gompas*, including all the Ge-lugs-pa ones in Zanskar. Not permanently resident at Likir, he comes occasionally for important *pujas*.

The two Du-khang are well maintained, with good recent murals. A small chapel upstairs, to which visitors may be admitted, has some images of great beauty, enclosed in marvellously carved wooden frames. Both here and in the outer chamber of the Gon-khang there are a large number of *thangkas*, new and

Devotees toiling up the trail to Ridzong Gompa.

old. Though some of the old ones have become tattered, others have been no more than mellowed by time, and are wonderful examples of their kind.

Ri-dzong: Founded as recently as the 1870s by a well-to-do layman turned lama, to give full expression to the Ge-lugs-pa ideal of monastic discipline, this *gompa* is up a gorge off the main road along the Indus, near the village of Ule-tokpo. It is the only one of the central Ladakh *gompas* that must be approached for several kilometres on foot, and is dramatically situated atop a ridge of glacial debris that blocks the gorge at its narrowest point. A kilometre or so further down is an associated *chomolling* or nunnery.

While it may not necessarily be on the agenda of those whose primary interest is in the *gompas*' paintings and ancient artefacts, Ri-dzong, by virtue of the strictness with which the Rule is observed, may come closer than some others to the ideals of Buddhism. The atmosphere of austerity, peace and dedication may prove an inspiration to anyone whose main quest is for the inwardness of the Buddhist Way.

Tingmosgang: Is a side valley some 3 miles (5 km) north of Nyurla on the main Khaltse-Leh road, Tingmosgang was an important royal residence – the most westerly of all – at least till the 17th century. Among the ruins of old fortifications are temples to Padmasam–bhava, Avalokiteswara and Maitreya, all of them containing images of very fine artistic quality.

Lamayuru: A detailed examination of the *gompa* here has relatively little to yield except to the most dedicated enthusiast. Given the extraordinary, almost uncanny, nature of the geological formations surrounding it, it is not surprising to know that Lamayuru (properly called Yung-drung, signifying Swastika) is reputedly one of the oldest religious sites in Ladakh, sacred long before the advent of Buddhism to the primitive animistic religion, the Bon-chos.

Tradition has it that the Buddhist monastery, which is today affiliated to the Dri-gung-pa, was founded by the sage Naropa during his wanderings. A more credible tradition associating the oldest of the temples with Rinchen Zang-po is buttressed by its murals which, although in poor condition, are squarely in the same manner as those at Alchi. The focal image is a well-preserved Vairocana, central of the five Dhyani Buddhas, whose cult was characteristic of Rinchen's period. His four companions occupy subordinate positions.

This temple is situated away from the main complex, down narrow alleys and steep flights of steps; the main Dukhang at the level of the entrance is built around the cave where Naropa is said to have meditated, and which contains images of the sage and of his disciples Marpa and Mila-Respa. The wall has fairly recent paintings, and the main image is of Jigsten Gonbo, founder of the Dri-gung-pa. The other main feature of interest is a butter-sculpture, a Tibetan art-form relatively little practised in Ladakh. A small temple on a higher level has another one. allegedly a century old, also images of Marpa and Mila-Respa, and three silver *chorten*.

Alchi Gompa: drying apricot fruit and kernels for winter.

ALCHI

Unknown except to a few specialists before the opening of Ladakh in 1974, Alchi has since then been recognized as an artistic site of global importance, and is the main or exclusive subject of several scholarly publications. The Alchi *chos-khor* (religious enclave) across the Indus from Saspol is a complex of five temples and associated *chorten*. Inscriptions tell us that the Du-khang, the earliest of temples, was founded by one Kal-dan Shes-rab, an aristocrat of Tibetan descent who had qualified as a lama at Nyarma near Thikse (now no more than a heap of rubble), one of the few monasteries positively established as having been founded by the great Rinchen Zang-po. He may have flourished in the second half of the 11th century. The founder of the Sum-tsek, the unique three-storey temple, was another scion of the same family, Lama Tshul-krims-Od, apparently an adherent of the Dri-gung-pa, and therefore active not earlier than about 1800. What is extraordinary about these and the later Manjushri Lha-khang, Lotsawa Lha-khang and Lha-khang Soma is the almost miraculous state of preservation of their 800-years-old murals. They are by far the most extensive surviving examples of the syncretic style which is presumed to have reached is highest level of development in Buddhist Kashmir, but which was obliterated there by the Muslim takeover from the 14th century onwards.

Characteristic of the period of the 'Second Spreading', the cult of the five Dhayani Buddhas is heavily stressed at Alchi. The Du-khang's central image is of Vairocana, the Buddha Resplendent, and its walls are adorned with six superb *mandalas* illustrating different aspects of the same manifestation of Buddhahood, and their relationships with aspects of the Doctrine. Even the most uninstructed can enjoy the curiously rococo decorative detail constituting a frieze along the tops of the walls, and filling up the space between the *mandalas*. On the front wall Mahakala struts above the doorway surrounded by a fierce goddess, heraldic-looking beasts, a mounted warrior and standing figures. Beneath and to one side a royal couple, their dress rendered in meticulous detail and with wine-cups in their hands, are attended by a prince and courtiers.

As the Du-khang must have ben the regular scene of worship in the *chos-khor*, its murals have suffered to some extent from the smoke of the butter-lamps, and also from the rubbing of bodies against them as the monks crowded into that small space. The Sum-tsek, on the other hand – its carved wooden facade so startlingly reminiscent of the temple architecture of Kashmir – although its decoration is even more elaborate – appears not to have suffered the same kind of wear and tear, even before the site was abandoned as a centre of living daily worship. It is true that an inscription records repainting and restoration in the reign of Tashi Namgyal in the 16th century; but even on those parts of the walls that scholars are positive have not been touched by the restorer's brush, the colours are for the most part as bright and fresh as though painted yesterday.

While the walls of all the three storeys are covered with magnificent *mandalas*, the most striking – and perhaps unique – feature of this temple are the three gigantic Bodhisatva figures in alcoves on the side and back walls, their legs and torsos visible from the ground-floor, while their heads extend through openings is the ceiling to the first-floor terrace. What is unusual about these figures is the garments they wear, draped about them from waist to mid-calf, each of them embellished with curious illustrations. Thus the robe of Avalokiteswara on the left depicts a

series of places and shrines, possibly representing important Buddhist places of pilgrimage, while on that of Maitreya at the back, scenes from the life of the historical Buddha are shown in roundels. To the right is Manjushri, whose garment, unique among the Alchi paintings, shows direct tantric influence, the 84 Masters of the Tantra being shown in some interesting poses whose religious significance may not be immediately obvious to the uninitiated.

Not an inch of wall-space is left unpainted, the Bodhisattvas' alcoves being filled up with gods and Buddhas, some of them shown being worshipped by people whose appearance gives a clue to contemporary dress and lifestyles. To the left of the Avalokiteswara, opposite his lower leg, there is an exquisitely refined rendering of a six-armed green goddess, identified variously as Prajnaparamita, Perfection of Wisdom, and Tara, the Deliverer, worshipped by a queen and a yellow-robe monk, and surrounded by four other manifestations of herself. Another beautiful, if less sensuous, portrayal of the same goddess appears on the wall of the upper storey between two of the *mandalas*, opposite a 22-armed Avalokiteswara.

The three lesser temples might be regarded as a sensation in the absence of the Du-khang and the Sum-tsek; in comparison with these they seem tame. The Manjushri Temple has murals of the Thousand Buddhas around an old but recently repainted image; the Lotsawa Lha-khang is one of the few anywhere dedicated to the Great Translator Rinchen Zang-po; and the Lha-khang Soma, the New Temple, as its name implies, is patently of a later date than the others, as the style of its murals confirms.

While scholars differ about the precise dates and styles of the Du-khang and Sum-tsek paintings, agreement is complete that they represent an extraordinary survival, and that no effort should be spared to preserve them – at risk now as perhaps never before from the stresses entailed by the passage of thousands of curious visitors before them every year. Their survival to date is no doubt a function of the abandonment of Alchi as a centre of living worship – at what period and for what reason, we shall never know. To this day Alchi *chos-khor* retains an atmosphere of peace and serenity which seems to derive from a magical blend of its idyllic remoteness – set in an oasis of green fields in a desert of barren mountains and gorges – and the rarefied spirituality expressed with such sophistication on the walls of its temples.

THE RESTRICTED AREAS

Ladakh's boundaries are unfortunately a sensitive political issue, forming as they do on the east and north India's international border with China and Tibet, part of which is under dispute, while to the west is the military Line of Control between India's state of Jammu and Kashmir and those parts of the state occupied by Pakistan. To the north-west, where the Line loses itself in a maze of peaks and glaciers, is the disputed territory of the Siachen Glacier and the Saltore Ridge. It is hardly surprising, then, that visitors, especially foreigners, are not permitted to stray anywhere near the borders.

Even if parts of the Pang-Gong Lake area are opened up, as it is rumoured, visitors will be permitted only in groups, on package-tours organized by the State Government's Tourist Department. The border question apart, there are good reasons for this. So trackless are the mountains and grassy valleys of Ladakh's far south and east, so inhospitable is the climate, its severe cold aggravated by the winds that rise regular as clockwork every afternoon, and so total is the absence of infrastructure – often of any kind of human habitation at all – that there can be no question of allowing single persons or even groups to wander off unaccompanied. To get lost would be only too easy – and would most likely have a fatal outcome.

While the Manali-Leh road is now open without restriction, **Rupshu**, the region to the east of it, continues to be closed. Comprising the area from the border between Ladakh and Lahaul a little north of the Bara-Lacha Pass, right up to the Indus, it is a land of fairly open high-altitude valleys bounded by bare rounded hills, its climate even drier and colder than that of central Ladakh, and said to feature an amazing frequency of dust-devils.

Even this bleak region, however, is home to a scattered population of nomadic herdspeople, the Chang-pa, whose wealth is in their flocks of Pashmina goats, yak and *chang-luk* – big-boned sheep valued for their load-carrying capacity as well as for their wool. These animals live on the various grasses, scanty no doubt but reportedly highly nutritious, that are found wherever there is a little water. The Chang-pa, who live in tents of coarse black cloth woven from yak hair, known as *ribo*, are a hardy and cheerful people, well adapted to the rigours of their environment. Their migrations are made according to a strict yearly routine, depending on the amount of grass and water and the possibilities of shelter that different pastures have to offer.

In the whole of Rupshu there is only one semi-permanent settlement, **Karzok**, at the northern end of the Tso-Morari Lake, where there is a small *gompa*. At over 14,850 ft (4,500 m), this must be one of the highest places in the world where crops are regularly grown – the ubiquitous naked barley – though there is no guarantee of their ripening every year. There are said to be the ruins of ancient human settlements, complete with irrigation channels, at levels even higher than Karzok.

The most important natural features of Rupshu are its lakes – the big **Tso-Morari** near the border with Spiti, with its satellite the Kyaghar Lake, and the **Tso-Kar** some 18 miles (30 km) south-east of the Thag-lang La. These are all drainage basins with no outlet; consequently their water is at least brackish, that of the Tso-Kar so salty that salt is procured from is margins, and was sold all over Ladakh and Kashmir until a few years ago by the Rupshu Chang-pa. Tso-Kar is partly fed by a channel from a smaller freshwater lake. All the lakes are breeding-grounds for a variety of birds, among them the Barheaded Goose, the Great Crested Grebe, the Brahminy Duck and the Brownheaded Gull. Some 31 miles (50 km) east of Tso-Morari, and the same distance from the Tibet border, is the important Drug-pa *gompa* of **Hanle**.

North of the Indus, and approached from Leh by the Chang La, a pass of about 17,820 ft (5,400 m), is another

eft, prayer lags and hrines often nark a nountain ass.

much bigger drainage basin, that of the **Pang-Gong Tso**. At an altitude of about 14,100 ft (4,300 m), this is an extraordinarily long and narrow basin, only 4 miles (6-7 km) at its broadest, and some 80 miles (130 km) in length. It is bisected by the international border between India and Tibet; the Chushul area on its southern shore was the scene of fierce fighting during the Sino-Indian war of 1962.

The lake itself, its expanse of crystal-clear water shading away to an astonishing range of greens and blues, set like a jewel among the bare many-hued mountains, presents a scene of stark but spectacular beauty.

Here, as in Rupshu, a scanty population depends mainly on the rearing of Pashmina goats and other livestock, but on a rather different system. More rain falls here than in Rupshu or central Ladakh, allowing a more plentiful growth of grass which enables the flocks to spend longer in any particular pasture. There is a scattering of villages along the lake's southern shore, where barley and peas are regularly cultivated,

and can be expected to ripen most years; it is only at the onset of winter that the villagers unfold their *ribo* and take the flocks out to the high pastures.

Until the 1950s they too engaged in the salt trade, their supplies coming from the salt lakes of western Tibet, where many of them made two trips a year to collect it.

Beyond the Pang-Gong to the north is the **Chang-chenmo** Valley, and further still the bleak and forbidding plateaux of **Lingzi-Thang** and **Aksai-Chin**, the latter now under Chinese occupation. In the pre-Independence period, these were the destination of the occasional *sahib* after wild yak, Tibetan antelope and other rare game; otherwise they have little to offer anyone, being bare expanses of sand and rock varied only by the occasional range of even barer mountains. The altitude of the plateaux is in the region of 16,500-17,500 ft (5,000-5,300 m).

Nubra: the district directly to the north of Leh over the Ladakh Range is reached in a day's drive over the 18,00- ft (5,500-

Camel caravan crossing the Shyok river.

m **Khardung La**, one of the highest motorable roads in the world. It is made up partly of the valley of the Nubra river, but mainly of the Shyok, a major river which rises in the vicinity of the Karakoram Pass, and joins the Indus beyond the boundaries of present-day Ladakh, in the neighbouring province of Baltistan. Where the Nubra, which flows down from the great Siachen Glacier, joins the Shyok at a strangely acute angle, both valleys open out, and it is in this central plain that most of Nubra's important settlements are situated. Most authorities agree that, though Nubra bears a general resemblance to the landscape of Purig and central Ladakh, on the whole it is a little softer and more kindly.

Moorcroft, for instance, writes in appreciation of 'the fields...green with barley, and the verdure, contrasting with the white stone faces of the terraces, the streams of clear water that surrounds them, the belts of apricot trees, interspersed with bushes of the dog rose, now in full bloom, with willows and here and there a walnut tree, the banks of the watercourses fringed with the dwarf iris and large tufts of lucerne, the neatness of the houses, and the cordial welcome of the inhabitants. Other writers agree that here was a most pleasant oasis for travellers to enjoy before or after the rigours of the Karakoram route.

Indeed, many of the trade caravans used to pause in Nubra for a few days' rest; in the 1930s an estimated 8,000 to 10,000 pack animals passed through every year. The Nubra people were thus able to supplement their subsistence economy by keeping some of their fields always under alfalfa (lucerne), a nutritious fodder for which there was a steady demand. Otherwise, the crops grown are the same as elsewhere in Ladakh – principally barley (which also found a ready sale to the caravans) and some wheat. As Moorcroft mentions, the climate also favours fruit – walnuts as well as apricots and apples; and lower down the summers are hot enough for melons and watermelons to ripen.

In central Nubra, the population is

The magnificent waters of Pang-Gong Tso stretch into Tibet.

almost exclusively Buddhist, their religious life centring on the *gompa* at **Deskit**. Far down the Shyok are the Muslim villages of Turtuk and Bogdang, which were part of Pakistan Occupied Kashmir from 1948 to 1971, but which were won for India in the war of 1971, when the Line of Control was pushed several miles west.

As well as constituting the approach to the Karakoram Pass and Central Asia, as it did in the days of the trans-Karakoram trade, Nubra is an important destination for mountaineers, and even now the occasional foreign expedition is permitted by the Government of India. (The liaison body is the Indian Mountaineering Foundation, to which applications are to be addressed.) The mountains of the eastern Karakoram to which it gives access, while hardly comparable in height or complexity with the mighty K2 massif further west, are still sufficiently impressive and challenging by any other standards.

Sia Kangri 24,350 ft (7,422 m), the **Teram Kangri** group (highest point 24,630ft/7,464 m) and the **Apsarasas** group (highest point 23,900/7,245 m), all to the north of the Siachen Glacier, are in territory claimed by both India and Pakistan, as is the Saltoro Ridge (**Saltoro Kangri** 25,550 ft/7,742 m) west of the glacier, where today Indian and Pakistani troops confront each other on the world's highest ever battlefield. In the 1970s and early 1980s, before the outbreak of the fighting, both India and Pakistan allowed or encouraged climbing expeditions to all these massifs, apparently as a means of asserting ownership and control.

As recently as 1986, an Indo-American expedition made a successful attempt on Sia Kangri, though the climbers' style is reported to have been somewhat cramped by artillery shelling on the glacier below.

Unequivocally within Indian territory is the spur of the Karakoram running south between the line of the Siachen Glacier and the Nubra river to the west, and the upper reaches of the Shyok to the east. This contains some fine sum-

Village traders use the double-humped Bactrian camel as a beast of burden in the Nubra valley.

200

mits, notably the **Rimo** group (highest point 24,370 ft/7,385 m) and **Mamostong Kangri** (24,800 ft/7,516 m) to the north of the Saser Pass, and the **Saser Kangri** group to its south. The Saser Kangri group contains five major peaks within a radius of 6 miles (10 km), and is the source of seven large glaciers draining into the Shyok and Nubra rivers. The first reconnaissance of this fascinating knot of mountains was made by T. G. Longstaff in 1909, during which he discovered the scale and complexity of the Karakoram glacier system.

It is unfortunate that the restricted areas of Ladakh include not only the outlying regions of Nubra, the Pang-Gong Lake and Rupshu, but also the Indus valley below **Khaltse**, where the villages of Da, Hanu, Garkhon and Darchiks are home to a minuscule ethnic group known as Drok-pa, Indo-Aryan by race in contrast with the Tibetan racial characteristics of the majority of Ladakhis, with their own distinct traditions and customs, and practising a form of Buddhism that has an intriguing intermixture of pre-Buddhist animist beliefs. The **Shagkar-Chigtan** valley, running north from Bodh-Kharbu towards the Indus, is also out of bounds. The Shagkar-Chigtan people are renowned for their *joie-de-vivre*, and also for having brought Ladakh's rich oral literature to its finest degree of development. Though Muslims, they retained till very recently traces of the Buddhism from which they were converted at an uncertain period during the last 400 years. The best versions of Ladakh's national folk-epic, the Kesar Saga, are said to have been those recited by the bards of Chigtan.

The casual visitor may not be too disappointed by being obliged to give Garkhon-Darchiks and Shagkar-Chigtan a miss, for neither has much in the way of obvious scenic or man-made beauty to attract the tourist. However, it would be the greatest pity if they should remain inaccessible to serious scholars until the processes of 'modernization' and 'development' have largely wiped out their unique cultural characteristics.

*eft, a
*Muslim
*oman from
*ubra.
*ight, a
*rokpa
der.

202

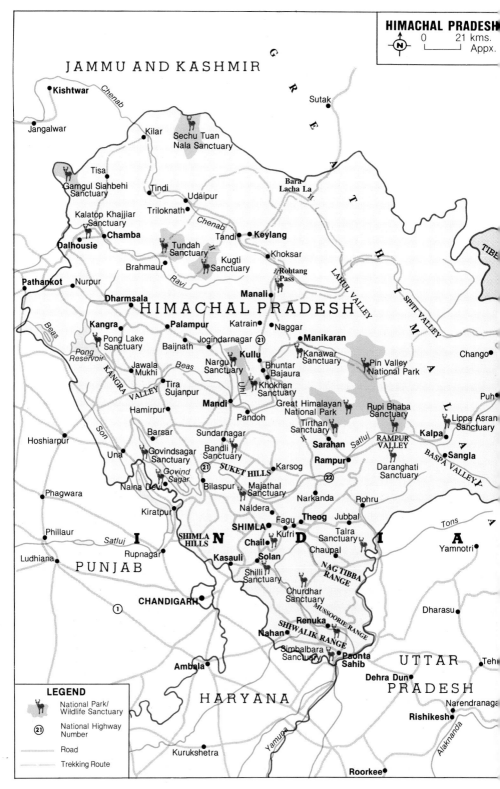

0   21 kms.
Appx.

JAMMU AND KASHMIR

Kishtwar

Sutak

Jangalwar

Kilar

Sechu Tuan
Nala Sanctuary

Bara
Lacha La

Tisa

Gamgul Siahbehi
Sanctuary

Tindi

Udaipur

Triloknath

Chenab

Kalatop Khajjiar
Sanctuary

Chamba

Tandi

Keylang

Dalhousie

Khoksar

TIBE

Brahmaur

Tundah
Sanctuary

Kugti
Sanctuary

Pathankot

Nurpur

Ravi

Rohtang
Pass

LAHUL VALLEY

SPITI VALLEY

Dharmsala

Manali

HIMACHAL PRADESH

Kangra

Palampur

Katrain

Naggar

Pong Lake
Sanctuary

Baijnath

Jogindarnagar

21

Manikaran

Chango

Pong
Reservoir

Kullu

Kanawar
Sanctuary

Puh

Jawala
Mukhi

Beas

Nargu
Sanctuary

Bhuntar
Bajaura

Pin Valley
National Park

Lippa Asran
Sanctuary

Tira
Sujanpur

Uhl

Khokhan
Sanctuary

Rupi Bhaba
Sanctuary

Kalpa

Hamirpur

Mandi

Pandoh

Great Himalayan
National Park

Hoshiarpur

Barsar

Sundarnagar

Tirthan
Sanctuary

Sarahan

Satluj

RAMPUR
VALLEY

Sangla

BASPA VALLEY

Una

Bandli
Sanctuary

Rampur

Daranghati
Sanctuary

Govindsagar
Sanctuary

21

SUKET HILLS

Karsog

22

Govind
Sagar

Phagwara

Naina Devi

Bilaspur

Majathal
Sanctuary

Narkanda

Rohru

Kiratpur

Naldera

Tons

Phillaur

Satluj

Fagu

Theog

Jubbal

SHIMLA

Kufri

Talra
Sanctuary

Ludhiana

Rupnagar

SHIMLA
HILLS

N

Chail

D

I

A

PUNJAB

Kasauli

Solan

Chaupal

Yamnotri

Shilli
Sanctuary

NAG TIBBA
RANGE

CHANDIGARH

1

Churdhar
Sanctuary

MUSSOORIE RANGE

Dharasu

Renuka

SHIWALIK RANGE

Nahan

Ambala

Simbalbara
Sanctuary

Paonta
Sahib

UTTAR

Tehi

Dehra Dun

PRADESH

National Park/
Wildlife Sanctuary

21

National Highway
Number

Road

Trekking Route

HARYANA

Narendranaga

Rishikesh

Kurukshetra

Yamuna

Alaknanda

Roorkee

206

HIMACHAL PRADESH

A holiday in Himachal typically begins somewhere on the drive to Shimla, when one is greeted by the first gust of fresh mountain air.

Given Shimla's proximity to the plains, it is the obvious choice for a first halt in Himachal. India's primary hill resort, Shimla continues to charm tourists with its unique ambience, a blend of the colonial and the Himachali. As one absorbs the vista from the top of Jakhu hill, it becomes apparent that Shimla is also ideally located to step into the rest of Himachal. Roads lead north to Kullu and Lahaul, east to Kinnaur and Spiti, and west to Kangra and Chamba. To the south lie the lower districts of Solan and Sirmaur.

The upper valley of the Beas is quite simply amongst the most beautiful places on earth. Known as Kullu-Manali after its popular tourist destinations, it offers bewitching countryside, excellent trekking and climbing routes, and a healthy crop of wild cannabis that ensure that the valley will always have a committed following.

Across the Pir Panjal range, north of Kullu-Manali lies Lahaul. Lahaul's rugged splendour has lent a singular character to the land and its people. Together with its twin sub–division of Spiti, this unspoilt mountain enclave is a preserve of ancient Buddhist heritage, and contains some of the most sacred centres of Tibetan Buddhism. Trekkers used to traverse Lahaul on their way to Zanskar and Ladakh, a dramatic journey that was made vicariously through books and photographs by those less inclined or able. But now the Manali-Leh Highway cuts through this high-altitude wonderland, served regularly by bus, and open to all who have permission.

In contrast to Lahaul and Spiti, two districts that have offered easy access both to the monsoon as well as to visitors are Kangra and Chamba. Kangra's rain-drenched slopes are dotted with numerous temples once renowned for their legendary wealth. Plundered by raiders from the plains in the 11th century, these shrines have since become milestones of an ever-strengthening faith, and are now amongst the most sacred places of pilgrimage in Himachal Pradesh.

Chamba, tucked away behind the Dhauladhar ranges, remained relatively insulated from strife and change. It nurtured an unbroken tradition of medieval Hinduism, symbols of which are still in evidence today. Over the centuries, it also fostered a unique style of Pahari art and architecture, a cultural heritage that has been carefully preserved.

Perhaps the star of Himachal is Kinnaur, that curious amalgam of Buddhist and Hindu customs, with its spectacular landscape, succulent fruits and exquisite local wine, the beauty of the Kinnauras and their dance and music. Linking arms with the Kinnauras in the serpentine chain dancing at dusk around the temple courtyard, heady with *anguri*, watching the alpenglow on the massif of Kinner-Kailash above: Himachali memories endure.

Preceding pages: a Pahari miniature from the Bhuri Singh Museum at Chamba; prayer flags on the Rohtang Pass.

SHIMLA

Few cities have had the distinction of luring an entire government away from its capital on the strength of their climatic charms. Shimla's ambience attracted the British in such measure that, come summer, it seemed justifiable to shift the complete administration of an Empire from Calcutta across the Gangetic plain to its environs.

A day's journey away from Delhi by road or rail, Shimla today is India's – and possibly Asia's – largest and most popular hill station. Spread along a 7.5 mile (12 km) long crescent-shaped ridge at a height of 6,700 ft (2,130 m), the city spills over the peaks and declivities of the crest onto its slopes. Alpine cottages, shopping promenades, recreational centres, restaurants and hotels cling to the sides of the Himalayan spurs, enveloped by dense woods of oak, pine, fir and rhododendron. A motorable road encircles the base of the town, above which traffic is restricted. That this unlikely hill town should once have been the seat of the British Empire in India seems remarkable. A glance at the city's short history reveals that many of its present attractions are actually ingrained in its past.

Perhaps the earliest visitor to pause in Shimla for a breath of fresh air was the mythical Lord Hanuman. On his flight to fetch the miraculous Sanjivni herb in a bid to save the life of Lakshman, the monkey god alighted on top of Jakhu hill for a moment of relaxation. A temple dedicated to him marks the spot. Aptly, a tribe of monkeys have established an unrivalled domain in the woods around the temple, and enjoy a protected status as manifestations of the deity.

Curiously, the modest village that existed on the ridge below Jakhu did not derive its name from this divine visitation, but from the goddess Shyamla, a manifestation of Kali, whose image was worshipped by the villagers. The first recorded reference to this village exists in the notes made by a British surveyor in 1817, in which Shimla is described as 'a middling-sized village where a fakir is stationed to give water to travellers.'

It was not to remain so for long. Officers from the British army had earlier been drawn to this cool, airy ridge for respite from the rigours of their campaign against the Gurkhas in the Satluj valley. Their accounts of its delightful environs attracted others, and in 1819 the first British home came up in the form of the modest cottage of the Assistant Political Agent to the area. His successor, Lt. Kennedy, erected the first permanent residence in 1822, which came to be dubbed 'Kennedy House' over the years, serving as a sort of summer home for an increasing number of heat-weary officers.

Others followed, and soon a fair-sized resort had materialised, occupied mostly by 'the rich, the idle, and the invalid', as one guest described it. Visitors included Lord Amherst, the Governor General in 1827, and Lord Combermere, the Commander-in-Chief of the British forces in India in 1828. These visits initiated the move to elevate Shimla's status from that of a settlement to one worthy of receiving the elite in British society. The Government did not find it difficult to convince the North Indian Rajas who owned this land to part with it, and 'Shimla Hill' became the property of the British in 1830.

With this acquisition, passing the summer in Shimla gained popularity by the season. Gradually, Shimla won recognition as an important political centre as well, with the virtual relocation of the Government taking place to its cool environs every summer. Eventually, this transmigration was given formal sanction in 1864. Shimla was declared the summer capital of the Government of India, and remained so till 1947, the year India achieved independence.

It was evident that Shimla's popularity lay in its ability to soothe those English souls who had suffered from "too much East." Unlike Calcutta, this was a city of their own making, which they developed carefully as a place of heath and pleasure, and more specifically, as a little England. Elegant country cottages as well as stately

Georgian manors were constructed to house the discerning Englishfolk. 'Auckland House' became the residence of the Governor-General, 'Peterhoff' the house of the Earl of Elgin, 'Bentinck's Castle' was built for Lord Bentinck, and 'Barnes' Court' was erected for Sir Edward Barnes, then Commander-in-Chief in India.

The western shoulder of Jakhu, known simply as 'The Ridge' was chosen as the site for Christchurch, the second church to be built in northern India, complete with murals and stained glass windows. Further west, on Observatory Hill, rose the imposing grey stone structure of the Viceregal Lodge, constructed at the behest of Lord Dufferin in 1885. A motorable highway from Kalka to Shimla was commissioned, and completed by 1857. The New Cart Road, as it was called, ran along the base of the town. From it rose the Mall, a glamorous shopping promenade arching up the sunny southern slopes towards the Ridge, then dipping away in a long crescent to meet the Cart Road once

again. The Mall became an avenue for the chic to be seen in their rickshaws, being drawn by pullers in uniforms conforming to the colours and crests of the occupants.

Along the Mall were the Davico's ballroom, as well as the Gaiety theatre, an echo of the old Garrick in London. Davico's was the venue of high teas and late-night dances before and after the plays staged in the summer at the Gaiety by the Amateur Dramatics Club. The theatre's green room, too, became a social club, yet another place of leisure. In time, the entertainment began to spill over from the ballroom to the residences of the officers. The summer sojourn in Shimla seemed to have become one continuous social whirl.

This revelry was made successful largely by the salubrious climate and environs of the hill city. Shimla, with its crisp, bracing air, lay amidst temperate Himalayan forests, an ideal location for invigorating outdoor excursions. Annandale, a grassy clearing near a glen 3 miles (5 km) away from the Ridge,

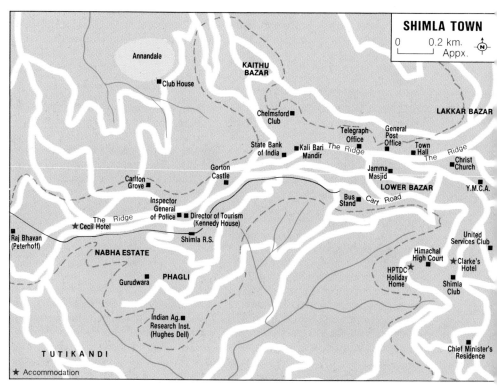

was a sporting venue for cricket and racing, as well as a favourite spot for picnics and fêtes. The Glen nearby was a quieter, more idyllic retreat, threaded by a clear stream. Across a spur were the Chadwick Falls, 215 ft/65 m high, and most spectacular during the monsoon. Dappled trails crisscrossed on the densely wooded dome of Jakhu, the central feature on the sub-Himalayan ridge.

The Forest Road circumvented the hill, passing through the eastern suburb of Sanjauli. It was in the summer a 6 km-long secluded track, springy with pine needles, and gave splendid views of the snow covered peaks towards the north. A steep 1 mile/2 km haul from the Ridge to Jakhu's summit culminated at the Hanuman temple from where the prospect was even better, and included a panorama of the town and its suburbs. Similar viewpoints within reach were the western crests of Summer Hill and Prospect Hill, both about 3 miles/5 km from the Ridge, and visited often during a leisurely afternoon's stroll.

Some preferred to retreat from this social merry-go-round. One of the first acts of Lord Kitchner on taking over as Commander-in-Chief was to build a magnificent residence for himself near Kufri, 11 miles/18 km away. With its extensive gardens landscaped amidst a pine forest, the mansion rivalled that of the Viceroy in Shimla. Lord Curzon is said to have personally supervised the laying out of a nine-hole golf course at Naldehra, 14 miles/23 km from the city. The Indian aristocracy, too, was similarly inclined. Maharaja Bhupinder Singh of Patiala founded a summer resort for his own State at Chail, complete with a cricket pitch, probably the highest in the world. Sited on a spur, his palace overlooked the distant Satluj river as it wound its way into the plains.

To the north rose the snow-clad ranges. At dusk, the lights of Kasauli and Shimla twinkled in the distance. The Maharaja is said to have made the move to Chail when his relationship with the bureaucracy in Shimla began to sour (he had been among the few Indian

exceptions whom the British elite chose to admit to their social circles). As a rule, the Mall and its charms were maintained as their exclusive preserve. Access to the promenade was denied not only to traffic but also, excepting the aristocracy, to all Indians.

Inevitably, the local bazaars began to mushroom in the backyard. Strings of shanty shops clung on to the sharp slopes falling away from the Mall towards the Cart road. Described by Rudyard Kipling as 'a crowded rabbit-warren', it came to be dubbed, with some accuracy, as the 'Lower Bazaar'. On the other side of the Ridge, a similar though smaller cluster of shops began to proliferate on Jakhu's northern slopes, occupied mostly by carpenters and wood-merchants, a trade that was booming in this rapidly growing town. Once again the name given to it was plain and descriptive – the 'Lakkar Bazaar'. It was described by the Committee on Shimla Improvement as 'an excrescence on the European quarter'. Thus, while the Mall and the British estates were developed with meticulous

care, the local bazaars were left alone. Over the years, Shimla acquired a second flavour, that of the hillsman. The crowded streets of the Lower Bazaar had their own distinct, unpredictable charm, as alluring as that of the Mall.

That continues to be the essence of Shimla to this day. **The Mall** still occupies centrestage, where most of Shimla seems to converge in the evening. While the rash of clubs, bars, restaurants and shopping complexes patronised by the tourists are ample reason to visit the high street, 'Mall-ing' itself has become quite a favourite pastime of the residents, who amuse themselves by strolling the length of the promenade to observe the visitors. **Scandal Point**, where the Mall touches the Ridge, is a prime rendezvous. The meeting place had earned its colourful name fifty years ago when a handsome Indian prince and the beautiful daughter of a senior British official met here for a long ride together on their horses. The story goes that their absence of a few days scandalised the town, though it has been written that 'none

Chapslee, one of Shimla's most interesting private hotels.

212

THE VICEROY'S TRAIN

The logistical difficulties of access to Shimla almost stymied the advantage of turning this hill resort into the summer capital of the British Raj. Every year, when the annual move to Shimla was to be made, hundreds of mules and local porters would have to struggle up from Kalka, at the foothills, with loads of official files, despatch boxes, officers' luggage and other paraphernalia. The Cart Road from Kalka to Shimla was completed in 1856, and the subsequent widening of this road led to the introduction of the *tonga* (horse carriage) service. However, the need for an efficient mode of transportation to the summer capital kept growing as the annual uphill exodus became bigger and matters of state grew more complex.

The obvious answer was a railway line between Kalka and Shimla. This was a daunting prospect, as the topography of the region was difficult with diverse rock strata being encountered along the survey route. In fact, a plan for the Kalka-Shimla railway was drawn up as early as in 1847, but was not acted upon, probably on account of the apparent impossibility of the task involved. Lord Curzon, the then Viceroy, proved to be the driving force behind this project and personally monitored the progress of the construction work. The laying of this 60 mile/96 km-long railway track was an engineering feat involving the construction of 103 tunnels and 24 overbridges, and the cost of construction worked out to about 17 million rupees at that time.

After two years of untiring labour, Shimla was on the rail map of the country. The line was inaugurated by the Viceroy himself and in 1891 opened to freight traffic. The first passenger train was flagged off in November, 1903. The railway provided a boost to the economy and trade of Shimla, enticing many to set up business and residence in this exclusive and elegant hill capital.

The Viceregal carriage in the train had the most opulent fittings and upholstery and was designed to meet every indulgence of the man who had made this seemingly impossible task a reality.

Even though Shimla is now efficiently connected by air and road with the plains, the train journey is immensely popular. The pace is gentle, affording ample opportunity to slowly take in the beautiful mountainscapes unfolding at each turn.

The train takes just over five hours from Kalka to Shimla, chuffing through verdant countryside and 18 tiny, old-world stations. The rail car, which is slightly faster, takes about four hours, and on account of its generous glazing, affords a better view of the passing landscape. Currently two pairs of trains and a pair of rail cars ply between Kalka and Shimla.

For the railway buff also, this narrow gauge track and its system of working offers an interesting subject for study. The trains here function on the basis of the ancient Neal's Token System – perhaps the only instance of this system still in use. A spherical metal token is carried in a leather pouch attached to a ring which is handed over at each station in exchange for another token for the next station. This is then inserted into an electro-mechanical contraption, which raises the signal allowing the train to pass on. At dusk the scene is especially intriguing as the exchange takes place in the light of a flaming torch or an old lamp.

The narrow gauge of the track necessitated the construction of very small carriages; similar 'toy trains' as they are called, ply between Siliguri and Darjeeling in the East, and Coimbatore and Ooty in the South, but the Kalka-Shimla train is the oldest and the most romantic of these.

could resist his equestrian charms'.

The British, of course, have left, to be replaced by the Government of Himachal Pradesh. The Tudor **Viceregal Lodge** now houses the Indian Institute of Advanced Studies, **Barnes' Court** has become the residence of the Governor, and **Bentinck's Castle** has been converted into the Grand Hotel. In fact, the economics of state tourism has dictated a similar commercial use for many of the colonial residences – a windfall for the visitor to Himachal. Lord Kitchner's retreat is now marketed as **Hotel Wildflower Hall**, and Patiala's summer palace as **Hotel Chail Palace**, with the Maharaja and Maharani suite on offer. Even the outhouses in these grand complexes are let out as independent 'log huts'. Other lodging facilities available to travellers are generously scattered across the labyrinth of sub-Himalayan ridges, thanks to the widespread network of rest houses and 'Inspection Bungalows' that the British system left behind.

This infrastructure has, in turn, been enhanced by the state tourism department. With almost the entire district falling within the reach of incorporating road-development, remote sites that were once considered retreats have now become destinations, a short drive away. The golf course at **Naldehra** is open to annual membership, or even a green fee, along with a choice of accommodation. **Mashobra** 8 miles/13 km, the site of the annual Sipi fair, is a popular day's excursion due to its enchanting forest trails. For those who wish to prolong their visit, refuge is available 2 miles/3 km away at the beautiful **Craignano rest house**, once the Himalayan home of the Italian Count of Craignano. **Fagu** 14 miles/22 km has yet another rest house sited to afford a superb view on either side of the ridge. Overlooking the Giri valley, Fagu's merits are heightened by the apple orchards that surround it. The fruit was introduced to the area by Samuel 'Satyanand' Stokes, an American who came to India in 1904 as a missionary, but ended up buying an estate in **Thanedar**, 51 miles/82 km

A spaniel seems to keep better shape than the soldiers it follows along Shimla's Mall.

214

from Shimla, after embracing Hinduism. He imported the 'Delicious' variety of apple from the USA, and began a lasting tradition by planting them in his garden. Today apples sustain hundreds of families commercially, and Himachal Pradesh markets ten million cases of high grade apples every year to the rest of the country.

All these destinations lie on the higher reaches of the same ridge system as Shimla, but the valleys lower down have places of interest as well. Thirty two miles (51 km) away, on the banks of the Satluj are the sulphur springs known as **Tattapani**, Hot Water. Upstream, 87 miles/140 km from Shimla, is **Rampur**, a commercial town with an interesting Buddhist monastery and an ancient Hindu temple. It comes alive in November during the annual Lavi *mela*, one of the biggest trade fairs of northern India. People from the remote mountain reaches of Kinnaur, Spiti and Lahaul congregate on the banks of the Satluj to trade local produce that includes wool, dried fruits, home spun blankets and shawls. Twenty one miles (34 km) beyond is **Sarahan**, reknowned for its exquisite pagoda-like Bhimakali temple. Another riverbank location is **Rohru** on the Pabbar, teeming with trout, and for inveterate anglers well worth the 65 miles/104 km drive.

Cool and refreshing during summer, these ridge-line venues come under a heavy blanket of snow during the winter months. While most of the summer resort attractions pale, two points on the ridge emerge as prime locations for winter sports. **Kufri** 11 miles/18 km and **Narkanda** 40 miles/64 km have excellent slopes for skiing, as well as facilities for a wintry refuge. Shimla has an ice skating rink beyond the Ridge, its glassy surface maintained between December and February. Shimla has quite a following in winter. Revellers drive up during December in anticipation of a white Christmas, and stay on to ring in the new year.

Not all find a warm night's stay, despite the scores of plush hotels in town. Shimla's popularity has soared over the years, and in prime time it caters to a floating population that outstrips the residents. A string of tourist bungalows along the three-hour drive from Kalka absorbs much of the disappointed crowd. In fact, several stations enroute deserve a stopover, especially one that is actually a bit of a detour. **Kasauli**, 48 miles/77 km short of Shimla, has managed to retain a quiet charm owing to its classification as an army cantonment town. From 'Monkey Point,' the distant lights of Chandigarh and the glint of the amber sky on the the meandering Satluj present a beautiful view at dusk.

For most, however, Kasauli is clearly a 'poor man's Shimla'. Up on Jakhu's shoulder is where they all want to be, despite the crowd. In recent years, the edge of the Ridge has begun to crumble, the charms of Davico's have been lost to a fire, and unplanned growth has predictable resulted in water shortages and choked peripheral roads. None of this has fazed the Shimla buffs. Merrymakers from the plains continue to be drawn to this hospitable hill city whose name has become a synonym for 'coolth'.

Deodar pines forest the slopes below Wildflower Hall.

THE KULLU VALLEY

Celebrated as the Valley of the Gods, Eden of apple and cannabis cultivation and cradle of the great Beas river, the Kullu valley is a long and narrow slice of lush verdure nestling between the Dhauladhar and Pir Panjal ranges. It is about 50 miles (80 km) in length, extending from the gorge of the Beas at Aut up to the Rohtang Pass, and rarely more than a couple of kilometres wide. According to available historical records the original name of Kullu was Kuluta, which finds mention in ancient Sanskrit texts like the Vishnu Purana, Ramayana and Mahabharata. However, folklore has it that the original name of this valley was Kulantapith, meaning 'the end of the habitable world' – appropriate enough if one stands at the Rohtang pass and views the fertile, inhabited Kullu valley on the one side and the stark, desolate moonscape of Lahaul on the other.

Kullu formed one of the oldest of the Punjab Hill States and was founded not later than the first or second century. Its original capital was Jagatsukh, from where the early Rajas ruled for twelve generations. Then it was shifted to Naggar and, much later in the 17th century, to what is now Kullu town.

In any historical account of this region, the reign of Raja Jagat Singh (AD 1637–1672) deserves special mention as it was then that the idol of Raghunathji was brought from Ayodhya and installed in Kullu. To expiate his having caused the death of a Brahmin, the king submitted his kingdom to the god by placing the image of Raghunathji on his *gaddi* (throne). Thereafter Jagat Singh and his successors regarded themselves as the regents of Raghunath, who remains the chief deity of the valley.

There are several other temples around Kullu which merit a visit for the legends associated with them and the stone carvings and images of gods found in them; these are **Jagannathi Devi**, **Vaishno Devi**, **Basheshar Mahadev** and **Bijli Mahadev**. The Bijli Mahadev temple is set on a spur across from Kullu town and sports a 60-feet-high staff, meant to attract divine blessings in the form of lightning which shatters the Shivaling into pieces. These are then meant to be put together by the temple priest and Shiva's image is restored to its original form till it is shattered again by the same divine energy.

Naggar is situated on the left bank of the Beas, roughly between Kullu and Manali, and commands a spectacular view of the valley. A splendid old castle here, built during the reign of Rajah-Sidh Singh (16th century AD) now serves as a hotel. There are some interesting temples scattered around Naggar like the sandstone **Gauri Shankar** temple and the **Vishnu** temple. A short walk above the castle is the **Roerich Gallery**, an elegant white-washed mansion displaying the works of the famous Russian painter Nicholas Roerich who, like many others, came to the valley and then stayed on.

Jagatsukh, again on the left bank of the Beas, is about 7.5 miles (12 km) upstream and towards Manali. The *shikhara* style **Shiva temple** and the neighbouring **Devi Sharvali temple** evoke the history of this ancient capital of Kullu. About 6 miles (10 km) south of Kullu lies **Bhuntar**, which has an airport serviced by a daily flight between Delhi and Chandigarh. From here one can take off into adjoining valleys like those of the Parvati and Sainj which branch off from the main Kullu valley.

The **Parvati valley** runs north-east from Bhuntar and is named after a consort the of the great god Shiva. The river that gives the valley its name ultimately merges with the Beas via a narrow gorge. The most frequented spot in this valley is **Manikaran**, a place of pilgrimage for Hindus and Sikhs, famous for its sulphur springs. A dip in the hot springs is meant to be good not merely for health but also for one's journey towards nirvana.

There is a legend associated with the hot springs which narrates that a serpent god stole the goddess' earrings while she was bathing; upon being threatened by Mahadev (Shiva), the mighty snake snorted the earrings out from his sub-terranean residence, causing holes to be made in the rock through which the hot water now bubbles out! **Kasol**, located right on the Parvati river, is an angler's dream. The rest house overlooks a grassy expanse scattered with cedars, with an inviting beach of white sand on the river's edge.

Located at the northern extremity of the Kullu valley, **Manali** is the prime tourist destination in Himachal Pradesh. Legend has it that the name combines the word 'Manu' and 'Alaya,' meaning the home of Manu, the father of mankind, and that this was where the world was renewed after the great mythical deluge.

Such legends are not difficult to believe when one is suddenly confronted with the mysterious and slightly forbidding **Dhungri temple** in the silent deodar forest above Manali village. Dedicated to the goddess Hadimba, this wooden temple has a four-tiered, pagoda shaped roof with a beautifully carved main door. This is said to be the spot where Bhima, the great Pandava of the Mahabarata epic, killed the cruel de-mon Hadimb. Bhima married his sister Hadimba, who later came to be wor-shipped as a goddess. There is also a morbid story of how the ruler who built the temple ordered the hand of the artist who carved the temple to be cut off so that he would not duplicate the work.

During the period when caravans of traders used the route through Manali and across the Rohtang Pass, Manali used to be called 'Dana,' meaning fod-der: this was the last point for mule trains to stock up before proceeding into the barren realm of Lahaul and beyond. The postal district used to be called **P. O. Duff Dunbar** after an enthusiastic forest officer of the same name who was posted here in the middle of the 19th century, and planted many of the forests in the region. He grew to love the place, its culture and people, and constructed his own house, Dunbar House, in Manali in the local architectural style.

The booming tourism industry has led to the mushrooming of hotels and guest houses in and around Manali. This

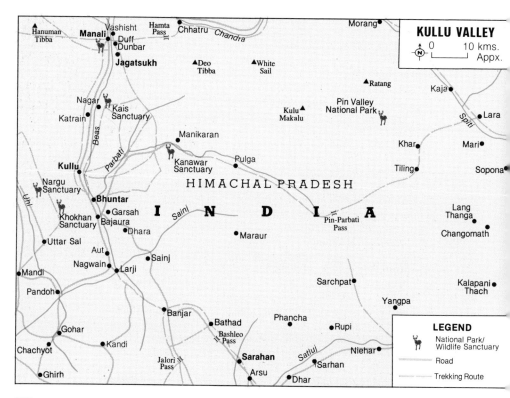

unplanned growth, especially along the main road and the bazaar, has resulted in a concrete eyesore. But the surrounding apple orchards and deodar forests serve as a green and soothing balm after one's senses have been ravaged by the cacophonic bazaar.

About 1.8 miles (2 km) away from Manali, on the left bank of the Beas, lie the **Vashisht** hot sulphur springs. Shower-fitted bathrooms in the Turkish style have made the springs a popular spot for visitors. About 7.5 miles (12 km) up from Manali, en route to the Rohtang Pass, one can stop at the pretty and quiet **Kothi** rest house; slightly further up the route are the **Rahalla Falls**. Between Manali and Kothi lies the **Solang valley** which has excellent ski slopes and is the hot spot during the cold and white skiing season. And finally, about 32 miles (50 km) from Manali, lies the famous **Rohtang Pass**, offering some of the most spectacular views of mountains in the Himalaya.

Lying near the Chandrakhani pass, and accessible through an invigorating trek, is the mysterious village of **Malana**. The village community here has its own unique culture and system of government. The language is different from the dialects of the surrounding region and the marriage rites and customs liberal, with no taboo on the number of times a person can get married. The system of resolving disputes involves the entire community, with appeals going to the village supreme court or Harcha, convened by the head priest on a tall platform of slate stones. The punishment is unusual: the defaulter is required to serve the entire village with a feast of mutton! The houses here have handsomely carved woodwork, some depicting soldiers in long armoured costume. This gives some credence to the prevailing belief that Alexander the Great came as far as Malana and some of his soldiers stayed behind, married local women and developed the distinctive Malana society.

Apart from the music of the Beas river and other streams and brooks which pervades this valley, it also resounds

A path winds through one of Manali's orchards.

with traditional songs and dance, laughter and celebration. The **Dussehra** festival, commemorating the victory of good over evil, is celebrated in spectacular style in Kullu. Gold and silver images of gods and goddesses are brought to the Dhalpur Maidan or field from all over the valley in colourful processions of palanquins and chariots. There is Hadimba from Manali, Raghunathji from Kullu – playing host, as it were – and Jamlu, the presiding deity of Malana village. According to a legend, it was Jambu who opened the casket containing the gods of Kullu on top of the Chandrakhani pass; a gust of wind sprang up and scattered them to their various abodes in the valley.

The festival is celebrated in October and continues for a week with much merry-making, music and dance. The traditional 'Natti' dance is also performed by several groups, and Dussehra provides a good opportunity to see this gentle and graceful dance. Dusshera time also means the springing up of many little shops and temporary markets which have on offer traditional clothes and handicrafts like the Kullu shawls and caps, *pattoos*, *namdas* and *gudmas* (all wool-woven), and *pullans* (footwear made from plant fibre and goat hair).

One of the reasons for the Kullu valley becoming an up-front tourist destination, apart from its inherent lure, is its easy accessibility by air. However, overland access via the national highway is preferable if one is not pressed for time, as the route weaves through Bilaspur with the magnificent Gobind Sagar Lake and then enters **Mandi**, a district town with a rich history and culture.

Scattered around Mandi are several old temples with beautiful stone carvings. The district itself, largely constituted by the two erstwhile princely states of Mandi and Suket, has several beautiful places which are almost unexplored by tourists. These include **Sundernagar** and the adjoining Balh valley, **Rewalsar Lake** with its floating reed islands and Buddhist, Sikh and Hindu shrines and

A procession carrying images of the village gods leaves a temple compound.

220

Janjheli which offers good trekking possibilities. The **Karsog** subdivision is prime apple orchard country and has an elegant rest house set in the midst of a thick forest. Thus, a drive through the Mandi region can be a rewarding experience in itself and sets the mood for the entry into the Kullu valley.

In recent years, apart from just walking around and drinking in the sheer beauty of this valley and the surrounding ranges, the tourist has access to well organised adventure sports activity. The mountaineering and sports institute at Manali offers training facilities for basic and advanced rock climbing, mountaineering and skiing. For those who can afford it, 'heliskiing' is an exciting option, in which a helicopter drops one off on ski slopes which may otherwise be inaccessible or too tedious to trudge up. White water rafting on the Beas is an exhilarating sport for the stout-hearted, and rafting tours can be arranged with expert river guides. The Beas, the Parvati and some of the other lesser rivers and streams of the valley abound in trout,

and fishing has become an immensely popular sport attracting angling enthusiasts from far and near. The valley also offers abundant trekking and mountaineering possibilities, of varying degrees of difficulty, encompassing the most spectacular Himalayan pastures, lakes, passes and forests.

An extremely pleasant and invigorating two-day excursion from Manali is the trek to **Brighu Lake** (13,780 ft/4,200 m), which nestles high above the valley just below Brighu Peak (15,423 ft/4,701 m) on the ridge separating the Beas and Hamta valleys. The lake can be approached from near Gulaba on the Rohtang Pass road, from where the climb is less demanding, or from Vashisht village near Manali, which is a far more arduous excursion.

This then is Kullu-Manali: heady and exhilarating, luring the traveller to succumb to its natural beauty, its cordial, artless folk (many visitors are compulsive 'regulars'): in a word, the best that the Himalayan treasure-house has to offer in any single place.

Roadside astrologer uses Rose-ringed parakeets to divine customer's fortunes.

THE MANALI-LEH HIGHWAY

The Manali-Leh road is open for less than three months in the year, from about mid-July to the beginning of October. Crossing the Pir Panjal, the Greater Himalaya and the Zaskar ranges, it attains a maximum elevation of over 17,400 feet (5,304 m) en route.

Manali, the starting point for a 297 mile (476 km) journey over four high passes and some of the most awe-inspiring terrain in the world, represents the last stop to savour the comforts of civilization. Up to **Palchan** the going is sedate, along the Beas, amidst apple orchards and scattered dwellings. Here begins the winding climb up to the Rohtang Pass, 32 miles (52 km) from Manali. Past **Kothi**, the last village in the valley, the road makes its way up through mixed forests of age-old pine and deodar, oak, rhododendron and horse chestnut, interspersed with newly planted poplar and willow, till it emerges above the tree line at Marhi. **Marhi** is a collection of restaurants housed in shacks, standing out against a backdrop of steep grassy slopes reaching up to the Rohtang Pass at 13,050 feet (3,978 m). **Rohtang**, which translates chillingly as 'heap of dead bodies', is the windswept divide between the serene and verdant beauty of Kullu and the stark expanse of rock and glacier on the other side, from where the moisture-laden monsoon clouds are held at bay by the Pir Panjal range. Visible opposite Rohtang is a labyrinth of high peaks and hanging glaciers enclosed between the Chandra and Bhaga rivers, including **Gyephang**, the presiding deity of the region.

From Rohtang to **Khoksar** is a series of continuous turns, on 12 miles (20 km) of road surface which never seems to recover from the ravages of winter, when the pass is closed for six months. Short of Khoksar, a dirt track branches off into a seemingly never-never land – up the Chandra valley, over the Kunzum pass and into Spiti. Khoksar is the first village in Lahaul, characteristic of the ones to

The Rohtang Pass divides the lush richness of the Kullu Valley from the harsher climate of Lahaul.

follow: groves of willow and poplar, potato fields irrigated by perennial glacial streams, and mud houses.

After crossing the Chandra at Khoksar, the road stays on the right bank, well above the river through **Khangsar**, **Sissu** and **Gondhla** before descending rapidly near Tandi, where the Chandra meets the Bhaga. **Sissu** has a charming creeper-covered rest house overlooking a shallow lake where the valley of the Chandra widens out in to a bowl. The road crosses the Bhaga at Tandi, and 5 miles (9 km) beyond lies **Keylong**, district headquarters of Lahaul and Spiti and the last pretension to anything approaching a town till Leh, 225 miles (360 km) away.

Beyond Keylong the road stays well above the narrow and constricted Bhaga valley till it opens out near **Darcha**. Darcha is well known in trekking circles with trails to Zanskar over the Shingu La (16,500 ft/5,029 m) and across to the Chandra valley. Ten miles (17 km) beyond Darcha the road crosses to the left bank of the Bhaga at **Patseo** where

there is a small resthouse. A sign-board nearby informs the traveller that he has seen his last tree for 150 miles (250 km). After passing through the exotically named Zingzingbar pastures, the road ascends through switchback turns up stony mountain sides to the **Bara Lacha La** (16,050 ft/4,892 m), 47 miles (75 km) from Keylong, after skirting the beautiful tarn of Suraj Tal, the source of the Bhaga.

Bara Lacha La, 'pass with crossroads on summit,' is perhaps the greatest of the four passes on the Manali-Leh road. Straddling the meeting point of gigantic ranges, its majestic sweep offers passage not only down the Bhaga and across into Ladakh but also to the Chandra valley and to Spiti. From the pass, curving around glacial ponds, the road descends through some of the roughest stretches of the route to the pastures of **Sarchu**, 67 miles (107 km) from Keylong. From here begins a passage across a lunar landscape – wide open spaces punctuated by rocky mountain faces and shattered boulders in a bizarre array of

ahauli hildren elax above he Chenab iver.

colours and shapes; a world which dwarfs mortal man and brings a piercing awareness of Nature's timelessness. At Sarchu, where the terraces above the Yonam and the Lingti Chu cover over 250 square km, a small colony of tents comes up these days, to provide basic amenities once the road opens. For the adventurous there is a trek from here to Phugtal monastery in Zanskar. The arrow-straight stretches of road beyond Sarchu are a speedster's dream till the crossing of the Tsarab and the climb for **Long Lacha La** (16,600 ft/5,059 m), 33 miles/54 km from Sarchu.

The dry and dusty ascent of the Longlacha La, the third pass on the road, is fatiguing for both man and machine. Past the bridge over the Tsarab are the 21 Gata loops over a six mile (10 km) distance. Approaching the top, the fantastic shapes and colours of rock faces and mountain tops begin to offer compensation. Once across the pass and driving down to Pang, two miles (3 km) away, the accompanying stream hurrying down to join the Doze river makes the journey pleasanter.

Pang, like Sarchu, is just another name marked on the map, distinguished only by a few derelict army built huts. The road crosses the Sumskyal, a deep, wide gash marking the edge of the Moray Plain, a massive plateau at an altitude of over 15,000 ft (4,500 m), and 28 miles (45 km) across. Climbing up from Pang, the road fringes at first a blinding white alkali basin, and thereafter the waterless plain ranging in width from 2-4 miles (3-7 km). It offers the adventurous some singular possibilities – chasing marmots for a closer view, looking for the elusive *kyang* (Tibetan wild ass) or the *nabu* (blue sheep), or simply stopping by with the nomadic *pashmina*-rearing shepherds of Rupshu.

Dibring, at the other end of the Moray Plain, is another sibling of Pang and Sarchu – just a few abandoned huts. From here begins a gradual ascent to **Taglang La**, 12.5 miles (20 km) away and at 17,469 ft (5,325 m) the highest point on the Manali-Leh highway. After Baralacha La, the only snow on the route is at Long Lacha La and around Taglang La; this is an index of the height of the permanent snow line in this arid land, where the sun beats down from the bluest and clearest of skies.

From Taglang La begins the descent to settled, inhabited Ladakh. **Rumtse**, the first village, is 13 miles (21 km) down, at a height of 14,500 ft (4,420 m). Past Rumtse, 56 miles (90 km) from Leh, the road meanders along the silt-laden Gya Chu till it meets the Indus at **Upshi**. From Upshi to Leh is a well travelled road, through Karu where a bridge across the Indus Leads to Hemis, the largest monastery in Ladakh, and another road branches off to such exotic locations as Changthang, Pang-gong Tso and Hanle. Further to the right are the ruins of Nyarma – a monastery founded in the times of Rinchen Tsangpo, and on the hill beside is the more imposing bulk Thikse Gompa. Shey Gompa follows and then, short of Choglamsar, the road leaves the Indus for the last few kilometres to Leh, where civilization beckons the weary traveller back to hot baths, soft beds and crowded bazaars.

Left, the turbulent Chandra river drains the Lahaul valley before joining the Bagha to form the Chenab. **Right**, potato fields occupy all cultivable areas in Lahaul.

KINNAUR, LAHAUL AND SPITI

The three tribal regions of Kinnaur, Lahaul and Spiti occupy about a third of the state of Himachal. Bordering Tibet and Ladakh, these areas straddle the loftiest mountains and valleys of the state.

Kinnaur is the easternmost and most accessible of the three tracts. This fabled land is said to take its name from the Kinners, original inhabitants of northern India, pushed into this mountain fastness by the Aryan hordes. Today's Kinnauras are not pristine representatives of that ancient race but an amalgam of the various people who have reached this sanctuary down the ages. There are few records of the early history of this region. It is surmised that, after the advent of Buddhism in the 8th century, the western Tibetan power of Guge held sway over Kinnaur. When Guge broke up, small local fiefdoms arose, and in the 16th century the Bushahr kings, who

trace their origin from Kamru in Kinnaur, welded the area together and it stayed part of this principality till Indian Independence. The mythological history of Kinnaur is contained in the *chironings*, a fascinating oral history of the origin and times of important deities, recited at all important events and festivals by the hereditary oracle of each deity.

Among the three tribal areas, Kinnaur displays the maximum variation in terrain, climate, vegetation and wild life, and in the people and their cultures. Broadly, it is possible to distinguish a lower, a middle and an upper Kinnaur.

Lower Kinnaur is a somewhat wilder and grander continuation of the preceding areas of Shimla district. On the left bank of the Satluj, forested mountain flanks slope down through fields and apple orchards before dropping steeply to the river. To enjoy the country, a walk along the old Hindustan-Tibet road is recommended. Starting from Sarahan in Shimla district, the track winds through some beautiful mixed forests of deodar, pine, oak and

Lahauli village near Gondla, above the Chenab river.

rhododendron, with night halts at resthouses in Taranda, Ponda and Nichar, before descending to the Satluj at Wangtu. This marks the limit for travellers without special permits to enter the rest of Kinnaur and all of Spiti which lies beyond. On the right bank of the river, lower Kinnaur is steeper, the peaks of the Srikhand range higher, the population is scantier and the walks far more adventurous. This area, called the Pandrabis, has the **Rupi-Bhabha Wildlife Sanctuary**, containing bear, antelope and numerous exotic pheasants, including perhaps the near-extinct Western Horned Tragopan. Treks to the west, cross the Tari Khango and Bhaba passes, lead to the Pin valley in Spiti. Comparatively little known, the upper Bhaba valley is in summer one of the most scenic areas of Himachal Pradesh. Snowy peaks and glaciers descend to miles of pasture dotted with sheep and carpeted with alpine flowers. Lower down, long grassy meadows amidst groves of birch and birdcherry bordering the silvery Bhaba on either side present ideal camping sites.

Middle Kinnaur, where the rainfall grows scantier and Buddhism begins to mingle with pantheist Hinduism, is dominated by the Kinner Kailash massif. To **Kalpa** (in the west) and its surrounding villages, the Kinner Kailash range offers the full impact of its majesty. Sweeping up 15,000 ft (4,500 m) from the left bank of the Satluj, the icy dome of Jorgandan is flanked by the rugged Kinner Kailash on the north and the needle-sharp Raldang to the south.

On its southern aspect, the Kinner Kailash range forms a sharp, rocky backdrop to the picturesque Baspa valley. The Baspa river is over 44 miles (70 km) long and, starting from the ridge marking the border with Tibet, it flows in a wide, wooded valley past some charming villages – Chitkul, Raksham and Sangla – before descending as a narrow torrent over the last 6 miles (10 km) to meet the Satluj at Karcham.

The Baspa valley contains the **Raksham-Chitkul Wildlife Sanctuary**, and some great treks over the Lamkhaga, Barasil, Lami, Rupin and Buranghatti passes to the catchments of the Yamuna, the Tons and the Pabbar. Another trek, also a pilgrimage route, is an abbreviated circumambulation of the Kinner Kailash range starting from Thangi village in the north, over the Lalanti Pass to Chitkul in the Baspa valley. Up the Satluj, its confluence with the Tedong stream marks the beginning of upper Kinnaur. Almost completely Buddhist in faith, and increasingly arid of climate, this area reflects its proximity to Tibet. Almost every village has its small monastary but there are no *gompas* of significant size or fame in the whole of Kinnaur. On the left bank, the valleys are short and ascend rapidly to the watershed ridge marking the Tibetan frontier. On the right the valleys are longer and offer beautiful walks to the villages of Asrang and Lippa up the Keerang stream, and Ropa and Sumnam up the Shyasu Khad. **Asrang-Lippa** is a small wild life sanctuary, with the only herd of ibex to be found outside Spiti in Himachal. Both valleys offer difficult treks to Spiti across the Srikhand range.

ahauli ouses are well onstructed o withstand he harsh nd long vinters.

By far, the largest tributary to join the Satluj in Himachal Pradesh is the Spiti. It flows its last 20 miles (32 km) through the Hangrang valley of Kinnaur to join the Satluj at Khabo, a few km after the latter enters India. Near Khabo, rising 13,000 ft (3,962 m) from the Satluj bed is the gigantic rocky mass of **Leo Pargyal II**. This immense expanse of cream-coloured rock is variously shaped into crenellated battlements, buttresses, spires and pinnacles. Snow and ice are visible only as specks here and there, evidence of the steep gradient and the howling winds which sweep across the mountain face.

The old Hindustan-Tibet Road continues north-east up the Satluj and over Shipki La into Tibet, while the Hangrang valley branches off to the north. The valley has numerous opportunities for the climber. **Nako**, high up on the left bank, with its lovely wooded lake, is on the route to Leo Pargyal, the highest mountain in Kinnaur. Further up the valley, again on the left bank, the beautiful village of **Chango** offers ac-

cess to the basin of the Chango glacier ringed by seven peaks over 20,000 ft (6,096 m), five of them still unclimbed.

Kinnaur, on the whole, is a summer paradise for the climber and trekker as well as the tourist. For the climber and trekker July-August are ideal, specially in the upper parts of Kinnaur where the monsoon seldom penetrates. For the tourist, June has the freshness of early summer, but September offers both the chance to enjoy the scenery and the opportunity to participate in the Phulech festival. It is celebrated in village after village, starting in late August from Rupi in lower Kinnaur and ending by the third week of September at Nesang in arid upper Kinnaur.

Phulech is a farewell to summer, symbolized by collecting the last flowers of the season in the pastures. It also inaugurates the annual long-distance migration of the flocks from the pastures to the plains for the winter. Phulech stretches over two to seven days, a carnival of dancing and drinking both in the village and in the pastures above.

Trilokinath Temple, Lahaul.

Though the women distill the local liquor, it is the men alone who imbibe the famous brews of Kinnaur made variously from apricot, grape and barley.

Bordering Kinnaur on the north-west is the Spiti sub-division of district Lahaul and Spiti. Located on the leeward side of the high ranges, the region receives virtually no rainfall. The lack of precipitation and minimum elevations of over 10,000 ft combine to produce a terrain seemingly devoid of vegetative cover and one of the harshest climates in the world. The region of Spiti was in one geological period the bed of the Tethys Sea which separated the continent of Gondwana from mainland Asia. The Tethys drained away, the Himalaya arose, and Spiti is today the premier geological museum of the world. Its mountain faces and river valleys document in pristine form every epoch from the pre-Cambrian to the recent. The poor vegetative cover and extremes of climate make the exposed rock and loose soils ideal subjects for the erosive potential of wind, water and snow.

Spiti is believed to have been settled for thousands of years, but little is known of its earlier history. After the 10th century it appears to have paid tribute to the principality of Guge and later Ladakh, and been subjected to occasional forays by the Kullu and Bushahr kings. The Spiti people were never warlike, and their resistance of extortionate demands took the form of subterfuge rather than pitched battle. Stories are told of a particular Ladakhi army being plied with liquor after overtures of friendship, and the inebriated force being massacred thereafter. Several *chorten* are said to have been constructed to commemorate the deaths of a viceroy of Ladakh and his retinue, who were murdered one winter (the king was informed that they had died of an illness).

The local chieftains in Spiti were called Nonos, and the Nono of Kewling traditionally exercised administrative and revenue collecting powers on behalf of the paramount power. When the British took over Spiti in the 19th century, they interfered little with the sys-

tem, and this isolated region, far from important trade routes and producing little of value, continued to live unchanged in a rhythm established over centuries.

The climate and terrain impose severe limits on spatial and demographic expansion in all the tribal areas. Unlike neighbouring Kinnaur and Lahaul which practiced polyandry, Spiti's traditional response to ensure an equilibrium between population and environmental resources was the evolution of a system of primogeniture. The eldest son inherited the major portion of the landholding, while the eldest daughter acquired all her mother's jewellery. Younger siblings were expected to become celibate monks and nuns.

Spiti can conveniently be divided into four units. The upper Spiti valley, called Tud, consists largely of high mountainous terrain, blending near the river valley into gently sloping terraces which end in sharp cliff faces along the river. The middle region opens out somewhat, with the riverside terraces gaining in extent.

On the left bank, steep rocky escarpments 2,000 feet (600 m) above the valley frown down from the edge of a greensward of rolling pastureland reminiscent of the *pashmina* homeland of Rupshu and Changthang in Ladakh. A little lower down, the river Pin, the largest tributary of the Spiti, meets its parent from the south. This valley forms the third region. Famous for its Chamurti horses and herbal wealth, Pin's terraces and pastures bear a striking resemblance to the Zanskar area of Ladakh. The lowest region of Spiti is called Sham. It stretches from the boundaries of Bhar to Sumdo, where the Parechu coming down from Tibet flows into the river Spiti, and includes the pretty villages of Poh, Tabo and Lari.

Spiti discourages visits by the timid. Its dirt roads, altitude problems and frugality of amenities invite only the robust and the adventurous. Yet for those who make it there, it is usually a worthwhile experience. The climber has a choice of a score of unclimbed, unnamed peaks over 20,000 ft (6,096 m). The highest peak in Himachal Pradesh, called Gya, is in Spiti, and it is still unclimbed. Closer to the road are better known mountains like the Shilla, at one time believed to be the highest in the world, and the Chau Chau Kang Nelda ('Snow Princess of the Moon and the Stars'). The trekker has the option of gentler walks to the lakes at Mane or Dhankar, the pastures of Langza or Demul or up the Paraiho stream into the Pin valley national park, to sight the ibex and the snow leopard. Venturing out of Spiti, over the high passes in the Srikhand range to Kinnaur or the Parbati valley in Kullu, or over the Prangla Pass to Ladakh, involve far more difficult treks. For the adventurous, there is also the option of white-water rafting on the Spiti and hang-gliding from the cliffs towering over the river.

More sedate travellers can enjoy the *gompas* of Spiti. Unlike Kinnaur, Spiti has a number of monastaries of considerable historical importance. **Tabo**, the oldest, is believed to have been built in the 11th century and contains the *chorten* of Rinchen Tsangpo, the great transla-

Lahauli potatoes in Manali market.

tor. The scholar Giuseppe Tucci ranked Tabo, along with Tsaparang and Tholing, as one of the holiest places in Tibetan Buddhism. The flat-roofed mud buildings of the monastery contain frescoes of exquisite beauty, their vibrant colours undimmed by age. **Lallung** in the Lingti valley and **Kungri** in the Pin valley also contain ancients frescoes of note. Of the major monasteries in the valley, Key, Dhankar and Tabo are Gelugs-pa, while Tangiud belongs to the Sakya sect and Kungri to the Nyingma. The annual festival, characterized by elaborate mask dances, occurs in summer at Key and Kungri, while at Tangiud it falls in October. Most village-level festivals and marriages are held in winter, when every evening becomes an occasion for the community to sing and dance. Winter is also the time for the Buchan, monks from Pin, to entertain. They move from village to village, enacting comic farces, singing old ballads and courting danger with acts of daredevilry involving swords and boulders.

Lahaul, located to the west of Spiti, forms the upper catchment of the Chandrabhaga or Chenab river. Enclosed within the high ranges of the Zanskar, Greater Himalaya and the Pir Panjal mountains, Lahaul is accessible only over a few high passes. Even though the Chandrabhaga, piercing through the Pir Panjal, leaves Lahaul at an altitude of only about 8,000 ft (2,438 m), its narrow gorge has always been a daunting prospect for all but the most intrepid. The passes across the Himalayan and Zanskar ranges lead merely to the aridity of Spiti and Ladakh. Only the Rohtang Pass, over the Pir Panjal, offers passage to the plains, through the verdant Kullu valley. Lahaul has no entry restrictions but the unpredictable Rohtang, closed for six months, is an awesome barrier.

The nomadic Gaddi shepherds have a legend about the origin of the Rohtang Pass and the fear it inspires to this day. In ancient times, it says, Lahaul had only an insurmountable mountain barrier to the south. The people of Lahaul learnt from the birds of a pleasanter

world beyond and wished to have access to it. After much entreaty, Lord Shiva agreed to create a passage but warned that for all time to come, those crossing must beware the swift change in weather and the winds blowing over the pass.

Lahaul, like its neighbouring regions, came under the influence of Buddhism in the 8th century and, like Spiti, came under the dominance of Guge and, later, Ladakh. But in the 6th century, with the waning of Ladakh's influence, Kullu established its rule over all of present Lahaul, a situation which continued till the British took over in the 19th century. At the local level, a few Thakur families ruled on behalf of the paramount power of the time till 1942.

The Lahaul social structure is more complex than that of either Spiti or Kinnaur. The valleys of the Bhaga, Chandra and the Myar are almost completely Buddhist, while the main Chandrabhaga valley has a peculiar admixture of the Hindu Swanglas (Brahmins by caste), a middle level of Buddhists, and then a number of lower castes with which both the upper strata and the middle have little social relationship.

Entering Lahaul from the Kullu side brings one into the Chandra valley. The Chandra, originating on the south east side of the Bara Lacha La, flows through barren, uninhabited territory for all but the last 18 miles (30 km) of its 70 mile (112 km) length. The upper portion is a boulder-strewn, moraine-banked valley overlooked by huge mountains and awesome hanging glaciers. The **Bara Shigri glacier** on the left bank is the largest in Himachal Pradesh. The road to Spiti covers a large portion of this terrain before crossing over the Kunzum pass. The high mountains between the Chandra and the Bhaga and the ranges on the left bank of the Chandra attract climbers. Trekkers enjoy walking across the Bara Lacha La via the beautiful Chandratal lake and also over the Hamta pass to Kullu.

The left bank is steep and bare even in the lower Chandra valley, but on the right it gradually broadens out, with

Chandra Tal at 14,000 ft (4270 m).

meadows above the road and villages along it. At Gondhla, one of the larger villages, there is an impressive fort of the old Thakurs with an eight-storey-high tower dominating the landscape. On a grander scale is Nature's effort on the opposite bank of the Chandra – sheer rock faces dropping 5,000 ft (1,524 m) from the snow-clad Pir Panjal. Further down, near the confluence of the Chandra and Bhaga at Tandi, is the ancient Guru Ghantal monastery associated with Padmasambhava, the sage credited with introducing Buddhism into the region.

From Tandi a little way up the Bhaga is **Keylong**, headquarters of district Lahaul and Spiti. This valley is shorter and generally narrower than the Chandra, but with villages on both sides of the river. There are three monasteries worth visiting in the lower valley – Kardang, Tayul and Shashur. For the adventurous, however, it is the upper valley which holds interest. From Darcha up the Zanskar Chu and over the Shingu La lies the Zanskar valley of Ladakh.

From Phuktal in Zanskar, it is possible to circle back to the Bhaga valley via Sarchu on the Manali-Leh highway.

The third portion of Lahaul is Pattan, the valley of the combined Chandra and Bhaga. Warmer, broader and more fertile than the valleys of the Chandra or the Bhaga alone, this is also the most thickly populated area of Lahaul. On the left bank, trails lead across the Pir Panjal to Bhramaur over the Kugti and other passes. Down-river are numerous large and prosperous villages, renowned for their produce of hops and the finest seed potato in India. At the far end of Lahaul is **Udaipur**, where the river curves around a lovely green bowl. The **Mirkula Devis** temple here is one of the finest examples of wood-sculpted temples in the hills. Nearby also is the **Trilokinath** shrine, revered by both Buddhists and Hindus, and to the north lies the secluded Myar valley. Shortly after passing through this charming vale at Udaipur, the Chandrabhaga enters a forbidding gorge and leaves Lahaul behind.

Crossing the Spiti river by yak in winter.

CHAMBA

Chamba – where rivers and rivulets abound, where deodar, oak and blue-pine forests cover the mountains, where daisies, narcissi and iris grow wild and where the snow-clad peaks dominate the skyline – is a nature lover's paradise and trekker's delight. Its charm also lies in its geographical variety as it extends from the Shivaliks, the foothills adjoining the states of Punjab and Jammu and Kashmir to the Dhauladhar, Pir Panjal and Zaskar ranges in the inner Himalaya. It also offers a rich cultural mosaic. Historically a Hindu kingdom, it has maintained a strong cultural entity and has some of the most ancient temples and bronzes of northern India. It is the homeland of the Gaddis, migratory shepherds, and the summer sojourn of the Gujjars, the nomadic Muslim milkmen, who descend to the plains as the Dhauladhar catches its first snow.

The shortest way to Chamba district is via Pathankot by train, followed by a 75 mile (120 km) drive on a broad and comfortable, albeit winding, road to Dalhousie. Alternately, one can fly from Delhi to Kangra by air and then travel by road via Nurpur (named after the empress Nur Jahan) to Chamba.

As one leaves the main road at Banikhet, and starts climbing the rhododendron-lined drive to **Dalhousie** through the Balun Cantonment, the old colonial hill station ambience begins to gradually unfold. Founded in the year 1853 and named after the famous Viceroy, the town was originally conceived as a sanatorium for Europeans. Dalhouse is dotted with churches, spacious colonial bungalows which still retain English names, and pleasant walks. The most popular walks are the twin rounds of Garam Sarak and Thanda Sarak ('warm road' and 'cold road'), so named because it is sunnier on one side than the other. These two circular walks join at Subash Chowk (originally called Charing Cross).

On a clear day, walking from the

Early 20th-century postcard.

Church & Mall Road
Dalhousie

234

Circuit House side towards Gandhi Chowk, one gets a magnificent view of the Pir Panjal range. Further on one reaches Upper Bakrota, a residential area with charming bungalows and a Tibetan carpet-weaving centre which sells fine carpets of traditional Tibetan design in rich colours. From Gandhi Chowk, a road leads to Panjpulla (Five Bridges) at a distance of 2 miles (3 km). It crosses Satdhara, a small fresh-water spring on the way. **Panjpulla** is a picturesque picnic spot with a stream and a Martyr's Memorial dedicated to Sardar Ajit Singh, a freedom fighter who died here. Another walk is from near the main bus stand – where a bridle path through a wooded area leads to the cantonment. On the right is a deserted British graveyard, many of whose epitaphs make interesting reading. Within the cantonment are two churches, one of which is imposing with its sandstone arches and stained-glass windows.

From Dalhousie, the more agreeable route to take to Chamba is via **Khajjiar**, 16 miles (26 km) away, where one can stop for a day or two. Trekking to Khajjiar can be exhilarating, as the walk is densely wooded with lovely views of snow-clad peaks. This area comes under the **Kalatope Wildlife Sanctuary**, and one may catch a glimpse of a barking deer or a leopard. After Bakrota a diversion leads to Kalatope, literally 'Black Cap,' so called because of the dense forest that surrounds it. There is a comfortable forest rest house here.

Khajjiar is an expanse of green bordered by tall deodar trees with a small lake in the middle. One can bask here in tranquillity as ponies gambol in the meadow and the tiny island floats in the lake.

A serpentine road leads to **Chamba** town, perched on the banks of the Ravi and Sal rivers. The view is dominated by the imposing facade of old buildings, particularly the Palace, now an educational institution, and the beautiful rectangular expanse of green called the **Chowgan**. The approach to the town is by a bridge over the Ravi. Alongside is an old suspension bridge, now used only by pedestrians.

The Chowgan is the heart of Chamba, the venue for sports and functions, and on summer evenings a meeting place for residents of the town. Traditions associated with it are woven into the life of the local inhabitants. Every year the Chowgan is closed to the public for a few months for maintenance and it reopens on the day of the Suhi festival with a procession. The origin of the town's name is traced to Champavati, the daughter of Raja Sahil Verman, who shifted his capital from Bhramaur to Chamba in the 10th century. According to one legend, she sacrificed her life so that water would be available to the public. At the Suhi festival women and children visit the temples and sing songs commemorating the event.

The geographical isolation of the Chamba state insulated it from outside influences and preserved its cultural entity. Ancient temples abound in Chamba, some with beautiful idols. The **Lakshmi Narayan temple** complex is located in the middle of the town: six temples built in the *shikhara* style, three

Embroidered image of solar deity used in a temple procession.

dedicated to Vishnu and three to Lord Shiva. The main idol of Lakshmi Narayan is made of white marble brought from the Vindhya hills at the time of Raja Sahil Verman. Also worth visiting is the temple of Hari Rai, which has an old bronze, and that of Chamunda, known both for its idol and for its beautiful view of the town.

The arts flourished in Chamba, and examples of Chamba miniature paintings, Chamba *rumal* (finely embroidered cloth) and silver jewellery can be seen in the **Bhuri Singh Museum**. The Museum also has beautiful stone inscriptions found at watering places, and carvings from old temples. The shops around the Chowgan offer traditional silver jewellery and the famous Chamba *chappals* or sandals, known for their unique designs.

The village of **Bhramaur** is 39 miles (62 km) from Chamba and serves as the headquarters of the area which goes by the same name. The road to Bhramaur is along the Ravi, past fields of maize and wheat and clusters of slate-roofed houses. As the valley becomes narrower, one sees single houses perched delicately on steep and treeless mountain slopes. En route one can visit the temple of **Chatrari** where one of the most exquisite bronzes of the area – Shakti Devi – is to be found. Bhramaur was the capital of the state for more than 400 years before it shifted to Chamba town. Its most interesting feature is the complex of temples called **Chaurasi** (literally, 'eighty-four') which owes its name to the fact that the king is said to have built the temples for the eighty-four saints who visited Bhramaur. Not many remain, but the Chaurasi has very old temples of Ganesh, Narsingh, Manimahesh and Larkana Devi. The artist who sculpted the idols of Ganesh and Narsingh as well as that of Chatrari was Gugga, whose hand, according to local legend, was cut off so that he could not replicate his wondrous works.

From Bhramaur one can trek to the **Manimahesh Lake**, situated at a height of about 11,000 ft (3,350 m) at the base of Manimahesh mountain, said to be

Participants in a temple festival.

one of the abodes of Lord Shiva. A level motorable road leads up to Hadsar from where the climb begins. Camping is possible at **Dhancho** before the final climb to Manimahesh. In July and August, the beautiful alpine flowers on the way are a treat for the eyes. The more adventurous can attempt to cross the Kugti Pass to the Lahaul valley or the Indrahar Pass to the Kangra valley.

To the north of Chamba across the Sach Pass lies the unspolit valley of **Pangi** – a land which remains completely snow-bound and unapproachable for the winter months, and which even in summer is only accessible on foot. The trek to Pangi valley takes one to a different culture, through varied terrain. The starting point of the steep climb is Satrundi, and as one nears the high pass the vegetation gets more sparse. Even in summer, snow covers the pass. The descent to **Brindabani**, where one halts for the night, feels much less arduous. From **Killar**, it is only 7.5 miles (12 km) away, and the river Chenab begins to form a familiar part of the landscape.

There is a comfortable rest house at Killar from where, after a day's rest, one can proceed towards the Lahaul valley, which is an easier route. A stretch of 5 miles (8 km) of 'jeepable' road has been constructed recently from Killar towards **Chairi**, where there is a place to stay. Another day's comfortable walk of 8 miles (13 km) leads to **Purthi** from where a jeepable road (18 miles/29 kms) goes on to **Udaipur** in Lahaul

In Chamba the folk tradition is alive and strong, and music and dance runs in the blood of the people. Folk songs vary with season and occasion and every important event triggers the composition of a new song, whether it be the inauguration of a dam or the death of a beloved. Festivals like Minjar in July/August throb with life and reflect the rich tradition of music, costumes and songs. Chamba's beautiful landscape, friendly people and strong culture leave no doubt as to the reason for this beautiful mountain region being described in an old adage as 'Chamba Achamba' – Chamba the Charming.

Drying maize in village rooftops for winter.

KANGRA VALLEY

Low hills and valleys dotted with small hamlets, terraced fields and sparkling snow-fed rivulets: the feminine beauty of the Kangra valley is set off by the mighty Dhauladhar range which dominates its backdrop. The beauty of the landscape is mirrored by the beauty of Kangra's people. Two centuries ago this region engendered a genre of miniature paintings celebrated for the richness and delicacy with which they represent all the nuances of human love.

The earlier history of Kangra is obscure, although legend dates it back 3,500 years to Vedic times. The area now included in the Kangra valley was originally a part of the kingdom of Trigarta with its capital at Kangra, then called Nagarkot. There are several fanciful derivations of the name Kangra. The most popular of these is Kangarh, the Fort of the Ear, referring to the legend that the fort stands over the ear of

the giant demon Jalandhara who was slain by Lord Shiva and buried under mountains. The area was exposed to frequent and successive invasions, and the fort was captured by the Mughal ruler Jahangir in AD 1620. The arts and crafts of the region continued to develop through repeated onslaughts and political upheavals.

The golden age of the kingdom began with Raja Sansar Chand, the most notable of the Katoch rulers of Kangra. At the age of 16 he recaptured Kangra fort and established himself as the supreme ruler of the valley. It was under his enthusiastic patronage that the Kangra school of painting grew and flourished. Although the cream of the Kangra miniatures is now in the Bhuri Singh museum in Chamba, Dharamsala has a museum with an art school attached to it where the painting of miniatures in the Kangra style is taught.

Overlooking the valley is **Dharamsala** (4,500 ft/1,500 m). Immediately above it rise dark, conifer-covered mountains reaching out towards the

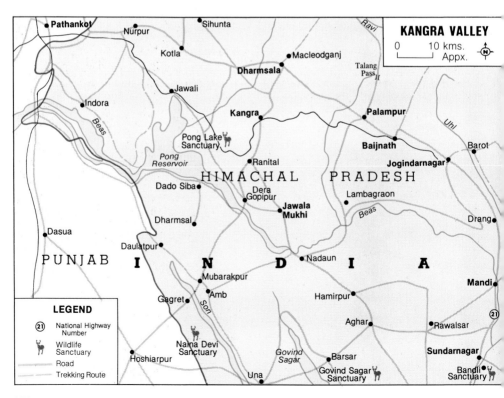

upper peaks of the Dhauladhars. One can trek up to the snow line comfortably and be back the same day. The starting point for the walk is the picturesque Dal Lake located in the middle of a forest of fir. It is right next to the Tibetan Children's village and is approachable from Dharamsala by road.

From here there is a trek to **Triund** (9,275 ft/2,827 m) at the foot of the Dhauladhar and another 5 miles (8 km) further up one reaches the snow line. The place offers a breathtaking view of the vast Kangra valley.

Mcleodganj or Upper Dharamsala is the abode of His Holiness, the Dalai Lama. Also called the Little Lhasa in India. It is primarily a Tibetan settlement, with a Buddha temple around which are situated a Tibetan monastery and nunnery. The Tibetan Institute of Performing Arts preserves a number of musical, dance and theatrical traditions of Tibet. For the lover of traditional arts and crafts there is a Tibetan handicraft centre. Mcleodganj is also a shoppers' delight for crafts and objects of Buddhist origin.

Quite near Mcleodganj, next to the traditional slate quarries of the area and also near the Dal Lake is situated the shrine of Bhagsunath, a scenic old temple next to a waterfall. **Dharamkot** is a popular picnic spot situated near Mcleodganj at a height of 6,890 ft (2,100 m). Between Dharamsala and Mcleod–ganj at Forsythganj is the elegant church of St John-in-the-Wilderness which has some interesting stained glass windows and a Christian cemetery. There is a monument to Lord Elgin, the eighth Viceroy of India, who died while holidaying in Dharamsala in 1862 and was buried here. Amidst the surroundings of a pine forest is situated the War Memorial at the entry point of Dharamsala.

Palampur, situated at a height of 4,000 ft (1,219 m), is one of the most beautiful hill stations of the Himalayas with its panoramic view of the snow ranges, salubrious climate, tea gardens with irrigation channels brimming with ice cold water, and its bungalows sheltered by pine trees. One can enjoy the several quiet walks among avenues of pine and cedar and tea gardens. A short walk takes one to the **Nigal Gorge**, a 1,000 foot (305 m) chasm through which flow the waters of Bundla stream, normally just a thin trickle but during the monsoons a roaring torrent. In fact, Palampur is an interesting place to visit in all seasons.

Eight miles (13 km) from Palampur is **Andretta**, a small rural haven amidst tea gardens, paddy fields and orchards. The pure springs and the solitude of the place are perhaps what lured Norah Richards, the late playwright and pioneer of rural theatre, and the late Sardar Shobha Singh, the famous painter who attempted to revive the Kangra school of painting, to settle here and draw other artists to form a community. The tradition of art lives on in Andretta. A potters' society is engaged in the revival of traditional pottery.

About 10 miles (16 km) away from Palampur is **Baijnath**, one of the foremost pilgrim destinations in the Kangra valley. The temple bears inscriptions dated AD 804 and is believed to be the

oldest extant Shiva temple in the country. Dedicated to Vaidyanath, the aspect of the god as Lord of Healing, this magnificent temple has some fine sculptures, including a unique composite image of Vishnu and Lakshmi. The Shivratri fair held every year nearby attracts thousands of pilgrims from all over the country.

To the south of Kangra and Dharamsala, situated picturesquely against a rocky cliff, is **Jwalamukhi**, one of the most revered Hindu temples in North India. The deity is not an image, but a blue flame fed by natural gas which shoots out of the rock in the sanctum. It is worshipped as the manifestation of the goddess of fire, Jwalamukhi. The temple has been visited over centuries by every notable who has passed through the Valley. Two important fairs are held here during the Navratras (equinoxes), when a large number of pilgrims from Punjab and Uttar Pradesh particularly flock to the temple.

A long, winding road leads to

Masroor, about 25 miles (40 km) from Kangra. It is known for its monolithic rock temple, richly carved in the Indo-Aryan style. A local legend says that the five Pandava heroes during their exile carved this temple overnight out of the mountain. Although this temple is lesser known than others in the valley, in architectural and sculptural conception and design it is superlative.

Another celebrated shrine is the **Bajreshwari Devi temple** at Kangra, near the confluence of the Banganga and Majhi streams. This goddess is held in great esteem by the Hindu worshippers of Shakti, the cosmic female principle. On account of the offerings of countless pilgrims, the Bajreshwari Devi temple became fabulously rich and was plundered in medieval times by several invaders, including Mahmud Ghazni and Mohammed bin Tughlaq.

It was a beneficiary of Maharaja Ranjit Singh, the ruler of the Punjab in the last century, who made an offering to the temple of an image in solid gold, in which he is shown paying homage to the Devi. The earthquake of 1905 completely destroyed the temple along with the town of Kangra. It was rebuilt in its present form in 1920.

Though in ruins, the **Kangra Fort** still dominates the valley and reinforces the impression of power and the struggle for it which characterised the feudal history of the state. Perched atop a cliff above the Banganga and Majhi rivers, the fort is accessible only by a narrow strip of land and protected by a series of gates.

Inside are temples to Laxminarayan and Ambika Devi and a small Jain temple with a stone image of Adinath. To the north of the fort stand the Dhauladhars and to the west, on a secluded cliff, the temple of Jayanti Devi. Even in its present state of ruin, the fort has a distinct majesty.

Kangra offers diverse possibilities to explore and enjoy its beauty: fishing, water sports and hang gliding at Pong Dam and Dehra Gopipur, trekking, mountaineering and bird-watching in the Dhauladhars. The mountains and valleys provide plenty of inspiration.

A young Tibetan nun at Dharamsala

'LITTLE LHASA'

In 1950, Tibet was invaded by the People's Liberation Army of Communist China. Routing the meagre Tibetan forces, the Chinese compelled the Dalai Lama, just turned 16, to administer a puppet government under their tutelage. Revolt was inevitable and, in 1959, following a massive uprising in the capital city of Lhasa, the Dalai Lama was forced to seek refuge in India. After a short stay in the hill resort of Mussoorie the Dalai Lama transplanted his vision of an exiled society to a new headquarters, an abandoned colonial hill station called Dharamsala. The British, beginning with a military cantonment on the shoulder of the tallest crest, Mun Peak, had gone 5 miles further to found a small town, Mcleodgunj, on a slender ridge facing the plains below. In May 1960, the Dalai Lama arrived in Mcleodganj to live and establish a government-in-exile.

Since the first days of the Dalai Lama's tenure, Mcleodgunj has undergone a dramatic change. The Tibetan population has swelled with hundreds of pilgrims, traders, government officials and foreign visitors in periodic residence. The serene colonial park at the town's centre has been obliterated to make way for rows of buildings housing shops, restaurants and hotels. At their centre rises a tall gold-crowned *chorten*, dedicated to fellow Tibetans still under the Chinese yoke. Outside of the town stand their homes – an impromptu jumble of tin and stone shanties, ascending floor over roof up the hill, graced by marigolds in the windows and hundreds of faded prayer flags strung between the trees overhead.

The Dalai Lama's residence in Mcleodgunj is called Thekchen Choling, Island of the Mahayana Teaching. It encloses an expanse of forest and hillside through which the Dalai Lama can stroll, tend his flower gardens and meditate. His modest private cottage dominates a kitchen complex, office building, security and secretarial quarters, all located at progressively lower levels to the front gate.

Across the flagstone *chora* or debating courtyard, stands the new Central Cathedral, a three-storey yellow hall topped by gold pinnacles and designed by the Dalai Lama himself. A battery of prayer wheels lines its outer walls, and inside are giant images of the Buddha. The secretariat compound of the government-in-exile called Gangchen

Kyishong, Abode of Snow-Happy Valley, is halfway to lower Dharmashala. Two white pillars frame its front gate with the government's emblem. Within, on a long flat, rise the monumental edifices of the Library of Tibetan Works and Archives and the Cabinet building. The Library has become a magnet for hundreds of Asian and Western scholars who previously had scant access to Tibetan culture. But by far the most extensive of the cultural projects initiated by the Dalai Lama is the Tibetan school system. It is viewed by the Tibetans as the most fundamental hope for the future of their cause. Advanced studies in Tibet's academic tradition are provided by the Institute of Higher Tibetan studies in Benaras as well as the Buddhist School of Dialectics in Dharamsala.

Even though Tibetans have settled in other parts of the country such as Byllakuppe near Mysore in South India, Mussoorie in the U.P. hills and Delhi, the soul of all Tibetans lies in Mcleodgunj where the Dalai Lama resides. With furry Lhasa Apsos running about, red-cheeked children bundled up in back packs, the aroma of *thukpa* (noodle soup), the sound of prayer wheels turned by the monks and the laughter and despair of an entire culture within a culture, 'little Lhasa' is a unique place to visit.

SIRMAUR – THE UNDISCOVERED SHIVALIKS

Lying in the southern region of Himachal Pradesh, this is one of the relatively less explored areas in the Shivalik hills. Sirmaur, one of the oldest erstwhile princely states, is characterised by a diversity of flora, fauna, landscape and culture. At one end lies the splendid Choor range and, at the other, the expansive Kyarda Dun valley. In between lie forests of the great deodar, oak and sal, inhabited by leopards, barking deer, ghural, black bear and an amazing variety of pheasants, including the beautiful Monal and Cheer.

The Shivaliks take off from the Haryana plains in successive ranges of increasing elevation, culminating in the Choor Dhar or range, which is crowned by the Choor Chandni peak at an elevation of 11,965 ft (3,647 m). Though dwarfed by the higher Himalaya, these ranges have their own delicate beauty: at dusk they fade one into the other in shades of blue and grey, like a succession of veils on an unknown face.

As in the case of most hill states, the history of Sirmau is a mosaic of tales of valour, deceit and romance. The major historical sources are the *Tarikh Riyaasat Sirmaur*, written by Kanwar Ranjor Singh in 1912, and the old district gazetteers. Starting from an era of perpetual warfare amongst local chieftains, Sirmaur's history weaves through a long line of rulers who bore the title of 'Prakash.' It is generally accepted that the ruling dynasty descended from Raja Shubh Bans Prakash, who ruled from 1195 to 1199, and formally ended with the merger of States in 1948 during the rule of Maharaja Rajinder Prakash who died without an heir in 1964.

Nahan was the seat of the state government under the princely regime, and is now the district headquarters of Sirmaur. Just a four-hour drive away from Delhi, it is one of the most beautiful hill towns in the region, situated on a wide ridge at an altitude of about 3,050 ft (930 m). From Nahan, if one looks towards the south and south-west one can see the sprawling plains of Haryana and the Paonta valley and towards the north, the rising Shivaliks.

Nahan was founded by Raja Karam Prakash in 1621 and was generally considered to be one of the cleanest and best planned of India's hill towns, boasting one of the oldest municipal committees in the country. Nahan has suffered somewhat from the malaise of over-construction, but by and large the town still has an orderly feel about it. The Nahan bazaar is located alongside a network of cobbled streets which could evoke a feeling of *déjà vu* in the European traveller.

Right in the heart of town is the quiet Ranital park and what is called the Pucca Tank, a largish body of water. One enters the town through an imposing gate called the Lytton Memorial and is greeted by the sight of the grassy Chaugan: this used to be the rulers' polo ground and is now a venue for sports activities and celebrations. A charming

Local wealth is often measured in cows.

pavilion has been built on the Chaugan recently, using elegant ornamental iron castings from the Nahan foundry, which was established by Raja Shamsher Prakash as long ago as 1864.

The town is built around three beautiful and relatively solitary walks (now paved paths) popularly known as the 'villa round,' the 'hospital round' and the 'military' or 'cantonment round.' The first is the prettiest and quietest of the three, meandering through a chir forest. The old graveyard and the *chhatri* are worth a visit along this walk.

Some of the other attractions in Nahan are the old palace, the adjoining Ranzore palace and the Jagannath temple, located in the bazaar. The Ranzore palace, which is the residence of hospitable descendant of the ruling family, has some exquisite wall frescoes about a century old. Within an hour's drive from Nahan, there are several interesting places which merit a day trip each. Located near Kala-Amb, the point from which the road up to Nahan takes off, is the **Saketi Fossil Park**. This displays rather surreal life-size fibreglass models of prehistoric animals whose fossils were discovered in this region. The Shivalik formations contain one of the world's richest collection of mammalian fossils, and a walk in this region offers the exciting prospect of discovering a fossil.

The **Trilokpur temple** built by Raja Deep Prakash in 1573 stands on a gentle isolated hillock about 16 miles (25 km) from Nahan. Twice a year, in May and October, a noisy and colourful fair is held around the temple when thousands of pilgrims throng to this place from the plains. Several kilometres down from the Nahan ridge, and towards the southeast, lies the Kyarda Dun or Paonta Valley. **Paonta Sahib**, located on the banks of the Yamuna river, is a small town sacred to the memory of Guru Gobind Singh, the tenth Sikh Guru. The Gurudwara here is amongst the most important Sikh religious centres.

There are two versions of how this place derived its name. It is said that since the Guru set his foot here and lived here for a while, the place is called

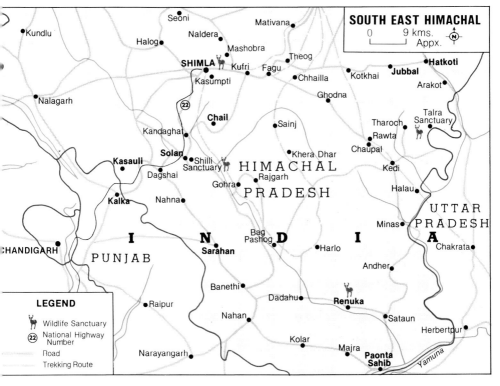

Paonta (derived from *paon*, foot, and *tikka*, mark). The second version has it that while bathing in the Yamuna, the Guru lost his foot ornament or *paonta* in the river.

On the southern bank of the Giri river and close to Paonta Sahib lies **Sirmur**, the old capital of Sirmur state. A local legend recounts that the Raja had promised a dancer half his kingdom if she could cross a river gorge on a rope. When the dancer achieved the feat, she was told by the Raja that she could have his entire kingdom if she would repeat her tight-rope walking act. She was half-way across when the Raja cut the rope and sent her hurling into the Giri river – but not before the girl cursed him and pronounced the imminent doom of Sirmaur town, which was soon destroyed by floods. Ruins of the bazaar, wells and a tank called Simauri Tal can still be seen here.

About 12 miles (20 km) north-west of Nahan, on the Nahan-Shimla route, lies the **Banethi** forest rest house commanding spectacular views of the

Haryana plains to the south, and of the Choor Dhar and the Sain Dhar to the north.

About 12 miles (20 km) north of Nahan, en route to the Renuka Lake, lie the twin peaks of **Jaitak hill** which is an important landmark in Sirmur's history: it was here that the most important battle between the British-led forces and the Gurkhas was fought.

Renuka Lake, about 28 miles (45 km) from Nahan, is perhaps the only relatively 'heard-of' place in this unexplored region, lying in a bowl formed by the surrounding hills. The foliage around it appears to be oddly tropical, with several palms leaning towards the water.

The local legend says that Renuka, wife of the sage Jamadagni, was killed by her own son Parsuram under orders from his father who was testing his son's obedience. The sage was pleased with his son and offered him a boon, whereupon the son asked for his mother to be brought back to life. Renuka is said to have then disappeared (probably disgusted with this chauvinist game), leaving behind this lake and attaining the status of a goddess. The contours of the lake do suggest the form of a sleeping woman.

Every year in November the Renuka fair is held in the grounds around the lake and Parsuram Tal, a mini-lake right next to the Renuka. This fair is a major attraction for the people of the surrounding villages and town as the emphasis is on festivity – singing and dancing, buying and selling, worshipping with purifying dips in the water and celebrating. At the northern end of the lake lies the **Renuka Wildlife Sanctuary**, covering an area of about 11.5 sq miles (30 sq km). There is a pride of Asiatic lions here which can be seen on a half-hour safari conducted in an official van, leopards, barking deer, ghurals, wild bear and jackals.

North and north-east of Nahan lie the **Sangrah** and **Shillai** regions of Sirmaur district. These are amongst the most underdeveloped areas of the state, inhabited by a hardy people eking out a difficult existence from the land. This region, especially the Sangrah area, has

Terraced fields.

a rugged beauty, with its sheer ravines and valleys dissected by streams and *nallahs*. In some areas around Sangrah, Haripur Dhar and Satahan, there are bursts of oak forest aflame with rhododendrons in early spring. These ranges are rich in limestone, and consequent mining activity has left unsightly white gashes on some slopes.

The Choor Dhar, topped by the **Choor peak**, dominates this region. The trek up to Choor peak goes through thick deodar forest rich in plant and bird life (including the Monal, the state bird of Himachal Pradesh). The peak and its immediate vicinity are covered with snow for a considerable part of the year. The summit has a statue of Chooreshwar Mahadev and on the western side, in a depression, a small stone-and-wood temple dedicated to Shirgul. The summit offers the awesome sight of the Himalayan ranges of Badrinath and Tibet. The Choor Dhar can be approached either from Nahan via Renuka and Sangrah or from the Solan side via Rajgarh. The take-off point for

the 87-mile (14-km) long trek is **Nohra**, a pretty village which grows prime vegetables, especially peas.

The diversity of this region is further exemplified by the **Rajgarh** sub-division which is the northern limit of Sirmaur, after which the Solan and Shimla divisions commence. This is orchard country: apple, peach and plum trees sprinkle the verdant hillsides and make a visit a heady experience, especially when the blossoms are out. Rajgarh is the administrative head–quarter and is more easily approachable from the Solan side via a good metalled road. Rewarding treks can be made with Rajgarh as base, to neighbouring places of interest like **Sarahan**, **Mangarh** and **Habban**.

In short, travelling through the Sirmaur region is a discovery of the Shivalik landscape, flora, fauna, history and culture. Exploration can be leisurely and peaceful, as this corner of Himachal Pradesh has not been overrun by commercial tourism and the accompanying din of frenzied construction.

Renuka
Lake, 28
miles
(45 km)
from Nahan.

HIMALAYAN TREKKING

The intricate mosaic formed by Himalayan rivers and ridges holds more possibilities for route-making than can be explored in just one lifetime. Our selection of routes through the west-Himalayan honeycomb has been made for varying abilities and inclination. Age is not a limiting factor on some of these walks given a reasonable degree of physical fitness. You can take the kids along to the lakes, for instance Gangabal and Beaskund, two that lie at the base of attractive peaks. The climb to Kansarnag, on the northern slopes of the Pir Panjal, gently tests your legs and lungs. Across the valley from it towards the northern rim of the Kashmir basin is Sheshnag, on the pilgrim path to the Amarnath cave. The glaciers of Kolahoi, on our itinerary to the twin lakes of Tarsar and Marsar, may just be out of bounds for children; but you could rendezvous with them at the end of the trek in Dachigam, a delight for lovers of wildlife.

A greater degree of difficulty may be experienced on the passes of the Dhauladhar and the Pir Panjal. The Rupin Pass links two very beautiful valleys, those of the Tons and the Baspa. The walk from Dharamsala to Keylong leapfrogs both the Dhauladhar and the Pir Panjal via the saddles of the Indrahar and the Kugti. Another journey once made by the mythical deities of Himachal was the crossing of the Hamta Pass, when some of them exercised their preference for Kullu's lush vistas over the rugged splendour of Lahaul.

The crossings of the Great Himalayan range itself are routes that were once used by daring traders and rulers alike, for commerce and for conquest. The Lonvilad Gali links the Warwan valley in Kashmir with that of the Suru, and the Umasi La is a glaciated pass that allows a tricky passage from Kishtwar to Padam. These classic routes take the trekker from the green, alpine valleys of Kashmir through a spectrum of changing vegetation to the dry and barren rain-shadow of Ladakh and Zanskar. One who has made these crossings will appreciate why Himalayan buffs insist that Ladakh and Zanskar should be approached on foot, and not on wheels or wings.

One across the Great Himalaya, we explore the interiors of the 'hidden kingdoms' of Zanskar and Ladakh. The trails link the nodal points of Padum, Panikhar, Stok, Hemis and Lamayuru, traversing the unique landscape and its isolated Buddhist cultural heritage. No time of year is 'out-of-season' for the walker who can face leeches and sub-zero temperatures with equanimity – and we have included a winter version of the Kargil-Lehinvan stretch on skis – but the Himalaya are best approached in fair weather, and with prudence. Hire a guide if necessary. And finally, don't leave any trash behind. Whatever you can carry up, you can all the more easily carry down.

Preceding pages: view from Namika La, Ladakh; skiers cross the Margan Pass. **Left**, mountain solitude.

THE VISHAW VALLEY

The Pir Panjal has for centuries been crisscrossed with trails laid down by shepherds and goatherds driving their flocks over the passes into the Kashmir Valley. Most of the glaciers on this range drain into the Valley to join the Jhelum; one of these is the beautiful Vishaw. Its valley stretches for about 40 km from the ever-frozen Konsarnag Lake to its mouth at Shopian. This short stretch is not only excellent trekking country with its abundant waterfalls, lakes and streams, forests and flowers, but also little frequented.

The duration of the trek is 5 to 6 days and the best season from mid-May to end-October. It begins with a 40 km drive south from Srinagar to Shopian, where pack-ponies can be arranged. The first stage 7.5 miles/12 km to the Aharbal falls is a short and easy walk: south from Shopian through paddy-fields for about 1-2 miles (3-4 km) and then sharply to the right through a pine forest down to the Vishaw. Cross the river over a wooden bridge and turn left immediately to the falls about a kilometer to the east, off the main route (there is a signboard indicating the way).

The river emerges through the beautiful gorge it has hewn out of slatey strata. Where the rock has resisted erosion, being harder, the river plunges over terraces, the highest and most vertical being the 50-ft high falls of Ahrabal. Looking up the ravine, one can see the Budil peaks clothed with pine forests, foaming rivers matching the whiteness of the snowy summits. A tourist hut overlooks the falls and its verandah affords a good view.

The second stage (8 miles/13 km), pleasant though at times taxing, leads to Kungwattan through a pine forest. From the falls the north side is quite inaccessible, but to the south-east there is a cattle track which descends into the ravine and winds up from the falls into the beautiful grassy valley above. First there is a gentle ascent and then a steep

Wind-twisted trees on a summer meadow.

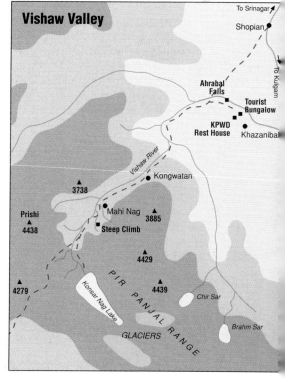

Vishaw Valley

To Srinagar
Shopian
To Kulgam
Ahrabal Falls
Tourist Bungalow
KPWD Rest House
Khazanibal
Vishaw River
Kongwatan
3738
Prishi 4438
Mahi Nag
3885
Steep Climb
4429
4279
4439
Chir Sar
Konsar Nag Lake
PIR PANJAL RANGE
Brahm Sar
GLACIERS

descent down to the river bank which is crossed by a bridge. The last part is an ascent of well over two hours and the sight of the rest house at Kungwattan in the distance is very welcome. This is a large meadow, typical of the Pir Panjal, and an excellent camping spot. An animal husbandry farm sits ostenta–tiously fenced off in the middle of the meadow, and at the further end of Kungwattan lies a rudimentary Forest Department rest house.

The third stage, to Konsarnag, is a vigorous climb of 10 miles (16 km). The pine forests are now behind you and the silver birch comes into view to be replaced a little higher up by juniper. The landscape becomes more and more rugged up to Mahinag where there are a few shepherd huts; brushwood needed for camping on the lake must be gathered here.

The track up from here is steep, though spectacular, and on one stretch strewn with boulders, making the way difficult for ponies. Snow bridges, icy streams and pools appear at intervals. The last stretch is up a mile-long snowfield, and over a hump at the top the lake finally comes into view. It lies in a large trough, its surface a mosaic of water and floating icebergs and on all sides lofty snow peaks of over 15,000 feet (4,572 m).

The lake is about 2 miles (3 km) long and shaped like a foot, toes towards you; the local name for it is Vishnupad, Vishnu's Foot, and it used to be a popular Hindu pilgrimage. At the further end is an extensive snowfield of great thickness. The barrier on which you are standing is not solid rock, as it appears, but a huge moraine, 500 ft (154 m) in height, and the water of the lake filters through it in small rivulets to form the Vishaw river just above Mahinag. Across the lake is a narrow glacial valley overlooking the plains of Jammu and Sialkot.

If you do not want to camp at the lake, you could pitch camp at Mahinag on the third day. The walk to Konsarnag and back to Mahinag could then be the fourth stage, and on the last day you could comfortably trek back to Shopian.

Konsarnag Lake, still frozen in June.

GANGABAL LAKE

At the northern end of the Great Himalayan range bordering Baltistan, this area in Kashmir has been given the title of Valley of Flowers. Throughout spring and summer a range of alpine flowers carpet the high meadows. This is the seasonal domain of shepherds and goatherds from as far off as Jammu in the south and Baltistan in the north.

A 3 to 4 hour drive follows the Sind river upstream to reach **Sonamarg** ,almost at the head of the valley. The trail to the Valley of Flowers starts 2 km short of Sonamarg from the **Thajiwas** meadow (8,900 ft/2,731 m), a good camping site just off the main road. A side excursion from here could be the Thajiwas glacier – a scenic walk of 2 to 3 hours.

Go back on the road for a few hundred metres to cross the Sind by a metal bridge to its true right bank. Start climbing up from the river, keeping on the upper trail, to a small ridge where the well marked shepherd trail veers off to the left. From here there are excellent views of the Thajiwas glacier looking back across the valley. Keep going up the meadow, at times steeply, passing shepherd huts. The trail then climbs through a dense jungle of pine and birch trees up to the meadow of **Shogari** – a perfect lunch stop. A hundred metres further up and the path veers off to the left through a beautiful birch forest before a short descent to the banks of the **Nichnai Nala** (stream). Follow the stream up, keeping to the true right bank. The path climbs gradually but seems to go on and on to the base of the **Nichnai Pass**, visible in the distance. There are good campsites next to the stream (11,800 ft/3,597 m). For the unacclimatized or less fit, this is a long day's walk of up to 8 to 9 hours involving a climb of almost 3,000 ft.

The next day starts with an optional route. The normal route follows the valley downstream for an hour before ascending steeply up the mountainside

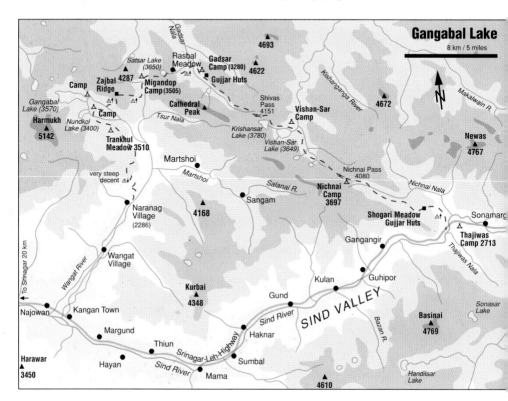

to **Zajmarg**, the ridge overlooking Gangabal Lake. Alternatively, if you are good at finding trails, look for a route from camp traversing the mountainside all the way to join the trail coming up from the valley. This avoids at least half the climb but is difficult to follow. It takes about four to five hours to Zajmarg (13,284 ft/4,050 m). From this vantage point there are grand views of **Mt. Harmukh** (16,870 ft/5,142 m) with the twin lakes of **Gangabal** and **Nundkol** at its base. A steep descent of about 1 to 2 hours leads all the way down to the lakes. There are good campsites near both lakes, though the lower Nundkol lake is generally preferred as it is well protected from the wind. This is an idyllic campsite and a full day could easily be spent exploring the two lakes. A walk up to a small hill overlooking Nundkol to the left just below Harmukh is highly recommended for breathtaking views of the mountain and the two lakes (about 2 hours to reach the top and probably less than an hour to set down).

Nundkol Lake and Gangabal Lake in the distance.

The last day of the walk is another long haul. Start by crossing the stream coming out of the Nundkol lake. From here the path keeps up on the hill traversing it all the way to the meadow of **Trankhul**, a large shepherd settlement (about 2 hours). Enter a pine forest and then climb for an hour before turning sharply around the mountain to the right. The path goes through a mixed pine, birch and juniper forest, climbing very gradually, then through a patch of open hillside before it takes a steep downward plunge through thick pine forest (about 3 to 4 hours). You could break up this long day by camping at Trankhul, the last campsite before reaching Naranag.

At the end of the long descent is the small village of **Naranag** on the roadhead. There are some old Hindu temples here which provide a resting place for pilgrims going up to Gangabal Lake. There is a daily bus service from here to **Wangat**, a town on the main Srinagar-Leh highway (10 miles/15 km), and from there a regular bus service to Srinagar, 25 miles (40 km) away.

PAHALGAM TO AMARNATH

The Amarnath yatra (pilgrimage) is made usually in July and August, in the interval between two full moons. Our walk begins at **Pahalgam** (7,200 ft/2,194 m). In the midst of the pious, carrying some of the cultural baggage of a *yatra* ourselves, we find it difficult to assert our identity as trekkers. Calling 'Jai Amarnath!' the pilgrims press forward, swathed in *dhotis* and saris, and wearing light canvas shoes, the well-to-do on mules, only the very old ferried on shoulder-borne *palkis*.

Through the village dwellings that skirt Pahalgam, we move towards **Chandanwari** (9,200 ft/2,834 m) our first halt, 10 miles (16 km) away. On our right, across the **Lidder**, the occasional sight of a meadow breaking through the trees brightens up an otherwise un–eventful stretch. Streams interrupt the path at intervals. Those close to villages and campsites are not potable, but you can sit by the side of a gushing rivulet at a small village shop at **Phraslun**, half-way to Chandanwari, and comfort your-self with swallows of cold, fresh water.

Car-loads of pilgrims roar past as you trudge along this 'jeepable' road, and Chandanwari finally comes into view, an extensive bustling campsite. Tents-and-beds, mules-and-muleteers, food-and-beverages – everything is available at a price. With varying degrees of ob-trusiveness, these support systems exist all along the route. But fortunately, the intrusion of the automobile ends here, and as you leave Chandanwari, walking over the rounded stones that edge the river bank of the East Lidder, the going is lively, the mountainside lush with trees. The track is carved into steps of earth and rock. Then the climb begins to **Pissughati** (10,700 ft/3,262 m) an unre-lenting 1,500 ft negotiated over barely a mile (2 km). Every now and again, a short-cut offers the lure of reaching the top faster.

At Pissughati, a meadowy pass, a sprinkling of tents, a distinct chill in the air. Over tea we are told that the walk to

Sheshnag lake is 5 miles (8 km) and will take three hours. It takes more like five, so it is only at dusk on our first day that we finally get a glimpse of the lake – deep in the valley, flanked on three sides by steep mountain ranges, a placid expanse of jade green. Hauntingly beautiful, it is overlooked by the **Sheshnag** campsite, a windswept meadow at 12,200 ft (3,718 m).

The next morning, on a path softened by the night's rain, we head for **Panchatarni**, 9 miles (14 km) away. As we climb up a thousand feet to **Wavbal**, the thin air makes us aware of the need to conserve our energies and pace ourselves. The landscape opens out; we are no longer walking along the mountain's edge, but through the vast undulature of its breadth.

Making our way over the perennially snowbound **Mahagunis Pass** (13,840 ft/ 4,218 m) we negotiate a descent on snow and ice: from here on to **Poshpather** (12,860 ft/3,920 m) we come down what is the largest single snowbed on this route. In an incessant

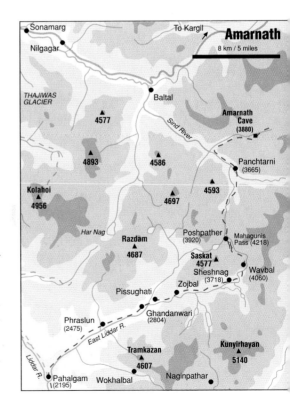

drizzle, the steady traffic of humans and mules churns up enough sludge and slush to make this an exercise in concentration and control.

From Poshpather the landscape gradually thaws into an expanse of green meadow. As the path meanders along its rim, we are transported into a pastoral world. Panchatarni lies across the vast expanse of the river-bed of the Sind; now, in July, the river is little more than a stream, easily waded by men and horses. Along its edge, in a linear spread, is the vast campsite. After the rigours of Mahagunis, the Panchatarni camp (11,900 ft/3,627 m) is almost Medi–terranean in its appeal.

Next morning, propelled by expect-ancy, we make our way to **Amarnath**, a little more than 3 miles (6 km) away. There are stories about the grandeur of the ice *lingam* in the cave-temple, said to wax and wane with the moon. Even as you see it, the approach is still something of a teaser, a roll in the land making the cave seem closer than it is.

Flanked by the **Amarnath-nar**

(river), the campsite is a bustling out-post of the Hindu heartland. It abounds with religious motifs: hermits in saffron, sadhus with matted hair, little shops selling religious offerings and marijuana, picture postcards of the ice lingam, and best of all, free *langars* (kitchens) run by wealthy patrons, which serve hot food to endless lines of hungry and tired pilgrims.

At the campsite you are confronted by yet another challenge: carved out of rock, a staircase of a few thousand steps leading to the mouth of the cave. In its recesses, you are face to face with the heart of this journey – rising from the ground, haloed by myth and legend, the phallic symbol of **Shiva**.

Separate from any other body of ice and snow, this ice-formation has been a source of wonder and religious inspira-tion for years. But standing before it, dampened by a steady dripping from the roof of the cave, we are open to the possibility that these same mundane droplets may in fact explain how the *lingam* came into being.

PAHALGAM TO DACHIGAM

The journey from Srinagar to Pahalgam (7,200 ft/2,194 m) by bus or taxi takes three to four hours, passing the temple ruins at Avantipur, built around the 8th century A.D. From Pahalgam, one may either take a taxi up to **Aru** (10,170 ft/ 3,100 m), 7 miles (11 km) upstream of Pahalgam, or trek this distance on the much less frequented track by the true right bank of the river. It is an exhilarating day's walk through dense pine forests and gentle hill slopes, the peace broken only by the chirping of birds and the rapid gushing of the frothy Lidder. Aru now has several hotels and campsites surrounding the small village it was not so long ago – all scattered across a massive meadow surrounded by ranges, with the Lidder flowing alongside, now somewhat lower. The grassy slopes are crossed by a maze of rivulets which at Aru gather to a confluence of two small rivers.

From here there are two routes to the Kolahoi glacier: one directly to Lidderwat along the Lidder and the other, much tougher, across the 12,729 ft/3,880 m high Harigali Pass via Armiun. The well defined trail from Aru to Lidderwat (7.5 miles/12 km) winds through forested pine and deodar slopes interspersed with meadows. The climb is initially steep but the track is wide and well trodden. Walking amidst the trees, you can sight a variety of birds –buntings, thrushes and many more. You leave the Lidder for part of the way to traverse the higher forested slopes and meet it again descending the bridge that leads to the rolling meadow of Lidderwat. Several campsites interspersed with a few basic hostelries dot this site, and to the north-east lie the icy peaks of the Kolahoi group.

We can start with a day's excursion to the **Kolahoi glacier**, 8 miles (13 km) from Lidderwat. The route runs along the true right bank of the Lidder for most of the way through pine forest. The slopes on either side of the river are

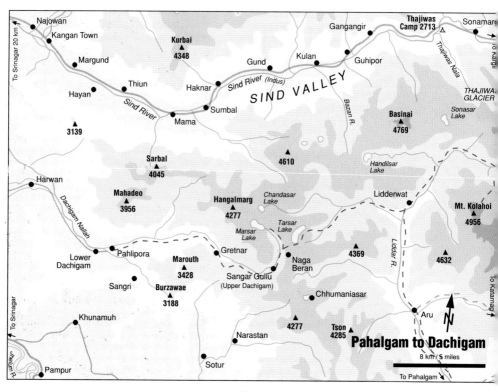

steep and, to begin with, well wooded. About two hours out of Lidderwat, to the right (or east, as one travels north), lies the Kallah waterfall; this steeply tumbling rivulet emerges after the winter snows melt from above Sosirwan from a high mountain bowl which is an expansive pasture. The Lidder must be crossed by a large snow bridge but the adventurous trekker can reach a high saddle above the pastures with unusual views of Kolahoi and its attendant peaks.

The route to Kolahoi continues along the Lidder to the meadow of Satlanjan where trekking parties often camp. A subsidiary valley to its west leads to the lake of Sonasar at 12,595 ft/3,816 m and a difficult pass, **Basmai Gali**, used sometimes by shepherds to cross from the Lidder valley to that of the Sind.

Past **Satlanjan** the terrain gets rougher; forests give way to abraded glacial topography, and the Lidder flows more turbulently. Patches of seasonal cultivation and scattered shepherd huts relieve the austerity of the landscape. We end up at a lake (11,154 ft/3,400 m)

beneath the glacier, an amorphous mass of ice and rock hanging down from the pyramid of **Kolahoi Peak** (17,995 ft/ 5,485 m). A quick return to Lidderwat can be made on the same day.

The serious trekker with proper equipment to camp out at relatively high altitude may be able to pick up traces of an old track which leads directly north from across the Kolahoi glacier over snowbeds to a pass at 14,422 ft/4,370 m which gives access to the Sind river at Saribal. During World War II, Britain's Royal Air Force ran a climbing school at Sonamarg which used the Thajiwas valley and this area for its training ground. It is also possible to do a circuit over the Kolahoi glacier and link up with the Armiun route to the glacier, but this requires mountaineering experience and the ability to climb over and possibly camp on the glacier.

The next day's walk leads upwards from Lidderwat to **Tarsar Lake** (12,998 ft/3,962 m), climbing rapidly along the true left bank of the stream which flows from the lake. Initially steep, the route

levels out as we approach the lake above **Dandabari**, just above the tree line. (The right or eastern fork leads to the pasture and camping ground of **Sekiwas** en route to Sonamarg; the two-day trek to the Sind valley traverses the **Yamhar pass** at 13,448 feet/4,100 m before descending into the thick forests of Zaiwan). The initial climb out of Lidderwat is steep and an early start is recommended, but gradually the angle eases and the valley opens up before the final incline to the lake itself. Tarsar is a relatively large spring-fed lake in a mountain bowl with steep sides, dominated by an unnamed rocky peak. There are camping sites in abundance for those continuing on, though it is possible to return quite comfortably to Lidderwat the same day.

Beyond Tarsar is a steep ridge with an indifferent trail traversing to its crest; beware of loose rock! Climbing 250 m up, we can see in the distance **Marsar Lake** (just over 13,100 ft/4,000 m), to the right, as well as Kolahoi, Mahadev and other peaks towering behind Tarsar.

According to local folklore, Marsar symbolizes death and Tarsar life.

Now entering the **Dachigam Sanctuary** (for which prior permission must be obtained from the Chief Wildlife Warden in Srinagar), we descend this ridge down to the Marsar lake about 2 miles (3 km) away, Marmots can be sighted frequently on this track. From Marsar, the larger lake of the two, flows the Dachigam Nallah, the river that supplies fresh water to Srinagar. The lake and the adjoining ridge form the northward border of the sanctuary. The land is now dotted with a variety of shrubs and grasses with now more frequent patches of vegetation.

A broad valley, the river flowing through its centre, descends into a narrower stretch curving west, with a prominent water fall. We descend the steep slopes into a broad open valley under a carpet of green studded with flowers and scattered white birch forests. We descend about 2 miles (3 km) before crossing the Nallah (either by a bridge or by wading through). We climb **Marsar Lake.**

through birch forests for about a mile (2 km) emerging at **Sangar Gullu** (9,300 ft/2,835 m), a campsite with a forest rest house: we are now in Upper Dachigam. From here we can view the entire expanse of this green valley, characterized by alpine meadows and stands of birch. Blankets of yellow buttercups and numerous other varieties of flora cover the slopes in early autumn.

From Sangar Gullu, one can either descend to **Gretnar** (5 miles/9 km), or to **Dagwan** (4.75 miles/7 km). The former route climbs steeply along a ridge to Leach Top (8,500 ft/2,590 m) then descends through dense forest to the rest house at Gretnar. En route on a clear day we can glimpse the main Kashmir valley and the ranges towards Baramullah. Gretnar is an excellent retreat for the nature and wildlife enthusiast. It is full of birds like orioles, ruby throats, tits, finches and the Koklas pheasant. The Himalayan langur also makes an occasional appearance. The route to Dagwan is more strenuous, traversing the folds of endless mountain slopes, with a high possibility of getting lost without a guide.

Pahlipora, (5,100 ft/1,555 m) is our next destination. From Gretnar the route is more difficult, traversing jungles of tall grass, dense forests and a profusion of tracks; a guide is essential for this part of the trek. We are now in Lower Dachigam and within the territorial range of the Himalayan black bear, a shy animal. The presence of wild cats, leopards and jackals can also be detected. There is a forest rest house at Pahlipora, and from here we catch a metalled road along the Numbal beat. The area is covered with trees – cherry, raspberry, plum, apricot, walnut, oak, willow and poplar. The slopes surrounding Lower Dachigam are grasslands with patches of dense vegetation. Bear and Hangul sightings are frequent here, and a rich variety of birds can be seen. A forest rest-house and an interpretation centre lie next to a trout hatchery, not far (about 2 miles/3 km) from the entrance to the Sanctuary, from where we can get a bus or taxi back to Srinagar.

Tarsar Lake.

LEHINWAN TO PANIKHAR

The trek from Lehinwan to Panikhar is ideally done in ten days, between the first week of July and the end of September when the first snow fall closes the passes leading to the valley. This trek is a rugged one, the terrain providing a dramatic contrast between the lush green valleys of upper Warwan and the steep barren ranges of Baltistan in the western corner of Ladakh.

The four hour drive from Srinagar to Lehinwan is via Anantnag and Kokarnag. Ponies can be hired at Lehinwan and the trek can commence on the same day to the first camp, a 3 to 4 hour walk to a site locally known as Do Pattri. On the second day the trail ascends steeply up a rocky path up to the **Margan Pass** (11,090 ft/3,380 m) (about five hours). A gradual descent over the grassy slopes leads to the camp site, **Chodromun**. The Warwan valley trail is through settled villages, alpine forests and fertile fields. It is a beautiful valley with its high altitude meadows, wooded and grassy slopes full of a variety of exquisite wild flowers, and snow-capped mountains.

The Warwan valley is cut off from the rest of Kashmir for the winter months. Although there is a road being constructed on this side of the pass, the shepherd's trail is recommended. From the camp at **Inshan**, a 5 to 6 hour trek from Chodromun, one gets an insight into typical Kashmiri village life.

On the fourth day, following the Warwan river, the trail passes through the scenic forests, villages and fields on to **Sukhnis** about 6 hours away across a bridge to the campsite. The Gujjars play an important role on the trail as they reconstruct bridges and clear the path which normally gets ruined by the severe winter conditions. On the fifth day, the route from Sukhnis onwards follows the Gujjar trail and climbs up towards the next campsite. About an hour after Sukhnis, a fast-flowing stream will have to be crossed on foot. Thereafter, the trail winds high along the grassy mountain side and descends onto a snow bridge, normally there till late in the season. Cross over to the other side and join the trail that leads to the campsite at **Police Kothi** (11,483 ft/3,500 m) set among silver birch trees. This is the old check post on the trade route across the Great Himalayan Range from Baltistan to Kashmir. This is a fairly tiring day and may well take about 7 to 8 hours.

The next day's climb to the wide grassy plains of **Humpet** 12,467 ft (3,800 m), upstream along the Kanital Nala, takes about 5 to 6 hours. This sweeping plateau is inhabited by the Gujjars during the summer months. All along the trail to Kanital you can hear the shrill cry of the Himalayan Long-tailed and Brown Marmots and perhaps glimpse them sunning themselves on the rocks. On the seventh day, a 6 to 7 hour ascent along the pastures leads to **Kanital** (13,123 ft/4,000 m) where camp is established on the last pasture below the **Brakhtiyan glacier**, on meadows covered with edelweiss. On this day, many streams have to be crossed on foot

Resting spot for tired trekkers.

and it is advisable to carry an extra pair of shoes. An early start is recommended, before the sun melts the snow and makes the streams more difficult to ford. Kanital is above the tree line and one can take a day off to acclimatise before the challenging climb over the Lonvilad Gali.

The **Lonvilad Gali** (15,420 ft/4,700 m) which is on the main Himalayan Range, lies on the left hand side as the glacier approaches. The trail through the moraine is difficult. As one walks along, the glacier turns sharply towards the north-east, at which point the trail ascends steeply westward towards the pass, normally snowbound. In the latter part of the season, the snow on the glacier melts, exposing the crevasses, and the route becomes much longer and more tricky. This is the longest and toughest day of the trek (8 to 9 hours).

The last steep climb of one hour up to the top of the pass is on soft snow, and can get rather tedious; but you will be rewarded with spectacular views of the peaks of Baltistan. From here, the trail crosses the heavily crevassed **Donoru**

glacier and descends into an arid world of brown and orange hues. Camp is on a small green pasture beside a little stream at **Donoru** (12,795 ft/3,900 m).

The next day begins by crossing the **Chellong Nala**. During the earlier part of the season, with luck there may be a snow bridge higher up. If not, the stream has to be crossed on foot. The water is deep and very cold. Thereafter proceed towards Panikhar (10,680 ft/3,255 m). The trail is a 5 to 6 hour walk through barren landscape with magnificent rock features and excellent view of the west face of Kun (23,251 ft/7,087 m). This last leg of the trek leads to the Suru Valley in lower Baltistan, inhabited by Shia Muslims. Mosques and minarets can be seen in the villages. Follow the dusty trail to the bridge on the outskirts of the town and cross over to pitch camp in a shady willow grove beside the **Chellong**.

Foreigners are required to register their passports at Panikhar. From here Kargil is 40 miles (64 km) away and takes about 4 ½ hours by jeep.

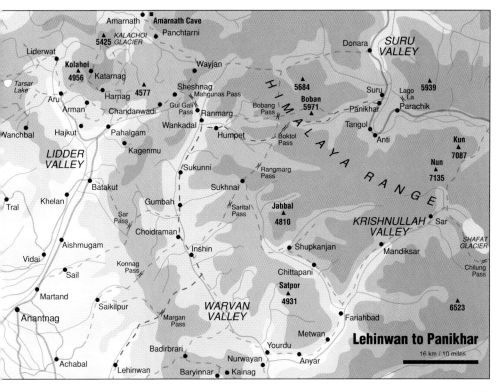

DRAS TO PANIKHAR

To reach Dras by road from Kashmir the traveller has to cross the Zoji La at 11,578 feet (3,530 m) from Sonamarg. As you move up the steep Zoji La road the lush, forest-clad hills of Kashmir disappear, and a rocky, stark and arid landscape takes its place. The black-topped road winds in tight curves to the Army checkpost at Gumri and glaciers become a common sight.

Ethnically Dards, the populace at **Dras** practise Islam. But the region is also rich in Buddhist cultural history, as seen from the statues at Dras, and at the further end of the trek, the rock carvings at Sanku (dating from the 7th and 8th centuries). Dras is at an altitude of 10,600 ft (3,110 m). Temperatures in winter drop to between -40° and -50°C, and snowfall is heavy. Through the months of May and October there is varied flora and fauna around Dras, and green-carpeted camping grounds, particularly below the adjoining village of Muradabad. The river Dras flows through the town. A bridge across the river leads south to the trekking trail.

It is an ascent all the way from this point to **Man-Man hill**, approximately 4 miles (7 km) away. The climb is steep, traversing a ridge and providing magnificent views of the mountain range beyond Dras in the north which the trekker is moving away from. The early stretch is quite relentless but after a few hours ascent, there are beautiful alpine meadows where Ladakhi shepherds camp in the summer months. These shepherds or their children are the only people you are likely to meet on the way, and your only guides to the correct trail forward in case you get confused and do not have a local guide with you. There are lots of clear streams on the way and after going uphill for five to six hours you camp at **Man-Man La**, about 12,500 ft (3,810 m), for the night, near one of the many springs, close to the pass.

On the second day you set out for Labar. This is a wind-swept valley 2–3 miles (3–4 km) short of the base of Umba. It is a hike of approximately 10 miles (16 km) from Man-Man La, first moving upwards across a large glacier, and then around an amazing variety of hills, with loose and sandy soil, rocks, boulders, clumps of grass. On the trail you see multitudes of flowers and the panorama of the Great Himalayan Range from the top of the valley, situated at about (13,500 ft/4,115 m). It is worthwhile spending a day here after the night's camp.

An early start is advised for the third day since it is a (12 miles/20 km) long haul to Sanku town via the **Umba La**. A small river by the valley needs to be crossed at the crack of dawn before the volume of the water increases with melting snow; then it is 2 miles (4 km) along the flat to the base of Umba with several glaciers to be traversed. A steep mile (2 km) uphill along a narrow track and you are at Umba top (14,800 ft/4,511 m), where a fierce wind blows unceasingly. The scene is stupendous – snow-covered peaks of the main

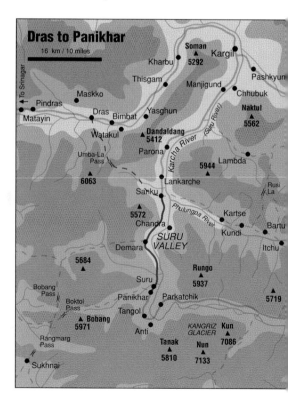

264

Himalayan Range glistening in the sunlight on all sides. The descent to Umba village on the other side is fairly hazardous, as the earth is loose and rock-strewn. So far, on the trail from Dras, no villages have been passed, and you can camp short of Umba village should you want to break up the third day's trek (which means reaching Sanku in the evening) into two days. The village is 2 miles (3 km) away from Umba top, and you can get a cup of tea at the local post office. After the village, there are several small settlements along the track (soon to be blasted into a jeepable road), which now moves above a silt-filled river to **Sanku**. The approach to Sanku is lined with wildflowers and plantations. There is more rainfall in this area now, perhaps due to the increase in vegetation and trees. There is a good camping-site near the Government guest-house in Sanku, and some tea stalls and shops with basic necessities in the main bazaar or 'high' street, and of course, dried apricots.

On the fourth and fifth days you follow the jeep road out of Sanku to Panikhar. The road runs more or less parallel to the Suru river and though there are tracks criss-crossing on either side it is best to trek along the road itself. As you walk south the road switches to the right side of the river 2.5 miles (4 km) past Sanku and continues for 5 miles (7.5 km) before changing back to the true left of the river towards Namsuru, so two bridges need to be crossed. It is a climb most of the way, and again you notice the contrasts of verdant hillsides and steep, rocky, arid patches. The Nun Kun massif becomes visible from the high points and if you can catch a sunset here you are lucky.

Panikhar is very similar to Sanku. Both have a Muslim population. The local inhabitants all along the trail are keen on medication, so it is a good idea to carry some analgesics for the adults and sweets for the children you meet on the route. From Panikhar you can either move on to Parkachik and Zanskar or catch the daily bus back to Kargil on the Srinagar-Leh highway.

Tired
trekkers.

PANIKHAR TO HENISKUT

The trek from Panikhar in the Suru Valley to Heniskut in Ladakh over the Kanji La begins from Baltistan, goes through Gulmatongus and crosses into the Buddhist area of Zanskar and Ladakh. The trail goes through dramatic semi-desert terrain, a continuation of the wild desolation of Ladakh.

Panikhar can be approached by road from **Kargil** (10,817 ft/3,297 m). The centre of the district, and lying on both banks of the Suru river, Panikhar is the meeting place of three routes: to Zanskar, to Yarkhand via Leh, and to Skardu. Inhabited by Shia Muslims, it has two beautiful mosques in the main bazaar which are over 400 years old.

The 40 mile (64 km) drive from Kargil to **Panikhar** takes about 4 ½ hours on a dusty road with willows and poplars growing along the water courses. At Panikhar, foreigners are required to register their passport details. Camp is on the outskirts of the town in a willow grove on the banks of the Chellong. Ponies can be hired from here.

The first day's trail from Panikhar to **Parkachik** takes about 5 to 6 hours. Begin by crossing the bridge directly in front of the camp, through the village and over the bridge spanning the Suru river. At the outskirts of the town, a steep climb leads to the top of a grassy ridge 13,200 ft/4,000 m from where one can get an impressive view of the Nun (23,408 ft/7,135 m) and Kun (23,251 ft/7,087 m) massif. This part of the trail is covered with exquisite wild flowers. Over the ridge, descend to Parkachik (11,483 ft/3,500 m), where camp is on a grassy plain beside the jeep track. The nearby village of Goma is the last Balti settlement; the treeless plateaus in the Suru valley were once the polo grounds of the Baltis.

On the second day, follow the motorable road to **Gulmatongus** (12,598 ft/3,840 m) which takes about 6 to 7 hours. On the way you get a spectacular view of the Parkachik gla-

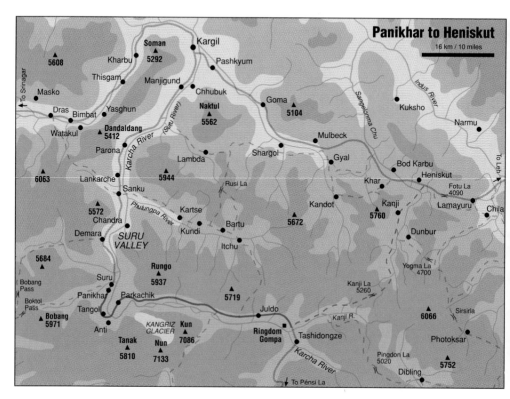

Panikhar to Heniskut

16 km / 10 miles

cier which comes from the Nun Kun massif, the highest in the region. The glacier is 21 km long, the longest in the Suru valley, and feeds the Suru river. Camp is set on a windy meadow opposite the Shafat Nala which is the approach to Kun.

From Gulmatongus the trail, once again on the jeep track (5 to 6 hrs) enters the remote Buddhist land of **Rangdum** (13,041 ft/3,975 m). Girdled by the Great Himalayan Range on one side and the mighty Zaskar range on the other, it has been called the "Hidden Kingdom." It experiences extremely cold winters; all its rivers freeze over – including the Zanskar river, on which the Zanskaris walk to get to Ladakh. **Yuldok** is the first village you pass on the way to the camp which is set on a grassy meadow carpeted with edelweiss, between the village and the Rangdum Gompa, about 200 years old, an imposing structure set on a hill.

From Rangdum, the trail goes up to the **Kanji Base** (13,910 ft/4,240 m) for about 7 to 8 hours through a wide gravel river bed. There are many streams to be crossed on this day and it is advisable to carry a pair of sneakers along. The stream short of the camp is best crossed on a pony, due to the depth of the water and the speed of the current. Camp is set on a rocky site beside the river, just large enough for one tent. There is no alternative campsite near the water point.

Start very early the next day so as to take the ascent at a comfortable pace. The path is snow-bound, rocky and barren but at the top of the **Kanji La** (17,225 ft/5,250 m) you will be rewarded with spectacular views of the Ladakh and Karakoram ranges. For about an hour after the top of the pass, the descent to **Kang Nar** (12,992 ft/3,960 m), the next camp site is on snow and scree, extremely steep; pony men find it difficult to bring the horses down to safety. The trail to Kang Nar takes about 4 hours and camp is set on a green patch near the **Kang Nala**. This is the longest day of the trek, about 9 to 10 hours.

The next day, follow the trail for about 6 to 7 hours along the valley downstream. Today, again, there are many cold streams to be crossed. The route is through magnificent gorges of granite and sandstone, right up to **Kanji** (12,424 ft/3,787 m), the first Ladakhi Buddhist village. Camp is beside the river short of the village where there are green fields of peas, wheat and barley.

The last day of the trek (5 to 6 hrs) to Heniskut (11,550 ft/3,500 m) is along a rocky path that is at many points washed away by the river; many streams have to be crossed en route. The trail is downstream along the Kang Nala through willow trees and rock gullies eroded into fantastic shapes. The route drops towards the river, and where it is crossed by a bridge the gorge opens up and meets the road. Heniskut is 7.5 miles (12 km) from **Fatu La** (13,386 ft/4,080 m), the highest point on the Srinagar-Leh highway. A cold, biting wind lashes the multi-hued, craggy peaks and plateaus. The drive towards Leh is 139 km. Visit the Lamayuru *gompa* en route, only 15 km from Fatu-La, the most mysterious and one of the oldest monasteries in Ladakh.

Rangdum Gompa.

KISHTWAR TO PADUM

The struggle starts right from the beginning: agility and endurance are what get you past the pushing and shoving crowd to a seat in the bus at the Jammu Terminus. After a long day's journey you reach **Kishtwar**, a small but populous town which greets you with blaring Hindi film songs. The road journey (on a different bus) can be continued still further up, depending upon how far the PWD (Public Works Department) and military engineers have been able to extend the roadway. Beyond this, you can hitch-hike on PWD trucks and jeeps, through dusty roads under construction, till you reach the point from where the track towards Itholi starts.

The racket of generator sets and construction machinery fades away behind you, giving way to the calls of unseen birds from patches of forests, the smell of damp earth, and the sound of your own footsteps. The trek starts here.

Through gaps in the trees you can glimpse fields below or across the ridge, as you walk along in merry tranquillity. The night halt can be made at a spartan log hut situated at the edge of a tiny settlement. Its inhabitants are friendly enough to cheer you up after the always-exhausting first day.

The second day's trek of 6 miles (10 km) takes you to the large, prosperous village of **Itholi** (also known as Arthal), situated at a height of about 3,500 feet (1,067 m) and at a distance of 30 miles (50 km) from Kishtwar. The village is situated at the confluence of the meandering Chenaits and its tributary the Bhut Nala. You could make a half-day visit to the nearly sulphur spring at **Tatta-pani** ('hot water') Like many such spots, it has some religious significance, and a point to note is that chicken or eggs are not to be consumed here. Of interest to the visitor are the beautiful white sand banks by the Chenab. The combination of warm sand and extremely cold water is bracing.

From Itholi you walk northwards on a

Legally felled lumber stacked beside the Chenab.

well defined path along the Bhut Nala. (This little frequented trail will finally lead you to **Umasi La**, the 17,370 ft / 5,294 m high pass across the Great Himalayan Range, which separates the Kishtwar valley from the Zanskar.) After an up-and-down trek of 9 miles (14 km) along the western bank of the river, you cross it to reach a tea-shop by the evening. Accommodation for the night can be found at the tea-shop, though camping out nearby is also possible.

The route further up leads into a beautiful wilderness with high peaks rising up jaggedly around. The wildly gushing Bhut Nala of the lower altitudes becomes oddly wider and more peaceful higher up. Oaks, pines, firs, crowd the hillside, and huge trees of silk-cotton line the path, their white tufts flying around you with each step.

By afternoon, the trail hits a small village 5 miles (8 km) from the tea-shop – an ideal place for lunch, and for hiring porters/guides for Umasi La. This is important, as the route is quite tricky, and even at times dangerous. The peo-

ple here are friendly, though a trifle inquisitive.

Machel (6,000 ft/1,828 m), a small settlement of about twenty odd huts, can be reached the same day by sundown after covering yet another 3 miles (5 km). It has a police checkpost, built to look after a sapphire mine nearby. The mine has long been in disuse, but the checkpost remains. Machel is the last place where one can be assured of finding porters and guides. It is helpful to spend some time here talking to the locals about weather conditions.

If you are carrying extra medicines or food, it is a good idea to distribute them to the villagers, who often suffer from chronic diseases due to deficiency, and lack of medical attention. In spite of their poverty and afflictions, these brave villagers will gather around when you leave, and smilingly wish you the best for your journey. You should be aware that the people of Kishtwar are in general friendly and hospitable but frankly curious. A city-bred person could very easily misinterpret this as intrusiveness

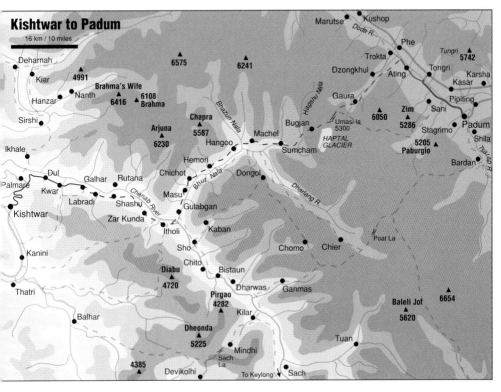

guided by ulterior motives. A brusque response would not invite trouble to the outsider, but certainly hurt some beautiful and innocent people.

The next day's trek through the forests is quiet and steady. As human settlements recede behind the ridges, you get the first intimations of isolation and real adventure. About 6 miles (10 km) up, you enter **Bhujwas**, a lush green grassland the size of twenty football fields, at an altitude of 9,000 ft (2,743 m). This astonishing expanse is strewn with boulders and has a stream flowing through it. Tongues of ice thrust down from the surrounding ridges. In clear weather, a more perfect camping ground would be difficult to come by elsewhere in the world. The day's walk might draw your eyelids down, but the unobstructed star-studded night sky and the velvet grass bathed in blue moonlight compel you to linger outside your tent till quite late. The name 'Bhujwas' is derived from the birch tree, whose bark (*bhoj-patra*) was used as parchment in the old days. (Today it is used as

roofing material, since it is water-proof too.

The next day's trek of 7.5 miles (12 km) is bisected by a lunch-break at the tree-line. Every trekker is advised to collect brushwood before starting out on the second leg of this stretch. The climb becomes tougher every minute from this stage onwards, and there is hardly any trail worth mentioning. The only trading that continues on this route is that of wooden snow-shovels being bartered by the Tibetans for rice. The beast of burden is sheep, thick bags slung across their backs.

You can now see various peaks stretch ahead of you, including **Mt. Brahma** and **Sickle-Moon**. It is an idyllic situation for a trekker: exquisite beauty in combination with rarefied air, but watch out for symptoms of altitude-sickness (if acclimatisation and toning up has not been thorough).

You halt for the high at the moraine, which will lead towards the pass the next day. You are at the base of the pass, just a few hours away from the climax **Not all river crossings are as easy as this!**

270

of the trek. Anxiety can be high, and comfort pretty low: the weather is unpredictable here, and the thunderous sounds of small avalanches on the opposite ridge can be unnerving. However, if you are on the correct side of the hill there is nothing to fear. The temperature drops suddenly and snowfall, even during May–June, is not uncommon. You are sharply aware of being up at 13,000 ft (3,960 m).

The next day is the longest day of the trek. Setting off as early as 5:30 a.m. is advisable, as the snow is firm then, and you should aim to cross the pass before the sun is high. The guide (or the shepherds, if you are following some) is in command today, and caution the motto. Crevasses may be open or hidden, depending upon snow-falls, and ropes will come in handy now and them.

The approach to Umasi La is in three stages. An initial climb of about a kilometre is of the same gradient as before. Then comes an immense snow-field stretching over 1.25 miles (2 km). The gradient suddenly drops and you can see ahead for quite a few kilometres. The sudden appearance of a stretch of flat whiteness makes is a dramatic change from the jaggedness of the previous terrain. Just about when you are tired of plodding over flat snow, comes the last and the most exhausting stage – the climb, with gradients as steep as 70° at times. Finding the right route around is of the utmost importance, as this part of the journey can be treacherous. An hour and a half of trail might get you to cover just about half a kilometre. Then, like magic, appears a tiny but distinct V-shaped crack on the ridge: **Umasi La**! The rest of the climb is fuelled by the surge of adrenalin.

If the ascent does not coincide with white-outs or heavy clouds, a marvellous view unfolds (although the lower valleys are too far below to be seen): a spectacle of whiteness of every possible shade, shape and size. You are standing on the Great Himalayan Range, home of the highest and the most glorious peaks on the planet!

The descent is steep and quick for about 2.5 miles (4 km), beyond which the decline becomes gradual, typical of the topography of Zanskar: a cold desert plateau, the altitude of which hardly varies, averaging 11 to 12,000 ft. There are no pines, streams or green-and-white mountains here. The dense vegetation of the Kishtwar valley has been replaced on this side of the pass by occasional patches of grass. If you have not been to a cold desert before, you will find the starkness of the region both overpowering and fascinating.

At 14,000 ft (4,267 m) you will pass by a few log huts where you may camp for the night, if you wish, or by sundown descend to the first green patch at about 13,500 ft/4,115 m. The shepherds prefer this, for the simple reason that their flocks haven't had anything to eat for the last two days. If you have the stamina, you can reach the village of **Atching**, a few kilometres below the green ledge. (If water is unavailable at the previous two sites, as sometimes happens, you may be forced to taken this option.)

The next day's trek of 11 miles (18 km) confronts you with the flatness of relief of Zanskar, with its bare rocks in subtle shades almost merging into one another. A sometimes dusty track takes you to **Sani** (12,000 ft/3,657 m). The trek is by now a relaxed affair, and you can take in the beauty of Zanskar at ease. The monastery here is an interesting one, and you can spend hours looking around and discussing philosophy with the monks. Padum can be seen about 10 km away. The last day of the trek whistles by as you cover almost 6 miles (10 km) of level ground. Its overriding features are again starkness combined with delicate shades and hues. The trail crosses the Zanskar river and finally enters **Padum**, the tourist headquarters of the region.

The trek has extended over two valleys, stretched over twelve walking days, and crossed over 17,370 ft (5,294 m). Your lasting impressions are likely to be variety, beauty, surprise and exhaution. By the end, you may even feel nostalgic about the beginning of the trek, for that seems years ago; the time in between has been filled with rich experiences, familiar and new.

DARCHA TO PADUM VIA THE SHINGU LA

The ten-day trek between Darcha and Padum can be done either way, from Darcha or from Padum. There are two possible routes for the first half of the trek and two for the second, with a short common stretch. These variations lend variety to what has now become one of the most popular treks in India. This account takes you along one of these routes, via the Shingu La.

Darcha is reached by road from Manali over Rohtang and then along the potato fields of Lahaul (the highest per hectare potato yield in the world). A stopover at **Keylong**, the district headquarters, might be necessary, and is certainly worthwhile for its three monasteries (each a good steep climb from the town), well-stocked shops and your last opportunity for fresh food on this journey.

Darcha, (10,827 ft/3,300 m) is about an hour by bus from Keylong. It consists of a police checkpost where you have to register, some hotels and a shop or two with essential supplies and lots of camping space (but no kerosene). From here, the dirt road goes on to complete the Manali-Leh highway.

The track runs to the north of Darcha, upstream along the true left of the river Kade. An hour's walk will get you to **Chikka**, a settlement of two villages: green fields, flowers, Lahauli folk. A sharp rise, then a gently rising track skirting a dusty hillside, still along the left bank. About four hours from Darcha, you come to a plank bridge just downstream of rapids and a waterfall: a bracing spot for a breather, overlooking gushing water. Nice camp, too, though much too soon for a ten-day trekker. At the beginning of the season you have to cross the bridge and continue along the true right bank. Later, after about mid-July, continue without crossing. Be sure to enquire at Darcha about this; the deciding factor is the location of a trolley bridge at Jankar Sumdo a day later.

Soon after, assuming you cross the bridge – a stream crossing which might

Ponies are often used to carry trekkers' baggage.

require a rope early in the season – walk on through potential camping greens, more of them on the right bank, until you decide to stop. The constraints for camping are few: space for your tent, water and, if you have ponies, grass. This last tends to reduce options drastically and might often force you to camp with the madding crowd.

The next day's walk takes you upstream along the Kade upto **Jankar Sumdo**. On the way, a minor stream crossing, a boulder-strewn stretch, and some lonely *bhoj* (birch) trees, with most of their bark peeled off as far as human hands can reach. Jankar Sumdo is a little over ten hours from Darcha, and can be done in one day if you are in a hurry. Or else you can plan your halts in such a way so as to avoid this uninspiring spot and camp an hour or two further on.

At Jankar Sumdo, you have to cross either the river Kade or the torrent from the Shingu La, depending upon which path you took. Until about mid-July, there is a trolley bridge across the Kade; later it is shifted to the other stream. This bridge is a bottle neck for package touring caravans, and you might be forced to camp here.

It is here that you find the next hotel. These "hotels" (small shacks, really), scattered at around one-day intervals along the standard treks in Zanskar, provide a sleeping space, very basic rice-dal meals, and the inevitable tea and biscuits. Many trekkers therefore carry a three-day supply of food, and flysheets instead of tents (since it rarely rains in Zanskar), and thus manage to avoid ponies or porters.

Starting from Jankar Sumdo, a steep initial climb, then a gentle meander up the true right bank of the Shingu La river. The valley is generally grassy with steep, towering rock faces – disintegrating rock, but safely on the other side of the stream. Again, there are many alternative places to camp. But if you intend to cross the pass the next day, walk on to **Chuminakpo** (14,107 ft/4,300 m), the last grassy spot before the pass. Here the altitude begins to assert itself. The air is crisp, rarefied,

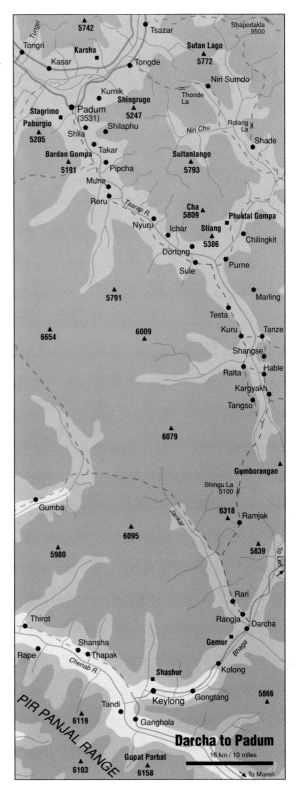

Darcha to Padum

18 km / 10 miles

filled with anticipation of the next day's entry into Zanskar, the Land of White Copper.

There is no natural entrance to the Zanskar valley. The two rivers which drain it, the Stod from the north and the Tsarap from the south, meet near Padum to form the Zanskar river, which leaves the valley via a long, inaccessible canyon. The only way to enter is over the Zaskar Range on the north, or over the Great Himalayan Range on the south. The Shingu La (16,732 ft/5,100 m), is the lowest of three passes over the latter.

The crossing over the Shingu La is the crux of the trek, also the only portion where you encounter snow: early July might find you sinking into it waist-deep. Ponies can get hopelessly stuck, and should start out well before dawn if snow is expected. The climb is steeper than before, the altitude higher. At the top of the pass, prayer flags flutter. The first breeze from Zanskar, laden with the chant "*Om Mane Padme Hum*" blows into your face. Lahaul is behind you, Gumborangan right ahead.

Follow the obvious way down: a stream crossing, later a grassy plateau. This is a useful camp for those coming from Padum, who have to cross the pass early the next day. For those going down, they might as well go further down, past a *chorten*, and camp by the river at **Lakong** (14,600 ft/4,450 m).

Ford the river early next morning and walk along the valley dominated by the **Gumborangan**, the solitary rock rising up many thousand spectacular feet from the valley floor. Always keep the river on your left as you walk downstream. The mountain-desert-fairyland character of the Zanskar landscape will accompany you all the way to Padum.

Six-odd hours away is **Kargiakh** village (13,320 ft/4,060 m), a pleasant camping green below a cluster of *chorten* just before the village, often crowded with technicolor tents. Alternatively, there is a windy plateau just across the bridge, where you will disturb a colony of marmots (called in Tibetan, Phyi, a name which echoes their shrill, whistling cry).

Autumn in Zanskar.

The ten-day trekker does Kargiakh to Purne in one long, dusty eight-hour haul. **Purne** is the small village near which the river that you have been following from Lakong meets the more important Tsarap river. About halfway there, the green fields, *chorten* and mud huts of **Shangse** village provide a change from the barrenness of the dusty yellow-brown Zanskar hills. Just before Purne, you are likely to miss the small sign painted on a stone, but, at every fork, just follow the path where you can make out trekking boot impressions in the dust. A narrow track leads off from the main trail and goes steeply downhill to a bridge, after which a gateway chorten marks the entrance to the tightly knit Purne village. Adjoining the village is a camping ground where you have to pay a nominal amount for each tent put up. (This camp is presently facing an escalating garbage crisis).

From here to **Phuktal** gompa and back is a four hour walk, easily the most beautiful part of your journey. Any description of this little excursion would be banal compared with the reality. One piece of advice: don't go there in a large group. The monastery nestles in the entrance of a huge cave. In the cave is an ancient pine tree, said to have been there even before the monastery was built, and a spring, which is the water source. The lamas' quarters come tumbling down the steep hillside below the gompa, and from there the track winds down past the chortens and main walls further below.

An alternative route continues from Phuktal and reaches Padum via Shade and the Thonde La.

Continuing from where we left off, the track from Purne now follows the river Tsarap. The first village, **Katge Lato** (12,450 ft/3,800 m), one hour from Purne, has a hotel and a camping space. Often the trekker's itinerary includes the trip to Phuktal and back and then on to Katge Lato, all in one day, chopping a day off the schedule. The track now skirts a gorge. The disintegrating track may force the horses into a detour through the villages above. Several small streams and seven hours of walking will get you to **Ishar**, with its fort and camping ground.

Soon after Ishar, cross a bridge and then continue along the left bank through a wider valley and a more comfortable track. You can camp at **Reru** village, about three hours from Ishar, or go on to **Mune** village, six hours away, with a hotel and an old *gompa*.

Padum is about six hours from here. Some ups and downs in the dusty track which continues along the true left of the Tsarap, and about halfway, the Bardan gompa, squatting on a big rock that projects into the river. Villages are more frequent now. Walk on till the valley widens into a large plain and into Padum.

Padum (11,873 ft/3,619 m), is a large village with camping grounds, hostelries and fresh food. Once the ancient capital of three provinces of Zanskar, it is now a roadhead – hence trucks, buses, jeep-taxis, and your getaway via the Pensi La and Kargil. Or you could continue your trek on to Lamayuru or Stok, the beginning of another story.

The Himalayan Blue Poppy.

PADUM TO LAMAYURU

The trek begins from Padum (11,873 ft/ 3,619 m), the erstwhile capital of Zanskar, where many ancient caravan routes once converged. It lies on the true left bank of Zanskar river, formed by the confluence of the Doda and the Tsarap Lingte. The town is well furnished with amenities and has numerous hotels; pack animals and porters can be arranged from here. The route from here runs north-west up the valley to **Sani Gompa**, one of the oldest monasteries in Zanskar. Beyond the monastery, we cross the Tungri bridge and camp next to the Pontse river, below the village of **Karsha**, having covered almost 9 miles (15 km) this day. Alternatively, we can cross a new bridge a few miles from Padum and trek directly to Pishu.

The *gompa* at Karsha is one of the largest in Ladakh, and is headed by the Dalai Lama's Lama's younger brother. Inside are two stupa gates with decorated ceilings, an old temple with *thangkas*, and a well preserved image of the 'God of grace,' whose incarnation the Dalai Lama is supposed to be.

The route to Pishu follows the river Stod upstream, remaining well above it, north-west into the Zanskar valley. A little more than halfway through this stretch, we view the Lingti, which joins the Stod. The landscape is harsh but magnificent: craggy mountain tops, brown valleys and sudden bursts of green cultivation. The Ladakhis have evolved a complicated system of irrigation to render the wilderness fertile. A network of channels brings river water to their scattered fields from lower levels through the technique of lift irrigation.

We follow the Zanskar river upstream, and as we pass the village of **Thonde** on the opposite bank, the valley gradually broadens out. There are streams en route, and the villages are islands of green amidst an arid wilderness. We camp below the village at **Pishu**, close to the river; this day we have covered nearly 8 miles (13 km).

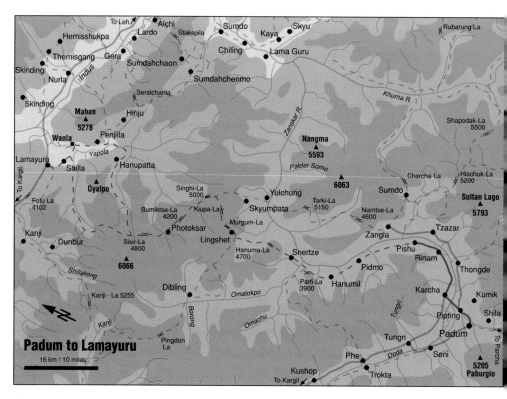

The next day's trail winds through the Zanskar valley, which gradually narrows. This stretch is mostly level, and a 4 mile (6 km) walk leads to a hanging bridge across the river to the village of **Zangla**, a possible day's excursion off our main trek. Zangla is the old capital of Zanskar and boasts a real palace and an eighty-year-old monarch.

There is a jeepable road from Padum to Zangla. Several trekking routes lead here, including one to the Markha valley and to Lamayuru via the Nirag La.

Back on the trail, the level walk takes us 4–5 miles (6–7 km) up to **Pidmu**. From here, the valley narrows and the route alternately climbs and descends for 3 miles (5 km) up to **Hanumil**, a village of just two houses, but with green farmlands providing a welcome change from the desert-like terrain. Camping sites here are excellent, with no problem of water.

The Zanskar gorge is at is narrowest from here, and the climb gets steeper. Four to five kilometers above the village we come across a sparkling blue stream

– the last before the **Parfi La** (12,795 ft/ 3,900 m). The climb is unrelenting, becoming quite steep closest to the top which is most often clear of snow. The other side of the pass presents an abundance of shrubs and bushes and a large stream called Uma-chu, a tributary of the Zanskar river. We cross it on a wooden plank bridge and soon after the path begins to climb again around a mountain, into a wooded valley abounding in willows and poplars, and up to a shepherds' campsite at **Snertze** about 2 miles (3 km) away. A good night's rest is advised here in anticipation of the long and arduous day to follow.

The next day we trek upstream, climbing steadily for about 1–2 miles (2–3 km) before the Uma-chu is joined by another small stream from the east. We follow this stream all the way to **Hanuma La** (15,420 ft/4,700 m), a long haul. The pass, snowbound for most of the year, is like a long, winding corridor rising sharply towards the end. From here we view the Lingshet Gompa at a

distance, and the wide sweep of the Ladakh and Zaskar ranges, including Nun and Kun. The path from the pass proceeds to another saddle, and then follows a long traverse along a mountainside, crossing **Lingshet** village 2-3 miles (3 -4 km) away. Lingshet has one of the most important monasteries of Ladakh, famous for its handicrafts, especially *thangkas*, and for a well stocked library of precious Buddhist manuscripts. The monastery is built compactly with many rooms, open courtyards, and a temple room for prayers. There are a few hotels run by monks here, and a pleasant camping spot close by.

The following day, we toil up a narrow, steeply winding path to a saddle, then descend close to the villages of **Yulchung** and **Gongma**. In a steady zig-zag climb we cross another small pass **Netuksi La** (13,860 ft/4,225 m), to traverse to the base of the **Singi La** (16,600 ft/5,060 m), partially covered in snow. The distance covered on this leg is not more than 6 miles (10 km) but

the going is tough. There is a campsite beside a small stream, where monks from Lingshet sometimes run a hotel. The next day involves another difficult two to three hours' climb to the top of the pass, the highest point we reach on this trek. We can view from here the whole valley up to the Sisir La, which we are to cross the next day, and its surrounding ranges. We then descend into a relatively green valley with myriads of flowers that bloom through spring and summer, and streams criss-crossing its full expanse – a perfect place to camp.

We ascend the following morning over a small pass called **Bhumtse La** (13,800 ft/4,200 m) a couple of kilometers away, from where we see the village of **Photoksar** perched pre–cariously over the Photang river, its rich green fields presenting a sharp contrast to the surrounding dry terrain. Accommodation is available either in the village or in excellent camping spots a little way off by the river. The next day, the mile-long climb to **Sisir La** (15,748

An easy day's walking and a comfortable campsite on the valley's edge.

ft/4,800 m), is quite severe, across a barren moonscape. On our descent, we leave the main track and strike north-west (the original track crosses the river and leads to **Hanupatta**). Continuing westwards, we cross a bridge and commence another ascent of 2.5 miles (4 km) to emerge at the base of **Nuche La** (15,700 ft/4,785 m). The campsite here is amidst green fields, generally occupied by shepherds.

The route next day climbs very gradually before reaching a magnificent blue mountain. The reason for its beautiful colour is unknown. The 2 mile (3 km) climb across the pass is gentler than those encountered thus far, though the descent of over a mile (2 km) down to the Shilla river is very steep. We can camp just before the river enters a gorge swerving prominently eastwards. The countryside and the river here are very beautiful. Carrying on the next day, we follow the Shilla into an awesome gorge, crossing it without bridges at least fif-teen to twenty times, shuttling from bank to bank. The depth, however, is not

threatening, and it is more convenient to trek inside the river for 2 miles (3 km) or so, until it becomes faster and deeper near Shilla village. This stretch covers nearly 7.5 miles (12 km).

We pass next through several patches of trees which offer the possibility of spotting wildlife. Soon after we arrive at **Shilla** village, close to the river. A short trip to **Wanla** Gompa, about 2 miles (3 km) away, can be made the same day or the next. The red *gompa*, visible from afar, is close to a thousand years old and has a stunning eleven-headed image, standing quite tall, and Tibetan frescoes.

Crossing the river on a bridge a mile or so (2 km) down from Shilla, we begin a 1-2 mile (2-3 km) ascent through another gorge to the top of **Prigati La** (12,224 ft/3,726 m), from where we can see the Lamayuru village and *gompa*, and the Srinagar-Leh road about a mile (2 km) away. After descending to Lamayuru, and exploring the village and monastery, we can either travel by road to Leh, or move on to Srinagar.

Lamayuru Gompa.

MARKHA VALLEY TO LADAKH

The Markha river runs parallel to the Indus across the Stok-Kangri massif. The starting point of the trek to the Markha valley is a 10-mile (15-km) long drive across the Indus from Leh to Stok village (11,500 ft/3,505 m). The village is picturesquely located and affords good views of Leh and the Indus valley from Thikse to Spituk.

From the village, towards the west, the peaks of the Stok Kangri massif are visible with the main peak (20,180 ft/ 6,153 m) looming over the others. The path leads in this direction and follows the dry true left bank of the Stok Nala. The climb is gradual for four to five hours, past the ruins of Stang-la-khar, a 19th century fort built when Ladakh was threatened by the Dogra general Zorawar Singh. The ramparts of the fort are above the path and so blend with the rocks around that it is easy to miss.

Cross a large willow grove at the foot of the fort before turning right up a subsidiary valley, climbing a little more steeply to the summer shepherd settlement of **Khilchay** (13,500 ft/4,115 m) at the foot of the Stok La. There are good climbing possibilities in this area. Some of the popular peaks are Stok Kangri, Parcha Kangri (19,895 ft/6,065 m) and Kantaka Kangri (1,300 ft/5,275 m). They do not require any technical mountaineering capability; a pair of good boots, crampons and a rope are enough. They are approached by following the Stok Nala almost to the base of the peaks. Two to three days at most are required from here to climb the peaks. A permit has to be obtained in advance from the Indian Mountaineering Foundation in New Delhi and a fee has to be paid, the amount depending on the height of the peak.

The second day starts with a steep climb to the top of Stok La (15,900 ft/ 4,848 m), following the trail which is conspicuously visible from the camp. At the top the path winds through a complicated knot of ridges keeping near the crest. The descent into the Rumbak valley an hour later starts steeply and is extremely dusty on account of loose rock and mud, but can be exhilarating for anyone who enjoys downhill scree running!

This day too is across barren landscape with hardly any vegetation to be seen. This is prime habitat for the snow leopard, an elusive animal rarely spotted even here. The trail keeps to the true right bank of the Rumbak Nala, through the small village of **Rumbak** (13,450 ft/ 4,100 m), and then, crossing to the true left bank, climbs up the valley of a subsidiary stream to the tiny settlement of **Yurutse**. Camping is possible here, or a little beyond, at the foot of the Kunda La – a long day's walk which could take up to 8 hours.

The climb to the Kunda La (16,100 ft/ 4,907 m) is not as steep as that of the previous day to **Stok La**, but it is longer. A clear day provides a spectacular view of mountains to the north merging into the distant Karakoram ranges. A steady descent next leads to the head of the Skiu valley, a small stream formed by

tiny rivulets. The valley narrows sharply from the broad grassy meadows at the top to the small opening at the settlement of **Sumdo** or **Shingo**.

The Skiu Nala, bordered by willows and wild roses, then flows through a series of gorges requiring quite a few river crossings all the way to the village of **Skiu** on the banks of the lower Markha. A little beyond the confluence of the Skiu Nala and the Markha river, the village (9,900 ft/3,017m) provides some good campsites. In the evening it is worth walking back on the trail to the confluence, to visit a small monastery cared for by an old nun who comes every morning and evening to light the butter lamps at the altar of Chamba – the future Buddha.

As a diversion, you could follow the Markha river downstream along the right bank from Skiu to reach its confluence with the Zanskar river, a long walk of five to six hours each way.

On the fourth day follow the river upstream from Skiu on one of the loveliest sections of the Markha, which broadens out and is spanned by several bridges. Woody bushes grow thickly along the river all the way to the charming village of **Thinlespa**. There are good campsites beyond the village.

Continue on the path, climbing steadily eastwards to the village of **Markha**, which has a monastery well worth visiting for its frescoes. Markha is at an altitude of 11,500 ft (3,500 m) and about six hours' walk from Skiu. A side valley from here leads to Zangla, the old capital of Zanskar, over the Rubering La through one of the least frequented regions of Ladakh.

From Markha the landscape changes from the warm, relatively wooded section of the lower Markha to the starker area past the village of **Umalung**. On to the twin villages of **Hankar** (13,100 ft/ 3,992 m) where there are good campsites, a total distance of only 6-8 miles (10-12 km) taking about 4 hours. Between the two villages is a ruined fort, the walls of which climb dizzyingly up a crag to an eyrie worth exploring for those with a good head for heights.

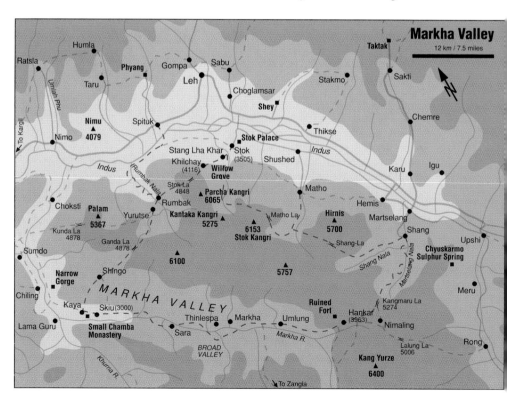

It is possible to continue on this day to the Nimaling plains in one long push of 5 to 6 hours. From just above Hankar, the trail veers off left (north-east) away from the Markha, up a narrow valley past villages smaller and seemingly poorer than those of the lower areas up to the **Nimaling plain** (16,100 ft/ 4,907m). This broad, undulating meadow slopes upward to the base of the ice-clad **Kang Yurze** peak (20,990 ft/ 6,400 m) the dominating feature of the area. Tiny springs and rivulets criss-cross the plain and provide pastureland to an astonishing number of animals – yaks, dzos, sheep, goats and horses from the villages all around. Himalayan marmots and white-tailed hares are seen in plenty, and it is not unusual to sight an occasional blue sheep or wolf. Camp is best by the main river flowing through the plain. At certain parts of the season, with water levels rising, great care must be taken crossing the stream. It is worth spending an extra day here lazing and wandering around the plain.

Crossing to the left hand valley, to-wards the north, you begin the climb up to the highest of the three passes on the trek, **Kongmaru La** (17,410 ft/5,306 m) with its wonderful views from the top. From here the trail descends steeply to the head of the Martselang valley, past the sulphur springs of **Chyuskarmo**, and follows the Martselang stream to the village of Sumdo or **Shang-Sumdo**, at its confluence with the Shang Nala. The route goes through narrow gorges and at times the horses have to be unloaded to let them pass through. The camp is in a beautiful grove, and there is a small *gompa* an hour away from the village.

Take the riverbed, as on the previous day and follow it till you reach a good footpath on the true left bank. You soon will reach a road (a dusty trail really, but suitable for motor vehicles) which you follow for some distance past a few *chorten* right up to **Martselang** on the Indus. This could take up to 4 hours to reach. To get to Hemis, leave Martselang on the right while still on the trail and follow a gently rising track to the *gompa*.

Part of Stok Palace is now an interesting museum.

SKI TREK: KARGIL TO LEHNIVAN

Many Himalayan trekking routes are suitable for skiing in winter. In the absence of organised expedition support, it is an adventure to pioneer these routes.

The Kargil-Inshan-Lehnivan route connects the three Himalayan regions of Ladakh, Kishtwar and Kashmir, traversing the Great Himalayan and the Pir Panjal ranges. It was first done by an Australian-Indian-Canadian expedition in 1990. The route is in good condition from late December to early March and should take 10 to 15 days to complete. From Kargil it is possible to make shorter skiing trips to Dras via Sanku, and to Rangdum Gompa via Panikhar. For proper acclimatisation it is advisable to fly to Leh from Srinagar after a few days' skiing in Gulmarg (8,956 ft/2,730 m), the premier ski resort of India. If flying to Leh directly from Delhi or Chandigarh, plan for adequate acclimatisation time in Leh. At 11,500 ft (3,505 m). Leh in winter is cold and dry (but picturesque). Guest houses run by families provide comfortable accommodation at off-season tariffs near the main bazaar. The shops are well stocked for winter and it is possible to buy kerosene and almost all provisions except high-tech expedition foods.

There is a bus connection from Leh to Kargil, but in case of poor road conditions you can hire a four-wheel-drive taxi for about 2,000 rupees. The 144 mile (230 km) road to Kargil passes through some spectacular country via Lamayuru, Fotu La (13,386 ft/4,080 m) and Namika La (12,198 ft/3,718 m). At Kargil it is possible to stay at the tourist bungalow if the hotels are shut. The road up the Suru valley toward Panikhar is usually open as far as Sanku, 16 miles (25 km) from Kargil.

Sanku-Panikhar (10,515 ft/3,205 m) 16 miles (25 km): Organize your gear and take a truck or taxi ride to Sanku where the skiing begins. Ski up the scenic Suru valley, following the gently rising, well travelled foot trail substituting the road in places, to reach Panikhar

easily in two days. Start early to avoid wet snow in the afternoon. Fantastic views of Nun and Kun will make the hard work bearable. The villagers of the Suru valley are friendly and hospitable and you may be invited to stay overnight in their homes.

Panikhar-Donara (11,975 ft/3,650 m) 10 miles (16 km): Start up the Chellong valley westwards from Panikhar and be prepared for a long day to Donara. The valley walls are steep, so keep next to the river which is almost entirely iced up. Start wearing your avalanche transceivers from this day onwards. The climb is gentle all the way to Donara, which is a wide plain where streams from Bobang and Lonvilad meet. Camp near the stream at the beginning of the valley leading southwards to Lonvilad Gali.

Donara-Lonvilad Gali (15,945 ft/4,860 m) 7 miles (11 km): The valley starts as a narrow gorge but widens after a steep climb about a kilometre from Donara. The climb to the pass consists of steep portions interspersed with

Left, drying out sleeping bags. **Right**, crossing a snow bridge.

gentler ground and takes you over a beautiful glacier abounding with frozen pools and formations of green ice. Most ice bridges over crevasses should be safe in winter. Near the end of the climb, be quick to pass under seracs high up on the right. Camp at the windy crest of the pass for good views.

Lonvilad Gali-Kanital (13,451 ft/ 4,100 m) (10 km): From the short crest of the pass the route drops sharply for 200 m to the Bhot Kol glacier, which sweeps down gently for 6 miles (10 km) to Kanital. This slope makes for excellent downhill skiing and you don't need to use skins on your skis till Kanital. Though the glacier is safe for skiing, lookout for crevasses and suspicious snow late in the season. Camp at Kanital or continue to Baziran.

Kanital-Baziran (3,960 m) 12 km: At Kanital the Kanital Nar, which is the main tributary of the Warwan river, originates from the snout of the Bhot Kol glacier. Follow the river on the left bank over the wide, undulating valley. Baziran is identifiable as a wide expanse before the valley narrows and turns left. Camping near the river will save you having to melt ice.

Baziran-Humpet (12,795 ft/3,900 m) 6.25 miles (10 km): After the narrow end, the valley opens up again till it is about a kilometer wide. The river branches off into small streams and route-finding can be interesting with narrow ice bridges, deadends and small stream crossings. Take care not to get the skins on your skis wet as it is much easier to carry skis over wet areas than to ski with ice clinging to your skis. Near Humpet the river enters into a gorge which is not very deep initially but drops rapidly. Try to be on the left of the river, or cross over early in the gorge and climb up the left wall to the large plateau which is Humpet. High up on the plateau look for a shepherds' hut, visible as a horizontal slit in the snow. It provides good roomy accommodation with a little improvisation.

Humpet-Sokhniz (9,022 ft/2,750 m) 9.5 miles (15 km): This is the most serious part of the route as you have to

Crossing the Margan Pass.

negotiate a long and narrow avalanche-prone valley to Sokhniz. An alpine start very early in the morning for better snow conditions is recommended. The first objective is to get down to the Kanital Nar about 1 mile (1.5 km) downriver from the shepherds' hut. Traverse down to the birch trees in the gorge and select a less steep slope where trees go down to the bottom. Ski, glissade and abseil through the trees to the river and ski along it using the ice bridges.

Reach the confluence of Kanital Nar and Sain Nar which form the Warwan river going southwards. At this turning, climb up about 100 m of steep slope on the left bank and then gently traverse down to meet the river. It is downhill all the way to Sokhniz and you can make good speed. Use both banks of the river, favouring the right bank. The slopes are prone to windslab avalanches, so be cautious and keep within shouting distance. Near Sokhniz the valley widens after a big avalanche chute. The village is on the right bank and is the last of the upper Warwan valley villages.

Sokhniz-Inshan (8,202 ft/2,500 m) 14.5 miles (23 km): Upper Warwan valley villages have a distinctive lifestyle and architecture. It is possible to stay with the villagers or in their community buildings. You can get baked potatoes, coarse millet *chapatis*, eggs and chickens for food. Sokhniz to Inshan can be done comfortably in two days.

It is also possible to get porters from Gumbar about 4 miles (6 km) from Sokhniz and make it to Inshan in one day from there. Snow is likely to get wet in the daytime. The well travelled track passes through the picturesque villages of Basmain and Choidraman. Inshan, situated opposite the base of the climb to the Margan Pass, is a big village with shops, a rest house, wireless station and police post.

Inshan-Margan Pass (11,975 ft/3,650 m) 8.75 miles (14 km): A jeep track is being built from Lehnivan to Inshan, over the Margan Pass. Make an Alpine start to climb up the steep forested hillside, on the right bank of the river right opposite Inshan, till you hit a trace of the jeep track. Keep on the track wherever possible, ascending through a delightful forest, traversing steep slopes and avalanche debris. Pass a rest house near the tree line and continue to the top of the pass to find a shepherds' hut; it is a good place to camp at the beginning of the 2.5 miles (4 km) long Margan pass.

Margan Pass–Lehnivan (9,418 ft/2,890 m) 7 miles (11 km): Cross the long flat pass to enter into Kashmir valley. Glissade and ski down the initial steep slopes for about 400 m to rejoin the jeep track and then ski on the track through the forest to Lehnivan village. Here it is possible to hire conveyance for Anantnag and then on to Srinagar.

The special characteristics of Himalayan ski mountaineering to be borne in mind are the extreme climate, high altitude, variety of snow conditions and the absence of organized support and rescue. It is advisable to have some experienced ski mountaineers in the team. Moreover all members should be committed, as abandoning the tour midway may not be possible.

Flocks of sheep leave for summer pastures.

A WALK TO BEASKUND

Between the Bara Banghal and the Pir Panjal ranges lies Beas Kund, the source of the river Beas, which, like all such sources in India, has a sacred aura. Our journey to this spot commences from Manali. The drive to Solang Nallah, about 7.5 miles (12 km) by road, takes us up the course of the river to the small isolated village of **Palchan**. The route from here to Solang is most beautiful, going through dense patches of vegetation and an assortment of streams and rivulets. **Solang** is a flat meadow, surrounded by steep hillsides to its north, around which a ski track and lifts have been constructed. One can either camp out or stay here in the log huts belonging to the Western Himalayan Mountaineering Institute.

The initial stage of the trek from Solang Nallah entails an easy day's walk, mostly along the true right bank of the river. The vegetation consists mostly of shrubs and bushes with dense forests along the hillsides above. As we move northwards, several valleys converge on the main river valley from the high ranges. More than once along this walk, we cross the river on improvised log bridges. This is a prime habitat for pheasants, Monal and Koklas. An assortment of other birds inhabit or migrate to these areas, like the Magpie Robin, woodpeckers, finches, martins, thrushes, tits and buntings and even some exotic species like the Black-throated Jay and the beautiful Nuthatch.

The trail ascends into dense conifer forests breaking into high-altitude alpine meadows. We now leave the heavily morained valley and trace our route upwards across high grassy hillsides. On either side lie untouched oak forests vibrant with bird life.

As we climb higher, the track becomes rather steep and gradually tapers off as we once again descend to **Dhundi Thaj** (9,000 ft/2,743 m), a small campsite in a network of streams. It serves mainly as a grazing ground for the Gaddis, who bring their herds up

from the valleys below. We also view the imposing massif of **Hanuman Tibba** (19,813 ft/6,039 m) filling the horizon with its sharp northern face.

The trek from here becomes tougher. A short climb leads to a snow bridge across the Beas, and firm ground gives way to loose scree. A wrong step here could lead to a freezing dip in the gushing Beas. The route ascends steeply along these scree slopes, with the river swallowed up by huge boulders more than once. After a 2 to 3 hour climb, we come upon a ridge, over which the river plunges as a waterfall. The route now bends northwest and the hillsides become craggier and barer. Hanuman Tibba still dominates the scene at **Lualli** (9,000 ft/2,743 m), close to the river; the silence is occasionally broken by thundering avalanches down the massif. With luck we could spot the Bharal or even the Ibex. Caves in the rocky cliffs surrounding us suggest the presence of the Himalayan black bear, pug marks and excreta confirming their existence.

From here, we can either climb the

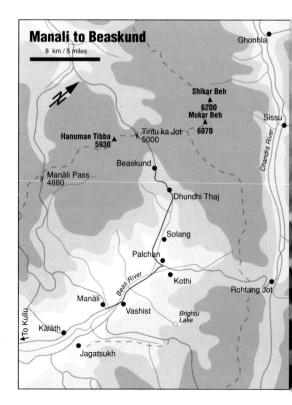

ridge directly above and descend into the narrow valley beyond, or climb the imposing hillside opposite to reach Lady's Leg (12,600 ft/3,840 m). The second alternative is much more enjoyable, though it could mean an extra day's walk. The trek goes up steep grassy slopes, criss-crossed by streams and waterfalls along its length. During September-October, alpine flowers cover the hillsides. After a 5 to 6 hour incline, we stumble across large tracts of meadows at the foot of **Mt. Friendship**. Impressive peaks can be sighted all around from here: **Mt. Indrasan** (20,410 ft/6,221 m), **Deotibba** (19,687 ft/6,000 m), **White Sail**, visible to the north-east, while to the west lies Hanuman Tibba.

A short walk up a rocky mountainside leads us to **Akhir-Goru** – a pass-like formation atop a ridge. From here one can spot the expanse of the valley below, its pastures large enough to accommodate several airfields. The route diverges to the right, in the direction of **Mt. Ladakhi** and **Mt. Manali**, and to the left is visible the Beas Kund, a pear-shaped lake in several shades of blue overlooked by high walls. Its perennial water supply comes from several springs located within its core, as well as numerous streams draining into it from glaciers up ahead. It is from here that the mighty Beas emerges in the form of a trickle that later swells along its course. A small shrine on the banks of the Kund testifies to its sanctity. Hanuman Tibba stands at the center of this valley; at its foot lies the ice-fall and heavily crevassed glaciers which also drain into the valley. All along the length of the Tibba's massif lie numerous hanging glaciers and cornices. To its right lies the **Tintu Pass**.

There are several alternatives for a return trek from this valley. One route leads via the Tintu Pass into the Chamba valley, but this is only for experienced trekkers. Another follows the direction of the Spiti valley across several high altitude ridges and passes. The easiest alternative, however, is to retrace our path back to Solang Nallah.

Sheep and goats on the move between winter and summer grazing areas.

TREKKING THE CHANDRA – BHAGA TRIANGLE

The triangle is formed by the valley of two phenomenally muddy, turbulent rivers, the Chandra and the Bhaga. They are in turn the headwaters of the Chenab, one of the five rivers of the Punjab, about which many a romantic ballad has been written and sung.

The Chandra and Bhaga flow through some of the most majestic mountains of the Himalaya. A trek through these two valleys takes you across high passes and into a world of textured rock, tumbling waterfalls, hidden green meadows studded with alpine flowers, and a mountain lake set like a jewel amid blindingly white snow-capped peaks and black rocks.

You can get to the start of your trek in the Chandra river valley by either of two routes: one across the Rohtang Pass (13,050 ft/3,978 m), a motorable road

from Manali, the other across the Hampta Pass (14,128 ft/4,306 m) on foot. The second starts from the village of **Prini**, just outside Manali, through pleasant forests and meadows. The first day has a stiff climb to the village of **Chika**; on the second day you camp across a stream close to the pass, and on the third day cross to **Chatru**. The pass is snow-bound in June, but clear in July and August. From here you can see **Indrasan Peak** (the seat of Indra, the God of Thunder) at 21,410 ft (6,525 m), and **Deotibba Peak** at 19,687 ft (6,000 m).

The drive across the Rohtang Pass climbs up in a series of steep turns, with wonderful vistas of the green, wooded valley of the Beas, which you are leaving. Across the Rohtang is the rain shadow belt, a completely new world of sheer, craggy heights above the muddy Chandra river. You come down to **Gramphoo**, which sports two tea shops and not much else. If it is early in the year (June), you start walking. If the road is open (July/August), you can drive up to **Batal** (approximately 25 miles/40 km upstream).

If walking from Gramphoo, your next camp is at Chatru (11,023 ft/3,360 m) – a 10 mile (17 km) walk, relatively level, along the Chandra river. Across the river to the right you can see rainbow-hued rocks rearing up into the sky; on the left, the mountains are greener, streams and waterfalls everywhere from the melting snows.

At **Chatru** there is a tea shop and a PWD rest house. Also visible are the ruins of the old village, devastated when a glacier-dammed lake burst and flooded the area. There is a place to sleep at the tea shop – quite basic, just a blanket-covered stone slab, but it's warm. The rest house has two rooms. It is advisable to stand the bed up and spread your sleeping bag on the floor. (These options are in case you decide not to camp.)

From Chatru to Chota Dhara (12,336 ft/3,760 m) is another 10 miles (17 km) of east walking, the river on your left and the **Bara Shigri glacier** on your right (the same that once blocked the river). In June you will encounter some snow on your route. The area presents the

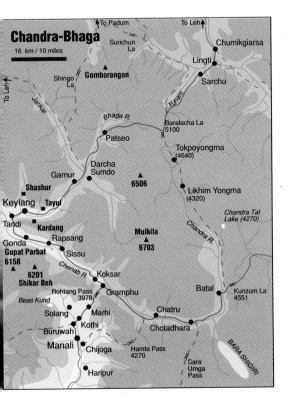

most wonderful contrasts – majestic, stark mountains and, suddenly around a corner, the brightest green meadow scattered joyously with flowers, with a sparkling stream bubbling through it. There is a rest house and tea shop here as well. (In June, the tea shops do not have much more than tea and biscuits; you would be well advised to carry all your own provisions.)

Chota Dhara to **Batal** (12,992 ft/3,960 m) is a steeper walk – lots of snow in June, rather dusty walking otherwise. There is a tea shop at Batal, too, and also a pleasant campsite.

Batal to the Lake of the Moon, **Chandratal** (14,009 ft/4,270 m), is a ten mile (17 km) walk. After the shepherds have crossed, it is a well defined route. It is still along the Chandra river, which in part spreads in little channels across a wide valley floor, and around the next bend narrows into a raging torrent trapped between ice floes. Just before the lake, the route levels out through meadows; you follow the pretty Chandratal stream and suddenly come

upon the lake. Its glassily calm surface early in the morning almost makes you believe in an upside-down world. The waters change color all through the day – from an implausible cobalt blue, through indescribable green, to molten silver at sundown.

Reflected in the waters is the lofty **Mulkilla Peak** (21,830 ft/6,654 m), which in Lahauli means 'Silver Fort.' Along the lakeside are shepherd shelters, and in July and August you can see the flocks on the hillsides and sit around the shepherds' fire for a chat. Birds abound, and the lake is also the breeding ground of the Brahminy Duck.

After Chandratal, you are climbing steadily. Rock and shale along the way are not easy on the feet. If the flocks have crossed, the path is well defined; otherwise you will be crossing mud slides and stretches of snow, discovering the path as you go. There are two rivers and a smaller stream to be crossed between Chandratal and the Bara Lacha pass.

Camp 1, after Chandratal, is in a

Breakfast on a cloudy morning at Chandra Tal.

meadow beside the first river, at **Likhim Yongma**. The river must be crossed very early in the morning before the melt starts, or you will be faced with a raging, unfordable torrent and a long walk up-river to a snow bridge or narrower ford.

Camp 2 out of Chandratal is by the next river at **Tokpo Yongma**. You now find yourself in a zebra-striped world of snow and bands of black rock: battlemented mountain tops, like abandoned forts guarding their vast unpeopled terrain. Set Camp 3 below the pass across the last stream, before hitting the snows.

The **Bara Lacha La** (16,050 ft/4,892 m) is a long, gradual pass, which must be crossed very early in the morning before sun-up, to avoid getting slowed down or stuck by softened snow. This is a unique three-way pass and the source of three rivers – the Chandra, the Bhaga and the Lingti, which flows into Ladakh.

Once across the pass, it's a quick easy descent to **Zingzingbar**. You pass another lovely lake, called **Surajtal** or Sun Lake. The Bhaga valley now unfolds before you. From July through to late September the road across the pass from Manali to Leh is open. Private transport could meet you here, or passing trucks could give you a lift. If walking, **Patseo** (14,091 ft/4,270 m) would be your next stop. This used to be the site of a large fair where traders from as far away as Tibet, Mongolia and Punjab used to barter their goods.

Jispa (10,892 ft/3,320 m) is nine miles (14 km) away from Pateseo and **Keylong**, the capital of Lahaul, another 13 miles (21 km). Your walk takes you along the Bhaga river. As you go lower, signs of vegetation start appearing – stunted pines and wild rose, all arranged like Japanese gardens amongst rock and trickling water.

Two Buddhist monasteries along the way make interesting visiting – the **Gemur** and **Tayul** *gompas*. Both have some very lovely frescoes.

Buses and taxis are available from Keylong to Manali and onward connections with the rest of the world.

Looking toward the Bara Shigri peaks from the Kunzum La.

ACROSS THE BASHLEO TO KULLU

The Kullu valley can be reached on foot by two routes. The picturesque **Jalori Pass** remains open only in summer but is motorable. The **Bashleo Pass**, on the other hand, is less frequented but more interesting in that there is no parallel motorable road. The best months for this trek would be May/June or September/October.

A convenient starting point for the trek is Shimla, the capital of Himachal Pradesh, easily accessible by air, train or bus from Delhi. It is here that one should stock up especially on tinned food and film; beyond Shimla, essentials like a sturdy pair of walking shoes become difficult to procure. The route has rest houses at convenient distances of a day's walk and, though it is not necessary to carry stoves etc, a sleeping bag is always useful.

En route from Shimla to Nirmand, one should look out for the mountain ranges of Kinnaur and Uttar Pradesh in the distance. Nirmand has some beautiful stone and wooden temples dating back to the 10th century. The following day you can either take a bus or walk to Arsoo and spend a night at the rest house just above the village, made in the old colonial style with high ceilings and an open verandah. It has two rooms and a chowkidar who, if the mood takes him, can cook for you.

An early start is advisable, as is a hearty breakfast. The first part of the walk is along the unmetalled road cut out of the hill and dotted with occasional pine trees. At **Baghipul**, 4 miles (6 km) away, the last few tea stalls appear before you begin your climb. The ascent is steep, and you see at a distance the terraced fields of rice, millet and maize of the valley below. The path is rocky in places but otherwise well defined. With the gain in height the vegetation starts changing and soon the deodar, the Himalayan cedar, begins to make an appearance.

The route opens upon a huge green

Rafting down the Satluj.

meadow with a crystal-clear brook against a backdrop of high mountains and a waterfall. To the right is the rest house of **Sarahan**, our camp for the night. The chowkidar could be persuaded to cook the meals. There is a good forest behind the rest house where you can collect brushwood for the evening camp-fire. Visitors breed curiosity, and soon the local headman and others may come to check you out. As the bonfire is under way the headman, spirited by the local brew, may tell stories in the flickering light about his village, its beautiful temple and their brave life.

After a good night's rest you can walk to the village in the morning. The main temple is a wooden structure situated among deodar trees with the characteristic verandah girdling it. Another small temple, dedicated to the goddess Kali, was built a century ago by the local Patwari (revenue official). A fair takes place in the month of April on this spot – the Jheeru Mela, to which all the inhabitants of the surrounding villages throng.

Situated at 11,000 ft/3,353 m, the pass, with peaks on either side, is visible even from Sarahan. The distance is only about 5 miles (8 km), but the climb is fatiguing. As one climbs through the deodar forest, on the right is a small spring with celebrated tonic properties. The track to the top is grassy with interspersed clumps of brown oak. When you reach the top you see the sharp-crested mountains in a riot of colours – gold, green, rust and yellow. A few colourful prayer flags flutter in the wind, fastened by travellers as a token of respect to the presiding deity. On the other side of the pass one may meet a Gaddi, a nomadic shepherd, from Bhramur in distant Chamba.

From the pass to **Bathad**, a distance of 5 miles (8 km), the descent is sharp but the glorious view makes up for it. Walking through the forest of fir, oak, horse-chestnut and walnut trees is a delight. It was here that the ruler of Kullu , Raja Ajit Singh who had been captured by the Sikh army in 1840 was rescued by the brave local inhabitants, the Sarajis. It is said that the Sarajis,

mountain goats that they are, climbed the hilltop and took the Sikhs by surprise by rolling down stones and boulders. Bathad comes into view – a small village with slate roofs on the bank of a stream next to a forest. The sight of the rest house revives your flagging spirits and tired limbs. You can luxuriate on the glazed verandah as the sun gently pours in.

From Bathad a motorable road leads to **Banjar**, 7 miles (11 km) away, but the walk is far more pleasant. The river is a constant companion for the trekker from here onwards. The village of **Goshaini** has an interesting temple with wooden carvings. As one approaches Banjar the valley opens: apple orchards, terraced fields and even concrete houses appear. The rest house commands a view of the valley down towards **Larji**. There is a comfortable rest house at Larji, just short of **Aout**, which is a favourite haunt for anglers (this place is famous for trout). Aout is a junction on the National Highway from where buses and a taxis ply to Kullu or Manali.

Rustic bridge.

A TREK THROUGH DODRA KWAR

The hills and mountains of Himachal Pradesh run along a roughly northwest-to-southeast axis, gaining progressively in altitude as one moves up from the plains towards the Tibetan plateau. The passes over the successive ranges and the river valleys cutting through them offer a wide variety of trekking opportunities. The lower Shivaliks have pleasant, gentle walks for those short of time and stamina while the higher passes in the Greater Himalayan and Zanskar Ranges provide a challenge best attempted by experienced climbers. The region in between provides the right blend of pleasure and perspiration for the enthusiastic trekker. In this middle ground, the trek to Dodra Kwar, in the upper reaches of the Rupin valley, is among the lesser known but more exciting walks.

The Rupin originates on the southern slopes of the mid-Himalayan range which on the north flanks the beautiful Baspa valley in Kinnaur. High offshoots from this snowy ridge border both sides of the Rupin along its short, torrential course. The only year-round access to Dodra Kwar is up the Rupin from Naitwar in Uttar Pradesh. The route generally followed in summer from Himachal Pradesh lies over the Chanshil Pass (13,000 ft/3,962 m), crossing the ridge on the right side of the Rupin from the gentler Pabbar valley. The passage through Dodra Kwar requires a minimum of three days' walking, stretchable to a week if the entire area is to be explored.

Chirgaon, a small town in the Pabbar valley 84 miles (135 km) from Shimla, is the best place for a night halt before the trek over Chanshil. This area was popular with anglers at one time but now the trout, dynamited and poached to extinction, is limited to a government farm. Log huts built for fishing at some idyllic locations in the valley downstream remain mute relics of the angling era. Chirgaon has an old forest resthouse and a larger, modern structure belonging to the state electricity board at Sandasu, 2 km further.

It is a charming drive from Shimla to Chrigaon. The initial 20 miles (32 km), part of the national highway to the Tibetan border, is along an unassuming ridge which marks the divide between the catchment of the Satluj, which takes its waters to the Arabian Sea, and the Yamuna, whose waters after merging with the Ganga, flow into the Bay of Bengal. At **Theog**, the road branches off the national highway, descending right to the river Giri. Thereafter it moves up the Giri valley to **Kharapathar** which at 9,000 ft/2,743 , 30 miles/49 km from Theog] straddles the divide between the Giri and the Pabbar catchment.

From Kharapathar, past the old town of Jubbal with its imposing palace, to the ancient temple of Hatkoti on the right bank of the Pabbar, is a downhill stretch of 16 miles (26 km). The road now turns up the Pabbar, past some 8th century stone temples in the Pratihara style, through **Rohru**, the most sizable township in the valley, to reach

Preceding pages, vantage point overlooking Himalayan foothills.

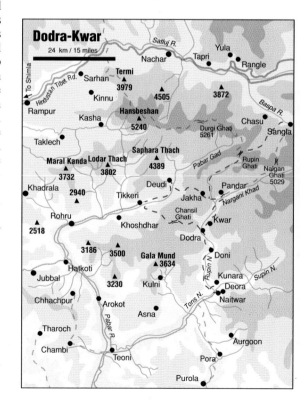

Dodra-Kwar
24 km / 15 miles

Chirgaon, 17 miles (28 km) away.

The upper Pabbar valley is called Chohara, a region whose culture and economy are still largely rooted in the past. Apple, the harbinger of money and modernity, has as yet only a limited presence. Paddy and *mash*, a black pulse grown on the irrigated tracts near the river, give way to buckwheat and amaranthus further up. The presence of village deities and assorted spirits is increasingly evident as one moves up the valley. The temples, square structures of rectangular stone slabs interspersed with large wood binders and topped with sloping slate roofs, are embellished with superb wood panels and sculptures of gods and goddesses, flora and fauna and ferocious mythical beings. This art is still extant among the lower caste artisan families and there are beautiful examples of recent work in the temples at Tikkeri and Dodra Kwar.

Four miles (6 km) up the motorable road from Chirgoan, **Tikkeri**, on the right bank of the Pabbar, is the starting point for the climb to Chanshil. Across a footbridge, a bridle path climbs up the mountain on the opposite side of the river to Larot, 5 miles (8 km) away. Forests of conifers and broad-leaved trees shade the steep foot ascent. **Larot** with its two-roomed forest rest house and a *dhaba* which dishes out basic fare of rice and dal, is the first day's halt.

From Larot it has to be an early start in the morning. Dodra, the next stage, is 16 miles (26 km) away across the **Chanshil**. In the early morning chill, the track winds for the first two or three hours through mixed forests of deodar, pine, high altitude oak and occasional maple, slowly giving way to birch and tall shrubs of rhododendron. At the edge of the tree line is a large meadow of gentle gradient with scores of tinkling, silvery brooks coursing over its mossy green surface. Further up, the meadows grow steeper and from late June to the end of August they are a riot of alpine blossoms, Gentian blue, the yellow of primula, the pink of the rhododendron bushes and a myriad other hues greet the eye, and the scented air is heady.

Breathtaking views.

Chanshil is an unpretentious divide at the end of a long, slanting traverse, marked by a small temple to the deity of the pass. It is customary to leave an offering of an iron article to appease the goddess and ensure a safe journey. Itself snow covered till late June, Chanshil offers a commanding view of the peaks ringing the Kinnaur boundary on the north and the even higher Swargarohini and Bandar punch ranges, across in Uttar Pradesh.

Down the other side are steep meadows again. One can tarry here a while for a glass of milk with the Gujjars, the pastoral nomad of the Himalaya. Make sure it's boiled, though, or it won't be the legs alone which will run down to Dodra. On the mountain face, across the narrow valley, it is possible to pick out Kwar on a clear day, before all views are shut out by the thick forest which covers the seemingly endless miles to Dodra, high up on the right bank of the Rupin. The region of Dodra Kwar has a mysterious aura. Its isolation, steep valleys, gigantic rock faces and the enormous landslips which threaten the existence of each village, all combine to lend a brooding grandeu to this rugged area. In the Pabbar valley inhabitants, it inspires a certain fear and awe. No outsider will eat in any of the houses in Dodra for fear of being sacrificed by poison to the local spirits. Fortunately, this quarantine does not extend to other villages in the area.

Dodra has a small ramshackle forest rest house with space to camp beside it. For those short of time, one long day's walk from here is the roadhead at Naitwar, 16 miles (26 km) away. The track lies down the Rupin valley, staying on the right bank all the way. Nearby is **Sewa** village in Uttar Pradesh, distinguished by an extensive area under poppy cultivation. A tea shop can rustle up an early lunch but it is more advisable to wait till the *dhaba* at **Dhaula**, about 6 miles (10 km) short of Naitwar. The track after Sewa follows a series of sharp ascents and descents before coming down to a wide riverbed just short of Dhaula. From here, through pine-covered hillsides, a broad path leads to the

Porters crossing the Baspa river.

confluence of the Rupin and the Supin, together called the Tons.

Across a bridge and a little way up the opposite hill is **Naitwar**, with roads leading to Dehra Dun or back to Shimla via Teoni, near the meeting place of the Pabbar and the Tons. Naitwar also offers access to some lovely treks up the Supin, to Har-ki-dun and Ruisher Tal.

Those with more time can visit the other villages of Dodra-Kwar and leave the Rupin valley by some other routes. The walk from Dodra to Kwar (8 miles/14 km) involves a steep descent to the Rupin, then a short distance up sandy beaches to the bridge at Gosango and a stiff climb up the opposite side. **Kwar**, headquarters of the area, is a series of hamlets stretched out half-way up the mountain, with a rest house, medical facilities and a wireless installation.

Kwar to **Jakha** (7.5 miles/12 km), the last village up the Rupin, involves crossing the river above Gosango and then climbing along the right bank of the Rupin, past the hamlet of **Jiskoon**, through a valley which gets progressively narrower. The inhabitants of Jakha in recent years have almost entirely converted to a religious sect practising abstention and vegetarianism – unusual for this cold and difficult region where limited arable land makes animal husbandry a significant economic activity. Dodra Kwar produces some fine local tweed (*patti*) made on the pit loom; the most celebrated is the *patti* from the small village of **Pandar** located up a tributary of the Rupin, between Jakha and Kwar, some 11 miles (18 km) from Jakha. From Pandar it is possible to cross over to the Supin catchment via the Manji Ban pastures, but it is a long way to the roadhead from there.

There are further options of two routes from Jakha out of Dodra Kwar. Up-valley, over the glaciers at the source of the Rupin, is the **Rupin Pass** (16,000 ft/4,877 m), leading to **Sangla** in the Baspa valley of Kinnaur. It is a long and arduous trek covering 30 miles (50 km), which (besides fitness and stamina) requires permits in advance to enter the restricted area of Kinnaur. Somewhat easier is a 15 miles (25 km) walk to **Deudi** in the upper Pabbar valley. Climbing up behind Jakha, the trail passes through thick forests of conifers and broad-leaved species including oak, walnut and birch, before crossing the same ridge which has the Chanshil pass further down. This less frequented track offers a chance to see the beautiful Monal pheasant, colonies of langur and, with luck, the brown bear. It is also a more difficult walk than over the Chanshil. After crossing the ridge to the Pabbar side, there is a second ascent of about 600 ft up a vertical rock face. Sheer drops occur frequently along this path, which has neither width nor gradient sufficient for horse or mule.

Deudi, on the right bank of the Pabbar, is reached after a rapid descent down mountain sides so steep that often one has to clutch at passing tree trunks to achieve a measure of control over pace and breath. It has a small forest rest hut for those too tired to walk the last 3 miles (6 km) to the roadhead at **Dhamwari**, about 7.5 miles (12 km) from Chirgaon.

Wooden temple towers in a remote village of S E Himalchal.

ACROSS THE PIR PANJAL

The Dhauladhar Range, seen from across the wide Kangra valley, is striking, rising straight up from the valley floor to heights of 15,000-18,000 feet (4,500 to 5,500 m). Set between the Dhauladhar and the Pir Panjal ranges is the lovely Chamba valley. The Ravi flows through this rich, green valley, a place of beautiful people and lilting music. Across lie the high mountains of the Pir Panjal, running almost parallel to the Great Himalayan Range from Chamba to Spiti. From the crest of this mighty range are visible the serried ranks of the Great Himalayas to the north-east – a cold, white, pristine world.

One of the most frequented routes across the Dhauladhar is via the **Indrahar** (or **Lakha**) **Pass**, 14,500 ft (4,420 m). The Dhauladhar crossings are mainly steep ascents from green forests and flowering meadows to ice, rock and snow. The treks are relatively short, but a few extra days en route are advisable for acclimatization.

Your trek starts from Macleodganj, a little above the town of Dharamsala: a beautifully located town, with views of the Kangra valley below and towering mountains above. Dharamsala is the permanent seat of the Dalai Lama in India and an important Buddhist centre, with monasteries, libraries and temples.

The first leg of your trek takes you along a well set path, through forests of oak, rhododendron and pine. The climb gets progressively steeper to your first camping option at **Triund** (5 miles/8 km). There is a picturesque forest rest house here but if you prefer a more quiet spot, there is one 3 miles (5 km) further on, in the lovely meadow at **Lakha**.

You are now getting beyond the treeline: ice, rock and snow ahead and, spread mistily below, the valley, a splendid sight in almost any weather with clouds boiling up its sides and magical glimpses of green in bright sunshine, or glitteringly competing with a starlit night. The pass is visible from Lakha and looks deceptively close and easy; in fact it is respectably steep. It is a good idea to spend an extra night in Lakha before attempting the glacier and pass up ahead.

A pre-dawn start is a must because by noon the weather worsens dramatically. Melting snow can turn treacherously slippery on the steep gradient. The climb can take between 4 to 8 hours. Once atop the pass, you leave ice and rock behind and face an interminable snowy, white world, sloping gently away into the distance with the green Chamba valley and the peaks of the Pir Panjal beyond.

The descent off the pass starts with a steep glissade. Approximately 5 hours of slip, slide and walk bring you to the meadow at **Mandhara**, the first of the alpine meadows of Chamba and Bhramaur, with the Ravi valley before you. The next day a short trek takes you to the village of **Kwarsi**, set amid green and gold fields surrounded by dense forests. The money economy hasn't quite arrived here, and barter is still practised. A *serai* (rest house) built on the precincts

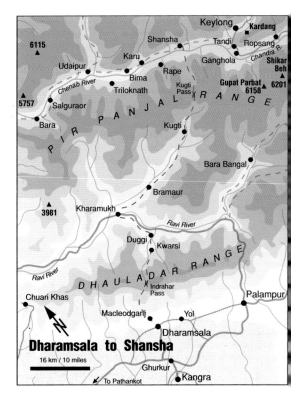

Dharamsala to Shansha
16 km / 10 miles

of the temple, offers shelter if you don't want to pitch camp.

An uneven 3-hour trek from Kwarsi, up hill and down dale, through meadows and forests, takes you to the roadhead at **Dalli**, another pretty village on the slopes above the forthing river. Here you can get a bus or have transport meet you to take you along a precipitous edge, all the way to the ancient temple town of Bhramaur. Some of the temples here date back to the 17th century.

From Bhramaur a jeepable track eastward takes you 8 miles (13 km) up to **Hadsar**, the start of your trek across the Pir Panjal via the **Kugti Pass** (17,000 ft/ 5,182 m) into Lahaul. (The westward road takes you to Chamba town and onward to Pathankot). Hadsar to **Kugti** village, the last settlement this side of the pass, is a tough 9 miles (15 km) of steep ups and downs. Your route is through green meadows dotted with herds of white sheep. Trees are sparser, allowing long views of the steep valley and the snows ahead. At Kugti village there are a few shops and a post-office.

The sun sets on a final campsite.

From Kugti to your next camp at **Duggi** continues to be a hard trek with sharp shale and stones, though peeping flowers and blooming shrubs provide respite. Duggi is a wide meadow with a tumbling stream, surrounded by the tall mountains. You might encounter your first yak here. This hardy animal provides food, fuel, apparel and transport for the mountain people, and is greatly valued.

Your last camp before crossing the pass is at the **Alyas** – about 13,500 ft (4,115 m). In early June this might be snow-bound, so you would camp a little lower. Gaddis and their herds will be encountered all along the way. They are a warm, friendly people and helpful in this wild mountain terrain.

To cross the pass a start is best made as early as 2 or 3 a.m. (the Gaddis start moving at midnight). The initial climb is gradual, but the rarefied atmosphere takes its toll: the last 1,000 ft are at a gradient of almost 60°. As you breast the last rise, all the effort is forgotten in the magic of the sight beyond – a tossing ocean of frozen peaks spreading to the horizon and beyond. Rejuvenate yourselves with the wild grandeur of the scene and prepare for a descent down 80° slopes of snow. Cutting steps helps – or you could go into a barely controlled glissade which may well end in a tumble. Rope and an ice axe are necessary items of equipment.

Camp off the pass must necessarily be on snow or a dry, rocky patch, unless you have enough stamina for an approximately 7 hour trek to **Khardu**. A zebra-striped valley of white snow and black rock carries you to the grassy plateau of Khardu, restful campsite. From here to the roadhead at **Shasha** is 10 miles (15 km) over loose rock and scree. But the enchantment of the mountains overrides all physical strain: sudden streams, silvery waterfalls and unexpected patches of green.

From Shasha the road takes you to Keylong in Lahaùl and thereon down along the Bhaga, up the Chandra, across the Rohtang Pass (13,050 ft/3,978 m) on to Manali and the pleasant green Kullu valley.

TRAVEL TIPS

GETTING THERE

BY AIR

The majority of visitors now arrive in India by air. While entry is possible through any of the four major international airports at Delhi, Bombay, Calcutta and Madras, Indira Gandhi International Airport at Delhi is certainly most convenient for visitors to India's Western Himalaya.

As a major stopover during flights between Europe and Asia, Delhi is well served with flights from most parts of the world. Many long-haul flights unfortunately arrive between midnight and 6 in the morning; apparently to suit the night landing regulations of European and Far Eastern cities, but in reality often because of the weight restrictions for a full plane taking off in the thin air of an Indian summer.

Indira Gandhi International Airport has been recently constructed and is constantly being improved. Left luggage facilities are available.

BY SEA

A few cruise ships such as *Cunard*'s Queen Elizabeth II do call but India is not a regular cruise destination. Some freighters offer passage to India and excellent accommodation is still available. The *American President Line*, *British India Steam Navigation Company*, *Eastern Shipping*, *Lloyd Triestino* and the *Shipping Corporation of India* are among the lines with regular sailings to and from Bombay, Calcutta and Madras. If you choose this mode of travel, it will become necessary to take a connecting flight or train to Delhi, Jammu, Srinagar, Leh or Kullu.

BY ROAD

The "hippy trail" through Turkey, Iran, Afghanistan and Pakistan has been little used in recent times, but when peace returns to this fascinating area, it will surely become popular with the more adventurous traveller. A few companies in Germany and the U.K. do still operate a few such voyages. In London, Trailfinders (42-48 Earls Court Road, London W8 6EJ Tel: 071-938 3366) can give advice.

The land border with Pakistan is open only at Waga, west of Amritsar in the Punjab. The land border with Nepal is open for non-Indian or Nepalese nationals at Bairwa, Birganj/Raxaul and Kakarbitta/Naxalbari.

TRAVEL ESSENTIALS

VISAS & PERMITS

All visitors to India, including Indian citizens, require a valid passport. All visitors, except Indians, require a valid entry, tourist or transit visa.

Single Entry visa is for people visiting India for reasons other than tourism, such as employment or business. If you plan to stay for a period longer than 3 months with such a visa, you must register with the nearest **Foreigners' Registration Office** within a week of arrival. You will then need an exit endorsement prior to leaving.

Multiple Entry visa may be obtained if you intend to exit and re-enter India during your visit.

Tourist visa is issued to visitors for a period of 3 months, to be used within 6 months of issue. Extension requests are considered by the Foreigners Registration Office in New Delhi (Hans Bhavan, Indraprastha Estate, Tel:331-9489 or 331-8179) or elsewhere or by the Superintendent of Police at the nearest district headquarters.

Transit visa is valid for 15 days, and must be used within 3 months of issue. This visa is strictly for those passing through India.

No special permission is required to visit the states of Jammu & Kashmir or Himachal

Pradesh. All foreign citizens entering Jammu & Kashmir, however, are required to register their arrival and departure with the Foreigners' Regional Registration Offices located at the airports and in the cities. The Srinagar office is located on Shervani Rd, Tel:74424 (10 a.m. - 4 p.m.) and the Jammu office on Canal Rd, Tel:42676. In Leh, the Superintendent of Police is responsible for foreigners' registration.

RESTRICTED AREAS

Both Himachal Pradesh and Jammu & Kashmir are sensitive border states adjacent to Pakistan and China. While you are free to visit the states *per se*, there are certain areas you cannot visit.

Broadly speaking, the area north of the Srinagar-Leh road and east of the Manali-Leh road is off limits. In Ladakh, while you are not allowed more than one mile north of the road running through Zoji-La, Dras, Leh and Upshi, many of the monasteries that lie beyond this line are indeed accessible. Major sections of Lahaul and all of Spiti require special permission to visit. Only groups are allowed to use the Manali-Leh highway, and that too with a police escort.

Permission to enter a restricted area must be sought from the Ministry of Home Affairs, New Delhi, preferably before entering India, as the procedure may take a long time, sometimes up to six months. Get advice from the nearest Indian mission.

MONEY MATTERS

Indian currency is based on the decimal system, with 100 *paise* to the rupee.
Rupee notes: 500, 100, 50, 20, 10, 5, 2, 1
Rupee coins: 5, 2, 1
Paisa coins: 50, 25, 10, 5

Major **credit cards** are accepted in the above average hotels and restaurants and many of the better shops. **Travellers' cheques** are also accepted at these places. Encashing travellers cheques, however, can take time, especially in banks, so change a few days' requirements at a time. In the more expensive hotels, hefty luxury taxes may be avoided by paying in hard currency or with credit cards.

Currency declaration: It is important to keep in mind various rules governing the use of foreign exchange. Any amount of foreign currency may be imported into India, provided you declare it on arrival in the **Currency Declaration Form**. This will enable you to take back unspent money, provided you retain the receipts from all banks and hotels where money was changed. Also, hotel bills, airline tickets and the like can be paid for in local currency only against proof of legal conversion. Currency must be exchanged only through banks or authorized dealers; the use of any other means is an offence.

Income tax clearance: Indians and foreigners domiciled in India for more than 90 days, or those who have worked in India during a 90-day visit, need an **income-tax exemption certificate** from Foreign Section of the Income Tax Department in New Delhi, to leave the country.

HEALTH

Visitors arriving from Africa and South America require an **International Health Certificate** with a record of a yellow fever inoculation valid for ten years. Remember that immunity is effective only ten days after vaccination.

No other vaccination certificate is needed, but for personal protection, a whole range of **injections** is recommended – cholera, typhoid, tetanus. Do consult your doctor for advice on *gama globulin* shots to boost immunity to hepatitis and for suggestions on anti-malarial pills. While the climate of the colder hilly regions is not exactly conducive to malarial mosquitos, you must take precautions in the plains and in the foothills .

A **personal medical kit** to take care of minor ailments is useful to have along. Anti-diarrhoeal medication, a spectrum of antibiotics, aspirin and something for throat infections and allergies would be a good idea. Also include Band-Aids, sterilized gauze bandages, sunburn salve, tweezers, antiseptic cream, insect repellent and water purification tablets. Salt pills to combat heat exhaustion are particularly necessary, especially if you visit in summer. A locally available powder, Electrolyte, containing salts and dextrose, is an ideal additive to water during summer months or if suffering from diarrhoea.

Stomach problems are somewhat inevitable for most visitors to India, because of the onslaught of spices and a different range of bugs and germs. However, "Delhi belly" can be avoided with a little care. When you arrive, rest on your first day and eat only simple food; well cooked vegetarian dishes, a South Indian *thali* and some fruit are perhaps best. An upset stomach is often caused by eating an excess of rich Indian meat dishes (which are often cooked with vast amounts of oil and spices). Let your body acclimatize.

Finally, drink plenty of **fluids** but never unboiled or unfiltered water. When in doubt, stick to mineral water, soda or the aerated drinks of standard brands. In smaller towns, avoid ice as this may be made with unboiled water. If you get **dysentery**, dehydration becomes dangerous. The more common *bacilliary* dysentery is nasty but fairly easily curable by antibiotics. The *amoebic* variety of dysentery, on the other hand, is more persistent and can result in serious damage if left untreated. Similarly, avoid uncooked food such as salads and cut fruit. All food should be cooked and eaten hot.

Altitude sickness is a danger in the high altitude regions of the Himalaya, especially Ladakh and Lahaul-Spiti. It mainly afflicts trekkers who disregard some simple rules of high-altitude acclimatization. As a rule, if you are climbing above 3,500 meters, at least one week should be spent for every 1,000 meters climbed. This is not an absolute limit, prohibiting you from intensive ascents such as climbing over passes, but refers rather to the height at which you camp. Altitude sickness is not merely an acclimatization problem, which can be solved by not going higher for a day or two, but a serious affliction which requires you to quickly descend 1,000 meters or more for recovery. The most important sign is water retention; others being extreme breathlessness, coughing up of fluid, severe headaches and nausea, blueness around the mouth, drowsiness and sometimes even derangement.

WHAT TO BRING

Light summer clothing is adequate for many Himalayan areas at the height of summer, although Leh and places far north can get chilly in the evenings. A couple of light sweaters or a jacket are therefore advisable.

Winter is, of course, freezing. You will need all the warm clothes you can get, as is evident from the temperature chart on page 310. Try to carry clothes that may be washed easily in mountain streams. Women should dress conservatively, avoiding shorts and revealing swim wear (even when swimming). Items suggested are T-shirts, shirts, walking shorts, walking trousers, warm jacket, trekking boots and insoles, tennis shoes, gloves, waterproof clothing, money belt, hat, sleeping bag. Cotton shirts, blouses and skirts are easily available throughout the country.

Unless you enjoy paying excess baggage charges on your return home, it is best to arrive light. The shopping possibilities are more often limited by space rather than cost.

If travelling away from the major cities or resorts it is worth carrying a medical kit, padlock and sewing kit among other items. Sun cream and sun block are not readily available so they should be brought. A hat is a sensible precaution. A bath plug is also useful in smaller hotels which often seem to have basins without them!

CUSTOMS

The international airports all have **red** and **green channels**. Tourists seldom have any trouble. Occasionally, customs officials ask to see one suitcase at random and make a quick check. **Prohibited articles** include certain drugs, live plants, gold and silver bullion and coins not in current use. **Firearms** require possession licenses, valid up to six months, issued either by Indian missions abroad or by a District Magistrate on arrival in India. For further details, check with the issuing authority. All baggage at Delhi is X-rayed prior to reaching the baggage collection area in the arrival hall.

Duty free imports include 200 cigarettes or 50 cigars, a bottle of alcohol, a camera with five rolls of film and a reasonable amount of personal effects such as binoculars, portable typewriter, sound recording instruments and so on. Professional equipment and high value articles must be declared or listed on a **TBRE form** on arrival which is a written undertaking to re-export them. Both the list and the articles must be produced on departure. This may be a lengthy process, so do allow time, both on arrival and departure, for this particular process.

With *Insight Guides* you can make the whole world your home. From Bali to the Balearic Islands, from Munich to Moscow, from Thailand to Texas, from Zurich to Zaire.

With *Insight Guides* the journey begins even before you leave home. With stunning photographs that put you in the picture, journalistic stories and features that give insight, valuable practical information and maps that map out your journey for you.

Insight Guides enrich the travel experience. They can be used before, during and after a journey — as a travel planner, as an indispensable companion and as a way of reliving memorable sights and moments.

We now have over 100 titles in print in various languages. Thanks to our extensive distribution channels your bookseller will have them available. Nevertheless, should you have problems purchasing certain titles, feel free to contact us:

"SEE YOU SOON!"

Höfer Communications
38 Joo Koon Road
Singapore 2262
Fax: (65) 8612755

A P A
INSIGHT
GUIDES

The Indian subcontinent encompasses some of the most mysterious and culturally independent countries in the world. **Insight Guide: South Asia** gives a vivid impression of the colourful kaleidoscope and the mythic-mystical depth of India. See Sri Lanka, jewel in the Indian Ocean, the Islamic nation of Pakistan, the mountains of Nepal, sandwiched between India and China, the extensive "rooftop world" of Tibet and the special travel experience presented by Bhutan and Bangladesh.

Or discover the unique wildlife and parks of the region with **Insight Guide: Indian Wildlife**.

Delhi—Jaipur—Agra
India
Kathmandu
Nepal
Pakistan
Rajasthan
South Asia
South India
Indian Wildlife
Sri Lanka

A P A
INSIGHT
GUIDES

For **unaccompanied luggage** or **baggage lost** by the airline, don't forget to get a landing certificate from customs on arrival. Also, Currency Declaration forms for amounts of cash in excess of US $1,000 must be completed at customs on arrival.

To avoid last minute departure problems, remember that the export of **antiques** over 100 years old, animal products (including ivory), jewelry valued more than Rs 2,000 (gold) or Rs 10,000 (otherwise) is banned. If in doubt about the age of semi-antiques, contact the Director, Antiquities, Archaeological Survey of India, Janpath, New Delhi.

ON DEPARTURE

Do remember to reconfirm your reservations for departure well in advance to avoid any last-minute difficulties. Security checks can be intensive and time-consuming, so allow two hours for check-in.

An **airport/seaport tax** of Rs 150 per person for departures to Afghanistan, Bangladesh, Bhutan, Burma, the Maldives, Nepal, Pakistan and Sri Lanka, and Rs 300 for departures to the rest of the world must be paid prior to check-in. Ensure that the name of your out-bound carrier is endorsed on the tax receipt.

For visitors with **Entry Permits**, exit endorsements are necessary from the office where they were registered. Should a stay exceed 90 days, an income tax exemption certificate must be obtained from the Foreign Section of the Income Tax Department in New Delhi.

GETTING ACQUAINTED

GOVERNMENT & ECONOMY

The Indian Union is a federation of 25 states and 6 Union Territories. The nominal Head of State is the President of India. Actual power, under the parliamentary system of government, rests with the Prime Minister and his Council of Ministers at the Center. These are responsible to the *Lok Sabha* (the Council of the People), a directly elected body, and to the *Rajya Sabha* (the Council of the States), an indirectly elected body. In function, these correspond roughly to the British House of Commons and House of Lords respectively.

In addition to the Center, each state has its own legislature from which a Chief Minister and his Council of Ministers are elected. The constitution distributes power between the Central and State governments. Elections are normally held every five years, but may be called earlier. India has had ten general elections since its independence in 1947.

With a well developed democratic structure, a large skilled labor force and an adequate communications structure, the country has made considerable progress since independence. Despite the agrarian bias of the economy, industry has grown enormously, making India one of the 15 top industrial nations of the world. If present rates of growth are maintained or increased, India could well join the ranks of the "miracle" Newly Industrialized Countries (NIC) in the next century. There are, however some serious problems that need to be overcome, although starvation is no longer one of them.

GEOGRAPHY

India's Western Himalaya occupy two of its northernmost states, Himachal Pradesh and Jammu and Kashmir. Himachal Pradesh is a mountain state; it encompasses an area ranging from the dusty plains and foothills of the Shivaliks to the towering Himalayan mountain ranges and onwards into the Tibetan plateau with its high altitude desert climate.

Jammu is the southern, transitional part of the state of Jammu and Kashmir and leads into the Vale of Kashmir, the geographically and culturally rich heart of Kashmir. To the east lie Ladakh and Zanskar; dry, cold deserts with extreme temperature ranges and an almost lunar landscape.

CLIMATE

Unlike the rest of India, the best time to visit the Himalaya is between April and July, when the plains become unbearably hot. Trekking opportunities open up as the snows melt and the verdant and relatively cool mountain areas become havens for trekkers and tourists. By June, the passes to Ladakh and the Keylong area open.

The trekking season is from May to October, since the monsoon does not really affect the region. After this, it becomes too cold to trek. The passes get blocked again, cutting off parts of the Himalaya. As the chart below shows, northern India can become extremely cold; abandon all preconceived notions of a tropical India.

Average Year Round Temperatures

		Jan	Apr	July	Oct
Srinagar	min°C	-2	7	18	6
	max°C	4	19	31	23
Leh	min°C	-14	-1	10	-1
	max°C	-3	12	25	14

CULTURE & CUSTOMS

While visiting temples, mosques or gurudwaras, it is essential to remove one's shoes prior to entry. Overshoes are provided in some places at nominal cost and stockinged feet are usually permissible. Avoid taking leather goods of any kind into temples as this can cause offence.

Photography is prohibited inside the inner sanctum of many places of worship. Do obtain permission before using a camera. Visitors are usually welcome to look around at their leisure and can sometimes stay during religious rituals. For visits to places of worship, modest clothing would be appropriate; this excludes brief skirts, skimpy tops and shorts. A small contribution to the donation box is customary.

The *namaste*, the greeting with folded hands, is the traditional form of greeting and its use will be appreciated though men, specially in the cities may offer to shake hands with you, if you are a man. A handshake may even be appreciated as a gesture of special friendliness.

Most Indian women would hesitate to shake hands with a man, Indian or foreign, and no offence is meant. Most would also be taken aback at the easy informality of interaction between the sexes common in the West.

In private, visitors are received as honored guests and your unfamiliarity with Indian ways will be accepted and understood. Should you be tempted to eat with your fingers in the Indian manner, remember to use only your right hand.

TIPPING

There is no harm in expressing your appreciation with a small tip. Depending on services rendered and the type of establishment, this could range from Rs 2 to Rs 10. In restaurants the tip is customarily 10 to 15 percent of the bill. Leading hotels add a 10% service surcharge and tipping in such places is clearly optional. Although tipping taxis and three-wheelers is not an established norm, it would not be taken amiss. Here too, 10% of the fare or leaving the change, if substantial, would be adequate. Porters at railway stations would expect around Rs 2 a bag. At airports, a rupee per bag in addition to the fee charged by the airport authority, though not essential, would be welcome.

If you have been a house guest, please check with your host whether he has any objections to your tipping any of his domestic helpers (e.g. a chauffeur who may have driven you around) before doing so.

TIME ZONES

Despite its size, India has a uniform time zone all over the country. Indian Standard Time (IST) is 5 ½ hours ahead of Greenwich Mean Time and 10½ hours ahead of U.S. Eastern Standard Time.

WEIGHTS & MEASURES

The metric system is uniformly used all over India for weight and for measure. Precious metals, especially gold, are often sold by the traditional *tola* , equal to 11.5 grams. Gems are weighed in carats (0.2 grams). Financial outlays and population are often expressed in *lakhs* (one hundred thousand) and *crores* (one hundred lakhs or ten million).

ELECTRICTY

India is on a 220 volt AC, 50 cycle system. Most larger hotels provide step-down transformers to provide voltage suited to your electrical appliances. The voltage often fluctuates in the hilly areas. Power cuts are not unknown, especially during the tourist season when demand for electricity shoots up.

Some areas depend either on captive hydro-generators or diesel generators. The electricity here may be supplied only in the evening. The main areas however are hooked onto a grid.

BUSINESS HOURS

Shops and offices are generally open from 10 a.m. to 5 p.m. **Banks** open from 10 a.m. to 2 p.m. on weekdays, but on Saturdays they close at noon. **Post office** hours are 10 a.m. to 5 p.m. except on Saturday, when they open only in the morning. Telegraph offices are open 24 hours. But remember that certain post office services terminate earlier in the day. During winter, some shops may close early.

HOLIDAYS

A multi-ethnic entity like India has no paucity of holidays. Since many dates are decided by a lunar calendar, it is not possible to pinpoint the exact holiday date. A list for 1992 follows:

January 26	Republic Day
February	Shivratri
March	Holi
	Good Friday
April 7	Mahavir Jayanti
April	Id-ul-Fitr
May 9	Buddha Purnima
June	Id-uz-Zuha
July	Muharra
August	Janashtami
August 15	Independence Day
October	Dussehra
October 2	Gandhi Jayanti
October/November	Diwali
November 2	Guru Nanak Jayanti
December 25	Christmas

RELIGIOUS SERVICES

There are few towns in India without temples, mosques and churches, although the church of your affiliation may not be available. Sikh gurudwaras exist in most major towns. There is one synagogue in New Delhi. Your hotel will give you more information as to the kind of religious institution you are seeking.

COMMUNICATIONS

MEDIA

With a large number of English dailies and hundreds of newspapers in Indian languages, the press in India provides a wide and critical coverage of national and international events. Among the better known English language dailies are the *Indian Express*, *The Times of India*, *The Telegraph*, *The Hindustan Times*, *The Hindu*, *The Statesman* and the *Independent*. There are also two Sunday papers, the *Sunday Observer* and the *Sunday Mail*, although all the major dailies also have Sunday editions. The prominent news magazines include *India Today*, *Sunday*, *The Illustrated Weekly* and *Frontline*. There are also excellent general interest magazines like *The India Magazine*.

English and foreign newspapers are available in New Delhi within 24 hours, as are most international magazines such as *Time*, *Newsweek*, *The Economist* and others.

There are several women's magazines, financial dailies and journals, city weeklies and an entire range of special interest magazines ranging from aviation to zoology.

TELEVISION

Both radio and television are government run and controlled, although there are moves afoot to introduce a measure of autonomy in both along the lines of the BBC. Both are huge networks with programmes in Hindi, English and the numerous regional languages. The single television company is known as *Doordarshan*. It operates two channels in major cities and one channel elsewhere.

The news in English is broadcast nationwide at 7.50 a.m. and 9.30 p.m. every day. There is also an excellent foreign news capsule every Friday at 10 p.m. hours called The World This Week. A useful teletext service called *Intext* is available. Many hotels also pick up CNN for their in-house cable service.

RADIO

Akashvani or All India Radio (AIR) broadcasts on shortwave and mediumwave, and in Delhi on FM. The frequencies vary so check with your hotel. Regional channels have different programmes. Some of the programmes on the National Channel are:

7.45 p.m.	Sports Roundup
11.10 p.m.	Financial Review
11.15 p.m.	Western Music

VIDEO MAGAZINES

A new form of news is in vogue with the introduction of monthly video magazines to balance the tilt of government electronic media. These can be bought or hired in most towns. The most established is undoubtedly *Newstrack* produced by Living Media, publishers of *India Today*. It gives 90 minutes of news and background that would never be shown on television. Its success has spawned a host of competitors such as *Business Plus*, *Observer News Channel*, *Eyewitness* and *Indiaview*.

POSTAL SERVICES

The mail service is generally good. The rate for **inland letters** is 60 *paise* for the first 10 grams and 40 *paise* for each additional 10 grams. Inland letter forms cost 50 *paise* each. For foreign destinations, **airmail letters** require Rs 6.50 for the first 10 grams. **Aerogrammes** cost Rs 5.

It is advisable to personally affix stamps to letters or postcards and hand them over to the post office counter for immediate franking rather than to slot them in a letter box. Sending a registered parcel overseas is a complicated and time-consuming process. Most parcels should be stitched into cheap cotton cloth and then sealed. There are often people sitting outside major post offices offering this service. Two customs forms need also be completed. Once the parcel has been weighed and stamps affixed, make sure they are franked and a receipt of registration is issued to you. Important or valuable material should always be registered.

Many shops offer to despatch goods, but not all of them are reliable. It is usually only safe when handled by one of the government run emporia.

Airfreighting purchases is possible but can be equally time-consuming. Whichever way you send your package, you will need the cash memo or bill, encashment certificate, passport and onward airline ticket. There are many airfreight agents available to help, and most travel agents will be able to provide assistance.

POST & TELEGRAPH

The main post and telegraph office addresses in some of the major towns are:
Central Post Office, near the Bund, Srinagar (Tel:76443, 76494)
Head Post Office and **Telegraph Office**, Leh
General Post Office, Pacca Danga Raja Ram, Jammu (Tel:5677, 43726)
Central Post Office, The Mall, Shimla

COURIER SERVICES

Most of the major international networks have agency agreements with Indian companies. DHL, UPS and Skypak work under their own brand name while Federal Express operates as Blue Dart. They all have offices in the major towns and, in addition to their international links, operate extensive domestic networks. The addresses are:

EMS Speedpost
Parliament Street, New Delhi
(Tel: 38-5605)

DHL
Hotel Asian International,
Janpath Lane, New Delhi 110011
(Tel: 331-8948, 332-2527/2534/2724)

Blue Dart Express
Plot No.8, Balaji Estate,
Kalkaji, New Delhi 110019
(Tel: 642-4308/6871/8950)

Skypak
17 Connaught Circle,
opp. Scindia House,
New Delhi 110001
(Tel: 332-6898)

Some courier companies have sub-agents in Srinagar and Shimla. In Srinagar, you must send parcels from the **Foreign Post Office** (Tel:76449) in the Air Cargo Complex on Shervani Road near the TRC. This is open from 10.30 a.m. to 3.30 p.m. except on Saturday, when it closes at 2 p.m. It is shut on Sunday.

TELEPHONE & TELEX

Making telephone calls to other Indian destinations from a telegraph or post office in the Himalayan region is nigh impossible, let alone making overseas calls. This is in contrast to the reasonably good telecommunications facilities in the rest of India. In Srinagar, for example, bad service and unruly queues compound your difficulties while trying to phone from the **Central Telegraph Office** on Maulana Azad Road (Tel:76549). If you must, make telephone calls outside usual rush hours, when it is also cheaper to phone.

Telex facilities are also available from the telegraph office, but are not reliable either. Telegrams too are problematic; a solution is to send two at a time, since they are not very expensive.

Check with your hotel as to the facilities it can provide. This can save a great deal of time and effort.

EMERGENCIES

In case of a serious emergency, such as theft or illness, turn either to your hotel or the nearest tourist office. They will help you on a priority basis, for example in contacting your embassy in New Delhi. All towns have a police station and a dispensary, with sophistication increasing with the size of the town. But remember, the Himalayan region does not exactly abound in facilities, except in the major tourist areas. Planning for possible emergencies is most essential.

Parts of Jammu and Kashmir, such as Srinagar and Gulmarg, have a Tourist Police. These are posted in areas of tourist interest, for assistance against attempts to cheat or harass. The office of the Tourist Police is at the TRC (Tel: 77228) in Srinagar. The tourism offices in other towns deal with cheating and harassment in the absence of a tourist police.

Some telephone numbers are:

JAMMU & KASHMIR

Srinagar	Police 100, 71362-5.
	Fire 101, 72222, 77555.
	Ambulance 76835, 76992.
Jammu	Police 100.
	Fire 101.
	Ambulance 5080, 42779.
Leh.	Police 18.

HIMACHAL PRADESH

Shimla	Police 100, 2444.
	Fire & Ambulance 101, 2888, 3464.
Manali	Police 26.

GETTING AROUND

FROM THE AIRPORT

Once through customs, the arriving passenger is often besieged by porters, taxi drivers and others. Choose one porter and stick to him. There is a system of paying porters a fixed amount per piece of baggage before leaving the terminal; a tip of Rs 5 is sufficient once the bags are aboard the bus or taxi. If a travel agent or friend is meeting you they may be outside the building. It is advisable to change some money in the arrival hall if you are taking a bus or taxi into town.

TAXIS

Delhi and Srinagar have a system of prepaid taxis to take you to your destination in town. This system prevents the occasional unscrupulous taxi driver from overcharging or taking an excessively long route. Other airports need not have such a system. If so, make sure the taxi meter is "down" before you start the journey. It is acceptable to share taxis for destinations in the same area. Depending on union fare agreements, some taxis may have fare charts which when applied to the amount shown on the meter give the correct fare. There is often a night surcharge of 10% between 2300 and 0600 hours and a charge of one or two rupees per piece of baggage carried.

BUSES

Some major hotels operate courtesy buses and a public service known as EATS (Ex-Serviceman's Transport Service) operates an airport bus service in Delhi. This stops at major hotels and selected points en route to the city center.

AIR TRAVEL

Indian Airlines (not to be confused with the international carrier, Air India) covers one of the world's largest domestic networks. It carries on average 30,000 passengers to 78 destinations in India as well as in Afghanistan, Bangladesh, the Maldives, Nepal, Pakistan, Sri Lanka and Thailand. Routes served by Airbus A-300 include an Executive Class but the others served by Boeing 737, Airbus A-320 and other aircraft only have a single Economy class.

There also exists a so-called third level "feeder" airline, **Vayudoot**. It operates smaller aircraft such as the Dornier 228 and HS-748. It mainly connects small towns not linked by Indian Airlines. Vayudoot also operates a charter service called "Rent-a-plane". Information may be obtained from the Commercial Department, Vayudoot, Safdarjung Airport, New Delhi 110 003 (Tel:69-9272).

In a virtual opening of the skies to the private sector, the government has now permitted the operation of "**air taxis**" (private airlines) from all airports in India. These are still in their infancy, with only a few operating presently. A large number of companies have, nonetheless, been permitted to begin operations, and this will eventually provide competition as well as an alternative to the state-owned airlines.

The previously lengthy and time-consuming **reservations** system has now been improved by the introduction of computers. This system is also linked to the international network, making confirmations easier. For travel during the peak season, from September to March, try and make reservations well in advance as flights are usually heavily booked.

Since **check-in** and security procedures can take time, it is advisable to reach the airport a good hour before departure time. Coach services to the airport are available and reliable.

In-flight service is generally adequate but unexciting. Snacks and meals are served but alcohol is available only on international flights. The **airport tax** for flights to neighboring countries is Rs 150. The baggage allowance per adult passenger is 20 kg for Economy and 30 kg for Executive Class. While the **cancellation charges** for tickets purchased locally are extremely high, they do not apply to domestic sectors issued on international tickets.

There are some attractive options available to air travellers in India. The **US $400 Discover India fare** is valid for 21 days of unlimited travel in a roughly circular direction. The **US $300 Tour India scheme** is valid for 14 days and limited to 6 flight coupons. Other concessional fares include a youth discount of 25 percent for students and travellers aged between 12 and 30 years. Groups of 10 or more are eligible for discounts of up to 50 percent, subject to certain conditions. Details will be available with either your travel agent or the nearest Air India office, or write to the Traffic Manager, Indian Airlines House, Parliament Street, New Delhi.

JAMMU & KASHMIR

Srinagar airport (Tel: 31521/9) is 14 km from the city. It is served by a morning flight from Delhi via Chandigarh, Amritsar and Jammu and an afternoon flight direct from Delhi. Both are daily flights in Indian Airlines' Boeing 737 aircraft. Indian Airlines has both an Airport Office (Tel: 30-163/194) and a city office at the Tourist Reception Center (Tel:73-270/538, 76-557). Air India has an office at Maulana Azad Road in the Hotel Broadway Annexe (Tel: 77-141). You can transfer to the city either by taxi or by coach.

Jammu airport is 5 miles (8 km) from the city center. It is served by the same flight from Delhi which goes via Chandigarh and Amritsar to Srinagar. Indian Airlines has an Airport Office (Tel:5745) and an office at the Tourist Reception Center, Veer Marg (Tel: 42-735, 47-577).

Remember that on entering the state of Jammu and Kashmir, you must register either arrival or departure with the Foreigners' Regional Registration Offices located at the airports and in the cities.

LADAKH

Leh airport is also an important military base, 5 miles (8 km) from the city. Since it is at an altitude of 3,500 meters, weather conditions often cause Leh flights to be cancelled. In such a case, you are NOT guaranteed a seat on the next flight. There are three direct flights a week each from Delhi, and twice a week via Srinagar and Chandigarh. An Indian Airlines office (Tel:76) exists.

HIMACHAL PRADESH

While Jammu, Kashmir and Ladakh are the preserve of Indian Airlines, Himachal Pradesh is served by Vayudoot. **Bhuntar Airport**, 6 miles (10 km) south of Kullu and 32 miles (52 km) from Manali, has a daily flight from Delhi. The HS-748 flies via Chandigarh where it halts for 25 minutes. The return flight leaves after a 25 minute wait. Sunday flights are one hour later. There is another daily flight from Delhi aboard a Do-228 aircraft in the morning, which flies via Shimla.

Jubbarhati Airport, 14 miles (23 km) from Shimla, serves the southern region. The daily Do-228 flight flies direct from Delhi. The flight returns home after a 25 minute halt.

There is also a recently introduced Dornier flight to **Dharamsala**, three times a week.

RAIL TRAVEL

Carrying about 11 million people every day to 7084 stations over 38,500 miles (62,000 kilometers) of track and with a work force of 1,618,000, the Indian Railways are the second largest system in the world and the largest civilian employer anywhere. Rail travel is safe and comfortable, but can be confusing. Of the many categories of accommodation available, those recommended are Air Conditioned First Class, two-tier Air Conditioned Sleeper and Air Conditioned Chair Car. Non air-conditioned classes, both first and second, can become dusty and uncomfortable, especially during the hot dry months in the plains. Advance reservation is advisable.

Trains are slow compared to those in the West, so if you are in a hurry, stay with the Expresses; fares are generally low. The **Indrail Pass**, paid for in foreign currency, offers good value for those on an extended tour of India. Prices range from US$190 on Air Conditioned First Class for 7 days to US$690 for 90 days in the same class, and from US$95 to US$345 on Air Conditioned

Sleeper and Chair Car for the same periods. An Indrail Pass gives total exemption from reservation fees, sleeper charges, supplementary charges on superfast trains and cost of meals. Passes may be booked either through leading travel agents or from **Railway Central Reservation Offices** in Delhi (Tel:34-4877/5080/5181), Bombay, Calcutta, Madras, Secunderabad and Hyderabad.

Before setting out on your journey, remember to check which station your train departs from. Allow at least an hour to find your seat/berth. Lists of passengers with the compartment and seat/berth numbers allotted to them are displayed on platforms and on each compartment an hour before departure. The Station Superintendent and the conductor attached to the train are usually available for assistance.

Food can usually be ordered through the coach attendant and, on some trains, the fare includes food as well. Snacks, tea, coffee and soft drinks are also usually available. Refreshment rooms are provided at big stations and stalls at others.

DELHI

Delhi has two main railway stations, Delhi Station in "Old" Delhi and New Delhi Station in New Delhi. The latter is next to Connaught Place and is easily accessible by bus. The No.6 bus connects the two stations. If you are staying in South Delhi, the Nizamuddin Station which is relatively less crowded and cleaner may be more convenient. However, not all trains stop here.

JAMMU & KASHMIR

The only major railhead in the state is at Jammu Tawi, 305 km from Srinagar. It is connected by rail to Delhi's three stations, Bombay, Ahmadabad and Lucknow among other places.

The *Jammu Tawi Mail* leaves Delhi station at 9 pm while the *Jhelum Express* leaves New Delhi station at 9.40 p.m.; both take 13½ hours to Jammu. They depart Jammu at 3 p.m .and 7.35 p.m. respectively for the return journey. The *Shalimar Express* departs New Delhi at 4.10 p.m. for a 15 hour journey to Jammu, and commences its return at 10.35 a.m.

The *Himsagar Express* from Cape Comorin passes through all three Delhi stations between 10 p.m. and midnight, taking 15 hours to Jammu. It starts its return journey at 8 p.m. The *Sarvodaya/Hapa Express* and the *Jammu Tawi Express* arrive at Delhi station from Ahmadabad and Bombay respectively. Both depart Delhi at 5.20 a.m. for a relatively quick journey of 11 hours. They depart Jammu at 10.35 a.m.

HIMACHAL PRADESH

Shimla is the only town accessible by rail, and to get there you must travel via Kalka, located in the foothills. The *Himalayan Queen* is a morning train which leaves New Delhi station at 6 a.m. and reaches Kalka at 11.25 a.m. The *Howrah-Kalka Mail* departs from Delhi station at 10.50 p.m .for an overnight journey to Kalka, arriving there at 6 am. The distance between Delhi and Kalka is 268 km.

From Kalka onwards, you take the delightful *Toy Train* on a narrow-gauge line to Shimla. The journey takes a little over 5 hours, covering 96 km and going via Barog and Solan. The train winds through scenic views and you pass through a series of 103 tunnels.

ROAD TRAVEL

Driving through the mountains of the Western Himalaya is an exotic experience, with roads wending their way round valleys, mountains, lakes, waterfalls, forests on a scale found nowhere else.

BY BUS

India has a comprehensive network of roads covering most of the country. The **Inter-State Bus Terminal** (ISBT) at Kashmiri Gate, old Delhi is where buses arrive and depart for destinations outside Delhi. ISBT is near the old Delhi railway station and there are many buses connecting the two. There is a plan to construct a second ISBT in Nizamuddin, near the railway station, but this may take some time yet.

In addition to the various government operated services, there are countless privately run buses. These vary in efficiency and quality, so you should make prior enquiries. The types of buses range from noisy, dilapidated bone-shakers to reasonably comfortable, air-conditioned express coaches. Some of these are part of the phenomenon known as 'video coaches'; these play commercial Hindi movies all night long at full volume during the journey. Travelling this way will considerably decrease your enjoyment of the journey, so stay far away from them.

Mountain travel can make you car-sick, especially on narrow, winding roads where you feel that there is nothing between you and the precipice plunging hundreds of feet down. Try to sit in front; take water and packed food with you. Keep an eye on valuables and luggage.

JAMMU & KASHMIR

The trip to Srinagar from Delhi takes a little over 24 hours. Enquire at J & K Tourism, Kanishka Shopping Plaza, New Delhi (Tel:332-4422 ext 2397). Private buses can be booked at Connaught Place and Janpath.

The **J & K State Road Transport Corporation**, TRC, Srinagar (Tel:72698) operates a number of buses between Jammu, Leh, Kargil, Pahalgam, Gulmarg, Sonamarg and Srinagar, graded Mini Luxury, Super Deluxe, A-class and B-class, as well as a Video Coach. Transport corporations from neighboring states also operate similar services. Rates are fixed.

In Jammu, all buses to Srinagar operate from the Railway Station, while all those to and from other states use the General Bus Stand. Buses operate from the TRC in Srinagar.

You can now travel to Leh from Manali as well, in addition to the usual route. This allows for a more varied itinerary.

HIMACHAL PRADESH

There are many buses between Delhi and Shimla, including Deluxe. Many of these are run by the **Himachal Pradesh Road Transport Corporation** (Tel: Delhi, 251-6725; Pathankot, 20088; Chandigarh, 20946). The buses again operate from the ISBT, Kashmere Gate, Delhi. Bookings to Delhi from Shimla may be made through the Tourist Bureau, The Mall, Shimla. The journey takes around 10 hours.

Other places connected with Shimla by bus are Kalka, Chandigarh, Amritsar, Jammu outside the state and Kullu, Manali, Dharamsala inside the state.

Kullu and Manali are both connected by a direct bus service with Delhi and Chandigarh, among other places. The services are operated by the state transport services of Himachal, Haryana and Punjab. The main bus station in Kullu is at Akhara Bazaar. Leh is also accessible by road from Manali.

BY CAR

Chauffeur driven cars can be rented through major agencies and most hotels. Self-drive cars have recently been introduced. Air-conditioned taxis too are available. Full information regarding road conditions, driving licences, **Tryptique** and **Carnet** can be obtained from the **Automobile Association of Upper India**, Lilaram Building, 14F, Connaught Circus, New Delhi 110 001 (Tel: 331 4071, 331 2323/2324/2325).

Do remember that in India you drive on the left of the road. A **third party insurance** is essential, and it must be either with a company registered in India or one abroad that has a guarantor in India.

JAMMU & KASHMIR

Both Srinagar and Jammu lie on National Highway 1A. This is an all-weather road open throughout the year. Between Jammu and Srinagar, you can make overnight halts at Jajjar Kotli, Kud, Patnitop, Batote, Ramban, Banihal and Qazigund. The distance between the two is 293 km.

Leh is 434 km from Srinagar along a state highway that crosses a series of high passes, such as Fotu La at 13,479 feet. The road is closed between October and May. Enquire about road conditions from Traffic Police Headquarters, Maulana Azad Road, Srinagar. You can stop on the way at Sonamarg, Dras, Kargil, Mulbekh and Saspol.

Some important distances from Jammu are : Amritsar 243 km, Chandigarh 436 km and Manali 428 km.

HIMACHAL PRADESH

The trip from Delhi to Shimla lasts about seven hours and covers 370 km. The highway drives via Haryana which has a number

317

of restaurants catering to motorists. Once inside Himachal, you drive slowly along the winding mountain roads.

Driving in Lahaul and along the Manali-Leh highway requires a Jeep.

WHERE TO STAY

HOUSEBOATS

Most foreign tourists in Srinagar prefer to stay in floating houseboats in Srinagar, in contrast to their Indian counterparts who prefer hotels on the shore. A houseboat is a flat-bottomed, stationary boat, between 65 feet and 130 feet long, and 10 feet to 20 feet wide, made of pine and cedar wood. Each contains a front veranda, living room, dining room, kitchen, rooftop sun-deck and two or three toilet and bath equipped bedrooms.

There is a range of houseboat categories, each denoting a different tariff and level of comfort.

The price includes accommodation, all meals, tea and transport to and fro aboard a *shikara*, a slim and elegant boat unique to Kashmir. The categories are, by no means, rigid, as you will soon find out. Some B-class boats may be better maintained than some A-class boats, depending on the owner, for example. In addition, the intense competition during the peak season means that you may well get a price somewhat lower than expected.

Bookings can be made at the TRC in Srinagar, but the prices here are the highest. Alternatively, you can try negotiating directly with touts or owners. A good idea may be to take a *shikara* ride and see for yourself which houseboat is worth renting. It is certainly acceptable to transfer from a particular houseboat if you are unhappy with service, facilities etc.

HOTELS

There is an immense variety of hotel accommodation in the main areas of tourist in the Himalaya. There are some excellent deluxe hotels as well as innumerable low-budget places for the backpacker. It is in the more remote regions that accommodation becomes a problem, although even here, the more intrepid can make arrangements.

JAMMU

4 & 3 STAR

Asia Jammu Tawi
National Highway.
Tel: 43930/2
Tlx: 0377-224 ASIA IN; (44 rooms)

Jammu Ashok
Ram Nagar.
Tel: 43127, 43864
Tlx: 0377-227; (48 rooms)

Cosmo
Veer Marg
Tel: 47561, 47169; (28 rooms)

MID-RANGE

Jagan Lodge
Raghunath Bazar.
Tel: 42402, 43243; (16 rooms)

Premier
Veer Marg.
Tel: 7450

Tourist Reception Centre
Veer Marg.
Tel: 5421; (128 rooms)

BUDGET

Tawi View Lodge
below Gumat.
Tel: 43752, 47301

Broadway Lodge
below Gumat.
Tel: 43636; (24 rooms)

SRINAGAR

DELUXE

Broadway
Maulana Azad Road.
Tel:71211/3, 79001/2
Tlx: 0375-212; (90 rooms)

Centaur Lake View
Cheshma Shahi.
Tel: 77601, 73135
Tlx: 0375-205 CLVH IN; (253 rooms)

Oberoi Palace
Boulevard.
Tel: 71241/6, 75617
Tlx: 0375-201 LXSR IN; (75 rooms)

MID-RANGE

Shahenshah Palace
Boulevard.
Tel: 71345/6
Tlx: 0375-335 SPEC IN; (80 rooms)

Shah Abbas
Boulevard
Tel: 77789, 74158
Tlx: 0375-273 YALI IN; (84 rooms)

Tramboo Continental
Boulevard.
Tel: 73914, 71718; (54 rooms)

Welcome Hotel
Boulevard.
Tel: 74010; (51 rooms)

Dar es Salaam
Nagin Road.
Tel: 77803

GUEST HOUSES

Raj Bagh contains several guest houses which offer good service and pleasant surroundings. These include the **Green Acre**, Tel: 73349; **Eden**, Tel: 78484; **Bazaz**, Tel:71228; and **Archana**, Tel: 73898

BUDGET

New Rigadoon
Dal Gate.
Tel: 76313; (30 rooms)

Hill Star
Buchwara.
Tel: 72512; (39 rooms)

Tourist Reception Centre
Shervani Road.
Tel: 73648, 77303/5
Tlx: 0375-207 TSM IN

LEH

DELUXE

Lha-ri-Mo, Tel:101
K-Sar, Tel:148
Shambala, Tel: 67
Kang-Lha-Chan, near Moravian Church

MID-RANGE

Kangri
behind Dreamland restaurant.
Tel: 51

Lung-se-Jung
near Dreamland restaurant.
Tel: 193

Dragon
Tel: 139

SHIMLA

DELUXE

Woodville Palace Hotel
Himachal Bhawan Road, Chota Shimla.
Tel:2722; (11 rooms)

Oberoi Clarkes
The Mall.
Tel: 6091/2/3/4/5
Tlx: 0391-206 OBCL IN; (33 rooms)

Chapslee
Lakkar Bazar.
Tel: 77319, 78242; (7 rooms)

4 & 3 STAR

Asia the Dawn
Tara Devi.
Tel:5858, 6464
Tlx: 0391-205 ASIA IN; (37 rooms)

Himland
Circular Road.
Tel:3595/6, 5328
Tlx: 0391-221 HITR IN; (34 rooms)

MID-RANGE

Shingar
The Mall.
Tel:2881, 4581; (30 rooms)

Samrat
The Mall.
Tel: 6172; (20 rooms)

Auckland
Lakkar Bazar.
Tel: 6315

BUDGET

Dreamland
The Ridge.
Tel:5057

YMCA
near Ritz Cinema.
Tel:3081

Tashkent
The Mall.

KULLU & MANALI

MID-RANGE

Silver Moon(HPTDC)
Kullu.

Span Resorts
Kullu-Manali highway, Kullu.
Tel: 38, 40; (23 rooms)

Sarvari (HPTDC)
Kullu.
Tel: 33

Ashok Travellers' Lodge
Manali.
Tel:31

Piccadilly Holiday Resort
Manali.
Tel: 114; (33 rooms)

Mayflower
Manali.
Tel: 104

Rohtang Manalsu (HPTDC)
Manali.

BUDGET

Bijleshwar View Guest House
Kullu.

Rohtang
Kullu.

Manalsu Guest House
Manali village, Manali.

Tourist Lodge (HPTDC)
Manali.

CHAIL, DALHOUSIE & DHARAMSALA

MID-RANGE

Chail Palace
Chail.
Tel: 43, 47

HPTDC cottages and log huts
Chail.

Aroma
Court Road, The Mall, Dalhousie.
Tel: 99; 20 rooms

Grand View
The Mall, Dalhousie.
Tel: 23

Tibet
Mcleod ganj, Dharamsala.
Tel: 2587

BUDGET

Himneel
Chail.

Youth Hostel
near bus stand, Dalhousie.

Shimla
opposite tourist office, Dharamsala.

Om
Mcleodganj, Dharamsala.

FOOD DIGEST

WHAT TO EAT

KASHMIR

Kashmiri food has basically the same roots as the North Indian food brought in from Central Asia by the Mughals. It is, however, a distinct variation with its own dishes. *Gushtava* consists of pounded and spiced meat balls cooked in a yoghurt gravy. The meat balls are made of mutton or goat. *Rishta* is lamb cooked in a similar way. *Rogan josh*, a dish also popular elsewhere in India, is mutton cooked to the bone in a spicy curry. A good rogan josh will be cooked in yoghurt with a carefully prepared blend of spices and ingredients. *Yakhni* is similar, but milder.

Karam sag is made with a spinach-like vegetable called *hak*, found in the Dal Lake. *Nedru yakni* is a dish made from lotus roots, cooked in yoghurt. *Marchwangan kurma* is a hot mutton curry while *tabak maz* is bland fried mutton. *Methi kurma* combines vegetables with chopped intestine, which tastes rather good. Kashmiri *nan* is different from the usual variety in that it contains chopped nuts and sultanas.

LADAKH

The staple of Ladakh is *tsampa*, a kind of roasted barley which is made into salty cakes. Often consumed with butter tea or *chang*, a local beer, the full meal is called *cholak*. *Pava* consists of peas and barley flour boiled in water until the peas become hard. *Thukpa* is wheat flour made into noodles which are then dropped into boiling water and finally served with meat sauce. *Gyatug* consists of strips of tsampa over which a flavored meat sauce is poured. The most popular dish is no doubt *mo mo*, or steamed tsampa dough served with a meat filling, much like a dumpling. *Skir* is a mix of meat, potatoes and grain cooked together.

Khambish and *kambir* are types of local bread. There is a biscuit made with sugar, grain meal and nuts called *holkur* which is often offered to guests. Local beverages are *chang*, *gugur chai* (tea made from green tea, with salt, butter, milk and soda added) and curd of yak milk. Ladakhi food is broadly related to Tibetan food.

HIMACHAL PRADESH

Himachal cuisine is similar to North Indian fare, with certain adaptations to hilly conditions. The diet is rich in protein, with pulses forming a far more important part than meat. Rice is normally eaten during the mid-day meal. *Chapattis* (wheat flour pancakes) replace rice for the evening meal during the summer months while *makki-ki-roti* (maize flour pancakes) is eaten almost exclusively in the winter months. Spices are conspicuous by their absence while garlic and onions are used sparingly. The use of yoghurt is important in the preparation of most dishes, though it isn't usually eaten plain. ***Madra*** (white gram cooked in yoghurt and *ghee*) and *palda* (vegetables or potatoes cooked over a slow fire in yoghurt so as to prevent it from curdling) are peculiar to the region. The standard dessert is *kheer*, a preparation of rice, milk and sugar.

WHERE TO EAT

Some of the best food available is found in the in-house restaurants of the major hotels. Often expensive, they guarantee quality as well as a variety of cuisines. Listed below are some restaurants that are not associated with any particular hotel.

JAMMU & KASHMIR

JAMMU

Cosmo Bar & Restaurant
Veer Marg (Tel:47561); Indian, Mughlai, Chinese, Continental; open noon to 10 p.m.

SRINAGAR

Ahdoo's
Residency Road (Tel:72593); Kashmiri; open 9 a.m. to 11 p.m.

Alka Salka
Residency Road; Chinese, Indian

Lhasa
The Boulevard (Tel:71438); Tibetan; open noon to 11 p.m.

Mughal Darbar
Residency Road; Kashmiri, Indian

LEH

Dreamland Restaurant
Fort Road; Tibetan, Chinese; open 8 a.m. to 10 p.m.

La Montessori
Chinese, Tibetan, Continental

Potala Hill Top Restaurant
Lal Chowk; Chinese, Tibetan; open 9 a.m. to 10 p.m.

Ecological Development Center

KARGIL

Naktul Chinese Restaurant
Chinese; open 7 a.m. to 10 p.m.

HIMACHAL PRADESH

MANDI

Cafe Shiraz
near Bhutnath shrine; Indian, Chinese, Continental; open 8 a.m. to 9 p.m.

Tourist Bungalow Restaurant
outside Mandi (Tel:2575); same as above, bar; open 7 a.m. to 10 p.m.

MANALI

Mount View Restaurant
near Tourist Information Office; Tibetan, Chinese, Indian, Japanese; open 8 am to 10 pm

DHARAMSALA

Toepa
main street of upper Dharamsala; Tibetan; open 8 a.m. to 9.30 p.m.

THINGS TO DO

GARDENS, RESORTS & PICNICS

HIMACHAL PRADESH

Shimla

The highest hill near Shimla, **Jakhu Hill**, offers a panoramic view of the town and a magnificent view of the snow-clad Himalaya. A temple of Lord Hanuman lies at the top of this hill, a mile (2 km) away from Shimla. The **Glen**, a wooded ravine with evergreen slopes, is a popular picnic spot 2.5 miles (4 km) from Shimla. A large spur separates the lovely 220-feet (67-meter) high Chadwick Falls from Glen. A picturesque suburb 3 miles (5 km) from the city, **Summer Hill** offers shady walks in quiet surroundings. Himachal University is located here. At a greater altitude, 3 miles (5 km) from Shimla, lies **Prospect Hill**, which offers views of the city, Summer Hill, Tara Devi and Solan district. You can witness a simultaneous sunset and moonrise from here on full moon eve.

Mashobra provides excellent picnic spots 8 miles (13 km) away from Shimla. Beautiful walks are possible amidst forests of oak and pine. **Kufri** is a hamlet 10 miles (16 km) away from the city where visitors can ski in winter. There is a picnic spot about a mile (2 km) above Kufri. **Wildflower Hall**, about 8 miles (13 km) away, is a lovely resort. **Fagu**, 13 miles (22 km) away affords extensive views of two valleys from a height of 8,283 feet (2,510 meters).

Kangra

With its location and natural wealth, Kangra has been associated with most historic events in the region. The **Nagarkot Fort** which perches atop an hourglass-shaped hillside is testimony to this. The area is surrounded by low, green hills.

Palampur

Neugal Khad is a gentle stream that turns torrential in the monsoon. The area has panoramic views of the Dhauladhar mountain range. Another stream is the **Bundla stream** which provides a pleasant walk along its banks.

A few kilometers away from Palampur is **Al Hilal**, the erstwhile palace and summer retreat of Maharaja Ranjit Singh who ruled Punjab till his death in 1839. It was later taken over by the Dogra ruler of Jammu & Kashmir and is now run as a modern hotel. The surrounding lawns and mango grove, European chandeliers and luxurious bedrooms put this palace in the top league of palaces-turned-hotels.

Manali

The **Vashisht Sulphur Springs** have been converted into Turkish baths with shower rooms and temperature controlled baths.

Chamba

Chaugan is a grassy *maidan* where townspeople congregate and where all social, religious, political and sports events are held.

Dalhousie

Satdhara is a popular picnic spot where seven springs cut across grassy, alpine meadows tufted with wild flowers. An easy mile-long climb takes you to **Subhash Bauli**, a spring which affords a spectacular view of the Dhauladhar mountains. Close by is **Jandri Ghat**, where the palace of the rulers of the erstwhile Chamba state lies amidst stately pines.

EXCURSIONS

Kullu

Kaisdhar is a secluded and quiet spot 15 km away from Kullu, across a steep mountain. It has magnificent scenery and quiet walks. **Bajaura**, also 9 miles (15 km) away, is famous for its orchards. An ancient temple, **Basheshar Mahadev**, is located here, with wonderful stone carvings and sculpture. **Manikaran**, 28 miles (45 km), in the Parbati valley, is known for its hot springs, trout fishing and Ramchanderji's temple. **Katrain**, at a height of 4,800 feet (1,463 meters), is halfway between Kullu and Manali. It has plenty of orchards flanked by forested hills. Katrain is famous for its bee-keeping and trout fishing in the swift torrents of the Beas river. **Naggar** is situated high above Katrain across the river on the east bank. Naggar castle is impressive, as is the Roerich Art Gallery above it. **Raison** camping site, 5 miles (8 km), has eight wooden huts where you can camp in solitary splendour.

Kangra

Nadaun is a quiet spot by the river Beas, 25 miles (40 km) away, where you can spend a quiet holiday fishing for mahseer.

Dharamsala

Not to be confused with the one in Srinagar, **Dal Lake** is a picturesque picnic spot connected by road to Dharamsala; it is also a trekking base. **Chinmaya Tapovan**, 6 miles (10 km), is a recently developed ashram complex. **Dharamkot** ,7 miles (11 km) is a picnic spot on the west side of a hill overlooking the Kangra valley. **Triund**, 10½ miles (17 km), is a trekking base and picnic spot barely 3 miles (5 km) from the snow line. It contains a forest rest house. **Masroor**, 25 miles (40 km), has 15 monolithic rock cut temples of the Indo-Aryan style, patterned after the great temple of Kailash at Ellora. **Trilokpur**, 26 miles (41 km) is a cave temple with stalagmites and stalactites dedicated to Shiva. **Nurpur**, 41 miles(66 km), has a ruined fort and a temple. The ruins still have carved stone relief work on them. **Sujanpur**, 50 miles (80 km), an ancient town, is famous for its ruined palace and temples.

Palampur

Andretta, 8 miles (13 km), the hometown of the artist Sardar Sobha Singh is a town straight out of a picture book. **Baijnath** ,10 miles (16 km) is a Shiva temple of great antiquity and is supposed to be the place where the evil king Ravana worshipped Shiva to gain immortality. It is thronged by pilgrims during the festival of Shivratri.

Shimla

Chail, 28 miles (45 km), is a haven in the Shivaliks at a height of 7,380 feet (2,250 meters). The road is motorable. There is also a sanctuary, to enter it, you need permission from the range officer in nearby **Janedghat**. Chail is supposed to have the highest cricket pitch in the world, as well as facilities for tennis, golf and squash.

Manali

Hadimba Devi is a temple believed to be 1,000 years old. It is approached by a walk through deodar forest. **Arjun Gufa** is a cave where Arjun, one of the five Pandava brothers from the epic Mahabharata, is believed to have meditated. **Kothi**, 7 miles (12 km), has magnificent views of snow-capped peaks. The **Rahla Falls**, 2½ miles (4 km) from Kothi, is the start of the climb towards Rohtang Pass. **Rohtang Pass** is the highest point on this road at 13,048 feet (3,978 meters), and has a little lake called **Sar Kund** nearby. This is reputed to have healing powers. **Keylong** 72½ miles(117 km) is the headquarters of Lahual-Spiti district, accessible by a motorable road. It is a village set amidst green fields of barley and buck wheat.

Mandi

Rawalsar, 15 miles (24 km) is a lake equally sacred to Hindus, Buddhists and Sikhs. A fair is held in honor of Lomas Rishi on April 13 every year. The lake is said to contain the spirits of departed saints and is highly revered by local people. Buses and taxis are available for visiting Rawalsar. **Prashar** contains a pagoda type temple of Prashar Rishi in a basin of green hills beside a small lake with a floating island in it. The snow peaks of Lahual-Spiti as well as a beautiful valley of rhododendrons is visible here.

Chamba

Salooni, 35 miles (56 km) is located atop a ridge at the entrance of the Bandal valley. Overnight accommodation is available. **Saho** 7½ miles (12 km) has an ancient stone temple at Chandrashekhar. **Bharmaur**, 43 miles (69 km) is the original capital of the ertswhile Chamba state. Several temples and monuments reflect its past glory. **Manimahesh**, (22 miles/35 km from Bharmaur) is a lake at the base of the Manimahesh Kailash peak. Thousands of pilgrims journey to its holy waters to bathe in it on the fifteenth day after the festival of Janmashtami.

Dalhousie

Kalatope, 5 miles (8½ km) at a height of 8,000 feet (2,400 meter) is ideal for a family trip. The route is jeepable, and overnight accommodation is available. **Dainkund**, 5 miles (8½ km), is 1,000 feet/304 meter higher and is a peak from where you can glimpse three rivers – Beas, Ravi and Chenab – winding their ways through low lands. **Khajjiar**, 16 miles (26 km) is a charming retreat in a saucer-shaped, green meadow with a golf course. It contains a natural turquoise lake held sacred by local people who worship at the nearby gold-domed temple of **Khajinag**. Accommodation is available.

WILDLIFE

JAMMU & KASHMIR

The state of Jammu & Kashmir ranges from the plains of Punjab to the Tibetan plateau. In the north it is bounded by the Karakoram mountains, in the east by Tibet and the Great Himalayan Range. The Indus river cuts through the state as it flows from east to west into Pakistan. Large areas of good wildlife habitat fall outside protected areas: the snow leopard range covers most of Ladakh; the Tibetan wild ass (*kiang*) and the black-necked crane survive in fairly secure but extremely small numbers near the Chinese border east of Leh. The west and southwestern parts of the state are affected by the monsoon while precipitation beyond the Great Himalayan range is generally limited to winter snowfall.

Conservation in Ladakh is fairly recent and there is little tourist infrastructure; the only way to see the area is by trekking. Many travel agencies and tour operators in Delhi can offer advice.

For further information contact: **The Chief Wildlife Warden**, TRC, Srinagar 190001, Tel:75411.

DACHIGAM NATIONAL PARK

Originating as a game reserve and then further developed to protect the catchment area for much of the drinking water supply of Srinagar, 13 miles (21 km) to the west, it now covers an area of 54 sq miles (141 sq km). The park today is famous as the home of the last viable population of **hangul**. Other species found include both the **brown** and **black Himalayan bear**, **musk deer** and **fox** and over 150 species of birds. A metalled road links Srinagar with lower Dachigam. Upper Dachigam (14,072 ft/4,289 m) should be reached on foot.

Best time to visit: May-August in Upper Dachigam; September-December in Lower Dachigam

Accommodation: 2 lodges and rest houses; hotels and house boats in Srinagar

Contact: Chief Wildlife Warden, Srinagar.

Nearest town and air: Srinagar (20 miles/ 32 km)

Rail: Jammu (196 miles/315 km)

HEMIS HIGH ALTITUDE NATIONAL PARK

Established in 1981 and covering 231 sq miles (600 sq km) of the Markha and Rumbak valleys. Most of the area is rocky and sparsely covered. Among the endangered mammals here are **bharal**, **ibex**, **snow leopard** and **marmot**. Over 50 bird species have been identified. The winters can be extremely cold, temperatures dropping to 8°F(-40°C).

Best time to visit: May-September

Accommodation: none, camping permitted

Contact: DFO, Hemis National Park, Leh.

Nearest town and air: Leh (19 miles/30 km from Nimu)

JASROTA SANCTUARY

Established in 1984, this extremely small area of 3.75 sq miles (10 sq km) supports a large population of **chital**, **barking deer**, **wild boar** and **rhesus macaque**. It is situated on the right bank of the Ujh river and has a large area under bamboo.

Best time to visit: September-January

Accommodation: 2 rest houses

Contact: Regional Wildlife Warden, near Jammu Ashok hotel, Manda (Ramnagar), Jammu.

Nearest town and rail: Kathua (15.5 miles/25 km)

Air: Jammu (40 miles/65 km)

KISHTWAR NATIONAL PARK

A new park established in 1981, encompassing almost 125 sq miles (400 sq km) at heights of 5,600-15,750 ft (1,700-4,800 m). Most of it is within the catchment area of the Chenab river. The forest is largely coniferous, including **neoza pine** and **deodar**. At higher altitudes, the forests give way to alpine meadows and scrub. A few **hangul**, **musk deer**, **markar**, **ibex**, **gray langur** and **leopard** can be seen.

Best time to visit: May-October

Accommodation: 2 rest houses

Contact: Regional Wildlife Warden, near Jammu Ashok hotel, Manda (Ramnagar), Jammu.

Nearest town: Kishtwar (37 miles/60 km)

Air & rail: Jammu (152 miles/245 km)

OVERA SANCTUARY & BIOSPHERE RESERVE

Established in 1981. Although only 12.5 sq miles (32 sq km), the area falls within the proposed Overa-Aru Biosphere Reserve of almost 154 sq miles (400 sq km). The sanctuary is located in the upper Lidder valley above Pahalgam. The area is largely forested and has a good **pheasant** population and other bird-life. Mammals include **hangul**, **musk deer**, **serow**, **langur** and **leopard**.

Best time to visit: April-October

Accommodation: rest house, camping sites

Contact: Chief Wildlife Warden, TRC, Srinagar

Nearest town and air: Srinagar (47 miles/ 76 km)

Other sanctuaries include Lungnag (Kargil district), Nandi (Jammu district), Ramnagar (Jammu district) and Surinsar Mansar

(Udhampur district). A second biosphere reserve at Gulmarg covering 112 sq miles (180 sq km) has also been proposed.

HIMACHAL PRADESH

This state rises from the plains of the Punjab to the Great Himalaya and the Tibetan plateau beyond. Because of the range in altitude, the state contains a wide variety of flora and fauna. Most of the sanctuaries are in the temperate and sub-tropical areas of the lower Himalaya.Twenty-eight areas are protected including one national park. Most of the sanctuaries are in areas unconnected by public transport. The most enjoyable and practical way to visit most of these areas is by trekking. It is possible to trek in much of Himachal and to buy food in many villages, although a couple of days' food should always be carried. One of the threats to Himachal's sanctuaries is human pressure and continued exploitation of the forests. The bird-life is rich and varied.

CHAIL SANCTUARY

Established in 1975, with 42 sq miles (108 sq km) of subtropical pine and temperate forest. Good bird-viewing, including **chir pheasants**, **martens** and **leopards**.
  Best time to visit: March-December
  Accommodation: 14-bed rest houses in the sanctuary; Palace Hotel, Chail, Tel:3743
  Contact: Chief Wildlife Warden, Shimla
  Nearest town: Shimla (28 miles/45 km)
  Rail: Kandaghat (7.5 miles/12 km)
  Air: Chandigarh (73 miles/118 km)

DARAN GHATI SANCTUARY

Established in 1974 with 64 sq miles (167 sq km) of temperate and mixed coniferous forest. Among the mammals are **leopards**, **musk deer**, **civets**, **martens**, **bears** and **gorals,** and **monal**, **kaleej** and **kokla pheasants**.
  Best time to visit: April-July, September-October
  Accommodation: 4 rest houses
  Contact: Chief Wildlife Warden, Shimla
  Nearest town: Rampur (37 miles/60 km)
  Rail: Shimla (100 miles/160 km)
  Air: Chandigarh (172 miles/277 km)

GOVIN SAGAR SANCTUARY

Established in 1974 to include the wetland and shore of the Govind Sagar reservoir. 38 sq miles (100 sq km). Migratory water birds.
  Best time to visit: October-December
  Accommodation: 5 rest houses
  Contact: Chief Wildlife Warden, Shimla
  Nearest town: Bilaspur (3.5 miles/6 km)
  Rail: Kiratpur (16 miles/30 km)
  Air: Chandigarh (44 miles/70 km)

GREAT HIMALAYAN NATIONAL PARK

Established in 1984, this is the largest of Himachal's protected areas, covering 669 sq miles (1,736 sq km) to the south-east of Kullu. The Sainj and Tirthan valleys are less disturbed than many parts of Himachal and hold good populations of many species. There is also a tremendous variety of birds.
  Best time to visit: April-June, September-October
  Accommodation: rest houses
  Contact: DFO, Wildlife Division, Kullu
  Nearest town: Kullu (37 miles/60 km)
  Air: Bhuntar (31 miles/50 km)

KALATOP KHAJJIAR SANCTUARY

Established in 1958, this small area, 18 sq miles (47 sq km), of mixed temperate forest is only a few miles from the hill station of Dalhousie. Ranges from 3,888 to 8,753 ft (1,185 to 2,668 m) above sea level. **Monal pheasants**, **woodland birds** and **hawks**.
  Best time to visit: May-June, September-November
  Accommodation: 5 rest houses
  Contact: DFO, Wildlife Division, Chamba
  Nearest town: Dalhousie (3.5 miles/6 km)
  Rail: Pathankot (53 miles/86 km)
  Air: Jammu (121 miles/194 km)

KANAWER BIRD SANCTUARY

Established in 1954 on 2.33 sq miles (6 sq km) of mixed forest with deodar, oak, pine etc., 22 miles (35 km) east of Kullu on the north side of the Parbati river.
  Altitudes range from 5,900 to 15,856 ft (1,800 to 4,833 m). **Tahr**, **serow**, **goral**, **bharal**, **musk deer** and **leopard** are among the animals, and **kokla**, **kaleej**, **chir** and

western tragopan are among the pheasants seen.

Best time to visit: May-June, September-October
  Accommodation: 4 rest houses
  Contact: DFO, Wildlife Division, Kullu
  Nearest town: Manikaran (2.5 miles/4 km)
  Air: Bhuntar (22 miles/35 km)

KUGTI SANCTUARY

Established in 1962 on 45 sq miles (118 sq km) of temperate forest with oak scrub at the higher levels (highest point: 19,600 ft/5,975 m). **Musk deer, tahr, ibex, barking deer, leopard** are seen.

Best time to visit: May-June, September-October
  Accommodation: 2 rest houses
  Contact: DFO, Wildlife Division, Chamba
  Nearest town: Chamba (54 miles/87 km)
  Rail: Pathankot (128 miles/206 km)

LIPPA ASRANG SANCTUARY

Established in 1962 with 68 sq miles (109 sq km) of temperate and coniferous forest. Permission is required for foreigners to visit this area. **Ibex, musk deer, bharal** and **leopard** are seen.

Best time to visit: April-October
  Accommodation: 3 rest houses
  Contact: Chief Wildlife Warden, Shimla
  Nearest town: Kalpa (16 miles/25 km)
  Rail: Pathankot (202 miles/325 km)

MANALI SANCTUARY

Established in 1954, 12 sq miles (31 sq km). **Tahr, serow, musk deer, leopard** are seen. **Snow leopard** have also been reported. **Tragopan, chir and monal pheasants** are present.

Best time to visit: May-June, September-October
  Accommodation: 5 rest houses
  Contact: DFO, Wildlife Division, Kullu
  Nearest town: Manali (2.5 miles/4 km)
  Air: Bhuntar (34 miles/55 km)

RAKCHHAM CHITKUL SANCTUARY

Established in 1962 and covering 86 sq miles (138 sq km) of Kinnaur district (highest point: 17,933 ft/5,466 m). Permission is required for foreigners to visit the area.

Best time to visit: May-June, September-October
  Accommodation: 2 rest houses
  Contact: Chief Wildlife Warden, Shimla
  Nearest town: Dalhousie (124 miles/200 km)
  Rail: Pathankot (198 miles/319 km)

While Himachal Pradesh has an impressive list of sanctuaries, many of them were established for shooting in the 1950s and 1960s, and little, if any, wildlife management has taken place since the introduction of the Wildlife Protection Act in 1972. None of these have been enlarged. The Western Himalaya is a magnificently forested area, but with the ever-increasing human pressure on the environment, strong administration is required to protect, conserve, and develop the remaining natural habitat.

CULTURE PLUS

Shergol, 123 miles (197 km) from Leh, on the Srinagar-Leh highway, has a tiny *gompa* on the eastern side of a village with the same name. This has a collection of beautiful wall paintings, tended by two monks and a nun. Some of the rooms are hewn from rock.

Mulbekh is 5 miles (7 km) down the same road. Situated above the village are two *gompas*, **Gandentse** and **Serdung**, which may or may not be open. You will have to search for a monk in the village to open these. Beyond the village is a monolithic bas-relief of a future Buddha. The Mulbekh *shuba*, a harvest festival, is a local attraction when the oracle of Mulbekh appears.

Lamayuru, 77 miles (124 km) from Leh is perched on a hilltop with the village at the bottom, a typical Ladakhi arrangement. During February-March and July, there is a festival when all the *lama*s gather for prayers, and a three-day long mask dance is performed.

Rizong, 44 miles (71 km) from Leh has both a monastery and a nunnery called **Chulichen**. It is possible to stay here overnight, men at the *gompa* and women in the nunnery. About thirty lamas of the **Gelugpa**, or Yellow Hat sect live and study here.

Alchi is 40 miles (64 km) away from Leh and unusually located in a low-lying area. The **Choskor** *gompa* is the biggest and most famous, with a collection of paintings and lavish wooden statues famous worldwide. You can stay in Alchi village, if you wish.

Likir is an ancient monastery, the first buildings of which were made 900 years ago. About 150 Yellow Hat lamas stay here apart from 30 pupils of the *gompa* school who live here part of the time. The approach and view from Lekir are outstanding. Likir is 32 miles (52 km) from Leh.

Spituk stands on a small mountain above the Indus, 6 miles (10 km) from Leh. It has 125 Yellow Hat lamas, the head lama of whom is also the Member of Parliament for Ladakh. The *gompa* has three chapels, the most impressive of which is the **Paldan Lamo** temple, or *gòn-khang*.

Sankar is an under-*gompa* of Spituk, and is small (inhabited by 20 monks) but interesting. 2 miles (3 km) away from Leh, it is open 7 to 10 a.m. and 5 to 7 p.m. only. The upper floor of the *gompa* has an impressive representation of Avalokitesvara, with 1,000 heads and 1,000 arms holding weapons.

Phiyang, 15 miles (24 km) from Leh, has 50 lamas and 7 novices belonging to the Red Hat sect. It contains an interesting old museum which displays Mongolian, Chinese, Tibetan and, possibly, Serasan weapons and armor. Phiyang is also the site of a festival (*see* **Festivals**) which rivals that of Hemis.

Shey is the old summer palace of the former kings of Ladakh. It was built 550 years ago. The palace *gompa* has the largest gilded statue of Buddha in Ladakh. The 12 meter high statue is made of gold and gilded copper sheets, and has blue hair. The lamas hold prayers between 7 and 9 a.m. and 5 and 6 p.m., which is also the best time to visit. Shey is 9 miles (15 km) from Leh towards Hemis.

Thikse, 10 miles (17 km) from Leh, is a rich *gompa* with 100 Yellow Hat monks.

The walls are painted red and are visible from far away. The *gompa* contains a 50-foot (15-meter) high Buddha figure in a chapel. Thikse also has an important festival held in winter.

Hemis is probably the most famous *gompa* in Ladakh. One reason is the Hemis festival, a spectacular pageant of mask dances and music. The general assembly room, or *Dukhang*, contains the throne of the **Rimpoche**, the spiritual overlord of Hemis. Nearby is the *lak-hang*, a chapel whose walls are covered with frescoes. Inside is a gilded Buddha statue surrounded by several silver *chortens* decorated with semi-precious stones. The *gompa* is 28 miles (45 km) away from Leh.

Matho contains 60 monks and 30 novices of the **Sakyapa** sect and is the venue for two fascinating festivals, *Nagrang* and **Nispetsergyat**. It is famous among Ladakhis for its oracle. The *gompa* has a small room called *gom-khang* which is filled with grain by every family in Matho at the first harvest.

Stagna *gompa* lies on the west bank of the Indus. The hill it stands on is said to look like a tiger jumping, the monastery being on its nose; hence the name Stagna or tiger's nose. The *gompa* contains many paintings, the most significant of which is one of Avalokitesvara from Assam.

Stok Palace, 200 years old, is the last inhabited Ladakhi royal palace. It has 80 rooms, of which only 12 are inhabited now. Three rooms comprise a museum open to the public, containing artifacts such as the royal family's jewelry and a collection of thirty-five 400-year-old *thangkas*. Another attraction here is the July archery contest.

TEMPLES & CHURCHES

SHIMLA

Christ Church. Situated on the Ridge, this is reputed to be the second oldest church in northern India. It has a majestic appearance, and inside contains stained glass windows representing faith, hope, fortitude and humanity, as well as other murals.

Tara Devi. There are two Hindu temples located here, 5 miles (8 km) away on National Highway 22. One temple is dedicated to Tara Devi, on top of the hill, and the other to Shiva, on the northern side.

KULLU

Raghunathji Temple. Half a mile (1 km) away from Dhalpur at Sultanpur, this temple of the principal deity of the Kullu valley was built in the 17th century.

Bijli Mahadev Shrine. This temple is remarkable in that it contains a 60 foot long staff which attracts blessings in the form of lightning. Once a year lightning strikes, shooting down the staff and shattering the Shiva *lingam* at its base. Each time, the priests restore the *lingam* and await the next recurrence of the 'miracle.' The temple requires considerable effort to reach, but is worthwhile also for its panoramic views.

Vaishno Devi Temple. This tiny cave contains an image of the goddess Vaishno Devi. It is 2½ miles (4 km) along the Kullu-Manali road.

KANGRA

Jwalamukhi Temple. A major center of pilgrimage for several centuries, this is considered one of the most sacred temples in North India. There is no idol here, instead, a flame which issues from a well around which the temple is built is considered a manifestation of the goddess.

Chintpurni. Another popular temple with a large following, it hosts a fair held around August which lasts ten days.

Chamunda Devi Temple. The temple is located by the Baner stream, with a backdrop of the mighty Dhauladhar mountains. Behind it lies a cave where a natural stone *lingam* is worshipped as a manifestation of Lord Shiva.

Brajeshwari. The shrine to this goddess is yet another famous place of worship associated with Kangra.

DHARAMSALA

St. John's Church. Located in a forest grove, it contains a memorial to Lord Elgin, a viceroy of India who died and was buried here in 1863. The church has some exquisite stained glass windows.

Kunal Pathri. This is a rock temple dedicated to a local goddess. It can be reached from Kotwali Bazaar.

MANDI

The temples of Mandi are constituents of the *shikhara* style viz. a cella surrounded by a spire and a porch which is usually decorated with carvings. Architecturally, **Triloknath** and **Panchavatara** are outstanding examples. The temple of **Bhutnath** is situated by the river in the old city and is the most frequented shrine. Another important *shikhara* temple has an idol which has on its right half the image of Shiva and on its left half that of Parvati, his consort. The **Shyamakali** or **Tarna Devi** temple on top of the west hill is yet another important shrine.

CHAMBA

There are numerous ancient temples here patterned in the local architectural style, as well as *shikhara* style temples. The main group of temples is **Lakshminarayan**, built between the 8th and 10th century, mostly dedicated to Vishnu and Shiva. The *Chaturmukh* is a major highlight of the **Hari Rai** temple. Other temples worth visiting are the **Bansi Gopal** temple, **Shri Bajreshwari** temple and **Chamunda Devi** temple.

MUSEUMS & ART GALLERIES

HIMACHAL PRADESH

Shimla
The Indian Institute of Advanced Studies (formerly the Viceregal Lodge). This six-storeyed building contains a good library and magnificent halls. It is open from 4 p.m. to 5 p.m. on certain days.

State Museum. Stone statues and miniature paintings, many from Himachal Pradesh, are on display here, including paintings from the Kangra school. This is a pleasant walk down from the church on the Mall. Open from 10 a.m. to 5 p.m., closed Mondays.

Chamba
Bhuri Singh Museum. The exhibits are interesting and pertain to Himachal's art and culture, especially the miniature paintings from the Kangra and Basohli schools. Open from 10 a.m. to 5 p.m. daily, except Sunday.

Naggar
Roerich Gallery is located on the hill above Naggar Castle. It is a small house containing the works of Professor Nicholas Roerich and his son.

Dharamsala
War Memorial. This beautifully designed monument was erected in honor of soldiers who died serving their country.

Dalhousie
Panjpulla. Here stands a memorial to the revolutionary freedom fighter Sardar Ajit Singh, who died on August 15, 1947, the day India attained independence. A picturesque area, water from a natural tank here flows under five small bridges from which the place takes its name.

JAMMU & KASHMIR

Srinagar
Shri Pratap Singh Museum, Lal Mandi, south of Jhelum river between Zero Bridge and Amira Kadal. This contains a collection of Kashmiri relics and exhibits. It is open between 10 a.m. and 5 p.m. every day. The museum remains closed on Mondays all day, and on Fridays between 1 and 2.30 p.m. Entrance is free.

Jammu
Amar Mahal Palace & Museum. A small private collection of Pahari and Kangra paintings. Open 8 a.m.-12 noon Sundays, 5-7 p.m. Tuesdays-Sundays.

Leh
Stok Palace. A small museum is housed in part of the palace.

FESTIVALS

HIMACHAL PRADESH

Dussehra. Celebrated in October by all of Himachal Pradesh for a week. Celebrates the victory of Lord Ram over Ravana, or of good over evil. Folk dances, exhibitions and cultural programmes are a part of the festivities, as are night-long community singing and dancing. Deities are brought to Kullu from neighbouring areas in colorful processions.

Minjar festival. A week long harvest festival to appease the God of Rain. The ritual-filled festival culminates in a procession leading to the immersion of *minjars* (corn tassels) in the Ravi river; July-August.

Doongri Forest fair. The goddess Hadimba is honored in this fair held in the Doongri forests of Manali. It lasts three days and the cedar forests provide a grand setting for the gathering of hill women in their colorful costumes. A winter carnival is also held here; May (Doongri forest) and February 10-14 (Winter carnival).

Shakti festival. Held in various temples of the Kangra valley, the events are festive. The largest is held at the Jwalamukhi temple; March-April.

Shivratri Mela. This is a unique fair held at Mandi. Hundreds of gods and goddesses are carried on palanquins on the shoulders of devotees, followed by a week-long programme of folk dances, songs and dramas by hill-folk; February-March.

Sipi fair. Villagers gather at Naldehra to sell handicrafts amidst a festive atmosphere; June.

Lavi Mela. The biggest hill trade fair in northern India is held at Hampur. The town comes alive with sports, culture and plenty of people; Second week of November.

Renuka Lake fair. The lake is shaped like a sleeping woman, and the fair celebrates the immortality of Renuka and her son. Locals gather here to chant praises of the two, worship at the temple and purify themselves by bathing in the sacred waters. There is much dancing and singing; November.

Sisu fair. This important fair is celebrated and observed by thousands at Lake Rewalsar; March-April.

LADAKH

Hemis festival. One of the largest and most spectacular of all *gompa* festivals, this commemorates the birth anniversary of Guru Padmasambhava (750-800 A.D.). Elaborate mask dances are performed over two days, symbolising the victory of good over evil, according to a simpler interpretation. The largest *thangka* in Ladakh is unfurled here once in twelve years (next in 1992). late June/early July.

Matho festival. There are, in fact, two festivals at the Matho Gompa. The two day Nagrang festival celebrates the Tibetan new year, with lamas acting mean and nasty on the first day and perfectly peaceable and friendly on the second! The Nispetsergyat, also called the festival of the oracles, displays possessed monks who perform amazing feats with knives and swords, and cavort blindfolded along mountains and high ramparts. February (Nagrang) and early March (Nispetsergyat).

Phiyang festival. A large and colorful festival which rivals that of Hemis in popularity and local attendance. Held previously in winter, the date for this has been moved to summer to coincide with the tourist season. July.

Spituk festival. The Spituk Gostor is celebrated with mask dances. The masks used are accurate imitations of the 'Jelbagh' dance masks seen hanging on the walls of Spituk Gompa. A statue of the goddess Kali is kept here, the face of which is revealed only once a year during the festival. Early to mid January.

Festival of Ladakh. An amalgamation of several smaller festivals, it is organised by the district's Tourist Office, 1st-8th August.

JAMMU & KASHMIR

Baisakhi. Also called the Blossom festival, this marks the end of winter and the beginning of the harvesting season. People throng parks and gardens, and in Jammu, there are festivities at the Nagbani temple. 13-14 April.

Id-ul-Milad. The birth anniversary of the Prophet Mohammad is celebrated with prayers all over. October/November.

Shab-e-Miraj. This festival commemorates the passing away of the Prophet Mohammad. Various relics, such as a hair of the Prophet at Hazratbal mosque, are put on display. March/April.

Amarnath Yatra. An important Hindu pilgrimage, it consists of a 3 to 5 day trek starting from Pahalgam to the Amarnath cave. The cave contains an ice lingam representing the God Shiva that waxes and wanes with the moon. The pilgrimage is undertaken in the lunar month of *Shravan* (July-August).

Bahu Mela. A major festival is held twice a year at the Kali temple at Bahu fort. March-April and September-October.

Purmandal Mela. This three day long festival is celebrated on Shivaratri at Purmandal, famous for its Shiva temples. Shivratri is also celebrated in Jammu in a big way at many temples. Purmandal is 24 miles (39 km) from Jammu. February-March.

Jhiri Mela. Commemorating the sacrifice of a farmer, Baba Jitu, who was killed by his greedy landlord, this festival involves a big fair at Jhiri, 9 miles (14 km) from Jammu. October-November.

Lohri. An important festival all over North India, Lohri involves *havan yagyas* (bonfires) in houses and temples. January 13.

Chaitre Chaudash. Another festival near Jammu, Chaitre Chaudash is celebrated at Uttar Baihni, 16 miles (25 km) away. March-April.

SPORTS

TREKKING

The best way to explore and experience the majestic Himalaya is undoubtedly on foot. The world's youngest and most rugged mountain system offers unparalleled trekking opportunities. For a successful trek, however, advance preparation is necessary, keeping in mind certain factors.

Most Himalayan treks demand six to eight hours of trekking every day, over a range of gradients and altitudes. Physical fitness and adequate acclimatization are thus essential. The greater the altitude, the more important is acclimatization. This problem can be alleviated by starting with short day treks initially.

In general, you can plan your trek in four ways: alone or in groups; hiring a porter; using a *sardar* and his crew; and through a travel agency. Trekking alone is inadvisable for those unfamiliar with the area or its people. Porters may be hired even in villages. They carry your baggage, enable you to communicate with local people, and, if a rapport is established, entertain you with stories and folk-lore. A *sardar* and his crew will free you from most logistical problems, but are more expensive. An experienced sardar is of great help in tackling problems such as hiring of cooks and porters and arranging provisions. More expensive but the most convenient are travel agencies specializing in adventure tourism, which take care of all your requirements, leaving you free to enjoy the trek. Various tourist offices will help you find suitable porters and sardars, or recommend a particular travel agency.

It is best to arrange your trekking equipment before you arrive in India, although most gear is available here.

Equipment: A tent may or may not be necessary, depending on where you are planning to trek and sleep. In the more remote areas, you will need to cook yourself, unless you have a sardar. Cooking equipment is available in India, although it is not as lightweight as imported equipment. Suggested items are a kerosene stove, fuel container, pots, spray-dried foods. A rucksack is a basic item, as are a medicine kit, toilet kit and paper, Swiss Army knife, sewing kit, water bottle, torch, sun block cream, lip salve, sunglasses and insect repellent.

MOUNTAINEERING

The Himalaya undoubtedly offer some of the most exciting and challenging mountaineering opportunities in the world. There is a diversity of ranges and peaks, many of them unclimbed. There is, however, a procedure you must follow, if you want to make mountaineering your dream of dreams come true.

The **Survey of India** has a list of peaks which are open for climbing. It includes unnamed peaks and those which have been attempted previously and unsuccessfully. Once you have decided upon a peak, the **Indian Mountaineering Foundation**, Benito Juarez Road, New Delhi 110021 (tel: 67-1211) will book it for you. You must book your peak as far in advance as possible; some are booked two years ahead. If the peak you want is booked and unavailable, the IMF will supply you with information about a peak roughly similar to the one you originally wanted to climb. The booking fee ranges from US$400 to $2,000, depending upon the location and height of the peak. A peak is not allotted to more than one expedition in a month. The climbing season extends from April to October. Permission is required from the Government of India before you climb a peak; the IMF will help you in this. Maps and surveys are available with the Survey of India in Dehra Dun, Uttar Pradesh.

Liaison Officer: Every expedition must be accompanied by an Indian Liaision Officer, selected by the IMF. He or she will usually accompany the expedition to base camp, and beyond if you wish. The officer is a mountaineer, is familiar with local language and customs, helps with administrative matters like arranging porters etc.

Equipment: The expedition must arrive with all its equipment – climbing boots, boot covers, crampons, downjackets, ice axes, sleeping bags, air mattresses, rucksacks, ropes, harnesses etc. One set of these will be for the liasion officer.

Safety and rescue: A wireless is essential for communication between the various camps, especially base camp. A radio set will prove useful in case special weather bulletins have to be arranged with All India Radio for tougher peaks; the IMF will arrange this. For accidents or emergencies, helicopters of the Indian Army and Air Force are on call. These have experienced rescue teams, some of whom have made daring and dramatic sorties in the past.

Acclimatisation: This is very important, and has been covered in great detail under Health. Most expeditions find that they need more time at base camp than planned for, making practice treks in neighbouring areas. Since peaks must be booked, it is not possible for you to make a practice ascent of a peak for acclimatisation. So plan well.

SKIING

One of the cheapest places in the world to ski in, India provides slopes which offer splendid views of the towering Himalayan range. Since the sport is government-run and therefore not fully commercialized, comparatively fewer people ski in India. Some of the resorts are highly developed, like Gulmarg in Kashmir, although this is still rudimentary when compared with, say, a premier Alpine resort. On the other hand, the spectacular views of mountain peaks and the untouched virgin slopes compensate for this.

JAMMU & KASHMIR

Gulmarg is India's main ski resort with well developed facilities for food, accommodation, instruction etc. There is a 1,650-foot (500- meter) **chair lift**, providing a ski run of 2,310 feet (700 meters). A **T-bar** giving a 660-foot (200-meter) run is available for beginners. A **gondola cable car** is under construction which will open up slopes as far as Apherwat. At a very advanced level, you can try **heli-skiing**. This has brought within access slopes previously impossible to reach.

The Indian Institute of Skiing and Mountaineering organizes 10 and 20 day courses imparted by trained instructors. Equipment such as skis, ski boots, ski poles, snow goggles, gloves, sledges, toboggans etc. is available on hire.

HIMACHAL PRADESH

Solang, near Manali, is another resort where you ski against a backdrop of icy glaciers and mountain peaks. **Ski courses** are run by the HPTDC which coordinates most adventure activities.

The slopes of Kufri and Narkanda near Shimla are easy and suitable for recreational skiing. Importantly, they are cheap and easy to access.

RIVER RUNNING

While it is a relatively young sport in India, white water **rafting** has gained popularity as a safe yet thrilling sport for people of all ages. The snow-fed rivers of the Himalaya offer tremendous possibilities for every river runner, from beginner to professional. Potentially, India is the river running capital of the world, with its endowment of rapid-filled rivers. **Kayaking** too is becoming a popular sport, and many foreign teams regularly visit. The season extends from October to late April, with a pause in January when the water becomes too cold.

JAMMU & KASHMIR

The most popular rivers in Jammu & Kashmir are the Indus (grade II and III), Zanskar (grade III) and Chenab (grade IV-V). The Indus, which passes through the barren wastes of Ladakh, consists of long stretches of rapids passing through gorges and unusual rock formations, which may be easily tackled at most places. The Zanskar is more challenging, and, at certain spots, dangerous. The latter sections are best negotiated in August and September, when water levels are low.

HIMACHAL PRADESH

In Himachal Pradesh, the main rivers are the Beas (grade III-IV), Satluj (grade IV-V) and Spiti. The Satluj is a fascinating river for rafting, with a spectacular staircase of rapids up to Tattapani. The scenery too is beautiful.

OPERATORS

Some of the companies specializing in river running are:
Himalayan River Runners
188A Jorbagh, New Delhi 110 003
Tel:61-5736

Snow Leopard Adventures
W-89A/104 Greater Kailash II,
New Delhi 110 048
Tel:642-6488

Markhor Adventures
F-108, Sector 21, NOIDA

Indian Rafting Company
606 Akash Deep, Barakhamba Road,
New Delhi 110 001
Tel:331-2773/3229/4115

Tiger Paw Adventures
D-383 Defence Colony,
New Delhi 110 024
Tel:61-6137, 62-4879

Mercury Himalayan Explorations
Jeevan Tara building, Sansad Marg,
New Delhi 110 001 (Tel:31-2008/2901)

GOLF

JAMMU & KASHMIR

Summer is the season for golf up in the hills. Kashmir has two well-developed golf courses, one in Srinagar and the other in Gulmarg. The Srinagar course has 18 holes with a par of 70, and is open most of the year. A relatively flat golf course, it is a popular venue for many all-India tournaments. The one at Gulmarg, situated 12,309 feet (3,730 meters) above sea level, is the highest green golf course in the world. Set amidst spectacular scenery, it was opened in 1904. There are hardly any flat stretches in this course, which has a par of 72, making playing here interesting and challenging.

You need not be a full-time member to play at either club; a daily membership facility is available. Should you wish to play regularly, a temporary membership too is available which allows you full access to the club house restaurant and bar. A golf set and balls can be hired, and professionals are on hand to help you learn or improve your play.

A number of **tournaments** are held here in the summer, open to all golfers with a handicap of 15 and under. Those recognized by the Indian Golf Union are:

The Northern India Wills Golf Open
The Northern India Amateur
  Championship
Sher-i-Kashmir Golf Open
Government of India Tourist Golf Open
Details are available at J & K Tourism.

HIMACHAL PRADESH

The only golf course of note in the state is the 9 hole course at Naldehra, near Shimla. One of the oldest courses in India, it is open from May to November. Equipment is available.

FISHING

JAMMU & KASHMIR

Kashmir is a veritable angler's paradise, with its network of rivers, streams and lakes abounding in trout, especially the famous rainbow trout. And, as is the case with most sports in India, it is cheaper to fish here than anywhere else in the world. The fishing season runs from March to October, although you can only trek to the high altitude lakes from July onwards. The best time to catch trout is either early morning or late evening.

For the intrepid angler, the most exciting fishing can be done at one of the high altitude lakes (4,000 meter/14,000 ft) in the mountains. This usually involves a trek, with full trekking equipment and food in addition to fishing equipment. A typical trek begins of

Sonamarg, visiting the alpine lakes at Vishansar, Kishansar, Satsar, Gadsar and Gangabal, and involving eight days of trekking. The rewards are tremendous, with spectacular views of lakes cradled by snow-clad mountains. The lakes mainly contain brown trout, and the use of spoons and spinners is allowed.

At a less arduous level, you can fish in rivers and streams, within your own exclusive beat. Most of these are within a two-hour drive from Srinagar. Each beat extends for over a mile (2 km), and you can fish exclusively at any point within it. Beat guards, two per beat, familiar with the habits of the fish, are on hand for help and advice. A permit is required, available for a small fee, one of which allows you to catch six fish. Six-day permits are also possible. You require only reels with flies, spoons and spinners being prohibited here.

The TRC, Srinagar, has a fishing counter where information about equipment, transport, location of beats and accommodation is available. The Department of Fisheries, responsible for overseeing the sport and maintaining the ecosystem of the rivers and lakes, is located on the first floor of the TRC. Many officials are keen anglers, and may offer advice.

HIMACHAL PRADESH

Trout may be found in the Beas river near Manali as well as the Pabbar river near Rohru, which is a day's trip from Shimla. You can try for *mahseer* on the Beas near Dharamsala. The tourist department in every district will be able to provide you with a license.

HANG GLIDING

Billing in the Kangra Valley hosts India's only annual international hang-gliding competition. The season extends from March to April and from mid-August to November. Courses may be taken through the HPTDC. All equipment is provided.

NIGHTLIFE

The nightlife of the West is a completely alien concept in the western Himalayan region of India. There are no discotheques or nightclubs; a hotel bar is the closest thing to the above. On the other hand, it is possible to witness local dances and festivals at night, especially if you get friendly with village folk.

Bars. Only the better hotels have visitable bars. In Srinagar, the best bars are at the **Oberoi Palace**, **Centaur Lake View** and **Lake Isle Resort**. These remain open till 11 p.m. An alternative is to buy your own alcohol in Srinagar, and to drink it in the evening on the veranda or roof of your houseboat. In Shimla, the best bar is at the **Oberoi Clarkes**, which remains open till 10 p.m. At **Chapslee** and **Woodville**, however, you get a nightcap in style.

SHOPPING

JAMMU & KASHMIR

Kashmir is famed for its wide variety of handicrafts. These include carpets, embroidered shawls, leather and fur clothing, jewelry, oak and walnut woodwork and *papier mâché* products. The Kashmiri **carpet** is perhaps the most expensive and desirable. These come in many sizes, made of wool, silk or a blend of both. The showrooms display spectacular collections of carpets. The **embroidered shawls** of Kashmir are another speciality. The finest are those made of *pashm*, which is made from the undercoat of goats that live higher than 13,000 ft (4,000 meters). Truly high quality *pashmina* shawls are very expensive; make sure that you distinguish them from *raffal*s, lower quality shawls. Embroidered **bags**, **coats** and **clothing** are also popular.

Leather and **fur products** can be made to measure quite easily. Tailoring quality suffers during the peak season; be clear about your requirements and insist on several fittings. This in fact applies to all tailoring. The fur trade, sadly, is wiping out much of the precious wildlife of the Himalaya. For this alone, it is not recommended that you buy fur products. The best furs, in any case, are exported.

The intricate **woodwork** of Kashmir is evident everywhere, from the most luxurious houseboat down to carvings on tables, chairs, chests and screens. The latter are cheap and easily available. Do not buy products inlaid with ivory; it's not very good for the elephants. The items most readily identifiable as Kashmiri are the boxes, trays and cups made of *papier mâché*. They are cheap, colorful and easy to carry. Some can be very intricate and beautiful, with gold leaf painted on. These items are manufactured in cottage industries to which visits can be easily arranged.

Some fixed price shops in Srinagar are the **Kashmir Government Arts Emporium** on Shervani Road and the **Government Central Market** on the Boulevard.

LADAKH

CAUTION. Many Ladakhi antiques such as *thangkas*, dance masks, swords and Buddha figures are prohibited from being sold. This is to prevent a damaging drain away from the monasteries. These rules are strictly enforced, so do not attempt to play smuggler. Since authentic items are in short supply, there is a flourishing trade in 'instant' antiques.

On the other hand, you can legally buy a number of items, like **Tibetan carpets** from Choglamsar, **silver cups** and **vessels**, **ornamental shells**, **prayer flags** and the expensive *perak*, a bejewelled ceremonial headgear. The monasteries themselves sell items like *dorjes*, or **prayer wheels**, small **bells** and **musical instruments**. You can now buy new *thangkas*, which are painted in Nepal or Darjeeling!

Fixed price shops in Leh are **Dragon Curios**, open 10 a.m. to 8 p.m., no credit cards; **Ladakh Art Palace**, open 9 a.m. to 7 p.m., credit cards accepted; **Lhasa Leh Curios**, open 9 a.m. to 6.30 p.m., no credit cards; **Tibetan Refugee Handicraft Centers** (there are two – one on the outskirts of Leh, the other on the Thikse road), open 10 a.m. to 4 p.m., no credit cards.

HIMACHAL PRADESH

SHIMLA

The Mall is the main shopping area of Shimla and also contains a number of restaurants. Two places worth visiting are the **Himachal Government State Emporium** and **Super Bazar**. Besides these, there are many privately run shops which deal in shawls, handmade shoes and decorative items. **Lakkar Bazar** is famous for its wooden toys, sticks and other wood-based decorative pieces. Shops are usually open 10 a.m. to 7 p.m. Most do not accept credit cards.

KULLU

Kullu has some distinct traditional handicrafts, many of them woollen. Among them Kullu shawls occupy pride of place. These are available in wool or *pashmina*, plain or designed with brightly patterned weaves for borders. *Pattus* are heavier and thicker than shawls; the rougher ones are used as blankets. The better quality variety is worn by women, fastened with brooches and long silver chains and tied around the waist with the patterns in front.

A local tweed made of very fine wool is used to make long coats worn by men. Kullu caps are colorful with a velvet circular band in the front. Other local specialities are embroidered felt rugs called *namdas*, colourful sandals made of fiber and goat hair and baskets made of a species of high-altitude bamboo. You can also buy an assortment of socks, mittens and hats. There are many shops in **Akhara Bazaar**, apart from the **Government Handicrafts Emporium**. Shops open daily from 9 a.m. to 8 p.m.

MANALI

Kullu shawls and caps, Tibetan handicrafts, *gudmas*, *pulas* and carpets are available in the **main market**, **Tibetan Bazar** and **Tibetan Carpet Center**.

DHARAMSALA

The **Kotwali Bazar** is where you can buy locally made handicrafts. Tibetan handicrafts, carpets and *thangkas* are sold in Mcleodganj. Visit the **Tibetan Handicrafts Center** which is open between 9 a.m. and 5 p.m. weekdays, closed Sunday.

MANDI

Bhutnath Bazar and **Seri Bazar** are the main shopping centers. Look for local handicrafts.

CHAMBA

Visitors will find that the embroidered *rumals*, or kerchiefs, of Chamba, and the leather slippers will make attractive souvenirs. The **Handicrafts Center**, a storehouse of the arts and crafts of Chamba, makes for good shopping.

DALHOUSIE

Local as well as Tibetan handicrafts may be bought at **Gandhi Chowk**.

SOME TIPS

Kashmiris are not only skilled craftspersons but also persuasive salespeople. Beware: never be pressurized into making a purchase. If you are dissatisfied for any reason, refuse to buy firmly and leave. Shopping in Kashmir is an enjoyable and satisfying experience if you are careful and do not get cheated or overcharged.

Ladakh is more expensive than Kashmir. Tibetan curios may be cheaper at other Tibetan centers in Dharamsala or Kashmir. If you plan to buy an expensive item like a Kashmiri carpet, check its price at home before leaving. Many good carpets are exported and sold abroad at competitive prices.

PHOTOGRAPHY

FILM

Film is not easily available in India and, when found, may not be of the type you are used to. The same applies to camera accessories. Carry more film than you will need as surplus film can always be used as a much appreciated gift.

Good and reasonably priced processing facilities exist in the larger towns and cities. Both Fujichrome and Ektachrome are in vogue, but Kodachrome film and processing is no longer possible in the country. E6 processing of varying quality may be done.

The desert regions of Ladakh and Lahaul-Spiti are at a great height, and the light is correspondingly more intense. The shadows are very dark, so many films may be unable to compensate for the extreme variations. A polarizing filter will help deepen the color of the sky. The *gompas*, on the other hand, are often dark and gloomy, and you will require fast film to capture the interiors. Do NOT use a flash inside the *gompas*.

EQUIPMENT

Protect your camera from heat, dust and humidity throughout your stay. Don't leave cameras and equipment on the back shelf of a car, which can get extremely hot. Ensure that exposed film does not go through a baggage scanner; sometimes these are not photo-proof.

There are few places in India where prompt and reliable camera servicing can be had, so equipment should be checked before coming here. Make sure that you are familiar with any new equipment you intend to use. Carrying an extra camera body may be a good idea if you intend to photograph a lot; apart from offering flexibility in using alternative lenses or film types, it also acts as a back-up in case of mechanical or electrical failure.

Nowhere are standard lenses adequate, especially if you wish to photograph nature and wildlife. Telephoto lenses from 180mm upwards are required for most people (it's unobtrusive, villagers are usually quite shy) and animal photographs, 35mm or 28mm wide-angle lenses are extremely useful for striking scenic or environmental pictures. When using telephoto lenses, a monopod or tripod is useful.

Fast film (ASA 400) is desirable in preference to flashes, especially inside the *gompas* of Ladakh. NEVER use a flash unit inside these; the delicate wall paintings and fabrics have not been exposed to direct light for hundreds of years and flash photography will inevitably damage these.

RESTRICTIONS

Photography is strictly prohibited at airports, sea ports and defense installations, and the authorities can be quite sticky at some railway stations, bridges etc. The Archaeological Department and various state museum departments are also strict about photographing monuments and exhibits; tripods and artificial lights may not be used without prior permission, which has to be applied for in writing.

Photography is also prohibited in certain tribal areas (especially in those where clothing is scant) as well as inside many places of worship.

At some airports, security officers may confiscate batteries or pencil cells from cameras, motor drives, torches and other electronic items. It is safest to put the cells in your checked baggage.

FURTHER READING

BIBLIOGRAPHY

Ali, Salim. *Indian Hill Birds*. Oxford University Press, Bombay.

Atkinson, E.T. *Religion in the Himalayas*. 1974. Cosmos Publications, New Delhi.

Barr, Pat & Ray, Desmond. *Simla*. 1978. Scholar Press.

Bates, R.S.P. & Lowther, E.H.N. *Breeding Birds of Kashmir*. 1952, 1991. Oxford University Press, New Delhi.

Buck, Edward J. *Simla Past and Present*. 1904. Thacker, Spink & Co., Calcutta. reprinted 1925. Times Press, Bombay.

Chetwode, Penelope. *Kullu, the End of the Habitable World*. 1972. John Murray.

Doux-Lacombe, Geraldine. *Ladakh*. 1978. Paris.

Drew, Frederick. *The Jummoo and Kashmir Territories*. 1875. London. reprinted 1976. New Delhi.

Duncan, Jane E. *A Summer Ride in Western Tibet*. 1906. London.

Enriquez, C.M. *Realm of the Gods: a tale of travel in Kangra, Mandi, Kullu, Chamba, Kishtwar, Kashmir, Ladakh and Baltistan*. 1915. Thacker, Spink & Co., Calcutta and Shimla.

Fairley, J. *Indus--the Lion River*. 1975. Allen Lane.

Francke, A.H. *Antiquities of Western Tibet*. Volume 1 1914, volume 2 1926. reprinted 1976. New Delhi.

Fraser, James Baille. *Journal of a tour through parts of the snowy ranges of the Himalaya mountains and to the source of the rivers Jumna and Ganges*. 1820. Rod Well and Mastin, London.

Goepper, Poncar-Lutterbeck & Poncar. *Alchi: Buddhas, Goddesses, Mandalas*. 1984. Koln.

Goepper, Roger. *Alchi*. 1984. DuMont Buchverlag, Koln.

Harcourt, A.F.P. *Himalayan District of Kullu, Lahaul & Spiti*. 1871. W.H.Allen & Co., London.

Harvey, Andrew. *A Journey in Ladakh*. 1983. Cape, London.

Heber A.R. & Heber K.M. *In Himalayan Tibet*. 1926. London. reprinted as *Himalayan Tibet and Ladakh*. 1976. New Delhi.

Hutchinson J. & Vogel, J.P. *History of the Punjab Hill States*. 2 volumes, 1933. Government Press, Punjab.

Iozawa, Tomoya. *Trekking in the Himalayas*. 1980. Yama Kei Poblishers Co. Ltd./ Allied Publishers Pvt. Ltd.

Jaitly, Jaya. *The Art of Jammu & Kashmir*. 1990. Mapin.

Jest, Corneille & Sanday, John. *The Palace of Leh in Ladakh: an example of Himalayan Architecture in need of conservation, reprinted from Momentum*. Volume 25 number 3. 1982.

Keay, John. *Where Men and Mountains Meet*. 1977. John Murray, London.

Keenan, Brigid. *Travels in Kashmir*. 1985. Oxford University Press.

Khosla, G.D. *Himalayan Circuit*. 1956, 1989. Oxford University Press, Delhi.

Moorcroft, William & Trebeck, George. *Travels in the Himalayan Provinces of Hindustan and the Punjab*. 1837. London. reprinted 1971. New Delhi.

Noble, Christina. *Over the High Passes*. 1988. Collins.

Peissel, Michel. *Zanskar, The Hidden Kingdom*. 1979. London.

Petech, Luciano. *The Kingdom of Ladakh 950 to 1842*. 1977. Rome.

Polunin, Oleg & Stainton, Adam. *Flowers of the Himalaya*. 1984. Oxford University Press, New Delhi.

Randhawa, M.S. *TravEls in the Western Himalayas*. 1974. Thomson Press, New Delhi.

Rizvi, Janet. *Ladakh: Crossroads of High Asia*. 1983. Oxford University Press, Delhi.

Saith, Sanjeev. *Himachal Pradesh*. 1991. UBSPD, Delhi.

Schettler, Margaret & Rolf. *Kashmir, Ladakh & Zanskar: a Travel Survival Kit*. May 1989. 3rd ed. Lonely Planet Publications.

Singh, Goverdhan. *Art and Architecture of Himachal Pradesh*. 1983. B.R.Publishing Corporation, Delhi.

Singh, Goverdhan. *History of Himachal Pradesh*. 1982. Yugbodh Publishing House, Delhi.

Singh, Madanjeet. *Himalayan Art*. 1968. Macmillan.

Snellgrove, David & Skorupski, Tadeusz. *The Cultural Heritage of Ladakh*. Volume 1 1977, volume 2 1980. New Delhi and Warminster (England).

The Gilgit Game. 1979. John Murray, London.

The Himalayan Journal. Volume 42 1984-85, volume 43 1985-86. Bombay.

Vigne, J.T. *Travels in Kashmir, Ladakh, Istardo, the countries adjoining the mountain course of the Indus and the Himalaya*. 2 volumes, 1844. Henry Colburn Publisher, London.

Wahid, Siddiq & Storm, Kenneth. *Ladakh, Between Earth and Sky*. 1981. Edita S.A.
Pallis, Marco. *Peaks and Lamas*. 1937, 1974.

Weare, Gary. *Trekking in the Indian Himalayas*. April 1986. 1st ed. Lonely Planet Publications.

USEFUL ADDRESSES

EMBASSIES & HIGH COMMISIONS

No country has representation in either Jammu or Kashmir or Himachal Pradesh. Most embassies and High Commissions are in New Delhi.

Afghanistan
5/50F Shantipath, Chanakya Puri,
New Delhi 110021.
Tel: 60-3331/3328

Argentina
B-8/9 Vasant Vihar,
New Delhi 110057.
Tel: 67-1345

Australia
1/50G Shantipath,
Chanakya Puri,
New Delhi 110 021.
Tel: 60-1336

Austria
EP-13 Chandragupta Marg,
New Delhi 110021
Tel: 60-1112

Bangladesh
56M Ring Road, Lajpat Nagar III,
New Delhi 110024,
Tel: 683-4065/4668/8405/9209

Belgium
50N Shantipath, Chanakya Puri,
New Delhi 110021.
Tel: 60-7957

Bhutan
Chandragupta Marg, Chanakya Puri,
New Delhi 110021.
Tel: 60-4076

Brazil
8 Aurangzeb Road, New Delhi 110011.
Tel: 301-7301

Burma
3/50F Nyaya Marg, Chanakya Puri,
New Delhi 110021.
Tel: 60-0251

Canada
Shantipath, Chanakya Puri,
New Delhi 110021.
Tel: 60-8161

China
50D Shantipath,
Chanakya Puri,
New Delhi 110021.
Tel: 60-0328/0329/0872

Denmark
2 Golf Links,
New Delhi 110003.
Tel: 61-6273

Finland
Nyaya Marg, Chanakya Puri,
New Delhi 110 021.
Tel: 60-5409

France
2/50E Shantipath, Chanakya Puri,
New Delhi 110 021.
Tel: 60-4004

Germany
6/50G Shantipath, Chanakya Puri,
New Delhi 110 021.
Tel: 60-4861

Great Britain
Shantipath, Chanakyu Puri
New Delhi 110021
Tel: 60-1371

Indonesia
50A Chanakya Puri,
New Delhi 110 021.
Tel: 60-2305/6/7

Iran
5 Barakhamba Road,
New Delhi 110001.
Tel: 332-9600/9601/9602/9603

Ireland
13 Jor Bagh,
New Delhi 110003.
Tel: 61-5485/7435

Italy
13 Golf Links,
New Delhi 110003.
Tel: 61-8311/8312/8313/8314

Japan
450G Chanakya Puri,
New Delhi 110021.
Tel: 60-4071

Kenya
E-66 Vasant Marg,
Vasant Vihar,
New Delhi 110057.
Tel: 67-2303/2280/2312

Malaysia
50M Satya Marg, Chanakya Puri,
New Delhi 110021.
Tel: 60-1291/1292/1296/1297

Mauritius
5 Kautilya Marg, Chanakya Puri,
New Delhi 110021.
Tel: 301-1112/1113

Nepal
Barakhamba Road,
New Delhi 110001.
Tel: 332-9969
Delhi 110021.
Tel: 67-7436/7460

New Zealand
25G Golf Links,
New Delhi 110003.
Tel: 67-7296/7318/7592

Netherlands
21 Olof Palmc Marg,
Vasant Vihar,
New Delhi 110057.
Tel: 67-0405/0446

Norway
50C Shantipath, Chanakya Puri,
New Delhi 110021.
Tel: 60-5982

Pakistan
2/50G Shantipath, Chanakya Puri,
New Delhi 110021.
Tel: 60-0601/0603/0604, 60-0905, 67-6004/
8467

Portugal
B-76 Greater Kailash,
New Delhi 110048.
Tel: 644-9648

Saudi Arabia
S-347 Panchsheel Park,
New Delhi 110017.
Tel: 644-2470/2471/5054/5419

Singapore
E-6 Chandragupta Marg,
Chanakya Puri,
New Delhi 110021.
Tel: 60-4162/8149/8527

Spain
12 Prithvi Raj Road,
New Delhi 110011.
Tel: 301-5892/3834/6359

Sri Lanka
27 Kautilya Marg, Chanakya Puri,
New Delhi 110021.
Tel: 301-0201/0202/0203

Sweden
Nyaya Marg, Chanakya Puri,
New Delhi 110021,
Tel: 60-4011/4021/4051/4055, 60-4961/
4963

Switzerland
Nyaya Marg, Chanakya Puri,
New Delhi 110021.
Tel: 60-4225/4226/4227/4323

Tanzania
27 Golf Links,
New Delhi 110003.
Tel: 69-4351/4352

Thailand
56N Nyaya Marg, Chanakya Puri,
New Delhi 110021.
Tel: 60-5679/5985/7289/7807

Trinidad & Tobago
131 Jor Bagh,
New Delhi 110003.
Tel: 61-8186/8187

Uganda
61 Golf Links,
New Delhi 110003.
Tel: 69-3584/9353

USSR
Shantipath, Chanakya Puri,
New Delhi 110021.
Tel: 60-6026/6137/6558

UAE
EP-12 Chandragupta Marg,
Chanakya Puri, New Delhi 110021.
Tel: 60-0466, 67-0830/0945

USA
Shantipath, Chanakya Puri,
New Delhi 110021.
Tel: 60-0651

Viet Nam
F-42 NDSE Part I,
New Delhi 110049.
Tel: 62-3088/3823/4586

Yugoslavia
3/50G Niti Marg, Chanakya Puri,
New Delhi 110021.
Tel: 60-4311/4312/4313

Zambia
14 Jor Bagh,
New Delhi 110003.
Tel: 61-9115/7779

Zimbabwe
B-8 Anand Niketan,
New Delhi 110021.
Tel: 67-7436/7460

GOVERNMENT OF INDIA TOURIST OFFICES

Australia
65 Elizabeth Street, Sydney NSW 2000.
Tel: (02) 232-1600

Austria
Opernring 1/E/11, 1010 Vienna.
Tel: 5871462

Canada
60 Bloor Street, West Suite No.1003,
Toronto, Ontario M4W 3B8.
Tel: 416962

France
8 Boulevard de la Madeleine,
75009 Paris.
Tel: 4265-83-86

Germany
Kaiserstrasse 77-111,
6000 Frankfurt Main-1.
Tel: 235423/24

Italy
Via Albricci 9, 20122 Milan.
Tel: 804952

Japan
Pearl Building, 9-18 Ginza,
7-chome Cho Ku, Tokyo 104.
Tel: (03) 571-5062/3

Malaysia
Wisma HLA, Lot No.203,
Jalan Raja Chulan,
50200 Kuala Lumpur.
Tel: 2425285

Singapore,
Podium Block, 5th floor,
Ming Court Hotel, Tanglin Road,
Singapore 1024.
Tel: 2355737

Sweden,
Sveavagen 9-11, S 11157 Stockholm.
Tel: 08-215081

Switzerland
103 Rue Chantepoulet, 1201 Geneva.
Tel: 022-321813

Thailand
Singapore Airlines Building, 3rd floor,
62/5 Thaniya Road, Bangkok.
Tel: 2352585

UAE
PO Box 12856 DNATA, Dubai.
Tel: 236870

United Kingdom
7 Cork Street, London W1X 2AB.
Tel: 01-437-3677/8

USA
30 Rockefeller Plaza, Room 15,
North Mezzanine, New York NY 10020,
Tel: 212-586-4901/2/3;

230 North Michigan Avenue,
Chicago IL 60601,
Tel: 312-236-6899/7869;

3550 Wilshire Boulevard, Suite 204,
Los Angeles CA 90010.
Tel: (213) 380-8855

JAMMU & KASHMIR TOURISM

Jammu & Kashmir Tourist Office
Kanishka Shopping Plaza,
New Delhi
Tel: 332-4422 ext. 2397

Jammu & Kashmir Tourist Office
Manekji Wadia Building,
129 Mahatma Gandhi Road, Bombay .
Tel:21-6249, 27-3820

Jammu & Kashmir Tourist Office
Pathankot.
Tel:57

Jammu & Kashmir Tourist Office, TRC
Veer Marg, Jammu.
Tel:5324;
Old Secretariat, Jammu.
Tel:5376

Jammu & Kashmir Tourist Office, TRC
Srinagar.
Tel:2449, 2927, 3648, 6209);
J & K Government Reception Center
Tel:72449, 72927, 73648, 76209

HIMACHAL PRADESH TOURISM

SHIMLA

Tourist Information Office
Panchayat Bhavan, near bus stand .
Tel:4589;
The Mall
Tel:3311, 3956;
Railway Station
Tel:4599

Himachal Pradesh Tourism Development Corporation (HPTDC)
Ritz Annexe .
Tel:3294, 5071

OTHER

HPTDC
Chandralok Building,
36 Janpath,
New Delhi.
Tel:332-5320;
Himachal Bhavan,
Sikandra Road,
New Delhi.
Tel:38-7473

HPTDC, 36 World Trade Center
Cuffe Parade, Bombay.
Tel:21-1123/9191/9284

HPTDC, Hotel Parvati,
Manikaran.
Tel:35,open 10 am to 5 pm, except Sunday

HPTDC
Kullu.
Tel:2349

HPTDC
Dalhousie.
Tel:36)

HPTDC
Kasauli .
Tel:5

Tourist Information Center
HPTDC Tourist Bungalow, Mandi.
Tel:2575, open 10 am to 5 pm, except Sunday

Tourism Information Office
Manali.
Tel:25, 116, open 9 am to 7 pm, except Sunday

Tourist Information Assistant
Dharamshala.
Tel:2363

Tourist Information Center
Hotel Iravati, Chamba.
Tel:94

BANKS

SRINAGAR

State Bank of India
Shervani Road.
Tel:76996, 77233

ANZ Grindlays
Shervani Road.
Tel:74092, 76935

Canara Bank
The Bund.
Tel:78598

American Express
Kai Travels, Boulevard

Bank of Baroda
Shervani Road.
Tel:78332

J & K Bank
Shervani Road.
Tel:72430

LEH

State Bank of India
Tel:52

J & K Bank

SHIMLA

State Bank of India
Tel:2480, 5503

ANZ Grindlays
Tel:2925

Punjab National Bank
The Mall.
Tel:3585, 5310

J & K Bank
The Mall.
Tel:3085

MANALI

State Bank of India
Tel:36

New Bank of India
Tel:64

MANDI

State Bank of India
Tel:2681

Punjab National Bank
Tel:2408

Canara Bank
Tel:2579

ART/PHOTO CREDITS

INDEX

E

F

G

H

I